ITCHING FOR TROUBLE

I saw him open his mouth and his lips begin to move, but something—a sound, a shadow—monopolized all my senses and I tried to move, duck and whirl, too late. I saw nothing. . . .

I pressed my cheek into the concrete of the alleyway and the heat of the day still cooked beneath the surface, along with a harsh, primal stink. I made a note to take it up with the city planners.

A voice with a smug drawl eddied into my consciousness. "Man get hurt talkin' up the sisters. . . . Hey, we keep in touch."

I tried to express my enthusiasm for the idea, but I sounded like a leaky faucet. . . . I took a little nap.

There was no sunset, no sun at all. . . . I lifted the head. What I saw was visceral pulp, a high-speed, car-crash face. He'd been left behind by someone who did not believe in leaving any hope of identification, but I recognized the luminescent curls and the sunshine shirt. I checked his hands.

Fingers and thumbs were charred stubs.

SCRATCH

Marc Savage

BANTAM BOOKS
NEW YORK • TORONTO • LONDON • SYDNEY • AUCKLAND

SCRATCH
A Bantam Crime Line Book / October 1991

Grateful acknowledgment is made for permission to reprint the following:
Excerpt from "Wild Thing" by Chip Taylor copyright © 1965 EMI Blackwood Music Inc.
All rights reserved. International copyright secured. Used by permission.

ISBN 0-553-29253-6

Published simultaneously in the United States and Canada

Bantam Books are published by Bantam Books, a division of Bantam Doubleday Dell Publishing Group, Inc. its trademark, consisting of the words "Bantam Books" and the portrayal of a rooster, is Registered in U.S. Patent and Trademark Office and in other countries. Marca Registrada, Bantam Books, 666 Fifth Avenue, New York, New York 10103.

PRINTED IN THE UNITED STATES OF AMERICA
OPM 0 9 8 7 6 5 4 3 2 1

For Sharon Lee,
who carried the flag

I would like to express my gratitude to Marjorie Braman, for her insights and enthusiasm.

1

It's not every day a man in my line of work sees a check for twenty-five thousand dollars. It was a plain check, a sensible blue one in the ledger-size corporations issue. I liked it. The company name, Thompson Avionics, sat up in the left corner and sort of purred at me.

I'm a licensed private detective whose income for the most part no longer depends upon tracking errant spouses or soliciting dubious information from unwashed gentlemen. Protection, not detection, is the name of the game these days. Antsy celebrities in town to perform or to visit. Professional athletes under death threats. Corporations whose guests are VIPs from some turbulent, accident-prone republic. You get the idea.

My office on the second floor of a shingle-sided two-story fronted on Queens Boulevard, and while the worst of rush hour was history, sounds of traffic still staggered in. It was a hot day that promised to become hotter. With the blinds up, sunlight furnished all the illumination the room required. It wasn't an ugly room, but it wasn't posh either; functional, that's the term. There was a big black leather swivel chair that was kind to my back, and across from my desk stood a pecan cabinet populated (but not crowded) with liquor bottles, and next to it there was an ancient white refrigerator with an asthmatic motor. Cece, before she divorced me, tried to spiff up the room with potted floor plants and lithographs that portrayed swanky jazz-age ladies and their gentlemen. The ladies all looked sophisticated to the point of

anemia, and there was something sly in the eyes of the
gentlemen—lust or ambition, or maybe someone had just
slipped them a check for twenty-five large.

The stylishly bearded party who had delivered the
check sat slouched a little in a wooden chair on the
client's side of the desk, an ankle hiked across his knee.
He was not a client, and I hoped he never would be. He
was lean and graceful, freshly graduated from Harvard,
and the double-breasted navy-blue pinstripe fit him like
a dream. Cranberry was the ascendant color in his tie,
a theme repeated in the silk display hankie that fluttered
from his breast pocket. The shirt he was wearing was as
white as any acolyte's collar. Black curls ran rampant
above a handsome face that was Mediterranean in coloring and feature. He looked every inch the son of Sal
DeLorio, and then some.

Sal DeLorio, Jr., coughed politely into his fist, then
shot me a grin that made the whole room seem brighter.

I pushed the check away, but not so far I couldn't
reach it in the event of fire or a tip from my broker.
"Well, handsome," I said, "next step is Harvard Law."

"You were missed at the party," he said.

"Sorry about that. Something came up. It's the nature
of this business, I'm afraid. Trouble never sleeps."

He gave me a look that hovered somewhere between
amusement and scorn. "Yes, I've heard that. Pop says
trouble has been relentless in its pursuit of you the past
six months."

Today was the twentieth of June, six months exactly
since the divorce. It was a junior partner in the firm of
DeLorio, Simon, Tortelli and Weitz who had represented Cece in the proceedings, and while the settlement
itself had been amicable, the guy had showboated in a
deposition at the expense of my office manager, Pat Conner. Vague, leering insinuations were made, linking Pat
and me. Almost thirty years I had known Sal DeLorio,
and when I got him on the phone, I expressed with perfect candor how much I did not appreciate his hired twit
badgering my employee. By the end of the conversation
we were both shouting, and the substance of our remarks
was pure school yard. We hadn't spoken since, although
from his wife, Meredith, there had been invitations to

functions, including young Sal's graduation party, which I passed on, not from any real enmity toward Sal, but because I wasn't prepared to confront certain memories yet. Meredith and Sal, Cece and I—we had been one tight gang once upon a time. There had been dinners, shows, a ton of laughs, vacations together to the Caribbean. And somewhere in there among the good times it stopped for one of us.

"How is the counselor?" I put in, before the silence became louder than the traffic outside. "I think I read in *Barron's* how he was keeping his name sweet on Wall Street."

"Pop's still acing them." A hand disappeared into his coat and came out with a thin tan box with some gold leafing on it. The box contained oval cigarettes, also tan. "You mind?" he asked, before lighting one.

I nodded at the chunk of heavy blue glass on the corner of the desk. "There's the ashtray," I said. "Pretty expensive poison you got there. Foreign?"

He let the smoke trickle slowly from his nostrils, Continental fashion. "Israeli. A gift from a friend."

"There goes your tennis game."

He shrugged, then leaned forward to drop some ash. "I'm taking up golf. Like Pop says, you can't do business across a net."

"Speaking of which," I said, "maybe we ought to get down to it. Pat told me, according to your father's secretary, the client's name is Holloway." I glanced down at the two signatures on the check sprawled upon the appropriate lines for president and comptroller. Neither officer could be accused of legibility. "Would that be one of the names here?"

"President of Thompson." Young Sal fanned smoke and gave me another of his irresistible grins. "That piece in *People Magazine*, I meant to write you, Ray: very impressive."

I scowled. Some months back at a forgettable bash I wound up in a corner with a lady writer, who flattered me into granting an interview. The upshot was a three-page spread in the magazine with a photograph of me in a black silk shirt, a shoulder rig, what's left of my black hair slicked back with some gunk the photographer happened to have along. My eyes were brazen slits and I looked like I belonged in a comic book; the text of the article had a similar breathless quality. To make matters worse, the lady took liberties, possibly to satisfy her alliterative urges. On the tallest day of my life I never surpassed six-foot-one, although in the article I am suddenly "a hunk, a heartthrob standing six-foot-three, a dangerous mix of menace and charm present in his jade-green eyes." My eyes in fact are hazel, and as to the hunk-and-heartthrob business, my widow's peak deepens by the year and the scales tell me my long flirtation with two hundred pounds has been consummated. I have one of those almost vertical noses such as you see on early Greek statues, which may be a genetical reverberation from a great-great-grandmother, said to be a full-blooded Cherokee. The quarter-moon scars beneath my right eye aren't the consequence of combat in Vietnam, as the article postulated, but resulted from a street fight with a kid from a nearby neighborhood, over a girl. The kid bit me, so I kneed him in the raisins and flagged a taxi that took me to the family doctor, whose offices were on Metropolitan Avenue, in his home. The bite required twenty stitches. The kid's name was Angelo Scorcese, a guy to be reckoned with these days, his father being a don whose shadow reached beyond the turf he pretended to limit himself to: Queens, the Bronx, Westchester County. If I deserved the teasing smile across the desk, I was not in a mood to prolong it.

"Pat saw the picture. She asked if I was the new Hathaway model. That about sums it up," I said. "So, if you're through having fun."

"I wasn't," he protested, but not convincingly. "Okay, maybe a little. But if I didn't know you, Ray, reading the list of luminaries you've handled, I'd be impressed. Honestly. This guy Holloway, he thinks you're one hombre. Pop said he told the guy you wouldn't be interested in the job, but he insisted."

"Power of the press for you. Suppose you tell me what the gentleman has in mind."

"I can do better than that." He stubbed out the tan cigarette, bent, hoisted the oxblood attaché case he'd brought with him onto his lap. A smell of spanking-new leather drifted across the desk. Sal DeLorio, Jr., held up a white plastic cassette and said, "How about letting the gentleman speak for himself?"

I brought out a tape deck, plugged it in, popped the cassette into place, and leaned a finger on the play button. The take-up spool revolved slowly at first, then sped up. Braked tires screamed on the boulevard and young Sal's eyes locked with mine. The refrigerator wheezed, coughing forth coolant. And then we were listening to Mr. Holloway.

A man could be heard clearing his throat. A prolonged growl luxuriating in its power to still whatever audience it had. Then came the voice—and what a voice. Even on the cheap cassette the enunciation emerged crisply, the delivery poised and commanding, the vowels shaped according to Ivy League precepts, every word a facet of light shimmering in the majestic river of his baritone.

"My name is Eric Holloway, Mr. Sommer, and I'm told you're a professional. I hope so. I am in no mood to tolerate failure. The matter I am about to discuss, as I trust you will agree, does not lend itself to calm and reason. I ask you to bear with me.

"Simply put, my business interests keep me absent from the country for prolonged periods of time, so that it is only now that I've learned I have a deeply . . . a deeply troubled daughter.

"It would appear that Julie has become a habitual runaway since the death of my wife. A day or two, a weekend, sometimes a long weekend, that's been the pattern. My guess is a combination of threats and bribes kept the housekeeper silent. Saw herself in a no-win situation, her word against Julie's. My daughter is a spirited, clever child, Mr. Sommer, no doubt an accomplished liar. And has, I'm afraid, more than a little of her father's manipulative nature. Even her mother found it difficult to control her.

"This time she's been gone for ten days. Naturally, before terminating her, I debriefed the housekeeper. What she confessed Julie's diary confirmed. In graphic detail. I . . . burned . . ."

The tape turned wordlessly. What might have been
sniffing was faintly audible. I touched the stop button
and dug my fingers into the back of my neck, thinking.
Young Sal flicked his eyes my way, then back down at
whatever was inside the briefcase. *Debriefed?* Holloway
didn't introduce himself with a military rank; possibly
he was with the foreign service in some capacity. Except
that he had said "business interests." All right. American
businessmen abroad, especially one sounding as inflated
as this bird, made it a point to imbibe with the embassy
types. Speak the lingo of the ambassador and his staff, it
paid dividends if you found yourself in a jam.

Young Sal, after depositing the briefcase on the carpet
beside his chair, seemed to be having a problem getting
comfortable. Finally, he took out one of his tan cigarettes and tamped it halfheartedly on the back of his
hand.

"This Holloway," I said. "How well's your father know
him?"

He shook his head. "From what I gather, there's some
history between them, but strictly business."

"Uh-huh." I took a hand from my cheek, let it drop.
"You don't know the guy, do you?"

"Ray, what I know about Pop's business you could fit
on the head of a pin and not disturb a single dancing
angel."

"Whatever that means," I said, "it doesn't exactly answer the question."

He fixed me with a frown, his face cocked a little, still
tamping the cigarette. "Guilty as charged. No, I don't
know anyone by the name of Holloway. Why should I?"

"No reason you should. No reason at all," I said. Maybe
I simply needed to hear the sound of a voice other than
Holloway's, something that wasn't pitched at me from
center stage. On the other hand, for a check like the one
on my desk, I guess if he wanted to do *Hamlet,* I'd sit
through it. I put the tape in motion, there was more of
the sniffing, then once again the sonorous Mr. Holloway.
But with an edge.

"She works the theater district," the voice went on,
"has a pimp—I believe that's the polite designation—by
the name of Ramone. No last name. She goes into Man-

hattan, uh, stays a few days, comes home. It's kicks, apparently, for spending money. From what I read in the diary, no hard drugs are involved, but they all fall prey to it sooner or later, do they not? It's how the sewer rats and bottom feeders operate, the Ramones of this world. Scavenging bastards.

"The point is, amigo—pardon me, Mr. Sommer—I do not yet believe the worst. I believe my daughter's alive, and I want your assistance. Her health, her whole future depend on it. I have contacted a doctor in Switzerland, who has agreed to take her case, but first we've got to find her.

"I need to know where she stays when she's not . . . where she stays when she sleeps. I'm not asking you, or any member of your agency, to perform a kidnapping. Simply locate her, and inform my attorney, Mr. De-Lorio. Arrangements have been made that do not expose you in any way to litigation.

"In your possession as you listen to this should be a check to cover your retainer. I happen to know it's more, considerably more, than your going rate, but I have found that urgent matters require extreme measures.

"I have enclosed an envelope of snapshots. The pictures aren't ones I would have chosen; however, they have the virtue of being the most recent. She is eighteen years old, Mr. Sommer. She is my life. I want her on a plane for Geneva within seventy-two hours. Time enough for a man of your abilities to assist me. Still time enough for me to stop payment on that check, if you don't."

Without a word young Sal passed the envelope across the desk.

The photographs were amateurish shots of a freckled, top-heavy young woman striking jailbait poses in a pair of cutoff jeans and what looked to be a man's tank-top undershirt scissored off to expose her flat, white tummy. The styles these days, the undershirt might have been a pricey item from Saks or Bloomie's. Her hair was a shade of red I hadn't encountered since acid went out of fashion. Chopped close around the ears, it bristled on top in a cockscomb effect, a coiffure you could duplicate instantly by grabbing the live end of one-ten. The eyebrows were something too: scarlet arches that peaked halfway up her forehead in a parody of astonishment. She had a nice little flipped-up nose, if you were in the market for that look. Her lips were worked into a naughty pout, but her eyes were flat, absent of shine, like coins that were almost as old as her profession.

I turned the photos over. The developer had stamped them in January of this year. I tossed the envelope of pictures across the desk to young Sal, asking him to look at them. While he did that I listened to the whine and roar on the boulevard and prodded the check absently with the pen I was using to take notes. A couple of red flags tickled my interest. One being the use of company funds to finance a strictly private investigation. The president of a corporation has some spending discretion certainly, but it stops a long way from funding a search for his daughter. I would have loved to eavesdrop on the conversation that persuaded a comptroller, a mouse by profession, to take the lion-size risk of putting his balls on the dotted line. But what was done was done. If I took the case, it was up to Holloway and his conscience, or a creative CPA, to explain the expenditure to the stockholders.

Something else intrigued me: no mention of the police. Not only had Missing Persons not been contacted, Mr. Holloway offered no rationale for avoiding the authorities (and there was considerable: bureaucratic foot dragging, public exposure, to name the most obvious). It was as if the law didn't exist. A curious citizen, our Mr. Holloway.

"I dunno, Ray," said young Sal. "The man sounds like a walking asshole, and I've had some experience with the type recently."

"A lot of clients start out sounding that way. To show me they're in charge. Of course, if they were in control of things, they wouldn't have come to see me in the first place. Most of them come around to behaving fairly human. The ones I go on working for do."

He moved his face, about the same distance he raised his eyebrows. "It would seem Pop told the guy wrong. You're taking the case, aren't you?"

"Somehow I don't picture the counselor sending you all the way to Queens on something he's writing off."

The grin was slow in coming, but it came. He was going to travel with a smile like that.

"You know Pop. Could be a client he doesn't want me to meet . . . or a clerk he's got some idea he's going to boff."

I glanced at the sly-eyed gentlemen on the walls and didn't say anything.

'I think he has some vague notion of challenging for a spot in *Guinness*," he said, and laughed a short, hollow laugh. There was an unsettled, squirmy air about him, as if he was having trouble getting comfortable in that chair again. "He can be such a crude bastard," he added bitterly.

"Yes," I said, "he can be. But look at some of the people he grew up with in Woodside. The Scorceses, their old man Joe, he's a capo now, got his fingers in every dirty pie in the borough of Queens. Guys on his street that go by names like Johnny the Geek, Lunchmeat Louie, Bald Frank. Angelo, Joe Scorcese's oldest, they call him the Angel of Death. Bad guys, Sal, professional bone-breakers. Your father has some old-world ideas about women, to be sure, but he's a picture of rectitude next to those guys, and he's had to work at it. I'd say he's done pretty good for a Woodside wop."

Young Sal stared at me. "Six months you don't speak to him, and now you sound like his publicity agent."

"Sometimes things need saying. Mr. Holloway, you heard what he said about his daughter on the tape, how she was his life? That's putting it mildly, how the wop feels about you."

He let his eyes drop, then reached for the stack of photographs, fanned them like playing cards. His lashes were long, almost feminine, dark fans hiding dark soulful eyes. "You think you can find her, the daughter?"

Any of a dozen of my people popped up as candidates to head up the operation. Several were pensioned cops with solid connections into Midtown West, pals still on the force that might have a useful file or snitch in exchange for the opportunity to warm my box seats at Shea, especially with the Dodgers coming to town. Scully, Moran, Venetucci, Boyle . . .

"If she's alive," I said, "and that's no small if."

Hendricks, Duvallier, Goldman . . . Still riffling names, but kidding myself. I wasn't going to use any of them. This was going to be my baby.

"Here," I said, dating and signing our standard contract. "You initial my copy as proxy for your father. I'll hang on to the cassette, in case Mr. Holloway proves to be all of that walking asshole you said he sounded like."

He picked up the sheets of verbiage and studied them. "You believe," he said, "in three years I'll be able to read this nonsense?"

"Uh-huh. And write better nonsense."

The prospect did not disenchant him. He packed it all away in the oxblood attaché case and stood up, and I came around the desk to get a handful of beard, slap him softly on the cheek.

"Maybe you'll get up to see us this weekend?" he suggested. "Some tennis, see if you can still lob me to death."

I touched my breast pocket, where the check from Thompson Avionics resided along with the pictures of Julie Holloway. "If I don't, here's twenty-five thousand reasons."

Going out my office behind the kid, I looked back over my shoulder, tapped by another thought. It wasn't the money at all. No, the reason had more to do with staring too long into the sly eyes of the gentlemen on the walls: every one of them looking just stupid enough to believe himself immune from the consequences of desire.

2

We went along the hall to the stairs at the back. There's a landing halfway down, where the staircase turns in on itself, and a window that overlooks a gravel parking area. Forsythia worth seeing swarmed up a slope at the far end of the lot, and below it, nosed against the back, was the same chocolate-colored van that was there when I arrived, when the yellow blossoms were virtually trembling from the activity of honeybees. The same legs in the same sloppy khaki trousers projected from beneath the rear bumper, and if the frame hadn't been glued to the building by successive layers of paint, I could have raised the window and probably heard the same inarticulate muttering that I was sure were curses rippling out across the gravel. The glass in the window needed cleaning, but it was serviceable enough to give us pause before the other thing of beauty below.

Red paint gleamed like a fashion model's lipstick. It was low-slung, all beveled surfaces, and as still as a stick of dynamite. It probably wouldn't top a hundred mph backing out of a garage. Just looking at it made the other parked vehicles blur, as if from the velocity of its beauty. My little gadabout coupe had the appearance of something looking for a hole to crawl into. The muttering mechanic beneath the chocolate-colored van must have been asleep or jealous not to grab the opportunity to gawk at a turbocharged Porsche.

"It's a 944," said young Sal, his head bent next to my shoulder, touching the flame from his lighter to a tan cigarette. "The budget Porsche. Or is that an oxymoron?

11

Personally, I think we underestimate the German sense of humor."

I looked at him. He was plugged into millions, and yet the kid had his head screwed on. "Graduation gift?" I said.

"From Pop. Take it for a spin?"

"Maybe another time." We started down the remainder of the stairs. "But if I were your age, a car like that, it'd be scary how good I'd feel."

We passed through the conference room and into the area shared by Martina and Pat. Martina—I called her Marty a lot—was a Czech émigré, who came in three mornings a week to relieve Pat of the more tedious bookkeeping chores. Pat Connor had been with me practically since day one, when the agency was a rented room with a phone and a post office box in Forest Hills, for the prestige, when most of the money came from serving papers in neighborhoods where warrants were as common as colds, but not that easy to pass on. Pat was all in black today, a short-sleeve ensemble big at the shoulders, the skirt snug beneath her knees. She had that milky, silken skin they are killing for these days in the fashion mags, along with long-lashed opulent eyes (the color determined by her choice of contact lenses), and a buoyant excess of flesh that was periodically starved off. She liked her happy hours and men with glib tongues, who vanished after a few dates, and that's what did her in. I looked at her hair—frosted, electric—and began to think a fellow could clean up with the right patter and a shiny cattle prod. Electroshock coifs were it. Martina, from her desk in the corner between a wall map and the safe, pretended to scrutinize her computer screen. "You haf an admirer, Patricia."

"Oh?" But Pat went on sorting the mail.

"The hair," I said. "Something new?"

"Not really, I've had it all my life."

Young Sal leaned over her desk, holding the cigarette behind his back. "I like feisty women."

"Be still, my heart," Pat simpered, feigning the part of a sitcom Southern belle.

I handed Pat the check with the deposit slip to put in the safe. Without looking up, she swiveled in her chair to pass the check across a partition of filing cabinets to Martina to put in the safe. Excellent. Our chain of command was intact.

I escorted Sal to the door that opened onto the waiting room. At her desk Pat pressed a button that electronically released the latch. The room wasn't much: a black leather love seat and director chairs, black leather stretched on tubular chrome. There was a low glass table with back issues of *Smithsonian* strewn about. Near the ceiling in two corners cameras were mounted for Pat to monitor visitors. Because most of our clients now are interviewed on their turf, for their convenience, the room had lapsed into a lounge for sore-ankled postmen, for meter readers seeking a haven from the elements. The ebony coat stand Cece acquired at an auction up in Connecticut stood coatless and skeletal next to Sal DeLorio, Jr., as he reached for the door to step outside. Morning light broke across his face, bright and harsh, leaching out the smile there. "Ray? Twenty-five thousand reasons don't add up to one good excuse. Unless you're just afraid I'll whip your ass."

The air outside smelled like a bled tire.

The door snapped sharply shut behind him. The coat stand cut a lean profile. A steal, Cece had said, pointing to the chased-silver inlay. Cece didn't pay top dollar for anything that wasn't a steal.

Pat held out a small stack of mail for me. I took it, glanced absently through it, stopped. There was a shade of blue about her eyes. "Pat?"

She moved things around on her desk, watching her hands do the moving. "I'll be up in a few minutes, huh?"

"Sure, fine." I looked once more through the photographs of Julie Holloway, selected one, and dropped it on her desk. "I want dupes of this for everyone in the agency. Another dozen for backup. I'll dictate the précis when you come up."

I went. I climbed the stairs, batting the mail against my hip, and paused on the landing as young Sal came into view below. Approaching his car from the opposite side were two men in white sneakers, dark Latin faces, gold chains, and designer jeans, the stitching on the denim almost as bright as the gold. One pumped a fist at the sky, and they rocked on their rubber soles in shared hilarity. Sal came around the rear of the Porsche, stopped to fish for the keys in the pocket of his navy-blue suit. The Latinos, still celebrating, danced closer, but there was another movement that drew my attention, and that's when reasoning caught up with common sense. A guy beneath a van and not a toolbox in sight. A guy that hasn't moved in all this time is suddenly scuttling out on the gravel, showing wood and blue steel.

I shot a foot into the lower window and the glass disintegrated and Sal was sharply visible in the jagged maw.

"Get outta there, Sally! It's a hit!"

The back doors of the van burst open. Two more of them crouched above the one with the sawed-off shotgun, only these were equipped with assault weapons, curved cartridge clips that were the signature of AK-47s, what Charlie used on us in Nam. The first blast from the shotgun knocked the boys in gold onto the hood of the Porsche. Sal dived away from the door. The second blast I only heard plummeting down the stairs. The AKs started their vicious chatter. Glass exploded on the landing.

Pat had 911 on the line, shouting our address, and Martina was fumbling the nine-millimeter from the safe.

"Three armed men," I said, and Pat repeated to the dispatcher. I chambered a round in the Beretta. "Brown van, fairly new. License number six-two-four Gamma Lambda something. V or W, Victor Walter. New York plates. And we're gonna want medics."

I plunged through the door onto the sidewalk of the boulevard, into the turbulent roar of ten lanes of fractious traffic. A 747 descending on LaGuardia drifted overhead with all the racket of a paper glider, its monster shadow slipping over me as I ran along the sidewalk away from the boulevard. Across the street, the barber, bald as my coat stand, covered a yawn, waved drowsily from his empty shop. Probably mistook the AKs, if he even heard them, for the sound of rap on somebody's ghetto blaster. I ran with the pistol pressed to my hip.

Gaining the corner of the office, I stopped, got my shoulder blades up against the gritty shingles, and breathed deeply through my mouth. I was conscious of tears in the corners of my eyes from running. I dropped to a crouch and swung out with my arms extended, the Beretta extended beyond my hands. I saw the back of the van, the doors closed, diminishing. I sprinted across the gravel and got my wrists on the roof of the Porsche to squeeze off three rounds at the driver's side of the van.

There was no sound in the world for a second or two except the yawing after-roar of gunfire—my own.

But the van kept going. I saw the tires smoke as it hit pavement. I saw it swerve and disappear.

Spent casings glittered in the gravel.

3

Shadowing the first squad car to arrive was an unwashed white station wagon equipped with enough aerial to intercept police dispatches anywhere in the five boroughs. Three men piled out. Two of them brandished Canons, camera straps slung bandolier fashion across their chests. They went to work quickly, kneeling and sighting and shooting and moving on. Both chewed bubble gum and produced impressive pink bladders. One of them was telling the other he didn't know shit if he didn't know Robert Frank. The third one, who wasn't much older, hung back.

His black eyes drooped beneath heavy lids, his black, crinkled hair had fled at the temples, prematurely stranding a swatch. He wore a seersucker suit, a narrow charcoal tie over his white shirt, smooth charcoal shoes with short laces and thin soles, a gold bracelet on his left wrist. He worked the nail of his pinkie behind a canine tooth, dug around a bit, brought the nail out for inspection. Whatever he'd extracted excited him enough to go on breathing. He shook out a cigarette and surveyed the carnage with a look of dismissal. Evidently, the death scene did not live up to his critical standards.

He sauntered over. "Arnold Wittgenstein," he said. "I'm a reporter for the *Daily Crusader*. And you would be?"

The boys with the Canons were having a field day with only two blues and both of them occupied keeping civilians from mucking up the crime scene. An EMS van arrived, conferred briefly with the officer on the sidewalk, wheeled away, reactivating its siren.

"Sir?" persisted Arnold Wittgenstein. "Uh, you there with the big gun in your hand?"

One of the photographers crouched, duckwalked toward Sal, where he lay facedown in the gravel, my coat over his head. What was left of it. After adjusting the lens, he took the camera from his eye, put his lean, eager face on his shoulder blade to look my way, issued another impressive bubble beneath his deadpan eyes. "This your coat?" he said.

I nodded.

"Paper'll pay for it," he said, reaching for it. "Whatever you say it's worth."

"How about your life?" I said, resting the nine-millimeter where he could see it on the roof of the Porsche.

"G'won, Lennie!" hissed Arnold Wittgenstein. "He's already popped two spics, you want he should go for the hat trick?"

The one called Lennie inhaled the bubble and retreated, muttering he wasn't any fucking war correspondent.

I said: "For the record, Arnold, I didn't put any of these bodies here. The name's Ray Sommer. Thanks for spooking Lennie."

"Nothing," said Arnold Wittgenstein, fitting a fresh cigarette between thin, bloodless lips. He flipped open a lighter, flipped it shut without touching off a flame, and peeled the cigarette from his lips. "Sommer . . . Ray Sommer . . . Why do I think I know that name?"

I looked at young Sal on the ground, the legs tangled grotesquely. He hadn't gotten far before the artillery caught up with him. The other two were sprawled where death had surprised them, across the hood of the Porsche. Glass from the shattered windshield powdered their corpses, a shroud that scattered the light like cheap sequins. The unforgettable odor of robbed life prompted some measured breathing even as I brushed at my eyes. Another blue-and-white with an arcade-game siren swung into the lot, continued turning, and took up a position on the sidewalk, its flashers pulsing, more video effects. I removed the clip from the butt of the Beretta, ejected the live round from the chamber, pocketed those, and put the gun in the hand of Arnold Wittgenstein.

"Fuck's this for?" he yelped.

"Wave it at Lennie, he even thinks about moving my jacket, and I'll give you an eyewitness account, exclusive, soon as I make a phone call."

His lips backed off his canines in what was meant to be a smile, although it conveyed all the warmth of a punctured hot-water bottle. Things like sympathy, trust, and the milk of human kindness had long ago leaked out of Arnold Wittgenstein.

"Deal," he said. His grin took on a wolfish cast. "Sommer. You're in the protection racket, aren't you? The heavy hitters hire you to protect their bods. Mind if I ask, any the stiffs here happen to be a client?"

"Mind if I ask how you'd like a nine-millimeter enema?" I said, and strode off, hearing the one called Lennie say, "Will you look at the gawkers? Arbus'd have a field day. Diane Arbus, Clyde. Jesus, where'd you learn to hold a camera, doing shoots for ladies' lingerie?"

In the crowd along the sidewalk I recognized the barber, frowning, and the Greek, who owned a coffee-shop newsstand that specialized in inedible fare, and his morning-shift waitress Kitty, which meant the Greek's fifteen-year-old son Costos had the run of the shop and his face buried in the latest *Penthouse*. Kitty gave a shy half wave. A little apart from the crowd, the mailman in his gray Bermudas and pith helmet lounged on the handle of his mail cart like a man of leisure looking over the back nine.

The ranking officer did not like the idea of my leaving the scene, but she relented, gave me five minutes to make the phone call.

As it turned out, I didn't need even that much time. I climbed the stairs. The glass underfoot sounded like delicate bones being broken. From my office I saw the traffic move in its relentless, predictable fashion. Fists shook through open windows, horns brayed, the human comedy hurtled on. I let some Jack Daniel's trickle down my gullet, but it didn't change the taste in my mouth. The smug gentlemen on the walls weren't much help either. I stared at the telephone, loosening the knot of my tie. "All right, smart guy," someone said, "talk to the man. See if you can't destroy Sal DeLorio in twenty words or less."

The someone was me. I talked to the man. I did it in less than ten.

4

The lieutenant in charge was polite, methodical, and for lack of a better word, dapper, which is no mean feat for a guy with a fifty-inch waist. A hard plastic name bar attached to the breast pocket of his cream-colored suit identified him as *Lt. Cox, Homicide.* He reviewed the jottings he'd made in his spiral pad and said, " 'Shooters—two Latins, one black. Possibly Jamaican.' " And looked up, pulling on his lip. Then went on: "Because of why, he had long hair?"

"Long," I said, "and it looked twisted, like dreads. Dreadlocks. Two, three seconds is all the look I got, Lieutenant, so if you're even wondering, from that distance, could I testify to it in court, the answer is no. Could have been a wig, or he was a flat-chested broad, Caucasian, spent a lot of time at the beach or a tanning parlor. Same story with the Latins. The license plate and van, I'd swear to those."

"That'll work. My book, witnesses suck. Even a half-ass attorney can do a number on them. What I like is evidence."

A pale fedora fit his head, his whole persona, so perfectly that it required an effort of will to imagine him hatless. Beneath the turned-down brim was a brow creased to depths to suggest something more went on under that hat than perspiration. He possessed a bulldog's mug: squashed nose, pendulous jowls, bottom lip riding the upper, especially as he contemplated me. He was a stout, slow-moving man wearing wide lapels and a wide paisley tie in a year when neither was fashionable.

He exhibited the Beretta, which he had confiscated

from Wittgenstein. Its eight and one-half inches of lethal steel rested lumpishly inside a transparent plastic bag. "You dropped this on the young journalist?"

"It's licensed."

"I'm certain it is." He held it up to his eyes. "Nine-millimeter parabellum, can be fired in double- or single-action mode. Nice balance. With the extra-large-capacity magazine. Fifteen rounds?"

"Plus a round in the chamber," I said.

He parted the plastic to sniff inside the bag. "Been fired recently."

"Three rounds at the van, trying to slow it down."

His lower lip overrode the upper. "And?"

"One slug might've struck glass."

Lieutenant Cox putted gravel soccer fashion with the side of his white patent-leather shoe, the stones skittering under the police line that separated us from the public.

"Well, you can tell me all about it down to the Hall," he said, sounding like it was a minor matter. The Hall was Boro Hall on Queens Boulevard, the seat of justice for the fiercely proud principalities that compose Queens. "You exercise use of deadly force, you got to tell the city why in triplicate."

"I understand," I said.

He made as if to swallow his upper lip for some moments, then fished a thin, red wafer from his suit pocket and put it in his mouth.

"Dried plum, isn't it?" I said.

A faint light of astonishment quivered in his eyes. "Yeah, as a matter of fact. Picked up a taste for 'em when I walked a beat in Chinatown. Loaded with vitamin C. Chinks feed it to their kids like candy. Guy Pauling, some kinda Nobel thinker, guy swears by the stuff. The vitamin C."

"Your finer Chinese restaurants use the dried plum in their sweet-and-sour. The clip joints use ketchup."

"You shittin' me."

"My ex-wife, she was into authentic."

"Huh. Fucking ketchup." He fed himself another wafer and scratched some more in the spiral pad. "Lessee. Young DeLorio visited your office, but not for personal reasons. Correct?"

"Correct. As I told you, simply to deliver a business offer, and if I accepted, to pick up the paperwork. Simple as that."

"The offer being?"

"Lieutenant, please. The 'private' in my job description, if it means anything, means my clients have a right to expect some protection, or at the very least, a degree of discretion. You show evidence to a judge to warrant a subpoena, we'll take it from there."

"Okay. Let's not get a hard-on. You want to jack me around, feel free. Oh," he added, feeling about in one of the lower pockets of his suit coat. He hefted the Beretta in the plastic bag once more, and smiled. It was the kind of smile that did not wish me health or happiness, and certainly not a good night's sleep. "Handing this to the boy reporter, that was cute. Not smart, but cute."

"Was it?"

"Muddy the prints on a potential murder weapon gonna be a pain in the ass for the DA, it comes to that. Tell me that train didn't pass through your station."

"Never."

His bottom lip crept north again and his eyes grew small. Even with my coat off, my white shirt was clinging in the heat, but Cox looked perfectly comfortable. I began to wonder if he wasn't a marvel of modern deodorants: a fat man who didn't sweat. He said, "Ray, you don't never want to say never. Even a asshole politician knows that."

As promised, Arnold Wittgenstein got his story, but an exclusive on the truth wasn't what he was shopping for. No, he was in the market for wild surmise. But because he had kept his camera crew away from Sal's body, I indulged him. The lad lived for insidious connections.

"But you wouldn't rule them out?" he said, suggesting another outfit from the academy of terrorism. No one, apparently, was to be excluded from the list of suspects. We had about covered the globe.

"Arnold, listen to the words: I . . . don't . . . know. Viciousness is the fashion today, whether it's drugs or politics."

"Hold that thought," he said, pinching off the remains of a cigarette and, with an absent flick, spinning it in the direction of the bodies on the hood of the Porsche. The butt landed and flared for an instant between the bloodied shapes, brief and harsh as an obscenity. "You hear or see something makes you think this was political? Ray, we talking local, or we talking international?"

"We aren't talking, Ace; you are. And what you're talking is garbage. What I said, the dealers and liberationists, they went to the same school. They kill with equal enthusiasm."

"So you don't want to say."

"Say what?"

"But you wouldn't rule them out, would you?"

I didn't say anything. He was pushing the microphone so close I could smell it. It was a whiff of the corruption power is said to beget. Hot plastic that was not new, not clean, that had recorded not just the words but the odor in the air of every dirty place it had been intruded.

"You are making me very tired, Ace."

"Fuck's that supposed to mean?"

"It means that in the interests of civility and plain common sense, you have decided to conclude the interview."

"This the thanks I get for risking my job?"

I thought about feeding him his microphone, but that'd be playing into his long suit. "Go on," I said, "practice your indignation somewhere else."

"Some fucking thanks," he said. For a man so incensed, he loped off toward the Greek's, where his buddies were holding down a pay phone, with a look of satisfaction. The public's constitutional right to be outraged and horrified had not been abrogated.

Another squad car, its cherry top throwing splashes of crimson across the sun-drenched brick of the barbershop, swung into view, a long gray Rolls purring behind it. The cop tapped the wha-wha pedal of the siren to clear the civilians. The chrome nose of the Rolls, its polished surface scattering sunlight like a drunken monarch awarding peerages, hove above the mangled bumper of the blue-and-white, swung inside of it, and lurched across the sidewalk onto the gravel. The chauffeur sprang nimbly from the front the instant the tires crunched to rest. Wearing a ruffled white blouse buttoned to the throat, black trousers that flared jodhpur fashion and buttoned at the ankles above chartreuse socks and black hiker boots. The lad wore a hat like a yacht captain's, except it was all black, but even so, some of his hair was visible, and it had been dyed to match the color of his socks. One of Meredith's arty protégés would be my guess. The rear door did not so much open in his hands as revolve with the flourish of a matador performing a perfect veronica. As television crews converged, pelting the air with the usual, shabby interrogation, out stepped Salvatore DeLorio.

Visible for an instant, he vanished behind a swell of reporters. Somebody with a minicam scrambled atop the bonnet of the Rolls for better vantage. The green-haired chauffeur, attempting to repel the invader, took a shoe in the chops for his trouble.

A phalanx of blues, holding their nightsticks in both hands, parted the press.

Sal crouched beneath the police line, between the bright orange pennants fluttering from it. Lieutenant Cox fell into step behind him.

He still had a good puss going for him, Sal. Fine patrician nose, the genuine article, not a rebuilt. Quick, ebony eyes that missed nothing, the saving grace of a Golden Gloves middleweight and inexhaustible womanizer. The full Sicilian lips always pushed a little forward, expectant, anticipating that whatever punches life threw his way he could deflect with a laugh, a lawsuit, or his fists. And for the most part it had worked. (Even his loss in the Golden Gloves finals on points remained an item hotly debated, twenty-five years later, in the betting parlors along Grand Avenue.) The only scar he had to show was an apostrophe of sleek white tissue knifing through the tweedy growth of his right eyebrow, and it hadn't come from boxing. I should know. Cece and I had been there the night Meredith unloaded—after two Bombay martinis, followed by several glasses of a robust Italian red with the scungilli and veal. The maid, Char-

lotte, was clearing away the crumbs of cheesecake, the coffee
cups, asking would we care for another Drambuie . . . Sal,
plucking a white rose from the centerpiece and placing
it behind his wife's ear, said, "How about some billiards
where I'm allowed to smoke?"—continuing his story
about some self-righteous state senator by the name of
Winslow, who was not simply an ass, but a philandering
one. Got that far when Meredith seized the neck of the
dead red, broke the body of the bottle across the edge of
the marble table, and went for him.

All Sal did was shake his head.

All she did was open him up enough that it required
seven stitches reluctantly zipped into place by their
neighbor, a specialist in tummy tucks, lifts, and bust im-
plants. And whose allegiance to the Hippocratic oath
faded considerably at the fashionable hour to be dining.

Meredith had said to her husband, clubbing him with
the wicked crown of glass, in her soft, cartoonish voice,
"Look in a mirror, you son of a bitch." Not shouting it,
almost in a tone that suggested concern for his grooming
habits.

And Sal had said as the blood gushed and he held her
wrists above her head, "I love a woman with spirit!"

Then said into the phone to the fancy-pants surgeon:
"Brent, I don't care who you're hosting from the Hamp-
tons, you gotta lady in Scarsdale her left nipple points
forty-five degrees off true, it looks like she suckled Bigfoot, and she's suing you right down to the short hairs.
She wins the suit, Brent, you'd have to be General Mo-
tors to afford your malpractice. How's my firm—excuse
me? Five minutes will be fine, Brent."

Now Sal said, "Ray." A hand on my shoulder, head
pressed against the knot of my tie.

Lieutenant Cox removed his fedora, discreetly shooed
the tape-and-string people away from the boy's body.
The hat left a mark like a welt. His brow was dusted
with freckles, and some reddish-blond hairs were flattened there, like snakes surprised on a thoroughfare.

Kneeling beside the body, Sal lifted my jacket, looked,
crossed himself, covered his son's head. He stayed there
awhile. The tailored suit couldn't hide the shaking. He
got to his feet, straightened the knot of his tie. Ruby cuff

links danced the light around. He approached with a kind of dignity, subdued yet suggesting he was capable of any street move: from horse trading to a shot in the nuts. Because of contacts my old man had, my brother Matt and I witnessed as kids the loss Sal took in the Garden on that long ago afternoon. He had lost a lot more than that this time, but I recognized the fine defiance in the glistening eyes.

"Sal," I said, "Lieutenant Cox."

"D. James Cox," the lieutenant put in.

They shook hands solemnly. D. James Cox put his hat back where it belonged, glanced past Sal's shoulder at an antsy type in a white shirt, black trousers, carrying a black satchel, and gave him a barely perceptible nod. The coroner fidgeted across the gravel, knelt beside the boy's body. His bald head bobbed as he worked. Two men in khaki uniforms started unloading body bags from the morgue wagon. Finished scribbling, the coroner removed one of Sally's shoes, then the sock. When he hastened off, I could see the tag attached to the naked toe. The work of a minute, recording the end of a lifetime.

"We have anything?" Sal addressed the question to Lieutenant Cox. "Something in the nature of a witness to this bloodbath?"

"Me," I said, and told him what I'd seen. D. James Cox, who had already interviewed me, listened as if he hadn't.

Sal nodded, listening, then picked at his eyebrow, where the scar was. "Assault weapons and a shotgun," he said. "No question about that, is there, Lieutenant?"

"Looks like, yeah. Awaiting ballistics is all."

Sal said, "The modus operandi certainly suggests it wasn't a mugging. You got Latins, and right across the boulevard you got Jackson Heights, and Jackson Heights, you might as well be in downtown Bogotá. Colombians, Cox. Inferences?"

The lieutenant adjusted his hat a millimeter. "Guy with the shotgun, according to Ray here, was black."

"So they hired a jig shooter."

"Uh-uh," I said. "The other way around."

"See, Mr. DeLorio, the way Ray tells it, the black guy is the outside guy. Hit like this, it's the outside guy is

running the show." He shrugged, looked at me, then Sal
DeLorio. "Just the way it's done."

Sal took a step toward the lieutenant, his chin inches
from Cox, and glared. "You patronizing me?"

Cox said nothing.

"I hope I'm not intimidating you, Lieutenant. Because
I've got juice. And I won't have any weenies handling
this investigation. I want fucking results. Me, I'm in your
shoes, I'd look real hard at the Colombians."

"All due regard for your present state of mind, Mr.
DeLorio, you say Colombians, that don't tell me boo.
Like, some guy in the Longshoremen's gets offed, every
wise guy says Mafia. So, I'm gonna do what, arrest Little
Italy, quarantine Woodside, Ridgewood, Rego Park,
Middle Village? Invade Westchester? Declare war on
New Jersey? Throw a net over Nassau County? Mr.
DeLorio, what I suggest, you grieve for your son with
your loved ones, don't dirty your feet trying to wear my
shoes. Ray, at the Hall, say inna hour?"

I said I'd be there.

Sal DeLorio was already striding away. I watched him
flick the dark glasses over his eyes before he knelt beneath the police line. I saw the reporters converge and
the cops closing ranks to screen them off. The green-
haired chauffeur with a discolored jaw held the door
of the Rolls with the flair of a fashion monger unveiling the
fall line. Ignoring the shouting, Sal bent inside, vanished.

5

First glimpsed from the boulevard, Boro Hall shapes up as a smooth-looking chunk of municipal architecture, white stone and tall dark glass situated in a field of emerald grass, a functionary's paradise. From a distance it is a sterile and forbidding presence, not unlike the mausoleums in our borough built for the bones of gangsters. Come a little closer and you see the cigarette butts, candy wrappers, the beer cans and shattered half-pints that embellish the lawn much as eczema could be characterized as a facial enhancer. Closer still, you notice the panel of glass in the far-right door radiating a cobweb of cracks. Entering, any vestige of hope, pride, or dignity dissipates. Marble floors and vaulted ceiling promote the majesty of the law; vandalized urinals flooding piss across the men's room represent a second opinion. Outside the courtrooms attorneys huddle with clients and family in passionate, even violent exchanges, while the bored articulation of clerks drones off the walls. Up close, being generous, about all you could say was that it was still a functionary's paradise.

I passed courtrooms one through four, dodging and weaving among knots of people, to reach the elevators. I rode up with a couple whose daughter had evidently been apprehended at the wheel of a stolen vehicle. The girl was a sulky but striking young thing, something Oriental about the eyes. She was fortunate her brains weren't splattered in a wreck or by a bullet, but you weren't going to tell her that: she knew her rights. Everybody does these days.

The room that I was deposited in came with recently

painted walls, soundproof tiles in the ceiling, fluorescent lighting behind plastic panels. Windowless, twelve feet on a side, it was the deluxe model. You could tell, because it was color-coordinated, brown on brown. And newly decorated. It lacked the patina of scrunge that is the indelible mark of firmly entrenched bureaucracy.

Brown metal desks faced opposite walls. I sat at one scrutinizing my fingernails, listening to the hum of the AC. With his penny loafers resting on the other desk, Cox's young partner leaned back on two legs of a wooden chair to groom his mustache, flip darts at the board mounted opposite the doorway. The mustache was slick, carefully shaped, modeled after Wyatt Earp. Unlike most cops whose stubby revolvers are clipped to their belts, he carried a nine-millimeter automatic in a shoulder harness beneath his armpit. More cops, the young ones especially, were packing automatics as a hedge against the day they might have to go up against some asshole with an Uzi. The young gunslinger's name was Wallace Fitzsimmons, but his close friends, if that's what Cox was, called him Wall.

I watched him stop the dart throwing long enough to torch the end of a Kool menthol with his butane, squint through smoke to adjust his aim. On corkboard that filled most of the wall facing the door were a host of mug shots to shoot for. Sharp steel and green plastic struck with authority between the eyes of a suspected child molester, who had jumped bail. An average-looking guy in a funny shirt, maybe a little fear showing, looked out from the photograph. Then I realized it wasn't a shirt: the man was a cleric.

"Nice place you got here," I said, to make conversation, take his mind off scumballs. "Decorate it yourself?"

He stroked the foliage on his lip with the tip of a dart and went on ignoring me. It must have been something new they were teaching at the John Jay School of Criminal Justice. Your normal New York cop will chatter like a shortstop.

I tried again, "Corkboard here shows the influence of Braque, I'd say. Little Picasso maybe. Helluva collage, Wall. May I call you Wall?" Guess not. So I studied the board. In addition to the mug shots it was cluttered with notices, the latest departmental regulations regarding arrest procedure, scraps of paper with phone numbers, reminders of court appearances. There were mug shots of Marilyn Buck, front and profile, the only one of the Nyack killers to escape. A cool customer there, with those fashion-model cheekbones that reminded me of my wife. Ex-wife. I noticed there were no dart holes in the lady assassin's portraits. She had escaped in a white Oldsmobile and was considered "armed and dangerous." The last time I saw Cece, her lawyer was assisting her into a yellow cab. She was wearing a black wool suit, the skirt with a daring split that gave me a glimpse of long silken leg before the door closed and the cab shot away from the curb. When I helped her lawyer up out of the snowbank, he said, "Ray, you sonuvabitch, that's felonious assault!" I said, "C'mon Larry, I'm buying. . . ."

I probably would have bought a round for the pathetic cleric in the mug shot not to be alone with the emptiness I felt that day. Or today.

"So," I said, "how long you been a detective, Detective?"

He made a production out of moving his feet from the desk to the floor. In polished chinos and washed-out blue work shirt, no tie, he came off as a snotty grad student slumming as a cop. "You're fulla questions, aren't you?" he said.

"I like the mustache. The longhorn look."

"You having fun, Sommer? Comfortable and everything?"

"Appreciate the concern, Wall. May I call you Wall?"

"No," he snarled, "you can't. What you can do, you can tell me how does a guy in your line of work let three shooters have a picnic right under his fucking nose. It's up to me, I wouldn't give you a license to carry a rake, much less a gun."

I took a deep breath, weighed the pleasure versus the price of slamming him up against a wall, and said, "Thank you for the vote of confidence. I'll remember it."

"You do that."

D. James Cox let the door swing shut behind him and

leaned against it, flattening the fedora's brim at the back, his bulldog nose up in the air. A smirk slithered out from under Wallace Fitzsimmons' mustache. "Hey, Lieutenant," he said, "Mr. Sommer's just telling me what it takes to be a celebrity. Guess what? In his case, the less the better. Sounds almost ecological, you ask me."

Cox said, "Sommer, you like a coffee, a tea, before we get down to it?"

"A coffee extra light would be nice."

"Mine black. Wall?"

"A black and light," grunted Wallace Fitzsimmons, rising.

"Extra light," I said.

"If you please," Cox injected, before the Wall could think of something suitably nasty.

When we were alone, the lieutenant said, "I don't know what it is, but some guys, they like to push your face in it. He bother you much?"

"He worked at it."

"Meaning?"

"He's a kid. He's entitled to a couple rounds gratis. After that, he gets in my face, could be he'd pay a price."

Lieutenant Cox straddled the chair recently vacated by his partner, fed himself a wafer of vitamin C, and rested his forearms on the back of the chair. "Sounds fair," he said. "Now let's talk about you. What goes into the deposition is voluntary, but on the basis of what you told me back in the parking lot there—three rounds at a van allegedly fleeing the scene of a crime, to slow it down?—you might want to think about having your attorney present. A rookie cop for chrissakes, he pulls his piece, it goes into the report there was some kinda threat. Fucking rookie knows that. Otherwise, your case, we're talking reckless endangerment, manslaughter, maybe even murder the DA gets a bug up his ass."

Cox climbed out of the chair and came across the room to perch his fanny on a corner of the desk. He jogged his hat, then peered down the flat ripple of his nose, the cop-to-civilian treatment, the eyes devoid of interest or anger. "My instinct, let a guy know where he stands, he might work with you."

"Three people," I said, "blown away. The van, I saw

something might've been a gun, I wasn't about to wait, see how accurate the dude was. Think a grand jury'd vote to indict?"

"Say it like that, with a straight face," he said, "grand jury'd never get called. Something you should know about me: I ain't interested in a cheap collar. Guys on the force here that specialize in it. My book, they're overpaid meter maids, but I don't run the department."

"It's still Moriarity, isn't it?"

Cox hesitated, like a man on suddenly unfamiliar turf. "You know the inspector?"

"My father . . . they worked together, same unit, robbery division. It was a long time ago. So. Who got dead?"

"Who said anybody got dead?"

"Reckless endangerment, manslaughter, murder—your words—can't apply to the three deaths I'm aware of. Ergo."

"Sign of age"—he sighed—"talking too much."

He reached into his apparently bottomless supply of dried plum and offered me a wafer. I took it.

"We got the van," he said. "Abandoned over on Eightieth Street, under the LIE there, place all the driving-school cars hang out. Gotta dead boy inside, Spanish descent, fits your description beautiful, bullet wound through the triceps, passed into the rib cage. Coulda been fatal, but it's a moot issue, since he got another one, a real beauty, in the right temple, powder burns like burnt toast, gun couldna been more'n a foot away. No question his pals did him, they didn't want excess baggage."

"ID him?"

"No wallet, no cards, nothin' so far. My gut tells me they can run his prints through the feds, Interpol, they won't find jack shit. He was an import. Some jungle rat drafted to do a job, then disappear into the bush."

"Sounds like you're buying into Mr. DeLorio's scenario. Any hard evidence?"

Cox pulled on his bottom lip and let his emotionless eyes roam the high corners of the room. "Well, for starters," he said almost dreamily, "the two dead Spanish boys, we found their car parked a block away. A black Trans Am with the smoked glass, flames painted on the hood. Registration says it belonged to one Teddy Peron.

Nothing on him. But the other dead boy goes by Jesus Hernandez aka Zero and there's a sheet on him, busted two three dozen times, used to sing like Pavarotti for a reduced plea. They're a coupla Puerto Ricans from the Bronx, we pop the trunk of the Trans Am, whadda you know, five kilos wrapped in plastic."

"There's some serious motivation," I said. "That's gotta fetch in the handsome six figures."

Cox's gaze drifted down to meet mine as the door opened and the scent of vending-machine coffee entered. "It's not that kinda scratch," he said. "We're talking five kilos of Garden State gold."

"Weed?" I said.

The Wall distributed the lukewarm, Styrofoam cups. After removing and carefully draping his blue blazer on the back of the chair, he tore a small notch in the plastic lid of his cup, left the lid in place, sipped his coffee through the notch. Cox drank his likewise, stakeout style.

"Weed?" I said again, and my voice sounded the same flutey note of disbelief. "What's to start shooting over?"

"Indeed," remarked Lieutenant Cox.

"That's your hard evidence?"

Lieutenant Cox did that business with his eyes again. He sighed. "Would you want to talk about—off the record—what young DeLorio came to see you for?"

I stayed sitting, but it wasn't easy. "The wandering-eyes act doesn't impress me. You got something on the boy, lay it out, let's look it over." As I spoke Wallace Fitzsimmons struggled to clear his throat. I said, "You might also give your partner here permission to go make wee-wee."

"Lieutenant!"

Cox waved at him absently, but his eyes were grim, intent, and focused on me. He said slowly, as if the effort cost him: "I ain't at liberty."

"Lieutenant, are we, or are we not taking this guy's deposition?"

Cox scratched up under the brim of his hat. "Sure, Wall, round us up a steno, tape machine, whatever."

The young gunslinger almost tore the arms off his blazer getting into it. The slamming door rattled the plastic light panels. A mug shot shuddered against the corkboard and drifted lazily toward the floor. It was the suspected child molester with the punctured face.

"Hotspur," I said, to be saying something.

"If that's Jewish for balls, yeah, the kid's got 'em." He jogged the brim of his hat an infinitesimal distance, then fed himself another wafer of dried plum. "Ray?"

"D.J.?"

"Two more years to my pension. I hear you're a right guy to work for."

I opened my hands, palms up. "I can be. Question is, how do we spend these few precious moments alone?"

6

When I left Boro Hall shortly before noon, I knew this about the victims in the parking lot: Teddy Peron owned a flower shop just off the Grand Concourse, not far from Yankee Stadium, a going concern by all appearances, and that his pal Zero was a career loser. And that in the glove box of Sal DeLorio, Jr.'s, Porsche, close to a pound of quality, uncut cocaine had been found.

Homicide had been instructed by the DA's office to sit on this last piece of information, no doubt until scowling Jimmy Skelton, the Queens district attorney, determined how best to release it to his advantage. A newspaper columnist, an old friend of mine by the name of Danny Belinski, once remarked that public figures must master the art of flashing meaningless smiles, but that Skelton was the only one he knew who flashed meaningless scowls.

By one o'clock Martina had returned from the fast photo shop on Broadway with the duplicates I requested. Julie Holloway straight on, chin at a jaunty angle, back arched, breasts lifting the T-shirt away from her rib cage. I gave Martina the background on the girl and the name of her pimp and told her to get on the phone. I wanted every agent, including those presently on assignment, to know the details and have a photograph before the day was out. Martina stared at the photographs and shook her head. "So hard she works at her depravity."

Pat and I then sifted through the phone calls that had come in while I was out, and I told her which ones I would handle. Finally, she laid her pen next to her stenographer's pad, stretched, and pinched the bridge of her nose, her eyes squeezed shut.

"That do it?" I said.

She nodded, her eyes still closed.

"How about let's phone the deli, have something sent up. See what Martina wants, huh?"

"Jesus, Ray, after this morning? I want to sleep for about forty-eight hours straight."

I looked at her and her eyes looked worse than earlier, and earlier she had looked about cried out. "Look, kiddo, two days from now, you wake up, it's going to be the same world. I'll take a cornbeef on rye, plenty of mustard, garlic dill on the side. Make it two cornbeefs."

She sat up straight in the chair across from me, the one Sal had used, and tried to level me with the violet eyes. For an instant I was reminded of the nineteen-year-old, no-nonsense Catholic girl with incredible breasts and a face out of Renoir. "You mind if I say something?"

"Why break precedent by asking?"

"I know you, Ray. You're pissed. And it's not because the boy was killed—okay, some of it is, awright?—it's because of where it was done. You're thinking about your reputation and I think that sucks."

The flow of flattery was interrupted by a brief electrical burp, followed by Martina's voice on the intercom, asking for permission to admit the glaziers. I gave it and got up to close the door of my office. I walked to the window overlooking the boulevard and watched two men in coveralls unloading glass from a van parked next to a fire hydrant. They looked legitimate.

Back in my chair, I studied her face, then leaned forward. "Anything else?" I asked.

Tears clung to her eyes. "I'd like to tear your heart out right now."

"You might not find one."

"Bastard!"

"Pat, talk to me. This isn't you."

She put her head down and pounded the desk, once, with her fist. "Dexter, Wells on Park Avenue South, they've been after me for months. Today, this morning, I was going to give you my notice. But now, shit . . ." She snatched pen and pad and went out the door sobbing, slamming it behind her. It banged open a moment later. "I think I forgot, or did I tell you there was a call for you from Meredith DeLorio?"

"You forgot," I said. "You did just fine."

"I'm sorry?"

"You did just fine, kiddo."

"That was two cornbeefs on rye and a garlic dill?"

"Yes," I said. "Now, if you'll excuse me."

I listened to her heels chopping along the carpet and descending, beyond hearing, and then I dialed the Manhattan exchange, told the receptionist when she answered who I was and wished to speak to. Wesley Havens Dexter, one half of Dexter, Wells Private Investigators, "We Specialize in Industrial Espionage," came on the line. Wesley and I had been fellow grunts in Vietnam, in I Corps with the Third Marines. I did my time and split, but word had it Wesley rotated into the Company to do a deep-cover tour. He surfaced, at least in my bailiwick, a couple years ago and formed a pricey Park Avenue security firm. "Raymondo," he said, "that really you?"

"Me, Wes."

"You dog-breath sonuvabitch, whatta you up to, sweatbro?"

"Surviving, sweatbro. And I don't like it, your company trying to steal my support, do you copy? Name is Pat Connor. Don't fuck with me on this one."

"Hey! Since when did you inherit King Kong's balls? Something you should know. She came to us, Raymondo."

I squeezed the phone hard, listened to the plastic almost buckle. "Wes?" I said. "Pal, I haven't forgotten your style. You inflated body counts. You were a guy who could lie about the dead, I should trust you about the living? In the 'Nam you had rank on me, but here you're just another asshole."

"And you're still a dumb fire-eater. Jesus, but you're simple." He laughed as only a man who's seen combat can, the laughter wicked and infectious and pitiless.

"That's me," I said cheerfully. "Oh, and one other thing: your ad in the Yellow Pages says you specialize in industrial espionage. See, I can't tell if you prevent it or perform it. Or do you just work for the highest bidder, like you did in Nam?"

I listened to forty-five seconds of insults and threats without hearing anything original, so I hung up.

Over sandwiches I tried the numbers of some people I knew in the Bronx, and one of them, Otto Cruz, recognized Teddy and Zero by name. Otto thought he knew Teddy's mother; she lived in a fancy apartment building overlooking Yankee Stadium. He'd check it out.

I went home to the four-bedroom Victorian in Kew Gardens to trash the bloodstained suit and put on light slacks, a comfortable pair of Brutini loafers. I dropped a notepad down the inside pocket of my jacket along with pen, penlight, and lock picks rolled in a plastic sleeve designed for Allen wrenches. In the garage I tested the alarm system on the F-10 coupe, a chipper little five-speed built by Nissan when they were sold as Datsuns. It was the perfect vehicle for the city: maneuverable, unassuming, park it in a space the size of a banana crate. But even though I covered the car phone with a beach towel and doctored the decor with crumpled beer cans, the extra aerial was unmistakable to the connoisseur. The alarm whooped off the walls of the garage and threatened to shatter the glass in the Mercedes convertible parked next to it.

I dodged along Metropolitan Avenue as far as St. John's Cemetery, then rode Woodhaven Boulevard to the Long Island Expressway, crawled up the ramp, and puttered along in second gear for a half mile before emerging from the congestion caused by a fender bender in the right lane. All the while I was on hold, or being transferred, in an attempt to track down Danny Belinski at the *Crusader*. The suspicion that he might be avoiding me picked up substance with each new relay.

Danny had fashioned a career in journalism as the working-class hero; his columns eschewed subtle allusions and academic balancing acts in favor of gut response, the flavor of the street. His idea of an office was a saloon, a ballpark, somewhere along the rail at Belmont. I would never forget how we worked together when Cece set a legal precedent by hiring a lawyer from Sal's firm to assist the prosecution in its case against her alleged rapist. On Sal's personal recommendation I was brought in to dig through the rapist's history as ruthlessly as the defense team would resurrect Cece's. In his column Danny kept our side of the story vividly before the public. It was a form of PR, no question about it, but given the weight we were up against, scruples were excess baggage. Because the defendant happened to be the son of a prominent financier, and a direct descendant of a legendary robber baron, the trial provided red meat for the tabloids, cost Cece a promotion at Shares of Life of America, a leading insurance conglomerate, as well as her influence within the silk-stocking district, where she had labored long and faithfully for the liberal-Democratic agenda. And there was a more profound, if not publicized, loss: Cece underwent an abortion, the issue from the night of terror. It was a fact never brought out at the trial, in spite of the prosecutor's strenuous efforts to convince Cece otherwise. We had the bastard nailed. We documented the blueblood's track record of assaults, dating back to an arrest his freshman year at Columbia. The jury came in with a unanimous verdict of guilty, and the judge levied the mandatory nickel, given the absence of aggravating circumstances. The attorney for the prosecution shrugged, Cece's attorney patted her hand, Cece did not take her eyes off her assailant. The guy walked on his own recognizance awaiting appeal. Two months later the appellate court unanimously refused to review, so the blueblood was sent up to Ossining to break bread with the felons from Harlem and Williamsburg and Red Hook. Shortly after that I proposed to Cece over cocktails at Jim Ray's in the Village, Danny in the booth opposite us. I kissed the tiny ripple where the bone had never been reset, at her insistence, on the bridge of her nose. We were married the following month, and Danny devoted a whole column to it. Years and pub crawls later left Danny and me not so much at odds as bored with one another. Danny accused me of sucking up to money; I grew tired of his knee-jerk sympathies, in which I detected less sinew than jerk.

To hell with him, I thought, an instant before I recognized the voice at the other end of the line.

"That you, Ray?"

"Me. How ya doin', Danny?"

"That's a bitch, what happened this morning. You talk to Sal?"

"A little."

"I know Sal, the one thing in his head right now, find the fucks and punch their ticket."

"Danny—"

"Old Joe could arrange it with a phone call."

"Yo, Daniel. I need some help."

He cackled, but the cackling quickly developed into a fit of coughing, then hacking, hacking, hacking. "That's a wise boy I'm listening to," he gasped finally. "I heard you blew the marriage."

"Not that. Chrissakes, I need advice, you think I'd ask a guy's gone into the tank, what is it, three times?"

"Four, it looks like. Makes me an expert."

"About a month ago—"

"Well, look at this. Sport, you made the late edition, front page. Your triple did any rate. The ghouls will want to frame this one. Oh-ho, and little Arnie, I see, they gave him space on page three, and a picture of the kid. Lessee: 'Terror that lasted seconds by the clock must have seemed an eternity to three young men in a Queens parking lot this morning.' You like it?"

I winced, and shifted down, coming upon the usual backup at the approach to the Midtown Tunnel.

"I thought you would. This boy writes with a blunt instrument. Jesus, listen to this—"

"Danny, about a minute I'll be in the Midtown Tunnel, end of conversation. What I wanted, a month ago you did a piece, it ran a few days, on runaways, kids in the life. You ever run across free-lancers, girls coming in for a day or two, a weekend, then going home, anything like that?"

"It happens. Everything happens in the street. I wouldn't say it's common. And there wouldn't be a whole lot of longevity. Some hawk would either own her or cut her."

"Uh-huh. His name would be Ramone, just the one

name, and hers is Julie Holloway. I guess she might have
changed it for the street, I hadn't thought of that."

"A lot do, or the street changes it for them."

I described her to him. "She's been at it about a year.
The pimp, I don't know when he got into the act. Any
of this light up a circuit?"

There was silence at the end of the line; then: "Kinda
foreign territory for you, sport. Since when did you become a finder of lost souls?"

"Since the daughter of a client, who happens to be
wealthy and impatient, turned up gone."

"Ah," was all Danny Belinski said, and it was perfect,
all the harangues and aspersions distilled into a single
syllable.

"Don't start with me," I said, "unless you want me
asking what your byline's doing in a sleazebag journal,
besides earning you a six-figure salary."

I listened to him wheeze. I suppose it was chuckling.
At my end it sounded like a barroom brawl. When he
could speak, and then only barely, he promised to check
his files. We agreed to touch bases in an hour, if he lived
that long. Three-pack-a-day humor.

7

At a parking garage on Forty-seventh Street near Ninth
Avenue, I gave the car jock my keys, adding how much I'd
appreciate a spot within view of his office. A little of the
folding fell into his palm and stuck there. A smile oozed
across his pockmarked face. According to the deejay on the
car radio, it was a perfect day for a stroll, sunny and
seventy-nine, but on Forty-seventh the air was freighted
with exhaust fumes, the unmistakable stench of simmering
asphalt, the discrete contributions of human and animal
waste. It was a block of parking lots and crumbling brown-
stones with signs in the windows advertising weekly ren-
tals. Catty-corner at the end of the block, an adult
bookstore with plywood for windows and a gate in the
doorway appeared to be the only viable retail operation.

I was old enough not to expect miracles, and my expectations were rewarded. The ladies of the street at that hour
fell roughly into two groups: those of an age where concrete is an essential element of their face powder, and then
the jailbait. Some of the latter looked like it was their first
time on high heels, but the awkwardness was less a product
of inexperience than pharmaceuticals; coltish, barely pu-
bescent, and stoned out of their heads, they looked, but did
not even see the picture of Julie Holloway, their level of
attention no higher than the fly of my pants.

As the time approached for me to get back to Danny,
I nosed about for a pay phone that hadn't been vandalized, and when I found one, it was occupied by a pair
of sweet young things who didn't look like they were
dialing home for permission to stay late at the library.
There was a news kiosk at the corner. I flipped a quarter

onto the one-legged newsie's rubber coin pad and reached for the late edition of the *Crusader*. I strolled up to the phone booth and leaned against it, glanced at the front page. It showed a pair of torsos on the hood of Sal's automobile, spotted and disfigured, faces wrenched into unreal configurations. The sweet young things did not quite know whether to resent my intrusion or welcome it for business reasons. They were both black, one in red satin shorts so tight they might as well have been transparent, the other in a white minidress and blond, antebellum curls. I turned to page 3 for the Wittgenstein piece. The picture stopped me. It was a photo of a third victim, son of a prominent attorney. He lay on the gravel, a foot pulled against his buttocks, hand thrown crazily above his head in a macabre salutation. His face that was no longer a face was completely visible.

The ink from the paper had blackened my fingertips by the time the girls had finished with the phone. The one in red turned to me and smiled, the beckoning bright as a theater marquee for an instant, then gone, replaced by fear and haste.

I slammed a quarter at the coin slot and watched it arc and spiral from my shaking fingers, go shimmering off the curb. I took a deep breath and coaxed another coin into the slot.

After a while a familiar, nasal voice answered: "Wittgenstein here."

"Ray Sommer, Arnold."

"Hey, pal."

"Somebody moved my coat."

"How about the fuckin' asshole puts a gun in my hand, my prints all over it? That fat detective ate my ass."

"We had a deal."

"Yeah? And I had a story to do."

"You got the story, Arnold. It was part of the deal. I kept my word and you didn't is what it is. Ask your chums there on the paper. Ask Danny Belinski, for one. I don't brag about conquests, just like I don't walk away from a screwing."

"Jesus, you know Danny B? The man is a fucking legend, the best. Ray, tell me what I can do to make this right with you."

"It's gonna be a long haul, Arnold. I'm talking years,

and here's why: the boy was facedown when he fell. He was facedown when homicide arrived. Your page three he's faceup. So what we're talking about is tampering with evidence at the scene of a murder. What we're talking about is a possible felony—to say nothing of the civil suit Sal DeLorio, Senior, is liable to slap you and your playmates and the *Daily Crusader* with once he comes out of mourning. The cops may or may not pick up on the discrepancy, but I have, and I'll use it if I have to. A simple phone call to Sal DeLorio is all it would take. Having your ass eaten by a New York detective, believe me, is pussy stuff next to the way Sal will come at you."

There was silence on the line. Then: "I think I fucked up," in a hoarse whisper.

I let him sweat.

"Ray?"

"Get humping, Arnold. That's all I can tell you. Pipe anything you learn about this morning's events to Danny. Come up with something, you still might have a career."

He was a suddenly humbled individual. When I gave him Danny Belinski's extension, so that he could transfer me, something like awe reduced the timbre of his voice to that of a twelve-year-old's.

"You got yourself a beauty," said Danny Belinski, "if we're talking about the same hawk."

"Let's hear it."

"Guy's been in the street a few years, into all the hustles out there, but he's still cherry so far as the cops know, never been pulled in. Lucky? You bet. The way I heard it, our boy got his start rolling fags in the Village, but here's where he shows some smarts: he only hits on out-of-towners, never locals. Cops down there like him for that mutilation killing, guy found in the Dumpster on Charles Street, year, year and a half ago. Nothing solid though, except Mr. Ramone moved his act into midtown about that time. Goes to work as an enforcer for Big Jim Lord, who fancies himself a kind of chairman of the board of the black pimps operating in midtown. Our boy, it seems, enjoys cutting chicks as much as guys. So he's vicious and he's got some smarts, but you could still lose him in the landscape until about the time I start to research my story, just after New Year's. He doesn't make a move, it's a quantum leap. Suddenly he's a player, got his own stable, some muscle, and not a shot fired, no bodies in the river. Like it, sport?"

"Ramone found himself an angel, it looks like. Not Lord?"

"Definitely not." Danny chuckled, but stopped before it developed into another brawl for air. "You locate Ramone, or the money behind him, we're even. Just so you understand the terms of this conversation."

"Yeah, yeah. Julie. Anything on her?"

"Nothing much. You mentioned she was a chemical redhead. Could be she's enhancing what nature gave her. One of the ladies I talked to referred to a freckled bitch said she was Ramone's main squeeze. If I'm not mistaken, red hair and freckles go together like syrup on pancakes. It's all I got."

"It's something," I said, gazing south down Eighth Avenue, throngs on both sides of the street. "You have an address for either of them?"

"Just the last one Ramone listed for welfare. Probably long gone from there."

"I gotta start somewhere." Then, before he could get off the line after telling me, I said: "Danny, I ought to mention, young Arnold that writes with a blunt instrument? He's taken a keen interest in Sal's killing. Whatever he learns, he'll bring to you. I'd appreciate hearing about it."

"You just never give up, do you, sport?"

"Never," I said. To hell with the wisdom of Lieutenant Cox.

The place was on Fifty-fourth Street, west of Ninth Avenue, not the toniest neighborhood in Manhattan. Past Ninth Avenue the street descends steeply toward the Hudson River. The facade of brick tenements was relieved, but not at all improved, by a couple of small, no-account parking lots. The residents were socializing on the stoops, white and black, mostly women, and most of them looking as faded as the clothes they wore. I passed empty tow trucks, their squawk boxes crackling between police transmissions. Behind some of the trucks, wrecks were still ahoist like twisted steel trophies. Wrecker pilots were pitching pennies against the wall of an ABC studio, the scent of cannabis uncoiling from their midst. But the late-night look in their eyes was not entirely due to reefer: you saw the same thing in the eyes of young cops, ambulance drivers, kids coming off their first serious combat. The eyes that said in spite of the swagger, the hip detachment—*I lost it.*

The address Danny gave me was a five-floor walk-up, the exterior given a recent coat of dark paint to gloss the firetrap as a brownstone. I climbed the steps of the stoop among what appeared to be three generations of residents. Most of the mail slots were absent names. The door onto the hallway did not look substantial enough to stop a stiff breeze. Let into the top half was a panel of clear, thin glass, the view into the building halfheartedly obstructed by some muslin curtains the color of old Scotch tape. A note affixed to a corner of the pane offered the following instruction to strangers: *We don't sell dope. That is the next billding not here. We don't sell it.*

I pushed on the door. A lock put up some resistance, about as much as a politician refusing a contribution. So I jerked the knob toward the hinges and nudged. I was inside. The light was grainy, and the perception of things yellowed—windows, the checkerboard tile, even the air itself—may have been colored by the wrenching aroma of animal urine and ammonia, to say nothing of the noxious emissions from baseboards drenched in roach poison. My eyes were watering before I knocked on the first door.

I introduced myself as an investigator for the law firm of DeLorio, Simon, Tortelli and Weitz. The firm, as I explained it, represented the interests of a wealthy Jamaican entrepreneur whose sudden demise left his only son, Ramone, heir to a fortune. The story excited some interest, but elicited no information until I waded to the third floor. There a damsel in a dirty housedress, barefoot, a corkcolored wen on her cheek, admitted me into a rancid foyer, from which the view of the next building's fire escape was almost cheerful next to the sight of a child too old to be, but still wearing diapers, his ankle shackled to a radiator by a dog's leash. The woman folded her arms across her bosom and demanded to see identification.

I handed her a card, a legitimate one, and waited

while her eyes trudged across it. The chained child made a sound like mooing.

"Mrs. . . . ?"

"Crutchner."

"Mrs. Crutchner, does Ramone still live here?"

She thrust the card back, still pinching it as she had when reading it . . . upside down.

"What's in it for me?" snapped Mrs. Crutchner.

"Mrs. Crutchner, you've been watching too much television. Either you answer my questions here, in the comfort of your home, or I get a subpoena, you go before a grand jury."

As a threat, it had all the substance of the Jamaican entrepreneur, but panic stirred in the whites of her eyes. "Jury? What'd I do? You can't put me on trial for nothin'. I got my rights."

"Sure you do. Where does, or where did Ramone live?"

"Fi'th floor, I think. Him and the white slut."

"They still live there, Mrs. Crutchner?"

"Gone. I dunno when. Been a while."

"The white girl," I said, producing the snapshot of Julie, "this her?"

She prodded the wen with a bitten fingernail. "She had the freckles, but not the hair like it is here."

"A wig maybe."

"Maybe." Over her shoulder she told the child to shut up its mouth. She moved her eyes around in a fashion that probably passed for coy in her circle. "You looking for a nigger, you show me a pitcher of a white girl. You think cause I use food stamps I'm automatically stupid?"

"Very good, Mrs. Crutchner. I see I'm traveling in fast company. I'll be candid," I lied. "The family had permitted Ramone to come to New York to study at Juilliard, he's a brilliant musician. The white chick is a hustler, finds out the guy is worth like millions, and makes the moves. He's totally in love, can't see a thing. Me, I'm the guy the family is sending to negotiate with the lady, if you understand what I'm saying."

"In love?" howled the Crutchner. "With his self maybe. Not no woman I ever seen him with. I give him that, he had some looks. And green eyes. A nigger with green eyes, can you beat that?"

"How about friends? Anybody in the building?"

She grinned. I have seen lovelier grins on jack-o-lanterns. "Friends? You kidding? In this building, you don't have friends, you just live here."

The child in diapers was chewing on the chain, drool running off the links.

Thinking about the fifth floor, I sucked it in, plowed up the steps through the stench and heat. The air in the stairwells vibrated with the sound of blackflies doing whatever it is flies do in the heat of the day. The Crutchner woman was right: nobody on the fifth floor claimed to be friends with Ramone. They recognized the picture of Julie without knowing her name, because the man pumped iron and was heard bouncing her off walls, speaking to her after she calmed down in a gentle, guttural voice, like you would use after spanking a child for toying with the burners on a stove. One tenant remembered the night before they left, he thought he heard two women in there, one of them with a kind of funny accent, like from the movies, but he couldn't swear to anything on account he had some brews around the corner on Ninth and was just settling into a mason jar of moonshine his brother, a trucker, had hauled up from Kentucky.

On the first floor, I tried the super's door once more, again without success. If anyone might know of a forwarding address, it would be the super.

Emerging from the building, I gulped the gritty air, grateful for it, and noticed a man on a stoop across the street. He wore some kind of tropical shirt, his knees spread, brooding over a can of beer. The shirt hung loose, untucked. It was sunshine yellow adorned with blue shapes like birds. What I could see of his face, it was the color of old copper, burnished like an Indian's. I rubbed the back of my neck. I didn't know what it was, but something about the man made me hesitate. Or maybe it was simply the weirdness of a guy in a party-time shirt, a beer in his hand, posing like that famous statue that Rodin did, I think it's called *The Thinker*.

8

For the next couple hours I put my considerable investigative talents to work on the street, and mostly what I picked up were shinsplints. Besides hookers, I braced the newsies, taxi drivers, the beat cops and the bag ladies, all the nickel-and-dime wise guys out strutting for their own amusement. Nobody knew anything, not even the ones who obviously recognized the girl in the photograph. It was early yet. Memories in the life tend to sharpen as the evening wears on. . . . And so it went: if it wasn't evasion, it was lip; or the newsies' indifferent shrugs, the bag ladies' hostile incomprehension, the expressions of regret from the hacks and flatfoots.

The sidewalks jammed up with the approach of evening, the enticements of the night. Milling among the street life, tourists elbowed one another, pointed like visitors at a zoo. There were the hotdogs, all zooted up, just in from Jersey, itchy to flush a week's wages down their idea of life in the fast lane. There were sailors, as there always are in this part of town in every city in the world. And young men with clean fingernails doing research for their doctorates in sociology. Also caught up in the mobs along Eighth Avenue were early theater patrons, making their way skittishly from the parking garages toward the bright marquees of Broadway and civilization. In the predusk, lights from the porno joints sifted on: faint carnival colors mottled faces and arms. Music pulsated from doorways where live sex was advertised, the music a lure, a kind of syrup for loose libidos.

Down the block, to slake my thirst, maybe grab a sandwich, I pushed open the door of a no-frills beverage house. When my eyes had adjusted, I decided to skip the sandwich.

The ceiling was low, cockroach-colored, made of tin that looked as if it had been run through an enormous waffle iron. The bar went back about half the distance of the room. Parallel to it was a pool table, faded green, a solemn game in progress, the lights over it in black shades shaped like the hats worn in rice paddies. A jukebox throbbed in the distance with an up-tempo lament, somebody not getting enough action. I stood at the end of the bar facing into the room and ordered a draft. There were some solitary mumblers along the rail, some working stiffs nursing a slow one before the subway home, a couple down toward the jukebox punishing their livers with boilermakers. The beer tasted like lubricant, more necessity than pleasure.

There were tables on tubular legs beyond the pool table, and whether by convention or some established rule, the area seemed reserved for the working women and their pimps. I watched the ladies come and go for a while, nibbling at my beer. There was a pattern. In through the door with the pebbled amber glass, pausing until they could see, then swinging their hips along the length of the bar and into the ladies' room. Some were quicker at tying off, more practiced at finding a vein, but one after another they would emerge from the patch of putrid yellow light, floating in a kind of private gravity, and sway toward the tables. That's how the pimps liked them—zonked, pastureland material.

Beyond the tables windowless walls offered more of the lovely shade of roach. What passed for illumination festered from shabby sconces, the total output per table being a spot of light about the size of a cold sore. An elderly gent with a gimp leg hobbled among the tables soliciting orders in a phlegmy voice. He wore a gray T-shirt clearly marked *Property New York Mets.* Bold blue lettering stamped back and front. The bartender called him Coach, which was about as witty as it got in here.

By the time the bartender found his way back with my change, I was showing empty. I rotated the glass on the counter and put a tenspot back in the field of play.

"Another of the same for me," I said, "and whatever you're drinking."

He slapped the tap, drew a beer for me. He was a sloppy gent in a black T-shirt, black leather vest, long black hair gone gray at the temples, a salt-and-pepper beard. Granny glasses tinted gray sat on a maroon nose, a great humped whale of wrecked blood vessels. His belly, white as fish flesh, hung out between the T-shirt and a thick silver belt buckle with a lot of turquoise worked into it. He bent low behind the bar to bring up a fifth of Johnnie Walker Black, even though directly behind him within arm's reach stood a fifth of same. His eyes tracked my gaze, and a sneer crawled into his beard. Well, maybe not the same. He trickled the true Black into a shot glass and the bottle disappeared below.

"You don't give the public much credit, do you?" I said. "I'll bet the Cutty tastes like the Chivas. Or the Johnnie Walker, either color."

He put his hands on the bar and leaned forward. "Assholes come in here, they wouldn't know it from horse piss, long as it's got the right label. Coors now, I sell the shit out of that, and what is it? Some Colorado spring water and trout sperm, far as I can taste. Tell you somethin'?"

"Tells me you sell a lotta horse piss."

There was a gleam in his evil, simple eye. "And trout jizz. Don't forget the trout jizz."

I lifted his shot glass and slipped the tenspot under it. "That should cover your losses," I said.

"Depends what I'm losin'."

"A minute of your time, the joy of my company forever."

"It's yer dime, Coach."

"Guy by the name of Ramone. A black dude, weightlifter type, with green eyes, specializes in turning out white tricks. One, anyway, that I know of." I showed him the photograph, moving it away when he reached for it. "Don't maul it, just look at it. Her name's Julie."

He straightened up, exposing his fish-white gut, and bitten nails worried the whiskers on his cheek. He was thinking. "The pimp and the pussy, what, they jack you up?"

"Ace," I said. I shook my head slowly, about the speed thought traveled between his ears, then snagged the bill from under his shot glass. I snapped it in front of his eyes. "If you would, please, can the scholarly curiosity. It's *my* dime, remember?"

"Up yers, Coach," he said, and pawed for the bill. And missed. And watched me down his shot of genuine Johnnie B.

"Righteous." I leered. "That's how I'm feeling. And there's nothing more dangerous than a righteous man. Kind of keep your hands up where I can see them. Otherwise . . ." I shrugged.

He did some more of that business with his beard, enough to where he could give thinking a bad name. "The broad I never seen, awright? The street's fulla jig pimps, they don't usually live long enough to make a name for theirselves, much less inneress me enough to akse 'em if they got one. Akse . . . hey, Dixie!"

One of the ladies over against the wall rolled her head for a languid glance.

I pocketed the rest of my change, the ten included, and dragged a chair up to the ladies' table.

There were two of them. They looked at me dreamily, as if we were all out in a meadow gathering wildflowers. They were young, but past puberty and at least one hit south of an overdose. The one who answered to Dixie wore a satiny tank top and matching hot pants. Her companion across the table opted for the virginal approach: snow-colored minidress and white heels. Her blond wig was embellished . . . with impossible antebellum curls. They were the sweet young things I had encountered at the phone booth, where I waited to call Danny. I said, "Bartender says you maybe can help me. You're Dixie, and you're . . ."

"Anything you want me to be," cooed the virgin, spreading her fingers, then closing them like a fan against her throat. "Name it, sugar."

"The name's Ray. Dixie, your lovely friend's got a coke, can I get you something—a spritzer, rum and cola?"

"Spritzer," she drawled, lifting a finger off the scar that ran from her cheekbone to the bone of her jaw. She smiled, which had the effect of turning the scar into a crinkly pink light like a strand of neon flashing on in the darkness of her skin. "You got some light eyes. I like a man with light eyes. Don't I know you from somewhere, Ray?"

"I think I'd remember a lady as lovely as you."

The virgin found my leg with her foot and was giving great ankle when the phlegm-voiced fellow limped up with a Campari and soda. I put a card next to Dixie's spritzer.

She lifted her false eyelashes, no small task. "Joleen, honey, stay easy. Ray an' me gonna get down. Be but a minute. Get youself comfortable at the bar. An' chile? Don't waste your time there. Ain't a one can pay for it, an' even if he could, ain't a one could get it up."

Joleen strolled off, not a word, just an airy smile before she whirled and put her fanny in motion. She certainly had a can that could.

"Like that, Ray?" said Dixie.

I shook my fingers as if they'd fallen asleep, when in fact they felt sensitive enough to crack a safe. "I'll plead the Fifth."

She fingered her scar. "Whachoo want?"

"A white chick about five-six or -seven, a redhead, got the chopped hair, like she just woke up. Name of Julie Holloway. She's done business on the strip is why I ask."

"The meat market," she said. "Lemme tell you about it. It be stone fuckin' cold out there, Ray. This homo disease got everyone bent outta shape."

"I want market reports, Dixie, I'll call Merrill Lynch."

"You lookin' to take this Julie stuff off'n the street, reduce my competition?"

"Her folks would like to see her."

"This a paint-by-number picture, but I ain't heard no numbers."

"Let's hear a picture."

"She got skinny legs for a white chick. Not just red hair, it like an explosion. Jailbait like Joleen. Got the big titties make up for the lack a smarts. They call her Julie Halloween, she such a witch."

I laid a photograph in the cold-sore light. "This her?"

"Be the witch herself."

"Word is she belongs to a pimp name of Ramone."

"You wanna new picture 'fore you pay for the last."

I folded a twenty lengthwise and set it next to her glass.

"I get more'n this for a straight-up."

"And you haven't told me anything I didn't know. But at least we've established your credibility."

I hunkered over the table to reach the fifty-dollar bill out of the sock on my ankle. I creased it lengthwise and dropped it between us. "Now tell me something I don't know."

"They a Ramone useta work for Big Jim Lord," she said. "He don't no more. People says he runnin' his own game now, buncha kinky white chicks. Somebody say he got a place in the Village."

"Somebody, huh? You know the guy, Dixie, this Ramone?"

Eyes down, hugging herself, she murmured, "Maybe. It was a long time ago . . ."

I reached out and touched her cheek, traced the silken tissue of the scar with my forefinger. "You going to sit there shivering or tell me the truth? Because what I'm thinking, you were cut by a man who likes to cut people. He would do it in the line of work for Mr. Big Jim Lord, or maybe just if the spirit moved him. Maybe he was a man you thought you loved. Or he marked you as a token of affection. But it wasn't long ago, darling. That scar is smooth as a baby's bum."

She let me lift her chin. Tears slipped from the corners of her eyes. "Ray? I'm feelin' pain."

"Sure you are. It's called being alive. But it doesn't earn you fifty."

"Horatio Street, corner a Washington. Way I hear it, be a duplex on the fourth floor."

I stared into her eyes, the pinpoint pupils, the muddle there to be manipulated if I didn't press, let pleasure or eagerness enter into it. "The duplex being where the girls crash after a hard day's night."

She nodded, spearing the tears with metallic fingernails.

"Kinky," I said. "You called them kinky white girls. Something they do over and above the call of duty?"

"Do anything, Ray. Like they high on somethin' the way they get for some porno movies. Like they on blow."

"Coke."

"They do anything."

I folded her fingers over the fifty. "How about Julie?"

"Ain't seen her inna week."

"She Ramone's lady?"

"Somebody say she say he say she is."

"Could you put a name on somebody?"

She sniffed and wrecked her makeup, but a tentative glow of triumph beamed from her face as she put the money out of sight, in a place about as private as Grand Central Station. "You ain't the only one wavin' money, Ray, lookin' for those two, but you the prettiest. They be up and down the strip since day before yestiday."

"How many's they?"

"Two. Oreo squad."

I lifted her fingers to my lips and kissed them. "A black gent and a white gent?"

"Umm. Mos' they offer any the sisters is twenty—ten now, ten they find who it is. Cheap shits. And mean? Redhead ma'fucka I talk wit', he talk real quiet, like he on top a things. But I tell him go walk the dog, I ain't got time for his petty bullshit, he near pull my arm off. Feel?"

On the inside of her right triceps the swelling was hard, like welts. A sound escaped her lips, an involuntary whimper of disbelief and remembered pain. "I just negotiatin' an' the man get so wild, his partner got to lean on him. That kinda team, I don't think nobody told 'em nothin'. They bad music."

"They leave a card, drop any names?"

We were holding hands, like a pair of teens back when guys wore crew cuts and a soda fountain was a place to be, and she said, "Redhead ma'fucka. He say his name is Holloway."

9

The pay phones were located between the jukebox and the ladies with a view down the length of the bar, a clear shot of the door with the pebbled amber glass. The new trade to come in were pretty much of a piece, with the mildly interesting exception of a lad in a shirt of sunshine yellow and blue, who eased up to the rail at the end of the bar, about where the barkeep and I held our Socratic dialogue.

The Stones were shaking it out on the jukebox, Mick vamping out "Honkytonk Woman," when Pat came on the line. I passed along what I'd picked up in the trenches, including a detailed description of Ramone by Dixie. "What's with you, anything?" I shouted, trying to compete with the jukebox.

"Otto Cruz called. Very excited. He'll be at the laundromat till ten or eleven. Want the number?"

I scratched it into my notepad. "That it?"

A pause. "Meredith DeLorio called . . . again."

Meredith . . . Sal, goddammit, would be too busy pushing his weight at the authorities, wanting action, answers, vengeance. But by now, certainly, Meredith's two sisters with their respective families should have arrived from Connecticut. And her parents, who summered on Cape Cod. And friends, neighbors, someone from the archdiocese. Cece, if she were in the city, would undoubtedly be there. Pat knew this as well as I did, which accounted for the cadence of her voice: *Meredith DeLorio called. Again.* Why you? her voice asked, without employing the words. Why, in the dead awful midst of her grief, is she reaching out for you? It was a question

I was asking myself, when the answer clicked in, clear and utterly comprehensible: I was the last to see her son alive, the final witness. Dear sweet generous Meredith, what dry crumbs my words will be. . . .

"Ray? You there, Ray?"

"Yeah." My voice sounded dissipated, listless.

"You okay?"

"I've been better, love. Listen, before you leave for the night, contact our answering service, leave a message in case Mrs. DeLorio calls, something to the effect that I'll try to make it up there tonight. If not tonight, tomorrow morning."

"Got it," she said. Then: "Oh. I don't think you can promise tomorrow morning. Lieutenant Cox called. He wants to see your body at ten A.M. in room 3020, the Argent Towers. It's right off Queens Boulevard on—"

"I know where it is, darling." It was ten stories of suites crawling with attorneys, bail bondsmen, process servers and skiptracers, the varied spawn of the law. The building was a five-minute stroll from Boro Hall. But it was a thousand miles from the procedural niceties fashioned by the courts. It was a place where men could speak candidly, even to cops.

"Anything else?" I said.

Silence.

"Pat?"

"Mr. Dexter called. I just got a raise. I'm not even working there, he bumped my salary five grand. You phoned him, didn't you?"

"That sonuvabitch."

"I told him I'd think it over. In case you wanted to talk to me, instead of him." Spoken with all the hauteur and high-bitch archness a Queens girl can muster.

"We'll talk. This isn't the time or place, though, all right?"

"Okay. But soon, Ray. Like I can't keep my life on hold, ya know?"

We hung up and I stood there staring down the bar at the boy in the blue and yellow shirt, the Thinker, hunkered over a glass of something and looking intently nowhere. I wondered if he was having fun too, or was I the only one.

From the time-warp jukebox came the sound of the
Troggs groaning out their classic sexual anthem: "Wild
thing/you make my heart sing/you make ev'ry . . . thing/
gah . . . roovy. . . . "
All the class of a backseat encounter and the timeless-
ness of things primitive, the song had to be older than
Joleen, whose sinuous approach was choreographed to
the simple raunchy sound. She invited me to burrow a
hand into her cleavage to verify the erectness of her nipples. I told her Dixie would personally remove my business if I did, and she floated off, a feather in the wind,
the curve of her can a gift from God.

The sun was low, far beyond New Jersey, when I
pushed my way onto the sidewalk and crossed Eighth
Avenue to start the trek back to the parking garage. I
had instructed Pat to arrange a stakeout on the intersec-
tion of Horatio and Washington immediately, even if the
chances of sighting the girl or the pimp much before
morning were negligible. For the money the guy Holloway was paying, he deserved the works, though his behavior on the strip bothered me some. Make that a lot.
Oh . . . what have we here? Out of the corner of my eye
I saw a sunshine yellow shirt emerge from the heavy
doors with the amber glass. I walked to the next inter-
section without looking back, and waited to recross the
avenue.
If the Thinker had a partner, or partners, on the street,
I didn't make them. Hands in his pockets, he dawdled
beneath a theater marquee, inspecting the posters, the
promise of raw, vicarious bliss inside. He was not tall,
maybe five-nine, and had some bulk in the shoulders,
but his wrists were narrow: too small-boned to be muscle, he was more than likely somebody's gofer, an errand
boy. When the crosswalk green vanished I stepped off
the curb. The Thinker dodged traffic to fall in half a
block behind me. I liked that. It meant he was operating
on his own, or if not, then his backup was truly behind
him. Advantage, Sommer. I eased along with the flow

of the citizenry. I recognized several of the ladies I had
interviewed earlier shrugged in doorways or resting their
prettiness against pay phones. We traded smiles, nods.
One even remembered my name, offered to do me a
kindness for the price of a straight-up. The substance
peddlers peeled by spieling their list of products in practiced mutters sounding eerily like incantations. As I came
to the cross streets I glanced west, looking for a block
with an inactive stretch. Beyond the Hudson River the
sun was descending in fiery splendor, the light almost
metallic in the gunpowder haze issuing from the refin-
eries. The Jersey riverfront, what you could see of it, was
the color of smoke, vague purple shapes of piers and
warehouses jutting into the water, waves that were molten in the last light of day. Then, at last, a quiet block.

I turned west onto it, directly into the dying blast of
the sun. I got my back up against the building. The
Thinker came around the corner and a hand leaped to
shield his eyes, blinded by the coppery light.

"*Qué pasa?*" I said, stepping beside him to get a grip
on his luminescent hair to crank his head back, my other
hand seizing his crotch. "If you would, please, put your
hands in your pockets. Otherwise you lose your two best
friends."

He did that. I could make out several people down the
block, just profiles in the sun. And an alley several yards
ahead. We went for it.

Fifteen feet into it, steel fencework had been erected,
and atop it strands of barbed wire canted over the alley.
There was a door in the fence that was padlocked and
the padlock meant business. Battered garbage pails were
ganged along one wall. Broken lathing, glass, even clothing spilled from burst plastic sacks dumped indiscriminately beyond the cans. There was a headboard with
head-sized holes in its rattan and a mattress slumped in
an awkward fold. The general air of havoc suited a
neighborhood not unfamiliar with violence and the messy
wake of a mostly transient population.

I heaved the boy in the sunshine shirt face-first into
the fence with the force of a day's frustrations, and
watched him claw and scramble to keep his feet, to turn
around. And collapse to his knees, a hand exploring be-

neath the fly of his jeans. His coppery face, some of it
anyway, came away with a tattoo of the fence, bruised
skin at first a violent red. The Thinker whimpered, "You
fuckeen crazy, man. Wha's it about? I fuckeen don'
fuckeen know you, you do zis to me?"

Maybe it was the angle, because it wasn't the light,
but looking at his face . . . I scratched the back of my
neck. I had seen him before, far from this neighborhood.
Far from a stoop on Fifty-fourth Street. I had seen him
for several rapid heartbeats and he wasn't wearing a par-
tytime shirt.

"Lemme look at your wallet, son."

"My wallah? Fuckeen flash ol' guy like you, you wan'
my wallah? Mus' be you a fuckeen cop." That cheered
him considerably. He reached behind him for the support of the fence to gain his feet. "I got a Miranda rights.
Mean you got no fuckeen bi'ness my wallah less my 'tor-
ney pre'nt."

"Oh?"

"So fuck off."

"Yeah, well." I moved close enough to smell his
moussed hair, his sweat too. "See, now we got a problem. Because you look like someone I mighta seen this
morning. And I'm not a cop." I hit him with a bare fist,
knowing I'd regret it, just beneath his eye, felt the cheekbone give with a sound like punching crushed ice. He
bounced off the fence screaming, hands to his face, hands
and face dark with blood. My knuckles throbbed. I told
him quietly to shut up. He tried. He still whimpered,
but not loud enough to arouse anyone.

I bent over him, crowding him against the fence. "Do
I have your attention?"

Tears wobbled down to mix with the blood running
from both nostrils. He nodded.

"Good. You want to tell me what all the shooting was
about this morning? The three guys in Elmhurst you
wasted?"

"Man, you crazy. I don' fuckeen know no guys in Elmhurst is wasted. Is a hones' truth."

"There was a black guy had a sawed-off twelve-gauge,"
I said, "you and your amigo used AK-47s. The amigo is
now a dead man, because if the police have it straight,

a nine-millimeter Beretta slug made him expendable. The Beretta belongs to me. I was the one in the parking lot this morning that put three rounds in your van."

It didn't seem to impress him. He wiped his hands on his jeans and sniffed, the blood beginning to clot in his nostrils. Pain was evident when he touched where I'd caught him. His dark eyes blazed at mine, then went away, then came back blazing once more. It was my turn not to be impressed.

"Let's see the wallet," I said. "Then we'll talk about the black guy."

I saw him open his mouth and his lips begin to move, but something—a sound, a shadow—monopolized all my senses and I tried to move, duck and whirl, too late. I saw nothing. Then what I saw was grainy crimson light that turned blood bright when I was kicked beneath the rib cage and realized I must have been dropped by some kind of blow. I spit up beer and bits of stuff I wasn't curious to analyze. I pressed my cheek into the concrete of the alleyway and the heat of the day still cooked beneath the surface, along with a harsh, primal stink. I made a note to take it up with the city planners.

A voice with a smug drawl eddied into my consciousness. "Man get hurt talkin' up the sisters too much. Could be you outta your league, pretty face. Hey, we keep in touch."

I tried to express my enthusiasm for the idea, but I sounded like a leaky faucet. . . . I took a little nap.

There was no sunset, no sun at all, only the street lamps and the neon and the flashbulb burst of passing head-lights by the time I got it together enough to stand up and survey the scene of my recent success. It was pretty much as I remembered it, except for the mattress, which lay flat out with someone resting on it, facedown. I lifted the head. What I saw was visceral pulp, a high-speed car-crash face. I recognized the luminescent curls and the sunshine shirt. The Thinker had been stripped naked from the waist down by someone who did not believe in leaving behind any hope of identification. Fingers and thumbs were charred stubs.

10

The green lights winked on up Third Avenue with a degree of orchestration so smooth as to create the illusion of a functioning, harmonious society. But they didn't fool me. Not Ray Sommer, who's seen some stuff in his two-score years and is not a man to be trifled with. Just ask the smarmy writer from *People*.

I swung the Datsun east across Eighty-sixth Street through Germantown, then cranked up York Avenue and onto the FDR. A tire struck a pothole and pain played "Chopsticks" on my rib cage.

Across the East River Astoria was just another field of lights in the flatlands of Queens. Illumination from the borough arched against the night sky, a bluish tumesence that testified to the excitement of human enterprise below. It was in Astoria that D. W. Griffith did his journeyman labor at the Biograph Studios with the likes of Mary Pickford, the Gish sisters, Lionel Barrymore. The nucleus of Hollywood. Birth of a notion. Just another field of lights beyond the Wards Island Psychiatric Center, the Triboro Bridge hovering over the island, a great swath of luminous steel suspended in the sky like a cinematic illusion.

I slipped off the FDR and took the Willis Avenue Bridge north to the Major Deegan. This was the bottom of the South Bronx, an area that looked like a lesson in carpet bombing. Hanoi twenty years ago was high-rent by comparison. Tenement walls, half-demolished, formed flimsy staircases into the sky. The few buildings left standing were windowless shells ablaze with graffiti—shelter for shooting galleries, crack merchants, rats

61

the size of footballs, and the flat-out crazies discharged from the state and city facilities to relieve the crowding. Right now the lunatics were the only ones visible on the sidewalks. They shuffled behind appropriated grocery carts filled with their earthly goods. Here and there one stopped to bellow at the sky as if an audience existed there. Fumes from the expressway overhead hung in these streets, stale and sordid, like my thinking.

By the book, I should be standing in an alley off West Fifty-first Street waiting patiently to be interviewed by a new gang of homicide suits instead of leaving an anonymous message on 911. The cops didn't appreciate citizens pedaling off from the scene of a crime, especially the crime of murder. And the way I was attracting dead bodies wasn't going to make them happy either.

All I knew was that I had suddenly become a magnet for mayhem. A queasy sense of disorientation, which I hadn't experienced since Nam, resonated in my nerves. Forget going by the book. Surviving was the name of the game.

If the poor faceless mess on the mattress had been one of the Latins wielding an uninhibited AK-47 this morning, I couldn't prove it. But if he was . . . The voice in the alley, the voice I faintly remembered before passing out, could have been the voice of a black man. And the guy with the sawed-off could've been . . . one and the same? If so, how did that connect to young Sal and all that uncut good stuff in his glove box? *If* it did. Ifs and maybes weren't sufficient reasons to surrender my independence.

The creature in the alley had promised to stay in touch. I hoped so. The next time, if I got lucky, it would be with a tire iron upside his head.

I dropped off the Deegan at 149th Street and dodged the potholes on River Avenue. Amid decor eloquent of ruin squatted a single edifice respectable if only by virtue of its intactness: this was the Bronx House of Detention. A packed house by the sound of it. Wives, lovers and ex-wives, parents, siblings, children and disputed progeny, all milled along the perimeter talking among themselves or reacting to remarks shouted from the interior: it was the end of visiting hours. This exodus of the unjailed proceeded with the wistful air parishioners exhibit upon departing a church picnic, except that even the most joyous expressions were wrapped in obscenities.

Down the avenue a few blocks, aglow but vacant for the evening, Yankee Stadium curved away into the night, an enormous wheel of concrete scuffed with shadows and the grit from every Lexington Avenue train grinding, groaning, squealing into the bay of tracks overhead. As a diehard Mets fan from day one (my office is fifteen minutes from my box seats at Shea), I still experienced a shiver at the sight of the House That Ruth Built. History has a way of dwarfing us. I felt like a nomad of the Sahara advancing upon the Great Pyramid at Giza.

I took a right beneath the El onto 161st Street, another onto Gerard, and halfway down the block Estadio Laundry, situated between a Dominican bodega and a Cantonese restaurant, bubbled with clientele. It was not your average laundromat, the Estadio. Live Boston ferns hung in glazed pots in the window; a deer's head with an eight-point rack was mounted above the bulletproof change window; beyond the fifty-pound dryers a bank of illegal gambling devices, in plain view of the street, entertained most of the sudspersons. Otto and two associates were leisurely sucking down Budweisers in the locked office. There was just enough space beneath the window to exchange cash for rolls of coins. I rapped the glass with my knuckles, which, considering the din of salsa throbbing off the walls from several ghetto blasters, struck me as something on the order of trying to drive a baseball with a bird's feather. Time passed. I knocked again. Where the laid-back spirit of *mañana* prevails, as it did in here, it is bad form to display impatience, so I entertained myself with a blind examination of the knot behind my ear. I had been sapped by somebody who had perfected the technique. Just touching the spot triggered nausea I had to clench my teeth against. More time passed. Finally, one of the companions lifted his eyes, moved his lips, and Otto's enormously bespectacled face swung around.

He motioned me to the back, where, beyond the gambling machines, a steel door admitted me to the office.

I was introduced to his companions, who then took off with their opened Buds, pinky fingers plunged in the tab opening for casual transport.

"You look li' shit," Otto said, bending behind his desk for an icy red, white, and blue can.

While we talked I dined on the remains of some plantain, refried beans, and gelid chicken studded with peppers. It tasted heaven-sent.

Like Lieutenant Cox, the most arresting feature on Otto's face was what adorned it: in Otto's case, it was a pair of glasses, the lenses, set in black plastic frames, looking almost bulletproof themselves. Together with the shadow rising from his jaw and long seashell ears, he projected the image of a possessed, turn-of-the-century anarchist, someone who might have haunted the streets of St. Petersberg with a bomb beneath his coat. But perched on the desk, blue jeans drawn up against his narrow chest, he appeared amiably owlish, raising a can of beer in salutation. "Here's mud in your ice."

I savored a slice of plantain. "Gotta be Juanita's cooking," I said.

He nodded. Tía Juanita, as she was known in the neighborhood, claimed, on the basis of charts no one understood, to be related one way or another to most everyone in that neck of the Bronx. Petite and flamboyant, she encouraged the impression of herself as a Gypsy, though in fact she worked in the Department of Motor Vehicles. She was one of the better-kept secrets of my success. Out of boredom she became a hacker, and such a proficient one that there wasn't a borough, county, or state department whose information she couldn't access; I had never asked her to infiltrate on the federal level with her trusty computer, but I had the scary suspicion it would be a piece of cake for her if I did. She was a lady: money never exchanged hands for her expertise, but gifts like perfume and theater tickets, designer clothing, and first-class flights to the Caribbean were always answered with thank-you notes, signed in a different hand by an aunt, uncle, niece, or nephew. Evidently Otto was one of her favorites. Shortly after Cece and I had separated, Juanita invited me up for an authentic home-cooked meal, having heard I was back in the bachelor mode ("Jeess, Ray, I dunno where, is jus' somethin' I hear"). She brought out a peach sherbet and espresso for dessert and made her pitch. A nephew, not one of the flashy types, but a serious boy with respect for his family, already finished one year at City College, had applied to John Jay out of a genuine desire to labor in law enforcement. Introduced to Otto, I was touched by his sincerity, no less by Juanita's belief in my clout. What I had was pitiful, but I filled the ear of a Queens assistant DA by the name of Dominic Amado and left several messages with the secretary of Inspector Moriarity. Possibly they made the difference. I'd like to think so. Otto was slated to enroll in September, and in the meantime I had been able to throw him several per diem opportunities like today's.

"Talk to me," I said, "and if you can spare another Bud, that too."

Before opening it, I pressed the cold can to the swelling behind my ear and tried to follow Otto's dramatization of all he'd accomplished. Hours of small talk and cold beers bought at the local bodega got him tight with the husband of one of Teddy Peron's sisters. According to the husband, Colombians in Jackson Heights were looking to connect up with the Bronx, form alliances, in order to check the action of some guy known in the streets as Peru. The guy was blowing the Colombians out of the market, cheaping them into extinction the way McDonald's and the nineteen-cent hamburg wiped out local drive-ins. Teddy Peron claimed a quasi-blood connection to the state senator, and according to Otto, traipsed into Queens in the guise of a broker. "The husband, name is Humphrey, say Teddy thing he got a future in politics."

I grunted and tipped the can to my mouth. "This Teddy, he runs a flower shop. Hell's he think he's got to offer the Colombians?"

Otto removed the thick-lensed glasses from his face and his black eyes looked liquid and blank. "Flowers ain't the only thin' he know about growing."

"Yeah, I heard. Cops found five kilos of weed in his trunk. So he deals. That's punk stuff to the Colombians."

The glasses having been returned to his face, Otto resumed the owlish pose. "You hearing me, Ray? I say growing. Growing, man. Means Teddy, he gotta buncha people. He got muscle in addition to the people it's good to know."

"What, he's gonna earn his spurs by hitting this one called Peru?"

"Humphrey don' say. Tell you the hones' truth, Ray, I don' thing he know. He like what they say in the newspapers, *especulación?* Speculating."

I treated myself to another swallow. "Then the theory is, Peru got wind of the meet and sent a message."

Otto nodded. Even his shoulders rolled toward his knees with conviction. "Zackly."

I thought about it. "Bodies ought to be released tonight, or sometime in the morning. Any talk about a viewing?"

"Up aroun' Tremont Avenue is where. I thing Humphrey say is tomorrow night."

"Stay next to him, if you can."

Otto belched—nothing showy, just a gentle, gastric diminuendo—and unlimbered himself, invited me to follow him to the change window. Through the bulletproof glass he pointed at one of the industrial-strength dryers.

"I got four generations a white shirts in there. On me. And Tía Juanita, she is having a seance in the bedroom of Teddy's mother, to reassure his spirit."

"I like the way you think," I said.

"Yeah?" he said. His owlish face brightened. "I thing so too. I put a shirts and one seance on my bill."

11

The DeLorios' paved drive wound down through a stand of blue spruce and wrapped itself around the shoulders of a multilevel fountain and flower treatment that was something to see in the moonlight, except that the house looming beyond it was so much more to see.

The place looked like the country seat of an English lord. Flagstone walkways undulated through the topiary. The flower beds were grouped and tended so that there would be color blooming throughout the season. Maples and oaks rose majestically at a discreet distance from the residence. Everything was barbered and trimmed and right up to snuff.

The house itself, surfaced in gray and white stone, rambled off two stories high to the east and west with private balconies, fenced with wrought iron, protruding from some of the second-floor rooms. There were brick chimneys and a pitched, slate roof and a portico from the drive to the formal entryway beneath which a marching band could have performed without feeling cramped. Ivy ascended the stone face of the house, pressed icy green leaves against the leaded glass of the second-floor windows. I had never taken time to count the rooms, but as I nosed in behind the line of cars already stretching around and beyond the fountain and back up the drive, it appeared there was a light on in every one of them.

Two men in suits, one with a flashlight, approached. I waited, inhaling the night air through the open windows. Thirty minutes' driving puts you a universe away from the electricity of the city. Here it was all cool and rich in the smell of earthbound growth. Visible in the light beneath the portico, men and a few women stood smoking, some in conversation, others just staring off. The men were in suits and the women in heels. Shawls adorned some of the women, and some of the shawls looked like fur.

A beam of light hit me in the face, held a few seconds, then went away. A voice said, "Ray Sommer?"

"You got it."

A hand came through the window, took mine, clasped it with another. My knuckles felt like they'd been mugged. "How you doin', you Kraut bastard!" said the voice with emotion.

"Ange!" I said, my eyes adjusting. "That you?"

"Me. Hey, say hello my cousin. Cato, Ray Sommer."

A large silhouette—larger even than Angelo Scorcese, which was saying something—extended a hand that imprisoned mine, and in a hoarse whisper, like a heavy body being dragged across gravel, said, "It is with much pleasure."

"Me and Ray," said Angelo as I climbed out of the car, "we grew up together, Metropolitan Avenue."

Some of the men beneath the portico drifted into the shadows that led in our direction. Several of the women not wearing shawls did likewise. Reporters.

Angelo Scorcese, even when he wasn't smelling like a vintner's floor, was not someone I wanted to stand around with batting my gums. But he could be useful.

"Looks like the family, friends, everybody's here," I said.

"Yeah. Even the old man, he come up say his condolences. Fuckin' bugs come outta the woodwork what they done to young Sally there." He upended a flask of a clear liquid for several seconds, gargled, swallowed, belched, and put the flask back beneath his suit. Angelo's strength under his father ran to extortion, loan sharking, the collection of difficult debts by methods that were as pitiless as they were surprisingly imaginative. He looped an arm over my shoulder, boozily confiding. His breath was fragrant with something that could be patented for paint remover. "I dunno," he said. "Old Joe, he's gettin' fruity, all the grape seeds he's importin'. Cato, he's like two months off the plane from Sicily. Every week it's another grape seed I gotta meet at JFK. Teach 'em how to talk. Like what am I now, some fuckin' English teacher?"

That might be worthy of meditation, Joe Scorcese suddenly importing fresh bodies, but not while Angelo was draped all over me. Grappa fumes ought to fall under the Geneva Convention.

Still confiding, he said, "Tell you what, gonna be some bugs get squashed, the old man finds who done Sally there. Take that to the bank. Got all these grape seeds gotta make their bones."

I managed to disencumber myself of the weight of his arm as well as his breath by leaning back into my car to roll up the windows. Over my shoulder I said, "Yeah, well. I guess there's no free lunch."

When I straightened up, he was no longer looking in my direction, but off into the shadows beyond the parked cars. In the moonlight I could make out his thick neck, the collar tight and flush to the skin, almost submerged in it. Not much forehead, more like a thin blank space between his hairline and his eyebrow—that's right, eyebrow, a single bushy bar between temples. A nose that looked like it had been through more bust-ups than Billy Martin and the shipbuilder. It was a hard, closed, cautious face, one that devoted the entirety of its limited cunning to looking out for number one. Below the neck he wouldn't feel anything softer than a wrecking ball, and then only if it hit him in a tender spot, like his flask. I watched him buy himself another snort and tuck it away.

"Yo, asshole," he addressed a gingerly approaching figure on the far side of the parked cars. "What, you lose your keys?"

"No, I'm looking for the missing link."

The nasal voice sounded familiar, even if the foolish bravado didn't.

Angelo Scorcese said, "They don't spray enough around here. I guess I got to go squash me a bug." He moved toward the shadows.

"Isn't that you, Sommer?" inquired the nasal voice. "Hey, it's me, Wittgenstein. Your very good friend, Wittgenstein."

He dodged from the shadows and into the moonlight between parked cars, and contrary to this morning's jaded countenance, there was real emotion in his face. Fear, foremost.

"It's all right, Ange. I know him. He's a reporter for the *Crusader*. Be nice, he might do a puff piece for your pizza joints. He ghostwrites a food column." Approaching young Arnold and confining his narrow shoulders with an arm, I added under my breath, "You got a death wish? Smarting off to a son of Joe Scorcese isn't real bright, Arnold."

His face groped for expression like a goldfish bumping up against a glass tank.

I nodded at the enormous presence of Cato, who had been closing on Wittgenstein from the drive. "Nice meeting you," I said, and steered Wittgenstein briskly along the pavement.

Angelo seemed mollified. He swayed behind my Datsun, whence came the sound of flatulence, followed by a manly torrent that threatened to cave in a fender.

"You're a stronger bastard than you look," Arnold breathed. "Could you lemme go? I'm a good Jewish boy, and these macho embraces, I gotta tell you, Ray, I'm not real comfortable being close enough to a guy to smell his after-shave."

We continued side by side toward the portico.

"You hear anything," I said, "about a serious player in Queens, we're talking cocaine, goes by the name of Peru?"

"Peru?" Arnold Wittgenstein shook his head. "Sounds bogus, you ask me. But I'll check it out. Something else, though, there's a lotta muscle up here, Scorcese people. Nobody's seen the don, but why else all the bodies."

I shrugged and said nothing.

"Which raises an interesting question, what is a Mafia kingpin doing in the home of a star attorney like Sal DeLorio?"

"It doesn't raise that question at all if he isn't in there."

"C'mon, Ray," he whined. "Caesar's army didn't march without Caesar. That missing-link person practically admitted as much to the bitch from channel five. How well you know him?"

I stopped for a moment. "Arnold, let me give you a piece of advice: stop trying to pick my brain and start using yours to get humping on the Peru thing."

At which point several of his colleagues in the news industry converged. They commenced to speak into their tape machines. I picked up the pace and ignored them, gaining the portico.

Hand-carved wood doors with a fanlight of stained glass greeted me at the formal entrance. The stained glass looked like a magnificent jewel exploding. I was admitted by a small, thin, lovely black woman in a powder-blue dress trimmed in white.

"How goes it, Charlotte?" I said.

"Oh, Misteer Sommer. 'Tis so sad, so sad. 'Tis a tragedy indeed. The missus been calleen you. Do you wish me to be findeen where she is?"

I was about to consent when the sliding doors off the library opened. "Not just yet, Charlotte," I said, "Thank you."

12

And there she was, wrapped in the light that swirled softly down from the crystal chandeliers.

I watched her close the library doors, shutting out the sound of muffled emotions, the sobs as well as the fugitive and fragile laughter over an anecdote, then turn, still not seeing me—not seeing anyone—her gaze off somewhere in the crystal. Her honey-colored hair was longer than I remembered it and was parted to the side, hung conspicuously forward, threatening to obscure one of her eyes. They were light green with slivers of gold in them, as if some shattered treasure lurked there. Straight from the office, she was dressed in a tailored, navy-blue skirt and double-breasted jacket, thinly pin-striped in crimson, the jacket loose at her slim waist with faintly padded shoulders. She was wearing a collarless, eggshell-colored blouse that looked like sueded silk the way the light caressed it. Lightly tinted stockings, and pumps to match the suit with some piping on the toes that played off the pinstripes. Somewhere hidden in the honey hair were earrings, because she never left the house without them. A necklace of unevenly shaped, deep blue stones and a lapis ring I had bought her were the only visible jewelry. The lapis, like her eyes, was shot with filaments of gold. Her lipstick needed touching up. She put her head back against the sliding doors and closed her eyes. Her breasts shifted faintly beneath the buffed silk.

Across from the library a pampered-looking lady emerged from a hallway and paused, eyebrows up, measuring me as I made my way toward my ex-wife. The pampered lady's face-lift wasn't the best I've seen, because whatever expression she was attempting to convey was trapped, locked in hard artifice. The magenta nails didn't help either.

When I was close enough, I said, "You look good, Cece." I touched her chin, lifted her face. She didn't fight it. "Tired, but wrapped tight."

The trace of a smile, and then she opened her eyes. "You are such a darling liar, darling."

"Can we go somewhere?" I asked. "I don't like having my back exposed to the Dragon Lady."

"Careful," said Cece. "I know politics was never your strong suit, but that's Pookie Winslow."

"Wife of the state senator?"

"Old Born Again. One of Albany's foremost chasers."

It all came back: the intimate dinner some years ago, Meredith whacking Sal with the busted wine bottle at mention of a man named Winslow. "Philandering asshole," Sal had called him. So this was the wife.

"What's she doing here?" I said. "This isn't Brian's district."

"Attending a social function. Chance to get her name in the paper, what else? It's what she does."

"Pookie," I said, taking my ex-wife's arm. "Jesus. One woman I never want to meet is a woman named Pookie."

Italian tile, octagons the color of a Madonna's breast, paved the formal entranceway. At the far end of it, French doors opened onto a patio overlooking red clay tennis courts and a bocce green. We went out the doors and onto the patio. The east and west wings of the house enclosed us. Beyond the bocce court the two tennis courts were swept with light, as if in anticipation of some elegant late-night competition. The clay looked as smooth and soft as a lady's facial powder. From the altitude of the banked lights to the sharp white chalk lines, a zone of theatrical emptiness hung in the night, like an unfulfilled promise. Down one wing of the home no light shone from a suite of windows. Young Sal's quarters: the one place it was pointless to try to keep out the darkness.

Tree roses bloomed in brick surrounds, delicately scenting the night air. Tables and chairs stained the color of cedar hunkered and squatted about the terrace. Light from the windows leavened the darkness, carving a corridor of dusky light for us to find our way in. We dropped down next to one another in a love seat.

I looked at Cece and thought her as beautiful now as the first moment our eyes met. She sat with her back straight leaning a little away from the back of the seat, her arms folded under her breasts, her eyes on the theater of light rising from the clay courts. She was marshaling her words. I drank in her profile, even the blip on the bridge of her nose, and waited.

"I knew you'd be coming," she said at last. "And to be honest, I've been dreading this moment. But it's not so bad. It's really not so bad. Do you know what, Ray?"

"What's that?"

"Possibly the only mistake bigger than our marriage was our divorce. Does that make any sense?"

I don't think, even if she had been looking at me, she could have seen my smile, or how sad it was. "Not a lot, precious," I said. "But I'll study on it."

She brought her face around then and unlocked her arms, and her right hand rose; one finger rested briefly at the corner of my eye and went away. She pressed it to her tongue, whatever the taste was, like taking Communion.

She pushed knuckles into her own eyes and said, "I saw the piece in *People*. I was happy for you. A man that's worked as hard as you have."

I thought: *And lost as much.*

She touched my shoulder in a familiar way, a gentle push. "But your hair. You looked so . . . film noir."

"Photographer's idea."

She tucked her chin and tangled her fingers, watched her hands wrestle in her lap. "He captured your element, then, didn't he?"

"She," I said, recognizing and already regretting the turn, the spin on the word. "The photographer was a woman."

"She understood you better than I," she said. "Evidently." Her eyes were fixed once more on the lighted courts, the emptiness there.

"It's possible," I said. "Which doesn't change the fact

that I loved you. Okay? So let's not get into a cocktail-party type of snit over something that doesn't concern you. We've got a successful divorce going here, let's not spoil it."

She looked at me and seemed to be blinking.

"You don't get it," I said.

She went on blinking.

"In love there's no second act. It's just words."

After a while she said, "For my part, I'm sorry you have such a limited understanding of love."

I said, "How's Meredith?"

"Maintaining. I think she finally gave in to all the free advice and took some Valium. When the priest wasn't looking. Aside from her parents, I think you're the only person she's called."

"Sal?"

"Locked in his office. Only heavyweights allowed. Skelton, the Queens DA, he's been in there, the assistant DA, Amado. According to Larry, your old friend Inspector Moriarity made an appearance."

"Larry? Who's Larry?"

"Levitsky. He's a junior partner in Sal's firm."

"Your lawyer," I said, "for the divorce."

She wrapped her arms beneath her breasts and stared off at the empty, lighted place. "That you shoved into a snowbank," she said, "no, punched. Yes, that's your style. The Queens approach to life."

"Jesus, Cece. You're seeing the guy."

"What?"

"You and Larry Levitsky . . ."

She lowered her face and closed her eyes, then stood up and pushed the honey-colored hair away from her eye. "What Meredith needs," she said, "is a lot more important than this. She's called you several times, Ray. Isn't that why you're here?"

13

I left Cece standing next to the love seat and found Charlotte inside. I followed her up the staircase to the east wing. A silver ankle bracelet snapped taut against her tendon, filament thin, catching the light like the blade of a knife. On her feet were namebrand jogging shoes with the logo writ large on the heel.

As we went down the hall pale plum carpeting muffled our footsteps. Acrylic beads swayed and clicked from Charlotte's cornrowed hair as she went from door to door, methodically turning each glass-faceted knob to inquire within. Light from wall sconces played off the oak dado, feathery and mutable as the glow from candles. Above it was grass cloth in which a color like sun-bleached barnwood predominated. Displayed among meticulously preserved samples of the children's early artwork was a selection of family photographs. A picture of the two Sals in front of the stone lodge on their property outside of Port Jervis the morning young Sal bagged his first buck, a tenpointer. Holding his Mannlicher high like he'd just scored the winning touchdown. Sixteen then, a world beater in knee-high boots, checkerboard cap turned backward, a beginner's mustache. Father and son stood on either side of the magnificent creature, hoisting it by the rack, the scarlet hole plainly visible in its snow-white breast: a heart shot.

Charlotte inched open another door, a wedge of light bronzing the side of her face. "Mrs. DeLorio?"

There were two daughters born after Sal. Genevieve had just finished her freshman year at Bennington with honors. In one photo she stood poised against ivory slopes, cradling her skis, cool and determined beneath a smooth blue sky. Zipped into scarlet Spandex, even with the freckles and hint of sunburn, she projected an image of austere beauty, a blend of tension and grace closer to music than flesh and bone. Little Christina, younger by a decade, suffered from Down's syndrome. A sawed-off tyke with the too big head, the flattened features they all seem to have, the uncertain gait as if their feet could not adapt to the hard surface of the planet. The greenhouse got refurbished when the family discovered her fascination with flowers. Sal's words, showing me a family portrait he kept in his office: "Sal and Genevieve, I get the prince and princess. It's a fairy tale, know what I mean? Next comes the troll. Life, Ray." Meredith's words: "She keeps us honest." A photograph showed Christina dancing on a tabletop in her overalls and Springsteen T-shirt, waving one of her father's cigars. Another of her transfixed before a bouquet of gladioli.

"Mrs. DeLorio?"

One of Sal seated down front of the dais at an Al Smith banquet with Wendell Reston of Magnabank, a couple of assemblymen whose names Cece would know, and Dominic Amado. One of Sal shaking hands with President Nixon. Sal in a yarmulke greeting Prime Minister Begin at some high-shekel sit-down. Sal in Kenya with the Weatherby planted against his hip, the impala he'd used it on draped at his feet, the horns rising like crooked parentheses. . . .

"Charlotte?"

She had crossed the hall, bypassing two doors.

"Young Sal's rooms, aren't they?"

"Misteer Sommer!" she hissed. "Show some respect. Ain't nobody in there."

The door opened on darkness, only faint light from the opposite windows sifting in. "Meredith?"

"Close it, Ray. Leave the lights off and lock it, will you?"

Her voice issued from across the room, from one of the two high-backed chairs facing and silhouetted against a window, the illumination hovering over the terrace. It was a small voice, so delicate and soft it invited parody. I picked out the shape of the bed, the dresser across from it, a coat tree slung with soft shapes, the archway into the adjoining room. There were tennis rackets and a full bag of golf clubs lazing in a corner. As I approached I saw the low table between the chairs, the ice bucket and bottles and glasses overturned on a tray.

"There's Jack Daniel's," she said, still a voice in a chair. "I'm drinking rum and soda."

Her hand rose with a glass in it. As soon as I could distinguish the bottles in the darkness, I doctored her drink, wrapped her fingers around it, splashed sour mash on the rocks for myself. I hoisted my poison, let the sweet heat seep into my senses. I found a coaster for my glass. Her perfume, a delicate jasmine, surprised me, like a sudden immersion. I placed my fingertips above her ears, stroked the flesh of her temples. She whispered a word, maybe several, that I could not hear. Then squeezed my hand, brought it across a cheek wet with tears, to her lips.

"Ray?"

It felt like a kiss.

"Yeah."

"You believe in God?"

"That's out of my league, sweetness."

"I don't either," she said, tipping the glass to her lips.

"That stuff and Valium could be bad news," I said.

"Not Valium. Xanax." She pushed her cheek against the back of my hand. "Oh Ray."

It went pretty much as I expected. She needed to hear every detail that I could remember of the morning, in order to hold on to her son that much longer. I stroked her temples as I spoke, still standing behind her, staring into the dusky corridor between the two wings. I took her through everything as far as the door, young Sal's cocky, parting challenge, the look on his handsome face as he stepped into the sunshine. . . . She let it go then, the denial that is love's last refuge, and her sobs washed her to the ends of the earth, to the place that is no place, the hard clear edge of solitude.

"I've lost my beautiful boy," she murmured, as if testing the veracity of her own words.

She tugged on my hand and I moved around the chair to crouch on one knee in front of her. Ringlets of blond hair enclosed her face, a rococo frame for her Yankee heritage: tipped-up nose, fine line of her lips, thin firm chin. Where Cece projected athletic vigor and tone, Meredith brought a dowry of zaftig curves. Her face, where the light touched upon it, looked almost incandescent.

"Ray, do you know what's been the greatest comfort to me, even more than family?"

"What's that?"

"Knowing he was in love, passionately so, and that he would never have to know the other, when all that's left are ashes and loathing. I think he met her in the last semester of his senior year. She had one of those fashion-model-sounding names—Alyshia? Yes, I'm certain that was her name. At least he died before his illusions did. I consider that a state of grace."

The whites of her eyes pressed feverishly against her lids. I helped her steer the glass from her lips to a coaster, and that done, walked to the windows overlooking the terrace.

"My husband says Sal was the victim of bad timing. Is that what . . . do you believe that, Ray?"

"I've heard some speculation to that effect."

"And the police?"

According to Cece, Sal Sr. had already met with the Queens DA, Skelton, master of the instant scowl. Sal might have enough juice to cut a stall with Skelton, but no way could they bury something as rich in publicity as the contents in the glove box of a Harvard boy's Porsche. I said, "It's one of the options they're looking at, certainly." I hesitated, stung by a pang of shame. "I'm sorry. I sound like some public-relations type. I just don't know that much, Meredith."

"I do. My son died seeing you. That's a form of divine irony or punishment, or maybe it's one and the same."

"Punishment?" I said. "Who's punishing who for what?"

"The God we don't believe in, that's who. Ray, I'm talking about *us*. What we had. It was—"

"It was two people on a vacation from reality," I said, with a harshness I hadn't intended. I tried to soften it. "Two friends who got foolish once."

"Ray? You'd lost Cece, and I had lost Sal long ago, ever since the birth of Christina. Suddenly I was flawed, undesirable. But foolish? It's a fool who honors a broken contract. I believe I'm quoting you, aren't I?"

"Word for word," I admitted.

She came out of the chair, a sudden desperate rush of jasmine and soft flesh, to fling her arms about my neck, to embed herself in my senses. "For years, I believed in you as a friend. That night in Haiti, I still believed in you. But

the way you've avoided me since, treating me like a one-
night stand, you're no better than my husband."

"It's a little more complicated than that. But you're
still right."

"Oh Ray. You aren't a bad man, I know that. It's just . . .
I used to think you were so much more than you are.
Maybe we were all better, once, than we are. Maybe we
were all, once, as good as my beautiful boy. Maybe this
is what we get for living."

"I don't believe that. We get what we get. It's how
you play your hand that matters."

Her shoulders squirming, she backed out of the embrace,
her lovely, if dazed face tilted up at mine, her features
sharpened by anger. "Really? You abandon me after one
night, no explanations. Then you watch my son being murdered and do nothing. You bastard!" Her hand swept back,
caught hold of the neck of a bottle, and brought it up with
the clear intention of rearranging my senses, but I caught
her wrist, worked the bottle from her fingers. I returned it
to its place on the tray beside her chair.

"C'mon, sweetness," I said, "this is a helluva way to
be thinking." I pressed her close and caressed her hair,
and pushed my wet eyes against her scalp.

"This is a helluva way to be living," she whimpered.

And like that, she went limp in my arms. I held her some
seconds longer, making sure, then lifted her onto Sal's bed.
Her breathing grew ragged with snores, then she coughed,
murmured something unintelligible. Rolled onto her hip, her
eyes squeezed shut against the faint light, like a child
pretending to sleep. Or an adult retreating into childhood.
I walked back to the window overlooking a deserted terrace. I thought about things. Haiti. One night. Not even
that: a few stolen hours. A lot can happen in that amount
of time. A war can erupt, a kingpin may die, a plane can
crash or a ship sink. A woman like Pookie Winslow could
probably have her nails done in that amount of time. And
a man can kid himself just about that long into believing
he's not a louse for seducing a friend's wife. But if he still
cares for the friend's wife, what then? I stared into the empty
love seat below, searching for something that wasn't there.

14

Downstairs I came upon Cece and Larry Levitsky, both looking out on their feet, drained by the day's events. She was nestled in his arms as they leaned against the wall outside the library. It was a little past ten, but there were still a considerable number of people mingling in there, coming and going. The front door swung in, admitting a small man with dark, jubilant eyes and a lady half his age and a head taller, their dress suggesting they had come straight from an evening at the theater. Beyond them I caught a glimpse of Pookie Winslow on the portico, a fur wrap on her shoulders and her garish fingernails flitting expressively, in animated conversation with the microphone held by the lady reporter from channel 5.

The small man winked and I nodded, watching him guide his lovely escort, his fingertips riding the base of her spine where it disappeared into her dress. It was Sydney Simon, number-two weight at DeLorio, Simon, Tortelli and Weitz. He stopped at the open entrance to the library to kiss Cece on the cheek and speak to Levitsky, but in the manner of someone delivering dictation. Behind his back Cece and Simon's companion made the best of an awkward situation by introducing themselves. Simon's fingertips returned to their accustomed place, about an inch north of the lady's derriere, and the two of them merged in the throng of distinguished mourners.

I approached the pooped-out lovers. "Meredith's out of it," I said. "Between Xanax, booze, and shock. Charlotte's sitting with her in Sal's room."

Cece grasped Levitsky's hand, saying, "Young Sal's?"

"It's where I found her."

"Shit. Goddamn Sal. Goddamn all you men, for that matter." Levitsky and I locked eyes. She pulled her hand away and we listened to Cece's heels ticking across the tile. "Larry?"

"In a moment, babe."

"*Babe?*" I muttered, all but choking. I actually liked Larry. He was a good-looking lad whose manners were a product of a Bronxville (not to be confused with the Bronx) upbringing. In his admiration for Sal, which bordered on idolatry, he was forever trying to parrot the sound of the street. Larry's weakness, when you got down to it, was an unshakable faith in the power of reason, to say nothing of a tin ear.

"Your DA, that ass-wipe mick, came up here dragging a bus load of reporters," he confided. "You got any idea what he's got he has to have this big meet with Sal?"

I shook my head no.

"It's been a real circus. Skelton playing to the cameras with that goddamn grimace of his, like he'd been handed the pope's stool sample. And then this bunch of semiliterates tramping over the grounds, putting flashlights in everyone's face. Scorcese goons, as I understand it. Jesus, Ray. Queens, the land that time forgot."

"Larry?" Cece crooned from the bottom of the staircase.

"Coming, babe."

I watched them ascend the stairs, an elegant twosome; they were going to go places in the society pages someday.

There was a guy on a stool outside the closed doors of Sal's office. He lowered the copy of the *Daily Crusader* he was reading and folded it neatly, placed it on the seat. By his costume he could have passed for an extra in a disco flick. He wore a shark-gray, double-breasted suit of a size a shark could swim in, and a midnight-blue V-neck that looked like velour. The open throat allowed him to display a fat gold necklace amid a field of unruly chest hair. His face had all the character of a stick of gum. His piece would be in a shoulder harness under his

armpit, or stuck in a holster down the groove of his spine.
On the other hand, maybe he didn't bother. A guy his
size had about as much fear of bullets as he did of dying
from his next breakfast.

"Hi, sport, you lost?"

Every hair on his head had been blow-dried into place,
two great swaths of it curving over his ears, thick and
stiff as fins.

"Sport?" I said. "What're you, the neighborhood
comic?" I was close enough then to drive a finger into
the band of gold on his throat. "I get a phone call from
Angelo, I'm on the first plane outta Phoenix. That give
you a clue, dummy?"

"You're his brother, Paul?"

"I'm not his sister, Paul, that's for sure."

The brute took a deferential step back, but no more,
his eyes becoming narrow. "For a guy lives all year in
the sunshine, you ain't got much color, sport."

"Because I don't live in it. You ever hear of skin cancer? Did you ever hear of that, dummy? Now you can
open that door for me or I can have Ange and Cato
throw you through it, whichever."

We traded glares a long moment, but on his side too
much thinking was involved, and acting independently
was foreign to his nature. He reached for the knob and
threw open the door, and his eyes expressed a kind of
bewilderment bordering on fury. I imagine Joe Scorcese
and his sons saw a lot of that look.

The ceiling in Sal's office was ten feet high and the
bookshelves behind his desk filled the wall to that height.
To one side of the desk a French door opened onto the
terrace. Several razor-thin Persian carpets, their intri-
cate designs as busy as the view of Manhattan from a
helicopter, adhered to the pegged pine flooring like gaudy
stamps. There were some chairs, leather seats and backs
the color of buckskin, loosely arranged in front of Sal's
desk. Beyond them was an informal couch, covered in
the same kin to buckskin, with pillows in pastel shades
piled along the back. A prunish-faced citizen wearing a
maroon windbreaker and gray pleated trousers, either

silk or some expensive blend, occupied the end of the couch nearest Sal's desk. He sat hunched up into the pillows, his feet not even reaching the floor, a gnomish shape that might easily be mistaken for a ventriloquist's doll.

This was Joe Scorcese, aka Joey Score, Joe the Baker, and in his venerable seventies now, simply the Baker. When he wasn't vacationing in the Caribbean, he could still be found every day at the bakery in Middle Village, where he had started out. Every day holding down his chair at the back at a table for two beneath the pay phone. Reading the sports, receiving respectful salutations from the customers. He always wore a felt hat, usually gray, that looked like something a television comedian would put on for effect, but in the presence of the Baker, even the feeblest intelligence would know better than to express amusement. The last I heard, there wasn't an agency local or federal that had enough credible information to take to a grand jury, though the market in rumors and speculation concerning the activities of the Baker remained bullish. Some hinted that just a few words into that pay phone he sat beneath could spell the end of a man's life. So the Baker had not merely a reputation and standing in the community, he possessed power beyond that of the mayor, the president of a borough, or its district attorney: people believed he dealt in death, which by inference conferred authority over its opposite, and all the perks that go with that. Danny Belinski observed, but never in print, that he had the face of a monkey and the clout of a Medici, and that was the truth.

A small bar with brass fittings and padded stools in pale leather occupied the end of the room opposite Sal's desk. I went there. In the mirror behind it, I saw Sal lift his face to the ceiling for the benefit of the Baker. There was a pad of yellow legal paper on his desk and not much else. A phone, an ashtray. I filled a glass halfway with water, drank it, enjoyed it so much I drank another half glass.

Sal put his shoes up on his desk, the half-moon lenses of his reading glasses shoved up in his hair, and remarked, "You come in here, interrupt a private conversation, just for a drink of water?"

I rinsed out the glass and left it upside down on a towel next to the sink. It was that or throw it at him. I had seen too many corpses in one day. I was in a mood to break things, but in a situation that dictated diplomacy—not always my strong suit.

"I apologize, Sal, to you, and to you, Mr. Scorcese, for the intrusion. Here's the thing: I understand you're under duress, Sal, but your client Holloway instructed me to inform you of any developments. Now, if you want me to deal with him directly, then hook me up, I'm outta here."

I moved up the room, past the Baker, who looked inanimate except for the light in the lethal black eyes that tracked my progress. Down the pad of yellow paper on Sal's desk ran what appeared to be a list of names and phone numbers. Every one of the names was flanked by checks; some had enough ink scratched to pass for cave paintings. Sal remained tilted back in his chair, feet on the desk, fingers manipulating the bluish flesh under his eyes. His beard was throwing shadow. The knot of his tie and the top button of his shirt had been loosened, the only notable concessions to sorrow.

I leaned on his desk and said, "I've been in the street, the Minnesota Strip to be exact, and a whole lot of people don't want to talk to me about your client's daughter. Tell you why: your guy behaves like a schizoid. Listen. On the tape he comes across as the Ivy League high roller with a messed-up daughter. I'm game so far. Lots of us with open sewers running through our private lives. But this is a guy so busy he sends me his tale of woe on a cassette, can't squeeze me into his hectic international schedule. The crowning touch, he sends me a check, you'd think he was trying to retire the national debt."

Sal pinched the bridge of his nose. "I don't see what's to complain about. The guy's paying you big money because it's a bitch of a job evidently. That's the way it works, Ray."

"Yeah," I conceded. "But two days earlier he was on the strip with a pal. Spends a whole day out of his international schedule to dicker with the street life, dan-

gling twenty-dollar bills. Plays hardball with a ninety-
five-pound hooker who tried to bump up the bidding.
Do you see the problem I'm having here, Sal?"

"He's desperate. Desperate men often do stupid things.
Almost guarantee it."

"I wonder. I don't know if the guy's scared or not
scared enough. What's he do for a living, you mind I
ask?"

Sal brought the half-moon lenses out of his hair, gentled them onto his nose. The glasses magnified and concentrated the stony look in his eyes. "I believe you were
hired to find the daughter, not investigate the father."

"Uh-huh." I glanced over at Joe Scorcese to see if there
was any sign of life. Not much. He was tugging listlessly
on the zipper of his windbreaker. He had a bad hand,
the knuckles swollen and the fingers bent dogleg fashion,
as if someone had literally caught his hand in the till and
slammed it on him. Kind of a private joke age was having on him. Possibly it was this that encouraged my recklessness, I don't know, but for no good reason I said,
"You know anything, Mr. Scorcese, about a party in
Queens is beating the Colombians at their own game?
Name of Peru. Said to be delivering quality product for
dimestore prices."

"Ray?" cried Sal, jerking his feet off the desk. "What're
we getting into here?"

"Mr. Scorcese," I said. "Does the guy exist? I mean I
don't see something like that going down without you
knowing about it is why I ask."

Sal came out of the chair then, and around the desk,
yanking off his glasses. "The fuck you talking about?"

"Salvatore," said the Baker, stressing all the syllables,
raising his hand with the crooked finger, "please. I am
a speak with Ray." The old man hiked himself forward
until his shoes touched the floor and said, "You ask about
this Peru. I too have heard the name. Why do you ask
this, Ray?"

I took a deep breath. "The list of names and numbers
on the legal pad there, if I had to guess, you're pumping
people in the know. Any luck?"

The Baker's eyes traveled to Sal and back to me.

"I'm a seventy-two years of age. Got my health, my bowels is good. Why am I so lucky?"

"Why?" I said.

"I never believe in luck. Brains. I hear somebody like you is using his brains, I'm a listen. Seventy-two, I'm a listen."

"For what it's worth, the business this morning might tie to this guy Peru. My information, the two boys from the Bronx got touched because they were in Queens to make an arrangement with some people from Colombia. The deal being they would combine forces with the Puerto Ricans to put this Peru operation out of business."

The Baker regarded me some seconds without any discernible emotion. Then: "What else can you tell me about this man?" There was a tension in his voice that was as quiet as a tiger crouching. It was a voice that expected people to think before they answered, and to think carefully.

"Nothing," I said. "That's it. Unless Sal can add to it." He was standing behind the bar now, a snifter of brandy in his hand, the liquor brightly streaking the glass as he swirled it in an easy, practiced motion. "I don't know how much Skelton or Moriarity took you into their confidence, Sal. Or how much they know. This morning, it didn't seem to be a whole hell of a lot."

"It still isn't," said Sal, coming away from the bar, "the putzes."

"Except what they found in the glove box of Sally's car."

Sal didn't stop or say a word until he was back in the chair behind his desk, his feet up and the snifter in his lap, the brandy moving with the motion of his hand. He extended his free hand in my direction. "Ray, you seem to be doing everything today except finding a missing daughter."

"There is one other thing."

"You hear that, Joe?" Sal uttered several sentences not in English, and the Baker, squirreled once more back among the throw pillows, nodded solemnly. "I told him you had probably discovered the remains of Amelia Earhart."

I turned my face to one side and nodded, and strolled

back up the room to the bar, and ran the tap. "The guy out there on the stool, I thought he was the house comedian, but you got him beat, Sal, hands down." I added ice cubes to my glass. The water in New York is famous for its flavor. All I tasted was death. I sloshed the contents into the sink and went to the door. I stopped there, one hand on the knob. "While I was digging through the mess your client Holloway made in the street, I drew a tail. I lured him into an alley, guess what? It's one of the boys in the van this morning, with the automatics. I'd swear to it."

Sal's hand with the snifter in it stopped moving, but it was the Baker who spoke first. "You Ray, where is this man?"

"Facedown in the alley if the police haven't scraped him up yet. Whoever coldcocked me made chopped liver of his face. And took the trouble to burn his fingers, make it impossible to get prints."

Sal looked across at Joe, then up at me. "That leaves just the jig with the shotgun this morning. You think he might be Peru?"

I described him to the Baker, the same description I gave Lieutenant Cox this morning, but nothing registered in the old man's face. It occurred to me that his eyes resembled nothing so much as the eyes of a good veteran cop: they had seen it all. They could look into hell without blinking.

Sal said, "Keep in touch. And Ray? I owe you." He put his eyes down, focusing on the shifting amber fluid in his glass, and when he brought them up, they were blurred, uncertain. "You know what I've got to live with as a last memory? He tells me this morning about this girl he's in love with, he's going to marry her, even though there's some difficulty, and what I told him was he was thinking with his dick. Stick to the game plan, I said. You can always get married, but right now there's law school, and with his looks, there'll always be ladies to lay. You know what he says, his last words to me?"

I put my hand on the back of my neck, and scratched there, and said nothing.

"He says, 'Maybe *you* ought to take this tape to Ray.

You might learn something about class while you're there.' "

"That was anger speaking, Sal. That's all that was."

"I got a priest, I want sermons. Now please get the fuck outta here. I need to make some phone calls."

"Sure."

I was across the threshold when he said, "If you see Meredith, tell her . . . well, you know what to say."

What was left of the news brigade converged when I stepped onto the portico. Microphones were thrust in my face and I was isolated in the will-o'-the-wisp glare of camera lights that made my hands, as I tried to fend off the blinding brightness, look eerie, almost skeletal against the night. Questions were lobbed out of the darkness from every direction, although I recognized one of the voices, perhaps because it was the shrillest. It belonged to the lady reporter from channel 5. She led a chorus of curiosity concerning the reported presence of "gangland mobster Joe Scorcese," pronouncing it *Scorceezi*. When my eyes had adjusted I was happy to see that Arnold Wittgenstein was not among my interrogators.

I flashed the lens of channel 5 my best smile. "Sorry, miss. I don't know any Scorceezi. Have a nice day."

15

The Hutchinson Parkway is a paved throwback to the era of horse paths. Narrow as the old gray mare's haunches, it winds and dips and lashes around outcroppings of granite, its only concession to the latter part of the twentieth century being the automated toll booths. I sped along the Hutch with the windows down, the radio up, the wind shuttling across the back of my neck, a cool pressure on my still tender nape. Headlights from the opposite lanes flared up on the windshield with the harsh redundancy of a police interrogation.

Once past the Bronx co-ops, the magnitude of the boroughs hove dramatically into view. It didn't seem to matter how many times I came upon it in the night, closing in on the Whitestone Bridge this way, the city always got the jump on my expectations. So much light, so much promise . . .

Like the prince in the fairy tale: young Sal with the lipstick-red Porsche, the ticket to Harvard Law, a lover with a fashion-model name. And a chunk of uncut cocaine in his glove box. That stunk. I didn't believe it, not because the boy had gone out and cornered the market on virtue, but for the simple reason he would not be so careless. The boy of this morning was not a driveling, twitchy, driven individual; he was in control. A little residue of anger there, alluding to his father as a walking asshole, but not bent out of shape by it. Even dummies didn't drive around with that much stuff hidden so casually. Only a publicity-hungry idiot of Jimmy Skelton's dimensions would be persuaded that he had compelling evidence of criminal activity on the part of someone with so much promise, and a Porsche to boot. The story would play big on local stations, with better-than-even odds to grab a sound bite on a network newscast. There would be blood in the water then. The piranhas would make short work of young Sal's life. Death by bullets was almost a kindness next to being buried by the media.

I rolled up the driveway, pressing the plastic dingus that raised the garage door, and came to a rest beside the Mercedes. And froze. Inside the house I could hear a heavy backbeat, the rippling of a guitar solo. I didn't remember leaving the radio on. And that loud?

Cece? I couldn't imagine the how or why, but I hadn't changed codes on the security system.

I crept from the garage and hiked up the street. A half block away I recognized a black compact with copper racing stripes and a bumper sticker that read *E.T., I Brake for Aliens.*

Going up the flagstone steps laid into the lawn, I sifted through memories of our encounters. And thought: Yes, that night, after I saw Cece slip into the taxi and dropped Levitsky on his butt in the snow, that was close. As close as it's ever gotten. We were practically hanging on each other.

A full moon drenched the slate roof in silver and brought the bank of Tropicana roses to attention: a sharp burst of salmon in front of the window boxes brimming with purple and white petunias.

I took off my shoes and eased through the front door, punched my code into the alarm panel, in case my visitor had reactivated the system. I checked the rest of the entryways. No one was lurking in the shadows to poke a weapon at me. I entered the room off the hall optimistically identified as the family room, where all the music was coming from. There were shelves for records and shelves for books and a working fireplace in the wall opposite the doorway. A large-screen television at one end and a bumper-pool table at the other, with cues in a rack mounted on the wall. A fawn leather couch and flanking armchairs were grouped to face the fireplace, and at one end of the couch a head of frosted, electric

hair jerked to the beat of "Just Another Night," Mick
Jagger gone solo.

"Housebreaking," I said. "Not just a career, but an
adventure."

Pat Conner maneuvered herself around on the couch,
got her knees beneath her, showed a sleepy smile, and
said, "You do keep a lady waiting."

"Ladies don't break into men's houses."

"Of course they don't. They use a key from the office
and the memory of the boss fumbling with the code to
the alarm."

I sank onto the couch beside her and inhaled the sour
aftermath of ashes left beneath the andirons for months.
I listened to Mick emoting, something about being lonely
in a hundred-dollar hotel or motel room, and I didn't
see the problem, compared with young Sal alone in a
ten-thousand-dollar casket. I was in a mood to punch
out district attorneys. I wasn't greedy. One would do.

"Ray?"

"Sorry. I don't think I'm going to be good company."

The leather squeaked and she was close enough for me
to detect the scent of a new perfume. She was still wearing her violet eyes. "I know what you need, Ray. Some
Bach. Some Jack D over shaved ice, Bach, and a bowl
of ice cream with Patty's surprise. How about it?"

"I've had enough surprises for the day, thank you."

She put her fingers to my cheek, then moved away,
and soon I was listening to the merriment and gusto of
the *Brandenburg Concertos*. Life before two world wars,
crematoria, gulags, Mafias, the plague of isms that pro-
moted murder as a matter of principle. Life before the
sewers backed up, flooding the streets of the world with
users and pushers and fashionable drug czars and dirty
little button men.

At my elbow there appeared a china bowl heaped with
vanilla ice cream sprinkled liberally with a dark, aro-
matic substance over which something the color of honey
had been ladled. A glass filled with shaved ice and the
rich amber of sour mash was fitted into my hand. Pat
said, "Enjoy."

The sprinklings on the ice cream, she explained, were

freshly ground coffee beans and the honey color happened to be her favorite scotch, Dewar's.

"A man your age," she said, licking her spoon, "needs to learn simple pleasures. What?" She put her half-finished bowl of ice cream on the glass cocktail table and leaned back, tucked her stockinged feet beneath her, and laid her cheek on her shoulder to look along the couch at me. "What'sa matter, Ray?"

I looked back at her. There'd been some drinking done, but she didn't slur her words and her eyes were open, clear. "This whole day's what's the matter." I told her what bothered me about Holloway, a guy playing fast and loose with a corporate checkbook, and yet goes berserk negotiating over an amount that would be pocket change to a man in his position.

"I don't see the problem," she said, lifting her face. "Everybody's generous when it's someone else's money. It's another story when it's their own. Ask Martina. Try collecting from some of the really rich assholes we've had for clients. They act like it's some kind of enormous favor they're doing us, paying a bill. This Holloway, he sounds like he's right off the assembly line."

"Could be," I said. I touched the slight swelling on the back of my neck and clenched my teeth an instant. I reached for the drink I hadn't touched and sought some relief there. "I still think he's some kind of screwball."

"Forget about it, already." She retrieved her bowl of ice cream. "You mind if I tell you something?"

"You mean, do I mind if the earth turns?"

"You been hanging out with these money types so long, this crowd Cece got you into, maybe you forgot how it is. Marty and me, you think they treat us any different'n a whore in the street, you're dreaming."

I looked at her, tipping my head a little. That milky complexion showed a rush of color. She stared into her lap a little longer, riding out the emotion, then shrugged and said, "You still love her."

"I don't know that, Patty."

"You do." She put her feet on the floor and snatched the empty bowl from my hands. "Ask me the difference between being foolish and being a fool, I can tell you. It's time. Don't you be a fool too, Ray."

I sipped my drink and listened to water running, plate-ware stacked with authority, drawers opened and shut, the teeming world of Bach. Pat came back into the room just as the needle was lifting off the record. She had freshened her makeup and her eyes appeared bright and reckless. She found her high heels beneath the cocktail table and sat on the couch to strap them on. Having accomplished this with a barely suppressed violence, she stood with her handbag clasped against a hip, a brittle smile fixed in her face. "Oh," she chirped, and poked about in the handbag. A shiny object tumbled next to me on the couch. A key. "There you go. You have any ideas where a girl can go these days to get laid?"

"You don't want . . ." I started to say, but the sharp edge to her face routed that argument. It wasn't a good one anyway. I got to my feet, feeling how tired I really was, and took a step toward her. The brittle smile trembled, but before it came apart completely, she turned and was gone from the room, the sound of her heels echoing in the hall. I thought about trying to stop her. Taking refuge in desire, given the events of the day, seemed an understandable, even sane thing to do. Except somewhere down the line it might leave me open to the charge of being one more of those who had treated her like a whore in the street. By not stopping her I thought I was choosing between her body and her respect, but in the long run I realized, as I shuffled down the hall to the door that was left open, the choice was probably narrower: between her resentment and her contempt. I stood in the doorway, hearing the angry acceleration of four cylinders, the bark of tires in the distance negotiating a turn. Moonlight combed the lawn with a luster that belonged to dreams.

Once, on a vacation to Rome with Cece, I toured St. Peter's and stood before Michelangelo's marble sculpture called the *Pietà*, still awesome despite the attack by a madman with a hammer. Christ with all his wounds is draped across a grieving Madonna's lap. When the phone rang, I was approaching a figure that I was certain was young Sal, his face intact, head reclined against a woman's bosom. Blood ran from his eyes like tears. For some reason I was appealing to the Madonna, whose face remained hidden. The phone kept ringing.

It was after one in the morning, and the reason the phone kept ringing and was not intercepted by my answering service was because someone had dialed my unlisted number. I fumbled for the instrument and pressed it to my ear.

"I'm here," I said.

Loud music, voices, the hurly-burly attendant upon active night spots came down the line along with Pat's voice: "Ray?"

"Yeah. How you doin'?"

"Great. Listen. Ray?"

"It's me, love."

"I'm doing great. I forgot to tell you. Noon, there's a lady coming to the office. To see you. She sounds like money, at least the accent does, but she was very definite, she'd come to the office. I guess I forgot what it's like to have a regular person for a client."

"Noon?" I said.

"She'll even wait if you're late," Pat said. "Listen. I'm sorry."

"Stop it. You need a ride, I'll come pick you up."

"I already got someone. Hey, wha's your name? Petey? Petey is a very sensitive person, Ray. He saw a foreign movie once. He sells Ford cars and golfs in the low eighties. Isn't that something?"

"Oh hell," I said.

"Sweet dreams," she said, and hung up.

16

It was a little past seven when I awoke, the wall above the headboard still in mauve shadow, the parquet of the floor the color of a buttermilk pancake. Through open windows the heat was already intruding, crowding the room like a party of uninvited fat people. I shut the windows and switched on the AC.

An hour later I had showered, shaved, retrieved the morning's paper, prepared an omelet to go with my Jamaican coffee. I sat outside at a table beneath the bedroom windows. For a few moments I gazed at the riot of roses, Don Juans and Star Whites in furious bloom. The *Times* gave the shooting major play (for the *Times*), placing a headline at the bottom of the front page, continuing the coverage on page 12. Most of the article was a rehash of standard history with regard to drug traffic in Queens, along with bios of the victims, a paragraph devoted to the mechanics of the shooting, some self-serving quotes from the office of the Queens district attorney. Lieutenant Cox was quoted too, but his remarks amounted to a courteous no-comment. Nothing about coke in a glove box.

Preparing myself for the meet with Lieutenant Cox in the Argent, I spent a peaceful quarter hour with a pair of scissors pruning the roses and scrutinizing for aphids. Since Cece and I had separated, I seldom cut any for display inside, content to enjoy them on the stem, chopping them when they turned blowsy. Clipping away among all that perfume and tender beauty brought me as close to answering Meredith's question of the night before as I would ever get. A person does not have to believe in God to know He exists.

But the guilt Meredith assumed went too far into metaphysics for my taste. A guy from Queens can get into trouble at that altitude. And trouble was something I already had plenty of.

Finished to resemble the pitted, travertine look of Boro Hall, from which it was a several minutes' walk, the Argent Towers had earned a reputation as a bordello of sorts: in the Argent loyalties, understandings, cherished values—yes, even blood oaths—got discreetly screwed. It was a building where deals were struck, and riding up in the elevator I reviewed my hand. It must have looked something like the one Caesar saw on the morning of the ides.

All of the doors were fitted with brass numbers, and below them in a metal sleeve were plastic inserts bearing the name of the enterprise operating within. I checked the note from Pat and stopped in front of room 3020: Long Arm Legal Services, Inc. The screw at the top of the "3" had worked loose and the brass hung upside down. Dust clung to the inverted numeral. Doubtless it was something that would be taken up at the next stockholders' meeting.

Sitting behind the receptionist's desk studying a copy of *Sports Illustrated*, young Wallace Fitzsimmons, Lieutenant Cox's understudy, treated me to a glare. He was wearing a clean white shirt today and a necktie that was mostly navy blue with thin crimson and canary stripes in it. A flush practically ignited his mustache, suggesting his bitterness at not having anything pointed to throw. "You're five minutes late," he said.

"That all? Long Arm, this is Izzy Stein's operation. His brother Abe's wife Zelda sits there. The Izman must really owe you guys to let you move in at this hour."

Izzy and Abe Stein were skip tracers, independent contractors who specialized in the capture and return of individuals that had jumped bail. Abe was methodical in his work, but Izzy was a betting man, inclined to look for the shortcut. His inspirations were famous for landing him in the soup.

The beauty of a meeting like this was that everyone concerned could deny that it took place.

"You know, Wall—may I call you Wall?—even if you got more hair on your face than Zelda, you are still prettier."

He rolled the magazine into a shape that suggested he might want to employ it as a pain enhancer. He struck his palm several times with it, then jabbed a button on his phone panel to announce my presence. A door beyond the reception area opened and the bony, olive face of Dominic Amado, the assistant district attorney of Queens, appeared.

His black eyebrows arched like thatchwork above his impatient eyes, and from a high forehead his hair tumbled away in black curls. He wore an off-the-rack navy suit with chalk-colored pinstripes, a scarlet tie with indigo shapes in it that resembled a computer printout. His black wingtips glowed with polish even if the heels had a slant to them like a seven iron. He was a small, proud man not getting rich fast.

"Nice to see you, Dom. Skelton busy trying to promote himself a sound bite as usual?"

His eyes sped north for an instant, but his roguish nature was very much in check, from the slope of his shoulders to the absence of snappy repartee. He was behaving very much like a man with a gun at his head.

The room into which I was introduced was about twice as deep as the reception area, and equally nondescript. A long table with lion's-claw feet and a poor imitation of a mahogany finish occupied most of the floor space, with eight high-back chairs attending it. There were filing cabinets. Plants that in their youth may have looked like pothos and a Wandering Jew were suspended in dull earthenware in front of the windows. The foliage belonged in a rest home, it had so many liver spots. A brown couch was backed against a wall, and three grown, really overgrown, men had managed to jam their behinds onto it, so that their dark trouser legs projected up and out, like appendages of a large beetle. The floor was covered in a nappy, off-colored carpet, and the little light that crept through the venetian blinds vanished into the shadows like decency at a bachelor's party. Smoke from cigarettes and pipes backed and filled against the fluorescent illumination. The skin of the men's faces had a greenish cast, as if viewed through a thin dollar bill.

I had come to this little confab in a lightweight cream suit with flecks of gray in it, a gray silk tie hanging pencil thin, a shirt pin-striped in white, lilac, Florentine blue, and mauve. I wore white suspenders, and a gray silk display hankie danced from my breast pocket. On my feet were a pair of white canvas slip-ons with rope soles, no socks. My cheek was smooth, my hair neatly parted. I thought I looked sober, professional, and sharp as a pickpocket at a policemen's ball, until I entered that room. To a man my companions were dressed in dark suits, heavy shoes. The expiring foliage in front of the windows exhibited more joie de vivre.

Dominic dispensed with the formalities with his customary abruptness. He snapped off introductions to members of the FBI, DEA, Justice Department, Treasury, and then with a flip of his hand, as if dismissing a witness for whom he had no more questions, he mentioned the members of the NYPD who happened to be present. That took care of everyone except the two gentlemen sitting opposite each other at the end of the table nearest me. The black guy wore dark glasses, a blue suit, a mostly blue tie wobbling out of his white collar and down his expanding chest and belly. He had the build of an offensive guard or tackle gone soft in retirement. He was chewing two or three toothpicks incessantly and there was something faintly askew about his Afro, which suggested a slipped rug. The white guy also affected the Secret Service look, wearing silver-rimmed granny glasses with gray lenses. His hair, which was the color of an orangutan's coat, erupted around his almost mime-pale face in unmanageable slivers and quills. Agent Orange, I thought. And his partner, the Rugman.

"These two gentlemen," I said. "I think we missed somebody."

"No, we didn't, because they aren't here," drawled Amado, pulling an eye shut as he sighted on the smoke swirling and crawling across the ceiling.

I looked down the table at the hulking figure of the chief inspector of detectives for the borough of Queens. His name was Patrick Moriarity. He wore his silver hair in a severe brush cut; a crisp white collar circumnavigated a seventeen-inch neck. His eyes were the color of ice turning to slush. As we traded looks his porcelain uppers made a noise like someone chewing dry cereal without the benefit of milk. "It's been a while, Chief," I said. "Good to see you."

"Same here, Ray."

"Okay," I said, turning to Dominic Amado, who was standing behind a chair occupied by Lieutenant D. J. Cox, "have it your way. These two aren't even present at a meeting that officially did not take place. Just remember: candor is as candor does."

The man from the Justice Department, Travis Bucknell, spoke up: "Blame it on Executive Order 12333, signed in eighty-one. It's legitimate for them to operate domestically under quote certain circumstances, end quote."

"Mr. Bucknell, it's not a matter of legitimacy, it's a matter of manners."

"Put a lid on it," said Amado. "We aren't here to argue etiquette. Sit down, Ray."

"I'll stand," I said. "I'm more comfortable staying uncomfortable."

"If discomfort is something you're looking for," hissed the redheaded man from behind his dark glasses, "that can be arranged."

I just shook my head. "I don't believe it. I pay taxes to support morons like this."

"Ray, please," urged Amado, "you aren't helping your case."

"My case?"

Amado refused to meet my eyes. "All right. What's in your best interests."

"My best interests. I'm listening."

He turned his back on me, another courtroom flourish, and appeared to address the three gentlemen on the couch, the beetle legs from the DEA. "Somebody by the name of Peru, you seem to think he had something to do with yesterday's business in the parking lot."

"Oh. Well, a guy gets down in the streets, he hears things. Used to be that's what cops did too." I looked at Moriarity, then Cox, nothing doing in either pair of eyes. "I dunno, Dom, but what I hear, if it isn't completely true, it still sounds interesting. I'm you, I'd run with it."

Amado dipped a shoulder as a prelude to swinging around, his face construed in a brief, wry expression. It was there, and then gone, replaced by the gun-at-the-head glaze. "Describe what you saw of the shooting, Ray. Only what you saw."

I did that. The men in the room listened.

"Thank you," said Dominic Amado. He addressed the room. "Any questions?"

There were none.

"Then I have one for you," said Amado.

"Sure," I said.

Amado veered along the table behind Agent Orange and approached. He did not lift his eyes, but addressed me as if a listening device lurked behind my lapels. "You gone public yet, like to your pal Belinski, with your ideas about Peru?"

I looked around the room and only the unidentified duo nearest us seemed at all interested in my answer. The rest were occupied with more pressing concerns, like fingernails, or the contents of their pipes, the line at Belmont, or in Bucknell's case, the shuttle schedule for D.C. out of LaGuardia.

I bent down and whispered in his ear, "I'm not wired. And to answer your question, no."

"No? You definitely have not spoken to the media?"

I shook my head. It seemed to buck Amado up a bit. He glanced over his shoulder in the direction of Agent Orange, then screwed his neck further, apparently for any reaction from Moriarity. If there was any change in the chief inspector's face, it was purely geological. There was a curious mix of relief and anger in the look Amado gave me, and he did not so much confide as spit his words: "Keep it that way, and you'll be sparing the DeLorio family a lot of grief."

I grinned, but not with any warmth. "We're talking cover-up, and you hate it. But you have your people to

answer to, and they have theirs, and somewhere up there
running this show, I bet I'd find our shy friends here."

Amado flushed and got up on his toes to press his argument. "Watch it, Ray. You don't want to get out of
your league. Take the deal, it's a good one. Going public
on the coke would be a waste of the taxpayer's money,
you and I both know that. It was a plant. Let the boy-
friends handle the ramifications. We're going to treat the
DeLorio shooting as a drive-by. Wrong people killed all
the time."

"You know it's a crock," I muttered.

"I know what I know," snapped Dominic Amado.
"Now don't fuck it up, Ray."

"You through?"

Amado shot his cuffs and picked at some invisible annoyance on his sleeve. "Yeah. You can go now."

"I don't think so." I brushed past him and got a hand
on Agent Orange's shoulder and put some weight on it.
I could feel the muscle spring into definition beneath my
hand. He lunged backward trying to rise from the chair,
so I leaned a little more. Gravity and the fact I can still
bench-press three hundred pounds persuaded him to relax. No one in the room, including his partner, moved
to his defense, although there was an edge in everyone's
eye, and the air was charged with a deceptive listless-
ness. "Now, Red, you come into Queens pushing your
weight, you must think you have a pretty good reason.
Way I look at it, Peru must be high up on your wish list,
am I right?"

"Mr. Sommer," he said in a raspy voice, directing his
gaze across the table at his partner, "people who dive
into unfamiliar waters are not merely stupid, they are
generally short-lived."

"That a threat, Red?"

"No—" and now he turned his head, the prickly hair
like a fire frozen to his polar complexion, his eyes absent
behind the gray lenses. "That's not a threat. It's a fact."

"I believe you," I said. "Must be your winning personality. Now, here's another fact. Two days before I was
hired to search for the runaway daughter of a client, the
client himself was playing detective, rousting hookers
along the Minnesota Strip for information. He didn't

learn much, because he had a personality like yours, Red, but he did make an impression. A vivid one. The description I got, the guy could've been your twin. Even had a partner like you do." I gave the black guy a nasty smile. "That rug slips much further, people're going to mistake it for a welcome mat, walk all over you, fatso."

The heavy black man's hand jumped toward his scalp and he growled something inarticulate, but definitely hostile.

I leaned a little more on Agent Orange's shoulder. "It was you," I said, "wasn't it?"

This time I let him push back his chair. Face-to-face we were about the same size, maybe he had an inch on me in height, twenty pounds trimmer. "Play the hero somewhere else," he said in a voice that sounded like a hand file working dry pine. He was wearing a dark suit with white checks in it, and a bow tie with all the colors of the flag was attached to his white collar. He said, "Do yourself a favor and stay out of my face."

I dropped a shoulder, pumped a fist between his ribs, followed up with a cross to the breastbone, just below the bow tie, that pushed the wind from his throat with a sound like a bad radiator valve. His knees folded and he went sideways, crashed onto a hip. Lieutenant Cox landed on one of my arms, Dominic Amado shook from the other. Both were shouting. Most everyone in the room was. Except Agent Orange. He was propped up on the carpet, gasping, his eyes bulging, face a bad color.

"Get him a wastebasket!" I yelled.

Just in time, his partner got one under his chin. Agent Orange pitched over it and lost breakfast. I yanked my arm loose from Amado, dropped to a knee next to the indisposed tough guy. "That was for a ninety-five-pound trick by the name of Dixie. Now listen: I'm going along with the deal Dominic's offered. I'm from dumb town. But if this Peru is responsible for young Sal's murder, all bets are off. I mean that."

Agent Orange put a hand to his mouth and coughed, very tentatively. "Get him out of my face," he said to his partner, who helped him to his feet even as he wrestled to keep his hairpiece in place.

17

Travis Bucknell, the gentleman from the Justice Department, slipped onto the elevator behind me, toting a battered briefcase with a triple-digit combination lock. Bifocals in gold Ben Franklin frames clung to the bridge of a narrow, elegant nose shot with radiant evidence of hard drinking. But pleasant, yearbookish features had survived time and liquor: sandy hair only beginning to recede, white teeth all in a row, sincerity radiating from twinkling eyes. With the doors closed and the elevator descending, he chucked a cigarette from a package and asked if I'd like one.

"Quit," I said. "Going on fifteen years."

"You mind?"

I hunched my shoulders.

"Thanks." He put a flame to the cigarette just as we touched down, the doors parted. "I overheard Inspector Moriarty, I think it was. You did a hitch in Nam?"

"Yeah."

The lobby walls were mauve and gray, and heavy gray curtains brushed the floor. Off to one side was a kind of conversation pit crowded with chairs and a couch covered in black Naugahyde. The chairs were maroon, the color of an overripe cherry, and the seats rose convexly as if from an excess of stuffing. There were ashtrays on octagonal mirrored columns. Dumb cane flourished behind the furniture. It was at once somber and flash, like a bordello pressed into service for a funeral.

We stepped off the elevator. Travis Bucknell said, "I was on staff at the embassy in Saigon, sixty-eight through seventy-two." There was a slow, easy cadence to his

voice, a lilt that suggested an educated Virginian. He
slung his gray coat over his shoulder, his pale blue oxford
shirt ballooning at his waist, where excess flesh rolled
above his belt, almost bobbed there. "I had as little truck
with spooks as was humanly possible, Mr. Sommer."

"Ray."

"Obliged. What always disturbed me about fellows like
the pair upstairs, they weren't our enemies, but they
didn't seem to be entirely in our camp either. They had
their own agenda."

"That's a polite way of saying they kind of make up
the rules as they go along. I know one or two of them."

"So do I," he drawled, "so do I." We had come as far
as the revolving doors and I told him I was staying behind to meet another party. He let his briefcase down
between his ankles and reached a handkerchief from his
hip pocket and ran it around the inside of his shirt collar.
He had the look of a man stealing up on an unpleasant
decision, unless it was simply the look of a man dying
for a hair of the dog. "Ray, what I'm about to tell you
is a violation of confidence. If you are not the man I
think you are, I'm scuttling years of cautious careerism.
To say nothing of a prodigious reputation as a closet sot.
I happen to know that the gentleman you assaulted is
not only CIA, his file bears the double-A designation.
Absolute Autonomy."

"A license to kill," I said.

Bucknell nodded. "A succinct definition, sir, and one
that you will never see in print. As to identity, in his few
appearances in closed committees, it has been Blades.
C. Boyd Blades. His most recent theater of operations
has been northern Latin America. Colombia, Venezuela,
Ecuador . . ."

"Peru," I murmured.

His blond eyebrows moved a trifle, but that was the
only change in his face.

"Anything on the partner?" I asked.

"Nada." We exchanged business cards and he said,
"Watch your ass, Ray. Blades is no gentleman."

"Mr. Bucknell, I was born and raised in Queens. That's
practically all I know are guys like Blades."

"New Yorkers," he said, shaking his head. *Noo Yaw-*

kahs. Whatever that meant seemed to invigorate him. He grasped my hand and shook it firmly. I watched him stride out the lobby, the back of his blue shirt darkly splotched from sweat. A black limousine glided into view and he got into it and was gone, vanished behind black glass. The motorcycle escorts cranked up their sirens and the limo drifted away.

The potbellied chair was surprisingly comfortable. It was obstructed from view of the elevator by an angle in the wall and tucked back among the shrubbery where I could sit in relative obscurity. A bell sounded. Elevator doors slid smoothly open, another bell rang, doors were sucked shut. Nobody I wanted to see flounced past, clerks and secretaries pursuing an early lunch. The bell again. The swoosh of hydraulics. Not a crowd this time. I listened to footsteps, leisurely, echoing: two men, not talking. Then I saw them: the stout one in the wide lapels, wearing yesterday's hat, and his companion, still looking college age in spite of the change of costume, the mustache all waxed, an extra-long Kool slanted rakishly from his lips.

"Lieutenant?" I said.

Cox touched his partner's sleeve, and the young man kept going. Cox came down the steps and approached in his slow, effortless manner, the hat so perfect he could retire and give lessons. He situated his fanny on the black Naugahyde, draped an ankle across the faded crease in his trousers. He performed some minor adjustments on the hat and popped a wafer of dried plum into his mouth. He regarded me with his small, unreadable eyes in a way that would have been offensive, except he was a cop, and didn't know any better. "You wanna know who told me you were a stand-up guy?"

"I'm betting it wasn't Amado."

"Danny Belinski. He said you aren't as smart as you think you are, but your instincts are good. Brother, I hope so. That show upstairs, Amado's still stewing over if he should slap you down for striking a federal officer. Moriarity's got him pretty much under control, but you took a chance there, Ray. You took some kinda chance."

"What, for punching a guy who wasn't at a meet that didn't even take place? Get real." Popping Agent Orange, or Blades, had felt good, real good, but it didn't loosen any bolts the way I hoped it would. Blades had stayed within himself, give him that. Got to his feet, brushed himself off, ignored the halfhearted apologies offered by Amado. Ignored everyone, really. My face the whole time stuck in his lenses, like we were the only two men in the room. He didn't have to express how much pleasure it would give him to kill me. The look on his face was scarier than that. Killing me—killing anyone— didn't matter enough to arouse an emotion like pleasure. "Mind if I ask you something?"

He turned his hands over on his thighs, palms up.

"Never mind," I said. "Only one of the people I mentioned Peru to would have a pipeline to the Queens DA. Of course. So let me ask you this: the stiff you found on Eightieth Street, in the van yesterday morning, you get anything from his prints?"

A flicker of conspiratorial light danced for an instant in the depths of his eyes. "We don't get nothing," he said, "because we don't get no prints. If I'm telling you anything."

"Fingers burned."

"Ten little crispy critters. Lab boys say it'd take about a minute. Put the guy's socks on his hands like mittens, douse 'em in lighter fluid, touch 'em off. How jah know?"

"Instinct."

Something parted his jowls, the thin remembrance of how it was to grin. He fed himself another wafer and hunkered forward on the couch. "Give." He snapped a finger.

"Have your guy Wall—I assume he performs some useful function aside from antagonizing everyone he meets— have him punch in the specifics on the computer, see what it kicks out. Ought to be at least one stiff in the past twenty-four hours in Manhattan that might suggest a similar MO."

He jogged his hat several millimeters without taking his eyes off me. "Serious?"

"West Fifty-first Street. The guy, I'm sure, was one of the shooters yesterday. The other Latino."

Cox pulled on his lip, thinking, his eyes all over my face. "I guess I just didn't hear a word you said."

"I know someone in the Scorcese family leaked what I'd been told about Peru."

"I don't know any a that, Ray."

"It wasn't to save the kid's reputation. That's just the bargain I'm supposed to think I made."

"Think what you want, you didn't do bad," he whispered, moving his eyes, taking in the lobby. "This is something you didn't hear a word of from me: coupla months ago at this college in Vermont the sister attends—what's her name?"

"Genevieve."

"Yeah, Jenny. Campus cop spots something suspicious in Sal's car. A baggy with white powder lying on a hand mirror on the seat. It was just a coupla grams, and the kid cries it's a plant. Daddy, according to the roommate that told us, squared it with the campus authorities before the police could be involved."

"On the seat," I said. "Lieutenant, this is a kid graduated cum laude from Harvard."

"That's the story. I don't say it ain't got an odor."

"This helpful roommate, you find him at Rent-A-Judas?"

"It's legit, Ray," said Cox. "One of the few fucking things in this case that we know is. Politics." He sneered. It was a whole speech in three syllables.

18

I swung onto the gravel behind the office building in the black Mercedes two-seater, a 450 SEL that Winston Bates, of Bates and Bates Europa Imports, provided the company for maintaining an open file on his brother's wife, some shapely fluff that Winston had had a go-round with and whose discretion he mistrusted. I had met Winston at a political soiree arranged by Cece and Meredith DeLorio. He had inherited Europa from his father, so he was smooth, educated, and because of it came across as a sincere guy who just happened to cuckold his own brother. For some reason this morning I did not feel so smart tooling around the streets in a Mercedes.

It was not quite noon. Every hair was in place and her makeup was immaculate, but one glance told me Pat was operating on caffeine and the diminished reserves of youth. She wore white today and her eyes were blue, almost neon. I asked her how she was and she said fine, but she'd feel a whole lot better if she could throw up. Then she told me the lady with the accent was waiting for me in the conference room.

An archway opened into the conference room. The walls were pale gray and the floor was covered in deep, slate-colored carpet. A long black table, highly polished, occupied a large portion of the room. The chairs were low-backed and comfortably padded and rolled easily on brass casters. There were file cabinets and shelves for law books and journals and some whacked-out lithographs Cece selected, done by Miró. It was a room so little used now that I generally passed through it without noticing a thing in it. The lady with the accent changed all that.

Sitting there at the far end of the table, scuttling a tan cigarette in an ashtray, she seemed to be the sole reason for the room's existence. Venetian blinds in the window behind her let in light as far as the nape of her neck, like a wedding train of platinum brightness.

She was young, early twenties, hair so radiantly blond it approached phosphorescent. It was chopped cleanly to hang just at her shoulders, then razor-cut on a slant toward her left eye, rakish but not punk. A bust in a pale blue moiré silk that looked healthy and segued nicely toward a narrow waist. The modest blouse composed a perfect foil for icy cheekbones, turquoise eyes, a mouth so desirable it hurt to look and would hurt more trying to forget. No jewelry to speak of, but her nails were lovely, tapered but not too long, and done to match the color of her lips, a red close to pomegranate.

I said: "I'm Ray Sommer. How can I help you?"

Upstairs in my office she gravitated to the chair Sal had occupied yesterday. The trek up and along the hall provided conclusive proof that nature had been generous in the extreme insofar as the lady's attributes. She wore washed-out gray trousers made to hide her shape with wide suspenders that dangled along her thighs and navy-blue cowboy boots, but the ensemble could not disguise the intoxicating grace with which she moved, the perfect flow of her in motion.

From my side of the desk I saw a beauty bordering on ethereal; at the same time there was something mannered about her, maybe out of touch, trying to get by on form alone. "You mentioned someone recommended me," I said, after we had enjoyed endless seconds of looking at one another. "I like to thank my references. Who's the friend?"

"I'd rather not say."

I pressed my lips together and looked at her, then picked up a pen, doodled on a pad to make sure the ink was flowing. "Suppose we start with less delicate matters, then. Your name, address, phone number: stuff like that."

"I should not like to say just yet. Do you mind awfully if I ask you some questions first?"

Her face was very still and erect, whether from habit or tension I could not tell, but her voice sounded cautious, even strained. I glanced at the sly-eyed gentlemen on the office walls, all smart guys like myself, but they didn't have a clue either.

I let the pen drop and eased back in my chair. "By all means," I said. "You want to know what you're paying for, I understand. Ask away."

She seemed to let her guard down a little. A tentative warmth entered her face, although she still gripped the gray leather hand purse in her lap, her painted nails lined up across the leather.

"I mean, calling on detectives isn't something one does as a matter of routine, is it?"

Since this wasn't really a question, I didn't really think about it.

She lowered her eyes. "And then you aren't what one would expect."

"What would one expect, or would you rather not say?"

If she was aware of the sarcasm, she did a good job of pretending not to be. "I mean to say," and now she was looking directly into my eyes, "you are certainly as handsome as the cinema would have us believe your sort are. You have warm eyes, trusting like. But . . . well, in real life, your ilk are rather shabby creatures, aren't they? And then, you don't even sound like someone from Queens."

I thought about who that would please and leaned forward, resting my forearms on the desk. "All it takes is a mother who came from the Midwest as an aspiring actress and wound up teaching English, and a cop father whose sons were going to do better than he did by sounding like Walter Cronkite. I got a brother teaches law at the University of Michigan if you wanna really hear someone doesn't sound like they're from Queens. Now that we have the source of my speech patterns clarified, was there something else?"

"You're making fun of me." She lowered her eyes once more and squeezed the leather purse tighter, if such a thing were possible. There was some acting being done now.

"Get off it." I laughed. "There isn't a man on the planet would do that."

"Why thank you," she murmured, still acting.

"Look," I said, "I don't mean to be rude, but most of my morning was taken up answering questions about a case the agency isn't even involved in. I have seventy-nine operatives currently at work on twelve separate assignments, which need my attention before the day is out. To say nothing of the fact I haven't had lunch yet. So the choice is yours: deli fare now or let's talk about why you're here."

She pursed that beautiful mouth of hers and used her turquoise eyes. "Tall, handsome, and remorseless," she said, "every bit as my friend described you, love, and more."

"Stop insulting my intelligence, little girl."

She cocked her face and the corners of her mouth curled with amusement. "Touché. All right, Mr. Sommer. I'm involved in a relationship that I can't seem to escape. My . . . the other half of the relationship is not willing to . . . There've been threats. And physical abuse."

"Threats," I said, "like what?"

"Just . . . threats."

"Like against your life?"

"No. No, he would never do that. Not against *my* life." Her lips curled at the corners once more. "He worships me, you see."

"You seem to think it's funny."

"No, I don't. I think it's sad, pathetically sad. And debasing and ugly and sick. Most of all sick."

I picked up the pen just to get the feel of something concrete. "Pardon me, but you didn't come here thinking you could hire a great big detective to sort of throw a scare in the guy, did you? Because intimidation isn't a service we offer."

Her eyes dropped and her voice followed. "I thought . . . I was led to believe you protected people."

"Correct. But usually for fixed periods of time. Your situation sounds kind of open-ended. That could be expensive. Around the clock, you'd be looking at seven-fifty a day minimum. That's three agents, three eight-hour pops. And that's minimum."

Back came the eyes for an instant, and then they went higher, searching, as she worried her bottom lip. "You do fetch rather a stiff sum," she murmured. She seemed vaguely put out.

"I pay for the best and so do you," I said. Gorgeous as she was, the absence of brains was getting to me. I was very close to escorting her as briskly as possible from the premises, and not learning the name of her friend was going to be one of those things that I would be able to sleep in spite of. "Or if you want to save a bundle, go to a judge, get a restraining order. Nine out of ten guys, they get served, amazing how they behave. Cost you nothing except your time."

It was sound advice, but to look at her you would have thought I had just expressed myself in Swahili. Her eyes fixed me in a sort of mooish stare, then she burst out laughing. It was a pleasant laugh, light and melodious, quite fetching actually, like a little snippet of Mozart to pick you up in spite of yourself. I grinned back at her. She was as screwy as anything Miró ever painted.

"Love," she said, "I'm sorry. But you simply don't know the man, or you'd realize how ludicrous that suggestion was."

I trundled back in the chair, put my hands on the arms about to rise, and tried to match firmness with courtesy. "That's me, ridiculous Ray Sommer, a ton of yuks for no bucks. If it would help, I can give you the names of some agencies that offer similar services. They're cheaper, and adequate up to a point. Since you're shopping anyway. I'll buzz my office manager, you can pick up the list on your way out."

She put the small purse beneath her arm, indicating her enthusiasm to end the interview. "That's very kind of you. Isn't this—didn't I read about you in the papers? You witnessed those murders yesterday."

"Yeah."

"And that lad, the lawyer's son, he had just been in your office."

"That's right."

"What in the world for, a chap with his sort of money?"

"To borrow a phrase, I'd rather not say."

"Given the rates you quote, love, I should certainly hope it wasn't for protection."

She stood then, and dismissed me with her turquoise eyes, a look as subtle as the work of a guillotine. I did not get up. I reached for the pen and looped spirals across the notepad, listening to the heels of her boots striking the carpet like fading heartbeats. Screwy. Evidently she got the agency's name from the newspapers, not some friend. Loonies are often the downside of publicity. At least in this one's case, all that got wasted was my time.

19

I had lunch in my office as I had the day before, the same thing as the day before: cornbeef on rye. It took me until 3:30 to learn that none of our operations had anything exciting to report, which normally was reason to celebrate, except today I had hoped for something to quicken the pulse from the crew monitoring the corner of Horatio and Washington. But no sign of Julie Holloway. And no sign of a muscular black guy with green eyes by the name of Ramone.

Pat came and went several times without mentioning last night, or the pitch from Dexter, Wells. She did give me a queer look, during one of our conferences, when I asked her to tell Meredith DeLorio, who was on the line, that I was out of the office, to try the car phone.

Between conversations with my people, I got through to Danny Belinski at Nesmith's Grill, on Third Avenue north of Forty-fourth Street. I asked him for a list of socially prominent Holloways in Westchester County, and he told me he'd cover every county in the state for the price of dinner at his favorite restaurant in Queens: Arpeggio's. "How's eight?" I said.

"Beautiful. Say, sport, I heard a funny story tied to your shooting yesterday. Skelton scheduled a news conference for noon concerning the case. Twenty minutes before it's supposed to take place, it's canceled. You believe it? Skelton walks away from publicity about as frequently as Danny Belinski refuses a free drink."

"Amazing," I said.

"Isn't it. All kinds of curious phenomena spinning off those murders. Take young Wittgenstein. He's on the case like a man possessed, yet he's a model of selflessness. There's no limit to what that boy won't share with me. Suddenly he's the Mother Theresa of journalism."

"Inspiring. Truly inspiring."

"Don't try to shit me, sport. You're stringing him with what, a rope around his neck? Ray?"

"Eight o'clock," I said, and hung up the phone.

Pat buzzed to say she had gotten through to Lieutenant Cox and he was on another line. I punched the flashing button on the face of the phone.

"Lieutenant? Ray Sommer. Is it comfortable for you to talk?"

"Unburden yourself to the old lieutenant."

"That story you told me about the couple of grams left on the seat of young Sal's car, up in Vermont. His sister attends Bennington, that's the college he was visiting. I wonder if you could get me the exact date, and the reason he was there, if he gave one."

There was a pause, about the time it might take to feed himself a wafer of dried plum, before he responded, "I hope you don't have any gaudy ideas about bypassing plain old-fashioned policework just to get you more ink. I don't think I'd want to be a part a that."

"Lieutenant. If something brilliant comes over me, you'll be the first to know. I want to make friends in law enforcement, not enemies."

"Friends?" he quipped. "Cheap labor, you mean."

I cradled the phone and put elbows on the desk, pinched the bridge of my nose, and glanced up at one of the smart guys on the wall, afternoon shadow making his eyes look bleak, jaded. It was close to how I felt, caught between not knowing enough and knowing too well how many people I cared about I had failed. Sunlight worked in the chunk of blue glass young Sal had poked his exotic cigarettes around in. It didn't stay long. The glass grew as dark as a fortune-teller's ball in the presence of a skeptic. I stood for a while at the window overlooking Queens Boulevard, Shea Stadium in the distance. Below, rush hour was under way, the pace such that however insane an individual driver might be, going full bore, the worst he could inflict upon even a pedestrian would be mild license-plate bruise. I was antsy. I grabbed my jacket off the back of the chair, slung it over my shoulder, and headed down the hall.

A majority of the gravel lot was stretched out in gray shadow, but the forsythia on the far bank was still making a party of the daylight. Downstairs in the conference room a sharp dry aroma prevailed, and with the blinds closed, the light was like the heat from two nickels rubbed together. My eyes adjusted to dwell upon the chair that the delectable screwball had inhabited. I picked up her ashtray and walked it to a wastebasket and emptied ashes and two darkish stubs into it. I ferried the empty weight to the bathroom beyond the archway and scoured the glass with hot water and an old toothbrush. I scrubbed with the determination of an ex-smoker. Pat's voice cut through my concentration like a breaking plate: "Ray? It's Meredith DeLorio. You don't seem to be answering your car phone."

I left the ashtray in the sink.

I leaned over Pat's desk and spoke through my teeth. "I'm not here. Period. Thank you. Darling."

Pat translated that diplomatically and again issued her condolences. When she had put the phone down, I said, "It seems to be a choice between policing the ashtrays here or going into the city, and I think we're already paying someone to clean the office."

The neon-blue eyes studied me with vague incomprehension. "You all right?"

"Three boys murdered right before my eyes, and I don't have a clue who or why. A morning wasted with the DA, who doesn't know any more than I do. A beautiful airhead shopping for a bodyguard under the impression we work for baby-sitter rates. No, I'm not all right, Pat. I'm going into the city and I'm going to rattle some cages."

"Airhead? The lady with the accent?"

"About enough brains to put out a cigarette when she's done with it, but not much more," I said. I straightened up and scratched the back of my neck. Something stirred, a thought as faint as the sound of dead ashes in a breeze.

Pat said, "That broad was no airhead."

I bent over the wastebasket and speared one of the oval stubs with a sharp pencil, blew the film of ash from it. I took the stairs two at a time. In my office I saw that I was right: we did pay someone to do the cleaning. The blue ashtray was bright and smooth and full of nothing.

20

I rode the local to Jackson Heights, crossed the platform and grabbed the first express, an F train, the car blowing air so cool it felt carbonated. The conductor proved to be one of those rare gems in the transit system: a gentleman who could speak comprehensible English. He announced our arrival at each station in a lucid, Jamaican lilt, his perfunctory "have a nice day" delivered with a wry touch that made me want to seek him out and shake his hand.

I got off at Forty-second Street in Manhattan and strode directly to the roach bar on Eighth Avenue.

The same barkeep was pushing the same watered liquor at the same washed-out, shadowy citizens. The same pool game seemed to be in progress, a couple of serious somnambulists circling the felt, oblivious of the dated music booming from the jukebox or the high level of wit circulating here or the willing women drifting in and out, their costumes loud with promise and their eyes suggesting sin as exciting as pushing a wheelbarrow of wet cement up a down escalator. My friend the barkeep soiled the air between us and took my order without any sign of recognition. Maybe it was the dark glasses I was wearing. All that was missing from yesterday's scenario were Joleen and Dixie. And of course the Thinker in the yellow shirt with blue bird shapes in it. He would stay missing forever. As the barkeep put a wrinkled paper napkin beneath my stein of flat beer, I touched the smooth worn wood of the bar top, the gouges and scars in it, the lonely graffiti that passed along news flashes

from the losing side of life. I pushed money at the barkeep and he went away.

Some great rockers bawled from the jukebox while I
nursed my beer. Little Richard. Jerry Lee Lewis. Couple
of Chuck Berry numbers. Roy Orbison, the sweet voice
escalating, could still whip up shivers. I was old enough
to remember when each of them dynamited the popular
consciousness. I probably wasn't the only one in there
old enough, but I may have been the only one conscious
enough. I ordered another draft. I listened to more music. Everybody wanted some kind of love—some for a
night, some a lifetime—but the general drift seemed to
be that no one was getting enough. Maybe they didn't
recognize enough when they had it. Maybe none of us
knows that and we're all fools and destined to bungle
this precious, tenuous arrangement.

Take the lady with the accent. Please.

There was a mirror beyond the tiers of bottles behind
the bar and in it I recognized a man in dark glasses,
much like myself, doing a good job of not amusing himself. A lady with an accent . . . I moved my fingers over
the scars in the wood, wondering why the phrase echoed. Maybe with a head as empty as mine felt, anything
would. I pulled off the dark glasses and eyed the man in
the mirror once more. He was about as far from amusement without being dead as a man can be.

I was about to try my luck on the street when the door
behind me swayed in, and I recognized her in the light
before the door crept back and she was just a profile
against the pebbled amber glass. Today's costume made
the provocative red of yesterday seem timid. She had
snaked herself into a canary-yellow outfit designed to in-
cite lust as far as Pennsylvania. She was alone, and when
she came out of the ladies', she was still that way. I
drifted up to her table along the wall and slipped onto
a chair across from her. "Spritzer?" I said.

"Do I know you, handsome?" she asked warily. Then:
"Ray?"

"Right both times," I said, and hailed the waiter.

She smiled and looked me over with a quiet, professional air more shrewd than sexual. The waiter with the
gimp leg and voice that sounded like he was late for his

black-lung checkup deposited her Campari and soda. I
put money in his gray hand.

"Be right back," he wheezed.

"Keep it," I said. "Just make sure whatever drinks the
lady here orders are honest."

Dixie emitted a low, slow whistle. "Suit an' tie, shirt
like that, you into the fine line, Ray. Yestiday, you got
by on handsome. Today I got to wonder what it is, the
business you in."

"Same as yesterday: looking for lost redheads."

"She a popular lady."

"Holloway and his friend been around again?"

"Say who?"

"The Oreo squad, you called them."

"Redhead ma'fucka? No. And tell you what, he best
not come 'round my ass, because I'll mace the fuck. Then
I'll kick his white balls 'bout as far as Harlem."

"You talk a helluva fight, beautiful. His buddy, the
black guy, was he big, like he was tough once, but several thousand gallons of ice cream made him the man he
is now?"

She took a dainty sip from her spritzer and touched
the corners of her mouth with her fingertips. "You talk
funny, you know that? Not funny ha-ha, but different.
Black gentleman you askin' about, yeah, he of a size, all
right. No missionary position with a boy like that. Uh-
uh. They something else about him."

I held my breath and watched her click her teeth with
a fingernail, thinking.

"Oh yeah." She leaned over the table. "His face, it
remind me of my mama's third husband."

"Oh," I said, deflating.

"Man used to peek on me when I be in the bathroom."

"Oh," I said again. "Dixie, you notice anything about
his hair, like the 'fro wasn't all his?"

"What 'fro? He got like his whole head shaved."

"No, not your mama's third husband. The brother that
was with Holloway."

"Ray?" She looked puzzled. "Tha's who I'm talkin'
about. The brother. The ice-cream man. He got a head
like Lou Gossett, Jr."

"Oh," I said.

The waiter, without being invited, dragged a leg up to our table and wheezed into Dixie's ear. The absent, dreamy look in her eyes focused sharply on me for a few moments, and then she seemed to lose interest, nodding, back in the dream once more. The waiter limped off. Dixie said, "You excuse me a minute, Ray, I got a phone call."

I nodded, trying to remember if I had heard anything remotely like the sound of a phone ringing. I didn't get very far down memory lane before a party in a chair at the table behind me said, in a drawl I recognized, "Feel that, pretty face?"

I felt it. It was sharp and cold and bore into me with the clear, surgical intent of skewering my kidneys.

"That Toledo steel," a smug and graveled voice informed me. "From Toledo in Spain, which is famous for they swords. What this be, that you feeling, is a stiletto. I can stick you quick and quiet and be outta here, nobody see a thing, jus' this flash Chuck sittin' his chair, waitin' his girl-friend. Tell you somethin', Chuck, whether you live or die, you got a long wait. She ain't comin' back."

This wasn't gloating. The man with the knife at my kidneys spoke with the patience of an adult addressing a child. There was even a note of weariness in his voice, as if from the burden of all his knowledge, but it was something I sensed he worked at. He was a punk, and he would always be a punk. At least as punks go, he wasn't a loose cannon. Selfish interest made him susceptible to negotiating.

"While I'm still breathing," I said, "how about listen-ing to a way you could make money, say nothing stay alive. Because you kill me, you're dead meat."

"Say what, Chuck? Say fuckin' what?"

"The name's Ray. I'm the guy you don't like talking up the sisters. I'm looking for Julie Holloway, and I'm going to find her. Unless you kill me, of course. But you do that, you lose out on the hundred you take me to her, and another hundred when I'm done talking with her. If that sounds like small change, consider the alternative. There's two guys, ask Dixie, looking for her as well. They don't pay shit, and one of them for sure is CIA. I know, because I spoke to him. I go down, they'll be on you so hard, you'd be happier with lung cancer. Believe me,

Ramone, I'm the boy you want to deal with, not them. It is Ramone, isn't it?"

There was a long, patient sigh and the biting pain behind my kidneys went away. "I like your style, Chuck. Lemme see your green."

I extracted bills from my sock.

"Don't turn around. Lemme see the century."

I pressed one against my shoulder, leaving just enough of it visible to assure him it was legitimate.

"I said, lemme see it."

"You're seeing it. That's as much as you're going to see until I see Julie. It's a hundred when I see her, another hundred once I've talked to her."

"I oughta stick you jus' for the practice."

I breathed through my mouth and lifted my heels from the floor, the muscles bunching in my thighs and calves. I clenched the glass that held Dixie's Campari and soda. I tried to sound calm. "If it's practice you need, buy yourself a Cabbage Patch doll. If you want me to believe you're as tough as you talk, you could start by not hiding behind my back."

"How about you keep your eyes on your dick and don't lip off. And sit right there."

I did that. The waiter limped past and stopped at the table behind mine. Whispers were exchanged. I scanned the room for someone in a canary-yellow sex-machine costume, but Dixie was nowhere to be seen. The urge to whirl and cream the smart boy behind me was barely overruled by the assumption that he would be more useful with his ego intact.

The music played and the ivory balls hiccuped off one another and the air crawled with a sinister smell very much like the reek of human bitterness. Attempts to engage Ramone in further conversation were rewarded with sudden stinging sensations alongside my spine. Time ceased to have meaning; there was just the waiting, the smell of bitterness, the sharp reminder that the man behind me killed people.

Then something new intruded upon the air, not exactly freshness, but a heady mix of soaps and lotions, and a perfume with all the subtlety of a predator's talons. A heartbeat later she flopped down in the chair opposite me, the one Dixie had vacated. She was dressed for business in a black

minidress covered with plastic, iridescent disks and black
panty hose, black high heels with sequins on the toes. Her
powder-keg hairdo was hidden beneath a spiky black wig,
and she was running on high voltage, her tongue snaking
over her lips, her trancelike face so pale the scarlet lipstick
looked almost obsidian. Her eyes skipped over me. She fitted a white cigarette, something in the 120 league, to her
lips and ignited a lighter beneath it, took several drags that
failed to slow her down. She was on the high wire.

"Julie? The name's Ray Sommer. How you doing?"

I held the hundred-dollar bill over my shoulder and it
was snatched away. "You got five minutes, Chuck. I be
right here, case you forget."

Even in the feeble light the definition of her clavicle was
sharp, skeletal. Her breasts beneath the glitz looked pendulous and her arms were all bone, and whatever spirit I
had detected in her face in the photograph had been si-
phoned off, something even expensive cosmetics could not
disguise. Smoke sifted up from her lips as she drummed the
end of her cigarette against the ashtray. Give her a few
more months on her present diet and she'd be ready for a
picture spread in *National Geographic*.

I reached into a pocket of my coat and dropped a copy
of a snapshot in the cold-sore light. "You've looked better," I said, "and it was only six months ago."

"Shit," she said. "Allie. That crazy bitch."

A mischievous smile played in her face, but not with
any vigor, and not for long.

"Allie," I said.

"She took the picture. This was before it got interesting. She took a bunch of them. Yeah. Me and Allie and
that weird old man of hers. You a friend of his?"

"I don't think so. I don't even know Allie."

Her eyes skipped about, taking that in. "Lemme get
this straight: you don't know Allie, you don't know her
old man, but you're looking for action."

"I'm looking for you."

"Then you're looking for action." She butted the remains of her cigarette and got another into her lips, fired
it up, dragged on it, then drummed away on the ashtray.
"So you know, I don't shave it no more."

I just leaned a little forward and stared at her. I felt old,

sad, almost ashamed. And more than anything, confused.
"You don't shave it no more, is that what you said?"

"Umm," she purred. "You window-shopping? Hey, I
had guys want that. Allie'd set them up, it was all they
could do was look, some of them. If that's your game, I
can get into it."

"No games, kid. Like I told your friend behind me,
this is strictly business." I showed her my card. "I was
hired by somebody very concerned about you."

She tore the card in half. "Just the detox blues," she
said. "You didn't take a check, did you?"

"Your father'd like to talk to you."

"Feeling's mutual," she said. She put a hand in her
false hair and curled a spike on her finger and closed her
eyes, let her breath out through her mouth so that I could
hear it, rippling with bitter amusement.

"Care to tell me where he could reach you?"

"Ray—is that your name?"

I said it was.

She put her bony elbows on the table and leaned toward me with a lunatic smile. "Ray, it's kinda tough
reaching me from Arlington."

Her eyes stopped for a moment and bore into mine,
making a point I was at a loss to understand. "Arlington," I said. "As in Virginia?"

"That's where the Veterans' Cemetery is. My mother,
when she's sober, suing the government is all she can
think about. It's like her religion. Daddy died four years
ago from some shit chemical they used in Vietnam. A
defoliant killed him." She shrugged and her face
drooped, a single obscenity tumbled from her lips. "I
don't even know what a fucking defoliant is."

A sharp, cold sting alongside the spine and a voice I
recognized: "You run outta time, Chuck."

Julie Holloway, with the resurrected mother and suddenly deceased father, disappeared much quicker than
her perfume. The only thing that hung in there longer
was the question: how good is a check from a dead man?

21

It was still rush hour when I boarded the train back to Queens, so that it didn't matter which car I entered, I would be sandwiched among strangers, pressed intimately fore and aft for the better part of a half hour. But I was betting it was quicker this way than by taxi. And I think better on my feet.

The air-conditioning in the car, a feeble breath at best, died altogether in the tunnel beneath the East River, as did the train. About a minute crabbed past before the bitching got under way. I used it and the rest of the spasmodic journey to Elmhurst to sort things out. It had bothered me that the daughter of an Ivy League–sounding guy like Holloway would tell me she didn't shave it no more, and now I understood why: the voice on the cassette was not the voice of Julie Holloway's father. Whose, then? Whoever the guy was, he was connected, or he wouldn't have had Sal DeLorio in his corner. Connected, and obviously on the far side of the law, given the handsome, fraudulent check deposited yesterday in my agency's account. Presumption: Sal somewhere in his career made the mistake of owing Joe Scorcese and the guy was an obligation the don was calling in. Owing the don was forever.

Another irritant, unlike Julie's lousy grammar, continued to resist understanding: Blades and the Rugman chasing up and down the strip for her. Presumption there: the guy who hired me under the guise of Holloway is someone they want. This Allie person's strange boyfriend. Not strange, weird. *Her weird old man.* It was something of a challenge to imagine what a girl of Julie's vintage and habits would consider weird.

Imagining it, I climbed the steps of the Elmhurst station, my mind awash with sewage. I needed a drink. I needed a long hot shower. I needed a nice clean occupation, like scraping drunks off the sidewalks or emasculating farm animals. Anything not to have to think about the twisted shape of some men's desires.

Because the office was empty for the night, I used keys to open the street door, manipulated camouflaged buttons alongside the doorframe to deactivate the alarm and at the same time release the electronic latch, admitting me into the area shared by Pat and Martina. The idea was to wash my face and shave in the sink off the conference room, then to select something fresh from the shirts and ties hanging in a closet off my office upstairs. Sweat glands can be murder on a shirt when there's a knife tattooing your back. I got as far as Pat's desk and stopped. No good reason for it. No good reason for gliding over to the safe and fetching from it a .22-caliber Beretta, a model 70S automatic. I chambered a round, the cocking action as smooth and soundless as a woman applying cold cream to her face. There was no good reason for the display of nerves, but the past two days had sharpened my instincts.

Spaced around each room were night-lights plugged into the baseboards, the illumination dying out as the eyes rose. I stepped into the conference room behind the barrel of the Beretta and saw two figures seated at the table. Nobody moved. Nobody uttered a word. I found the light switch on the wall with my elbow.

Agent Orange and the Rugman.

"You guys are good," I said, not lowering the Beretta. "I'd appreciate it someday if you'd show me how you disarmed my alarm and deciphered my code."

The Rugman tucked his head in, working a half-dozen toothpicks in his mouth, "Piece of cake, Mr. Sommer, if you want to know the truth."

Agent Orange, or Blades, if that was his name, sat at the end of the table farthest from me. He sat with his pale hands clasped on the table and dark glasses over his eyes. Both men were dressed as I remembered them from this morning, except the Rugman wasn't wearing his shades. He had small brown eyes with an eager light in them, as if he were pleased with the situation. They were the eyes of a man I could learn to like in spite of his occupation. I said to him, "Your partner here, Stevie Wonder in whiteface, I bet he even sleeps with his shades on, am I right?"

The black man did not take the bait. He nudged the toothpicks into a corner of his mouth. "We're all Americans here, Ray. Put the gun down."

I dropped it in a pocket of my coat along with a hand on it and hitched a shoe up on the arm of the chair opposite Agent Orange. "Next time you're going to pull a B and E, call ahead. That way I could put on a pot of coffee, leave some lights on so you wouldn't have to sit around in the dark."

Blades spoke in his grinding, raspy voice: "You're a Marine, Sommer."

"You asking or insisting?"

"Neither. I'm counting upon it. So is your country. Semper fi and all that good stuff."

"Uh-huh."

"You did a tour in Vietnam, up in I Corps with the Third Marines."

"That's right, Boyd, I did." The forest of toothpicks stopped dead in the Rugman's mouth. Blades leaned a little forward and grinned, although as looks go it conveyed all the pleasure of a stress fracture. "I humped the bush with a guy you might know by the name of Wesley Dexter. Good old Wesley. A tough enough lad, but his real talent was self-promotion. Unlike myself, Wesley reupped, and rumor has it he went with you guys. Say," I said, and looked into the small, bright, brown eyes, "since we're on a first-name basis, big guy, what do they call you besides 'sir'?"

First the black man started in on his toothpicks, then turned his head, passing the decision to answer on to Mr. C. Boyd Blades. Blades said, "Gerald. You'll answer to Gerald, won't you, Gerald?"

Gerald said, "I mos' certainly will, Boyd." He still seemed to be enjoying himself.

"You two are cute enough to be a lounge act in Atlantic City."

"Ray," said the man with the mime-white face, whose emotions, if he had any, did not run to pleasure, "the purpose of our visit is to put some facts on the table. We know a little about you now, and what we know we like. You served with distinction. You came out, you graduated from John Jay, some sort of police academy, as I understand it. FBI recruited you. A hotshot sergeant in Queens pulled some strings to get you assigned to him, but you turned that down, just like you did the Bureau. Instead, you go to work as a bouncer, a taxi driver, a night watchman in the diamond district. Spend close to a year and a half doing dead-end time. We don't think it's a coincidence that during this year and a half, a legal challenge had been mounted to overturn a verdict in a cop killing. A cop who worked under a hotshot sergeant of detectives by the name of Moriarty. A dead cop who happened to be your father. Those are some of the facts we want to put on the table."

I took my foot off the arm of the chair and my hand off the gun and worked on my breathing. "He was clerking a jewelry store as part of a stakeout. When the gang hit, his backup jumped the gun, my old man caught four rounds in the chest and face."

Blades ran a pale tongue along his upper lip. "For eighteen months you kept a low profile in the event you should have to take action. Classic terrorist strategy. It calls for patience and commitment. That's another thing we like about you."

"Just what did you have in mind, Ray, if his killer walked?" This from Gerald, his bright eyes serious, the toothpicks going.

"But he didn't, did he? A lawyer for the family by the name of Sydney Simon convinced the appellate court of that. And the Supreme Court bounced it back without comment."

Gerald said softly, "Merely a hypothetical question."

"I thought we were putting facts on the table."

"All right." Blades's voice scraped against the tension.

"The man who hired you to find Julie Holloway, he's a giant in our business. I should say, the last giant. He started in Nam before you, in Special Forces, training the Montagnards, a Stone Age people old Ho wanted to Leninize or neutralize. He worked through the Canadians in Iran to free some of our people. He did critical spadework in Libya to give Qhaddafi a whiff of the grape. The man has been around, and he's suffered for it. But he's always come through, which is why he was given as close to carte blanche as it gets. Less than a month ago he vanished with Agency money, a lot of it, and that isn't kosher. Even if you're a giant."

"How much he sting you for, you mind I ask?"

"Sorry."

"You don't know the meaning of the word, pal. To you it's the politic way of telling me to fuck off. I don't see what we have to talk about."

"Money," he said, "for starters. If you took a check from Thompson Avionics, and I'm betting you did, then you'll be sorry to learn the company no longer exists. And pride, we could talk about that, because you're a marine. I don't see you sitting still for being conned out of both your pride *and* hard cash."

Blades was not an individual I would ever feel entirely at ease with, without a gun in my pocket, but he hit every note in a tune I liked. "Gentlemen, there's liquor in my office upstairs. I think a drink might make us all a little more human."

Fresh toothpicks occupied the corner of Gerald's wide, happy mouth, and his eyes were moist with appreciation, savoring a sip from the bottle of Molson's. Blades had requested Russian vodka, but settled for British over ice with a lemon-peel twist. I poured my usual and let it sit while I changed shirt and tie.

Blades did the talking. It occurred to me, listening to his voice scratch and claw the air, that he might have a damaged larynx, possibly the fruit of his winning personality.

"You were on the mark this morning," he said. "Gerald and I have been pursuing Miss Holloway. It is Miss

Holloway, is it not? Red hair, about five-six or -seven, built, goes with a boy by the name of Ramone. On the street her *nom d'amour* is Julie Halloween."

I plunked down in the chair behind my desk in a clean shirt, a different tie, and let some of my drink minister to my nerves. "Sounds like the same lady. Except the voice on the cassette wasn't her father. Her father's a dead Vietnam vet."

"Cassette?"

"It's how I was hired. A taped voice and some photographs delivered to Sal DeLorio."

Blades and Gerald exchanged glances. Again it was Blades who did the talking. "We've been operating at a disadvantage, apparently. All we got was a phone call and description, with the hint he might negotiate if we could produce the girl. Photo'd be a big help."

I let in a little more liquor and looked at Blades, at the faintly reflective glass concealing his eyes. I looked at Gerald. He was scrunched comfortably back in his chair, and his shirt collar riding up on his nape nudged his wig just enough to tip it into a ludicrous position vis-à-vis his face. All they needed was a third partner wearing a rubber nose and they'd be a team to rival Nixon's plumbers. I stared into my glass. "Money was mentioned," I said.

"Ten thousand dollars cash. Small denominations. Rumpled and handled." Blades raised a hand, teased his thumb against his first two fingers. "Our work, with the occasional exception, such as the man you know as Holloway, consists of interpreting satellites and publications, and drawing upon indigenous sources. People familiar with the turf, in other words. Like you. The understanding between us, in addition to the money, is absolute discretion on both sides. All you have to do is locate Julie for us and keep your mouth shut about it. Or if we find her first with the help of a photograph, the agreement stands."

"Okay," I said. "The money's there. You don't produce it, I talk."

"To whom? About what? Upon what evidence? You're blowing smoke, Ray. Go along with the program, you'll reap the benefits."

"You want Julie, basically, as a bargaining chip?"

"She's safe with us."

"Like any other ninety-five-pound trick—right, Boyd?"

Gerald speared an arm across Blades's chest, restraining him. He set down his empty bottle. His eyes were still bright, but unamused. He pushed the toothpicks into the corner of his mouth. "Way you two go at it," he growled, "you oughta be married. Ray, goddammit, this is serious business. We're here asking for your help, politely. There are other methods at our disposal, but seeing this morning what a stickler you are for manners, we thought we'd try it the nice way, first."

"First," I grunted. I finished my drink and went to the window overlooking Queens Boulevard. Sunlight had all but bled from the sky and some stars were visible, brilliant in the distance, clear as a baby's conscience. I could see the jumble of high rises that constituted Lefrak City, and farther off, a faint wash of light from Shea Stadium. Traffic whirred below, an uneven dynamo of human questing. I touched the back of my neck. "Would our working relationship include a description of this ace agent, in case I happen to bump into him?"

"Sorry." Blades, as deeply contrite as ever.

"Yeah. Your ace guy, you said something about he'd suffered. Would that include a deceased wife?"

Silence for several moments. Staring into the glass overlooking the boulevard, I caught the reflection of a vigorous pantomime, a furious, silent exchange. Finally, "Yes." Blades again. "A suicide," he volunteered.

"Recently?"

There was no debate. "Recently." It was Gerald this time. "You going somewhere or just making conversation?"

"Skilled liars always build from a grain of truth. On the cassette he mentioned the death, suggesting it ignited, or at least fueled his daughter's disturbance. The daughter that is not his daughter. I suppose it was suicide without a doubt."

"She left a note." Back to Blades. "And we know for a fact where he was at the time."

"In South America?"

"Sorry."

"I thought we were all Americans." I approached the desk, fussing with the knot of my tie. Because the two of them had all the investigative finesse of a marching band, I reached into a desk drawer and dropped a snapshot on the desk between them. Blades snatched it up. "Your Miss Holloway," I said. "If you boys find her, with or without this, she's yours, you don't owe me the ten big ones. If I find her, I'll let you know, provided you leave a number. But I won't turn her over. Holloway, whoever he is, will have to deal with me."

I glanced at the sly-eyed gentlemen on the walls, struck by a thought. They seemed to share the same low opinion of my faculties as I did. Whatever I had been using for brains was the equivalent of a clubfoot.

"It must be the heat," I said, "or the booze, or the no food for too long. Or maybe it's keeping company with bozos like the two of you. I've gone stupid, haven't I? Holloway. In some circles he's known as Peru. The guy you leaned all over the Queens DA for. The guy you chilled a murder investigation for. Holloway and Peru are one and the same." I leaned across the desk, my eyes going from Gerald to Blades, a desperate face doubled in his lenses, a dangerous face too, if you knew its owner as I did. "Guys?"

Blades planted his hands on his thighs, preparing to stand. "Sorry."

I came over the desk after him, but he must have seen it in my eyes, because he pivoted from the chair, escaping my momentum. Before my feet struck the carpet, Gerald introduced his shoulder to my rib cage and bulldozed me back across the desk. A flailing hand caught hold of the blue glass ashtray, but I didn't use it. Gerald was just a guy trying to help a partner and hang on to his hairpiece. Between wheezy gulps of air he screamed at Blades to please put the fucking gun away. An icy pressure, about the circumference of a D battery, which I assumed was the silencer, withdrew from beneath my earlobe.

Slowly Gerald lifted his two-hundred-plus pounds off me. "Ray, you best learn who it's safe to fuck with and who it's not. We're not."

22

A little past eight found me in Arpeggio's in Forest Hills
bellied up to the brass-rail bar in the long, narrow lounge
off the dining area. My ribs creaked still from Gerald's
embrace and my mind reverberated. It wasn't too
crowded given the hour and the evening, maybe twenty
citizens waiting for a table. Nobody seemed to mind the
wait. They stood and sat in groups with the drinking
portion of the meal firmly in hand. Smoke undulated
overhead, like something washed in from a bad dream.
The talk was the usual talk: smutty stories, office politics,
sports, the day's tension chipping off in chunks of brittle
laughter. A couple at the bar on stools next to me chewed
languidly on each other's faces.

At the entryway to the tables I could see Mario, the
host, standing behind his lectern scanning the guest list,
then snatching off his reading glasses to check the progress of a Mets game on a television elevated above the
bar.

With scarlet flocked walls, heavy swagged curtains
with more folds than a fat cardinal's vestment, prepos-
terous nudes on dark velvet, Arpeggio's wouldn't win any
prizes for ambience, but like so many restaurants in the
city, it didn't give a fig for looks. It had Mario, and it
had chefs.

A tall cadaver by the name of Paulie, who had the
grave manners of a head butler, interrupted Mario's concentration on the ballgame to whisper in his ear. Paulie
was the odd man out in Arpeggio's, where the crew ran
to impishness and displayed a weakness for spontaneous
outbursts of song.

Even now, warming to piped-in Dean Martin, busboys could be heard warbling above the crash of stoneware in the kitchen: "When the moon hitsa your eye like a big pizza pie. . . ."

And then I heard the voice of a man who numbered among his "personal friends" probably a quarter million New Yorkers named Sport. He hollered greetings to several of those before he stopped in front of me, arms spread wide, loopy smile curling around the wings of his nose. It was an open, ingratiating face that had taken some punishment and didn't seem too concerned about it. The eyes were as black as the cumulus of hair was white. Eyebrows ascended from the bridge of his nose and ended in rakish, snowy tufts. The nose inside the smile, the nose of a onetime Fordham fullback, was as pink as raw hamburger and ugly as a car wreck. We embraced.

Danny Belinski said, "Handsome as ever."

"How about you? You're down to one chin. Look at this character: pin-striped suit, polished shoes, no ashes anywhere. What, you take up the Jane Fonda program?"

"No, that was the South Vietnamese," he growled. Giving his drink order to the barkeep, Vincent, Danny looked past my shoulder, monitoring the activity around him. It was a habit of his profession, but one that so annoyed his second wife that she divorced him chiefly because of it. With his eyes still off somewhere, he said, "Mario and his phony specs. Wears them because his girlfriend told him they make him look intellectual. Mario, I says, you think anybody comes in here because the maître d' is a guy that looks like a guy who writes sonnets by candlelight, you got to lay off the tomato sauce. Whadda ya gonna do, huh? Everybody wants to be somebody else. The American dream. Me, I starve fifty pounds off my bones in order to look good for my divorce. Miss Fonda wants to be a world-famous exercise instructor who didn't do anything Tokyo Rose didn't do, except win an Oscar."

"You lost me back there with the divorce."

"Thank you, Vincent." We knocked glasses. He winked at someone past my shoulder, then brought his eyes back

into the conversation. "Know something, sport? All
crooners to the contrary, we don't want love. Love's
deader than the beasts in La Brea. It's attention, that's
what we crave. Can't get it from God because He's been
pronounced dead, so all we have left is fame, the lowing
of the envious mob."

I watched him smack down his empty glass, Vincent
already moving our way. He had put the drink down
like a beat-upon lineman flushing his system with Gat-
orade. "When a man starts talking about love," I said,
"to another man, in a bar outside the Village, I know
I'm listening to a well-oiled guy. You better slow down,
Danny, or you'll fall asleep in your salad."

He pulled on his wrecked proboscis, savoring a sip from
his second drink, his eyes darting merrily. "I don't think
you ever met my fourth. Denise Louise Pemberton of the
Rhode Island Pembertons. English stock, terribly old,
don'tchu know? Got a leg up in the slave trade and never
looked back. Worth a fortune. Look them up in the Social Register, it says something to the effect that it was a
shipping and insurance consortium. Nothing about
chained labor. But her old man got tight one night on
the brandy he keeps hidden in the library. He says, Yes,
the family did quite well off those monkies."

"Her old man," I said, not quite knowing why.

"So I says, Your coloreds are all right, provided they
keep the Limeys out of the woodpile. The old coot doesn't
even blink. He says to me, My daughter has always had
a weakness for lost causes and coarse men. Whadda ya
gonna do? The guy is fucking immune. I bet the old
bastard drinks rat poison as a mild laxative. Jesus!"

Danny jackknifed, slapping the bar rhythmically, the
laughter cascading out of his rubicund face, having such
a hell of a good time it sounded like he was going to
cough blood. Vincent handed him a tall glass of ice water. When he had finished it, Danny stoked up a cigarette, clutched his glass of Chivas Regal, and solemnly
touched my glass with it. "Hail and farewell to lost
causes," he murmured.

Vincent leaned across the bar and said, "Mario, he'sa
say Paulie got a table for you and the Danny B."

I thanked him and drained my glass. "Send another

one along with Paulie, please, Vincent," I said, pushing what was left of my change across the bar.

Mario touched his black bow tie before moving out from behind the lectern to flick off his glasses and embrace Danny. They slapped backs and exchanged endearments. Danny asked what was truly fresh tonight. Then Mario and I shook hands.

"I don't see you in some time," he said gravely. "You or your beautiful wife. She is well?"

"*Bene*, Mario," I said. "*Grazie.*"

Before we reached the booth in the rear, Danny had stopped at several tables to shake hands, buss cheeks, introduce me as one of his oldest personal friends.

Tony Bennett or someone who sounded awfully like him was becoming pretty worked up over misplacing his ticker in San Francisco, and several of the waiters, already whistling, seemed prepared to leap into the fray. Paulie brought my drink and distributed menus and drifted away to give us time to study them. The seating wasn't perfection, unless black leatherette stretched across parking-lot gravel is your idea of comfort. But the linen tablecloth was clean and crisp, the color of a wedding gown, and rising from a cut-glass vase, a fresh red rose puckered gently, like a bride's expectant lips. I folded my menu and gazed up the room. Red carpeting, which when new complimented the billowy curtains, ran under tables and chairs and up a step to a landing where the tables were larger and the light was brighter and the carpeting wasn't. In the aisles it had been ground the dry color of brick. The light fixtures that hung on stalks from the gilded ceiling were composed of black metal concentric hoops emanating from the bulb, probably pretty daring in Frank Lloyd Wright's day. They hung there now like pooped-out ideas, acquiring dust and shedding little light. I knew the feeling.

We ordered. Danny sat back in the booth and tasted his breadstick, followed it with a larger bite, and still chewing, said, "Speaking of lost causes, you got something else you want me to waste my time on for a free meal? I turned up zip on Holloway."

"I know. I met the daughter. Of a dead father. Who

wrote a check to my agency yesterday in the amount of twenty-five thousand dollars."

Paulie arrived with the salads and a dozen raw oysters for me. He knew how I liked them. Fresh lemon was squeezed over the delicacies, and the pepper mill got churned a precise quarter turn over each. When Paulie had faded away, I filled Danny in on the encounter with Julie in the roach bar. He heated up another cigarette and chased a cherry tomato around the plate with his fork. "So the name's smoke," he said.

"Yeah, a cover. But it's also a connection. The guy using the name is a big in the CIA. The real Mr. Holloway, according to the daughter, died four years ago, possibly from exposure to some of the chemical shit we used in the Nam. It could be this big was assigned the name, but then why hire me to find the daughter? Not only me, but there's a couple of Agency people he's got trucking down the same road. From them I know the guy using the name also did a tour in the Nam, so possibly that's another connection. You know what yanks my short hairs?"

"Having the little mystery girl disappear on you ought to rank right up there."

"Before that. The deal was screwy from the gitgo. The funds for a private investigation were being drawn from a corporate account. I knew it was improper, but I shrugged it off. Makes me think I'm losing my edge, Danny."

"The guy strung you a little. Forget about it. Your vanity got bruised, but bruises heal."

I finished the last of the oysters a happier man than when I started. "Vanity, huh? I thought Cece walking out on me would have extinguished any of that, but maybe you're right. Patty's accused me of the same thing, more or less. I must have it in spades. Remind me to weep into the deep hours of the morning over it. Thompson Avionics mean anything to you?"

"Not a thing, sport." He caught the eye of Paulie hovering in the distance and pointed to his empty glass, then pushed away his plate of half-eaten salad to get his elbows onto the table, another cigarette going. "But I have this journalistic instinct you're going to enlighten me."

"Not by much." I dug into the salad. "It's the company Holloway was supposed to be president of, that the check was drawn against. About an hour ago I had the pleasure of chatting with a pair of dildos from the CIA. They kind of invited themselves into my office to wait for me. The way they explained it, Holloway snookered the Agency out of some funds, possibly through this Thompson Avionics, but they didn't say that. They more or less admitted it was a dummy organization that had been dissolved the moment the fancy pants came to light. Means my check for twenty-five grand is a joke." Danny's eyes got large and his tufted brows danced up and down. "What?"

"Just waiting for the punch line," he said. "Like how much they offered you to do what."

"Ten grand for the girl, for bait. But you see I want her for the same reason." I waited for Paulie to clear the plates and agreed with his selection of wine for the meal. Not that I had ever disagreed. It was a little ritual we observed, a bow in the direction of the social graces. Paulie trundled solemnly off through a wave of filial sentiment as one after another of the waiters chimed in to assist Eddie Fisher through "Oh, My Papa." I leaned over the table. "I don't have anything solid, but whoever this Holloway character is, I think he connects to the shooting yesterday."

Danny Belinski straightened up and spread his arms across the top of the booth, a low, slow whistle escaping his lips.

"Off the record," I said.

Danny just looked at me, his black eyes no wider than hyphens. "You share any of this with Lieutenant Cox?"

"The police aren't interested in speculation."

"According to young Arnie, they aren't interested period. Yesterday, besides his partner, Cox had four detectives under him working on your triple. They've all been reassigned. Moriarity, that bag of flatulence, told channel five tonight every lead is being pursued. Bullshit." He stubbed out a cigarette angrily in the ashtray and got another one going. "Who's putting money in the streets for information is the Scorcese family."

"Sure," I muttered, something ugly crawling about inside me. "Joe squibs the shooters as a favor, Sal's got his revenge. The cops, they've avoided the paperwork, they're happy. Taxpayers don't get beat out of the expense of a trial, say nothing of the investigation, so they should be happy. How come I'm not?"

"Vanity? Sport, everybody does business with the Scorceses of this world. Even Cox, who is a fairly honest cop, understands that. We all make the best deals we can." Danny drew his lids together for the hyphenated stare. "Wittgenstein's been busting his ass on this, some lead you gave him on a guy named Peru. The kid overwrites like all kids do, but unlike most of the putzes around him, he's got a modicum of talent. More important, he's got guts and a love for his craft. I'd hate to see you screw him out of a chance to be a good reporter. Speaking of deals."

"I'm touched," I said. "I may just need this entire tablecloth to soak up the emotional fallout."

"You and old man Pemberton." A loopy grin curled around his nostrils. "Remind me to send you a case of rat poison for Christmas."

"Actually," I said as Paulie arrived with the veal for Danny, the broiled bluefish for me, "there's nothing to bargain over, in that respect. I like the kid's spunk."

"Serious?"

I waved a hand. "He's paying his dues. He got caught off base. If I threw a scare into him, good, maybe I've saved him some grief down the road." I savored the wine Paulie had trickled into my glass. Another ritual. "Perfection," I said, "as always."

"*Grazie*, Mr. Sommer. Mr. Belinski?"

"Please," said Danny. He asked after Paulie's family. The family was well. And the brother with the tumor? Benign. The bottle of wine was left tilted in a basket, the glass swaddled in a cloth of red and white checks. Danny lifted his glass and swirled it beneath his nose. "Straight goods, you won't pull the plug on Wittgenstein?"

"I said I liked him, what do you want?"

He winked. "That's enough."

We watched each other chew and moan and exclaim over the righteousness of the meal.

After a while Danny said, "I heard there was some quality coke found in Sally's Porsche."

I didn't say anything.

"As I understand it, it's happened before. Not long ago. Up at Bennington, where his sister attends school. Any of this interest you?"

"I've heard the story," I said.

"I thought you might've." He devoted himself to the veal once more, forking it in and making little sounds of pleasure. His passion for the plate seemed somehow contrived, a deliberate act for an obvious purpose. He reached for the basket with the bottle in it. "More wine, sport?"

I watched him pour, his eyes steadfastly refusing to meet mine. "Thanks," I said. "Now you going to tell me what it is, or is the object of this little exercise to make me feel like that German emperor the pope made hang around in the snow for days, waiting for an audience?"

Danny's eyebrows did another two-step. "Pope Gregory the something. I think we made him a saint for it. Don't tell me divorce has turned you toward religion."

I lapped up some wine. "About Sal."

"Oh. The way it came down at Bennington, it was a security cop acting on a tip happened to observe the suspicious substance in Sally's car. He contacted the local authorities, who obtained the warrant. Lemme ask you, when was the last time you heard about a campus cop being tipped off to a bust? That matter, when was the first time?"

"The boy was set up, that's obvious."

Danny's eyes glittered with delight. "The campus cops are employed by a security agency under contract to the university. I made some phone calls. This is one of those agencies that hires nickel-and-dime guys for nickel-and-dime wages, even deducts the cost of the uniforms from their pay. The police up there didn't have a file to pull, because no complaint was made, and anyone who was anyone at the school was either on vacation or attending a faculty tea or doing something too damn genteel to come to the phone. But I did get through to an impressionable young lady in the security agency's home office in Boston. She grew up in Queens, the little sweetheart,

which made her susceptible to my boyish charm. All she
could do was give me the names and addresses of every
stiff that worked security at Bennington, going back to
the first of the year. One name hits me in the face because of the address, here in Queens, Long Island City.
The rest of the stiffs, they live in Vermont or Massachusetts. But here's a guy by the name of Leo Saperstein
making a long commute for bupkus. Recognize him?"

"Sure. The younger brother of Manny Saperstein. Mad
Manny of Tip Top Tech." Mad Manny, as he liked to
promote himself, operated an enormous electronics
warehouse in Queens and had personally installed a
"state of the art" security system in my house in Kew
Gardens as partial payment for a favor I did him once,
removing an obnoxious growth from his back by the
name of Tony Knucks. "Leo's a bright enough boy, but
with a big monkey riding him around. I didn't know
there was much call for junkies in the security business."

"Unless it's their keen appetite for dope makes them
such good ferrets."

"More and more it looks like someone trying to get to
Sal through his son. I mean, what could a kid do to bring
on the kind of heat we're looking at? I think I need to
have a heart-to-heart with Sal."

Danny shrugged. "Sure. But why not start with Leo?
I know for a fact he's back in the city. Hit the places he
hangs out. Ask him about that night in April."

I grinned. "You telling me how to run my business?"

"I don't see Patty here, so somebody better."

Paulie appeared between us. "Excuse me. Mr. Belinski, there is a phone call for you. The house phone, next
to Mario."

In Danny's absence I went downstairs to use the men's
room. There were pay phones outside the bathroom. I
rang up my answering service for messages, wrote down
names and numbers—and one number, no name. From
Information I obtained the number of Tip Top Tech on
Queens Boulevard in Long Island City and dialed it and
listened to a screaming recorded message from Mad
Manny that might well have incited Ghandi to violence.

Tip Top Tech was closed for the evening. I pried the receiver from my fingers and scratched the back of my neck, trying to recall what I knew of the Saperstein brothers. I climbed the brick-colored stairs and found Danny back in the booth, a fresh scotch in his fist, and his hundredth cigarette of the day going down to defeat. I slipped into the booth opposite him, ready to ask about the Sapersteins. I didn't. He sat there like a man going through the motions and his eyes were lost, off somewhere.

"Danny?"

"Wittgenstein. Little Arnie. He's in emergency, Physicians' Hospital in Jackson Heights. Found him dumped in a garbage pail. Broken jaw, lost some teeth, concussion, possibly some brain damage. We're such smart fuckers, you and I."

23

Arpeggio's faced out on a service road that was separated by a concrete island from Queens Boulevard. The island wasn't much, five car lengths deep at its base and equipped with wooden benches arranged at oblique angles, almost vacant now, but during the day the stark seats were filled with opinionated geriatrics enjoying the sun, knitting, smoking, bitching in Yiddish, some Polish and German thrown in, some Neapolitan. Even some English. Only one of the benches was occupied when I came out, after paying the check and leaving Danny downstairs barking questions into the mouthpiece of a pay phone. The night air was warm, but not adhesively so, garlic from the restaurant combating the fumes off the snarling boulevard. A full moon with a feverish pallor hung up there, cookie-cutter crisp against a sky of ink. Apartment buildings and condos soared overhead, high black shapes with random and faintly trapezoidal patches of light in them. People were out taking the night air, couple of joggers, lovers arm in arm drifting beneath the pinkish glow of a street lamp: here the world was safe and vigorous and sweet. You wouldn't find any small, tightly knit, spunky men lying around here with their faces bashed in. A bunch of teens crossed the boulevard and surrounded the solitary figure on the bench with sounds of teasing and laughter, and departed as abruptly as they'd appeared.

If I remembered correctly, the Saperstein brothers frequented the neighborhood haunts around Tip Top, and in Leo's case, the sleazier the joint, the better the chance of finding him in it. Introducing Leo to the field of play

had intrigued me more than I let on to Danny, and his
suggestion to look him up was like a weak echo of my
intention. The Tony Knucks that caused Manny Saperstein such a problem happened to be a loan shark, nom-
inally under Angelo Scorcese, but a loose cannon in the
organization, a crazy. In a pay-phone-to-pay-phone conversation the Scorcese family's *consigliere* assured me
there would be no gnashing of teeth if Mr. Knucks were
persuaded to relocate. Charlie Rip, one of my agents and
a former linebacker for the New York Giants, introduced
Mr. Knucks to the fear of God, and shortly after he
limped out of Beth Israel, the shark torched his records
and left town. But the deal left a sour taste. It had begun
by my trying to help a guy—not gratis, but as a favor—
and ended because the Scorcese family had acquiesced
in the favor, with the Saperstein brothers owing the don.
Tip Top, according to my informants, functioned as a
front for a fencing operation, high-tech stuff that got
highjacked from LaGuardia or JFK. It was difficult to
imagine why anyone on the Scorcese payroll would need
to moonlight as a rent-a-cop. Difficult, but maybe not
without its rewards.

The Mercedes was parked around the corner and down
the block from the boulevard, nestled beneath a magnificent maple. As I approached the corner the party on the
bench stirred. He was just a shadow standing there, but
I would have recognized him without hearing the voice
that growled my name. Anything that big that didn't
breathe would have an awning in front of it.

"How's tricks, Cato?"

He took his time crossing the street, moving with that
easy grace some fat men possess, as if all the world is a
ballroom. His elbows chopped the air smoothly and precisely. No suit tonight. Tonight he was wearing a cutoff
Jets jersey, gray warm-up trousers with elastic ankles,
black sneakers with white soles that winked as he walked.
On his head was a watch cap rolled low over his eyes. He
hauled with him a heavy scent of onions and peppers,
warm dough, smoke. "*Prego*," he said, nudging me in
the direction of my car.

Two vehicles beyond the Mercedes was a black Chevy
van, its engine idling, nobody visible beyond the dark

glass windows. I got a glance at the plates: ARP 180.
Behind the door on the shotgun side was a panel door
with a porthole window in it that Cato rapped his
knuckles on. The door slid back. Joe Scorcese said, "I'm
a hope, Ray, you still usin' your brains. Get in."

A partition had been erected between the front seat
and the two behind it. Something that looked like carpeting covered the partition on our side, completely concealing us from the party (or parties) in front. Nearest
this was a half seat that Cato lowered his bulk into, sitting so that he faced the porthole. I shared the larger
bench seat with Joe, who communicated with the driver
through something resembling a pilot's headset, although the earpieces were smaller. He appeared to be
wearing the same costume as the night before, including
the comedian's felt hat, crumpled even more by the
headset clamped over it. Attached near the top of the
partition was a tubular light that Joe controlled with a
rheostat. The light gave off a dim, bluish glow, not
enough to read by, but sufficient to show me the ugly
shape of a snub-nosed revolver that came out of Cato's
waistband and now rested flat on his thigh. It rested
there with no more attention given to it than if it were
a ring of keys.

The driver maneuvered us from the curb. Joe uttered
a few words into the mouthpiece that were not English.

Then, screwing himself around in the corner where he
sat, he addressed me: "You hadda father was a cop. It is
my loss I only know him by his name, his *reputazione*.
It is a good name he carried and you are increasing it.
That is good. Salvatore showed me your business is already in the magazines. You are smart and tough, and
from last night I see you have good sense and show Sal
the respect for his loss and do not stop thinking if a man
insults you. I admire you for a businessman. I am a businessman."

"Does that mean I can still aspire to father children?"

The don muttered more words into the mouthpiece.
"You have a way of speaking I bet is good for magazines."

Uh-huh. But maybe not so good when addressing a businessman in the business Joe Scorcese was in. I dummied up.

The van was traveling now at what seemed to be expressway speed. My guess—and it was only that—was that we were whipping along on the LIE, heading east. But from where I sat, the porthole window was almost opaque, a pane of hard dark blue intermittently smeared with streaks of yellowish illumination.

"You mind if I ask, Mr. Scorcese, what this ride is about?"

"For a private conversation, Mr. Sommer."

"Well, if Cato would just step outside."

"That is magazine talk again. Let us be serious. It will save time."

He spoke quietly, with a tiger's crouch in his voice. I said nothing at all, once more.

"Good," he observed. "You know it is time to listen. This murder of Salvatore's son, you take it very hard. You have guilt, because it happened so close and you have a name, and anger that you could not give justice to his killers. As a man I respect you. But your opportunity is done. It is the business of others now."

"I understand that," I said.

"I do not think so. A reporter you say is a friend last night, he is become very busy today, all kinda questions about the situation."

"Wittgenstein?"

"The name I do not hear."

"He's in a Jackson Heights hospital right now with a broken jaw, possible brain damage."

"These are details, Mr. Sommer, that are not of my concern. I speak to you as a man of business now. So you will understand where your responsibilities end. Who hurts Salvatore hurts me. I take care for myself. Are you understanding this better?"

"Absolutely."

"Good."

"I have just one question, Mr. Scorcese: if I could give you the identity of the man responsible for young Sal's murder, would you be interested?"

It was the don's turn not to speak.

"Put me in touch with Sal," I said, "and I think I can deliver."

The monkey-faced man with the deadly eyes opened his mouth and a sound that might have been laughter rattled in his throat, a vicious little sound, like a stone violating a church window. "Ray," he said, "you gonna have your chance. Sal is a reason for this ride."

The sliding door rolled back on itself and I was prodded into the night, down upon thick damp grass with a view of what appeared to be the Whitestone Bridge roped off in lights against the sky. We were in the Bronx, in a cemetery. I could smell the unmistakable wash of sea air, the tang of the beach sifted through foliage. Cato followed me across the grass among the granite and marble headstones so I could take a leak. There were sounds of traffic in the distance.

Approaching the van, I recognized Angelo resting his backside against the grille, the heel of his steel-toed boot locked on the chrome bumper. He appeared to be wearing camouflage fatigues and a baseball cap, the bill reversed. His arms were folded beneath his pecs with an air of satisfaction.

"Ange," I said, "you squashed that bug after all, didn't you?"

"You said he wrote a food column."

"I said he ghosted one. Maybe I lied a little."

"Not no more you didn't."

The van was parked on pavement and the impulse to grab Angelo and bounce his face off a hard surface was almost irresistible. But I just stood there feeling like a fool, or worse, as parking lights crept along the ribbon of asphalt, approaching the van. The silhouette of a Jaguar, a late-model two-seater with the top up, purred within a dozen or so yards and extinguished its lights. The asphalt curved before reaching the van and the car was stopped on the far side of the curve. Joe Scorcese came around from the rear of the van in white socks and cheap sandals, the rubber soles producing soft raspberries in the damp grass. A figure climbed slowly from the Jag. He moved like an athlete who has pushed himself beyond capacity, playing on adrenaline, who felt pain now in all of his parts. He even seemed to hesitate taking Joe Scorcese's hand. Then, just as I became certain I recognized him, the man bowed over the hand, pressed the twisted fingers to his lips. They began to speak. The breeze carried fragments, but they weren't using English. Then the Baker uttered my name.

I waded off into the grass. It was Sal DeLorio; rather, the wreck of him. The man, who even last night was in fierce control of himself, now stood in the moonlight, his unshaven face colored blue and yellowish, hands trembling, his clothing soured by sweat and the effects of long drinking. He looked older than Joe would ever be. The brilliant eyes were just spots in his face. There was about him the cruel, always shocking transformation reserved for corpses: he looked so much smaller inside his clothes. He was a man robbed of a dream.

I put out my hand, but either Sal did not see it or he was beyond such gestures. In the light of the moon he seemed to be functioning in a delirium. He dug his fingers into my arms just above the elbows and peered up, as if desperately trying to recognize me. "So you're the golden boy," he croaked. "You better be. I am in no condition to hear bullshit."

Standing to one side and behind Sal, Joe muttered something not in English, in short, harsh syllables.

Sal took his hands away and pushed them into the pockets of his suit coat.

"I don't know what you mean by golden boy," I said, "but I do have something to run by you. You don't look too good, Sal, you want to sit down, lean against the car maybe?"

"You want to tell me who the fuck killed my son? Just tell me that."

"You got it turned around," I said. "You're going to tell me."

Sal showed me a clenched fist, made strangling noises in his throat. I held up an open hand. "Sal. You're a little crazy right now. Listen. Last night you accused me of going after everyone except the person I'd been hired to find. The fact of the matter is I wasn't going after them so much as stumbling into them, and maybe the reason has to do with the fact that the man who hired me to find Julie Holloway isn't her father. What he is, Sal, is a guy the CIA wants to talk to about some missing money. Two agents took the trouble tonight to break into my office to wait for me, in order to explain their interest in this beautiful creature. They weren't exactly strangers, these two, because they sat in on a conversation I had with Dominic Amado this morning. Moriarity was there, Cox was there, a bunch of feds too. All that weight, given what I knew about yesterday's shooting, struck me as overkill, unless you pulled some strings, Sal, or Joe—Mr. Scorcese—did." I glanced past Sal's shoulder and the don waved a hand, the twisted fingers dismissing my gaffe, forgiving my lapse of respect. "But the crowd wasn't there on your account," I went on. "They were there because of a man I asked you about last night, Mr. Scorcese. The one known in the street as Peru."

"I remember this," the don murmured, his eyes meeting mine.

"So do I," snapped Sal, "so do I. The guy's moving drugs. Maybe the two boys from the Bronx thought they could move on him and paid the price, or maybe not. You're drifting into the hypothetical, Ray."

"Wrong. You are, Sal. But that's easy to do in a case like this, with as little as we know. So indulge me a bit. Skelton, the Queens DA, what do you know about him?"

Sal rolled a shoulder and glanced at the don, who nodded. "What's to know? He's a politician. He'd disown his mother if the polls showed it'd get him elected. He comes up to the house last night—this is before you are there, Joe—he wants his personal photographer to sit in on the conversation."

"The man's a believer in publicity," I said.

"I told that mick the photographer could sit anywhere, including on the mick's face, but not while he was talking to me. Guy's a stiff."

"Skelton's office offered a deal to me this morning. Because I accepted, Skelton canceled a scheduled news conference. And it wasn't any juice you might have, Sal. It was weight from above. The trade-off being Skelton won't go public with the stash in the Porsche's glove box so long as I keep my mouth shut about the existence, or possible existence, of someone named Peru."

"That dope," Sal said through clenched teeth, "was a plant."

"And not the first time, either—right, counselor?"

He shuddered visibly. "Get on with it, golden boy."

"Assumptions, hypotheses, you work with this stuff as much as I do, probably more. It is hardly an assumption, almost a given, that a man in your position has acquired his share of enemies. Some known, some not. How well do you know the man who misrepresented himself on the cassette as the father of Julie Holloway?"

"I know him exceedingly well, as a matter of fact."

"I don't think so," I said. "The man you introduced me to as Holloway happens to be known in other circles as Peru. We're talking a big in the CIA who's rumored to be moving major quantities through Queens. We're talking maybe murderer, or person behind the murder of your son. Could we put a name on him, Sal? You're among friends."

"Name's Thompson Grace," he murmured.

The don caught Sal's sleeve in his small, crabbed hand. "Say the name was, Salvatore?"

"Grace, Joe. Tommy Grace. Think I introduced you once, the track, Belmont last summer."

"Sal, can you tell me what this little girl, Julie Holloway, is to this guy? Her father, she says, died from exposure to a defoliant in Nam, probably Agent Orange. I know Grace spent time in the Nam too. Is it only coincidence?"

"He—I don't know. I received my instructions the same way you did: on a cassette. Package arrived by courier at the house, the evening before yesterday."

His eyes had begun to sharpen and he seemed to be gaining his focus, a grasp on the present. That encouraged me, because if he was capable of lying, which he obviously was now, he could be manipulated toward the truth, or what part of it he knew.

"That's it, that's all the contact you had?"

"All," he said, sullenly.

"Listen a Ray, Sal," counseled Joe Scorcese. "I think we gonna have a meet with Mr. Grace."

"*Padrino*," said Sal, almost a whisper.

"Gimme the address. I'm a make some calls. Set it up."

Because I needed to speak to Sal alone, I did not suggest that Grace's home was the one place he would *not* be. The Baker squeaked off through the grass. I watched him climb into the front of the van, where the phone would be.

"You're looking better," I said. "Coming off the ropes a little. You look like you're even strong enough to separate fact from fiction. Yesterday morning your son told me you had advised your client, this Holloway-Grace, that I wouldn't be interested in a lost-and-found job. Since you can't advise a cassette, either you had a conversation with the man or you lied to your son. Or your son lied to me. There's a lie in there somewhere. Maybe more than one."

Sal's eyes brightened and locked on mine for several seconds, then he bent over the door of the Jag, dug around behind the passenger seat, came up with a clear, squat bottle of expensive brandy. He uncorked it and had a pull, as indifferent to etiquette as, say, Angelo Scorcese.

"The fucking golden boy." He sneered. "Yes, he phoned me. The rest came by courier."

"But Sally said you told him I wouldn't be interested. Something changed your mind."

Sal had a lost look about him that was cutting to see, because he had always been the measure, a tough kid from the streets of Queens who had become a class act, senior partner of a Park Avenue firm, a citizen with clout and style.

"Was Julie somebody you recognized, Sal? Or turn it around, somebody who might recognize you?" It wasn't exactly a blind lob, and it split the plate. He clutched the squat bottle with both hands, his haggard face full of pleading. "I spoke to Julie today. I got the impression that part of her career involved being a party girl to older men. She mentioned a wild time with a girlfriend's old man. I assumed she meant the girl's boyfriend. But maybe it wasn't a boyfriend. Old man could mean the girl's father, couldn't it? Which in the context of the conversation makes more sense."

He pushed the neck of the bottle against his lips, and when he was done with that transaction, his voice was a dull, distant, reportorial sound: "For years Tommy and I've had a lucrative quid pro quo. His information on defense decisions helped our stock plays, and our understanding of real estate in the boroughs guided his investments. There were a number of deals to celebrate, and Tommy, he arranged the entertainment. There were always young girls, that seemed to be his specialty. Well, you have a few drinks, it's right there. So was a video camera, I find out later."

I said nothing. This guy Grace was a piece of work, all right, but if what Sal said was true, I was grabbing at smoke once more. It didn't make sense, if he already had the leverage of a compromising tape, to go after Sal's son, unless the act was an escalation in a war of threats. Maybe Sal had something on the man. No. The Scorceses wouldn't have been running down snitches all day if Sal even suspected who had ordered the hit. My head began to feel like a lab rat on a treadmill. The moonlight made apparitions of us, pale semblances of men.

"Ray? Nothing to Joe about . . . the girls, huh?"

"It's all yours," I said. I started off through the grass toward the van.

"Schmuck!" he snarled. "Who anointed you? First, you stand with your thumb up your ass while my boy is being murdered, then I learn you fucked my wife in Haiti. You don't walk with the angels either, golden boy."

He was right. I just kept walking through the cemetery grass. I needed a drink for medicinal purposes in someplace sleazy, the sleazier the better. I was looking for a soul mate.

24

There were two bucket seats in the front of the van, and I occupied shotgun for the ride back to Queens. Angelo drove, wearing a headset to communicate with his father. A police scanner burped out a continuum of mayhem: a floater in the East River; a sideswipe on the Brooklyn Bridge, perpetrator in a dark Camaro, no license number; stickup of a liquor store in progress; report of a multiple rape in Jamaica, Queens; a call for backup at the scene of a domestic quarrel. . . . Angelo, when he wasn't squinting to listen to the don, expounded on various ethnic groups. I stared straight into the night, saying nothing, remembering how much Cece bitched about the company I kept. She was a great believer in guilt by association. I began to think she had a legitimate fear.

It was close to midnight when the van rolled around the corner past Arpeggio's and stopped, facing the Mercedes. The static on the scanner sounded like distant gunfire, the sound of evil and stupidity happening to someone else. Angelo was putting the finishing touches to a scholarly monologue on the subject of Jews as I climbed out. I said, "Ange, you ought to write that stuff down. Those papers they sell in the grocery store checkout lines, they pay money for shit like that."

Long Island City isn't one of the lovelier districts in the borough of Queens, with its welter of anonymous warehouses, scaling billboards, the din and permanent shadow of the elevated train snaking through its heart.

By contrast, sandwiched between an all-night coffee shop and a bar that advertised topless dancers, Tip Top Tech exuded an air of prosperity. I parked the car beneath the tracks of the El and crossed the street. Through the steel grating that protected the storefront I could see in the dim light various displays of electronic gadgetry piled pyramid fashion around the floor, signs in front of them reading PRICES SLASHED!: everything from computers to televisions that fit in the palm of your hand. And of course, the bread and butter: security systems. Back in the depths of the store I could make out a pair of Dobermans prowling the aisles, their motion sleek, fluid, surging like enormous nightmares. Now, there was a security system.

I pushed the buzzer to the door that led to the floor upstairs, where Manny and Leo Saperstein lived. I waited. I gave the buzzer two more long shots, and when still no voice crackled over the intercom, I started with the nearest local bistro, the go-go bar next door.

It was everything an operation of this kind aspires to be: boisterous and crowded, garishly illuminated, a swamp for raw emotions to muck about in. Right now piped-in Pointer Sisters was shaking the room, sassy and unstoppable, and so excited. A horseshoe-shaped bar faced the entrance and dancing upon it with a sedated rhythm was a barefoot blonde, adorned in a black velvet bow tie and the bottom half of a string bikini. In front of her most of the troops were congregated, brawling along the bar as she moved, a fun-loving bunch with a loud, if restricted, vocabulary. Unlike her sisters, who were bathed in crimson light and shook their hips on opposing platforms, the blonde kept her eyes very much open, to avoid tripping on a drink or the hands of her admirers. A nice face, not much going on in it, processing her surroundings. Sturdy, peasant body. Dollar bills drooped from the crotch of her bikini and her skin gleamed, not entirely from exertion. Several fans had sprayed her with shaken beer bottles. I found Leo on the other side of the horseshoe, perched on a stool, brooding over his Seven and Seven. He was outfitted for ogling in gold lamé trousers pegged at the ankles and a matching sleeveless getup with a stiff clerical collar, zipper tight

from navel to throat. Any more after-shave and he'd be
a candidate for emissions testing. I leaned over him and
said, "Leo, what, you dating someone from *Star Wars*?"

He lurched forward on his stool, almost overturning
his drink, and looked for an instant like he was going to
cry. He drew the back of his hand across his lips. "Jesus,
Ray. You don't want to do that to a guy who's falling in
love. Will you look at those balloons?"

It was so loud in there I had to point at the bottle of
Jack Daniel's, then at the sink. The barkeep delivered
my Jack and water, and exchanged my tenspot for a flock
of soggy singles.

"So how's it with you and Manny?"

"Can't kick."

"Business good?"

"Dynamite."

"That's what I hear," I said. "Makes me curious how
come you're moonlighting as a campus security cop.
Can't be the money."

Leo jabbed his plastic stirrer intently into the ice in
his drink. "It was a favor to a guy, no big deal."

"Let's talk upstairs," I suggested.

"Hey, c'mon," he pleaded, "she's coming this way.
Connie! Hey, Connie!" He sprang from a rung on his
stool to add to the bouquet of currency dripping from
her crotch, an act of generosity she rewarded by dropping to a crouch, fondling her breasts listlessly, large
brown eyes concentrating upon a spot above the pawing
crowd. Leo made inarticulate noises in his throat chasing
a nipple with his lips.

"Let's go," I said, and hauled him away from the bar
by the back of his stiff collar, Leo squirming a little for
show, but generally going along with the program.

Outside, I put the arm about his shoulders and bustled
him off to his doorway.

"What's with the heavy hand?" he protested. "Fuck's
a matter?"

Once in the vestibule I backed him against the wall.
Tears leaked from the corners of his eyes. "You gonna
hit me, Ray, don't hit me in the gut. Please. I got a bad
gut already."

I pinched the plastic zipper on his gold lamé sleeveless

jacket and ran it down. A heavy gold chain shone on his white chest, between almost womanish breasts. It was eighteen carat, arranged in a herringbone pattern. A cool, palpable weight on my finger as I lifted it away, let it drop upon his throat. "This thing must weigh almost as much as you do," I said. "Quit crying, I'm not going to hit you. But lie to me, Leo, you're light enough to toss out a window real easy. You might want to keep that in mind. Kind of focus on it."

At the back of the vestibule arose a narrow staircase that looked as if it had been built fifty years ago and then forgotten. What remained of a black rubber runner suggested that the inhabitants routinely wore cleats instead of shoes. The banister wobbled like a loose tooth. The stairs struck left at a ninety-degree angle, and at the top of them we encountered a hallway to our right that led away from a large room overlooking both the boulevard and the El, stitched across the sky like a scar. A heavy musk of furniture polish presided in the room. The hallway went back with rooms off it Pullman fashion. We went that way.

Leo kept a tidy kitchen for a junkie, but then, as I thought about it, I hadn't much experience sitting around the hearth with people who stuck themselves with needles for pleasure. The porcelain sink shone with the brightness of sunlight off snow, and the stove didn't appear to have been used for anything messier than boiling water. Since Manny was a notorious slob, this had to be Leo's doing. As if to confirm it, he fussily doled out coasters before offering me a drink.

"A beer," I said, "if you have one."

"Should. It's all my brother drinks." He reached into the refrigerator and brought out a cold brown bottle with a long neck and opened it on the counter next to the sink. "Glass?"

"Right out of the bottle's fine."

He placed it on a coaster in front of me and went about preparing a Seven and Seven. The beer was good and cold. I sat at a round oak veneer table, practically squinting from the glare off polished surfaces.

"Where's Manny tonight?"

"I should know? Card game somewhere, most likely."
He sat down across from me and ran a hand through his
stringy hair, then tasted his drink. He had the face of a
cherub once you got past the unhealthy eyes. He essayed
a convivial look. "Throw me out the window. You were
good in there, Ray. If I didn't have a gut full of knots, I
prob'ly woulda filled my shorts. Now, why'd you wanna
go and scare a guy like that?"

"Some guys, it clarifies their thinking. And don't be
too sure I was kidding."

He waved a small, chubby hand. "Go on with you.
You talk too much to be a real thug. Besides, you're a
celebrity now. I couldn't believe it. I'm sitting there in
my doctor's waiting room reading this coverless copy of
People, and there's your ugly face. I even tore the pages
out to show my brother. I think he'd kill me, his own
flesh and blood, for publicity like that, know whadda
mean?"

I put my bottle down carefully on the coaster and
leaned forward and slapped his face with the flat of my
hand. There was more wrist than arm in the blow, but
Leo spun sideways off his chair, taking his drink with
him, ice cubes and booze washing across shiny linoleum
that was new about the time Eisenhower was sworn in
for his first term. It was a shade of mucus green with
Chinese-red squiggles worked into it, like aborted road
maps. Leo crawled around on his hands and knees
whimpering and plucking up ice cubes. The glass fetched
up in one piece against the baseboard. I handed it to
him and told him to get up and sit down, he didn't want
to ruin his Ziploc suit, did he? He sat down, still whimpering. One of his cherub cheeks was flushed, and he
cupped a hand over his ear, complained about his hearing.

I tilted the bottle to my lips and emptied it. "Leo, shut
up. It's past one in the morning and I'm tired, and when
I get tired, I get cranky. So stop waltzing me around.
Let's talk about this favor you were doing by becoming
a rent-a-cop. I know you and your brother are into the
Scorcese family. So's a big part of the borough. Maybe
you'll get rich, maybe you'll wind up in the slam or the

trunk of a car, it's your life. I'm not a crusader, Leo.
Live and let live, I say. Just tell me about this favor you
did for the family."

"Who said anything about it was the family?"

I showed him my index finger. "Leo. Don't waltz me.
Don't even think about it."

"It was a lady," he said, and winced, ducking his head
and fighting for breath. "I got whacha call a spastic co-
lon," he explained. "That sucker knots up, I can't hardly
breathe."

"About the lady," I said.

"As a favor to the old man, I was supposed to keep
tabs on her nights. Security job was just a cover."

"The old man."

"The Baker is the way I got it."

"So you weren't hired or asked to stick packets of cocaine onto the seats of empty sports cars."

"Ray, you can hit me all you want. It isn't the same
as winding up in a Jamaica landfill." He winced once
more, a hand diving inside his trousers. "I need a nightcap, you mind?"

He reached into a drawer next to the sink. I watched
him break open the cellophane seal on a fresh syringe,
mix and cook his solution in a spoon, draw the stuff up
through the needle.

"Before the nightcap," I said, "tell me about the lady.
Was she a student?"

"C'mon, Ray."

I raised my index finger, I showed him my hand.

"Yeah, she was a student. Somebody a men's magazine
would do a centerfold on, no question about it. I fell in
love with her day one, but she's taller than me, five-nine,
maybe -ten. Talk about a wilted erection. She had blue
eyes, blond hair, balloons, the works. I assumed she was
the don's private stock, know whadda mean?"

"The name wasn't Genevieve, was it?"

"No," he said. He looked like he was truly in pain. He
peeled the sock off his foot, moved his hands across the
sole, pinching and squeezing. He isolated a vein in his
arch, just behind the ball of his foot. "Do me," he
pleaded.

There were other marks in the neighborhood, but his

foot was as scrubbed as any surface in the kitchen. I picked up the syringe, squeezed a drop off the tip to clear it of any air, then locked onto his wasted eyes. "How about the name," I said.

"It was a funny last name. Like a duchess-sounding one. Kane-Wells. That's it. Allie Kane-Wells."

"Allie," I said.

I tapped the vein, a simple exercise of motor skills, then watched my thumb descend. Blood, no more than a thorn would draw, bubbled from the puncture. Holding the needle to the light, I witnessed a drop, two drops wobble free and roll down. Before the blood reached my hand I tossed the syringe into the snow-white sink.

25

Back in the mausoleum in Kew Gardens I mixed a weak brandy and soda and carried it upstairs to run a bath. I stripped, the bone-white tile cold and refreshing against my bare feet. Sitting on the side of the tub with the drink in my hand, I could see in the mirrored closet doors most of the bedroom. Cece's look: white carpet and tile, white walls, exposed beams, plenty of foliage—bromeliads and ferns, spider plants suspended in the windows, a bonsai queen palm—that I paid the housekeeper an extra stipend to keep watered. It looked like an oasis and offered all the comfort of a mirage.

I sank into the steaming water, the ticklish heat. I submerged the back of my head where there was still a little swelling. Even some pain, but the pain kept me from becoming comfortable, logy. Leo all but admitted to laying the stuff on Sal Jr. at Bennington, the implication being he was acting upon Scorcese family wishes. That didn't make sense for a number of reasons, not only in light of subsequent events, but primarily because if the don had some reason to go after the boy, he had both a more direct and less public means of doing so. First piece of nonsense. Second: the don boffing a coed. Angelo yes, but not . . . okay, it was possible, but not probable. One thing seemed to be incontrovertible: this Allie person had a yen for old men. I thought about the other major player in this tangled mess—the guy Sal identified as Tommy Grace—and the entertainment he provided: young girls. Young girls to set up men who should know better. Sure. With men, the adage about two heads being better than one is pure foolishness where the opposite sex is concerned, because while one head may be thinking, the other's already made the decision.

I toweled myself down standing in the tub, staring across at a partially fogged mirror, looking for any sign of intelligent life. The cool tile still felt refreshing to the soles of my feet. I threw on a light cotton robe, brushed my teeth, brushed my hair, dumped the remains of my brandy in the toilet. At the end of the bed was a chest composed of hammered copper and wood that had the aspect of having washed up from a shipwreck, which Cece had "stolen" in an auction somewhere, and which seemed to attract all my discarded clothing with the power of a vacuum. From an inner pocket of the jacket I had worn, I dug out my notebook, the list of names and numbers I had gotten from my answering service when I called them from Arpeggio's. Since I was already running on empty, I dialed the number with no name. A weary voice answered after a half-dozen rings: "Sneaky Pete's here. Five minutes to last call."

"Sneaky, somebody gave your number to my answering service. Could you check if anybody there wants to speak to Ray Sommer?"

The voice of Sneaky checked. Nobody did.

I said, "Sneaky, thank you. You mind telling me, where are you located?"

Almost Nineteenth Street on Eighth Avenue.

"Manhattan?"

"Fuck you calling from, Nome fucking Alaska? Yeah, the city. And hey, guess what? It's closing time. Night, Nome."

Nineteenth and Eighth placed the anonymous caller in Chelsea. Just north of the Village. Not that far, maybe a ten-minute walk, from Horatio Street. A ten-minute walk from many places.

I dialed information for the number of Physicians' Hospital and got myself patched through to a nurse in intensive care with a sweet, deep warble in her voice, as if she were just taking a breather between gospels, and while it wasn't the policy of the hospital to respond to phone inquiries, her heart prevailed to the extent that she would admit that a patient named Arnold Wittgenstein was on her floor and that his condition was stable.

Any further questions would have to be directed at his doctor, and the doctor was not in. I thanked the lady and hung up. Stable. So was the chest at the end of the bed. So was death. Death was about as stable as it gets.

I fell into bed and into a sleep that was dark and dreamless. I awoke feeling like a man buried alive, a faint gray light sifting into the room, the phone burring in my ear like a tocsin. It was not quite six in the morning. I lifted hundreds upon hundreds of pounds of earth to answer that phone.

"Ray? Is . . . Ray?"

"Meredith?"

"I couldn't—I haven't been able—I keep, I keep waking, Ray, in spite of the medication. I want, I wanted some fresh air—some fresh air, I thought. I found him in the drive. And Ray, there's blood everywhere!"

My feet hit the carpet and I was squeezing the receiver in an effort to keep a clamp on my emotions. "Meredith, please," I said, "who is it you found?"

"My—my"—she fought for breath—"Sal, Salvatore, my husband."

"No," I said, before I could stop myself, "no fucking way."

"What? What did you say?"

"Are you certain, sweetness?"

"There's blood everywhere."

I grabbed a pillow from the bed and pushed it into my mouth, bit down hard, and raged into it. I had a taste of the madness and futility that was the daily diet in the Nam, where death lived in the fast lane. Even the first thought to pulse through me had its origin in Nam: *It wasn't you, at least it wasn't you.* I pressed the receiver against the mattress and shook, until the worst of the craziness had worked itself out of my system. Meredith did not need to hear my panic in the midst of her despair. Finally, I lifted the receiver to my ear.

"Ray?" she cried. "Are you there?"

"I am," I said. I surprised myself. There was in my voice a brutal calm that I remembered coming over me after combat, after a crude scrutiny assured me of the presence of my body parts. "Call the police," I said. "I'll be up shortly. With my people for security, not a bunch of hoods."

"Police are already here," she said. "I had my sister call. I killed him, Ray."

"Yeah? Then have your sister call Sydney Simon, would you do that for me?"

"Why?"

"To keep you from confessing to any crime, except living. The girls need you. They're the survivors, Meredith. They need you more than the dead do."

I listened to her crying into the phone for a while, then told her I was on my way. But just in case, I phoned Sydney Simon myself before calling Charlie Rip.

26

Charlie Rip liked to introduce himself as Charles A. Ripley, the name he was born with, and when someone asked, as someone invariably did, what the "A" stood for, he delivered it deadpan in a soft Georgia growl: "The 'A' is for Armageddon—believe it or not." People believed it.

Charlie went two-seventy when he was lean and earned his living terrorizing NFL quarterbacks. Now that he worked for me, instead of a helmet he sported an array of natty chapeaus. He wore them with the aplomb of a man who knew there weren't too many objects on the planet that he wasn't bigger than. This morning he was topped off in a rather modest scarlet beret. There were three diamond studs arranged in his right ear and his bottom lip swelled faintly from the plug of tobacco stored there. He wore a double-breasted navy-blue trench coat over navy-blue sweats and held a black umbrella against the lightly falling rain.

A clear plastic tarp had been spread over the Jaguar and an officer from the Westchester County Sheriff's Department was posted beside it to ensure its integrity from the elements and anyone not outfitted in the uniform of the Westchester County Sheriff's Department. In other words, me.

In spite of the weak light and the distortion brought about by the folds in the plastic, I got a good idea of how bad it must have looked to Meredith. Although the body had been removed, the blood and even bits of flesh were visible. And the window on the shotgun side had been shattered by the bullet that had done its damage to

Sal. He had pulled the Jag off alongside the stand of blue spruce, at least two hundred yards from the house, to do his dying. An unregistered Colt .380 automatic had been found on the floor of the car beneath his legs, which was the only piece of information the sheriff had seen fit to share with me, and that only because Meredith told me she had seen the gun there when she opened the door. I circled the car one more time, Charlie shielding me from the spitting weather with the umbrella, then dug my hands in the deep pockets of my khaki trench coat, chewed my lip, and studied the sky. The rain had begun to trickle down just before I left the house.

The sheriff's officer stood next to the door on the driver's side in a bright orange rainslick with a hood to protect his cap. He stood with his arms folded beneath the slick, as if he were about to deliver a verdict. He had a small, prim mouth, a fiery zit in the region of his Adam's apple and the general air of a man badly in need of some castor oil.

"Everybody in place?" I said.

"Chain of command, the works," Charlie Rip murmured, cutting his eyes in the direction of the officer, who was yawning even as he strolled a step or two our way. He raised his voice to say, "Sheriff don't much appreciate our presence. Why would that be, do you suppose?"

Before I could answer, Charlie Rip loosed a glob of chew that smacked the wet asphalt like grease in a hot pan, sending the officer in the orange slick up on his toes and prancing backward, as if to dodge the fallout.

"I don't know," I said. I glanced over at the officer settling down beneath his bright slicker like an exotic bird come to rest. His prim little mouth got primmer and the color climbed alarmingly in his face; he looked like a pimple about to burst. "What would you say, Officer?"

"I ain't the sheriff," he volunteered. "I don't guess it's none a my business if a person wants to pay a hotshot like you to come up here and hold her hand. Just so's you don't get in the way of the people who have to do the real work."

I put a hand against Charlie's chest. But Charlie did

no more than expel another glob of tobacco, this one landing harmlessly in the middle of the drive.

"I thank you for your candor," I said.

"Yeah," Charlie Rip added, "you the boy, all right. You keep that car guarded real good, hear?"

Charlie and I moved slowly up the drive toward the house, neither of us speaking. Once we reached the portico, I removed my khaki hat and wrung it out and found a handkerchief to mop my face. There were five county cars parked in among the cars belonging to the DeLorio family and friends, in addition to the one parked across the entrance to the drive as a deterrent to members of the press. Every one of the official vehicles was nosed in at a crazy angle, as if to underscore that urgent business was afoot. But cops parked that way even if they were stopping for a frankfurter. Maybe it was disorienting to ride around all the time in such conspicuously ugly vehicles, or maybe, because they were the law, they thought they could do any damn thing they pleased.

"It's your call," said Charlie Rip, the rolled-up umbrella stuck beneath his arm, "how long you want us to stay. I hear the sheriff making noises it's a suicide, which, if that's the case, I don't know—"

"It wasn't suicide, Charlie."

"Then we stay."

"Not you," I said "You've got the people in place. I want you to take a fresh eye back to Horatio Street, look it over for any seams. How about the rooftop, we have anybody up there?"

"Shit," said Charlie Rip. "I'll see who Patty's got for me."

"Let's blanket the goddamn place for twenty-four hours. You get that set up, I want you to start in a bar in Chelsea, name is Sneaky Pete's, say you're wondering if Ramone's been in lately, anybody seen him around. Make friends if you can. Give them drinking money to hit another bar, asking the same questions. With any luck we can network the bars between there and Horatio Street. Patty'll have the cash for you."

"You want this guy bad."

"I want him, just once, face-to-face."

Charlie Rip grinned and scratched his ear, the one

loaded with diamonds. "I hope you invite me to the party. I ain't never seen you when you're pissed off. I bet it's a sight."

I spent the rest of the morning being ignored by the sheriff and giving whatever comfort I could to Meredith, who, between the medication and her grief, was hardly coherent. Her sister Jean stayed with her, and Sydney Simon popped in when he wasn't conferring with the sheriff or touching bases with the office. I found Christina in the kitchen with Charlotte and the cook, Brigitte, a stout charmer with rosy cheeks. Both women were surreptitiously dabbing at their eyes as Christina, cigar in fist, strutted about impersonating her father. A deputy posted outside the exercise room informed me that it was Genevieve's request to be left alone. I honored the request.

By noon the rain had stopped and sunlight was leaking into the sky, although tentatively. It felt like a truce in the weather more familiar to the Catskills, where there will be hours of aggressive sunshine suddenly and with little prelude succeeded by a deluge, and then a night of clear and icy starlight. The sheriff and his men were gone along with the Jaguar transported on a flatbed. In place of the official car, Sal's Rolls now traversed the entrance of the drive with one of my crack media guys in the driver's seat, Rocky Lee Chang, who spoke better English than most New Yorkers, but did an obtuse Oriental bit that was Oscar level, bringing to the part the authority of a sixth-degree black belt. I was standing beneath the portico inhaling the riot of aromas the dying rain had unleashed, scratching around the small swell on the back of my neck, as the yellow taxi murmured through the patch of blue spruce and descended in front of me. I opened the back door for my ex-wife.

She came into my arms the way I had choreographed it in my dreams, although in my dreams death hadn't been part of the bargain. "Oh my darling," she cried, "oh Ray. This isn't fair. Life is such a bastard."

I paid the hack and escorted her into the house. I helped her out of her hooded raincoat, a light silvery something, and handed it to Charlotte, who took it off somewhere. Cece was in gray today, skirt and jacket smartly cut, the folds of a silk handkerchief knifing out of her breast pocket, the color a perfect match for her peach silk blouse. A string of pearls lay at her throat. I had never bought her pearls, associating them with older women, but these looked as if they had been selected exclusively for her. In removing her coat, I had caught the scent of her perfume and it lingered with me still, working its spell. I stopped her at the bottom of the staircase and turned her around, and ventured my fingers in the hair above her ear. "Don't blame life, Cece. We're all of us sinners. It's just a matter of degree."

I met her lips with mine. I met them and met them and met them, greedy for the feel of her, selfish as a sixteen-year-old, and desperate as only a man of forty can be.

She pulled her face away and pressed it to my chest, her hands moving, straining against my back, her body shaking against mine. I stroked her hair and opened my eyes. Meredith DeLorio in a long black gown stood at the head of the stairs, one hand gripping the corner of the wall, looking devastated, and maybe what was more painful to witness—looking betrayed.

"Ray?" she called down in a tiny, quavering voice. "Cece, is that you? Please do come up. It seems ages since we've seen you. Come. We'll have a drink on the balcony overlooking the courts while Salvatore finishes bathing and primping. Male vanity."

Speeding along the Hutch in the Mercedes, I put through a call to Boro Hall and lucked out. Lieutenant Cox was in the building, in courtroom three, to testify in the case of a billiards-hall stabbing in Richmond Hill.

The courtroom was laid out something like an amphitheater, the seating for the spectators fanning up and away from the focal point, the area beyond the rail: here were the opposing attorneys' desks, desks for the bailiff and court recorder, the jury box off to the right filled with serious faces, and the elevated proscenium where Judge O'Meara presided, the flag rippling lifelessly from a standard behind his right shoulder. O'Meara was listening to arguments from the district attorney and the attorney for the defense as I entered the courtroom. I noticed the fingers of his left hand drumming on his desk, and I suspected it wasn't from impatience so much as boredom, which gave him an opportunity to practice his fingering on a folk guitar, music being one of his passions. Food being another. I had bumped a few glasses with J.D. (for Julius David, a Jewish Irishman, an unbeatable combination in Queens) in Arpeggio's, where the O'Meara clan were wont to join in on a refrain or two with the waiters. I liked him. He was a hearty, educated man, in whose presence you were bound to learn something. He ran his courtroom like an amiable despot, taking shit from no one.

Lieutenant Cox was sitting in the row immediately behind the rail, on the prosecution's side of the aisle, a pale blue fedora in place today, a camel-colored double-breasted suit with a blue, almost indigo shirt, another wide tie with pale blue quarter moons floating in it. Crouching in the aisle beside him, Wall had put himself together in an acceptable Rutgers teaching-fellow costume. When the conference ended, the Wall sauntered up the aisle shaking a cigarette loose from his pack. I slid into a seat behind the lieutenant and leaned forward. "It's me, Lieutenant—Ray. Just wondering what you learned from the Bennington bust."

Cox got his elbow on the back of the seat and cranked himself ninety degrees so that he was facing the aisle, the side of his mouth available to me. "Bust is the word. The alleged offense, because it occurred on campus grounds and no complaint was filed, it didn't get written up. There ain't even a jacket, just what the two officers on the scene could remember, which—sonuvagun—ain't much."

"Uh-huh. Here's something to take out on a rainy day and chew on: the security cop that reported the stuff in Sal's car was Leo Saperstein. I can't prove it, but I know it."

"That little shitwad?"

"Commuting every day to Vermont. How soon before you testify?"

"That little shitwad probably planted the stuff!" Cox blurted angrily.

The sound of the gavel stung the air. Judge O'Meara was smiling paternally, but it was the kind of smile that precipitated a trip to the woodshed. "Gentlemen, this court is not interested in your salty speculations, nor will it tolerate them. Are we of one mind on this?"

"Yes, yer honor," snapped Lieutenant Cox.

"Mr. Sommer?"

"Absolutely. One mind. Take it to the bank, your honor."

The eyebrows bunched above O'Meara's eyes, black as his robe, and he leaned forward, his head lowered, and there was junkyard dog written all over him. "Another thing the court will not tolerate is insolence, Mr. Sommer."

"It's . . . I apologize, your honor, if—I've had a shock, that's all. My apologies to the court." Under my breath I said to Cox, "Any idea how long before you're going to testify? Because we got to talk."

"I already testified. The DA's boy asked me to take notes on this witness for him."

I put my hand up to his ear. "Tell him to hire a new secretary. Somebody murdered Sal DeLorio, Senior, last night."

Lieutenant Cox fussed with the brim of his fedora a little longer than usual and still did not look satisfied. He stood up abruptly, ignoring the entreaties of the attorney prosecuting the case, and mounted the aisle with a slow, somber stride. Outside the courtrooms tall glass tinted close to black overlooked the grounds, and even on a bright day, like today was trying to be, the glass offered a vision of a world that was smooth and full of menace.

I stood behind Cox, who was staring through the black glass. "I was there for Sal's last match in the Garden," he said.

"So was I," I murmured.

"He was a class act, that left jab of his. The nigger was just stronger."

"The black guy was just a little more in every area, Lieutenant. It was an honest fight. Unlike the one Sal took on last night."

Lieutenant Cox jogged his hat around and slipped another wafer of dried plum into his mouth. "What do you want?"

"Whatever you can learn from the Westchester County sheriff's office. I was up there all morning, and they froze me out. Sal was my friend. His wife, she's lost a son and a husband in three days, she flipped out this morning. I owe her some explanations."

We rode the elevator. The color-coordinated office was pretty much as I remembered it, the wall-to-wall bulletin board with the thousand and one items stuck to it. Young Wall was on the phone, a cigarette in the corner of his mouth, negotiating with his lady over which movie to attend tonight. While Cox worked his sources in Westchester I feigned interest in the FBI photos affixed to the corkboard. Marilyn Buck, even discounting the shabby quality of the reproduction, couldn't touch Cece, and the difference between them had nothing to do with lighting and everything to do with disposition. Miss Buck, evidently a punk at heart, bore a résumé that included murder. The intangible ingredient, call it spirit, or heart, or grace, it wasn't there in the lovely outlaw: she was just an exquisite surface.

Cox, hunched over his phone and listening, slipped himself a wafer, grunted, and thanked someone named Bernie. He shifted his buttocks around in the chair and poked out another number, jabbing his blunt finger with a deliberation that was almost maddening to watch, as if he were operating under the impression that the right combination was going to make him the instant-lottery winner. Wall continued to lobby for a slam-bang, body-count movie, one that portrayed his profession as an almost unending succession of violent confrontations, whereas in real life it's a cop's typing finger that develops calluses, not the trigger finger. And homicide boys arrive on the scene *after* the mayhem. I got out of there and found a pay phone in the corridor.

I spoke to Charlotte, who assured me that Mrs. DeLorio was resting comfortably and that Genevieve, accompanied by one of my agents, had driven to the pharmacy to fill a prescription the doctor had left. I asked to speak to the agent in charge, listened to her recitation of the layout, then asked if my ex-wife were available.

Time passed. A recorded voice requested more coinage if I wanted to maintain the connection. Cece came on the line at last. "Ray?"

"What's the doc's prognosis?"

"You amaze me. Where are you calling from?"

"Boro Hall. A cop here is making some phone calls for me, find out what the county boys know about Sal's murder."

"Same old same old." She sniffed. "Listen, Ray, I'm sorry to sound bitchy. You were an ace in there, carrying Meredith back to the bed, the words you used. But then you vanished. I turn around and you're gone. Talk about déjà vu."

"I hear you."

"I don't think you do. I don't think you ever will."

"People I care about are being murdered, Cece. I kind of have a hard time accepting the idea there's nothing I can do about it."

"People I care about are still alive. And it would mean something to feel that they cared as much as well."

"I do," I said. "Jesus, I do. But I can't stop being who I am. I wasn't born in Bronxville."

There was silence for a few moments and then a titter of rueful laughter. "You dear sweet bastard," she said. "As for Meredith, the doctor did not prognosticate, but he shook his head and frowned quite impressively. The malpractice risks these days, you don't get a doctor, you get a mime authorized to prescribe drugs. I don't suppose it will influence you one way or another if I ask you to be careful."

"Careful's my middle name."

"Funny. It never appeared on the marriage license."

I listened to dial tone.

Lieutenant Cox said: "The sheriff's office is looking at suicide, severe depression over the murder of his kid. Evidence in favor: fingerprints on the butt of the Colt, nitrates on the fingers, autopsy confirms it was a close-range trauma. Bullet trajectory also confirms it was short range. There was brain tissue smeared all over the fragments from the shotgun window."

I said: "Bullshit."

Cox said: "You got any evidence?"

"It's not in Sal's nature. He's a fighter."

"You don't think the Japs are, that stick themselves?"

"Seppuku? That's all about shame, I think, or loss of honor. Nothing to do with revenge. Another thing: he stops the car way up by the road. What, so he won't wake everyone up? A guy's gonna do himself, he isn't thinking like that. A murderer might think like that, though."

Lieutenant Cox helped himself to a wafer of dried plum and trundled a foot or so back in his chair in order to lace his fingers on his belly. The seating arrangements had been reversed since my last visit. It was my turn to sit on a corner of the desk. The Wall, having mapped out his entertainment plans for the evening, turned his considerable talents to tossing darts at mug shots, his loafers up on his desk. Just another day in the slam-bang, body-count life of a cop.

Cox cranked his head around to inquire of his partner: "You hear anything he said that sounded like evidence?"

The Wall drilled a dart home and said: "I just heard a guy talking. Not even a smart guy. Just a guy talking to make the air conditioner work a little harder."

"So far," I said, "that's the only work being done in this room. Okay, Lieutenant. If Sal blew his brains out, he'd use his gun hand, the hand he favored. Not the hand he jabbed with. And the only way he blows out his brains *and* the shotgun window is with his left hand. I don't care if you found it loaded with nitrates, I don't believe it."

Cox just looked at me and blinked. His eyelashes were so pale that all you saw were lids, like the wink of some large amphibian. "No nitrates found on the left hand. The right, yes."

"You saying he took the trouble to stick the pistol into his left ear or temple?"

"Nope. Into his mouth."

I stared at the board with the thousand and one notes, sorting my thoughts. "I have to tell you, Lieutenant, I saw the car. It's a two-seater convertible. Roominess isn't what it's about. For Sal to poke a barrel in his mouth and blow out the shotgun window means he either rolls down the window on his side, or opens the door. The window was up and the door was closed, because Meredith, his wife, had to open it to see the gun on the floor. Ergo."

"Dead men don't have time to close doors. I know," said Cox, unlacing his fingers and digging about on his desk. "That's why I asked my old friend Bernie Weiss, the coroner up there, to take another look at Sal's mouth. Suicides, generally, if they're going to eat the gun, like it looks like with Sal, at the last instant they bite down on the barrel. The heat from the barrel fries their lips. Bernie called back a few minutes ago. The lips were intact."

"Excuse me. It sounds like we agree. It was murder."

Lieutenant Cox pulled his bottom lip out, let go of it. "Yeah. He was shot at close range, his mouth open, possibly screaming. That'd be my deduction. But that ain't my jurisdiction."

27

I grabbed a hot lunch in a bistro near the courthouse. I ate London broil medium rare and au gratin potatoes that came from the earth and not out of a box and washed everything down with draft beer in ice-cold mugs. For a while I felt better than I had any right to feel.

Just as I was finishing up, Dominic Amado and several of his cronies bustled in, and when he saw me, he came over to the table to ask if I was being a good boy, sticking to our understanding. Evidently he knew nothing of the murder this morning. I said, "Speaking of sticking things," and made a gesture with my finger. We both laughed and then he told me a smutty joke and we laughed some more, then I paid my check and I left. For all I knew, Amado despised me, but it wasn't something I was going to give a whole lot of thought to. We were just two guys working in the same toilet.

It was a green-eyed Patty that greeted me at the office, her nails done a closely matching shade of jade. She looked well rested, if a little uneasy. She was wearing a canary-yellow jumpsuit of some gauzy, translucent material with flaps on all the pockets and glove straps on the padded shoulders, what the military might design for the troops if ever the strategy shifts from waging war to waging sex. Camouflage was hardly the guiding principle behind her costume.

She started to stand as I came through the door, then sat, her fingers tripping about the front of her jumpsuit looking for something to adjust.

The toilet flushed in the bathroom off the conference room.

"Martina," Patty said, her eyes suddenly wet. "I can't focus real good you know, all that's happened. I asked her to stay on the afternoon, help me get through it. Jesus, Ray. They just announced it on the radio. Saying it's suicide."

"He was murdered," I said. "Shot at close range. My guess is by a person he knew. Meredith, when she called me this morning, she tried to confess to it, but since her son's death, she's been trying to assume responsibility for every evil event starting with the Cross."

As I was speaking Martina came into the room and slipped behind her computer screen and fell to crunching information, but even from a distance I could see she had been crying. There seemed to be a whole lot of emotion in the room and not all of it related to the DeLorio tragedy. Martina barely knew the family.

I asked Pat to come upstairs to my office.

We reviewed the caseloads. Charlie Rip had signed out for five hundred dollars in small bills. We discussed potential new accounts. We jawed and jawed and Pat avoided my eyes. "Now let's talk about the real reason Martina's here."

She ducked her head, only for a few moments, then brought her face up, trembling but game. From her notepad she produced a folded sheet of office stationery. She had run it through the computer, but I could feel the force of her signature with the ball of my thumb. It felt like ground glass dragged across my heart.

"I'm sorry it had to be this way," she said. "But this is my notice. Two weeks, and I'm going with Dexter, Wells. I'm telling you, Martina could take over tomorrow, and she'd like to, but I thought you'd feel better with a transitional period. But it's up to you. I don't wanna tell you your business."

"If you don't, who will? I'm going to miss you like all hell, Pat, but it's a step up, no question about it."

"I'll meet people is the thing."

"It's a big organization."

"And travel. I'm being hired as Mr. Dexter's personal assistant."

"Really?" Several words of wisdom occurred to me concerning the character of Mr. Wesley Dexter, but I left them where they belonged. "I guess I'm just going to have to get up off my butt and congratulate you."

Pat shoved her fingernails over her eyes. "Then why do I feel so lousy?" she blurted.

I came around the desk and persuaded her to stand and gentled her against my chest. God, was I going to miss her. I was hell with the women. I was the man they hated to leave, that was what they protested, but they left me anyway. I didn't think my cologne was entirely to blame.

"Ray?"

"I think you're right. If you can give me two weeks, if that won't jeopardize things over at Dexter, Wells, it would be a big help."

"No, not that. I mean, I can do that for you. I'd like to ask a favor of you."

"Ask it."

"I'd like to be kissed."

When Martina buzzed to say there was an express package delivered by messenger to my attention, we had just finished finding the last article of clothing, one of Pat's heels. I went down the stairs putting the finishing touches to the knot of my tie. Martina had signed for the package and it lay squarely in the middle of Pat's desk, a ten-by-fourteen mailing envelope lined with plastic bubbles. The contents felt like a cassette, but it could also be something made to feel like a cassette, so I took it upstairs, told Pat to go with Martina down to the Greek's, buy a magazine or a Coke.

She had refurbished her makeup in the cramped water closet off my office and her eyes tickled lazily over me, as if whatever I was saying was just background music for her thoughts.

"Nine years," she drawled. "You do make a lady wait."

"I'm shy," I said. I patted her robust fanny. "Now please, love, explain the changing of the guard to Martina at the Greek's."

She had to fuss with my tie before she went, and when

she was gone, her absence was something almost tangible, like a fragment of something plucked from my heart that I could feel between my forefinger and the ball of my thumb, like a mote of ground glass.

I stood behind my chair and stared at the package on the desk, wrestling with my nerves. I could hear the laughter already all the way to Boro Hall if I phoned in a request for a bomb detail. There was an electromagnetic scanner downstairs, but it wouldn't detect plastique. Furthermore, if the package was what it seemed, the scanner would erase the tape. The sly-eyed gentlemen on the walls seemed to be taking a sadistic pleasure in my predicament.

The way my luck was running the only direction was up. Do it.

I plucked the staples loose with a plastic-handled gizmo with pairs of opposing metal fangs, and a cassette I recognized, because its twin resided in a drawer of my desk, sidled out of the package. Cassette and player merged with the indifferent ease of love by the clock. I recognized the magnificent voice with the melodramatic, sniffling pauses. It was Mr. Holloway. Or it was Mr. Grace. At any rate, it was the man I most wanted to hear from.

"Sommer!" it began, going straight into the peremptory mode, no fussing to sound civil. "Sommer," it repeated, "you have so far proved to be a mixed blessing. You evidently are what any marine permitted to do his own thinking is—namely, a double-edged sword.

"You were hired to find a missing person expeditiously and discreetly, but by all accounts you are more obsessed with my identity than with the job at hand. I think you are a stupid man."

There was a pause, but the tape kept running, transmitting the sound of someone bothered by bad sinuses. I heard other voices faintly in the background, although these could have issued from a radio or television. The magnificent voice again: "Lest you misunderstand, Sommer, I credit you with energy. You seem to have run with the ball. You have more guts than brains, but that's not entirely a bad thing. Brains tend to manufacture excuses, amigo. Guts get it done. As I'm sure you know by now, getting things done is my profession. I have taken

pride in most of what I have done. I say this, because
bowing to a single imperative, I am risking my reputation, my honor, very likely my life. And I am staking all
of this on what little I know of you.

"Here is all I ask: hear me out. There will be an envelope at Arpeggio's with your name on it and a thousand in cash if you show up there tonight at nineteen
hundred hours. With the money will be instructions. If,
after we've spoken, you want to cancel the mission,
you're gone, with the thousand for your time. Ball's in
your court, amigo."

28

I listened to the cassette several more times that afternoon between taking phone calls and fielding inquiries
over the intercom. I watched the sunlight flare up and
work its way out of the blue glass ashtray, in about as
much time, measured against eternity, as the human race
has been around. So what were a couple of lives, father
and son, in such a heinous, incomprehensible equation?
It required only a belt of bourbon to straighten that out.
They mattered to the living, to that within us which for
practical reasons will not be terrorized by our insignifi-
cance. I'm glad I figured that out, because I wasn't feeling altogether human. Danny Belinski returned my call
to say that young Arnold's condition had been upgraded,
a brain scan reflecting complete activity. But he would
have to undergo reconstructive surgery for his jaw and
nose. I asked Danny to fax a copy of Arnold's insurance
policy to Cece's company, to her attention. Whatever
was the deductible, my agency would pick up. Danny
felt as low as I did, or he wouldn't have closed off the
conversation with a cheap shot about buying absolution.
I said what a man could be expected to tell another man,
but without heat, and hung up.

I phoned Cece to explain the purpose of the fax that
she would find on her desk Monday morning. We talked
small talk for a few minutes, nothing at all intimate, but
falling into the shorthand developed over years of intimacy.

I listened to the cassette one more time, after bidding
Pat and Martina good night. There was an insidious al-
lure to the man's words, along the lines of something

offered through the mail, a promise that you could not possibly pass up but probably should. I suppose it was un-American of me, but I still did not believe in something for nothing, whether you called it free admission, a lottery, or an envelope stuffed with cash.

There is a safe beneath the floor under the master bed in the house in Kew Gardens. I took a long hot shower and dressed carefully. I wore loose gray cotton slacks, scuffed Reeboks, a washed-out blue work shirt over which I slipped on a leather shoulder rig rubbed dark with neat's-foot oil. From the floor safe I removed a .357 Colt Magnum called a Python with a six-inch barrel and the stopping power of a cement truck. I checked the load and parked the Python alongside my rib cage. Also from the safe I withdrew a .22-caliber Beretta automatic in a custom rig, checked its load, then strapped it to my calf, shook down the pant leg, beautiful, you'd never know. I put on a gray cotton padded jacket that cost me almost four bills because it had the name of a pasta designer sewn in it and looked in the mirror. Still a slight bulge, the Python's grip. Some adjustments. There.

I hesitated before the mirror, feeling just a bit foolish wearing all this artillery. The feeling passed. It was better to be alive and foolish, than dead because of it.

It was almost 6:30. I went downstairs and made myself a weak drink. I walked to the back patio with my glass. The roses danced in the twilight, their bloom like the skirts of ballerinas. The neighbor's Labrador unloosed a howl in response to a siren. It was several seconds before I recognized the sound of the phone ringing.

Charlie Rip said, "Somebody got the jump on us, about this Ramone boyfriend. There ain't a bar in Chelsea or the north part of the Village but it didn't hear from some brothers. Mostly I get a familiar picture. Some shaved-head old fat-ass.

"That's the bad news. The good is I jus' touch bases with Horatio Street, and they got a live one. Be the little girl Julie herself. She come in across the rooftops. Not five minutes later she out the same route. Sammy J ridin' her ass even as we speak."

Sammy J was shop speak for a young actress who had some off-Broadway credits and did not want to do porn

to survive, by the name of Samantha Jewison. I had recruited her at one of Meredith DeLorio's soirees. She was
feisty and resourceful, one of my best free-lancers.

"The bald guy," I told Charlie, "is CIA. Anybody
mention a white guy with wild red hair and shades?"

"Nope. Jus' the brothers."

"They must have gotten to Dixie, unless . . ." Unless
they had a tap on my phone, the bastards. I said to
Charlie Rip, "Forget Ramone, for now. Get on down to
the Village, give Sam whatever backup she needs. This
may not be a secure phone, Charlie, so just listen. I've
got a seven o'clock appointment. When that's over, I'll
contact you at the phone booth we agreed on. Don't
move on the girl unless someone else tries to. Got it?"

"I almost hope somebody tries," Charlie said wistfully.
"It's been a long time since I got paid to flatten someone.
Lord, but I do miss the contact, Ray."

I drove the Datsun in case parking was a problem.
Every space was taken alongside the curb in front of the
restaurant, as I had expected, but I found a spot just
beyond the island of benches. I eased in among the patrons, winked at the bartender Vincent, who knew what
I wanted, and approached Mario. He removed his glasses
to listen. No, he was sincerely apologetic, he knew nothing about an envelope. But it was still five minutes before the agreed-upon hour.

I went back to the spot where my drink waited and
nibbled at it, looking over the citizens waiting for a table. Since it was not even seven, there was breathing
space along the bar; by eight, there would be a line outside. I didn't see anyone I recognized or anyone that
seemed to recognize me. I saw Mario pick up the phone
next to the lectern, adjust his eyeglasses, nodding as he
listened. On the television mounted over the bar Sugar
Ray Leonard and Marvin Hagler were battering each
other courtesy of videotape. I checked my watch. It was
a few minutes past the magical hour. I tossed back the
rest of my drink and pushed my glass across the glossy
wood for Vincent to snag on his next pass. Somebody
touched the back of my elbow. Mario.

"A man come to the kitchen, say this for you."

A white envelope emerged from a breast pocket inside his black suit. It felt the right kind of thickness for a thousand dollars in small bills. I slipped it inside my jacket and put a hand on his shoulder to thank him. I patted his cheek and descended the brick-colored carpet to the rest rooms, locked myself in a stall, and crouched on top of the toilet to look inside the envelope. There was money. There was an address in Long Island City and a time to be there: midnight. I recognized the address. It was a place of employment for nude dancers, right next to Tip Top Tech.

I laid a twenty-dollar bill on the lectern in front of Mario and told him to spend it on his favorite charity.

"*Grazie,*" he said.

"*Ciao,* Mario."

I stood aside so that two couples, fumbling with the door and laughing, could enter, then I slipped into the spidery dark of the night. There were some strollers down the block and the roar of automobiles on the boulevard, like last night, and the benches on the concrete island were almost deserted, like last night, except instead of one there were two solitary shapes residing there, separated by several benches. Neither of them looked to be the intimidating size of Cato. Both, however, stood up as if on the same wavelength and began walking my way. I moved up the sidewalk on the diagonal, closing on the curb, the cars parked alongside it. The far guy picked up his pace to a jog and that's when I dived for it, getting the magnum out before I landed on my chest next to a Lincoln. Sharp blue light stabbed the air and chewed up the sidewalk just behind my feet. The far guy mounted the curb, maybe six cars down, as I squirmed to a sitting position next to the Lincoln's fender and sighted on him. I squeezed off two rounds and he did a wicked Baryshnikov kind of dance and wound up on the sidewalk in a broken heap. Gunfire slammed into the Lincoln and glass erupted overhead, filling the air with bits and pieces. I scampered to the car ahead of the Lincoln and crawled along the grille, trying to hear over the sound of traffic and my own heartbeat. I could not hear footsteps. I peered beneath the chassis, saw nothing in the street. I ducked my head out to look down the sidewalk just as a car without lights sped up the block and braked hard, opposite where there had been a body. The body wasn't there. I wheeled and poked my face out the other side of the car. The door of a dark sedan was flung open and shapes moved behind it. I kept most of myself behind the car and let the Python speak. I heard screams. The sedan backed furiously, its lights still off, the door still open, the driver covering most of the block in reverse before his luck ran out and he was forced to cut the wheel sharply to avoid ramming a BMW that was turning onto the street. The maneuver was almost a success, except for the open door that raked and ate German steel for a split second before it exploded off its hinges. The party in the BMW belatedly leaned on the horn. The sedan landed on the concrete island, uprooting one of the benches there before shifting gears, shooting back into the street and around the corner the still honking BMW had just negotiated. Down the block the strollers were picking themselves up from the sidewalk. Nobody had ventured from Arpeggio's.

I holstered the Python and moved up the street, willing myself to walk, not run. When I reached the Datsun, I glanced over my shoulder. No one was pointing excitedly my way. I started the engine, considered leaving the lights off, but turned them on. People were apt to remember better a car pulling away with no lights than one they could plainly see.

I took the first side street, and once around the corner I developed a heavy foot. My shirt stuck to me like wet newspaper. I took a deep breath and howled. I was a wild man under the influence of tides and moon. I was a red-blooded carnivore, a mad dog, and Grace was the meat I hungered for.

29

I carried reloads in the pocket of my jacket, six cartridges inside a plastic baggie, and several baggies in the pocket. Given the speed of traffic working its way off the Fifty-ninth Street Bridge into Manhattan, I used the leisure time to empty the jackets from the Python and reload. Kids with squeegees and scrapers approached the car, offering to clean the already clean windshield for a dollar, a form of creative extortion that a firm sense of humor could always combat. But I was a crazed man tonight with an envelope full of unspent money and a keen appreciation of my own mortality. If the truth be told, I was a scared man too; I was trying to maneuver in a situation increasingly unclear. Nothing was as it appeared, and nobody gave a shit, so long as Mr. Grace was spared the embarrassment of going public. Fuck Mr. Grace, I thought. I fluttered bills out the window, two twenties, if the squeegee force would block the lane to my right so that I could slip across Sixtieth Street.

They did that and I made my way into Manhattan five minutes faster.

Christopher Park sits in the heart of Sheridan Square, a pie-slice piece of property begirded by a cast-iron fence with a sturdy, medieval air about it. The park itself consists of a sprinkling of lofty trees, benches bolted to the concrete, some trash baskets conspicuously ignored, and toward the rear a statue of General Sheridan stands on a pedestal amid a swarm of unlovely foliage. He is in full military costume with a hand fixed sternly to a hip, as if all he surveyed did not quite pass muster. No surprise, that. Christopher Park on a Friday night would not sit well with a military disposition.

At the hour I pulled alongside it, a mostly festive air pervaded the park; the drunks were all behaving themselves. A female juggler was entertaining a circle of spectators while out front three older gents were harmonizing for a small crowd. A queen dressed up in scarlet and white to look like a cheerleader whisked past on roller skates and shook a mean hip at a couple of the leather boys, then sailed off to flirt with a cop on horseback. A mob of bodies emerged from the Sheridan Square station and dispersed into the night.

I was double-parked across from the Lion's Head Pub, waiting for Charlie Rip to finish whatever business he was conducting via walkie-talkie. Then he folded himself into the Datsun. We caught the green light at Seventh Avenue and percolated along Christopher Street with the windows down, the night warm but not uncomfortable, the sidewalks on either side surging with citizens that were predominantly male. Charlie outlined the surveillance he had arranged for the building into which Julie Holloway had disappeared. I said it sounded good. We crossed Bleeker and drew up next to a coffee import shop, where Sammy J was loitering. She bounced off the curb and leaned on the windowsill next to Charlie, hunched and cramped as he was, to observe how much he resembled the fetus of a bear implanted in an insect. Charlie threatened to drown her in tobacco juice.

I backed the Datsun until I reached a curb painted yellow, a bus-stop zone, and asked Sam to get behind the wheel. She was dressed in a pink jogging suit with high white sneakers and a Knicks headband. Once she had the seat adjusted forward so that she could reach all the pedals, we reviewed our procedure, who was where, descriptions of Julie, of Ramone, of the two bozos from the CIA, of Dixie. "Any questions?" I said.

"No questions, Chief," she said. "But next time, if I'm going to sit in a car, I vote for the Mercedes. I got an image to maintain. Cartoon car like this, I keep looking over my shoulder, make sure Goofy isn't sitting in the backseat."

I blew her a kiss watching Charlie let himself into the

coffee import shop. I crossed the street to the limestone building that Julie Holloway had entered. Aromas from the coffee emporium paved the way, a rich and heady mixture. I opened a red door that was last painted about the year the "Miracle" Mets won it all and found myself on a few square feet of pale gray tile. Tile steps led to a tile landing and a gray door that was locked, with a pane of glass the size of a magazine and something like chicken wire embedded in the glass. On the wall to my left was a stainless-steel panel of buttons, one for each apartment, and a speaking grille. A piney scent of disinfectant hung in the air. There was no name that I recognized. I started with the top-floor apartments for no good reason, except that I had to start somewhere. Where there was a response, I simply said that I needed to speak to Julie. That brought me nothing on the top floor, but the very first stab on the next landing was more encouraging. A female answered: "Yes?"

"Julie, please."

"One moment." Then: "May I ask who it is?"

"This is Ray Sommer. We spoke briefly yesterday."

"Did you?"

Something in the tone, or delivery, of that question rang a familiar note, although that seemed a lot of mileage to get from two words. Still, there was an air of precision to the voice that made me certain it wasn't Julie's.

"Yes, we did, as a matter of fact. And it's rather important that I speak to her now. Make that *vitally* important."

Silence. But the burring of the intercom continued, which meant the communication was still open.

"Hello?"

I could hear the buzz of electrical current releasing the lock. The voice said, "Do come up."

If I thought I had gotten too much mileage out of the question, I was wrong. The invitation gave me ideas a man in my condition should not have, not with a Colt under my arm and a Beretta beneath a trouser leg.

I rode the elevator to the fourth floor and the door to

the apartment I wanted stood directly opposite. There
was a glass peephole for security and I could feel myself
being scrutinized through it after I knocked. When it
was opened, I put on a game smile and said, "Hello,
Julie. Remember me?"

It was a pleasure to see her in something that didn't
shop her parts. A baggy blue sweatshirt, sweat pants,
her head wrapped in a melon-colored towel. She wore
no makeup and she smelled of soap. She was something
more than a trick now; she was somebody's daughter.
Somebody's daughter whose nose and eyes advertised a
habit that didn't come cheap.

"Sure," she said glumly, "I know you. Sommer. The
fuckin' fuzz."

So much for small pleasures. "*Mister* Sommer to you,
child. Would there be anybody here, I wonder, wanting
a big strong detective tonight?" I raised my voice.
"Somebody with an accent part foreign and part fake?
With platinum hair and a pair of eyes and lips a man
would be willing to die for, anyone meeting that description?"

"Let him in, love," came a voice from a person I could
not see—the same voice that had addressed me over the
intercom. It sounded as if its owner was exceedingly
weary, or resigned, or so bored with the issue of how she
felt that she no longer was interested in the problem.

Before I could cross the threshold, little Julie clutched
a sleeve, tugged at my wrist to whisper, "You seen my
man?"

"Ramone?"

She wagged her face pitifully.

"I'd like to, child."

She stood on her toes to whisper: "Ask her. Ask the
bitch in there. She gets the stuff. She runs him. I think
she's setting him up. You're a dick, you got a gun."

"Sorry," I said.

"I'd even shave it," she said. "Anything you want. Just
don't let her set him up."

I had worked my way inside by now in the give-and-
take of conversation, so that I could see a door leading
to a small bedroom, and I nudged the girl that way. "I'll
do what I can, okay?" I had steered her inside the bed-

room with my hands on her shoulders, and now it was
my turn to bend over and whisper: "The stuff we're talking about, is it blow?"

She nodded, trembling.

"Quantities?"

She did more of the same.

So the lady I was about to meet was Ramone's angel,
the mysterious person who had given him a leg up in the
slave trade. I knew something else, or thought I did.

I urged Julie down on the side of the bed, stroked her
cheek, asked her to give me a chance.

"Just don't let her," she hissed. "I'll do anything. Ramone never hurt me unless I asked for it. He loves me."

I listened to a guy a while ago at a dinner party given
by the DeLorios go into rhapsodies over all the satellites
in the sky that were going to turn us into a single, global
village, the implication being the whole planet was on
the brink of civilization. Evidently he didn't get down
in the streets of the city much. Only an idiot would
equate information with being civilized. It was just another tool. And so long as a lonely kid believed love took
the shape of beatings, it was not merely a useless tool, it
was a joke, a slap in the face, a contusion on the conscience.

30

There was a hallway with oak-plank flooring. There was a cumbrous black lacquer chest with bookshelves rising from it, the flanks of the chest curved as if groaning under some unimaginable weight. Oriental artifacts posed serenely on the chest; others rested on sconces affixed to the walls. A luxurious runner of Chinese carpet, pastels sculpted on a field of royal blue, cushioned the journey to a small living room, two windows jammed with foliage overlooking Christopher Street. Between the windows a low dark love seat faced a black lacquer table with bowed legs much like the curvature afflicting the chest in the hall. There was a working fireplace in a brick wall, a couple of armchairs, a small television, a phone, a circular table that looked like it had been appropriated from one of the outdoor bistros in the Village. There were more bookshelves in the room, more doodads in the Oriental mode—scrolls, Buddhas, a coromandel lacquer screen, its four panels arranged at angles reminiscent of a child's drawing of lightning. A galley kitchen faced the room over a narrow bar top with a butcher-block surface. Two cane stools hugged the kick space beneath the bar. A wok was visible, resting on a burner of the white enamel stove. Whoever collected Oriental obviously liked to cook that way. Somehow the divine creature sitting on the far end of the love seat with her legs crossed did not strike me as someone who cooked Oriental, or any way. I had been very wrong about this lady, and Pat had been very right. She regarded me with unconcealed arrogance. "Tea, Mr. Sommer? Spirits perhaps?"

"Nothing, thanks. Your apartment?"

"I'm subletting from a friend who's taking the year off to wander about Asia. Evidently there's some of it she hasn't purchased."

She brought out a cup for herself, poured tea into it, inhaled the fragrance with her eyes closed, holding the cup with both hands, the gratification simple and complete, and somehow eloquent. I was willing to bet her face softened in the same way when she slipped into a hot bath or new lingerie. Surrendering to the pleasure entirely. The teapot had gilt-colored dragons painted on it. She put her cup down and leaned back in the love seat with a tan cigarette perched between her index and middle fingers, flame springing from a platinum lighter.

"You played that nice yesterday," I said. "I wrote you off as an airhead, some ghoul curious to get a whiff of murder."

She studied me with the turquoise eyes. Tonight she was wearing a white cotton button-down shirt and some baggy, bleached-out jeans, and she was barefoot. Very little makeup and no jewelry. She looked wholesome enough to invite to a church social, leaving aside the cigarette for a moment. I revised my estimate of her age downward from yesterday; she might not even be twenty.

"I should think there's a great deal we have to talk about, you and I. Why don't you sit down?" She patted the space next to her, and when I took it, she smiled. It was a nice smile if you didn't mind the kind a dog receives for being obedient. "Do you get many ghouls, as you call them, in your business?"

"Publicity attracts all kinds of people. Most of our business involves shielding public figures from nuisances, and the occasional threats. But no, to answer your question, we don't get many. We aren't in the business of solving murders."

"But if you did solve one, that would certainly be a feather in your cap, would it not?"

"Frankly, young lady, it would be closer to a hot poker up the keester."

That ruffled her about one percent of nothing. She didn't lose even a fraction of her good-doggie smile. "I see. In your rude way you are saying you still cannot help me."

"I did not hear anyone asking for help. I just answered what I assumed to be a hypothetical question. Are you needing help?"

She averted her eyes and the smile dropped away and she ate smoke. I used the opportunity to ask her for a cigarette. She extended her hand with a thin box of them. The box was tan with gold leafing on it. I thanked her and rotated the cigarette under my nose. This was a leaf with body, no question about it. She passed me her lighter. I sprang a flame, looked at it, snuffed it out. I handed back lighter and cigarette. I had her attention.

"You smoked a couple of these in my conference room before I arrived yesterday," I said. "Later, I happened to notice the butts, and they looked familiar. But I had nothing to match them against. But the cigarette I remember. Israeli, aren't they?"

She shrugged. "A friend who works at the UN brings them in duty free. It is a little luxury I indulge myself in."

"You get my age—Allie, isn't it?"

She bought time, narrowing her eyes as she inhaled more smoke. She could have all the time she wanted. What she couldn't buy, by stalling, was much credibility.

"Like I was saying, Allie, you get my age, the memory's not so sharp. Good for a few days; in fact, incredibly good that far back. The dead boy you were inquiring about, Sal DeLorio, he was smoking these same cigarettes the morning he was murdered. Said they were a gift from a friend. Small world, huh? Hard to believe you and he shared the same connection at the UN. I'd believe it easier if you were his friend. It would even make some sense out of yesterday's performance if Allie were in fact short for Alyshia."

She unlimbered herself and was on her feet in a single, fluid motion, palm and thumb scraping the long side of her haircut away from her cheek, her eyes tremulous and pleading. "Please, wait here." She strutted on the balls of her bare feet along the runner. Words were exchanged behind the bedroom door, Julie's sounding edgy, strung out, Allie's full of comfort and balm. Five minutes passed. I used some of that time to dial the Datsun and give Sammy the phone number of the apartment, ask if there was anything doing in the street. While she touched bases, I roamed over the pantry and observed all the requisites for an authentic Oriental preparation, from the dried mushrooms to peanut oil, and everything hither and yon. Sammy said there was nothing doing and we hung up.

I heard the bedroom door click shut. I was sitting on my end of the couch, so that I saw her stop, nearly at the end of the runner, just abreast the kitchen, and smile. "I'm having a brandy," she cooed. "Is there anything?"

"If you can make a pot of decent coffee to go with it."

"I can do," she said.

I got up from the low love seat to watch her work, leaning on the butcher block. "You were the lady Sal wanted to marry."

She stopped, did something with her hand, flipping it away from her waist. "He thought so. He didn't listen to me. There were difficulties. My father is a very protective man."

"I imagine I'd be the same if you were my daughter. Fathers are that way."

She looked at me for a long, withering moment. She put water on to boil and fitted the Melitta with a paper filter. She trickled brandy into two snifters. She set one snifter on the butcher block for me, cut her eyes in such a way that even a sober man might construe them as provocative, then turned her back on me to scan the pantry. "May one ask how you learned my name? Julie denies telling you."

"I would hope so, because she didn't," I said. The time to discuss the photograph of Julie and what she had to say about it had not yet arrived. "But if you will credit me with some intelligence, several coincidences conspired to give me the idea. It was a great deal of comfort to Sal's mother to know he had experienced a real passion before dying, Alyshia being the name of that passion. No description went with the name because you had never been introduced to the family. But I learned things within twenty-four hours of the murder, and one of the things was that Sal almost got nailed for possession at Bennington a month or two ago, a situation that

smelled of a setup. The substance was cocaine. This is a
careless kid for a cum laude graduate from Harvard. I
don't believe it. One of the reasons I don't, last night I
talked to a dirtball who had been paid to keep tabs on a
student at Bennington by the name of Allie Kane-Wells.
I think he was the one who planted the stuff in Sal's car.
He wouldn't admit it, and I wasn't inclined to beat it
out of him, even if I thought I could have. Sometimes,
if you pay attention, you learn as much from what a
person doesn't tell you, or won't. He did, however, describe you, and damned accurately."

I watched her spoon dark coffee into the filter and
snatch the boiling kettle up. Water filled the Melitta with
a chocolaty froth, which almost immediately commenced to drip through the filter and into the glass pot.
She added water steadily, continuing to favor me with a
view of her back. That was fine by me. It was easier to
keep my mind where it should be. The scent of the coffee
raveling through the room was distraction enough.

"Take them separately, the two incidents might not
have meant much to me. But your little visit was the
bridge. Two people smoking the same exotic cigarette.
And one of them with the name of the other on her beautiful lips. I've been told I'm a stupid man, but if enough
things come together with the force of a hammer between the eyes, they're going to get my attention. What
I still haven't figured out is the motive behind the visit,
what you hoped to accomplish through that soap-opera
performance you turned in."

She had turned around to lean against the sink, her hands
at her hips gripping the white porcelain lip of the sink. Her
eyelashes without mascara were long and practically transparent, and the way she worked them, every man jack at
the church social would have been doing handsprings. On
me it was wasted. I can appreciate modesty, but not when
it's passed off as the Dance of the Seven Veils.

"One thing I found out, you are not stupid," she said
at last. "Was I really that poor an actress?"

"You were in a class by yourself," I said, and left it at that.

She pushed out her bottom lip and momentarily ceased
trying to seduce me. I took my demitasse of coffee and
the brandy back to the love seat and she joined me there.

She put her bare feet up on the table and pretended to take an interest in her toes. At the peak of her fascination, she said, "But how did you locate me, may I ask?"

"Tell me what you know," I said, "about the Zen art of archery."

She placed her cheek alongside the back of the love seat to evaluate my response. "This is a joke, right? Knock knock, who's there?"

"No. It goes something like this: in order to hit the target, you do not aim for it."

"I've never done acid, love. I thank God I didn't have to live through the sixties. A whole generation of sheep."

"At least they knew Zen wasn't about acid, and vice versa." I held the snifter up as if to touch glasses, then tipped it to my lips. As brandy goes, it was a little on the youthful side. I was glad for the coffee. "My point is this: I found you by not looking for you. I was hired two days ago, actually the morning Sal was murdered, to locate a girl by the name of Julie Holloway, said to be a runaway. It was Sal who delivered the offer along with photographs of Julie. Now, I got into this business by serving paper—subpoenas, to be precise—and it could be interesting, because people don't like to appear in court, and some of them were masters at not appearing in court, because nobody could find them to serve them. Or maybe it was a case where the subpoenaed party was known to have a violent disposition and a large neck size. Me, I specialized in the masters and the big-neck boys, being a little crazy at the time. I haven't been down in the streets for years, but when this invisible father offered me twenty-five grand to look for his daughter, I thought it was time to come out of the closet. Besides, I was bored. Today, one of my agents recognized her and followed her here. All it took was the grind of hours of watching, and a little bit of luck. And here I am and here you are. Zen, my dear."

She wrinkled her nose and laughter trickled out, as sweet as I remembered it. She let her fingers linger briefly on the back of my hand. "Whoever called you stupid, love, shouldn't be free to roam the streets. They haven't the mental capacity to be left alone. It's a terrible brandy, isn't it?"

"Yes. But the coffee's excellent."

"Another?"

"Thank you."

I rose when she did and watched from the far side of the butcher-block bar as she poured into her cup and mine. She put down the pot and turned just her face to look at me. "Afraid I'll add more than coffee to your cup?"

"Thought never crossed my mind."

"Really."

"Absolutely."

She placed the pot of coffee on a wooden tray in front of me. "Be a love then, carry this to the table. That way you can keep your eye on it and I won't have to trek back and forth with you for a shadow."

We got comfortable once more. I sat forward, hunkered over the table, my wrists on my thighs, my face cocked her way. With her legs extended, her feet on the table, she was nestled on the small of her back, her hands embracing the demitasse, her whole face lit with a kind of wicked merriment. "You are so brilliant," she said, "and yet you look rather befuddled. My father has accused me of instability, and I prefer to think of myself as unpredictable. For me it is a weapon of defense."

"A beautiful lady, you get hit upon, what, more times in a day than you can remember. I was married to a beautiful lady once. Whatever works for you, use it, I say. My ex-wife was raped before we were married, and it colored everything between us, including a kind of terror toward conception. The guy that raped her got her pregnant, and she had an abortion." I stopped, and reached for the remainder of the raw brandy. I put it to rest. I said, "You are the first person I've told that to, Alyshia."

She did not do anything with her eyes this time except meet my gaze. "I'm listening."

"There's nothing more to tell. Except that beauty like hers, like yours, it might give you a little edge in life, but it's no insurance policy."

She took her feet off the table and reached for the slim box of cigarettes. "Oh?" she said, settling back into the couch, an eyebrow lifted. "I do hope you aren't under the impression that you've enlightened me in any way."

"Not really," I said, "but I thought I'd give it a shot. Because I think you're playing in a dangerous league."

"How is that, love?"

"Several months ago an enforcer for a major midtown pimp by the name of Big Jim Lord suddenly quit on Big Jim to run a stable of white walkers. And he didn't do it the usual way, by muscling someone out of business. He started with fresh recruits, which means he had money behind him, and enforcers don't earn the kind of money it would take to break in like that. So he had an angel, somebody to pay for the costumes and the protection. What makes this enforcer turned pimp so interesting, he not only turns on his walkers with cocaine, he sends them to work high on the stuff. It's like he's got so much of it he can afford to be careless. His name in the street is Ramone. One of his walkers is Julie Holloway, the strung-out girl in your bedroom, the girl my agency was paid twenty-five thousand dollars to locate.

"What I meant by dangerous league, the guy who hired me to find Julie said he was her father. Wrong. Her father has been dead for four years. The man who in fact hired me is a heavy hitter, or was, in the CIA. Seems he stiffed the Agency for some major money. There are Agency people spread out all over the city—people who have left their table manners at home—and they're looking for Julie or for Ramone. My guess is you are connected rather intimately with both of them."

She poured coffee for us and did it with a steady hand. I might have just finished offering an opinion on the weather.

"Look, some stuff I've heard suggests you're the power behind the throne, the one running Ramone, Julie, the rest of the walkers. In which case, whoever's interested in Julie and Ramone may be a whole lot more interested in you. Or is that why you came to see me yesterday?"

"Do you know, love, there's a funny story behind that. When Sal and I started . . . to see one another, and the trouble began, he advised me to seek you out. For *my* protection. He was the one being threatened and harassed and beaten, but it was my safety he was concerned about. It was all very romantic, and so very naive."

"I'd like to know who was giving Sal all the grief."

"I told you my father is very protective. He has friends—or should I say, associates—that regard violence as just another way of doing business. And he has enemies whose business is violence. Most of my life has

been spent in boarding schools abroad for that reason. I
was forced to change names and schools every couple of
years for that reason. When he finally permitted me to
study in the States, it was under the usual conditions of
falsehood, but with one extra restriction: no serious relationships until I had gotten the green light. I agreed,
of course, believing he was on a sensitive assignment, but
when months passed, and the months became a year,
and the year stretched toward a second one . . . Well,
Sal's sister and I were on the same ski team. The thing
about Sal, he was the first boy who didn't ditch me when
my father stepped in, either personally or in loco par-
entis. Sal just kept coming back, no matter what was
thrown at him, even that coke left in his car. He had a
certain flair, Sal did. And beautiful eyes."

"Flair," I said. "How about backbone, guts, balls.
How about integrity? I'm listening to you, I wonder if
that beautiful skin of yours isn't pure Teflon."

I got up and strode to the butcher-block bar, a distance of three strides, and turned around to face her, a
hand at the back of my neck, scuffling around there. I
looked at her and thought I saw down in there, in the
turquoise depths of her eyes . . . nothing. Yesterday she
had spoken of a relationship she couldn't escape and had
laughed bitterly at my advice. And when Sal alluded to
walking assholes, it wasn't his father after all, I was certain, but Allie's. I had misunderstood damn near everything put in front of me, and the only virtue I could
claim in the case so far was having survived to realize it.

Alyshia leaned forward to rest her forearms on her
thighs. Her face was a gorgeous map of indifference. She
spoke matter-of-factly. "You were correct about one
thing: the man who hired you to find Julie Holloway is
really after me. He's the man behind Sal's murder, if it
would interest you to solve it. He was once my lover and
is still my father. I expect it's why Mum killed herself."

31

Alyshia set her demitasse down and snatched up a cigarette and touched a flame to it. The phone rang beneath
my elbow. I picked it up. "Yeah?"

"Ray?"

"Speaking, Sammy."

"Guy looks very much like Ramone coming up the
block from Hudson. With two pals."

"One a redhead?"

"And another black dude with a 'fro."

"Get the car running, and as close to the door as you
can. We aren't out in five minutes, it's Charlie's call."

I nestled the receiver and told Alyshia to find some
shoes because Ramone had chosen to work the other side
of the street. "He's coming with two Company types.
Tell Julie to crawl under the bed and stay there for the
next five-to-ten minutes. You wouldn't happen to have
any mace, would you?"

She said she didn't.

"Hairspray?"

She said she did.

"Get me that," I said, "and a wet hand towel."

And thank God for an ex-wife into authentic. I lifted
the nearly full plastic bottle of peanut oil from the pantry. The staircase ran next to the elevator shaft. I
splashed peanut oil across the steps.

Back in the apartment I found Alyshia struggling to
get into a blue leather jacket, showing some emotion at
last. I held the jacket for her. The leather was as soft as
a safecracker's fingertips. She handed me the wet towel
and I wrung it out and wrapped it around my right

hand. I told her what to do with the hairspray. Then I put my arms around her, because she was shaking, and said it was going to be a piece of cake. We went down the hall and out the door and closed it. Footsteps echoed up the stairwell, someone coming fast and making no effort to disguise it. I stood with my back to the door next to the elevator and Alyshia crouched directly in front of it. The sound of the elevator whirring toward us mounted, and then stopped, and there was a brief silence, punctuated by pounding footsteps. Then the doors of the elevator were sucked apart. Alyshia sprang. I heard a scream. I stepped around the corner and saw a young black man with his hands on his eyes and drilled him on the bridge of his nose. He crashed into the back of the elevator and sat down hard, his legs splayed, blood flooding from his nostrils. He groaned, partly conscious, probably just enough to wish he weren't. From the staircase came a yelp, a sudden cry of surprise and confusion, and then: "Oh! Oh! Oh! Oh shit! Oh!"

I pressed the down button and glanced at Alyshia. She stood with her back against the side of the car, the back of her hand to her lips, her eyes on the crumpled figure on the floor. He looked like he might be a tough lad after some bedrest. I couldn't see the color of his eyes.

I bent over him. "This is Ramone, isn't it?"

The attack of nerves Alyshia had back in the apartment was evidently an aberration. Her voice sounded as hard as pavement. "It is, yes."

Over a black T-shirt he wore a lemon-yellow satin costume that resembled the warm-up dress of a pro basketball player. Rather modest togs for a midtown pimp. He wore his hair in cornrows. His fingernails gleamed with clear polish, and the nail on the little finger of his right hand was extra long, presumably to scoop blow. I managed to find someplace on the front of his jacket that he hadn't bled on yet and grabbed hold and dragged him into a corner at the front of the elevator. He groaned and blinked his eyes, and when they were open, I showed him the butt of the Python. "The next few minutes, the only thing you better open your mouth for is to breathe. We'll talk some other time, handsome. If you live that long."

The elevator came to rest on the main floor. I said to

Alyshia, "Give me the hairspray. There's one more guy, he's either going to be right outside the elevator or in the vestibule between the doors. They're looking for Julie, not you. Get next to him, and dump your purse. Here, loosen a couple buttons on your blouse. It'll help you keep his attention."

The elevator doors swept apart. I occupied the corner with Ramone, listening to rubber soles twitch across the tile. The sound of the knob turning was sweet: whoever was out there was on the far side of the door. I heard Alyshia cry "Damn!" before the door went shut. And not a moment too soon, because the stairwell was echoing once more, and whoever was coming was coming fast. If Alyshia didn't have the guy in the vestibule ogling her cleavage by now, we'd switch to Plan B. Trouble with that, there was no Plan B. I stuck my face out, saw nobody looking in through the chicken-wire glass, and edged up next to the corner of the stairs. When the steps were close enough that I could hear the gasps for breath, I moved away from the corner with my left hand extended, the can of hairspray in it. It was Blades, his red hair flaming out from his face. He leaped. I ducked, getting rid of the hairspray, which wasn't going to do me any good. A foot caught me just below the ribs and slammed me onto my hip, but Blades hit the floor facefirst, the sound of it amplified in the open area. I shook loose the towel, because I wasn't going to need it either. The floor had landed a punch more vicious than any I could throw. An arm, a leg moved, but not with any conviction. Blades was a man having a bad dream.

I looked into the elevator, saw that Ramone was behaving himself, and punched the buttons to send him back to the fourth floor. Nursing him might give Julie something to do besides shoving death up her nose.

I turned the knob slowly and slowly brought the door back from the vestibule. My reward was a view of Gerald's rear end in the same blue trousers he was wearing yesterday, the material stretched to a hue close to that of a washed and polished grape. He was being a good scout, helping Alyshia retrieve the contents of her purse.

I could only imagine where his eyes were. I put the barrel of the Python between the cheeks of his ass and said, "Gerald, this is a .357 Magnum. Your career as a man is history if you don't plant your hands on the wall, right above the intercom there."

"Sommer?" he grunted, rising.

"Plant 'em, Gerald."

He did that. Alyshia, kneeling below him, gave me a look and winked. I went over him with my left hand and found a stubby-barreled revolver clipped on his belt over his left hip.

Gerald said, "I just been transferred. I haven't even been on the target range, Ray."

"I thought they issued you guys Uzis or MAC-10s. I know cops in Queens that carry more firepower." I dropped the revolver in a coat pocket. "I'd like it if you told me how you found Ramone, because I know you couldn't have done it with the money you were putting out."

"Ray, you know I can't—"

I ratcheted the hammer on the Python back to the half-cock mode. "Just for tonight, Gerald, I'm a dangerous man. I was set up by the boy you're looking for and two cowboys tried to shoot me dead outside a restaurant in Queens. I killed one of them, and possibly both, and I did it with this gun. To borrow a phrase, I'm not a man to fuck with."

"You crazy?"

"You bet." I could see sweat rippling out of the hairpiece and into his collar. I brought the hammer back to full cock without mentioning that the safety was still in place.

He spat an amorphous mass of toothpicks between his legs. "Was the little sister, the hooker, Dixie, she told us what she told you. We took it from there."

"Now, why would she do that, or did Boyd use his punching-bag personality on her?"

"No, no rough stuff. The little sister's scared what Ramone might do to her for what she told you. We explained how we could be like an insurance policy."

"A little friendly coercion."

"You got to use what you got to use."

"What'd you use on Ramone once you found him?"

"A little this, a little that, you know. Ray, if you could

just uncock that sucker so we don't have an accident here, I'd appreciate it."

I used the trigger to release the hammer, letting it snick back to rest. I moved the barrel up his spine. "You got something in your eyes, Gerald, that tells me you're in the wrong sort of work. Maybe it's the light of sanity. I hope so. My advice, you look into a new career, starting tomorrow. For now, if you would please, with your left hand, undo the belt, unzip the fly." He did that, and I helped him out of his trousers and handed the pants to Alyshia, who wadded them up under her arm. He was wearing boxers with blue stars on a field of white cotton. "Now the shorts," I said.

"This is embarrassin'," he said.

"This is staying alive," I said to him.

I prodded him with the barrel of the Python and he stepped out of the boxers. I told him to continue holding up the wall. When he seemed to have that under control, I nodded at Alyshia, and we went through the door to the street and into the Datsun, Sammy driving. She revved it out through three gears along Christopher Street and made the corner heading north on Hudson. After several blocks, with no headlights dancing up on us, I told her to pull over. I gave her the name of the strip joint in Queens with instructions for Charlie Rip to meet me there by midnight. I climbed into the driver's seat, and Alyshia surged from the back and onto the shotgun side.

"How you doing?" I asked, popping the clutch and nosing us back into the traffic.

"Was that the truth, about you killing some chaps?"

I said it probably was, one of them certainly looked dead enough, and anyone hit by a Python through a window, even the window of an expensive-looking sedan, would be happier dead than living in the cobwebs of life left to them. She laid her neck back against the seat and looked out her window, so that I couldn't see her face. "If a man," she said, "raped you repeatedly, and the man was your father, would killing him be a crime in your book, Mr. Sommer?"

32

It was not yet ten o'clock when Alyshia and I pulled into a parking space beneath the El, across the boulevard from the dance emporium for naked ladies next to Tip Top Tech. A train shambled overhead. There was a diner on the other side of Tip Top Tech, and I suggested she might prefer to kill some time in there, but she felt she'd really like a strong drink. I took her elbow and we maneuvered among the cars. We went through the doors and into the pounding backbeat, the wail of exuberant falsettos. The girl with the peasant body that Leo Saperstein lusted after was traipsing along the bar, a crowd moving as she moved, this one if possible even a little louder than last night's. The dancers from last night were absent, although on one of the small stages a blonde with small breasts had her own group of admirers taken by the lady's talent for smoking cigars with something other than her mouth. The air of degeneracy in the place would have given Darwin pause.

I found us a table next to the inactive stage, as far from the revelers as possible. From what I had seen, Alyshia was the only woman in the place with clothes on. If it bothered her, I couldn't discern it. Our waitress wore a skimpy black apron, presumably to match the black bow tie at her throat, and tattoos. A pale blue ram about an inch long was bounding across the northern slope of her left breast, and on her wrist a pink unicorn of the same size stood alertly surveying her knuckles. Narrowing her eyes at Alyshia, she sucked in her tummy and practically socked me in the eye with the tattooed bosom. "Having fun, honey?" She leered.

"Not yet," observed Alyshia. "I'd like a Chivas on the rocks, love. Make it a double, water on the side."

"Jack and a splash," I said, eyeing the ram. "Let me guess: you're an Aries."

The waitress wobbled back a step on her four-inch heels. "Wow. You're like the first guy's ever guessed that. You oughta be a detective."

"Like wow," Alyshia deadpanned, resting her chin on the heel of her hand and following the waitress with her eyes. "You're missing something, Mr. Detective. The ones on her derriere."

I glanced, but she was too far and the light was too low. I turned back around and shrugged. "My loss, no doubt."

"Flags," she said. "One cheek the old Union, Confederate on the other. Quite well done, if you like that sort of thing. I don't happen to. Women get marked in enough ways as it is."

"We can still leave."

"Not at all. This place has the sort of bracing quality of a truth one wants to shy away from. I like it."

Our waitress came back with the drinks, set the glasses on napkins, quoted the price.

"You don't keep a tab here?" I said.

She put her tattooed hand on my shoulder. "Honey, I'd like to. For you. But the manager takes it out of my pay, anyone stiffs me, and I fall for guys too easy. I don't care if you're the pope, you pay as you go."

I handed her a twenty and she made change and I returned some of it to her as a tip.

"Thanks a bunch," she said, and leaned over the table, her hand still on my shoulder, but her attention on Alyshia. Her fingernails were bitten and dirty, and it had been a long time since a razor had visited her underarms. "Listen, honey, the manager, his name is Dave, he says to me, if you're looking to make some easy money, he'd guarantee a bill a night."

"A bill?"

"That's a hundred dollars. Dancers here get minimum wage, drinks at half price, and a percentage of their tips. On a Friday or Saturday night, after the bar takes its percentage, a really hot act might still pull in a hundred, a hundred fifty, but during the week, it's diddly. And you're always screwed on the drinks. But a guaranteed hundred, be honest with you, I've never heard an offer that sweet."

"And from a man who cheats on the drinks," I added.

Alyshia showed me drop-dead eyes for a moment, then raised them to caress the waitress. "Tell whatever his name is I'm enormously flattered, but my sex-change operation isn't complete yet. Maybe next year."

The waitress's chin just barely missed colliding with her kneecaps. When she stumbled away, I watched the flags of two Americas flex and shift in a unique fashion.

We sipped our drinks. I did at any rate.

I said, "I like to watch you work."

"Do you?"

"When it's on someone else."

"Meaning?"

"On me it's wasted. Tonight especially. I'm up to my eyebrows in trouble. Leaving the scene of a shooting, I could have my license suspended, possibly revoked, my whole business down the tubes. It's not the greatest business, but it's mine, I'm still my own man. And that's the bright side of my thinking for the moment. Because I have a bad feeling about this night."

Evidently she didn't share my apprehension. As I spoke she got one of her cigarettes going and then let her gaze wander, surveying the room and its inhabitants with a regal eye.

I tried again. "Part of this bad feeling has to do with you. I don't get a clear picture. All the way here you were working on my emotions, the gist of it being that since Ramone had sold you out, I might qualify for the part of Galahad. You need protection, and your idea of that is for the protection to be permanent. The way you were playing it, the whole thing could be negotiated without either of us uttering the word 'murder.' You are a tough, intelligent lady. Normally, I'm a sucker for that variety. But there's something elusive about you, something out of focus."

"Really?" She dropped the remainder of the double down her gorgeous throat and found a handkerchief in her purse to touch the corners of her mouth. She let the water ride. "Do get me another of the same," she said, tapping off the ash that had accumulated on her cigarette. The tattooed waitress, whether from the size of the tip or Alyshia's supposed sexual orientation, did not let us out of her sight for more than a few seconds, so that my two fingers in the air were swiftly acknowledged. "How clear would you like the picture to be, love? My father seduced me when I was barely twelve. He called it having safe sex. That way, we were keeping ourselves pure for our loved ones. In his case, presumably, my mother. And in mine, it was the knight on the white horse that would become my husband. This was my father telling me this, you understand. That was a time in my life when I was still fairly innocent, if you believe in innocence. Do you?"

Her eyes flared at me.

"If you have to ask, you probably wouldn't buy the answer. What I do believe is that I've got very little time to decide how much or if I can help you. A lot depends upon how straight you can be with me. Slowing down on the scotch would be a beginning."

Our lady of the tattoos arrived with the tray of drinks, distributed them. She looked a little out of breath. "Dave says, depending a course how far along you are, you know, with the change and all, he might be able to guarantee a bill and a half. Honey, I'm tellin' you."

The regal eye for an instant looked stunned, then deferred to me, someone more acquainted with trash. "I'm sorry," I said, "there isn't any place on your costume to pin a name tag and I didn't catch your name."

"Cherry," she said. "Cherry Power. It's my stage name. My real name that I was born with is Phyllis."

"Well, Phyllis, I happen to be the lady's surgeon. You tell Dave that if he's looking for geeks, he might start by looking in the mirror. Would you do that for me, darling?"

"Look in a mirror," she repeated, uncertainly. "Yeah," she said, when I added to the tip, "yeah, I think I could remember that."

"Do it, then."

I watched the two flags wave until the smoke and dim light gobbled them up. I said to Alyshia, "Contradict me

if I'm wrong, but the way I put it together, at some point
in the relationship your father persuaded you to recruit,
no other word for it, young girls for sexual favors. My
guess being they were the daughters of Vietnam Vets,
like Julie. Through various veteran functions. How else?"

Alyshia ignored my advice about the scotch and pushed
at least half her drink into oblivion.

She put her face into her hands, her lovely fingernails
gracing the corners of her eyes, stroking her temples.
"Ray? Welcome to the real world. Yes, I pimped for my
father and did it willingly. Julie was fourteen when she
started. She loved it. There were gifts and money, but
most of all they were treated nicely by the men and made
to feel by my father that they were doing something
incredibly important. When all it was they were performing for powerful men that Tommy—that is, my father—
he could flash a videotape, a cassette, they were in the
palm of his hand. Or as he would phrase it, their testicles
were. I was a little girl eager to please, and I was duped
as much as the others, because I believed there was some
ultimate, right reason for what we were doing. I believed implicitly, given what I knew of his employment,
that what we did was sanctioned at the highest levels. Is
that so difficult for you to believe?"

I watched her put to bed the rest of her second double
before I had finished my first watery shot. "No," I said,
"it's not difficult. Blind faith has been around for a while.
And what exactly did you think your father did?"

"Exactly was precisely what I didn't know. I knew,
because it was necessary for me to attend boarding
schools abroad under a false identity, and periodically
to change schools, that he was employed in some sort of
hypersensitive position within the government. By twelve
I knew it was the Central Intelligence Agency, because
my parents sat me down to tell me. But beyond that,
what he did, I knew nothing. The impression left was
that he worked beneath somebody who was nearly the
equivalent of God."

I fished inside my jacket and laid the photograph of
Julie Holloway in the jailbait pose on the table, facing
Alyshia. "Would you know anything about this?"

She considered it, her eyes going away somewhere,

then coming back to the picture. "It was taken over the holidays, Christmas break last." She turned the photo over and pushed it away. "Be a dear, love, and buy us another."

She kept her eyes on the back of the photograph and her face looked stone cold, had that scraped quality of hysteria.

I chanced it. "Julie, before she knew who I was really, and before I even knew you existed, I showed her this picture, she said Allie took it. A name that meant nothing to me then. She said something about Allie and her weird old man. Now, old man could be boyfriend or father. You erased that confusion by confessing he was both. I'm not interested in the sordid details, because I have an active enough imagination, but this isn't just another photo in the family album. He doesn't hand out a photo of you, his true target, because he's devoted years to your protection, and certainly isn't going to reveal your identity to a civilian, who might sell the story, once he got a hold of it, to the press. Never mind that's not my style, he had every right to believe it might be. So he points me in the direction of someone who is innocent, but may have guilty knowledge. Julie. The first time I talked to her, she said something to the effect that this picture was taken before it got interesting. I am just wondering if she meant something more than sexual configurations."

"My father wasn't doing just lines of cocaine, it was closer to freeways. Riding that ego surge it gives you. Boasting of the men he controlled, boasting of his accomplishments, many of which I am sure he had no business disclosing, especially to two young girls."

She stopped then, and concentrated her energy upon attracting the attention of our waitress. A double arrived within the minute, no charge, courtesy of Dave. Dave had business potential: all the sensitivity of a tire iron. I had underestimated him.

This time Alyshia sipped her drink, as if she had some idea of staying coherent for a while. "I can pretty well imagine what Julie meant by interesting. You see, I had, until that night, I had been under the impression that . . . what went on between my father and me, that was our private aberration. It was our bond. But that night was *my* introduction to the real world. He bragged to her, in my presence, about how it was between us. He actually . . . to that little whore . . ."

Her turquoise eyes went off somewhere.

"That was the night you said he . . . did it again and again, against your will."

She looked at me, almost startled, and laughed and lowered her head and shook it, a brew of reactions in which contempt was the active ingredient. She brought her face up, and it had that scraped quality once more. "Ray, you remind me of actors in old movies, when men wore hats and actually removed them in the presence of ladies. Even if the women weren't, strictly speaking, ladies. They ganged up on me, Ray. It was his idea. He accused me of having an attitude, being unfaithful, all of it garbage. They stripped me naked and he injected me with something that made me very whoozy until I threw up. After that, I was simply a spectator."

"Heroin," I said.

She closed her eyes, then opened them, and they looked bleak, and freshly wounded. "So they did what they did. They had me everywhere. I can put it in fine print, if you'd like."

Because her emotion for once seemed grounded and real, I was touched. I said, "It isn't necessary. Were you involved with Sal, then?"

"We had been introduced, he had made overtures, but no. The only man who interested me then, you see, was this brute that Julie lived with. She told me about him the morning after. . . ." Her fingernail prodded the overturned photo.

"Your Galahad for hire."

"Something like that."

I leaned forward, my forearms on the table. "You became his angel, the lady with access to real money. Your father is in the business of importing cocaine, some back-channel piece of thinking the Agency can safely deny. But you took him off, you and Ramone did. That's what this whole thing's about, isn't it?"

She moved her shoulders around, easing back in her chair, and said nothing.

"Tell me something," I said. "Did Sal ever understand your predicament?"

"No. He was just a walk-on. A pretty boy with all the moves. And speaking of walk-ons, Ray, that's all you are, sitting here waiting for a phone call. I can take you to Tommy right now. If you think you have it in you."

I said I thought I did. I excused myself and went to the men's. In there, I removed every round from Gerald's revolver but one.

It was block after block of shabby storefronts and warehouses a few stories high. Ghosts of aerosol paint snarled across shingles and scabrous mortar and brick with names and dates and profane messages. Occasionally there was a street lamp still intact and working. We were a little north of Astoria Boulevard, and we could see the beams of light from LaGuardia Airport groping the sky. The windows were rolled down and Alyshia smoked nonstop. Borne on the clammy ether off the East River, smells intruded, the rank atmosphere of empty night streets, sweet with rot and edged by acrid confinement. I glanced at Alyshia smoking, her face moving from side to side as she spoke, totally composed. She told me about the time her father had brought her here, shortly after Christmas, and about the warehouse where women worked over Formica tabletops with plastic wrappers and scales, silent dark women (mostly Hispanic, but some East Indians with enormous brown eyes, the red dot on their foreheads), each with an electric space heater and wearing surgical gloves, and wearing nothing else, their nipples distended from exposure to December downdrafts. Their naked ankles were shackled by handcuffs. Men had been present in the room as well, dressed and armed. The men made many remarks.

"Enlighten me a little, if you will," I said. "What's your father doing, showing you his operation?"

She did not answer right away. Then she said, "Flaunting his power. This was the night after . . . the night we talked about. He made me wear dark glasses and cover my hair with a scarf, and I was not to speak, only observe. He explained that in the event of his death, his lawyer had a key for me to his safe-deposit box, and inside it would be keys to the warehouse, and to the product stored there. He said it was my secret inheritance, as opposed to whatever would be left in the estate, which, thanks to my mum's gambling habits, wouldn't be much."

"But you made an early withdrawal, with Ramone's assistance."

"Even a man of my—of Tommy's capacity has to sleep sometime. I found a locksmith, and possibly I led the chap on a little. I had duplicates of all of Tommy's keys in an hour. *Then*, I interviewed Ramone. He was perfect."

"Hungry and brutal and sly," I said.

"Precisely."

"The two of you got into the warehouse, stole a quantity of cocaine plus weapons and ammunition, which, because of your father's erratic schedule, he didn't discover until fairly recently. Correct so far?"

"Yes," she hissed. "I had to have something to negotiate my freedom with. If my fa—if Tommy's led you to believe that love or reason plays any part in his thinking, you are making an enormous mistake. He's way beyond a state of mind one could characterize as sane."

"I can believe that," I said. "But you suggested that your father, and not bad luck, was behind young Sal's murder. Why?"

"The same stunt he pulled at Bennington: leaving cocaine in Sal's car."

"Oh," I said. Except that the district attorney's office never released that information; that was the deal Dominic Amado and I struck, at the encouragement of Agent Orange. "Oh yeah," I said.

"There." Alyshia pointed suddenly. "There it is."

The building occupied dead center in the block, the entrance set back and down from the sidewalk, windows on either side girded with metal shutters that were heavy enough to stop a small-caliber bullet. The place rose four stories, standard for the area, and had acquired its quota of aerosol commentary. In a moment of abandon the contractor had fitted the upper-story windows with facsimiles of the Roman arch and extended the lintel to cre-

ate a postage-stamp porte cochere, enough to shelter one
foot patrolman or a family of stray felines. The contractor evidently awoke from his orgy and cheaped the facade with shingles the color of jaundice. The building
shared a common wall, Siamese fashion, with a structure
of even less enchantment. Narrow alleys little wider than
I am tall ran abreast of the buildings. There were several
cars parked along the block, most of them absent tires
and probably radios and engine blocks as well. Alyshia
did not recognize any of them as belonging to her father.
We circled the area with the same result. We made a
second pass, and I turned right at the next corner and
set the brake. I made a show out of checking Gerald's
revolver and handed it to her. "Lock the doors," I said.
"You don't need me. Keys are in the ignition. There's a
phone. Use this only if you don't have a choice. Anybody
hassles you, just put the car in motion and get gone. I'll
find a way home."

She took the gun without hesitation and handled it in
a manner that suggested experience. "I'll be here," she
said. "I've come this far. I'll be here until I can be certain. . . ." She hesitated, letting the turquoise eyes do
the pleading. They did a job of it. "Ray? He kills people."

I touched her cheekbone with a finger, drew it across
her skin to the corner of her mouth. "I do too," I said.

She caught my hand in hers and drew it beneath her
blouse. Her lips were cool, but her tongue pushed hungrily. Her nipple was erect, which might have been a
consequence of passion, if indeed she felt any, but I was
more inclined to chalk it up to the clammy night air. She
was one for the books.

33

I climbed out of the Datsun and she crawled over the gearshift to occupy the driver's seat. I could taste her lipstick with the tip of my tongue. She pulled the door shut. I told her to roll up the windows, leave just a crack, that's all. She took my hand in both of hers and rested her cheek for a moment against my knuckles. "I wish I had had the presence to bring along the keys I had made. It would be so much simpler for you."

"I have my ways," I said. "You're sure about the door in the back?"

"Sure," she whispered. "One thing I ought to tell you: whatever you're going to do in there, you better get done quickly. Ramone knows about this place as well."

I stood looking at her in the deserted, harsh-smelling street, struck by sadness at her transparency. It is one thing to see you've been played with in retrospect; it is quite another when you can see it coming.

"Ramone," I said. "Won't that be nice? He kills people too. We'll have a lot in common to talk about. Or maybe I'll just shoot him. I'd be one of the last to argue you don't have a body worth killing for."

She started running up the window, then stopped. "You are a nasty, brutal man," she said. "I don't wonder you lost that beautiful wife of yours."

I smiled, or maybe it was just a grimace. "I can be. Especially when I'm being waltzed around. I know who killed young Sal. And who didn't."

Her face went away and the window went up. She reached for the tan box of cigarettes in her purse, resting the revolver in her lap. Because the sidewalks were empty

when I turned the corner, there was nothing to melt into;
I was obvious whether I did a drunken stagger or performed like a guy in a ballet, doing scissor leaps in tights.
I tucked my chin, pocketed my hands, tried to walk as
if this were part of a nightly ritual: no rush, and no
curiosity.

I slipped down the alley next to the building Tommy
Grace was supposed to occupy. Overhead, in a switch-
back pattern, the fire escape ascended past blind glass.
There were window wells for the basement and visors of
three-quarter-inch plywood bolted where the glass should
be. In back an unlit private street serviced two blocks of
buildings, each equipped with enough yard for a tractor
trailor to crab itself into. My nostrils drank in the pitch-
thick fumes laid down by the trucks, a familiar, cloying
residue, the suck of transience. I crept onto the loading
platform, found the door Alyshia had described, a hollow metal one. The beauty of this one was there was
only one lock. I secured the penlight between my teeth,
the beam on, and studied my options in the plastic sleeve
for Allen wrenches. I started with a tension bar and rake,
because with any sort of luck, that would bring the
quickest success. I tried several rakes. They worked the
pins, popping some and losing others that my touch was
not soft enough to counter with the bar. I turned to a
pick with a deep tooth and probed the pins one at a time.
It was just a matter of patience. The final pin dropped
and the tension bar swiveled slowly, but no matter how
slowly, there was still a faint click of the lock surrendering. I put away the picks and the penlight and crouched
to one side of the door, breathing through my mouth,
gliding the Python from its holster. The seconds passed.

I reached for the knob and turned it in the same spirit
of caution as I had the lock. When the door was ready
to open, I lay belly down, my left hand on the knob, the
Python aimed into the opening that would appear when
I nudged the door inward. I nudged. No light raced out,
and very little filtered in from the common area. Best of
all, nobody with guns was waiting to greet me, unless of
course they were hovering behind the door. I squirmed
forward on my stomach to cross the threshold, the Python in both hands now, shouldering the door ahead of

me, and then away, propelling it with a foot until the knob glanced off the wall. Nobody behind the door. I closed it and dusted myself off as well as I could under the circumstances. There was a raw smell of abandonment, of failed plumbing, of studs behind damp plasterboard on the road to rot, of rodents taking over. It smelled almost as bad as a detox cell on Saturday night.

When my eyes had adjusted enough to discriminate in shades of charcoal, I could make out levers and a loading belt and an open elevator toward the front. I moved that way along a narrow aisle and emerged onto a catwalk that overlooked the darkened ground floor, a chiaroscuro of vague shapes into which one of the network of pipes overhead dripped slowly, a periodic pinging. I stood there for a while, listening, and heard nothing except the tiresome sound of slow disintegration. I slipped the penlight from my pocket. Its knitting-needle beam touched upon a doorway to a room to the left of the aisle, and two more on its right. And on two men standing between the doors, both wearing night-vision goggles, although only one pointed a weapon. It was a Russian assault rifle, an AK. This was my week for them. An AK was not something I was prepared to argue against, even with the Python, although I kept it aimed as a bargaining chip.

"Gentlemen," I said, "the name's Ray Sommer. I was told I might find Tommy Grace here. I work for the man is the thing. Tell you what, I'll tuck away the Magnum, if Shorty there, he would drop the barrel, or raise it, I don't care, just so if he sneezes, he doesn't put a burst through me."

"Amigo," the taller, unarmed one said, touching the shoulder of his comrade, and the first word after that that I understood was *bobo*, foolish. I heard hombre, and right next to it, *peligroso*, which I hoped meant dangerous, if the subject of discussion was me and my Magnum. When the short guy lowered the barrel, I immediately shelved the Python.

The taller one worked a knob and light strayed out from a room. "Mr. Sommer," he said, wrestling off the goggles and stepping into the light, "you are a man of some tenacity. If you would enter my crude quarters."

I did that. The little guy, whose name was Felipe, accompanied me. In the lit room I made out a dark brown face, possibly mestizo, a nose with the flat curve of a teaspoon, pale lips and black eyes, jet-colored hair greased to look like an arrangement of quills. Felipe wore a blue-jean jacket over a canary tank top. His jeans bunched at his ankles in accordian folds above unlaced, white hightops. A black mustache, clipped even with the corners of his mouth, almost completely obscured his upper lip. He looked nineteen and a little nervous. There was a walkie-talkie crammed in his rear pocket.

The room itself resembled a bunker. It was long and narrow with plasterboard walls, the four-by-eight sections just nailed to the studs and left there, no taping or caulk. Fluorescent lights hung four to a pod from the exposed ceiling. Toward the back sat a wooden desk with a green banker's lamp upon it, two black telephones, an inverted infantry helmet. Behind it stood a refrigerator that had seen some years, a cast-iron sink, a small stove with legs and a porcelain finish overrun with cracks. Open, metal shelving bracketed to a wall swelled with provisions, everything from coffee to liquor to canned stews. The taller party, who by intonation and Alyshia's description could only be Tommy Grace, instructed me to place my hands flat on the desk. Felipe reached under my coat and liberated the Python. He moved away and offered it butt-first to the boss man, who took it, spun the cylinder, sighted with it somewhere over my head.

It was a show, but it gave me time to look him over. He was a solid customer. Even in bulky black exercise pants, black sweatshirt, and black nylon windbreaker, powerful thighs and broad shoulders were clearly defined. The man's weathered neck was the neck of a weight lifter. His hair looked coarse and was cut close to his scalp, just long enough to influence with a brush; it was chestnut in color with some gray fetching up in his temples and sideburns and in random flashes along a retreating widow's peak. His was a seaman's face: worked dark by sun and by exposure made leathery and radiant with creases. It was clear where Alyshia had inherited the sharp, predatory nose and striking eyes, although hers were of a deeper, more unreadable blue. He exhibited the composure of a man it would be smart to be nice to. Too bad. I was tired of being a smart guy.

I turned around to check out the surroundings. A console television lurked up near the doorway with a VCR atop it. John Wayne was emoting on the television screen without benefit of sound. A table beside the television was piled with plastic cassettes. I wondered if any of them reprised evenings when wealthy men embarked upon simulated incest for the camera.

He popped the cylinder on the Python, caught the cartridges in his palm, dropped them on the desk, and left the empty Colt next to a telephone. I watched him open a monogrammed gold compact, spoon something from it up his nose. He snapped the lid on the gold box. "Drink?" he said, gesturing toward the shelves.

"Whatever you're having."

He brought glasses, a dusty bottle of Haig & Haig, and we drank it neat.

"Tommy?" I said.

He unlimbered a captivating smile. "It's one of the names I'm known by. I'm not one that is easily impressed, but your zeal in finding me quite takes the breath away."

There were several chairs in front of the desk, wooden ones. "You mind?" I said, and sat down without waiting for permission. "The feet, they're a little tired from running. An hour ago it was from your pals in the Agency, who otherwise give you high marks, but don't like the idea of you absconding with their money. And earlier, say shortly after seven, what I was running from were bullets. Quite a lot of them. Some goons in a dark sedan. Or wouldn't you know anything about that?"

We exchanged looks for a few moments, gauging one another, and then he spoke rapidly to Felipe and Felipe hauled the walkie-talkie out of his pocket and mashed a button with his thumb. Static prickled the air. Felipe conferred with the party at the other end, but not in the dictatorial accents Tommy Grace employed. A guttural voice crackled from the walkie-talkie. Tommy Grace, listening, said to Felipe: "Yes, both of you on the roof. Pronto."

The boy with the AK sauntered up the room past a

couch and some armchairs. He moved with a pinched gait, as if he might be pigeon-toed.

When the door closed, Tommy Grace put his eyes on me. From beneath the black jacket he hauled out a heartstopper of a gun: it was a .45 automatic. He laid the barrel beneath his nose, caressing his lips with it, looking like a man having amusing thoughts. His eyes grew dreamy. "Let us assume, for the sake of argument, you are correct about the earlier incident. Have you a death wish? Coming in here alone, gung-ho to rip my heart out, either you're crazed or you've stretched the definition of stupid beyond anything in the dictionary."

"Possibly," I agreed. "But it's not your heart I'm after. It's the money you promised me. Sending me after Julie was a means of pressuring Alyshia. Because you knew they had someone in common: Ramone. And you have a bone to pick with him, as well as with your real daughter. They ripped you off. What would Alyshia be worth to you, Tommy, in round numbers?"

"You're posturing, Sommer."

I moistened a fingertip and pushed it along my upper lip and held the smear of color up to the light. The tremor in his hand, the ache that washed over his face bespoke recognition. But I could be as swinish as the next guy. "If you think I came in here without backup and something to negotiate, you make a stupid Marine look like Harvard material. Speaking of which, Sal DeLorio, Junior, was Harvard material. You might have read about it. He was ripped apart by AK-47s, like the one Felipe has. What you didn't read is that a stash of cocaine was found in his car. Just like a stash left on the seat of his car up in Bennington, few months back, when he was calling upon your daughter. Evidently you don't approve of Harvard boys."

Tommy Grace advanced on the desk, laid the automatic flat on top of it, and lifted the Python with a finger in the trigger guard. He watched the Magnum rock on his finger for the better part of a minute. He kept his eyes on the Magnum, even as he spoke. "Believe it or not, Ray, the boy was harassed for his own good. The hope being he would back off, extricate himself from Alyshia's fantasies. You see, she has had to matriculate so long under so many false identities, she has rather lost a clear picture of herself. Her mother was more drawn to the casinos of Europe than the rewards of motherhood. With that kind of emotional abandonment, is it surprising, the intensity of her fantasies? To be honest, I'm not confident my wife's death was suicide. And since she hooked up with this Ramone parasite, Alyshia's been increasingly a danger to herself and to anyone associated with her. That's the truth, Sommer. So also is the existence of an analyst willing to treat her, although not in Switzerland. Now you know our dirty secrets." He trundled a swivel chair back from the desk and deposited himself in it. "I'm sorry about the DeLorio boy, but it was none of my doing."

"I believe you," I said. "I'll tell you something else. I believe your daughter arranged young Sal's murder. She didn't pull the trigger, but she might as well have. Who else besides you and his father could reasonably be expected to know of the appointment with me that morning? Answer: someone he was intimate with. Someone who associated with the likes of Ramone. Someone who with a single act severs a link to herself and possibly shines a light away from herself. It's the only way I can make sense of planting so much high-grade powder. And I tell you what, I turn this over to the police, your daughter will never see that fancy analyst. Now, what you have to think about is how badly you want to see your daughter, that you've spent a lifetime trying to protect. You might want to factor in that I'm not out of here in one half hour, the whole story on tape, and some in her words, is delivered to the Queens DA."

I watched him spoon more of the white stuff into his nose and listened to his sinuses reacting, a sound I was familiar with from the two tapes. He seemed to be waiting for something, or somebody. And he clearly relished having an audience to wait with him, although what I had told him appeared to put him through some emotional changes. The chill of the night seeped into the room, almost as cold as the light in Tommy Grace's eyes.

"So what's the price," he said, "for delivering my daughter?"

I smiled. It was a genuine smile. I think it was my first

of the day. "Tell me something: how much did you take
the Agency for?"

He laughed. He laughed as if he had heard the fun-
niest joke of the week. Then he hooked a finger in the
trigger guard of the Python and picked it up, sprang the
cylinder, and inserted a single cartridge. Snicked the cylinder shut and spun it. "It wasn't money per se, amigo.
It was a few kilos transported by Thompson Avionics.
Actually more than a few. No point in being coy, one
businessman to another: it was five hundred kilos."

He let me ponder that with the barrel of the Mag
pointed in the general direction of my chest cavity.
"Now, what's the price you're asking for Alyshia?" he
said.

I leaned a forearm on the desk, my other hand scrambling around on my ankle for the Beretta. "As you might
expect, Tommy, we no longer honor checks from
Thompson Avionics or any other dummy company you
might have accounts for. And we aren't set up to convert
cocaine into dollars. So I'm afraid what we're talking
about is solid cash. Twenty-five thousand if you get her
out of the country immediately and I have the name and
address of the analyst. Otherwise, you have twenty-four
hours to raise a million, in cash. Then you do what you
want. But I don't think you have twenty-four hours."

"You amuse me, Sommer," he said, placing the muzzle
of the Mag beneath his chin. He winked, and the hammer banged against an empty chamber. "How about the
twenty-five in cash, no questions asked?"

And the barrel swept down aimed at my chest with
his finger on the trigger, and the color jumped in his
knuckle, and I heard the snap of the hammer as if it
came from the next room, a sound happening to somebody else. I blinked, feeling the heat roar up in my face,
and let myself down in the chair, one hand holding both
Beretta and underside of the seat. My eyes stung.

"You are fucking certifiable," I said, when I could
speak. The raw taste of vomit soiled the back of my
mouth.

"I'm a man willing to run risks. A man capable of anything, amigo. I've been out on the edge so long. . . . It
isn't worth talking about. The country's got its heroes

that go to the moon, and then it's got me, who's been to the dark side of the moon and returned. I'm expendable. I accepted that going in. But Alyshia wasn't part of the bargain. Do you have children, Sommer?"

"No."

"Pity. They're the second chance life gives us. Having a daughter, it's an opportunity to watch your wife growing up, becoming young again. It's quite astonishing really. And I assure you, it is an experience you would steal or kill for."

"Nothing," I said, "I know about you would dispute that."

"Good. Bear that in mind, amigo. Now let me tell you a quick story. *Sendero Luminoso* mean anything to you?"

"Group of Maoists, operate out of Peru. A small bunch, but vicious. Shining something or other in English."

"Shining Path," he said. "Very good, Sommer. I've spent close to two years sucking up to those bastards, brokering all the crop they controlled or could confiscate. It's given the Agency considerable insight into how the left is proceeding in this hemisphere. But the enthusiasm for spending cuts, believe it or not, afflicted the Agency more than it did, say, HUD. About a year ago, a directive came down from the Committee, a board of senior officers reporting to the director, designating specific operations as Distant Cousins. My op became one of them. Simply put, we were no longer in the system; each of us reported verbally to a rabbi within the Agency, but no records were to be kept. In other words, we were unfunded, forced to be self-sufficient. As my rabbi put it: time for some old-fashioned free enterprise."

"Sure," I said. "Who'd believe it? And even if they believed it, who could prove it? It's a rogue operation."

"Instead of paying for it, and destroying it, we turned a profit. Think about it. Where'd you rather see the money go—up the chimney or to the good old U.S. of A.?"

"Another way of looking at it: you guys are funding the enemy that you're set up to shut down. Give bureaucrats a problem, they'll find a way to prolong it. But bottom line, you guys are just pushers."

"It's a dirty world, amigo, I don't know what else to tell you."

I eased the Beretta back under my pant leg and pretended to think it over. "All right. Show me twenty-five, you can have your daughter. But remember, get cute, and the Queens DA will party on your ass."

His eyes went wide and he tucked a shoulder, suggesting less than respect for the threat. He got a spoon up one nostril just as someone rapped on the door, two times quickly, two times slow.

Tommy Grace spooned cocaine up the other nostril as they came through the door, hands locked behind their heads. Directing traffic were Felipe and another dark-faced guy, this one taller and bulkier, all chest and arms in a blue-and-white-checkered shirt with mother-of-pearl snaps. He wore black Spandex gloves and a weathered straw hat with a high round crown and funneled brim, a striped necktie for a hatband that trailed down his back. He had a squat face, eyes that reflected the light like metal, and his wide cheeks were stippled with pox or acne scars. There was an automatic pistol in his left hand that he carried by the barrel and laid on the desk in front of Grace. He needed a bath. Nothing could be done for his clothes that burning wouldn't do better. Grace did not seem to notice. The squat-faced, smelly man went back up the room and out the door, leaving Felipe to guard the two men sitting on the couch with their fingers still laced behind their heads. From the shape of their faces it appeared the two men had recently been in an accident. Not a bad one, because after all they were still walking, but one they might remember for a while.

I was their accident.

"Ramone," I said, "Boyd. Small world, huh? You guys know Tommy?"

34

There were several seconds of hostile silence. The fluorescents washed Blades's pale face a mushroom shade, except where it had struck the lobby floor. At the point of impact the skin was bloated, purple beneath the eye, running to crimson at the edges. I could not see his eyes because he was wearing the gray, reflective glasses, which, due to the swelling, sat askew on his face. There were abrasions along his jaw and what looked like spots of blood on the collar of his shirt. His ring and pinkie fingers had been hastily taped together on his left hand. Although I could not have hit Ramone anywhere near as hard as Blades hit the floor, the pimp did not look much happier. His eyelids were purple with blood, parted about the width of a coin slot. His nose was a smear of cartilage on his right cheek and his upper lip stuck out, as if he were storing a frankfurter beneath it. Now I knew why my knuckles still throbbed. I had done good work.

Evidently, once he finished sniffling and enjoying the early glow of the drug, Tommy Grace was making a similar observation. "Sommer," he said, grinning, "did you?"

"I had help."

The grin stayed in place a while longer as he nodded, studying me. With his mesmerizing eyes still on me, he rattled something off and Felipe grunted words I could not hear. Footsteps approached. Behind me Blades's raw voice said, "Tommy, can we cut the Mickey Mouse with the hands here? You contacted us and we came in good faith."

Grace flipped his hand negligently, a gesture of imperial indifference, and Blades took up a chair to my right, off the end of the desk. A sparse beard bristled along his jaw, reddish gold in the light, and lay across his upper lip like fragments of shattered glass. His reflective lenses flung back images of my face. I didn't have anything to fling back except a smile. Blades turned away.

"How's D?" said Grace.

Blades gestured in my direction. I could see the tips of the taped fingers and they were hot red in color, suggesting he had jammed them crashing into the floor. He growled, "You think, with him sitting here?"

"I asked you a question."

"Not thrilled, but he can live with the terms. The Committee doesn't even have to know. It's my op now, Tommy. I'll control the flow, the payouts, like our friend Ray here. The files will of course be purged."

"Of course. Felipe show you the fifty kilos in the locker?"

"I didn't count down to the last gram, but you've always been a man of honor. It's the only reason D rescinded the directive on you."

"Honor." Tommy Grace sneered. "Don't jerk me off. I'm walking because you guys got ninety percent of the product, my silence, and because you know if you fuck with me, I can take down some important people. I groom you what—three, almost four years?—you try to peddle white bread like that. You disappoint me."

Grace was showboating again. It didn't impress Blades, although it might have alarmed some to know how hard Tommy Grace was hitting the nose candy. He was out there, in my opinion, capable of anything.

"So what's the game plan, Tommy?"

"Simplicity itself. Everybody comes out a winner." He winked and leaned forward in the swivel chair, snatched up the auto pistol. He chucked a live cartridge onto the desktop, then picked it up pinched between thumb and forefinger, as if it were a jewel to be examined for flaws. "Well, *almost* everybody."

"I thought—"

Tommy Grace told him calmly, "Shut up," showing Blades a view of the barrel that would gain his attention. He barked a terse command at Felipe, and Felipe, waving his AK, murmured words we couldn't hear. Ramone took his hands off the back of his head and shook them, flexing the fingers, then squeezing himself up and down each arm, he approached the desk in his shiny yellow and bloodied costume. He walked with a swagger that looked like something remembered, not felt. Felipe did not follow, but crossed the room to switch off the VCR, then took up a position next to the door.

Ramone stopped and stood midway between Blades and myself, maybe a little nearer Blades. He tried out a smile beneath the coin-slot eyes. "Wha' say, Chuck? You goin' work for the guvmint too?"

I looked back at him and shook my head.

Tommy Grace said, "Hey, amigo," and shot Ramone in the neck, severing the carotid artery. The room was all sound and blood. It sprayed from the wound, Blades scrambling sideways from his chair, but not fast enough. In the noise and confusion the corpse of Ramone staggered woodenly about for several seconds before the adrenaline was gone and he went to his knees. Felipe came up the room and slammed the stock of the AK into the back of Ramone's head to make the corpse lie flat.

I gave Blades a handkerchief to go along with the one he had while Tommy Grace spooned more cocaine. Felipe resumed his post next to the door.

"Now then," Grace announced, "as we've disposed of the garbage, let us get on with the good stuff. My apologies for the mess. Boydo?"

"You mind, Tommy, let me use the sink, get this shit out of my hair? It was like standing next to a fire hydrant."

"No can do, Boydo." He waved the pistol negligently. "Find a chair and sit down. Drink?" And before Blades could answer, the pistol swept my way. "He's a Cutty man, Sommer. I believe there's some on the shelf there. He'll drink it neat."

I brought bottle and glass and set them in front of

Blades. I kept my eyes on Grace the whole time. He was out there so far I could feel his craziness coming up from behind. I sat down, arranging my chair so that I was ninety degrees to the desk, able to keep an eye on all of the present participants. As casually as possible, I leaned forward to park my elbows on my thighs. The Beretta was still at least two seconds away. To give my posture credence I addressed Blades: "Where's Gerald? Not still searching for his pants, I hope. We left them on the curb. Of course, in that neighborhood . . ."

Blades inhaled some of the Cutty and tried to straighten his glasses, an impossible task. The door to the room opened as Blades answered, the blood-smeared lenses moving in Grace's direction. "Gerald? He's my insurance policy. In case you get cute, Tommy."

The lady with the blue jacket bundled beneath an arm came through the door holding something familiar and black in her hand. It was Gerald's hairpiece.

"If I heard you correctly, love, your policy's been canceled."

35

I thought: *She's farther out there than he is.*

From out of the shadows behind her sifted the radiant hair, the pale impeccable skin, and turquoise eyes of Alyshia Grace. She shifted the wadded coat so that it rode against her hip as she strode toward us, the motion of her long legs almost gliding, a skater's supple carriage. Her eyes dropped an instant, surveying the mess on the floor that was once Ramone, but she did not break stride. She circled the desk on the side away from Blades, behind me, and stopped just short of Tommy Grace, who had pushed himself out of the chair, a look of triumph in his weathered face. She pitched Gerald's hairpiece onto the desk and shifted her coat once more, this time cradling it beneath her breasts. I could see that her right hand was inside the wadded shape and I knew why.

"Baby love," Tommy Grace said, opening his arms, inviting her to step into them.

She didn't approach him. She just stood there. An eerie smile crept into her face. "I walked up to him sitting in the car, the jacket just like this, and he rolled down the window. I shot him right through the jacket. You showed me how to do it with a pillow, to muffle the sound, but a jacket works just as well. See?" She unfurled the blue leather so that we could see the multiple holes in it, each with its aureola of sooty black from the heat of the muzzle. We could also see the stubby revolver, once Gerald's, hanging from her right hand.

"Tommy," snapped Blades, "who is this? D will—miss? Miss, are you telling us Gerald, that you shot him? You terminated a federal officer?"

229

Alyshia showed him her drop-dead eyes. "I've never shot a man before, love, so I'm no expert. But I shot him up close, the way Tommy says it should be done. He certainly looked dead. Dead as the chap there on the floor."

"Tommy," Blades pressed, "we've got a problem here."

"Shut up!" said Grace, whirling, the Mauser in his hand. "Just shut the fuck up a moment, all right? We'll work it out." He swung his attention back to his daughter, who was still standing there, maybe five feet from him, the jacket in one hand, the revolver in the other. "Baby love, tell me, what did the man do? What did the man say?"

"Do?" she said. "He rolled down the window."

"Did he—"

"He rolled down the window and said, 'Miss?,' and I said, 'I don't think I will,' and I didn't. I can take care of myself, Tommy." She brought the revolver up, aimed at her father. "You are through running my life."

"Alyshia."

"All I asked you to do was leave the stuff in the Starion, and leave me alone. A clean, easy arrangement. But evidently, your ego got in the way." She turned her face just enough to let me know she was favoring me with an explanation. "And you advised me to obtain a restraining order. My father is a looney tune. I have tapes of some conversations that I could turn over to *The Times*, the *Washington Post*, they would be political dynamite."

"Alyshia, think about what you're saying."

"I am, Daddy. Absolutely every word of it. Ray, all I asked in exchange for them was a paltry ten kilos. A chance for me to have a new life. Was that so unreasonable, given what you know about him?"

Grace moved his eyes my way, grinning. "Indeed. And what is it you know about me, amigo?"

"That you're a dangerous man, basically," I said. "That Ramone made a big mistake hooking up with Alyshia to steal guns and cocaine. He made an even bigger one by going along with her on the extortion deal." I turned to Alyshia. "I take it the theft was something of a disappointment."

"Aside from the rifles, about three kilos. The chap there

on the floor, he was ecstatic. He thought in terms of the street. I was thinking in terms of my freedom, and it wasn't nearly what I needed."

Tommy Grace looked like a man aging with every turn of the minute hand. "If I can do better than ten kilos, would you put the gun down? And try to understand something: shoot me and Felipe will put a dozen rounds through you before you even hear the echo of the round you fired."

I had slipped the Beretta from my calf and squirreled it beneath the waistband above my left hip without anyone screaming dirty pool. So I said, "Before anybody thinks about shooting anybody, the gun you have, Alyshia, only had a single bullet. It was all I was willing to trust you with, and even then, I can see I miscalculated."

"Oh?" She swung the barrel around, sighted on my chest, and squeezed off an aborted round. "Aren't you the clever bastard?"

Tommy Grace closed the gap between them and wrestled the revolver from her. She tried to kick him where it would hurt, but he was quicker, caught her ankle, and twisted, forcing her to grab the edge of the desk to avoid landing on her face. He hooked the swivel chair with a foot and shoved it at her, told her to sit in it and shut up. She did that.

He sprang the cylinder and rotated it, and then looked at me. "You are a cold son of a bitch," he said. "The one round, you said you knew she had arranged young Sal's murder. You gave her the gun to use on herself."

I thought about how I should answer that, or even if I had an answer, my thinking being a little crazed at the time. I said, "You might have something there, Tommy."

Crow's-feet fanned away from the corners of his slit eyes. He continued to wave the Mauser around in a negligent fashion. Finally, he shook his head, and it sounded like he was laughing softly and against his will. "I underestimated you, Sommer," he said. "In the category of sons of bitches, you're just about my equal. Coming from me, that's a compliment."

I just looked into his eyes and said nothing.

Blades said, "I think I figured how we can finesse this. She's your daughter, Tommy?"

"Yes."

"Give me the gun, or you do it yourself, fit it in the pimp's hand. Christ, he's still warm. Be beautiful prints. Pimp's dead, Gerald's dead, it's a wash. But I think we got to get moving on this. D suspects anything, you know he's going to renege on the deal. Vengeance being next to godliness with him."

"What deal is that, Daddy?" wheedled Alyshia, her elbows propped on the arms of the chair, her fingers linked beneath her chin.

"We'll talk," he said.

"I can remember when you didn't make deals. I can remember when you stipulated conditions. I think you're losing it."

Grace ignored the taunt, handing the stubby revolver to Blades and ordering him to do the grisly work of acquiring a print. "Was he left- or right-handed?" he asked Alyshia. Because she was facing him, her back to me, I could not see how she was using her eyes, but I would have been willing to bet Grace got the equivalent of Shakespeare in silent turquoise.

I searched my memory of the moment the long-haired black guy emerged from beneath the van, the shotgun visible, the shotgun . . . raised . . . the stock pressed against—"He's right-handed," I said.

Grace's eyes lingered a little longer, in a duel of wills with his daughter. "Boyd," he said, "you see or know any reason Sommer could be wrong?"

Blades, having enough difficulty finding a spot to place his feet that wasn't wet with blood, did not devote a great deal of attention to the question. "Nope," he grunted. "And if I did, I'd still go with the statistical probability." I noticed it was my handkerchief he handled the barrel of the revolver with, so that when he was finished contriving evidence, I requested its return. He handed it back and I asked Alyshia for her platinum lighter, which she happened to be using to light one of her Israeli cigarettes. I watched white linen wisp into ash inside the overturned infantry helmet. I returned her fancy lighter. Neither of us said a word.

Tommy Grace said to Blades, who had returned to his chair close to the corner of the desk nearest Alyshia, "You have the first fifty. At the end of the month, for the next eight months, you will receive by mail a bus, rail, or airlocker key, and in that locker will be fifty kilos. In the first envelope, besides the key, there will be names of contacts, a cover letter, and my diary of operations."

In spite of the swelling on the side of his face, Blades eked out a grin, a sly, knowing one. "Give the plastic surgeons just enough time to remodel you."

Tommy Grace winked, the compact open in his hand, the Mauser hanging casually from a finger as he spooned cocaine into his nose.

"You fool," said Alyshia. She rose slowly from the chair and paced for several seconds, her arms folded under her breasts. "Tommy, you're letting the coke do your thinking. What did you always tell me? The Agency doesn't make deals with people who try to screw it; it only makes promises it has no intention of honoring. They're going to come after you whether you keep a kilo or one hundred of them. Darling, you're holding the guns and the merchandise. Smiley there, with the puffed face, according to Ray he's a double-A, which means you're bargaining with the very chap who likely will be the most eager candidate to find and murder you. Since they're going to come after you in any event, why give them a thing? Why even discuss it? Either they kill you and me in six months, a year, or we kill them now. Don't you see that?"

By the time she was finished she was parked alongside him, her pelvis pressed against his thigh, her two hands stacked on his shoulder.

He turned his face away from Blades toward his daughter for a moment, and something indescribable overtook his features, a wave of horror, of sorrow, there, then gone. "Amigos," he said, his face moving our way, Blades's and mine, "the lady has a point. Boyd, tell D, nice not doing business with him."

Tommy Grace tried to bring it off with a light touch, but there was an air of exhaustion, of overwhelming fatigue about him. He had the look of a man being used up, diminished. A cornered creature. He raised his voice to Felipe, who nodded and hauled out the walkie-talkie. Alyshia picked up the cigarette she had left burning on a corner of the desk, perched her fanny there, and swung her intoxicating eyes my way, evidently feeling a little flirtatious. I glanced at Tommy, but he was speaking into the phone now, gesturing with the pistol in his hand. That pistol seemed to have Blades's undivided attention.

"So you found your keys," I said.

She nodded. "So I did. When I saw Ramone and this red-haired person being admitted to the building, I thought it likely you would need assistance."

"Assistance. Like pointing what you assumed was a loaded gun at me and pulling the trigger. Straight out of the Girl Scout handbook, I suppose."

"Why, love, it was you said the gun was empty. I believed you."

"No, I'll tell you your reason for coming. You suspected, correctly, that arrangements were being made, and you're here for your piece of the action."

She cocked her beautiful face, her cheek nearly touching her shoulder, her eyes clear and serene. They were eyes like infants are supposed to have, not murderers. "Either one uses or is used in this life," she said. "I've had quite enough of the latter, thank you."

Tommy Grace glanced up the room and cut short his phone conversation. "Gabriel," he said, "welcome," and they were the last words he spoke in English. Gabriel was the squat-faced man who needed a bath. Evidently, Alyshia understood what her father was saying, because she butted her cigarette in the helmet and sprang from the desk. "You're just going to leave them here?" she cried.

"Yes," he said, "I'm going to leave them here. And we'll be far, far away."

"Why don't you shoot them, you fool?"

Grace backhanded her so hard she stumbled and landed, skidding on her backside up against the shelving. Blood gushed from her nostrils. "Permit someone to call you a fool more than once, and you deserve to be called one," he said. "Gentlemen, I'd like you to make yourselves comfortable on the sofa there. Gabriel and Felipe will attend to your seating."

"Tommy," said Blades, rising to his feet, "you know what this means: you've crossed the line."

"I crossed it long ago. So long ago the wherefores don't even interest me. Sommer, what, your feet fall asleep?"

"No," I said, standing. "I think you broke her nose. If that interests you."

Grace barked words and Gabriel came up the room, drawing from the back of his belt two pairs of handcuffs. I thought of the women made to sit naked, diluting and weighing drugs under the eyes of strange men. Because he evidently spoke no English, Gabriel pointed solemnly. Blades and I stood back-to-back, Gabriel first snapping the cuffs on Blades's wrists, then looping the short chain between my cuffs over his, and clamping the cuffs on my wrists. With a grunt he prodded us onto the couch, pulled our legs out and over the arms at opposite ends. We were a couple. Not a happy couple, but happier when Gabriel, satisfied with his work, moved toward the door, taking his smell with him. It was a smell entirely compatible with the warehouse, sour with neglect.

I watched Grace crouch and raise his daughter with a single arm, and situate her over his shoulder in a fireman's lift. I could hear her coughing and spitting, trying to clear her throat. She seemed to be trying to speak. As they came toward us I could decipher some of what she was saying. It was a mix of childish pleas and obscenities, fear and desperation. They passed out of my range of vision, but I could hear Tommy speaking to Felipe and Gabriel. Then I heard him say, "Easy, baby love. It's going to be all right. Everything's going to be all right."

This was a pro, Tommy Grace, a master of deception. Possibly Alyshia believed him. I know I didn't.

When the door closed, Blades said, "You don't speak the language."

"No," I said, "only bits and pieces."

"We're alone. Tommy's instructions, the greasers stay on the other side of the door for thirty minutes, shoot anybody that tries to leave. Us, in other words."

"That's damned unsociable."

"That's Tommy. He plays hard, but I think the daughter's right, he's lost something. The old Tommy would have shot us."

"Then I'm liking the new one better," I said. "Which isn't much. He keeps his own daughter as a concubine."

"Sommer," he snorted, "among the Montagnards, he was rumored to dine on human flesh, when it was offered. I told you, he's out there, but he's always delivered. The thing with his daughter is penny ante compared to crossing D, believe me."

"No, I'd say it's about the ultimate violation of trust, Boyd. Boffing you and D, that would come under the heading of just desserts. Tell you something else: there's no one he holds more sacred than the daughter he's defiled. And I don't think he knows how to balance that in his mind any longer."

"Meaning?"

"He's a guy on a ledge."

"That's dated news, Sommer. Try to surprise me."

"I can get us out of these cuffs, but I need to get my hands in front of me. You game?"

"That puts me in a vulnerable position, doesn't it? Vis-à-vis a man who doesn't like me."

"Boyd, most of the people I work for I don't like. Most of the people you work with, would you invite them home for a barbecue? We're talking common ground here. I go back a long way with the DeLorios. I want satisfaction. You don't want to lose five hundred kilos of prime product, to say nothing of landing Tommy Grace. He's your white whale, isn't he?"

"Let's do it," he grunted.

I kicked off my shoes. "Get your legs crossed and tucked against your crotch."

"Got 'em."

"Going up," I said. Pushing against one another's back, we rose to our feet, took a breather, then stepped off the couch, moved away from the coffee table. "Okay," I said, "the idea is to get the cuffs past my hips and as close to the floor as we can so that I can step through them a leg at a time."

I felt weight on my wrists, Blades slowly lowering himself to a crouch. It was painful getting the cuffs below my hips, because I had to screw my shoulders forward and at the same time swivel my legs, jerking on his cuffs, which did not contribute to his comfort either. Succeeding at that maneuver, Blades sank to his knees, then gradually onto his hip. I brought a leg up, ankle against thigh, perched like an awkward ostrich, until I had drawn my knee through, and then was straddling the linked cuffs. Liberating the other leg was simple enough, although I could feel the toll the first leg had taken in my left shoulder. The pain was suddenly exquisite. I jammed the heel of my right hand into the front of the shoulder in an effort to correct its relationship with the socket, and shortly the pain subsided, but tears had been shed in the process.

"I have picks," I said. "I trust you have some experience."

"Some."

"We're doing so well here for two guys who don't like each other, tell you what: I'm going to open your cuffs. Then you open mine."

We were unencumbered within a matter of minutes. He loaded his piece from the desk and cocked it and I did the same with the Beretta. We lip-read and we pointed. He crouched next to the doorframe. I rotated the knob slowly, yanked it inward, and dived for the floor. Blades punched two rounds into the dank, dark, empty air of the desolate warehouse.

Nobody there. Just Sommer and Blades.

"Help," he said, "is lousy everywhere. Thank God."

When my heartbeat had slowed to a pace that would permit me to speak without squeaking, I said, "He's making his run. Does he have a chance?"

"Tommy's a monster," he said, "the best we have out there. But solo, he can be brought down. I give him a year, tops."

Blades's prediction was generous in the extreme. I found my car with the keys in it and drove home to the house in Kew Gardens. I took some Jack D over ice into the family room and sat in the fawn leather couch to stare into the fireless fireplace, wondering what I might

have done smarter or swifter that would have saved even
a single life. A numbing, humbling sense of futility set
in, not unlike beating about the bush in a far country
for a purpose unclear, after an enemy that was at once
invisible and everywhere. I had helped no one there as I
had helped no one now. I had started from scratch and
wound up there. I had simply survived, to remember.
And to mourn. Oddly, just before I passed out, my sympathies turned in the direction of a murderer: of Alyshia,
whose life had been stolen before she ever had a chance
to experience it. I awoke in my clothes to the sound of
mockingbirds cavorting in a chestnut tree. I padded
barefoot out to retrieve the banded copies of *The New
York Times* and *Daily News*, the copies thick as the
stepping-stones in the driveway. Along with cups of black
Jamaican and a purely egg omelet smothered in ketchup,
I read about a fire in a warehouse in Astoria, a body
burned beyond immediate recognition. A disagreement
over drugs was suspected. I went out and pecked among
the roses. I stayed there longer than usual, feeling the
entire time like a criminal in a house of worship.

I might have stayed longer, but the phone was ringing.
I picked it up in the kitchen.

A voice I would never forget that belonged to a mime-
white face said, "Sommer?"

"You know it is."

"It might make the papers, it might not. A determination hasn't been finalized. Just thought you'd like to
know a silver Mitsubishi Starion swerved off the Henry
Hudson at a high rate of speed and plowed into a shelf
of granite. Occupants tentatively identified as Thomas
Grace and daughter killed instantly. About one in the
morning, which puts it a little after they left us at the
warehouse. You were right about him too: no skid marks.
Tommy punched his own ticket."

I had nothing to say.

"Guy did everyone a favor, taking that psychopathic
daughter with him."

"Gerald, was he . . ."

"Oh yeah. He's in a body bag on ice down at Langley.
Got caught thinking with his dick. Goddamn budget
cuts, that's what we get: inexperienced field men like

Gerald. Listen, after last night, I'd give my left nut for a partner like you. Anyway. At least Tommy had the class to clean up his own mess. No hard feelings?"

"You and Wes Dexter," I said.

"What's that supposed to mean?"

"You wouldn't understand if I explained it," I said, "and neither would he. Have a nice life. And Boyd? Don't even think about running Distant Cousins through this borough."

Ugly, chiseled laughter rattled in my ear. "Ray, I'm afraid you're talking in riddles."

36

The DeLorios, father and son, were laid to rest in a single, impressive ceremony. Services were conducted in Latin and English within the solemn walls of St. Patrick's Cathedral, and if there was an empty pew in the place, I didn't see it. The mayor and chief of police occupied the pew immediately behind the one reserved for the family. I sat off in an alcove with the rest of the bearers watching Meredith brave the ceremony, flanked by her daughters, each with a hand in hers. Conspicuous among the mourners were the society-page reporters, who thought nothing of murmuring into their tape machines and scanning the pews with tiny binoculars.

We emerged from the cathedral with the caskets into a circus of television crews, boom mikes, shouting reporters, and blues on horseback attempting to shield us from the maelstrom. There was a good deal of shoving and jostling as we made our way down the steps to the waiting cortege. I saw one of Sal Jr.'s bearers, a Harvard classmate, snatch a pesky female reporter by the front of her silk blouse and drag her along for several steps, employing oratory decidedly un–Ivy Leaguish.

More words were spoken at the cemetery, more tears shed. It was a balmy enough day for June, temperature in the high seventies, but quirky gusts played havoc with hemlines and hats, and the green-and-white-striped awnings above the caskets swelled and snapped. Both Sals, I reflected, would have enjoyed the sight of buffeted skirts, surprised thighs, the good Lord giving them a last wink of human pulchritude. I retreated to a small knoll twenty yards off, beyond earshot of the archbish-

240

op's words. A man with a bad conscience should never stand too close to a man of the cloth. Besides, Sal and I had said our good-byes in a cemetery already, and once was enough.

Limousines returned us to the DeLorio estate for the wake. Bouquets, a riot of them, occupied every niche and corner, and spilled out over the terrace, wreaths and sprays of glorious color. The most ornate, a forest of roses that put my backyard to shame, arrived from an anonymous well-wisher, delivered by a florist I knew to be in the Scorceses' debt. The don, I thought, was a most extravagant mourner. But perhaps he had reason to be.

I saw Cece long enough to brush cheeks and to learn that she and Larry were going away for a week in Italy, to visit Rome and Florence. Roma and Firenze: the same cities we toured when we were young and in love. I wondered vaguely if Cece hadn't the idea that such a trip would vanquish the past. Sooner try to outrun your own shadow.

Meredith caught up with me at one of the open bars on the terrace. She linked her hand to my arm and we walked.

"You have been a friend," she said, without looking up, but squeezing my elbow. "Ray?"

"You want to know what I know about the murders," I said, "and what I know, Meredith, is nothing." I could lie like the big boys. It was not my proudest moment, but wisdom argued for it, and perhaps not a little compassion. Of course, that's probably what the big boys believed as well: "I'm sorry . . . ."

She kept her pace, her eyes still averted. "I will pay you."

"Sweetness, try to understand something: my business has to do with protecting, not investigating. Now, if you're adamant about this, I can give you the names of some highly regarded investigators. But I'd leave it to the police for a few weeks anyway. They've got the resources."

"I want . . . you."

"Meredith."

"Ray!" Gone was the cartoon-soft voice. Up came the eyes. "I have been around politicians long enough to read between the words. There's a cover-up in the works. Turn it around. If it was me that had been killed, and Sal were standing here, would he take no for an answer?"

I did not tell her that her husband would not have come to me with her request, having resources infinitely superior to mine in the person of Joe Scorcese. That would have meant explaining things I did not want to get into. Like my suspicion that the don arranged her husband's death. I was almost certain I understood the reasoning, but like everything else in this network or web of atrocities, I didn't have proof. And there was another consideration that someone of Meredith's wealth might not comprehend. Where there was a conspiracy of silence of this size, exposing it had its price. And it would be far in excess of what a rich woman, even of Meredith's means, could pay me.

The dirty truth of the matter was that I still wanted to work in the five boroughs.

I lifted Meredith's hand to my lips. "Sweetness," I said, "I'll do what I can."

Several days after the funeral a padded mailing envelope, stapled shut, was delivered to the office, to my attention, "Private and Confidential." I had to show identification to the messenger and sign a receipt. Pat Connor, less than a week away from transferring to Dexter, Wells said, "You mind if I say something, Ray?"

"Christ, Patty. After nine years?"

"Almost ten," she corrected me. "I don't like it there's no return address."

"I don't either, Pat. But it's got nothing to do with anything that should worry you. However, if you and Martina want to stroll to the Greek's, fine by me."

They conferred. They decided to stay. I took the package upstairs and laid it on the desk, got settled in my chair, and prodded it with a chrome letter opener. I had a pretty good idea of what the lumpy package contained. I swiveled in the chair to look out the boulevard window into a limitless and lovely blue sky. There was a tremulous quality to the air that morning, almost like something young lovers bring to a first kiss. Young love: now there was a subject Ray Sommer could write a book on. He was the expert; he had seen it all. It would not be a pretty thing to read. I glanced at one of the gentlemen on the wall. His leer looked shopworn. He knew all about the subject too.

I snapped my wrist and the chrome letter opener smashed the glass over the lithograph and tumbled to the carpet. The leer was gone.

I tore open the envelope and emptied its contents on the desk. Tens and twenties, with an occasional worn century. When I had finished counting, I had ten thousand dollars in untraceable cash, just as Agent Orange had promised. And if what he told Tommy Grace was true, Blades was the new boy in charge of Distant Cousins, my warning notwithstanding. Ray, I thought, who are you to issue threats? You're just one more guy treading water in the toilet. This is Queens, Ray, try to remember that. I put in a phone call, businessman to businessman, but not to Blades.

Thirty minutes later I managed to find a parking place on a side street about a block and a half away from Perfect Pizza on Austin Avenue. It was ten in the morning, the vigor of the city distilled across the street in a pickup game of basketball, four on four fighting over a half court and a netless hoop, while the other half of the concrete court had been chalked off with bases for a heady Whiffleball game among enthusiastically cursing prepubescents. Turning the corner onto Austin, I inhaled the air from a vent of a dry-cleaning establishment, a ghastly mix of machine heat and some essence of breath mints. Nobody but the Korean greengrocer and fruit vendor, Sing Lee, seemed to be doing much business at this hour, and most of his customers appeared to be elderly citizens, the hardcases looking to shave a few cents off the bill for finding a bruised fruit, a yellowing leaf. As I passed, spirited negotiations were under way over some plums, Sing Lee's comprehension of English diminishing in an inverse ratio to the number of his nods per minute. A sun-faded red awning stretched from the front of his storefront to the curb, shading the bins of fruit he paraded out each morning at six and dragged inside at midnight. Next to Sing Lee's, Perfect Pizza looked like the

Trump Tower. There was brick facing, black glass, an
enormous red neon sign, polished brass fittings on the
door and throughout the inside. None of this plastic seating: the booths and every chair within were cushioned
and covered in black leatherette. There was a bright yellow jukebox inside, to the right as you entered. Two pool
tables, several arcade games. A trio of computerized cash
registers ranged along a stainless-steel counter. The place
was empty now as I made my way past the track-lit
booths, smelled the ovens heating up, paused to watch
Johnny Cantaloupo toss a wheel of dough already pro-
cessed and cut to shape in a plant in New Jersey.

Johnny Cantaloupo seemed to be happy this morning,
singing "Strangers in the Night." It was probably the
extent of his wit. Johnny Cantaloupo was a man who
managed a pizza shop and kneecapped guys who couldn't
meet the sharks' weekly interest payments.

In the back room among the packages of paper napkins,
pizza-box flats, towers of paper cups, Angelo Scorcese and
a couple gentlemen I did not know were having their in-
tellects tested by a game show that featured lots of lights
and buzzers and a host with a lupine grin. Contestants
were asked questions of tabloid significance—"Imagine you
found Bigfoot in your bedroom"—and the responses were
voted upon by the studio audience.

Angelo reluctantly took his eyes away from the screen to
pat me down. I showed him the contents of the padded
envelope. He gave me a look, but said nothing. I unbut-
toned my shirt to demonstrate that no way was I wired.

He frowned at the gesture. "C'mon, Ray. Whadda ya
doin'? You and me, we grew up together. I got to do the
feelie-touchie because I got to do it. We know you're a
stand-up guy."

He led the way back out to the street, to a navy-blue
Mercedes limo, no doubt part of a fleet owned indirectly
by the family, much like the van that had ferried me to
the cemetery for the last conversation I would ever have
with Sal DeLorio. The windows in the Mercedes were
all up, and as darkly tinted as the law would permit.
Across the roof I watched Sing Lee, smiling like he had
an entire Frisbee in his mouth, foist a spray of green
grapes on the party in the backseat. Angelo opened the

curbside door for me to get in, and I saw Joe Scorcese, the grapes in his lap, run the window up, saying, *"Grazie,* Sing, *grazie,"* saw Cato sitting in the front seat with his huge hands on the wheel, erect as a harbormaster.

Joe was in a somber charcoal suit this morning, white shirt buttoned up to his thin, wattled throat, no tie, no Dumpster hat on, black patent hair parted down the middle. The hair was his, all right, but the color came out of a bottle. A faint scent of cloves drifted off him. The black eyes glittered, and I tried to imagine they looked kindly on me, searched my experience for the memory of a benevolent gun barrel pointed my way, and came up empty. The don rattled off some dialect and Cato eased the Mercedes away from the curb and drove about the way I thought he would: stiffly, as if conducting an ocean liner through the Panama Canal.

Joe Scorcese said something else and the air-conditioning was kicked up a few notches. The beautiful morning sky through the tinted glass had a twilight glaze to it, as if it were in the power of money or evil to change day to night. The people on the street took on an air-brushed quality, their features sharp and questing and characterless, like lab rats. With his little dogleg fingers Joe Scorcese plucked the grapes, buffed each one in his silk handkerchief before submitting it to his shrunken, predatory lips. His concentration and the way he chewed, quickly and hungrily, bore an eerie resemblance to behavior I had witnessed in the Bronx Zoo. I thanked him for honoring my request to meet.

He put a hand up without looking my way, his eyes feasting on the fruit in his lap. Sitting back in the seat as he was, the soles of his smooth black shoes barely grazed the carpeting. "Speak," he said. "I'm a listen."

"Basically, Mr. Scorcese, I'm here because I'm a guy who wants to go on doing business in this borough, without doing business with certain parties in this borough."

Another grape polished, he popped it in. "Go on."

"You once were kind enough to credit me with having some brains, so I'm hoping you have an equally high opinion of my discretion."

Another grape shined, another grape gone. "Could be.

Ray, we are two men here. I don't bring my *consigliere*. Say what you have in your head."

I took a deep breath, hoping it wasn't one of my last. "All right. My thinking is this: there isn't anything goes down in this borough you don't know about. Like, take one example, if someone wants to move weight through Queens bypassing the Colombian network. So you know, the book's closed on your old friend Tommy Grace."

"Friend? Tommy Grace, he don't got no friends. Sal, how many people show up his funeral? Hundreds. He was buried beside his son with respect, all kindsa friends. How many people pay the respects for this Tommy Grace, a man who blackmails respectable people? Maybe done worse things'n that, I hear, his own daughter. Do not call such as this my friend."

"I apologize, Mr. Scorcese," I was quick to say. "Poor choice of words."

He screwed his black eyes in my direction. "You know who pay the respects, at this man's funeral?"

If Meredith hadn't told me, I think I would have guessed it, given the tone of outrage in his voice.

"Genevieve DeLorio," I said. "And possibly a man with red hair."

"Yes," he hissed, and went back to the business of his appetite.

"She and Alyshia were on the same ski team. Genevieve introduced her to young Sal back in December, January, and nature took its course. Genevieve and Sal, they didn't have a clue as to the truth of Alyshia's life. And in the end, neither did Alyshia. She set the kid up, Mr. Scorcese. She arranged Sally's murder in order to put pressure on Grace to cut a deal. All she wanted was the money to get free of him, and all he wanted, really, was her, his daughter. He was burnt out. He had made his daughter a wife. They were both . . . they were lost."

The Baker turned his face to the roof of the Mercedes and uttered a stream of dialect. He said, in English, "Between me an'a Grace, was strictly business."

"I understand," I said.

His lips curled unpleasantly. "Tell you somethin', Ray, who put the boy's father in the ground is you."

I thought about the last thing Sal said to me.

"You don't bring a Grace into it, he don't gotta be clipped, Sal. But you bring him in, Sal gonna want satisfaction. I love Sal. But he don't come before business. Nobody comes before the business."

Sal's last words: *You don't walk with the angels either, chum.* You got that right, Sal. I've got dirt on my hands and blood on my conscience and a favor to ask of a killer.

"I call him from the van. I tell him, the Grace, you gotta problem, you take a care."

"Tommy Grace did Sal," I said woodenly.

The small man shrugged. "It is not of my concern."

I felt very cold very suddenly and stared hard out the tinted glass. There was not a damn thing I could do but what I came to do. I emptied the padded envelope on the seat between us. "It's ten thousand dollars," I said. "See it gets back to the new party you'll be doing business with. If you would, tell them I can't be bought, but I can be realistic. Would you do that for me?"

Joe Scorcese looked at the money, looked at me, then at the grape perched in his handkerchief. Without answering the request, he reminded me of the night of young Sal's murder. Telling me how after I'd left, Meredith had confronted her husband in the study, hurled accusations, then made a confession of her own. About a night in Haiti.

"Mr. Scor—"

He raised a hand full of bent fingers. "I'm a say this only once: you owe Salvatore."

"All right," I said, "I owe him, Mr. Scorcese."

"*Padrino,*" he said, hoisting his crabbed killer's hand for me to kiss. "It is how you may call me now."

I stared at the twisted flesh, the bent offering, without any more illusions of being my own man. "You're pulling my chain," I said, a form of gallows wishfulness.

He screwed his horrible little face up at me, his eyes without a flicker of anything in them, and said, "You the man with brains. You think I'm a pull your chain?"

I didn't. I seized the frail hand and squeezed it firmly, saw the pain sharpen the color of his eyes, then brushed the desiccated back of his hand with my lips. I would save my business and worry about my soul later. "*Padrino,*" I said.

ABOUT THE AUTHOR

MARC SAVAGE grew up in Kalamazoo, Michigan, graduated from the University of Michigan, and later from Columbia University in New York. He currently lives in Phoenix, Arizona, with his wife Sharon and a parrot named Garp. His next novel will be published by Bantam next Spring.

Three Brides for Three Grooms...

Laurel and Damian, two strangers, collide with each other and discover a red-hot passion...
Could it be love, though?

Annie and Chase were married to each other once before but it failed...
Is this their second chance?

Stephanie and David realize
they need each other—a fake engagement
is the perfect answer...
But is it only pretend?

How will it all end?

The beginnings take place at the...

WEDDING *of the* YEAR

Dear Reader,

I love weddings. I'll bet you do, too. Blushing brides, handsome grooms, people having fun…most of the time. Weddings, especially big ones with flowers and music and lots of guests, can be stressful. Sometimes it's not just excitement that puts color in the bride's cheeks!

Come with me to *The Wedding of the Year*. The bride's divorced parents spend the day smiling, but those smiles are as phony as the butter-cream roses on the cake. The bride gets cold feet. How can she expect to be happy if her parents couldn't make their marriage succeed? Annie and Chase don't know what to do. Maybe they should pretend to fall in love all over again. Sure, it's a sacrifice, but devoted parents will do anything for their beloved daughter—won't they?

What about the rest of the wedding party? Things are happening to them, too. Damian, the rich and gorgeous best man, brings his mistress to the wedding only to find himself distracted by a beautiful stranger. All he can think about when he sees Laurel is how much he wants to take her to bed. His mistress is angry. So is Laurel, who wants no part of the game—until she and Damian are alone.

Don't take your eyes off the guests, either. The bride's mother plays matchmaker. She seats a very eligible man and a widow with a dubious reputation at the same table in hopes that David and Stephanie will find each other fascinating. They do. Sparks fly, except they're not the kind the matchmaker had in mind—but oh, are they fun to watch!

Trust me. This is going to be the best wedding you ever attended. You're in for excitement, romance and enough heat to start a fire.

Here's to love and marriage!

With all my warmest wishes,

Sandra

SANDRA MARTON

WEDDING *of the* YEAR

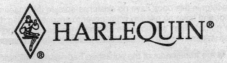

HARLEQUIN®

TORONTO • NEW YORK • LONDON
AMSTERDAM • PARIS • SYDNEY • HAMBURG
STOCKHOLM • ATHENS • TOKYO • MILAN • MADRID
PRAGUE • WARSAW • BUDAPEST • AUCKLAND

HARLEQUIN BOOKS

by Request—WEDDING OF THE YEAR

Copyright © 2002 by Harlequin Books S.A.

ISBN 0-373-18509-X

The publisher acknowledges the copyright holder of the individual works as follows:
THE BRIDE SAID NEVER!
Copyright © 1997 by Sandra Myles
THE DIVORCEE SAID YES!
Copyright © 1997 by Sandra Myles
THE GROOM SAID MAYBE!
Copyright © 1998 by Sandra Myles

This edition published by arrangement with Harlequin Books S.A.

Visit us at www.eHarlequin.com

Printed in U.S.A.

CONTENTS

THE BRIDE SAID NEVER!

CHAPTER ONE

DAMIAN SKOURAS did not like weddings.

A man and a woman, standing before clergy, friends and family while they pledged vows of love and fidelity no human being could possibly keep, was the impossible stuff of weepy women's novels and fairy tales.

It was surely not reality.

And yet, here he was, standing in front of a flower-bedecked altar while the church organ shook the rafters with Mendelssohn's triumphal march and a hundred people oohed and ahhed as a blushing bride made her way up the aisle toward him.

She was, he had to admit, quite beautiful, but he knew the old saying. All brides were beautiful. Still, this one, regal in an old-fashioned gown of white satin and lace and clutching a bouquet of tiny purple and white orchids in her trembling hands, had an aura about her that made her more than beautiful. Her smile, just visible through her sheer, fingertip-length veil, was radiant as she reached the altar.

Her father kissed her. She smiled, let go of his arm, then looked lovingly into the eyes of her waiting groom, and Damian sent up a silent prayer of thanks to the gods of his ancestors that it was not he.

It was just too damned bad that it was Nicholas, instead.

Beside him, Nicholas gave a sudden, unsteady lurch. Damian looked at the young man who'd been his ward until three years ago. Nick's handsome face was pale.

Damian frowned. "Are you all right?" he murmured.

Nick's adam's apple bobbed up and down as he swallowed. "Sure."

It's not too late, boy, Damian wanted to say, but he knew

9

better. Nick was twenty-one; he wasn't a boy any longer. And it *was* too late, because he fancied himself in love.

That was what he'd said the night he'd come to Damian's apartment to tell him that he and the girl he'd met not two months before were getting married.

Damian had been patient. He'd chosen his words carefully. He'd enumerated a dozen reasons why marrying so quickly and so young were mistakes. But Nick had a ready answer for every argument, and finally Damian had lost his temper.

"You damned young fool," he'd growled, "what happened? Did you knock her up?"

Nick had slugged him. Damian almost smiled at the memory. It was more accurate to say that Nick had tried to slug him but at six foot two, Damian was taller than the boy, and faster on his feet, even if Nicholas was seventeen years younger. The hard lessons he'd learned on the streets of Athens in his boyhood had never quite deserted him.

"She's not pregnant," Nick had said furiously, as Damian held him at arm's length. "I keep telling you, we're in love."

"Love," Damian had said with disdain, and the boy's eyes had darkened with anger.

"That's right. Love. Dammit, Damian, can't you understand that?"

He'd understood, all right. Nick was in lust, not love; he'd almost told him so but by then he'd calmed down enough to realize that saying it would only result in another scuffle. Besides, he wasn't a complete fool. All this arguing was only making the boy more and more determined to have things his own way.

So he'd spoken calmly, the way he assumed his sister and her husband would have done if they'd lived. He talked about Responsibility and Maturity and the value in Waiting a Few Years, and when he'd finished, Nick had grinned and said yeah, he'd heard that stuff already, from both of

Dawn's parents, and while that might be good advice for some, it had nothing to do with him or Dawn or what they felt for each other.

Damian, who had made his fortune by knowing not just when to be aggressive but when to yield, had gritted his teeth, accepted the inevitable and said in that case, he wished Nick well.

Still, he'd kept hoping that either Dawn or Nick would come to their senses. But they hadn't, and now here they all were, listening to a soft-voiced clergyman drone on and on about life and love while a bunch of silly women, the bride's mother included, wept quietly into their hankies. And for what reason? She had been divorced. Hell, *he* had been divorced, and if you wanted to go back a generation and be foolish enough to consider his parents' marriage as anything but a farce, they were part of the dismal breakup statistics, too. Half the people here probably had severed marriages behind them including, for all he knew, the mealymouthed clergyman conducting this pallid, non-Greek ceremony.

All this pomp and circumstance, and for what? It was nonsense.

At least his own memorable and mercifully brief foray into the matrimonial wars a dozen years ago had never felt like a real marriage. There'd been no hushed assembly of guests, no organ music or baskets overflowing with flowers. There'd been no words chanted in Greek nor even the vapid sighing of a minister like this one.

His wedding had been what the tabloids called a quickie, an impulsive flight to Vegas after a weekend spent celebrating his first big corporate takeover with too much sex and champagne and not enough common sense. Unfortunately he'd made that assessment twenty-four hours too late. The quickie marriage had led to a not-so-quickie divorce, once his avaricious bride and a retinue of overpriced attorneys had gotten involved.

So much for the lust Nick couldn't imagine might masquerade as love.

A frown appeared between Damian's ice-blue eyes. This was hardly the time to think about such things. Perhaps a miracle would occur and it would all work out. Perhaps, years from now, he'd look back and admit he'd been wrong.

Lord, he hoped so.

He loved Nick as if he were his own flesh and blood. The boy was the son he'd never had and probably never would have, given the realities of marriage. That was why he'd agreed to stand here and pretend to be interested in the mumbo jumbo of the ceremony, to smile at Nick and even to dance with the plump child who was one of the bridesmaids and treat her with all the kindness he could manage because, Nick had said, she was Dawn's best friend and not just overweight but shy, too, and desperately afraid of being a wallflower at the reception afterward.

Oh, yes, he would do all the things a surrogate father was supposed to do. And when the day ended, he'd drive to the inn on the lake where he and Gabriella had stayed the night before and take her to bed.

It would be the best possible way to get over his disappointment at not having taught Nick well enough to protect him from the pain that surely lay ahead, and it would purge his mind of all this useless, sentimental claptrap.

Damian looked at his current mistress, seated in a pew in the third row. Gabriella wasn't taken in by any of it. Like him, she had tried marriage and found it not to her liking. Marriage was just another word for slavery, she'd said, early in their relationship…though lately, he'd sensed a change. She'd become less loving, more proprietorial. "Where have you been, Damian?" she'd say, when a day passed without a phone call. She'd taken his move to a new apartment personally, too; he'd only just in time stopped her from ordering furniture for him as a "surprise."

She hadn't liked that. Her reaction had been sharp and angry; there'd been a brittleness to her he'd never seen before—though today, she was all sweetness and light.

Even last night, during the rehearsal, there'd been a suspicious glint in her dark brown eyes. She'd looked up and smiled at him. It had been a tremulous smile. And, as he'd watched, she'd touched a lace handkerchief to her eyes.

Damian felt a twinge of regret. Perhaps it was time to move on. They'd had, what, almost six months together but when a woman got that look about her…

"Damian?"

Damian blinked. Nicholas was hissing at him out of the side of his mouth. Had the boy come to his senses and changed his mind?

"The ring, Damian!"

The ring. Of course. The best man was searching his pockets frantically, but he wouldn't find it. Nick had asked Damian to have it engraved and he had, but he'd forgotten to hand it over.

He dug in his pocket, pulled out the simple gold band and dropped it into Nick's outstretched hand. Across the narrow aisle, the maid of honor choked back a sob; the bride's mother, tears spilling down her cheeks, reached for her ex-husband's hand, clutched it tightly, then dropped it like a hot potato.

Ah, the joys of matrimony.

Damian forced himself to concentrate on the minister's words.

"And now," he said, in an appropriately solemn voice, "If there is anyone among us who can offer a reason why Nicolas Skouras Babbitt and Dawn Elizabeth Cooper should not be wed, let that person speak or forever—"

Bang!

The double doors at the rear of the church flew open and slammed against the whitewashed walls. There was a rustle of cloth as the guests shifted in the pews and turned to see what was happening. Even the bride and groom swung around in surprise.

A woman stood in the open doorway, silhouetted against the sunlight of the spring afternoon. The wind, which had torn the doors from her hands, ruffled her hair wildly around her head and sent her skirt swirling around her thighs.

A murmur of shocked delight spread through the church. The minister cleared his throat.

The woman stepped forward, out of the brilliance of the light and into the shadowed interior. The excited murmur of voices, which had begun to die away, rose again.

And no wonder, Damian thought. The latecomer was incredibly beautiful.

She looked familiar, but surely if he'd met her before, he'd know her name. A man didn't forget a woman who looked like this.

Her hair was the color of autumn, a deep auburn shot with gold, and curled around her oval, high-cheekboned face. Her eyes were widely spaced and enormous. They were...what? Gray, or perhaps blue. He couldn't tell at this distance. She wore no jewelry but then, jewelry would only have distracted from her beauty. Even her dress, the color of the sky just before a storm, was simple. It was a shade he'd always thought of as violet but the fashion police surely had a better name for it. The cut was simple, too: a rounded neckline, long, full sleeves and a short, full skirt, but there was nothing simple about the body beneath the dress.

His gaze slid over the woman, taking in the high, rounded breasts, the slim waist, the gentle curve of her hips. She was a strange combination of sexuality and innocence, though the innocence was certainly manufactured. It had to be. She was not a child. And she was too stunning, too aware of herself, for it not to be.

Another gust of wind swept in through the open doors.

She clutched at her skirt but not before he had a look at legs as long and shapely as any man's dream, topped by a flash of something black and lacy.

The crowd's whispers grew louder. Someone gave a silvery laugh. The woman heard it, he was certain, but instead of showing embarrassment at the attention she was getting, she straightened her shoulders and her lovely face assumed a look of disdain.

I could wipe that look from your face, Damian thought suddenly, and desire, as hot and swift as molten lava, flooded his veins.

Oh, yes, he could. He had only to stride down the aisle, lift her into his arms and carry her out into the meadow that unrolled like a bright green carpet into the low hills behind the church. He'd climb to the top of those hills, lay her down in the soft grass, drink the sweetness of her mouth while he undid the zipper on that pale violet dress and then taste every inch of her as he kissed his way down her body. He imagined burying himself between her thighs and entering her, moving within her heat until she cried out in passion.

Damian's mouth went dry. What was the matter with him? He was not a randy teenager. He wasn't given to fantasizing about women he didn't know, not since he'd been, what, fifteen, sixteen years old, tucked away in his bed at night, breathing heavily over a copy of a men's magazine.

This was nonsense, he thought brusquely, and just then, the woman's head lifted. She looked directly up the aisle, her gaze unwavering as it sought his. She stared at him while his heartbeat raced, and then she smiled again.

I know what you're thinking, her smile said, and I find it terribly amusing.

Damian heard a roaring in his ears. His hands knotted at his sides; he took a step forward.

"Damian?" Nick whispered, and just at that minute, the

wind caught the doors again and slammed them against the whitewashed walls of the old church.

The sound seemed to break the spell that had held the congregants captive. Someone cleared a throat, someone else coughed, and finally a man in the last pew rose from his seat, made his way to the doors and drew them shut. He smiled pleasantly at the woman, as if to say there, that's taken care of, but she ignored both the man and the smile as she looked around for the nearest vacant seat. Slipping into it, she crossed those long legs, folded her hands in her lap and assumed an expression of polite boredom.

What, she seemed to ask, was the delay?

The minister cleared his throat. Slowly, almost reluctantly, the congregants turned and faced the altar.

"If there is no one present who can offer a reason why Nicolas and Dawn should not be wed," he said briskly, as if fearing another interruption, "then, in accordance with the laws of God and the State of Connecticut, I pronounce them husband and wife."

Nick turned to his bride, took her in his arms and kissed her. The organist struck a triumphant chord, the guests rose to their feet and Damian lost sight of the woman in a blur of faces and bodies.

Saved by the bell, Laurel thought, though it was more accurate to say she'd been saved by a C major chord played on an organ.

What an awful entrance to have made! It was bad enough she'd arrived late for Dawn's wedding, but to have interrupted it, to have drawn every eye to her...

Laurel swallowed a groan.

Just last week, during lunch, Dawn had predicted that was exactly what would happen.

Annie had brought her daughter to New York for the final fitting on her gown, and they'd all met for lunch at Tavern on the Green. Dawn, with all the drama in her eighteen-year-old heart, had looked at Laurel and sighed over her Pasta Primavera.

"Oh, Aunt Laurel," she'd said, "you are so beautiful! I wish I looked like you."

Laurel had looked across the table at the girl's lovely face, innocent of makeup and of the rough road that was life, and she'd smiled.

"If *I* looked like *you*," she'd said gently, "I'd still be on the cover of *Vogue*."

That had turned the conversation elsewhere, to Laurel's declining career, which Annie and Dawn stoutly insisted wasn't declining at all, and then to Laurel's plans for the future, which she'd managed to make sound far more exciting than they so far were.

And, inevitably, they'd talked about Dawn's forthcoming wedding.

"You are going to be the most beautiful bride in the world," Laurel had said, and Dawn had blushed, smiled and said well, she certainly hoped Nick would agree, but that the most beautiful woman at the wedding would undoubtedly be her aunt Laurel.

Laurel had determined in that moment that she would not, even inadvertently, steal the spotlight. When you had a famous face—well, a once-famous face, anyway—you could do that just by entering a room, and that was the last thing she wanted to do to the people she loved.

So this morning, she'd dressed with that in mind. Instead of the pale pink Chanel suit she'd bought for the occasion, she'd put on a periwinkle blue silk dress that was a couple of years old. Instead of doing her hair in the style that she'd made famous—whisked back and knotted loosely on the crown, with sexy little curls tumbling down her neck—she'd simply run a brush through it and let it fall naturally around her shoulders. She hadn't put on any jewelry and she'd even omitted the touch of lip gloss and mascara that was the only makeup she wore except when she was on a runway or in front of a camera.

She'd even left early, catching a train at Penn Station that was supposed to have gotten her into Stratham a good hour before the ceremony was scheduled to begin. But the train had broken down in New Haven and Laurel had started to look for a taxi when the station public address system announced that there'd be a new train coming along to pick up the stranded passengers in just a few minutes. The clerk at the ticket counter confirmed it, and said the train would be lots faster than a taxi.

And so she'd waited, for almost half an hour, only to find that it wasn't a train that had been sent to pick up the passengers at all. It was a bus and, of course, it had taken longer than the train ever would have, longer than a taxi would have, too, had she taken one when the train had first ground to a halt. The icing on the cake had come when they'd finally reached Stratham and for endless minutes, there hadn't been a cab in sight.

"Aunt Laurel?"

Laurel looked up. Dawn and her handsome young groom had reached her row of pews.

"Baby," she said, fixing a bright smile to her face as she reached out and gave the girl a quick hug.

"That was some entrance," Dawn said, laughing.

"Oh, Dawn, I'm so sorry about—"

Too late. The bridal couple was already moving past her, toward the now-open doors and the steps that led down from the church.

Laurel winced. Dawn had been teasing, she knew, but Lord, if she could only go back and redo that awful entrance.

As it was, she'd stood outside the little church after the cab had dropped her off, trying to decide which was preferable, coming in late or missing the ceremony, until she'd decided that missing the ceremony was far worse. So she'd carefully cracked the doors open, only to have the wind pull them from her hands, and the next thing she'd known she'd been standing stage-center, with every eye in the place on her.

Including his. That man. That awful, smug-faced, egotistical man.

Was he Nicholas's guardian? Well, former guardian. Damian Skouras, wasn't that the name? That had to be him, considering where he'd been standing.

One look, and she'd known everything she needed to know about Damian Skouras. Unfortunately she knew the type well. He had the kind of looks women went crazy for: wide shoulders, narrow waist, a hard body and a handsome face with eyes that seemed to blaze like blue flame against his olive skin. His hair swept back from his face like the waves on a midnight sea, and a tiny gold stud glittered in one ear.

Looks and money, both, Laurel thought bitterly. It wasn't just the Armani dinner jacket and black trousers draped down those long, muscled legs that had told her so, it was the way he held himself, with careless, masculine arrogance. It was also the way he'd looked at her, as if she were a new toy, all gift-wrapped and served up for his pleasure. His smile had been polite but his eyes had said it all.

"Baby," those eyes said, "I'd like to peel off that dress and see what's underneath."

Not in *this* lifetime, Laurel thought coldly.

She was tired of it, sick of it, if the truth were told. The world was filled with too many insolent men who'd let money and power go to their heads.

Hadn't she spent almost a year playing the fool for one of them?

The rest of the wedding party was passing by now, bridesmaids giggling among themselves in a pastel flurry of blues and pinks, the groomsmen grinning foolishly, impossibly young and good-looking in their formal wear. Annie went by with her ex and paused only long enough for a quick hug after which Laurel fell back into the crowd, letting it surge past her because she knew *he'd* be coming along next, the jerk who'd stared at her and stripped her naked with his eyes…and yes, there he was, bringing up the rear of the little procession with one of the bridesmaids, a child no more than half his age, clinging to his arm like a limpet.

The girl was staring up at him with eyes like saucers while he treated her to a full measure of his charm, smiling at her with his too-white teeth glinting against his too-tanned skin. Laurel frowned. The child was positively transfixed by the body-by-health club, tan-by-sunlamp and attitude-by-bank-balance. And Mr. Macho was eating up the adulation.

Bastard, Laurel thought coldly, eyeing him through the crowd, and before she had time to think about it, she stepped out in the aisle in front of him.

The bridesmaid was so busy making goo-goo eyes at her dazzling escort that she had to skid to a stop when he halted.

"What's the matter?" the girl asked.

"Nothing," he answered, his eyes never leaving Laurel's.

The girl looked at Laurel. Young as she was, awareness glinted in her eyes.

"Come on, Damian. We have to catch up to the others."

He nodded. "You go on, Elaine. "I'll be right along."

"It's Aileen."

"Aileen," he said, his eyes still on Laurel. "Go ahead. I'll be just behind you."

The girl shot Laurel a sullen glare. "Sure." Then she picked up her skirts and hurried along after the others.

Close up, Laurel could see that the man's eyes were a shade of blue she'd never seen before, cool and pale, the irises as black-ringed as if they'd been circled with kohl. Ice, she thought, chips of polar sea ice.

A pulse began to pound in her throat. I should have stayed where I was, she thought suddenly, instead of stepping out to confront him...

"Yes?" he said.

His voice, low and touched with a slight accent, was a perfect match for the chilly removal of his gaze.

The church was empty now. A few feet away, just beyond the doors, Laurel could hear the sounds of laughter but here, in the silence and the lengthening shadows of late afternoon, she could hear only the *thump-thump* of her heart.

"Was there something you wished to say to me?"

His words were polite but the coldness in them made Laurel's breath catch. For a second, she thought of turning and running but she'd never run from anything in her life. Besides, why should she let this stranger get the best of her?

There was nothing to be afraid of, nothing at all.

So she drew herself up to her full five foot ten, tossed her hair back from her face and fixed him with a look of cool *hauteur*, the same one she wore like a mask when she was on public display, and that had helped make her a star on runways from here to Milan.

"Only that you look pathetic," she said regally, "toying with that little girl."

"Toying with...?"

"Really," she said, permitting her voice to take on a purr of amusement, "don't you think you ought to play games with someone who's old enough to recognize you for what you are?"

The man looked at her for a long moment, so long that she foolishly began to think she'd scored a couple of points. Then he smiled in a way that sent her heart skidding up into her throat and he stepped forward, until he was only a hand's span away.

"What is your name?"

"Laurel," she said, "Laurel Bennett, but I don't see—"

"I agree completely, Miss Bennett. The game is far more enjoyable when it is played by equals."

She saw what was coming next in his eyes, but it was too late. Before Laurel could move or even draw back, he reached out, took her in his arms and kissed her.

CHAPTER TWO

LAUREL SHOT a surreptitious glance at her watch.

Another hour, and she could leave without attracting attention. Only another hour—assuming she could last that long.

The man beside her at the pink-and-white swathed table for six, Evan Something-or-Other, was telling a joke. Dr. Evan Something-or-Other, as Annie, ever the matchmaker, had pointedly said, when she'd come around earlier to greet her guests.

He was a nice enough man, even if his pink-tipped nose and slight overbite did remind Laurel of a rabbit. It was just that this was the doctor's joke number nine or maybe nine thousand for the evening. She'd lost count somewhere between the shrimp cocktail and the *Beouf aux Chanterelles*.

Not that it mattered. Laurel would have had trouble keeping her mind on anything this evening. Her thoughts kept traveling in only one direction, straight towards Damian Skouras, who was sitting at the table on the dais with an expensively dressed blond windup doll by his side—not that the presence of the woman was keeping him from watching Laurel.

She knew he was, even though she hadn't turned to confirm it. There was no need. She could feel the force of his eyes on her shoulder blades. If she looked at him, she half expected to see a pair of blue laser beams blazing from that proud, arrogant face.

The one thing she *had* confirmed was that he was definitely Damian Skouras, and he was Nicholas's guardian. Former guardian, anyway; Nick was twenty-one, three years past needing to ask anyone's permission to marry. Laurel knew that her sister hadn't wanted the wedding to take place. Dawn and Nick were too young, she'd said. Laurel had kept her own counsel but now that she'd met the man who'd raised Nick, she was amazed her sister hadn't raised yet a second objection.

Who would want a son-in-law with an egotistical SOB like Damian Skouras for a role model?

That was how she thought of him, as an Egotistical SOB, and in capital letters. She'd told him so the next time she'd seen him, after that kiss, when they'd come face-to-face on the receiving line. She'd tried breezing past him as if he didn't exist, but he'd made that impossible, capturing her hand in his, introducing himself as politely as if they'd never set eyes on each other until that second.

Flushed with indignation, Laurel had tried to twist her hand free. That had made him laugh.

"Relax, Miss Bennett," he'd said in a low, mocking tone. "You don't want to make another scene, do you? Surely one such performance a day is enough, even for you."

"I'm not the one who made a scene, you—you—"

"My name is Damian Skouras."

He was laughing at her, damn him, and enjoying every second of her embarrassment.

"Perhaps you enjoy attracting attention," he'd said. "If so, by all means, go on as you are. But if you believe, as I do, that today belongs to Nicholas and his bride, then be a good girl, smile prettily and pretend you're having a good time, hmm?"

He was right, and she knew it. The line had bogged down behind her and people were beginning to crane their necks with interest, trying to see who and what was holding things up. So she'd smiled, not just prettily but brilliantly, as if she were on a set instead of at a wedding, and said, in a voice meant to be heard by no one but him, that she was hardly surprised he still thought it appropriate to address a woman as a girl and that she'd have an even better time if she pretended he'd vanished from the face of the earth.

His hand had tightened on hers and his eyes had glinted with a sudden darkness that almost made her wish she'd kept her mouth shut.

"You'll never be able to pretend anything when it comes to me," he'd said softly, "or have you forgotten what happened when I kissed you?"

Color had shot into her face. He'd smiled, let her snatch her hand from his, and she'd swept past him.

No, she hadn't forgotten. How could she? There'd been that first instant of shocked rage and then, following hard on its heels, the dizzying realization that she was suddenly clinging to his broad shoulders, that her mouth was softening and parting under his, that she was making a little sound in the back of her throat and moving against him...

"...well," Evan Something-or-Other droned, "if that's the case, said the chicken, I guess there's not much point crossing to the other side!"

Everybody at the table laughed. Laurel laughed, too, if a beat too late.

"Great story," someone chuckled.

Evan smiled, lifted his glass of wine, and turned to Laurel.

"I guess you heard that one before," he said apologetically.

"No," she said quickly, "no, I haven't. I'm just—I think it must be jet lag. I was in Paris just yesterday and I don't think my head's caught up to the clock." She smiled. "Or vice versa."

"Paris, huh? Wonderful city. I was there last year. A business conference."

"Ah."

"Were you there on business? Or was it a vacation?"

"Oh, it was business."

"I guess you're there a lot."

"Well…"

"For showings. That's what they call them, right?"

"Well, yes, but how did you—"

"I recognized you." Evan grinned. "Besides, Annie told me. I'm her dentist, hers and Dawn's, and the last time she came by for a checkup she said, 'Wait until you meet my baby sister at the wedding. She's the most gorgeous model in the world.'" His grin tilted. "But she was wrong."

"Was she?" Laurel asked, trying to sound interested. She knew what came next. If the doctor thought this was a new approach, he was sadly mistaken.

"Absolutely. You're not the most gorgeous model in the world, you're the most gorgeous woman, hands down."

Drum roll, lights up, Laurel thought, and laughed politely. "You'll have to forgive Annie. She's an inveterate matchmaker."

"At least she didn't exaggerate." He chuckled and leaned closer. "You should see some of the so-called 'dream dates' I've been conned into."

"This isn't a date, Doctor."

His face crumpled just a little and Laurel winced. There was no reason to let her bad mood out on him.

"I meant," she said with an apologetic smile, "I know what you're saying. I've been a victim of some pretty sneaky setups, myself."

"Matchmakers." Evan shook his head. "They never let up, do they? And I wish you'd call me 'Evan.'"

"Evan," Laurel said. "And you're right, they never do."

"Annie wasn't wrong, though, was she?" Evan cleared his throat. "I mean, you are, ah, uninvolved and unattached?"

Annie, Laurel thought wearily, what am I going to do with you? Her sister had been trying to marry her off for years. She'd really gone into overdrive after Laurel had finally walked out on Kirk.

"Okay," Annie had said, "so at first, you didn't want to settle down because you had to build your career. Then you convinced yourself that jerk would pop the question, but, big surprise, he didn't."

"I don't want to talk about it," Laurel had replied, but Annie had plowed on, laying out the joys of matrimony as if she hadn't untied her own marriage vows years before, and eventually Laurel had silenced her by lying through her teeth and saying that if the right man ever came along, she supposed she'd agree to tie the knot....

But not in this lifetime. Laurel's mouth firmed. So far as she could see, the only things a woman needed a man for was to muscle open a jar and provide sex. Well, there were gizmos on the market that dealt with tight jar lids. As for sex...it was overrated. That was something else she'd learned during her time with Kirk. Maybe it meant more to women who didn't have careers. Maybe there was a woman somewhere who heard music and saw fireworks when she was in bed with a man but if you had a life, sex was really nothing more than a biological urge, like eating or drinking, and certainly not anywhere near as important.

"Sorry," Evan said, "I guess I shouldn't have asked."

Laurel blinked. "Shouldn't have...?

"If you were, you know, involved."

"Oh." She cleared her throat. "Oh, no, don't apologize. I'm, ah, I'm flattered you'd ask. It's just that, well, what with all the traveling I do—"

"Miss Bennett?"

Laurel stiffened. She didn't have to turn around to know who'd come up behind her. Nobody could have put such a world of meaning into the simple use of her name—nobody but Damian Skouras.

She looked up. He was standing beside her chair, smiling pleasantly.

"Yes?" she said coldly.

"I thought you might like to dance."

"You thought wrong."

"Ah, but they're playing our song."

Laurel stared at him. For the most part, she'd been ignoring the band. Now, she realized that a medley of sixties hits had given way to a waltz.

"Our sort of song, at any rate," Damian said. "An old-fashioned waltz, for an old-fashioned girl." His smile tilted. "Sorry. I suppose I should say 'woman.'"

"You suppose correctly, Mr. Skouras. Not that it matters. Girl or woman, I'm not interested."

"In waltzing?"

"Waltzing is fine." Laurel's smile was the polite equal of his. "It's you I'm not interested in, on the dance floor or off it."

Across the table, there was a delighted intake of breath. Every eye had to be on her now and she knew it, but she didn't care. Not anymore. Damian Skouras had taken this as far as she was going to allow.

"You must move in very strange circles, Miss Bennett. In my world, a dance is hardly a request for an assignation."

Damn the man! He wasn't put off by what she'd said, or even embarrassed. He was amused by it, smiling first at her and then at the woman who'd gasped, and somehow managing to turn things around so that it was Laurel who looked foolish.

It wasn't easy, but she managed to dredge up a smile.

"And in mine," she said sweetly, "a man who brings his girlfriend to a party and then spends his time hitting on another woman is called a—"

"Hey," a cheerful voice said, "how's it going here? Everybody having a good time?"

Laurel looked over her shoulder. The bride and groom had come up on her other side and were beaming at the tableful of guests.

"Yes," someone finally said, after some throat-clearing, "we're having a splendid time, Nicholas."

"Great. Glad to hear it." Nick grinned. "One thing I learned, watching the ladies set up the seating chart, is that you never know how these table arrangements are going to work out." He looked at Laurel, then at Damian, and his grin broadened. "Terrific! I see that you guys managed to meet on your own."

The woman opposite Laurel made a choked sound and lifted her napkin to her lips.

Damian nodded. "We did, indeed," he said smoothly.

Dawn leaned her head against her groom's shoulder. "We just knew you two would have a lot to talk about."

I don't believe this, Laurel thought. *I'm trapped in a room filled with matchmakers.*

"Really," she said politely.

"Uh-huh."

"Name one thing."

Dawn's brows lifted. "Sorry?"

"Name one thing we'd have to talk about," Laurel said pleasantly, even while a little voice inside her warned her it was time to shut up.

The woman across the table made another choking sound. Dawn shot Nick a puzzled glance. Gallantly he picked up the slack.

"Well," he said, "the both of you do a lot of traveling."

"Indeed?"

"Take France, for instance."

"France?"

"Yeah. Damian just bought an apartment in Paris. We figured you could clue him in on the best places to buy stuff. You know, furniture, whatever, considering that you spend so much time there."

"I don't," Laurel said quickly. She looked at Evan, sitting beside her, and she cleared her throat. "I mean, I don't spend half as much time in Paris as I used to."

"Where do you spend your time, then?" Damian asked politely.

Where didn't he spend his? Laurel made a quick mental inventory of all the European cities a man like this would probably frequent.

"New York," she said, and knew instantly it had been the wrong choice.

"What a coincidence," Damian said with a little smile. "I've just bought a condominium in Manhattan."

"You said it was Paris."

"Paris, Manhattan..." His shoulders lifted, then fell, in an elegant shrug. "My business interests take me to many places, Miss Bennett, and I much prefer coming home to my own things at night."

"Like the blonde who came with you today?" Laurel said sweetly.

"Aunt Laurrr-el!" Dawn said, with a breathless laugh.

"It's quite all right, Dawn," Damian said softly, his eyes on Laurel's. "Your aunt and I understand each other—don't we, Miss Bennett?"

"Absolutely, Mr. Skouras." Laurel turned to the dentist, who was sitting openmouthed, a copy of virtually everyone else at the table. "Would you like to dance, Evan?"

A flush rose on his face. He looked up at Damian.

"But—I mean, I thought..."

"You thought wrong, sir." Damian's tone was polite but Laurel wasn't fooled. Anger glinted in his eyes. "While we've all been listening to Miss Bennett's interesting views, I've had the chance to reconsider." He turned to Dawn and smiled pleasantly. "My dear, I would be honored if you would desert Nicholas long enough to grant me the honor of this dance."

Dawn smiled with relief. "I'd be thrilled."

She went into his arms at the same time Laurel went into Evan's. Nick pulled out Evan's chair, spun it around and sat down. He draped his arms over the back and made some light remark about families and family members that diverted the attention of the others and set them laughing.

So much for Damian Skouras, Laurel thought with satisfaction as she looked over Evan's shoulder. Perhaps next time, he'd think twice before trying to play what were certainly his usual games with a woman.

Gabriella Boldini crossed and recrossed her long legs under the dashboard of Damian's rented Saab.

"Honestly, Damian," she said crossly, "I don't know why you didn't arrange for a limousine."

Damian sighed, kept his attention focused on the winding mountain road and decided there was no point in responding to the remark she'd already made half a dozen times since they'd left Stratham.

"We'll be at the inn soon," he said. "Why don't you put your head back and try and get some sleep?"

"I am not tired, Damian, I'm simply saying—"

"I know what you're saying. You'd have preferred a different car."

Gabriella folded her arms. "That's right."

"A Cadillac, or a Lincoln, with a chauffeur."

"Yes. Or you could have had Stevens drive us up here. There's no reason we couldn't have been comfortable, even though we're trapped all the way out in the sticks."

Damian laughed. "We're hardly in the 'sticks', Gaby. The inn's just forty miles from Boston."

"For goodness' sakes, must you take me so literally? I know where it is. We spent last night there, didn't we?" Gabriella crossed her legs again. If the skirt of her black silk dress rode any higher on her thighs, Damian thought idly, it would disappear. "Which reminds me. Since that place doesn't have room service—"

"It has room service."

"There you go again, taking me literally. It doesn't have room service, not after ten o'clock at night. Don't you remember what happened when I tried to order a pot of tea last night?''

Damian's hands flexed on the steering wheel. "I remember, Gaby. The manager offered to brew you some tea and bring it up to our suite himself."

"Nonsense. I wanted herbal tea, not that stuff in a bag. And I've told you over and over, I don't like it when you call me Gaby."

What the hell is this? Damian thought wearily. He was not married to this woman but anyone listening to them now would think they'd been at each other's throats for at least a decade of blissful wedlock.

Not that a little sharp-tongued give-and-take wasn't sometimes amusing. The woman at Nicholas's wedding, for instance. Laurel Bennett had infuriated him, at the end, doing her damnedest to make him look foolish in front of Nicholas and all the others, but he had to admit, she was clever and quick.

"'Gaby' always makes me think of some stupid character in a bad Western."

She was stunning, too. The more he'd seen of her, the more he'd become convinced he'd never seen a more exquisite face. She was a model, Dawn had told him, and he'd always thought models were androgynous things, all bones and no flesh, but Laurel Bennett had been rounded and very definitely feminine. Had that been the real reason he'd asked her to dance, so he could hold that sweetly curved body in his arms and see for himself if she felt as soft as she looked?

"Must you drive so fast? I can barely see where we're going, it's so miserably dark outside."

Damian's jaw tightened. He pressed down just a little harder on the gas.

"I like to drive fast," he said. "And since I'm the one at the wheel, you don't have to see outside, now do you?"

He waited for her to respond, but not even Gabriella was

that foolish. She sat back instead, arms still folded under her breasts, her head lifted in a way he'd come to know meant she was angry.

The car filled with silence. Damian was just beginning to relax and enjoy it when she spoke again.

"Honestly," she said, "you'd think people would use some common sense."

Damian shot her a quick look. "Yes," he said, grimly, "you would."

"Imagine the nerve of that woman."

"What woman?"

"The one who made that grand entrance. You know, the woman with that mass of dyed red hair."

Damian almost laughed. Now, at least, he knew what this was all about.

"Was it dyed?" he asked casually. "I didn't think so."

"You wouldn't," Gabriella snapped. "Men never do. You're all so easily taken in."

We are, indeed, he thought. What had happened to Gabriella's sweet nature and charming Italian accent? The first had begun disappearing over the past few weeks; the second had slipped away gradually during the past hour.

"And that dress. Honestly, if that skirt had been any shorter…"

Damian glanced at Gabriella's legs. Her own skirt, which had never done more than flirt with the tops of her thighs, had vanished along with what was left of her pleasant disposition and sexy accent.

"She's Dawn's aunt, I understand."

"Who?" Damian said pleasantly.

"Don't be dense." Gabriella took a deep breath. "That woman," she said, more calmly, "the one with the cheap-looking outfit and the peroxide hair."

"Ah," he said. The turnoff for the inn was just ahead. He slowed the car, signaled and started up the long gravel driveway. "The model."

"Model, indeed. Everyone knows what those women are like. That one, especially." Gabriella was stiff with indignation. "They say she's had dozens of lovers."

The car hit a rut in the road. Damian, eyes narrowed, gave the wheel a vicious twist.

"Really," he said calmly.

"Honestly, Damian, I wish you'd slow—"

"What else do they say about her?"

"About...?" Gabriella shot him a quick glance. Then she reached forward, yanked down the sun visor and peered into the mirror on its reverse side. "I don't pay attention to gossip," she said coolly, as she fluffed her fingers through her artfully arranged hair. "But what *is* there to say about someone who poses nude?"

A flash fire image of Laurel Bennett, naked and flushed in his bed, seared the mental canvas of Damian's mind. He forced himself to concentrate on the final few yards of the curving road.

"Nude?" he said calmly.

"To all intents and purposes. She did an ad for Calvin Klein—it's in this month's *Chic* or maybe *Femme*, I'm not sure which." Gabriella snapped the visor back into place. "Oh, it was all very elegant and posh, you know, one of those la-di-da arty shots taken through whatever it is they use, gauze, I suppose." Her voice fairly purred with satisfaction. "She'd need it, wouldn't she, seeing that she's a bit long in the tooth? Still, gauze or no gauze, when you came right down to it, there she was, stark naked."

The picture of Laurel burned in his brain again. Damian cleared his throat. "Interesting."

"Cheap is a better word. Totally cheap...which is why I just don't understand what made you bother with her."

"You're talking nonsense, Gabriella."

"I saw the way you looked at her and let me tell you, I didn't much like it. You have an obligation to me."

Damian pulled up at the entrance to the inn, shut off the engine and turned toward her.

"Obligation?" he said carefully.

"That's right. We've been together for a long time now. Doesn't that mean anything to you?"

"I have not been unfaithful to you."

"That's not what I'm talking about and you know it." She took a deep breath. "Can you really tell me you sat through that entire wedding without feeling a thing?"

"I felt what I always feel at weddings," he said quietly. "Disbelief that two people should willingly subject themselves to such nonsense along with the hope, however useless, that they make a success of what is basically an unnatural arrangement."

Gabriella's mouth thinned. "How can you say such a thing?"

"I say it because it's true. You knew that was how I felt, from the start. You said your attitude mirrored mine."

"Never mind what I said," Gabriella said sharply. "And you haven't answered my question. Why did you keep looking at that woman?"

Because I chose to. Because you don't own me. Because Laurel Bennett intrigues me as you never did, not even when our affair first began.

Damian blew out his breath. It was late, they were both tired and this wasn't the time to talk or make decisions. He ran his knuckles lightly over Gabriella's cheek, then reached across her lap and opened her door.

"Go on," he said gently. "Wait in the lobby while I park the car."

"You see what I mean? If we'd come by limousine, you wouldn't have to drop me off here, in the middle of nowhere. But no, you had to do things your way, with no regard for me or my feelings."

Damian glanced past Gabriella, to the brightly lit entrance to the inn. Then he looked at his mistress's face, illuminated by the cruel fluorescent light that washed into the car, and saw that it wasn't as lovely as he'd once thought, especially not with petulance and undisguised jealousy etched into every feature.

"Gaby," he said quietly, "it's late. Let's not argue about this now."

"Don't think you can shut me up by sounding sincere, Damian. And I keep telling you, my name's not Gaby!"

A muscle knotted in his jaw. He reached past her again, grasped the handle, slammed the door closed and put the Saab in gear.

"Wait just a minute! I'm not going with you while you park the car. If you think I have any intention of walking through that gravel in these shoes..." Gabriella frowned as Damian pulled through the circular driveway and headed downhill. "Damian? What are you doing?"

"What does it look like I'm doing?" He kept his eyes straight ahead, on the road. "I'm driving to New York."

"Tonight? But it's late. And what about my things? My clothes and my makeup? Damian, this is ridiculous!"

"I'll phone the inn and tell them to pack everything and forward it, as soon as I've dropped you off."

"Dropped me off?" Gabriella twisted toward him. "What do you mean? I never go back to my own apartment on weekends, you know that."

"What you said was true, a few minutes ago," he said, almost gently, "I do have an obligation to you." He looked across the console at her, then back at the road. "An obligation to tell you the truth, which is that I've enjoyed our time together, but—"

"But what? What is this, huh? The big brush-off?"

"Gabriella, calm down."

"Don't you tell me to calm down," she said shrilly. "Listen here, Mr. Skouras, maybe you can play high-and-mighty with the people who work for you but you can't pull that act with me!"

"I'd like us to end this like civilized adults. We both knew our relationship wouldn't last forever."

"Well, I changed my mind! How dare you toss me aside, just because you found yourself some two-bit—"

"I've found myself nothing." His voice cut across hers, harsh and cold. "I'm simply telling you that our relationship has run its course."

"That's what *you* think! What *I* think is that you led me to have certain expectations. My lawyer says…"

Gabriella stopped in midsentence, her mouth opening and closing as if she were a fish, but it was too late. Damian had already pulled onto the shoulder of the road. He swung toward her, and she shrank back in her seat at the expression on his face.

"Your lawyer says?" His voice was low, his tone dangerous. "You mean, you've already discussed our relationship with an attorney?"

"No. Well, I mean, I had a little chat with—look, Damian, I was just trying to protect myself." In the passing headlights of an oncoming automobile, he could see her face harden. "And it looks as if I had every reason to! Here you are, trying to dump me without so much as a by-your-leave—"

Damian reached out and turned on the radio. He punched buttons until he found a station playing something loud enough to drown out Gabriella's voice. Then he swung back onto the road and stepped down, hard, on the gas.

Less than three hours later, they were in Manhattan. Sunday night traffic was sparse, and it took only minutes for him to reach Gabriella's apartment building on Park Avenue.

The doorman hurried up. Gabriella snarled at him to leave her alone as she stepped from the car.

"Bastard," she hissed, as Damian gunned the engine.

For all he knew, she was still staring after him and spewing venom as he drove off. Not that it mattered. She was already part of the past.

CHAPTER THREE

Jean Kaplan had been Damian Skouras's personal assistant for a long time.

She was middle-aged, happily married and dedicated to her job. She was also unflappable. Nothing fazed her.

Still, she couldn't quite mask her surprise when her boss strode into the office Monday morning, said a brisk, "Hello," and then instructed her to personally go down to the newsstand on the corner and purchase copies of every fashion magazine on display.

"Fashion magazines, Mr. Skouras?"

"Fashion magazines, Ms. Kaplan." Damian's expression was completely noncommittal. "I'm sure you know the sort of thing I mean. *Femme*, *Chic*...all of them."

Jean nodded. "Certainly, sir."

Well, she thought as she hurried to the elevator, her boss had never been anyone's idea of a conventional executive. She permitted herself a faint smile as the doors whisked open at the lobby level. When you headed up what the press loved to refer to as the Skouras Empire, you didn't have to worry about that kind of thing.

Maybe he was thinking of buying a magazine. Or two, or three, she thought as she swept up an armload of glossy publications, made her way back to her employer's thirtieth floor office and neatly deposited them on his pale oak desk.

"Here you are, Mr. Skouras. I hope the assortment is what you wanted."

Damian nodded. "I'm sure it is."

"And shall I send the usual roses to Miss Boldini?"

He looked up and she saw in his eyes a flash of the Arctic

coldness that was faced by those who were foolish enough to oppose him in business.

"That won't be necessary."

"Oh. I'm sorry, sir. I just thought…"

"In fact, if Miss Boldini calls, tell her I'm not in."

"Yes, sir. Will that be all?"

Damian's dark head was already bent over the stack of magazines.

"That's all. Hold my calls until I ring you, please."

Jean nodded and shut the door behind her.

So, she thought with some satisfaction, Gabriella Boldini, she of the catlike smile and claws to match, had reached the end of her stay. Not a minute too soon, as far as she was concerned. Jean had seen a lot of women flounce through her employer's life, all of them beautiful and most of them charming or at least clever enough to show a pleasant face to her. But Gabriella Boldini had set her teeth on edge from day one.

Jean settled herself at her desk and turned on her computer. Perhaps that was why Mr. Skouras had wanted all those magazines. He'd be living like a monk for the next couple of months; he always did, after an affair ended. What better time to research a new business venture? Soon enough, though, another stunning female would step into his life, knowing she was just a temporary diversion but still hoping to snare a prize catch like him.

They always hoped, even though he never seemed to know it.

Jean gave a motherly sigh. As for herself, she'd given up hoping. There'd been a time she'd clung to the belief that her boss would find himself a good woman to love. Not anymore. He'd had one disastrous marriage that he never talked about and it had left him a confirmed loner.

Amazing, how a man so willing to risk everything making millions could refuse to take any risks at all, in matters of the heart.

*   *   *

Damian frowned as he looked over the magazines spilling across his desk.

Headlines screamed at him.

Are You Sexy Enough to Keep Your Man Interested?
Ten Ways to Turn Him On
Sexy Styles for Summer
The Perfect Tan Starts Now

Was there really a market for such drivel? He'd seen Gabriella curled up in a chair, leafing through magazines like these, but he'd never paid any attention to the print on the covers.

Or to the models, he thought, his frown deepening as he leafed through the glossy pages. Why did so many of them look as if they hadn't eaten in weeks? Surely, no real man could find women like these attractive, with their bones almost protruding through their skin.

And those pouting faces. He paused, staring at an emaciated-looking waif with a heavily made-up face who looked up from the page with an expression that made her appear to have sucked on one lemon too many.

Who would find such a face attractive?

After a moment, he sighed, closed the magazine and reached for another. Laurel's photograph wasn't where Gabriella had said it would be. Not that it mattered. There'd been no good reason to want to see the picture; he'd directed his secretary to buy these silly things on a whim.

Come on, man, who are you kidding?

It hadn't been a whim at all. The truth was that he'd slept poorly, awakening just after dawn from a fragmented dream filled with the kinds of images he hadn't had in years, his loins heavy and aching with need...

And there it was. The photograph of Laurel Bennett.

Gabriella had been wrong. Laurel wasn't nude, and he

tried to ignore the sense of relief that welled so fiercely inside him at the realization.

She'd been posed with her back to the camera, her head turned, angled so that she was looking over her shoulder at the viewer. Her back and shoulders were bare; a long length of ivory silk was draped from her hips, dipping low enough to expose the delicate tracery of her spine almost to its base. Her hair, that incredible mane of sun-streaked mahogany, tumbled over her creamy skin like tongues of dark flame.

Damian stared at the picture. All right, he told himself coldly, there she is. A woman, nothing more and nothing less. Beautiful, yes, and very desirable, but hardly worth the heated dreams that had disturbed his night.

He closed the magazine, tossed it on top of the others and carried the entire stack to a low table that was part of a conversational grouping at the other end of his office. Jean could dispose of them later, either toss them out or give them to one of the clerks. He certainly had no need for them, nor had he any further interest in Laurel Bennett.

That was settled, then. Damian relaxed, basking in the satisfaction that came of closure.

His morning was filled with opportunities for that same feeling, but it never came again.

There was a problem with a small investment firm Skouras International had recently acquired. Damian's CPAs had defined it but they hadn't been able to solve it. He did, during a two-hour brainstorming session. A short while later, he held a teleconference with his bankers in Paris and Hamburg, and firmed up a multimillion dollar deal that had been languishing for months.

At twenty of twelve, he began going through the notes Jean had placed on a corner of his desk in preparation for his one o'clock business luncheon, but he couldn't concentrate. Words kept repeating themselves, and entire sentences.

He gave up, pushed back his chair and frowned.

Suddenly he felt restless.

He rose and paced across the spacious room. There was always a carafe of freshly brewed coffee waiting for him on a corner shelf near the sofas that flanked the low table where he'd dumped the magazines.

He paused, frowning as he looked down at the stack. The magazine containing Laurel's photo was on top and he picked it up, opened it to that page and stared at the picture. Her hair looked like silk. Would it feel that way, or would it be stiff with hair spray when he touched it, the way Gabriella's had always been? How would her skin smell, when he put his face to that graceful curve where her shoulder and her neck joined? How would it taste?

Hell, what was the matter with him? He wasn't going to smell this woman, or taste her, or touch her.

His eyes fastened on her face. There was a hands-off coolness in her eyes that seemed at odds with her mouth, which looked soft, sexy, and heart-stoppingly vulnerable. It had felt that way, too, beneath his own, after she'd stopped fighting the passion that suddenly had gripped them both and given herself up to him, and to the kiss.

His belly knotted as he remembered the heat and hardness that had curled through his body. He couldn't remember ever feeling so caught up in a kiss or in the memory of what had been, after all, a simple encounter.

So caught up, and out of control.

Damian's jaw knotted. This was ridiculous. He was never out of control.

What he had, he thought coldly, was an itch, and it needed scratching.

One night, and that would be the end of it.

He could call Laurel, ask her to have drinks or dinner. It wouldn't be hard; he had learned early on that information was easy to come by, if you knew how to go about getting it.

She was stubborn, though. Her response to him had been fiery and he knew she wanted him as badly as he wanted her, but she'd deny it. He looked down at the ad again. She'd probably hang up the phone before he had the chance to—

A smile tilted at the corner of his mouth. Until this minute, he hadn't paid any attention to the advertisement itself. If pressed, he'd have said it was for perfume, or cosmetics. Perhaps furs.

Now he saw just how wrong he'd have been. Laurel was offering the siren song to customers in the market for laptop computers. And the company was one that Skouras International had bought only a couple of months ago.

Damian reached for the phone.

Luck was with him. Ten minutes later, he was in his car, his luncheon appointment canceled, forging through midday traffic on his way to a studio in Soho, where the next in the series of ads was being shot.

"Darling Laurel," Haskell said, "that's not a good angle. Turn your head to the right, please."

Laurel did.

"Now tilt toward me. Good."

What was good about it? she wondered. Not the day, surely. Not what she was doing. Why did everything, from toothpaste to tugboats, have to be advertised with sex?

"A little more. Yes, like that. Could you make it a bigger smile, please?"

She couldn't. Smiling didn't suit her mood.

"Laurel, baby, you've got to get into the swing of things. You look utterly, totally bored."

She *was* bored. But that was better than being angry. Don't think about it anymore, she told herself, just don't think about it.

Or him.

"Ah, Laurel, you're starting to scowl. Bad for the face,

darling. Relax. Think about the scene. You're on the deck of a private yacht in, I don't know, the Aegean.''

"The Caribbean," she snapped.

"What's the matter, you got something against the Greeks? Sure. The Caribbean. Whatever does it for you. Just get into it, darling. There you are, on a ship off the coast of Madagascar.''

"Madagascar's in Africa.''

"Jeez, give me a break, will you? Forget geography, okay? You're on a ship wherever you want, you're stretched out in the hot sun, using your Redwood laptop to write postcards to all your pals back home.''

"That's ridiculous, Haskell. You don't write postcards on a computer.''

Haskell glared at her. "Frankly, Laurel, I don't give a flying fig what you're using that thing for. Maybe you're writing your memoirs. Or tallying up the millions in your Swiss bank account. Whatever. Just get that imagination working and give us a smile.''

Laurel sighed. He was right. She was a pro, this was her job, and that was all there was to it. Unfortunately she'd slept badly and awakened in a foul mood. It didn't help that she felt like a ninny, posing in a bikini in front of a silly backdrop that simulated sea and sky. What did bikinis, sea and sky have to do with selling computers?

"Laurel, for heaven's sake, I'm losing you again. Concentrate, darling. Think of something pleasant and hang on to it. Where you're going to have supper tonight, for instance. How you spent your weekend. I know it's Monday, but there's got to be something you can imagine that's a turn-on.''

Where she was having supper tonight? Laurel almost laughed. At the kitchen counter, that was where, and on the menu was cottage cheese, a green salad and, as a special treat, a new mystery novel with her coffee.

As for how she'd spent the weekend—if Haskell only knew. That was the last thing he'd want her to think about.

To think she'd let Damian Skouras humiliate her like that!

"Hey, what's happening? Laurel, babe, you've gone from glum to grim in the blink of an eye. Come on, girl. Grab a happy thought and hang on."

A happy thought? A right cross, straight to Damian Skouras's jaw.

"Good!"

A knee, right where it would do the most good.

"Great!" Haskell began moving around her, his camera at his eye. "Hold that image, whatever it is, because it's working."

A nice, stiff-armed jab into his solar plexus.

"Wonderful stuff, Laurel. That's my girl!"

Why hadn't she done it? Because there'd already been too many eyes on them, that was why. Because if she'd done what she'd wanted to do, she'd have drawn the attention of everyone in the room, to say nothing of ruining Dawn's day.

"Look up, darling. That's it. Tilt your head. Good. This time, I want something that smolders. A smile that says your wonderful computer's what's made it possible for you to be out here instead of in your office, that in a couple of minutes you'll leave behind this glorious sun and sea, traipse down to the cabin and tumble into the arms of a gorgeous man." Haskell leaned toward her, camera whirring. "You do know a gorgeous man, don't you?"

Damian Skouras.

Laurel stiffened. Had she said the words aloud? No, thank goodness. Haskell was still dancing around her, his eye glued to his camera.

Damian Skouras, gorgeous? Don't be silly. Men weren't "gorgeous."

But he was. That masculine body. That incredible face,

with the features seemingly hewn out of granite. The eyes that were a blue she'd never seen before. And that mouth, looking as if it had been chiseled from a cold slab of marble but instead feeling warm and soft and exciting as it took hers.

"Now you've got it!" Haskell's camera whirred and clicked until the roll of film was done. Then he dumped the camera on his worktable and held out his hand. "Baby, that was great. The look on your face..." He sighed dramatically. "All I can say is, wow!"

Laurel put the computer on the floor, took Haskell's hand, rose to her feet and reached for the terry-cloth robe she'd left over the back of a chair.

"Are we finished?"

"We are, thanks to whatever flashed through your head just now." Haskell chuckled. "I don't suppose you'd like to tell me who he was?"

"It wasn't a 'he' at all," Laurel said, forcing a smile to her lips. "It was just what you suggested. I thought about what I was having for dinner tonight."

"No steak ever made a woman look like that," Haskell said with a lecherous grin. "Who's the lucky man, and why isn't it me?"

"Perhaps Miss Bennett's telling you the truth."

Laurel spun around. The slightly amused male voice had come from a corner of the cavernous loft, but where? The brightly lit set only deepened the darkness that lurked in the corners.

"After all, it's well past lunchtime."

Laurel's heart skipped a beat. No. No, it couldn't be...

Damian Skouras emerged from the shadows like a man stepping out of the mist.

"Hello, Miss Bennett."

For a minute, she could only gape at this man she'd hoped never to see again. Then she straightened, drew the robe more closely around her and narrowed her eyes.

"This isn't funny, Mr. Skouras."

"I'm glad to hear it, Miss Bennett, since comedy's not my forte."

"Laurel?" Haskell turned toward her. "You know this guy? I mean, you asked him to meet you here?"

"I do not know him," Laurel said coldly.

Damian smiled. "Of course she knows me. You heard her greet me by name just now, didn't you?"

"I don't know him, and I certainly didn't ask him to meet me here."

Haskell moved forward. "Okay, pal, you heard the lady. This isn't a public gallery. You want to do business with me, give my agent a call."

"My business is with Miss Bennett."

"Hey, what is it with you, buddy? You deaf? I just told you—"

"And I just told you," Damian said softly. He looked at the photographer. "This has nothing to do with you. I suggest you stay out of it."

Haskell's face turned red and he stepped forward. "Who's gonna make me?"

"No," Laurel said quickly, "Haskell, don't."

She knew Haskell was said to have a short fuse and a propensity for barroom brawls. She'd never seen him in action but she'd seen the results, cuts and bruises and once a black eye. Not that Damian Skouras didn't deserve everything Haskell could dish out, but she didn't want him beaten up, not on her account.

She needn't have worried. Even as she watched, the photographer looked into Damian's face, saw something that made him blanch and step back.

"I don't want any trouble in my studio," he muttered.

"There won't be any." Damian smiled tightly. "If it makes you feel better, I have every right to be here. Put in a call to the ad agency, tell them my name and they'll confirm it."

Laurel laughed. "You're unbelievable, do you know that?" She jabbed her hands on her hips and stepped around Haskell. "What will they confirm? That you're God?"

Damian looked at her. "That I own Redwood Computers."

"You're *that* Skouras?" Haskell said.

"I am."

"Don't be a fool, Haskell," Laurel snapped, her eyes locked on Damian's face. "Just because he claims he owns the computer company doesn't mean he does."

"Trust me," Haskell muttered, "I read about it in the paper. He bought the company."

Laurel's chin rose. "How nice for you, Mr. Skouras. That still doesn't give you the right to come bursting in here as if you owned this place, too."

Damian smiled. "That's true."

"It doesn't give you the right to badger me, either."

"I'm not badgering you, Miss Bennett. I heard there was a shoot here today, I was curious, and so I decided to come by."

Laurel's eyes narrowed. "It had nothing to do with me?"

"No," Damian said, lying through his teeth.

"In that case," she said, "you won't mind if I…"

He caught her arm as she started past him. "Have lunch with me."

"No."

"*The Four Seasons*? Or *The Water's Edge*? It's a beautiful day out, Miss Bennett."

"It was," she said pointedly, "until you showed up."

Haskell cleared his throat. "Well, listen," he said, as he backed away, "long as you two don't need me here…"

"Wait," Laurel said, "Haskell, you don't have to…"

But he was already gone. The sound of his footsteps echoed across the wooden floor. A door slammed, and then there was silence.

"Why must you make this so difficult?" Damian said softly.

"I'm not the one making this difficult," Laurel said coldly. She looked down at her wrist, still encircled by his hand, and then at him. "Let go of me, please."

Damian's gaze followed hers. Hell, he thought, what was he doing? This wasn't his style at all. When you came down to it, nothing he'd done since he'd laid eyes on this woman was in character. The way he'd gone after her yesterday, like a bull in rut. And what he'd done moments ago, challenging that photographer like a street corner punk when the man had only been coming to Laurel's rescue. All he'd been able to think, watching the man's face, was, Go on, take your best shot at me, so I can beat you to a pulp.

And that was crazy. He wasn't a man who settled things with his fists. Not anymore; not in the years since he'd worked his way up from summer jobs on the Brooklyn docks to a Park Avenue penthouse.

He wasn't a man who went after a woman with such single-minded determination, either. Why would he, when there were always more women than he could possibly want, ready and waiting to be singled out for his attention?

That was it. That was what was keeping his interest in the Bennett woman. She was uninterested, or playing at being uninterested, though he didn't believe it, not after the way she'd kissed him yesterday. Either way, the cure was the same. Bed her, then forget her. Satisfy this most primitive of urges and she'd be out of his system, once and for all.

But dammit, man, be civilized about it.

Damian let go of her wrist, took a breath and began again.

"Miss Bennett. Laurel. I know we got off to a poor start—"

"You're wrong. We didn't get off to any start. You're

playing cat-and-mouse games but as far as I'm concerned, we never even met.''

"Well, we can remedy that. Have dinner with me this evening.''

"I'm busy.''

"Tomorrow night, then.''

"Still busy. And, before you ask, I'm busy for the fore-seeable future.''

He laughed, and her eyes flashed with indignation.

"Did I say something funny, Mr. Skouras?''

"It's Damian. And I was only wondering which of us is pretending what?''

"Which of us…'' Color flew into her face. "My God, what an insufferable ego you must have! Do you think this is a game? That I'm playing hard to get?''

He leaned back against the edge of the photographer's worktable, his jacket open and his hands tucked into the pockets of his trousers.

"The thought crossed my mind, yes.''

"Listen here, Mr. Skouras…''

"Damian.''

"*Mr.* Skouras.'' Laurel's eyes narrowed. "Let me put this in words so simple even you'll understand. One, I do not like you. Two, I do not like you. And three, I am not interested in lunch. Or dinner. Or anything else.''

"Too many men already on the string?''

God, she itched to slap that smug little smile from his face!

"Yes,'' she said, "exactly. I've got them lined up for mornings, afternoons and evenings, and there're even a couple of special ones I manage to tuck in at teatime. So as you can see, I've no time at all for you in my schedule.''

He was laughing openly now, amusement glinting in his eyes, and it was driving her over the edge. She *would* slug him, any second, or punch him in the very center of that oh-so-masculine chest…

*Or throw her arms around his neck, drag his head down
to hers and kiss him until he swung her into his arms and
carried her off into the shadows that rimmed the lighted
set...*

"Laurel?" Damian said, and their eyes met.

He knew. She could see it in the way he was looking at
her. He'd stopped laughing and he knew what she'd
thought, what she'd almost done.

"No," she said, and she swung away blindly. She heard
him call her name but she didn't turn back, didn't pause.
Moving by instinct, impelled by fear not of Damian but of
herself, she ran to the dressing room, flung open the door
and then slammed it behind her. She fell back against it
and stood trembling, with her heart thudding in her chest.

Outside, in the studio, Damian stood staring at the closed
door. His entire body was tense; he could feel the blood
pounding through his veins.

She'd been so angry at him. Furious, even more so because he'd been teasing her and she'd known it. And then,
all at once, everything had changed. He'd seen the shock
of sudden awareness etch into her lovely face and he'd
understood it, felt it burn like flame straight into the marrow
of his bones.

She'd run not from him but from herself. All he had to
do was walk the few feet to the door that sheltered her,
open it and take her in his arms. One touch, and she would
shatter.

He would have her, and this insanity would be over.

Or would it?

He took a long, ragged breath. She was interesting, this
Laurel Bennett, and not only because of the fire that raged
under that cool exterior. Other things about her were almost
as intriguing. Her ability to play her part in what was
quickly becoming a complex game fascinated him, as did
her determination to deny what was so obviously happening
between them. She was an enigma. A challenge.

Damian smiled tightly. He had not confronted either in a very long time. It was part of the price he'd paid for success.

Perhaps he'd been wrong in thinking that he could get her out of his system by taking her to bed for a long night of passion. Laurel Bennett might prove a diversion that could please him for some time. And he sensed instinctively that, unlike Gabriella, she would not want nor ask for more.

The thought brought another smile to his lips. The women's libbers would hang him from his toes, maybe from a more sensitive part of his anatomy, and burn him in effigy if they ever heard him make such a cool appraisal of a woman, but they'd have been wrong.

He was no chauvinist, he was merely a man accustomed to making intelligent assessments. Laurel was a sophisticated woman who'd had many lovers. Even if Gabriella hadn't told him so, one look at her would have confirmed it. A brief, intense affair would give pleasure to them both.

He would go about this differently, then. He would have her, but not just once and not in a grimy loft. Damian ran his hands through his hair, straightened his tie and then made his way briskly out to the street.

CHAPTER FOUR

LAUREL'S APARTMENT took up the second floor of a converted town house on the upper east side of Manhattan. The rooms were sun-filled and pleasant, and the building itself was handsome and well located.

But it was an old building, and sometimes the plumbing was a problem. The landlord kept promising repairs but the handful of tenants figured he was almost as ancient as the plumbing. None of them had the heart to keep after him, especially when it turned out that Grey Morgan, the hunky soap star in apartment 3G, had been a plumber's apprentice back in the days when he'd still been known as George Mogenovitch of Brooklyn.

His pretty dancer wife, Susie, had turned into a close friend, but she was another in what Laurel thought of as a legion of inveterate matchmakers. At least she had learned to read the signs. When Susie made spaghetti and invited her to supper, she accepted happily. When the invitation was for Beef Stroganoff and a good bottle of wine, it was wise to plead an excuse.

Laurel smiled to herself. Susie and George were the most warmhearted people imaginable, which explained why she was sitting on the closed lid of the toilet in her bathroom with a bunch of tools in her lap while George stood in her bathtub and tried to figure out why no water at all was coming out of the shower.

"Sorry it's taking me so long," he said, grunting as he worked a wrench around a fitting. "But I think I've almost got it."

"Hey," Laurel said, "don't apologize. I'm just grateful you're willing to bother."

George flicked back his blond mane and shot her a grin.

"Susie wouldn't have it any other way," he said. "She figures it keeps me humble."

Laurel smiled. "Clever Susie."

Not that George needed to be kept humble. He was a nice guy. Success hadn't gone to his head the way it did with some men. Hand them some good looks, some money, fame and fortune, and what did you get?

A man like Damian Skouras, that's what. Laurel's mouth thinned. Or like Kirk Soames. What was it about her that attracted such superficial, self-centered bastards?

Of course, she hadn't seen it that way, not at first. She was a woman accustomed to making her own way in the world; she'd learned early on that many men were threatened by her fame, her independence, even her beauty. So when Kirk—powerful, rich and handsome—came on to her with wry certainty and assurance, she'd found it intriguing. By the time he'd asked her to move in with him, she'd been head over heels in love.

Annie had told her, straight out, that she was making a mistake.

"Move in with him?" she'd said. "What ever happened to, 'Marry me?'"

"He's cautious," Laurel had replied, in her lover's defense, "and why wouldn't he be? Marriage is a tough deal for a man like that."

"It's a tough deal for anybody," Annie had said wryly. "Still, if he loves you and you love him..."

"Annie, I'm thirty-two. I'm old enough to live with a man without the world coming to an end. Besides, I don't want to rush into anything, any more than Kirk does."

"Uh-huh," Annie had said, in a way that made it clear she knew Laurel was lying. And she was. She'd have married Kirk in a second, if he'd asked. And he *would* ask, given time. She'd been certain of that.

"Laurel?"

Laurel blinked, George was looking at her, his brows raised. "Hand me that other wrench, will you? The one with the black handle."

So she had moved in with Kirk, more or less, though she'd held on to her apartment. It had been his suggestion. He'd even offered to pay her rent, though she had refused. If she kept her apartment, he'd said, she'd have a place to stay when she had shoots or showings in the city because he lived thirty miles out, in a sprawling mansion on Long Island's North Shore.

"Bull," Annie had snorted. "The guy's a zillionaire. How come he doesn't have an apartment in the city?"

"Annie," Laurel had said patiently, "you don't understand. He needs the peace and quiet of the Long Island house."

In the end, it had turned out that he did have a Manhattan apartment. Laurel closed her eyes against the rush of painful memories. She'd learned about it by accident, fielding a phone call from a foolishly indiscreet building manager who'd wanted to check with Mr. Soames about a convenient time for some sort of repair to the terrace.

Puzzled, telling herself it was some sort of mistake or perhaps a surprise for her, Laurel had gone to the East side address and managed to slip inside when the doorman wasn't looking. She'd ridden the elevator to the twentieth floor, taken a deep breath and rung the bell of Apartment 2004.

Kirk had opened the door, dressed in a white terry-cloth robe. His face paled when he saw her but she had to give him credit; he recovered quickly.

"What are you doing here, Laurel?"

Before she could reply, a sultry voice called, "Kirk? Where are you, lover?" and a porcelain-skinned blonde wearing a matching robe and the flushed look that came of a long afternoon in bed, appeared behind him.

Laurel hadn't said a word. She hadn't even returned to

the Long Island house for her things. And when the story got out, as it was bound to do, the people who knew her sighed and said well, it was sad but they'd have sworn Kirk had changed, that once he'd asked her to move into that big house on the water they'd all figured it meant he'd finally decided to settle down...

"You got a bad diverter valve," George muttered, "but I've almost got it under control. Takes time, that's all."

Laurel gave him an absent smile. Everything took time. It had taken her months to get over the pain of Kirk's betrayal but once she had, she'd begun thinking about their affair with the cold, clear logic of hindsight and she'd found herself wondering what she'd ever found attractive about a man like that to begin with.

She'd mistaken his arrogance for self-assurance, his egotism for determination. She, who'd always prided herself on her control, had been stupidly taken in by sexual chemistry, and the truth was that not even that had really lived up to its promise. She'd never felt swept away by passion in Kirk's arms.

But Damian's kiss had done that. It had filled her with fire, and with a longing so hot and sweet it had threatened to destroy her.

The tools Laurel was holding fell from her suddenly nerveless fingers and clattered on the tile floor.

"You okay?" George said, glancing over at her.

"Sure," she said quickly, and she bent down and scooped up the tools.

Damian Skouras was not for her. He was nothing but an updated copy of Kirk, right down to the sexy blonde pouting in the background at the wedding.

"Gimme the screwdriver, Laurel," George said. "No, not the Phillips head. The other one."

Had the man really thought she wouldn't notice the blonde? Or didn't he think it mattered?

"Egotistical bastard," she muttered, slapping the screwdriver into George's outstretched hand.

"Hey, what'd I do?"

Laurel blinked. George was looking at her as if she'd lost her mind.

"Oh," she said, and flushed bright pink. "George, I'm sorry. I didn't mean you."

He gave her the boyish grin that kept American women glued to their TV sets from two to three every weekday afternoon.

"Glad to hear it. From the look on your face, I'd hate to be whoever it is you're thinking about."

She'd never been able to bring herself to tell Annie the truth of her breakup with Kirk, not because Annie might have said, "I told you so," but because the pain had been too sharp.

"You were right" was all she'd told her sister, "Kirk wasn't for me."

Maybe I should have told her, Laurel thought grimly. Maybe, if I had, Annie and Dawn and everybody else at that wedding would have known Damian Skouras for the belly-to-the-ground snake he was.

"Got it," George said in triumph. He handed her the screwdriver and flipped the selector lever up and down. "Just you watch. Soon as I get out of the tub and turn this baby on—"

"Just be careful," Laurel said. "Watch out for that puddle of water in the..."

Too late. George yelped, lost his footing and made a grab for the first thing that was handy. It was the on-off knob. Water came pouring out of the shower head.

"Damn," he shouted, and leaped back, but it was too late. He was soaked, and so was Laurel. Half the icy spray had shot in her direction. Sputtering, George pushed the knob back in, shut off the water and flung his dripping hair back from his eyes. He looked down at himself, then eyed

Laurel. "Well," he said wryly, "at least we know it works."

Laurel burst out laughing.

"Susie's going to think I tried to drown you," she said, tossing him a towel and dabbing at herself with another.

George yanked his soaked sweatshirt over his head and stepped out of the tub. His sneakers squished as he walked across the tile floor of the old-fashioned bathroom.

"I guess you'll have to phone old man Grissom," he said with a sheepish smile. "Tell him that valve's just about shot and he'd better send a plumber around to take a look."

"First thing in the morning," Laurel said, nodding. She mopped her face and hair, then hung the towel over the rack. "I'm just sorry you got drenched."

"No problem. Glad to help out." George draped his arm loosely around Laurel's shoulders. Together, they sauntered down the hall toward the front door. "As for the soaking—I was planning on entering a wet jeans contest anyway."

Laurel grinned, leaned back against the wall and crossed her arms.

"Uh-huh."

"Hey, they have wet T-shirt contests for women, right?" he said impishly as he reached for the doorknob. "Well, why not wet jeans contests for guys?" Grinning, he opened the door. "Anyhow, you know what they used to say. Save water, shower with a friend."

"Indeed," a voice said coldly.

Damian Skouras was standing in the doorway. He was dressed in a dark suit and a white shirt; his tie was a deep scarlet silk, and his face was twisted in a scowl.

Laurel's throat constricted. She'd been kidding herself. The man wasn't a copy of anybody, not when it came to looks. Kirk had been handsome but the only word that described Damian was the one she'd come up with this morning.

He was gorgeous.

He was also uninvited. And unwelcome. Definitely unwelcome, she reminded herself, and she stepped away from the wall, drew herself up to her full height and matched his scowl with one of her own.

"What," she asked coldly, "are you doing here?"

Damian ignored the question. He was too busy trying to figure out what in hell was going on.

What do you think is going on you idiot? he asked himself, and his frown deepened.

Laurel was wearing a soaked T-shirt that clung to her like a second skin. Beneath it, her rounded breasts and nipples stood out in exciting relief. She had on a pair of faded denim shorts, her feet were bare, her hair was wet and her face was shiny and free of makeup.

She was more beautiful than ever.

"Laurel? You know this guy?"

Damian turned his head and looked at the man standing beside her. Actually he wasn't standing beside her anymore. He'd moved slightly in front of her, in a defensive posture that made it clear he was ready to protect Laurel at all costs. Damian's lip curled. What would a woman see in a man like this? He was good-looking; women would think so, anyway, though he had too pretty a face for all the muscles that rippled in his bare chest and shoulders. Damian's gaze swept down the man's body. His jeans were tight and wet, and cupped him with revealing intimacy.

What the hell had been going on here? Laurel and the Bozo looked as if they'd just come in out of the rain.

Unfortunately, it hadn't rained in days.

He thought of what the guy had said about showering with a friend. It was, he knew, a joke. Besides, people didn't shower with their clothing on. Logic told him that, the same as it told him that they didn't climb out of bed wet from head to toe, but what the hell did logic have to do with anything?

Coming here, unannounced, had seemed such a clever

idea. Catch her by surprise, have the limousine waiting downstairs with a chilled bottle of champagne in the built-in bar, long-stemmed roses in a crystal vase and reservations at that restaurant that had just opened with the incredible view of the city.

It hadn't occurred to him that just because the telephone directory listed an L. Bennett at this address was no guarantee that she lived alone.

"Laurel?"

The Bozo was talking to Laurel again but he hadn't taken his eyes off him.

"What's the deal? Do you know this guy?"

"Of course she knows me," Damian snapped.

"Is that right, Laurel?"

She nodded with obvious reluctance. "I know him. But I didn't invite him here."

The Bozo folded his arms over his chest. "She knows you," he said to Damian, "but she didn't invite you here."

"I don't know how to break this to you, mister...?"

"Morgan," George said. "Grey Morgan."

Damian smiled pleasantly. "I don't know how to break this to you, Mr. Morgan, but I understood every word she said."

"Then you'll be sure to understand this, too," Laurel said. "Go away."

"Go away," the Bozo repeated, and unfolded his arms.

His height, and all those rippling muscles, were impressive. Good, Damian thought. He could feel the same sense of anticipation spreading through his body again, the one he'd had this afternoon when he'd wanted nothing so much as to take that photographer apart.

Maybe he'd been sitting in too many boardrooms lately, exercising his mind instead of his muscles.

Laurel was thinking almost the same thing, though not in such flattering terms. What was with this man? She could almost smell the testosterone in the air. Damian's jaw was set, his eyes glittered.

George, his buffed torso and his tight jeans, was oozing muscle; Damian was the epitome of urbanity in his expensive dark suit...but she didn't for a second doubt which of them would win if it came down to basics.

Arrogant, self-centered, accustomed to having the world dance to his tune, and now it looked as if he had all the primitive instincts of a cobra, she thought grimly. How in hell was she going to get rid of him?

"Laurel doesn't want you here, mister."

"What are you?" Damian said softly. "Her translator?"

"Listen here, pal, Laurel and I are—"

"We're very close," Laurel said. She moved forward, slipped her arm through the Bozo's, looked up and gave him a smile that sent Damian's self-control slipping another notch. "Aren't we, George—I mean, Grey?"

"Yeah," the Bozo said, after half a beat, "we are. Very, very close."

Damian's brows lifted. Maybe George or Grey or whoever he was, was right. Maybe he did need a translator. Something was going on here but he couldn't get a handle on it. He felt the way he sometimes did when he was doing business in Tokyo. Everyone spoke some English, Damian could manage some Japanese, but once in a while, a word or a phrase seemed to fall through the cracks.

"So if you don't mind, Mr. Skouras," Laurel said, putting heavy emphasis on the *mister*, "we'd appreciate it if you would—"

"George? Honey, are you done up there?"

They all looked down the hall. A pretty brunette stood at the bottom of the steps, smiling up at them.

"Hi, Laurel. Are you done borrowing my husband?"

Damian's brows arced again. He looked at Laurel, who flushed and dropped the Bozo's arm.

"Hi, Suze. Yeah, just about."

"Great." The brunette came trotting up the stairs. "Did he do a good job?"

Laurel's color deepened. "Fine," she said quickly.

"You see, George?" The brunette dimpled. "If the ratings ever go into the toilet, you can always go back to fixing them."

Laurel swallowed hard. Damian could see the movement of the muscles in her throat.

"He fixed my shower," she said, with dignity.

Damian nodded. "I see."

"Suze," George said, clearing his throat, "Laurel's got a bit of a problem here…"

"No," Laurel said quickly, "no, I don't."

"But you said…?"

"It's not a problem at all." She looked at Damian. "Mr. Skouras was just leaving. Weren't you, Mr. Skouras?"

"Yes, I was."

"You see? So there's no need to—"

"Just as soon as you change your clothing," he said. He leaned back against the door jamb, arms folded, and gave her a long, assessing look. "On the other hand, what you're wearing is…rather interesting. You might want to put on a pair of shoes, though. You never know what you're liable to step in, on a New York street."

He had to bite his lip to keep from laughing at the expression that swept over Laurel's face.

"I know what *you've* stepped in," she said, her chin lifting and her eyes blazing into his, "but I promise you, I've no intention of going anywhere with you."

"But our reservation is for eight," he said blandly.

A little furrow appeared between Laurel's eyebrows. "What reservation?"

"For dinner."

The furrow deepened. "Dinner?"

Damian looked at Susie. They shared a conspiratorial smile. "I'd be insulted that she forgot our appointment, but

I know what a long day she put in doing that Redwood Computer layout."

"Redwood?" Susie said.

"Redwood?" George said, with interest, "the outfit that makes those hot portables?"

Damian shrugged modestly. "Well, that's what Wall Street says. I'm just pleased Laurel's doing the ads for the company." He smiled. "Almost as pleased as I am to have had the good fortune to have purchased Redwood."

"Redwood Comp...?" Susie's eyes widened. "Of course. Skouras. *Damian* Skouras. I should have recognized you. I was just reading *Manhattan Magazine*. Your picture's in it." A smile lit her pretty face. "George?" she said, elbowing her husband in the ribs, "this is..."

"Damian Skouras." George stuck out his hand, drew it back and wiped it on his damp jeans, then stuck it out again. "A pleasure, Mr. Skouras."

"Please, call me Damian," Damian said modestly.

George grinned as the men shook hands. "My wife and I just bought a hundred shares of your stock."

Damian smiled. "I'm delighted to hear it."

I don't believe this, Laurel thought incredulously. Was it a conspiracy? First Annie and Dawn, her very own flesh and blood; now Susie and George...

"Laurel," Susie said, "you never said a word!"

"About what?"

"About...about this," Susie said, with a little laugh.

"Suze, you've got this all wrong."

"You're not posing for those ads?"

"Yes. Yes, I am, but—but this man—"

"Damian," Damian said with a smile.

"This man," Laurel countered, "has nothing to do with—"

"My advertising people selected Laurel. With my approval, naturally."

"Naturally," Susie echoed.

"Imagine my surprise when we bumped into each other at my ward's wedding yesterday." His smile glittered. "In the flesh, as it were. We had a delightful few hours. Didn't we, Laurel? And we agreed to have dinner together tonight. To discuss business, of course."

Susie's eyes widened. She looked at Laurel, who was watching Damian as if she wished a hole in the ground would open under his feet.

"Of course," Susie said, chuckling.

"At *The Gotham Penthouse*."

"*The Gotham Penthouse*! I just read a review of it in—"

"*Manhattan Magazine*?" Laurel said, through her teeth.

Susie nodded. "Uh-huh. It's supposed to be scrumptious!"

Damian smiled. "So I hear. Perhaps you and—is it George?"

"Yeah," George said. God, Laurel thought with disgust, it was a good thing there was no dirt on the floor or he'd have been scuffing his toes in it. "It is. Grey's my stage name. My agent figured it sounded better."

"Sexier," Susie said, and smiled up at her husband.

"Well, perhaps you and your wife would like to join us?"

"No," Laurel said sharply. Everyone looked at her. "I mean—I mean, of course, that would be lovely, but it isn't as if—"

"You don't have to explain." Susie looped her arm through her husband's. "It's a very romantic place, *The Penthouse*. Well, that's what the reviewer said, anyway."

Her smile was warm. It encompassed both Damian and Laurel as if they were a package deal. Laurel wanted to grab Susie and shake her until her teeth rattled. Or slug Damian Skouras in the jaw. Or maybe do both.

"You guys don't need an old married couple like us around."

"Susie," Laurel said grimly, "you really do not understand."

"Oh, I do." Susie grinned. "It's business. Right, Damian?"

Could a snake really smile? This one could.

"Precisely right," Damian said.

"It would be lovely to get together for dinner some other time, though. At our place, maybe. I do a mean Beef Stroganoff—which reminds me, George, if we don't get moving, everything will be burned to a crisp."

George's face suddenly took on a look of uncertainty. "Laurel? You're okay with this?"

A muscle worked in Laurel's jaw. At least somebody was still capable of thinking straight, but why drag innocent bystanders into the line of fire? This was a private war, between her and Damian.

"It's fine," she said. "And thanks for fixing the shower."

"Hey, anytime." George held out his hand, and Damian took it. "Nice to have met you."

"The same here," Damian said politely.

Susie leaned toward Laurel behind her husband's broad back.

"You never said a word," she announced in a stage whisper that could have been heard two floors below. "Laurel, honey, this guy is *gorgeous*!"

This guy's a rat, Laurel thought, but she bit her tongue and said nothing.

Susie had been right. The restaurant was a winner.

It had low lighting, carefully spaced tables and a magnificent view. The service was wonderful, the wine list impressive and the food looked delicious.

Laurel had yet to take a bite.

When she'd ignored the menu, Damian had simply ordered for them both. Beluga caviar, green salads, roast duck glazed with Montmorency cherries and brandy and, for a grand finale, a chocolate soufflé garnished with whipped cream that looked as light as air.

Neither the waiter nor Damian seemed to notice her hunger strike. The one served each course, then cleared it away; the other ate, commented favorably on the meal, and kept up a light, pleasant conversation in which she refused to join.

"Coffee?" Damian said, when the soufflé had been served. "Or do you prefer tea?"

Even prisoners on hunger strikes drank liquids. Laurel looked across the table at him.

"Which are you having?"

"Coffee. As strong as possible, and black."

Coffee was what she always drank, and just that way. Laurel gave a mental sigh.

"In that case," she said, unsmiling, "I'll have tea."

Damian laughed as the waiter hurried off. "Is there anything I could do to make you less inclined to insult me?"

"Would you do it, if there were?"

"Why do I have the feeling your answer might prove lethal?"

"At least you got *that* right!"

He sighed and shook his head, though she could see amusement glinting in his eyes. "That's not a very ladylike answer."

"Since you're obviously not a gentleman, why should it be? And I'm truly delighted to have provided you with a laugh a minute today. First Haskell, then George and Susie, and now here I am, playing jester for the king while he dines."

"Is that what you think?" Damian waited until their coffee and tea were served. "That I brought you here to amuse me?"

"I think you get your kicks out of tossing your weight around."

"Sorry?"

"You like to see people dance to your tune."

He pushed aside his dessert plate, moved his cup and saucer in front of him and folded his hands around the cup.

"That is not why I asked you to join me this evening."

"Asked? Coerced, you mean."

"I had every intention of asking you politely, Laurel, but when you opened the door and I saw you with that man, Grey…"

"His name is George."

"George, Grey, what does it matter?" Damian's eyes darkened. "I saw him, half-dressed. And I saw you smiling at him. And I thought, very well, I have a choice to make. I can do as I intended, ask her to put aside the words that passed between us this morning and come out to dinner with me…"

"The answer would have been no."

"Or," he said, his voice roughening, "I can punch this son of a bitch in the jaw, sling her over my shoulder and carry her off."

The air seemed to rush out of the space between them. Laurel felt as if she were fighting for breath.

"That—that's not the least bit amusing."

"It wasn't meant to be." Damian reached across the table and took her hand. "Something happened between us yesterday."

"I don't know what you're talk—"

"Don't!" His fingers almost crushed hers as she sought to tug free of his grasp. "Don't lie. Not to me. Not to yourself." A fierce, predatory light blazed in his eyes. "You know exactly what I'm talking about. I kissed you, and you kissed me back."

Their eyes met. He wasn't a fool; lying would get her nowhere. Well, her years before the camera had taught her some things, at least.

"So what?" she said coolly. She forced a faintly mocking smile to her lips. "You caught me off guard but then, you know that. What more do you want, Damian? My admission that you kiss well? I'm sure you know that, too— or doesn't your blond friend offer enough plaudits to satisfy that ego of yours?"

"Is that what this is all about? Gabriella?" Damian made an impatient gesture. "That's over with."

"She didn't like watching her lover flirt with another woman, you mean?" Laurel wrenched her hand free of his. "At least she's not a total idiot."

"I broke things off last evening."

"Last...? Not because of..."

"It was over between us weeks ago. I just hadn't gotten around to admitting it." A smile curled across his mouth. "It hadn't occurred to me that you'd be jealous."

"Jealous? Of you and that woman? Your ego isn't big, it's enormous! I don't even know you."

"Get to know me, then."

"There's no point. I'm not interested in getting involved."

"I'm not asking you to marry me," he said bluntly. "We're consenting adults, you and I. And something happened between us the minute we saw each other."

"Uh-huh. And next, you're going to tell me that nothing like this has ever happened to you before."

Laurel put her napkin on the table and slid to the end of the banquette. She'd listened to all she was going to listen to, and it wasn't even interesting. His line was no different than a thousand others.

"Laurel."

He caught her wrist as she started to rise. His eyes had gone black; the bones in his handsome, arrogant face stood out.

"Come to bed with me. Let me make love to you until neither of us can think straight."

Color flooded her face. "Let go," she said fiercely, but his hand only tightened on hers.

"I dreamed of you last night," he whispered. "I imagined kissing your soft mouth until it was swollen, caressing your breasts with my tongue until you sobbed with pleasure. I dreamed of being deep inside you, of hearing you cry out my name as you came against my mouth."

She wanted to flee his soft words but she couldn't, even if he had let her. Her legs were weak; she could feel her pulse pounding in her ears.

"That is what I've wanted, what we've both wanted, from the minute we saw each other. Why do you try to deny it?"

The bluntness of his words, the heat in his eyes, the memory of what she'd felt in his arms, stole her breath away and, with it, all her hard-won denial.

Everything Damian had said was true. She couldn't pretend anymore. She didn't like him. He was everything she despised and more, but she wanted him as she'd never wanted any man, and with such desperate longing that it terrified her.

Her vision blurred. She saw herself in his arms, lying beneath him and returning kiss for kiss, wrapping her legs around his waist as she tilted her hips up to meet his possessive thrusts.

"Yes," he said fiercely, and she looked into his eyes and knew that the time for pretense was over.

Laurel gave a soft cry. She tore her hand from Damian's, shot to her feet and flew from the restaurant, but he caught up to her just outside the door, his fingers curling around her arm like a band of steel.

"Tell me I'm wrong," he said in a hoarse whisper, "and so help me God, I'll have my driver take you home and you'll never be bothered by me again."

Time seemed to stand still. They stood in the warmth

and darkness of the spring night, looking at each other, both of them breathing hard, and then Laurel whispered Damian's name and moved into his arms with a hunger she could no longer deny.

CHAPTER FIVE

THEY WERE INSIDE the limousine, shut off from the driver and the world, moving swiftly through the late-night streets of the city. The car, and Damian, were all that existed in Laurel's universe.

His body was rock-hard; his arms crushed her to him. His mouth was hot and open against hers, and his tongue penetrated her in an act of intimacy so intense it made her tremble. She felt fragile and feminine, consumed by his masculinity. His kiss demanded her complete surrender and promised, in return, the fulfilment of her wildest fantasies.

There would be no holding back. Not tonight. Not with him.

Wrong, this is wrong. Those were the words that whispered inside her head, but the message beating in her blood was far louder. *Stop thinking*, it said. *Let yourself feel.*

And she could feel. Everything. The hardness of Damian's body. The wildness of his kisses. The heat of his hands as he touched her. It was all so new... and yet, it wasn't. They had just met, but Damian was not a stranger. Was this why some people believed they'd lived before? She felt as if she'd known him in another life, or maybe since the start of time.

Her head fell back against his shoulder as his hand swept over her, skimming the planes of her face, stroking the length of her throat, then cupping her breast. His thumb brushed across her nipple and she cried out against his mouth.

He said her name in a husky whisper, and then something more, words in Greek that she couldn't understand. But she understood this, the way his fingertips trailed fire over her

71

skin, and this, the taste of his mouth, and yes, she understood when he clasped her hand and brought it to him so that she could feel the power and rigidity of his need.

"Yes," she said breathlessly, and he made a sound low in his throat, pushed up her skirt, slid his hand up her leg and cupped the molten heat he found between her thighs.

The shock of his touch, the raw sexuality of it, shot like lightning through Laurel's blood. A soft cry broke from her throat and she grabbed for his wrist. What she felt—what he was making her feel—was almost more than she could bear.

"Damian," she sobbed, "Damian, please."

"Tell me what you want," he said in a fierce whisper. "Say it."

You, she thought, I want you.

She did. Oh, she did. She wanted him in a way she'd never wanted any man, not just with her body but with something more, something she couldn't define...

The half-formed realization terrified her, and she twisted her face away from Damian's seeking mouth.

"Listen to me," she said urgently. Her fingers dug into his wrist. "I don't think—"

"Don't think," he said, "not tonight," and before she could respond, he thrust his hands into her hair, lifted her face to his and kissed her.

It was not the civilized thing to do.

Damian knew it, even as he took Laurel's mouth again.

The same wild need was beating in her blood as in his. He felt it in her every sigh, her caresses, her hungry response to his kisses. But she'd started to draw back, frightened, he suspected, of the passionate storm raging between them.

Hell, he couldn't blame her.

Something was happening here, something he didn't pretend to understand. The only thing he was sure of was that whatever this was, it was too powerful, too elemental, to deny. He'd sooner have given up breathing than give up this moment.

Minutes ago, when he'd touched her, when he'd felt the heat of her and she'd given that soft, keening cry of surrender, he'd damn near ripped off her panties, unzipped his fly and buried himself deep inside her.

That he hadn't done it had had little to do with propriety, or even with reason, though it would have been nice to tell himself so. The truth was simpler, and much more basic. What had stopped him was the burning need to undress her slowly, to savor her naked beauty with his eyes and hands and mouth.

He wanted to watch her face as he slowly caressed her, to see her pupils grow enormous with pleasure, to touch her and stroke her until she was wild for his possession. He wanted her in bed, his bed, naked in his arms, her skin hot against his, climbing toward a climax that would be more powerful than anything either of them had ever known, and though the intensity of his need was setting off warning bells, he didn't give a damn. Not now. His body was hot and hard; he wanted Laurel more than he'd ever wanted anything, or anyone, in this world.

She'd told him, in the restaurant, that he wasn't a gentleman but hell, he'd never been a gentleman, not from the moment of his birth. Now, as he cupped her face in his hands and whispered her name, as her eyes opened and met his, he knew that he'd sooner face the fires of hell than start pretending to be a gentleman tonight.

He lived in an apartment on Park Avenue.

It was a penthouse duplex, reached by a private elevator that opened onto a dimly lighted foyer that rose two stories into darkness. If he had servants, they were not visible.

The elevator doors slid shut, and they were alone.

Shadows, black-velvet soft and deep, wrapped around

them. The night was so still that Laurel could hear the pounding beat of her heart.

There was still time. She could say, "This was a mistake," and demand to be taken home. Damian wouldn't like it, but what did that matter? She was neither a fool nor a tramp, and surely only a woman who was one or both would be on her way to bed with a man she'd met little more than twenty-four hours ago.

Damian's hands closed on her shoulders. He turned her toward him, and what she saw mirrored in his eyes drove every logical thought from her mind.

"Laurel," he said, and she went into his arms.

He kissed her hard, lifting her against him, his hands cupping her bottom so that she was pressed against his erection. His mouth teased hers open. He bit down on her bottom lip, then soothed the tiny wound with his tongue, until she was trembling and clutching his jacket for support.

"Say it now," he said in a savage whisper. "Tell me what you want."

The answer was in her eyes, but she gave it voice.

"You," she said in a broken whisper, "you, you—"

Damian's mouth dropped to hers. Heart surging with triumph, he lifted her into his arms and carried her up the stairs, into the darkness.

His bedroom was huge. The bed, bathed in ivory moonlight, faced onto a wall of glass below which the city glittered in the night like a castle from a fairy tale.

Slowly Damian lowered Laurel to her feet. For a long moment, he didn't touch her. Then he lifted his hand and stroked her cheek. Laurel closed her eyes and leaned into his caress.

Gently he ran his hand over her hair.

"Take it down," he said softly.

Her eyes flew open. She couldn't see his face clearly—

he was standing in shadow—but there was an intensity in the way he held himself.

"My hair?" she whispered.

"Yes." He reached out and touched the silky curls that lay against her neck. "Take it down for me."

Laurel raised her hands to the back of her head. Her hair had already started coming loose of the tortoiseshell pins she'd used to put it up. Now, she removed the pins slowly, wishing she could see his face as she did. But he was still standing in shadow, and he didn't step forward until her hair tumbled around her shoulders.

"Beautiful," he whispered.

He caught a fistful of the shining auburn locks and brought them to his lips. Her hair felt like silk against his mouth and its fragrance reminded him of a garden after a gentle spring rain.

He let her hair drift from his fingers.

"Now your earrings," he said softly.

Her hands went to the tiny crystal beads that swayed on slender gold wires from her earlobes. He could see confusion in her eyes and he knew she'd expected something different, a quicker leap into the flames, but if that was what she wanted, he wouldn't, hell, he *couldn't,* oblige. His control was stretched almost to the breaking point. He couldn't touch her now; if he did, it would all be over before it began, and he didn't want that.

Nothing would be rushed. Not with her. Not tonight.

One earring, then the other, dropped into her palm. Damian held out his hand, and she gave them to him. Her hands went to the silver buttons on her silk jacket, and he nodded. Seconds later, the jacket fell to the floor.

He reached out and caught her wrists.

"Nothing more," he whispered, and brushed his mouth over hers. "I want to do all the rest."

She heard the soft urgency in his voice, the faint tone of command. His eyes glittered; there was a dark passion in his face, a taut pull of skin over bone that made her heart beat faster.

But his touch was gentle as he undressed her. And he did it slowly, so slowly that she thought she might die with the pleasure of it, first her blouse, then her skirt, her slip and her bra, until she stood before him wearing nothing but her high-heeled sandals, sheer stockings, a garter belt and panties that were a lacy wisp of white silk.

She heard his breath hitch in his throat. He stepped back and looked at her. She felt a flush rise over her skin and she started to cross her arms over her breasts, but he stopped her.

"Don't hide yourself from me," he said thickly. "Laurel, *mátya mou*, how exquisite you are."

She wanted to ask him what it meant, the name he'd called her; she wanted to tell him that no matter what he thought, this night was a first for her, that she'd never given herself to anyone this way, never wanted anyone this way.

There were a hundred things to say, but she couldn't bring herself to say anything but his name.

"Yes," he said, and he lifted her in his arms again, kissed her deeply and carried her to the bed.

He undid the garters, rolled down her stockings and dropped them to the floor. He lifted each of her feet and kissed the high, elegant arches; he sucked her toes into his mouth. Then he knelt beside her and undid the tiny hooks on the garter belt. His hands shook as he did, which was strange because while he'd never counted them, he'd surely undone a thousand such closures before. He had done all these things before, taken a woman to his bed, undressed her…and yet, when Laurel finally lay naked before him, he felt his heart kick against his ribs.

He whispered her name and then he put one arm beneath her shoulders and lifted her to him, kissed her mouth as she curled her hands into the folds of his jacket. There was a tightness growing deep within him, one that threatened to shatter what little remained of his control. He knew it was time to stop touching her. He needed to rip off his clothing and bury himself inside her or risk humiliating himself like an untried boy, but he couldn't.

Nothing could keep him from learning the taste and feel of her skin.

He kissed her breasts, drawing the beaded nipples deep into his mouth, and when she cried out his name and arced toward him, her excitement fueled his own. He ran his hand along her hip, his fingers barely stroking across the feathery curls that formed a sweet, inverted triangle between her thighs, and the tightness in his belly grew.

"Laurel," he said. "Look at me."

Her lashes fluttered open. Her eyes were huge, the blue irises all but consumed by the black pupils. She was breathing hard; her face, her rounded breasts, were stained with the crimson flush of passion.

He had done this to her, he thought fiercely, he had brought her this pleasure. He said her name again, his gaze holding hers as he moved his hand lower and when, at last, he touched her, she let out a cry so soft and wild that he thought he could feel it against his palm.

He rolled away from her and stripped off his clothing. His hands shook; it was as if he was entering into an unknown world where what awaited him could bring joy beyond imagining or the darkness of despair. He didn't know which right know, and he didn't give a damn.

All that mattered was this moment, and this woman.

Laurel. Beautiful Laurel.

Naked, he knelt on the bed beside her. She was watching him, her face pale but for the glow on her cheeks, and the urgency deep within him seemed to diminish. Just for a moment, he thought it might almost be enough to take her in his arms, kiss her, hold her close and listen to the beat of her heart against his the whole night through.

But then she whispered his name and held her arms up

to him, and he knew that he needed more. He needed to penetrate her, to make her his in the way men have done since the dawn of time.

"Laurel," he said, and when her eyes met his, he gave up thinking, parted her thighs and sank deep into her heat.

Laurel rose carefully from the bed.

It was very late, and Damian was asleep. She was sure of it; she could hear the steady susurration of his breath.

Her clothing was scattered across the room. She gathered up the bits and pieces, moving quietly so as not to wake him, and she thought about how he had undressed her, how she'd let him undress her, how she'd wanted him to undress her.

A hot, sick feeling roiled in the pit of her stomach.

The apartment was silent as she slipped out of his bedroom, though the darkness had given way to a cheerless grey. It made it easier to see, at least; the last thing she wanted to do was put on a light and risk waking him.

What in heaven's name had she done?

Sex, she told herself coldly. An experience, a seduction, the kind other women whispered about, even joked about. That was what had happened to her, a mind-blowing night of passion in the arms of a man who obviously knew his way around the boudoir.

Laurel's hands trembled as she zipped up her skirt.

She had given up all the moral precepts she'd lived by. She'd humiliated herself. She'd…she'd…

A moan broke from her throat. She'd become someone else, that was what had happened, and the knowledge that such a woman even existed inside her would haunt her forever.

The things she'd done tonight, the things she'd let Damian do…

What had happened to her? Just the sight of him, kneeling between her thighs, had made her come apart. He was so magnificent, such a perfect male animal, his broad shoulders gleaming as if they'd been oiled, his hair dark and tumbling around his face. The tiny gold stud, glinting in his ear, had been all the adornment such a man would ever need.

And then he'd entered her. She'd felt her body stretching to welcome him, to contain him...and then he'd moved, and moved again, and a cry had burst from her throat and she'd shattered into a million shining pieces.

"Damian," she'd sobbed, "oh, Damian..."

"I know," he'd whispered, his mouth on hers, and then she'd felt him beginning to move again, and she'd realized he was still hard within her. The flames had ignited more slowly the second time, not because she'd wanted him less but because he'd made it happen that way, pulling back, then easing forward, filling her and filling her, taking her closer and closer to the edge until, once again, she'd felt herself soar into the night sky where she'd blazed as brightly as a comet before tumbling back to earth.

She'd found paradise, she'd thought dreamily, as Damian's arms closed around her. She'd blushed as he whispered soft words to her and when, at last, he'd kissed her forehead, and her mouth, and held her close against his heart, she'd drifted into dreamless sleep.

Hours later, something—a sound, a whisper of breeze from the window—had awakened her. For a moment, she'd been confused. This wasn't her bedroom...

And then she'd remembered. She was in Damian's arms, in his bed, with the scent of him and what they'd done on her skin, and suddenly, in the cold, sharp light of dawn, she'd seen the night for what it really had been.

Cheap. Tawdry. Ugly.

Paradise? Laurel's throat constricted. A one-night stand, was more like it. She'd gone to bed with a stranger, not just gone to bed with him but—but done things with him she'd never...

...felt things she'd never...

"Laurel?"

She gasped and spun around. The bedroom door had opened; Damian stood in a pool of golden light that spilled from a bedside lamp. Naked, unashamed, he was a Greek statue come to life, hewn not of cold marble but of warm flesh. There was a little smile on his lips, a sexy, sleepy one, but as he looked at her, it began to fade.

"You're all dressed."

"Yes." Laurel cleared her throat. "I—I'm sorry if I woke you, Damian. I tried to be quiet but—"

God, she was babbling! She'd never sneaked out of a man's apartment before, but she'd be damned if she'd let him know that. Anyway, there was a first time for everything. Hadn't she proved that tonight?

"I apologize if I disturbed you."

"Apologize?" he said, his eyes narrowing.

"Yes. Oh, and thank you for..." *For what? Are you crazy? What are you thanking him for?* "For everything," she said brightly.

"Laurel..."

"No, really, you needn't see me out. I'm sure I can find my way, just down the stairs and through the—"

"Dammit," he said sharply, "what is this?"

"What is what? It's late. Very late. Or early, I don't really know which. And I have to go home, and change, and—" The quick, brittle flow of words ended in a gasp as he reached out and brought her against him. "Damian, don't."

"Ah," he said softly, "I understand." He laughed softly, bent his head and took the tip of her earlobe gently between his teeth. "Morning-after jitters. Well, I know how to fix that."

"Don't," she said again. She could hear the faint rasp in her own voice; it said, more clearly than words, that though her head meant one thing, her traitorous body meant something very different. She could feel him stirring against her and a warm heaviness settled in her loins.

"Laurel." Damian spoke in a whisper. He wasn't laughing now; he was looking at her through eyes that had darkened to silvery ash. "Come back to bed."

"No," she said, "I just told you, I can't."

His smile was honeyed. Slowly he dipped his head and kissed her, parting her lips with his.

"You can. And you want to. You know that you do."

She closed her eyes as he kissed the hollow of her throat. He was right, that was the worst of it. She wanted to go with him into that wide bed, where the scent of their lovemaking still lingered.

Except that it hadn't been lovemaking. It had been... There was a word for what they'd done, a word so ugly, so alien, that even thinking it made her feel unclean.

His hands were at the top button of her blouse. In a moment, he'd have them all undone, and then he'd touch her, and she wouldn't want to stop him...

"Stop it!" Her hands wrapped around his wrists. His brows, as black as a crow's wings, drew together. She'd taken him by surprise, she saw, and she made the most of the advantage and pressed on. "We had—we had fun, I agree, but let's not spoil it. Really, we both knew it was just one of those things that happen. There's no need to say anything more."

His eyes narrowed. "I thought we might—"

"Might what? Work out an arrangement?" She forced a smile to her lips. "I'm sorry, Damian, but I'd rather leave it at this. You know what they say about too much of anything spoiling it."

He was angry, she could see that in the flush that swept over his high cheekbones. His ego had taken a hit but that was too damn bad. What had he expected? An if-it's-Tuesday-it-must-be-your-place kind of deal, the sort he'd no doubt had with the blonde?

She waited, not daring to move, knowing that if he took her in his arms and kissed her again, her pathetic show of bravado might collapse—but he didn't. He studied her in silence, a muscle bunching in his cheek, and then he gave a curt nod.

"As you wish, of course. Actually you're quite right. Too much of anything is never good." He smiled politely, though she suspected the effort cost him, and turned toward the bedroom. "Just give me a minute to dress and I'll see you home."

"No! No, I'll take a taxi."

Damian swung toward her. "Don't be ridiculous."

"I'm perfectly capable of seeing myself home."

"Perhaps." His voice had taken on a flinty edge, as had his gaze. He folded his arms over his chest and she thought, fleetingly, that even in the splendor of his nudity, he managed to look imposing. "But this is New York City, not some little town in Connecticut, and I am not a man to permit a woman to travel these streets, alone, at this hour."

"Permit? *Permit?*" Laurel drew herself up. "I don't need your permission."

"Hell," he muttered, and thrust a hand into his hair. "This is nothing to quarrel about."

"You're right, it isn't. Goodbye, Damian."

His hand fell on her shoulder as she spun away from him, his fingers biting harshly into her flesh.

"What's going on here, Laurel? Can you manage to tell me that?"

"I have told you. I said—"

"I heard what you said, and I don't believe you." His touch gentled; she felt the rough brush of his fingertips against her throat. "You know you want more than this."

"You've no idea what I want," she said sharply.

He smiled. "Tell me, then. Let me get dressed, we'll have coffee and we'll talk."

"How many times do I have to say I'm not interested before you believe me, Damian?"

His eyes darkened. Long seconds passed, and then his hand fell from her shoulder. He turned, strode into his bedroom, picked up the telephone and punched a button on the dial.

"Stevens? Miss Bennett is leaving. Bring the car around, please."

"Why did you do that? There was no need to wake your chauffeur!"

He looked at her, his lips curved in a parody of a smile as he hung up the phone.

"I'm sure Stevens would appreciate your thoughtfulness, but he's been with me for years. He's quite accustomed to being awakened to perform such errands. Can you find your own way to the lobby, or shall I ring for the doorman?"

"I'll find my own way," she said quickly.

"Fine. In that case, if you'll excuse me...?"

The door shut gently in her face.

She stood staring at it, feeling a rush of crimson flood her skin, hating herself and hating him, and then she spun away.

Would she ever forget the stupidity of what she'd done tonight? she wondered, as she rode to the lobby in his private elevator.

More to the point, would she ever forget that the only place she'd ever glimpsed heaven had been in Damian Skouras's arms?

In the foyer of the penthouse, Damian stood at the closed doors to the elevator, glaring at the tiny lights on the wall panel as they marked Laurel's passage to the lobby. He'd put on a pair of jeans and zipped them, but he hadn't bothered closing them and they hung low on his hips.

What the hell had happened, between the last time they'd made love and now? He'd fallen asleep holding a warm, satisfied woman in his arms and awakened to find a cold stranger getting dressed in the hallway.

No, not a stranger. Laurel had metamorphosed back into who she'd been when they'd met, a beautiful woman with a tongue like a razor and the disposition of a grizzly bear. And she'd done her damnedest to make it sound as if what had gone on between them tonight had no more importance than a one-night stand.

The light on the panel blinked out. She'd reached the lobby, and the doorman, alerted by the call Damian had made after he'd closed the bedroom door, would be waiting to hand her safely off to Stevens.

Still glowering, he made his way to the terrace in time to see Laurel getting into the car. Stevens shut the door after her, climbed behind the wheel and that was that.

She was gone, and good riddance.

Who was he kidding? She wasn't gone, not that easily. Her fragrance still lingered on his skin, and in his bed. The sound of her voice, the way she'd sighed his name while they were making love, drifted like a half-remembered tune in his mind.

He had lied to her, when he'd said Stevens was accustomed to being roused at all hours of the night. Being at the beck-and-call of an employer was something he'd hated, in his youth; he'd vowed never to behave so imperiously with those who served him.

Besides, waking Stevens had never been necessary before.

No woman had ever risen and left his bed so eagerly, Damian thought grimly, as he strode into his bedroom. His problem was usually getting rid of them, not convincing them to stay.

Not that he really cared. It had been pleasant, this interlude; he'd have been happy to have gone on with it for a few more weeks, even for a couple of months, but there were other women. There were always other women.

Something glittered on the carpet. Damian frowned and scooped it up.

It was Laurel's earring.

His hand closed hard around it. He remembered the flushed, expectant look on her face when he'd taken the earrings from her, when he'd begun undressing her, when she'd raised her arms to him and he'd knelt between her thighs and thrust home...

"Home?" he said. He laughed, then tossed the earring onto the night table.

It was late, he was tired, and when you came right down to it, the only thing special about tonight had been the sheer effort it had taken to get Laurel Bennett into his bed.

Whistling, Damian headed for the shower.

CHAPTER SIX

SUSIE MORGAN sat at Laurel's kitchen table, her chin propped on her fist as she watched Laurel knead a lump of sourdough batter.

Actually, Susie thought with a lifted eyebrow, Laurel was closer to beating the life out of the stuff than she was to kneading it. Susie glanced at her watch and her brow rose another notch. Laurel had been at it for fifteen minutes, well, fifteen minutes that she knew of, anyway. Who knew how long that poor mound of dough had really been lying there? When she'd come by for Laurel's if-I'm-home-and-haven't-gained-any-weight-the-camera-might-notice Friday morning bread-baking session, there'd already been a dab of flour on Laurel's nose and a mean glint in her eye.

The flour was one thing, but the glint was another. Susie frowned as Laurel whipped the dough over and punched it hard enough to make her wince in sympathy. She'd never known her friend to look so angry, not in the three years they'd known each other, but that was the way she looked lately…though there were times when another expression chased across her face, one that hinted not so much of anger but of terrible unhappiness.

Laurel had alternated between those two looks for four weeks now, ever since the night she'd gone out with Damian Skouras, whose name she hadn't once mentioned since. He hadn't come by again, either, which didn't make sense. Susie had seen the way he'd looked at Laurel and, whether Laurel knew it or not, the way she'd looked at him. Any self-respecting scientist caught between the two of them would have had doubts about carbon emissions being the only thing heating up the atmosphere.

Susie had given it another try, just the other day.

"How's Adonis?" she'd said, trying to sound casual.

Laurel had tried to sound casual, too. "Who?"

"The Greek," Susie had replied, playing along, "you know, the one with the looks and the money."

"How should I know?"

"Aren't you seeing him anymore?"

"I saw him once, under protest."

"Yeah, but I figured—"

"You figured wrong," Laurel had answered, in a way that made it clear the topic was off limits.

"Well, if you say so," Susie had said, "but, you know, if anything's on your mind and you want to talk about it…"

"Thanks, but there's nothing worth talking about," Laurel had replied with a breezy smile, which, as Susie had tried to tell George that night, was definitely proof that there was.

"I don't follow you," George had said patiently. So she'd tried to explain but George, sweet as he was, was a man. It was too much to expect he'd see that if there truly was nothing worth talking about, Laurel would have said something like, "What *are* you talking about, Susie?" instead of just tossing off that meaningless response. She'd even tried to explain that she had this feeling, just a hunch, really, that something had happened between Laurel and the Skouras guy, but George's eyes had only glazed over while he said, "Really?" and "You don't say," until finally she'd given it up.

Susie's frown deepened. On the other hand, even George might sense there was a problem if he could see Laurel beating the life out of that poor sourdough. A couple of more belts like the last and the stuff would be too intimidated to rise.

Susie cleared her throat.

"Uh, Laurel?"

"Yeah?"

"Ah, don't you think that's about done?"

Laurel gave the dough a vicious punch and blew a curl off her forehead.

"Don't I think what's about done?"

"The bread," Susie said, wincing as Laurel slammed her fist into the yeasty mound again.

"Soon." She gave the stuff another whack that made the counter shudder. "But not just yet."

Susie's mouth twitched. She sat up straight, crossed her long, dancer's legs and linked her hands around her knee.

"Anybody I know?" she said casually.

"Huh?"

"Whoever it is you're beating to death this morning. I figure there's got to be a face in that flour that only you can see."

Laurel ran the back of her wrist across her forehead.

"Your imagination's working overtime. I'm making bread, not working out my frustrations."

"Ah," Susie said knowingly. She watched Laurel give the dough a few more turns and punches before dumping it into a bowl and covering it with a damp dish towel. "Because," she said, going with instinct, "it occurred to me, it might just be Damian Skouras you were punching out."

Laurel turned away and tore a piece of paper towel from the roll above the sink. She thought of saying, "Why would you think that?" and looking puzzled, but she'd barely gotten away clean the last time Susie had raised Damian's name. Susie knew her too well, that was the problem.

"I told you," she said flatly, "I'm making bread."

"That's it?"

"That's it."

Susie cleared her throat again. "So, have you heard from him?"

"Suze, you asked me that just the other day. And I said that I hadn't."

"And that you don't expect to. Or want to."

"Right again." Laurel took the coffeepot from the stove and refilled Susie's cup. She started to refill hers, too, but when she saw the glint of oil that floated on what remained, her stomach gave a delicate lurch. Wonderful. She had definitely picked up some sort of bug. Just what she needed, she thought, as she hitched her hip onto a stool opposite Susie's. "So, where's that handsome hunk of yours this morning?"

"At the gym, toning up his abs so he can keep his devoted fans drooling. And don't try to change the subject. It's *your* handsome hunk we were talking about."

"My...?" Laurel rolled her eyes. "What does it take to convince you? Damian Skouras isn't 'my' anything. Don't you ever give up?"

"No," Susie said, with disarming honesty. She lifted her cup with both hands, blew on the coffee, then took a sip. "Not when something doesn't make any sense. You are the most logical, levelheaded female I've ever known."

"Thank you, I think."

"Which is the reason I keep saying to myself, how could a logical, levelheaded female turn her back on a zillionaire Apollo?"

"It was 'Adonis' the last time around," Laurel said coolly. "Although, as far as I'm concerned, it doesn't matter what you call him."

"You didn't like him?"

"Susie, for heaven's sake..."

"Okay, okay, maybe I'm nuts—"

"There's no 'maybe' about it."

"But I just don't understand."

"That's because there isn't anything *to* understand. I keep telling you that. Damian Skouras and I went to dinner and—"

"Do you know, you do that whenever you talk about him?"

Laurel sighed, shook her head and gazed up at the ceiling. "Do what?"

"Well, first you call him DamianSkouras. One word, no pause, as if you hardly know the guy."

As if I hadn't slept with him, Laurel thought, and she felt a blaze of color flood her cheeks.

"Aha," Susie said, in triumph. "You see?"

"See what?"

"The blush, that's what. And the look that goes with it. They always follow, right on the heels of DamianSkouras."

Laurel rose, went to the sink and turned on the water. "I love you dearly, Suze," she said, squeezing in a shot of Joy, "but you are the nosiest thing going, did you know that?"

"George says I am, but what does he know?" Susie smiled. "Men don't understand that women love to talk about stuff like this."

"Stuff like what? There's nothing to talk about."

"There must be, otherwise you wouldn't turn into a clam each time I mention Damian's name."

"I do not turn into a clam. There just isn't anything to say, that's all."

"Listen, my friend, I was here that night, remember? I saw the way you guys looked at each other. And then, that was it. No further contact, according to you."

"Hand me that spoon, would you?"

"You can't blame me for wondering. The guy's gorgeous, he's a zillionaire and he's charming."

"Charming?" Laurel spun around, her cheeks flushed. "He's a scoundrel, that's what he is!"

"Why?"

"Because—because…" Laurel frowned. It was a good question. Damian hadn't seduced and abandoned her. What had happened that night hadn't been a Victorian melodrama. She'd gone to his bed willingly and left it willingly. If the memory haunted her, humiliated her, she had no one to blame but herself. "Susie, do me a favor and let's drop this, okay?"

"If that's the way you want it…"

"I do."

"Okay, then. Consider the subject closed."

"Great. Thank you."

"It's just that I'm really puzzled," Susie said, after a moment's silence. Laurel groaned, but Susie ignored her. "I mean, he looked at you the way a starving man would look at a seven-course meal. Why, if Ben Franklin had come trotting through this place that night, he wouldn't have needed a kite and a key to discover that lightning bolts and electricity are the same thing!"

"That's good, Suze. Keep going like that, you can give up dancing and start writing scripts for George's soap."

"You make it sound as if you didn't like him."

"You clever soul." Laurel flashed a saccharine smile. "How'd you ever come up with an idea like that?"

"Yeah, well, I don't believe you."

"You don't believe me? What's that supposed to mean?"

Susie rose, went to the pantry cabinet and opened it. "It means," she said, taking out a box of Mallomars, "that lightning must have struck somewhere because I've never known you to come traipsing in at dawn." She peered into the box. "Goody. Two left. One for you, and one for me."

Laurel glanced at the chocolate-covered marshmallow cookie Susie held out to her. Her stomach lifted again, did a quick two-step, then settled in place.

"I'll pass."

"I can have both?"

"Consider this your lucky day. And how do you know what time I came in?"

Susie bit into a cookie. "I went running that morning," she said around a mouthful of crumbs, "so I was up at the crack of dawn. You know me. I like the streets to myself.

Besides, these old floors squeak like crazy. I could hear you marching around up here. Pacing, it sounded like, for what seemed like forever.''

Not forever. Just long enough to try to believe there was no point in hating myself for what I'd done because it was already part of the past and I'd never, not in a million years, do anything like it again.

''Where'd he take you that night, anyway?''

''You know where he took me.'' Laurel plucked a cup from the suds and scrubbed at it as if it were a burned roasting pan. ''To dinner.''

''And?'' Susie batted her lashes. ''Where else, hmm?''

To paradise in his arms, Laurel thought suddenly, and the feeling she'd worked so hard to suppress, the memory of how it had been that night, almost overwhelmed her.

Maybe she'd been a fool to leave him. Maybe she should have stayed. Maybe she should have taken up where the blonde had left off...

The cup slipped from her hands and smashed against the floor.

''Dammit,'' she said fiercely. Angry tears rose in her eyes and she squatted and began picking up the pieces of broken china. ''You want to know what happened that night?'' She stood up, dumped the pieces in the garbage and wiped her hands on the seat of her jeans. ''Okay, I'll tell you.''

''Laurel, honey, I didn't mean—''

''I slept with Damian Skouras.''

Susie took a deep breath. ''Wow.''

''I slept with a guy I didn't know all that well, didn't like all that much and didn't ever want to see again, because—because—''

''I understand the because,'' Susie said softly.

Laurel spun toward her, her eyes glittering. ''Don't patronize me, dammit! If *I* don't understand, how can you?''

"Because I slept with George, the first time we went out. That's how."

Laurel sank down on the edge of a stool. "You did?"

"I did. And I'd never done anything like it before."

"Well, then, why did you, that time?"

Susie smiled. "Who knows? Hormones? Destiny? It happened, that's all."

Laurel's smile was wobbly. "See? I was right, you ought to be writing for the soaps."

"Mostly, though, I did it because my body and my heart knew what my brain hadn't yet figured out. George and I were soul mates."

"Yeah, well, I don't have any such excuse. Damian Skouras and I are definitely not soul mates. I did what I did, and now I have to live with it."

"The bastard!"

Laurel laughed. "A minute ago, he was Adonis. Or was it Apollo?"

"A minute ago, I didn't know he'd taken advantage of you and then done the male thing."

"Trust me, Suze," Laurel said wryly, "he didn't take advantage of me. I was willing."

Susie plucked the remaining Mallomar from the box. "That's beside the point. He did the male thing, anyway. 'Wham, bam, thank you, ma'am—and maybe I'll call you sometime.'"

Laurel stared at her friend. Then she rose, yanked a piece of paper towel from the roll, dampened it in the sink and began to rub briskly at the countertop.

"I told him not to call."

"What?"

"You heard me. He wanted to see me again. I told him it was out of the question, that I wasn't interested in that kind of relationship."

"You and Damian made love, it was great and you told him you never wanted to see him again?"

"I.didn't say that."

"That it wasn't great? Or that you never wanted to see him again?"

Laurel stared at Susie, and then she dropped her gaze and turned to the sink.

"What's your point?" she said, plunging her hands into the water.

"It's *your* point I'm trying to figure out here, my friend. Why did you make love with the guy and then tell him to hit the road?"

"I didn't 'make love' with him," Laurel said sharply. "I slept with him."

"Semantics," Susie said with a shrug.

"No, it's more than that. Look, Susie, what you did with George was different. You loved him."

"Still do," Susie said, with a little smile.

"Well, I didn't love Damian. I can't imagine loving Damian. He's such an arrogant, egotistical, super-macho SOB…"

"Sigh," Susie said, rolling her eyes.

Laurel laughed. "The point is, he's not my type."

"Nobody's your type. Name one guy since that bastard, Kirk Soames, who you've given more than a quick hello and I'll eat whatever it is you think you're gonna make out of that poor overbeaten, overkneaded, overpounded sourdough."

"And I'm not his type," Laurel finished, refusing to rise to the bait. She shut off the water, dried her hands on a dish towel and turned around. "That's the sum, total and end of it, so—so…"

Susie had just taken a bite of the Mallomar. A smear of dark chocolate and marshmallow festooned her upper lip.

"You only think so, babe. I saw the way you guys looked at each other."

Laurel swallowed hard. "There's a—a smudge of chocolate on your mouth, Suze."

"Yeah?" Susie scrubbed a finger over her lip. "Did I get it?"

"Most of it. There's still a little bit…" Laurel's stomach rose slowly into her throat. "That's it," she said weakly. "You've got it now." She turned away and wrapped her hands around the rim of the sink, waiting until her stomach settled back where it belonged.

"Laurel? You all right?"

Laurel nodded. "Sure. I'm just—"

"Tired of me poking my nose where it doesn't belong," Susie said. She sighed. "Listen, let's drop the subject. You want to talk about it, I'm here. You don't…?" She gave an elaborate shrug. "Tell you what. How about having supper with us tonight? George is making *pirogi*. Remember his *pirogi*? You loved 'em, the last time."

"Yes, I did. They were—they were…"

Laurel thought of the little doughy envelopes filled with onion-studded ground beef. She *had* loved them, it was true, but now all she could think about was how they'd glistened with butter, how the butter had slid down her throat like oil…

"They were delicious," she said brightly, "but—but this bread is my last extravagance for a while. I'm going on a quick diet. You know how it is. I've got a layout coming up and I need to drop a couple of pounds. Give me a rain check, okay?"

Susie leaned back against the counter. "Well, have supper with us anyway." She patted her belly. "It wouldn't hurt me to lose some weight, and you know those close-ups they give George. Forget the *pirogi*. We'll go wild, take out a couple of Lean Cuisine Veggie Lasagnas and zap 'em in the microwave. How's that sound?"

Lasagna. Laurel imagined bright red tomato sauce, smelled its acidic aroma. Saliva filled her mouth, and she swallowed hard.

"Actually, I may just pass on supper altogether. I think

I've got some kind of bug. I did a shoot in Bryant Park last week. Everybody was coughing and sneezing like crazy, and I've felt rotten ever since."

"Summer colds," Susie said philosophically, as she popped what remained of the Mallomar into her mouth. "The worst kind to shake. A couple of aspirin and some hot chicken soup ought to…Laurel? What's the matter?"

A bead of jelly, glistening like blood at the corner of Susie's mouth, that was what was the matter.

Laurel's belly clenched.

"Nothing," she said, "noth—" *Oh hell*. Her eyes widened and she groaned, clamped her hand over her mouth and shot from the room.

When she emerged from the bathroom minutes later, pale and shaken, Susie was waiting in the bedroom, sitting cross-legged in the middle of Laurel's bed, a worried look on her face.

"Are you okay?"

"I'm fine," Laurel said with a shaky smile.

"Fine, my foot." Susie looked at her friend's face. Laurel's skin was waxen, her eyes were glassy and her forehead glistened with sweat. "You're sick."

"I told you, Suze, it's just some bug I picked up."

"The one that had everybody on that photo session coughing and sneezing?"

"Uh-huh."

Susie uncrossed her legs and stood up. "Except you're not."

"Not what?"

"Coughing. Or sneezing."

"Well, it hit me differently, that's all."

"Have you been out of the country or something?"

"Not in weeks."

"I mean, there's all kinds of nasties floating around this old planet. Weren't you in Ghana or someplace like that a couple of months ago?"

"It was Kenya and it was last year, and honestly, I'm okay. You know what the flu can be like."

"Uh-huh." There was a long silence and then Susie cleared her throat. "My sister had the same symptoms last year. Nausea in the mornings, tossing her cookies every time somebody so much as mentioned food and generally looking just about as awful as you do."

"Thanks a lot." Laurel speared her hands into her hair and shoved it off her forehead. Her skin felt clammy, and even though her stomach was completely empty, it still felt like a storm-tossed ship at sea. "Listen, Susie—"

"So she went to the doctor."

"I'm not going to the doctor. All I need is to take it easy for a couple of days and—"

"Turns out she was pregnant," Susie said quietly, her eyes on Laurel's face.

"Pregnant!" Laurel laughed. "Don't be silly, I'm not…"

Oh God! The floor seemed to drop out from beneath her feet.

Pregnant? No. It wasn't possible. Or was it? When had she last had her period? She couldn't remember. Was it since she'd been with Damian?

No. No!

She sank down on the edge of the bed, feeling empty and boneless. Everything had happened so quickly that night. Had Damian used a condom? Not that she could remember. She certainly hadn't used anything. Why take the pill, when sex was hardly a major item in your life? She knew some women carried diaphragms in their handbags but she wasn't one of them. You needed a whole different mind set to do that. You had to be the sort of woman who might find herself tumbling into a man's bed at the drop of a hat and she had never—she had certainly never…

A little sound tore from her throat. She looked at Susie's

questioning face and did what she could to turn the sound into a choked laugh.

"I can't be," she said. "How could I possibly have gotten pregnant?"

"The method hasn't changed much through the centuries."

"Yes, but just one night…"

One night. One endless night.

"You need to make an appointment with your doctor," Susie said gently.

"No," Laurel whispered. She lifted her head and stared at Susie. "No," she said, more strongly. "It's ridiculous. I am not pregnant. I have the flu, that's all."

"I'm sure you're right," Susie said with a false smile. "But, what the heck, you want to make certain."

Laurel rose from the bed. "Look, how's this sound? I'll spend all day tomorrow in bed. I'll down aspirin and lots of liquids and if I'm not feeling better by Monday or Tuesday, I'll call my doctor."

"Your gynecologist."

"Really, Susie." Laurel looped her arm around the other woman's shoulders. Together, they headed for the foyer. "Give that imagination of yours a rest and I'll do the same for my flu-racked bones. And be sure and tell George I'm taking a rain check on dinner."

"I'm getting the brush-off, huh?"

"Well," Laurel said with forced gaiety, "if you want to hang around and listen to me upchuck again, you're welcome."

"Listen, if you need anything… Aspirin, Pepto-Bismol…" Susie flashed a quick smile. "Just someone to talk to, I'm here."

"Thanks, but I'm fine. Truly. You'll see. These bugs are all the same. You feel like dying for twenty-four hours and then you're as good as new."

"Didn't you say you'd been feeling shaky all week?"

"Twenty-four hours, forty-eight, what's the difference?" Laurel swung the door open. "It's flu, that's all. I'm not pregnant. Trust me."

"Uh-huh," Susie said, without conviction.

"I'm not," Laurel said firmly.

She held a smile until the door shut and she was safely alone. Then the smile faded and she sank back against the wall, eyes tightly shut. "I'm not," she whispered.

But she was.

Four weeks gone, Dr. Glassman said, later that afternoon, as Laurel sat opposite her in the gynecologist's sunny, plant-filled Manhattan office.

"I'm glad we could fit you in at the last minute like this, Laurel." The doctor smiled. "And I'm glad I can make such a certain diagnosis. You are with child."

With child. Damian's child.

"Have you married, since I saw you last?" A smile lit Dr. Glassman's pleasant, sixtyish face again. "Or have you decided, as is becoming so common, to have a child and remain single?"

Laurel licked her lips. "I—I'm still single."

"Ah. Well, you'll forgive me if I put on my obstetrical hat for a while and urge that you include your baby's father in his—or her—life, to as great a degree as possible." The doctor chuckled softly. "I know there are those who would have me drawn and quartered for saying such a thing, but children need two parents, whenever it's possible. A mother and a father, both."

There was no arguing with that, Laurel thought, oh, there was no arguing with—

"Any questions?"

Laurel cleared her throat. "No. None that I can think of just now, anyway."

"Well, that's it for today, then." The doctor took a card from a holder on her desk, scribbled something on it and handed it to Laurel. "Phone me Tuesday and I'll give you your lab reports, but I'm sure nothing unforeseen will arise. You're in excellent health, my dear. I see no reason why your baby shouldn't be healthy and full-term."

Dr. Glassman rose from her chair. Laurel did, too, but when the doctor smiled at her, she couldn't quite manage a smile in return.

"Laurel?" The doctor settled back behind her desk and peered over the rims of her reading glasses. "Of course," she said gently, "if you wish to make other arrangements..."

"I'm four weeks pregnant, you say?"

"Just about."

"And—and everything seems fine?"

"Perfectly fine."

Laurel gazed down at her hands, which were linked carefully in her lap. "If I should decide... I mean, if I were to..."

The doctor's voice was even more gentle. "You've plenty of time to think things through, my dear."

Laurel nodded and rose to her feet. Suddenly she felt a thousand years old.

"Thank you, Doctor."

The gynecologist rose, too. She came around her desk and put her arm lightly around Laurel's shoulders.

"I know what an enormous decision this is," she said. "If you need someone to talk to, my service can always reach me."

A baby, Laurel thought as she rode down in the elevator to the building's lobby. A child of her flesh. Hers, and Damian's.

Babies were supposed to be conceived in love, not in the throes of a passion that made no sense, a passion so out of character that she'd tried to put it out of her mind all these weeks. Not that she'd managed. In the merciless glare of daylight, she'd suddenly think of what she'd done and hate herself for it.

But at night, with the moonlight softening the shadows, she dreamed about Damian and awakened in a tangle of sheets, with the memory of his kisses still hot on her lips.

Laurel gave herself a little shake. This wasn't the time for that kind of nonsense. There were decisions to be made, although the only practical one was self-evident. There was no room in her life for a baby. Her apartment wasn't big enough. Her life was too unsettled, what with her career winding down and an uncertain future ahead. And then there was the biggest consideration of all. Dr. Glassman was right; some people might think it old-fashioned but it was true. Children were entitled to at least begin life with two parents.

The elevator door slid open and she stepped out into the lobby. Her high heels clicked sharply against the marble floor as she made her way toward the exit.

A baby. A soft, sweet-smelling, innocent bundle of smiles and gurgles. A child, to lavish love upon. To warm her heart and give purpose to her existence. Her throat constricted. A part of Damian that would be hers forever.

She paused outside the building, while an unseasonable wind ruffled her hair. Gum wrappers and a torn page from the *New York Times* flapped at her feet in the throes of a mini-tornado.

What was the point in torturing herself? She wasn't about to have this baby. Hadn't she already decided that? Her reasoning was sound; it was logical. It was—

"Laurel?"

Her heart stumbled. She knew the voice instantly; she'd heard it in her dreams a thousand times during the past long, tortured weeks. Still, she tried to tell herself that it couldn't be Damian. He was the last person she ever wanted to set eyes on again, especially now.

"Laurel."

Oh God, she thought, and she turned toward the curb and saw him stepping out of the same black limousine that had a month ago transported her from sanity to delirium. All at once, the wind seemed to grow stronger. Her vision blurred and she began to sway unsteadily.

And then she was falling, falling, and only Damian's arms could bring her to safety.

CHAPTER SEVEN

WHAT KIND OF MAN wanted a woman who'd made it clear she didn't want him?

Only a man who was a damned fool, and Damian had never counted himself as such.

And yet, four weeks after Laurel Bennett had slept in his arms and then walked out of his life, he had not been able to forget her.

He dreamed of her—hot, erotic dreams of the sort he'd left behind in adolescence. He thought of her during the least expected moments during the day, and when he'd tried to purge his mind and his flesh by becoming involved with someone else, it hadn't worked. He had wined and dined half a dozen of New York's most beautiful women during the past month, and every one had ended her evening puzzled, disappointed and alone.

It was stupid, and it angered him. He was not a man to waste time mourning lost opportunities or dreams. It was the philosophy that had guided his life since childhood; why should it fail him now? Laurel was what his financial people would have termed a write-off. She was a gorgeous woman with a hot body and an icy heart. She'd used him the way he'd used women in the past.

So how come he couldn't get her out of his head?

It was a question without an answer, and it was gnawing at him as his car pulled to the curb before the skyscraper that housed his corporate headquarters...which was why, when he first saw her, he wondered if he'd gone completely over the edge. But this was no hallucination. Laurel was real, she was coming out of the adjacent building—and she was even more beautiful than he'd remembered.

103

He stepped onto the sidewalk and hesitated. What now? Should he wait for her to notice him? He had nothing to say to her, really; still, he wanted to talk to her. Hell, he wanted more than that. He wanted to go to her, take her in his arms, run his thumb along her bottom lip until her mouth opened to his...

Damian frowned. What was this? The feverish glow on her cheeks couldn't hide the fact that her face was pale. She seemed hesitant, just standing there while pedestrians flowed around her like a stream of water against an immutable rock.

Dammit, she was weeping!

He started toward her. "Laurel?"

She had to be ill. She'd never cry, otherwise; he knew it instinctively. His belly knotted.

"Laurel," he shouted, and she looked up and saw him.

For one wild, heart-stopping instant, he thought he saw her face light with joy but he knew it had only been his imagination because a second later her eyes widened, her pallor became waxy and she mouthed his name as if it were an obscenity.

His mouth thinned. To hell with her, then...

God, she was collapsing!

"Laurel," Damian roared, and he dove through the crowd and snatched her up in his arms just before she fell.

She made a little sound as he gathered her close to him.

"It's all right," he whispered, "I've got you, Laurel. It's okay."

Her lashes fluttered. She looked at him but he could tell she wasn't really focusing. His arms tightened around her and he pressed his lips to her hair while his heart thundered in his chest. What if he hadn't been here, to catch her? What if she'd fallen?

What if he'd never held her in his arms again?

"Damian?" she whispered.

There was a breathy little catch in her voice, and it tore

at his heart. She sounded as fragile as Venetian glass. She felt that way, too. She was tall for a woman and he would never have thought of her as delicate yet now, in his arms, that was how she seemed.

"Damian? What happened?"

"How in hell should I know!" The words sounded uncaring. He hadn't meant them to be, it was just that a dozen emotions were warring inside him and he didn't understand a one of them. "I was just getting out of my car... You fainted."

"Fainted? Me?" He watched the tip of her tongue slick across her lips. "Don't be silly. I've never passed out in my..." Color flooded her face as she remembered. The doctor. The diagnosis. "Oh God," she whispered, and squeezed her eyes shut.

Damian frowned. "What is it? Are you going to pass out again?"

She took a deep breath and forced herself to open her eyes. Damian looked angry. Well, why not? He'd never expected to see her again and now here he was, standing on a crowded street with her in his arms, playing an unwilling Sir Galahad to her damsel in distress and, dammit, *he* was the reason for that distress. If she'd never laid eyes on him, never gone to dinner with him, never let herself be seduced by him...

It wasn't true. He hadn't seduced her. She'd gone to bed with him willingly. Eagerly. Even now, knowing that her world would never be the same again no matter what she decided, even now, lying in his arms, she felt—she felt—

She stiffened, and put her palms flat against his chest.

"I'm not going to pass out again, no. I'm fine, as a matter of fact. Please put me down."

"I don't think so."

"Don't be ridiculous!" People hurrying past were looking at them with open curiosity. Even in New York, a man standing in the middle of a crowded sidewalk with a woman in his arms was bound to attract attention. "Damian, I said—"

"I heard what you said." The crowd gave way, not much and not very gracefully, but Damian gave it no choice. "Coming through," he barked, and Laurel caught her breath as she realized he was carrying her back into the building she'd just left.

"What are you doing?"

"There must be a dozen doctors' offices in this building. We'll pick the first one and—"

"No!" Panic surged through her with the speed of adrenaline. "I don't need a doctor!"

"Of course you do. People don't pass out cold for no reason."

"But there was a reason. I—I've been dieting." It was the same lie she'd tried on Susie hours ago, but this time, she knew it would work. "Nothing but tomato juice and black coffee for breakfast, lunch and dinner," she said, rattling off the latest lose-weight-quick scheme that was floating through the fashion world. "You can drop five pounds in two days."

Five pounds? Damian couldn't imagine why she'd want to lose an ounce. She felt perfect to him, warm and lushly curved, just as she'd been in his dreams each night.

"You don't need to lose five pounds."

"The camera doesn't agree."

His smile was quick and dangerously sexy. "Maybe the camera hasn't had as intimate a view of you as I have."

Laurel stiffened in his arms. "How nice to know you're still the perfect gentleman. For the last time, Damian. Put me down!"

His eyes narrowed at the coldness of her voice. "My pleasure." He put her on her feet but he kept a hand clamped around her elbow. "Let's go."

"Go? Go where? Dammit, Damian..."

She sputtered with indignation as he hustled her through

the door, across the sidewalk and toward the limousine. Stevens was already out of the front seat, standing beside the rear door and holding it open, his face a polite mask as if he were accustomed to seeing his employer snatch women off the street.

Laurel dug in her heels but it was useless. Damian was strong, and determined, and even when she called him a word that made his eyebrows lift, he didn't loosen his hold.

"Thank you, Stevens," he said smoothly. "Get into the car please, Laurel."

Get into the car, *please?* He made it sound like a polite request, but a request was something you could turn down. This was a command. Despite her struggles, her protests, her locked knees and gritted teeth, Damian was herding her onto the leather seat.

She swung toward him, eyes blazing, as he settled himself alongside her.

"How *dare* you? How dare you treat me this way? I am not some—some package to be dumped in a truck and—and shipped off."

"No," he said coldly, "you are not. You're a pigheaded female, apparently bent on seeing which you can manage first, starving yourself to death or giving yourself a concussion." The car nosed into the stream of traffic moving sluggishly up the avenue. "Well, I'm going to take you home. Then, for all I give a damn, you can gorge on tomato soup and black coffee while you practice swan dives on the living-room floor."

"It's tomato juice," Laurel said furiously, "not soup. And I was not doing swan dives." She glared at Damian. Her skirt was rucked up, her hair was hanging in her eyes, a button had popped off her knit dress and there he sat, as cool as ice, with a look on his face that said he was far superior to other human beings. How she hated this man!

"A perfect three-pointer," he said, "aimed right at the pavement."

"Will you stop that? I just—I felt a little light-headed, that's all."

"At the sight of me," he said, fixing her with a stony look.

Laurel flushed. "Don't flatter yourself."

"Tomato juice and black coffee," he growled. "It's a toss-up which you are, light-brained or light-headed."

Laurel glared at him. She blew a strand of hair off her forehead, folded her arms in unwitting parody of him and they rode through the streets in silence. When they reached her apartment house, she sprang for the door before Damian could move or Stevens could get out of the car.

"Thank you so much for the lift," she said, her words dripping with venom. "I wish I could say it's been a pleasure seeing you, but what's the sense in lying?"

"Such sweet words, Laurel. I'm touched." Damian looked up at her and a half smile curled over his mouth. "Remember what I said. You don't need to lose any weight."

"Advice from an expert," she said, with a poisonous smile.

"Try some real food for a change."

"What are you, a nutritionist?"

"Of course, you could always get back into the car."

"In your dreams," she said, swinging away from him.

"We could go back to the *Penthouse*. Maybe you'd like to see what you missed last time. The caviar, the duck, the soufflé…"

Caviar, oily and salty. Duck, with the fat melting under the skin. Chocolate soufflé, under a mantle of whipped cream…

Laurel's stomach lifted. No, she thought, oh please, no…

The little she had eaten since the morning bolted up her throat.

Dimly, over the sound of her retching, she heard Damian's soft curse. Then his hands were clasping her shoulders, supporting her as her belly sought to do the impossible and turn itself inside-out. When the spasms passed, he pulled her back against him. She went willingly, mortified by shame but weak in body and in spirit, desperately needing the comfort he offered.

"I'm so sorry," she whispered.

Damian turned her toward him. He took out his handkerchief and gently wiped her clammy forehead and her mouth. Then he swung her into his arms and carried her inside the house.

She was beyond protest. When he asked for her keys, she handed him her pocketbook. When he settled her on the living-room couch, she fell back against the cushions. He took off her shoes, undid the top buttons on her dress, tucked a pillow under her head and an afghan over her legs and warned her not to move.

Move? She'd have laughed, if she'd had the strength. As it was, she could barely nod her head.

Damian took off his jacket, tossed it over a chair and headed for the kitchen. She heard the fridge opening and she wondered what he'd think when he saw the contents. Her seesawing stomach had kept her from doing much shopping or cooking lately.

Laurel swallowed. Better not to think about food. With luck, there just might be some ginger ale on the shelf, or some Diet Coke.

"Ginger ale," Damian said. He squatted down beside her, put his arm around her shoulders and eased her head up. "It's flat, but that's just as well. Slowly, now. One sip at a time."

Another command, but she still didn't have the energy to argue. Anyway, it was good advice. She didn't want to be sick again, not with Damian here.

"There's a chemistry experiment in your kitchen," he said.

"A chem...?"

"Either that, or an alien presence has landed on the counter near the sink."

Laurel laughed weakly and lay back against the pillow. "It's sourdough."

"Ah. Well, I hope you don't mind, but I've disposed of it. I had the uncomfortable feeling it was planning on taking over the apartment."

"Thanks."

"How do you feel now?"

"Better." She sighed deeply, yawned and found herself fighting to keep her eyes open. "I must have eaten something that disagreed with me."

"Close your eyes," he said. "Rest for a while."

"I'm not tired."

"Yes, you are."

"For heaven's sake, Damian, must you pretend you know every…"

Her eyes closed. She was asleep.

Damian rose to his feet. No, he thought grimly, he didn't know everything, but he knew enough to figure that a woman who claimed she'd been on a diet of tomato juice and black coffee wasn't very likely to have eaten something that made her sick…especially not when she was carrying around a little white card like the one that had fallen from her pocket when he'd put her on the couch.

He walked into the kitchen and took the card from the table, where he'd left it: Vivian Glassman, M.D., Gynecology and Obstetrics.

It probably didn't mean a thing. People tucked away cards and forgot about them, and even if that was where Laurel had been today, what did it prove? Women went for gynecological checkups regularly.

His fist clenched around the card. He thought of Laurel's face, when she'd seen him coming toward her a little while ago—and he thought of something else.

All these weeks that he'd dreamed of her, relived the

night they'd spent in each other's arms. The heat, the sweetness—all of it had seemed permanently etched into his brain. Now, another memory vied for his attention, one that made his belly cramp.

In all that long, wild night, he'd never thought to use a condom.

It was so crazy, so irresponsible, so completely unlike him. It was as if he'd been intoxicated that night, drunk on the smell of Laurel's skin and the taste of her mouth.

He hadn't used a condom. She hadn't used a diaphragm. Now she was nauseous, and faint, and she was seeing a doctor whose specialty was obstetrics.

Maybe she was on the pill. Maybe his imagination was in overdrive.

Maybe it was time to get some answers.

He took a long, harsh breath. Then he reached for the phone.

Laurel awoke slowly.

She was lying on the living-room couch. Darkness had gathered outside the windows but someone had turned on the table lamp.

Someone?

Damian.

He was sitting in a chair a few feet away. There was a granitelike set to his jaw; above it, his mouth was set in a harsh line.

"How do you feel?"

She swallowed experimentally. Her stomach growled, but it stayed put.

"Much better." She sat up, pushed the afghan aside and swung her legs to the floor. "Thank you for everything, Damian, but there really wasn't any need for you to sit here while I slept." He said nothing, and the silence beat in her ears. Something was wrong, she could feel it. "What time is it, anyway?'' she asked, trying for a light tone. ''I must have slept for—''

''When did you plan on telling me?''

Her heart thumped, then lodged like a stone behind her breastbone.

''Plan on telling you what?'' She rose to her feet and he did, too, and came toward her. Damn, where were her shoes? He was so tall. It put her at a disadvantage, to let him loom over her like this.

''Perhaps you didn't intend to tell me.'' His voice hummed with challenge; his accent thickened. ''Was that your plan?''

''I don't know what you're talking about,'' she said, starting past him, ''and I'm really not in the mood for games.''

''And I,'' he said, clamping his hand down on her shoulder, ''am not in the mood for lies.''

Her eyes flashed fire as she swung toward him. ''I think you'd better leave.''

''You're pregnant,'' he said flatly.

Pregnant. Pregnant. The word seemed to echo through the room.

''I don't know what you're talking about.''

''It will be easier if you tell me the truth.''

She twisted free of his grasp and pointed at the door. ''It will be easier if you get out of here.''

''Is the child mine?''

''Is...?'' Laurel stuffed her hands into her pockets. ''There is no child. I don't know where you got this idea, but—''

''How many men were you with that week, aside from me?''

''Get out, damn you!''

''I ask you again, is the child mine?''

She stared at him, her lips trembling. No, she wanted to

say, it is not. I was with a dozen men that week. A hundred. A thousand.

"Answer me!" His hands clamped around her shoulders and he shook her roughly. "Is it mine?"

In the end, it was too barbarous a lie to tell.

"Yes," she whispered, "it's yours."

He said nothing for a long moment. Then he jerked his head towards the sofa.

"Sit down, Laurel."

She looked up and their eyes met. A shudder raced through her. She stepped back, until she felt the edge of the sofa behind her, and then she collapsed onto the cushions like a rag doll.

"How—how did you find out?"

His mouth curled. He reached into his pocket, took out a small white card and tossed it into her lap. Laurel stared down at it. It was the card Dr. Glassman had given her.

She looked up at him. "She told you? Dr. Glassman *told* you? She had no right! She—"

"She told me nothing." His mouth twisted again. "And everything."

"I don't understand."

"The card fell from your pocket. I telephoned Glassman's office. The receptionist put me through when I said I was a 'friend' of yours and concerned about your health."

The twist he put on the word brought a rush of color to Laurel's face. Damian saw it and flashed a thin smile.

"Apparently your physician made the same interpretation. But she was very discreet. She acknowledged only that she knew you. She said I would have to discuss your medical condition with you, and she hung up."

Laurel's face whitened. "Then—then you didn't really know! You lied to me. You fooled me into—into—"

"I put two and two together, that's all, and then I asked a question, which you answered."

"It wasn't a question!" Laurel drew a shuddering breath. "You said you knew that I was—that I was—"

"I asked if it was my child." He moved suddenly, bending down and spearing his arms on either side of her, trapping her, pinning her with a look that threatened to turn her to ice. "My child, damn you! What were you planning, Laurel? To give it up for adoption? To have it aborted?"

"No!" The cry burst from her throat and, as it did, she knew that it was the truth. She would not give up the life within her. She wanted her baby, with all her heart and soul, had wanted it from the moment the doctor had confirmed that she was pregnant. "No," she whispered, her gaze steady on his. "I'm not going to do that. I'm going to have my baby, and keep it."

"Keep it?" Damian's mouth twisted. "This is not a puppy we speak of. How will you keep it? How will you raise a child alone?"

"You'd be amazed at how much progress women have made," Laurel said defiantly. "We're capable of rearing children as well as giving birth to them."

"A child will interfere with the self-indulgent life you lead."

"You don't know the first thing about my life!"

"I know that a woman who sleeps with strangers cannot possibly pretend to be a fit mother for my child."

Laurel slammed her fist into his shoulder. "What a hypocritical son of a bitch you are! Who are you to judge me? It took two of us to create this baby, Damian, two strangers in one bed that night!"

A thin smile touched his lips. "It is not the same."

"It is not the same," she said, cruelly mimicking his tone and his accent. She rose and shoved past him. "Do us both a favor, will you? Get out of here. Get out of my life. I don't ever want to see your face again!"

"I would do so, and gladly, but you forget that this life you carry belongs to me."

"It's a baby, Damian. You don't own a baby. I suppose that's hard for someone like you to comprehend, but a child's not a—a commodity. You can't own it, even if your name is Damian Skouras."

They glared at each other, and then he muttered something in Greek and stalked away from her.

Dammit, she was right! He was behaving like an ass. That self-righteous crap a minute ago, about a woman who slept with strangers not being a fit mother, was ridiculous. He was as responsible for what had happened as she was.

And now she was carrying a child. His child. A deep warmth suffused his blood. He had always thought raising Nick would be the closest he'd come to fatherhood. Now, Fate and a woman who'd haunted his dreams had joined forces to show him another way.

Slowly, he turned and looked at Laurel.

"I want my child," he said softly.

Laurel went cold. "What do you mean, you want your child?"

"I mean exactly what I said. This child is mine, and I will not forfeit my claim to it."

His claim? She felt her legs turn to jelly. This kind of thing cropped up in the papers and on TV news shows, reports of fathers who demanded, and won, custody. Not many, it was true, but this was Damian Skouras, who had all the power and wealth in the world. He could take her baby from her with a snap of his fingers.

Be calm, she told herself, be calm, and don't let him see how frightened you are.

"Do you understand, Laurel?"

"Yes. I understand." She made her way toward him, her gaze locked on his face, assessing what to offer and what to hold back, wondering how you played poker with a man who owned all the chips. "Look, Damian, let's not discuss this now, when we're both upset."

"There is nothing to discuss. I'm telling you how it will be. I will be a father to my child."

"Well, I'm not—I'm not opposed to you having a role in this. In fact, Dr. Glassman and I talked a little bit about—about the value of a father, in a child's life. I'm sure we can work out some sort of agreement."

"Visiting rights?"

"Yes."

His smile was even more frightening the second time. "How generous of you, Laurel."

"I'm sure we can work out an arrangement that will suit us both."

"Did I ever tell you that my father played no part in my life?"

"Look, I don't know what the situation was between your parents, but—"

"I might as well have been a bastard."

"Damian—"

"I have no great confidence in marriage, I assure you, but when children are involved, I have even less in divorce."

"Well, this wouldn't be the same situation at all," she said, trying not to sound as desperate as she felt. "I mean, since we wouldn't be married, there'd be no divorce to worry ab—"

"My child deserves better. He—or she—is entitled to two parents, and to stability."

"I think so, too," she said quickly. "That's why I'd be willing to—to permit you a role."

"To permit me?" he said, so softly that she knew her choice of words had been an error.

"I didn't mean that the way it sounded. I won't keep you from my—from our—child. I swear it."

"You swear," he said, his tone mocking hers. "How touching. Am I to take comfort in the word of a woman who didn't even intend to tell me she was pregnant?"

"Dammit, what do you want? Just tell me!"

"I *am* telling you. I will not abandon my child, nor be a father in name only, and I have no intention of putting my faith in agreements reached by greedy lawyers."

"That's fine." She gave him a dazzling smile. "No lawyers, then. No judges. We'll sit down, like two civilized people, and work out an arrangement that will suit us both." She cried out sharply as his hands bit into her flesh. "Damian, you're hurting me!"

"Do you take me for a fool?" He leaned toward her, so that his face was only inches from hers. "I can imagine the sort of arrangement you would wish."

"You're wrong. I just agreed, didn't I, that a father has a place in a child's life?"

"Ten minutes ago, you were telling me you never wanted to see my face again."

"Yes, but that was before I understood how deeply you feel about this."

"You mean, it was before you were trapped into telling me you were pregnant." He laughed. "You're a bad liar, Laurel."

"Damn you, Damian! What do you want from me?"

There was a long, heavy silence. Then his arms wound around her and his hands slipped into her hair.

"Don't," she said, but already his mouth was dropping to hers, taking it in a kiss that threatened to steal her sanity. When, finally, he drew back, Laurel was trembling. With hatred, with rage—and with the shattering knowledge that, even now, his kiss could still make her want him.

"I have always believed," he said softly, "that a man should have children only within the sanctity of marriage. But that is a paradox, because I believe that marriage is a farce. Nonetheless, I see no choice here." His hand lifted, as if to touch her hair, then fell to his side. "We will marry within the week."

"We will...?" She felt the blood drain from her face. "Marry? Did you say, *marry*?"

"We will marry, and we will have our child, and we will raise him—or her—together."

"You're crazy! Me, marry you? Never! Do you hear me? Not in a million years would—"

"You've accused me of being arrogant, and egocentric. Well, I assure you, I can be those things, and more." A muscle beside his mouth tightened, and his eyes bored into hers. "I am Damian Skouras. I command resources you'll never dream of. Oppose me, and all you'll gain is ugly notoriety for yourself, your family and our child."

Laurel began to tremble. She stared back at him and then she wrenched free. Angry tears blurred her eyes and she wiped them away with a slash of her hand.

"I hate you, Damian! I'll always hate you!"

He laughed softly, reached for his jacket and slung it over one shoulder.

"That's quite all right, dearest Laurel. From what I know of matrimony, that's the natural state of things."

Damian opened the door and walked out.

CHAPTER EIGHT

FIVE DAYS LATER, they stood as far apart as they could manage in the anteroom to a judge's chambers in a town just north of the city.

Judge Weiss was a friend of a friend, Damian had said. He'd begun to explain the connection, but Laurel had stopped him halfway through.

"It doesn't matter," she'd said stiffly.

And it didn't. For all she gave a damn, the man who was about to marry them could be an insurance salesman who was a justice of the peace in his spare time.

The only thing she wanted now was to get the thing over with.

She hadn't asked anyone to attend the ceremony. She hadn't told Susie or George or even Annie that she was getting married. Her sister had seemed preoccupied lately and anyway, what was there to tell? Surely not the truth, that she'd made the oldest, saddest female blunder in the world and that now she was paying the classic price for it by marrying a man she didn't love.

She'd decided it would be better to break the news when this was all over. She'd make it sound as if she and Damian had followed through on a romantic, spur-of-the-moment impulse. Susie might see through it but Annie, good-hearted soul that she was, would probably be thrilled.

She glanced over at Damian. He was standing with his back to her, staring out the window. He'd been doing that for the past ten minutes, as if the traffic passing by on the road outside was so fascinating that he couldn't tear his gaze from it.

She understood it, because she had been staring at a bad

oil painting of a man in judicial robes with mutton-chop whiskers for the same reason. It was a way of focusing on something other than the reality of what was about to happen.

Laurel took a deep breath. There was still time. Maybe she could convince him that his plan was crazy, that it was no good for him or her or even for their baby.

"Mr. Skouras? Miss Bennett?"

Laurel and Damian both looked around. The door to the judge's office had opened. A small, gray-haired woman smiled pleasantly at them.

"Judge Weiss is ready for you now," she said.

Laurel's hands tightened on her purse. It was like being told the dentist was ready for you. Your heart rate speeded up, your skin got clammy, you had to tell yourself to smile back and act as if that was exactly the wonderful news you'd been waiting for.

Except this wasn't the dentist's office, and she wasn't going to have a tooth drilled. She was going to hand her life over to Damian Skouras.

"Laurel."

She looked up. Damian was coming toward her, his expression grim.

"The judge is ready."

"I heard." She swallowed hard against a sudden rise of nausea, not from the pregnancy—that had ended, strangely enough, the day Damian had learned of her condition. This churning in her gut had to do with the step she was about to take.

I can't. God, I can't.

"Damian." She took a deep breath. "Damian, listen. I think we ought to talk."

His hand closed around hers, tightening in warning, and he smiled pleasantly at the clerk.

"Thank you. Please tell the judge we'll be along in a minute."

As soon as the door swung shut, Damian turned back to Laurel, his eyes cold.

"We have discussed this. There is nothing more to be said."

"We've discussed nothing! You've issued edicts and I've bowed my head in obedience. Well, now I'm telling you that it isn't going to work. I don't think—"

"I haven't asked you to think."

Color flew into her cheeks. "If *you'd* been thinking, we wouldn't be in this mess!"

It was an unfair attack, and she knew it. She was as responsible for what had happened as Damian, but why should she play fair when he didn't? Still, he didn't deny the accusation.

"Yes." A muscle tightened in his jaw. "You are correct. We are in, as you say, a mess, and since it is one of my own making, the solution is mine, as well. There is no other course to take."

"No other course that meets with your approval, you mean." She tried to shake off his hand, but he wouldn't let her. "If you'd be reasonable—"

"Meaning that I should permit you to do as you see fit?"

"Yes. No. Will you stop twisting everything I say? If you'd just think for a minute... We have nothing in common. We hardly know each other. We don't even like each other, and yet—and yet, you expect me to—to marry you, to become your wife."

"I expect exactly that."

Laurel yanked her hand from his. "Damn you," she whispered. She was trembling with rage, at Damian, at herself, at a situation that had gotten out of control and had brought this nightmare down on her head. "Damn you, Damian! You have an answer for everything and it's the same each time. You know best, you know what's right, you know how things have to be—"

Behind them, the door swung open.

"Mr. Skouras? The judge has a busy schedule this morning. If you and Miss Bennett wouldn't mind…?"

Miss Bennett minds, very much, Laurel thought…but Damian's hand had already closed around hers.

"Of course," he said, with a soft-as-butter smile that had nothing to do with the steely pressure of his fingers. "Darling? Are you ready?"

His smile was soft, too, but the warning in his eyes left no room for doubt. Make no mistake, he was telling her; do as I say or suffer the consequences.

Laurel gathered what remained of her self-composure, lifted her chin and nodded.

"As ready as I can be," she said coolly, and let him lead her into the judge's office.

It was a large, masculine room, furnished in heavy mahogany. The walls were paneled with some equally dark wood and hung with framed clippings and photos of politicos ranging from John F. Kennedy to Bill Clinton. Someone, perhaps the clerk, had tucked a bouquet of flowers into a coffee mug and placed it on the mantel above the fireplace, but the flowers weren't fresh and their drooping heads and faded colors only added a mournful touch to the room. An ancient air conditioner wheezed in the bottom half of a smeared window as it tried to breathe freshness into air redolent with the smell of old cigars.

"Mr. Skouras," the judge said, rising from behind his desk and smiling, "and Miss Bennett. What a fine day for a wedding."

It was, Laurel supposed. Outside, the sun was shining brightly; puffy white clouds sailed across a pale blue sky.

But weddings weren't supposed to be held in stuffy rooms like this one. A woman dreamed of being married in a place filled with light; she dreamed of flowers and friends around her, and of coming to her groom with a heart filled with joy and love.

*If only this were real. If only Damian truly wanted her,
and loved her...*

A sound of distress burst from Laurel's throat. She took
a quick step back. Instantly Damian's arm slid around her
waist.

"Laurel?" he said softly.

She looked up at him, her eyes dark and glistening with
unshed tears, and he felt as if a fist had clamped around
his heart.

She didn't want this. He knew that, but it didn't matter.
He'd told himself that a dozen times over. The child. That
was the only thing that mattered. They had to marry, for
the sake of the child. It was the right thing to do.

Now, looking down into the eyes of his bride, seeing the
sorrow shimmering in their depths, Damian felt a twinge
of uncertainty.

Was Laurel right? Was this a mistake?

She had offered to share the raising of their child with
him, and he had scoffed. And with good cause. It didn't
take a genius to see that what she really wanted was to get
him out of her life forever. Still, a clever attorney could
have made that an impossibility and he had a team of the
best. A child should be raised by two parents; his belief in
that would never change. But what good could come of
being raised by a mother and father who lived in a state of
armed truce?

Why, then, was he forcing this marriage?

Why was he taking as his wife a woman who hated him
so much that she was on the verge of weeping? Damian's
throat tightened. This wasn't the way it should be. A man
wanted his bride to look up at him and smile; he wanted
to see joy shining in her eyes as they were joined together.

If only, just for a little while, Laurel could look as if she
wanted him. As if she remembered how it had been, that
night...

"...always beautiful but you, my dear Miss Bennett, are

a treat for an old man's eyes. And Mr. Skouras.'' The judge, a big man with a belly and a voice to match, clasped Damian's hand and shook it heartily. ''I know you by reputation, of course. It is a pleasure to meet you, and to officiate at your wedding.''

Damian cleared his throat. ''Thank you for fitting us into your schedule, Your Honor. I know how difficult it must have been, but everything was so last minute...''

Judge Weiss laughed. ''Elopements generally are, my boy.'' He smiled, rubbed his hands together and reached for a small, battered black book. ''Well, shall we begin?''

''No!'' Laurel's cry was as sharp as broken glass. The judge's smile faded as he looked at her.

''I beg your pardon? Is there a problem, Miss Bennett?''

''There is no problem,'' Damian said smoothly. ''We made our decision so quickly...my fiancée is simply having a last-minute attack of nerves, Your Honor.'' Damian slid his arm around Laurel's waist. She looked up at him and he smiled. It was an affectionate smile, just as the way he was holding her seemed affectionate, but she knew better. ''I suppose,'' he said, flashing the judge a just-between-us-boys grin that made the older man chuckle, ''I suppose that no bride is calm on her wedding day.''

''Damian,'' Laurel said, ''it isn't too late—''

''Hush,'' he whispered, and before she could stop him, he tilted her chin up and kissed her.

It was a quick, gentle kiss, nothing more than the lightest brush of his mouth against hers, and she wondered, later, if that had been her undoing. Perhaps if he'd kissed her harder, if he'd tried, with silken tongue and teasing teeth, to remind her of the passion that had once consumed them, everything would have ended in that instant.

But he didn't. He kissed her the way a man kisses a woman he truly loves, with a sweet tenderness that numbed her senses.

''Everything will be fine, *kalí mou*,'' he murmured. He

lifted her hand to his lips, pressed a kiss to the palm and sealed her fingers over it. "Trust me."

The judge cleared his throat. "Well," he said briskly, "are we ready now?"

"Ready," Damian said, and so it began.

The words were not as flowery, but neither were they very different from the ones that had been spoken in the little Connecticut church, barely more than four weeks before. The sentiments were surely the same; the judge had told Damian, over the phone, that he prided himself on offering a little ceremony of his own creation to each couple he wed.

He spoke of friendship, and of love. Of the importance of not taking vows lightly. Of commitment, and respect.

And, at last, he intoned the words Laurel had been dreading.

"Do you, Laurel Bennett, take Damian Skouras to be your lawfully wedded husband?"

A lump seemed to have lodged in her throat. She tried to swallow past it. The judge, and Damian, were looking at her.

"I'm sorry," she said, stalling for time, "I didn't—I didn't hear…"

The judge smiled. "I asked if you were prepared to take Damian Skouras as your lawfully wedded husband."

"Miss Bennett?"

Laurel shut her eyes. She thought of her baby, and of the power Damian held…and then, though it was stupid and pointless, because she didn't love him, didn't even like him, she thought of the way he'd kissed her only moments ago…

She took a shaky breath, opened her eyes and said, "Yes."

The car was waiting outside.

"Congratulations, sir," Stevens said, as he opened the

door. He looked at Laurel and smiled. "And my best wishes to you, too, madam."

Best wishes? On an occasion such as this? Laurel felt like laughing. Or weeping. Or maybe both but then, the chauffeur was as much in the dark about this marriage as everybody else.

It wasn't easy, but she managed to summon up a smile. "Thank you, Stevens."

Damian seemed to find that amusing.

"Nicely done," he said, as the car swung out into traffic. "I'd half expected you to assure Stevens that you were being carried off against your will."

Laurel folded her hands in her lap and stared straight ahead.

"Stevens was just being polite, and I responded in kind. I can hardly hold him responsible for the dilemma I'm in."

"The dilemma you're in?"

There was a soft note of warning in his voice, but Laurel chose to ignore it.

"We're alone now, Damian. The judge isn't here to watch our performance. If you expect me to pretend, you're in for an unpleasant surprise."

"I refer to your attitude toward my child. I will not have it thought of as a dilemma."

"You're twisting my words again. This travesty of a marriage is what I meant. I want this baby, and you damn well know it. Otherwise I wouldn't be sitting here, pretending that—that all that mumbo jumbo we just went through is real."

"Pretending?" His lips compressed into a tight smile. "There's no pretense in this. I have a document in my pocket that attests to the legitimacy of our union. You are my wife, Laurel, and I am your husband."

"Never!" The words she'd kept bottled inside tumbled from her lips. "Do you hear me, Damian? In my heart, where it matters, you'll never be my husband!"

''Such a sharp tongue, sweetheart.'' He shifted in his seat so that he was leaning toward her, his face only inches away. ''And such empty threats.''

''It isn't a threat.'' She could feel her pulse beating like a fist in her throat. ''It's a statement of fact. You may have been able to force me into this marriage but you can't change what I feel.''

He touched the back of his hand to her cheek, then drew his fingers slowly into her hair. The pins that held it up worked loose and it started to come undone, but when she lifted her hand to fix it, he stopped her.

''Leave it,'' he said softly.

''It's—it's messy.''

He smiled. ''It's beautiful, and it's how I prefer it.''

It was difficult to breathe, with him so close. She thought of putting her hands against his chest and pushing him away, but then she thought of that night, that fateful night, and how they'd ridden in this car and how she'd wound her arms tightly around his neck and kissed him...

...how she longed to kiss him, even now.

God. Oh God, what was happening to her?

''Really,'' she said, with a forced little laugh, ''how I wear my hair is none of your business.''

''You are my wife.'' He ran his hand the length of her throat. Her pulse fluttered under his fingers like a trapped bird, confirming what he already suspected, that though his bride seemed to have recovered her composure, she was not quite as calm as she wanted him to believe. ''Is the thought so difficult to bear?''

''I learned something, when I was first starting in modeling. I never asked a question unless I was sure I wanted to hear the answer.''

He stroked his thumb across the fullness of her bottom lip. A tremor went through her, and her eyes darkened.

''Don't,'' she whispered—but her lips parted and her breathing quickened.

His body quickened, too. She wanted him, despite everything she'd said. He could read it in the blurring of her eyes, in the softening of her mouth.

Now, he thought. He could have her now, in his arms, returning his kisses, sighing her acquiescence against his skin as he undressed her.

He bent his head, pressed his mouth to the slender column of her throat. She smelled of sunshine and flowers, summer and rain. He shut his eyes, nuzzled her collar aside and kissed her skin. It was softer than any silk, and as warm as fresh honey.

"Laurel," he whispered, and he drew back and looked into her face. Her eyes were wide with confusion and dark with desire, and a fierce sense of joy swept through him.

He ran his thumb over her mouth again. Again, her lips parted and this time, he dipped into the heat that awaited him. A soft moan broke from her throat and he felt the quick flutter of her tongue against his finger. Her hands lifted, pressed against his shoulders, then rose to encircle his neck. Damian groaned and pressed her back into the seat.

God, how he wanted her! And he could take her. She was his wife, and she wanted him. She was a sensual, sexual woman and now there would be no other men for her.

What choice did she have, but to want him?

He pulled away from her so quickly that she fell back against the leather seat.

"You see?" he said, and smiled coldly. "It will not be so bad, to be my wife."

Her face reddened. "I hope you go to hell," she said, in a voice that trembled, and as he turned his face and stared out the window at the landscape rushing by, he wondered what she would say if he told her that he was starting to think he was already there.

He had to give her credit.

He had told her they'd be leaving the country but she

didn't ask any questions, not where they were going, or why, and she didn't blink an eye when they boarded a sleek private jet with Skouras International discreetly stenciled on the fuselage.

She settled into a seat, buckled her seat belt, plucked a magazine from the table beside her and buried her nose in it, never looking up or speaking except to decline, politely, when the steward asked if she'd like lunch.

But not even an actress as good as Laurel could keep up the deception forever. Four hours into the flight, she finally put the magazine down and stirred.

"Is it a matter of control?" she said. "Or did you just want to see how long it would take me to ask?"

He looked up from his laptop computer and the file he'd been pretending to read and smiled politely.

"Pardon?"

"Stop playing games, Damian. Where are we going?"

He took his time replying, signing off the file, shutting down the computer, stuffing it back into its leather case and laying it aside before he looked at her.

"Out of the country. I told you that yesterday."

"You told me you had business to attend to and to bring along my passport. But we've been flying for hours and—" *and I'm frightened* "—and now, I'm asking you where you're taking me."

"Greece," he said, almost lazily.

His answer shocked her. She'd been to Greece once; she remembered its stark beauty as well as the feeling that had come over her, as if she'd stumbled into another time when the old rules that governed behavior between the sexes were very different than they were now.

"Greece?" she said, trying not to let her growing apprehension show. "But why?"

"Why not?"

"I'm not in the mood for games, Damian. I asked a

question, and I'd like an answer. Why are we going to Greece?''

There were half a dozen answers to give her, all of them reasonable and all of them true.

Because I own an island there, he could have said, and there was a storm last month and now I want to check on my property. Because I have business interests on Crete, and those, too, need checking. Because I like the hot sun and the sapphire water...

''Because it is where I was born,'' he said simply, and waited.

Her reaction was swift and not anything he'd expected.

''I do not want my child born in Greece,'' she said hotly. ''He—or she—is going to be an American citizen.''

Damian laughed softly. ''As am I, dearest wife, I assure you.''

''Then why...?''

''I thought it would be a place where we could be free of distraction while we get to know each other.''

Catlike, he stretched. He'd taken off his jacket and tie, undone the top two buttons of his shirt and folded back the sleeves. His skin gleamed golden in the muted cabin light, his muscles flexed. Laurel felt a fine tremor dance down her spine. Whatever else she thought of him, there was no denying that he was a beautiful sight to behold.

And now, he was hers. He was her husband. The night she'd spent in his arms could be a night lived over again, on the sands beside a midnight sea or on a wild hilltop with the sun beating down on the both of them. She could kiss Damian's mouth and run her hands over his skin, whisper his name as he pleasured her...

Panic roughened her voice.

''I don't want to go to Greece, dammit! Didn't it ever occur to you to consult me before you made these plans?''

Damian looked at his wife's face. Her eyes glittered, with an emotion he could not define.

Fear. She was terrified, and of him.

God, why was he being such a mean son of a bitch? He had forced her into this marriage for the best of reasons but that didn't mean he had to treat her so badly. She was right, he should have consulted her. He should have told her, anyway, that he was taking her to Greece, to his island, Actos. He should have told her that for some reason he couldn't fathom, he wanted her to see where he had lost the boy he'd been and found the man he'd become.

He felt a tightening inside him, not just in his belly but in his heart.

"Laurel," he said, and touched her shoulder.

She flinched as if she'd been scalded.

"Don't touch me," she snarled, and he pulled back his hand, his face hardening, and thought that the place he was taking her was better than she deserved.

The plane landed on a small airstrip on Crete. A car met them and whisked them away, past hotels and streets crowded with vacationers, to the docks where sleek yachts bobbed at anchor.

Laurel smiled tightly. Of course. That was a Greek tradition, wasn't it? If you were what Susie had called a zillionaire Adonis, you owned a ship and, yes, Damian led her to one—but it was not a yacht. The *Circe* was a sailboat, large, well kept and handsome, but as different from the huge yachts moored all around her as a racehorse is from a Percheron.

"Damian," a male voice cried.

A man appeared on deck, opening his arms as they climbed the gangplank toward him. He was short and wiry; he had a dark beard and a bald head and he wore jeans and a striped T-shirt, and though he bowed over Laurel's hand and made a speech she sensed was flowery even though she couldn't understand a word, he greeted Damian with a slap on the back and a hug hard enough to break bones.

Damian reciprocated. Then, grinning, the two men turned to Laurel.

"This is Cristos. He takes care of *Circe* for me, when I am away."

"How nice for you," Laurel said, trying to look bored. Not that it was easy. Somehow, she hadn't expected such relaxed give and take between the urbane Damian Skouras and this seaman.

Cristos said something. Damian laughed.

"He bids you welcome, and says to tell you that you are Aphrodite come to life."

"Really?" Laurel smiled coolly. "I thought it was Helen who was carried off against her will."

If she'd thought to rile Damian, she hadn't succeeded. He grinned, told her to stay put, clattered below deck and disappeared.

Stay, she thought irritably, as if she were a well-trained puppy.

Well, she wasn't well trained. And the sooner he understood that, the better for them both.

She rose from the seat where he'd placed her and started forward. Instantly Cristos was at her side. He smiled, said something that sounded like a question and stepped in front of her. Laurel smiled back.

"I'm just going to take a look around."

"Ah. No, madam. Sorry. Is not permitted."

So, he spoke English. And he had his orders. What did Damian think, that she was going to dive overboard and swim for her freedom?

Actually it wasn't a bad idea.

Laurel sighed, wrapped her hands around the railing and gazed blindly out to sea.

It was too late for that.

She was trapped.

She didn't recognize Damian, when he reappeared.

Was this man dressed in cutoff denims, a white T-shirt

and sneakers her urbane husband? And why the change of clothing? It was hot, yes, and the sun beat down mercilessly, but surely it would be cooler, once they set sail.

But Damian's change of clothes had nothing to do with the climate. Every captain needed a crew, and Cristos's crew was Damian.

Except she had it backward. In seconds, she realized that Damian was in charge here, not just in name but in fact. There was a subtle change that took place between the two men as soon as Damian came up the ladder. Even she could sense it, though the men worked together easily. Still, there was no question about who was the leader.

It was Damian, and he led not by command but by example.

She watched him as he took the boat through the narrow channel that led to the open sea. His dark, wind-tossed hair curled around his face. Sunlight glinted on the tiny stud in his ear and when the sun grew too hot, he pulled off his T-shirt and tossed it aside.

Laurel felt her breath catch. She'd blocked the memory of how he'd looked, naked, during the night they'd spent together. Now, she was confronted with his perfect masculinity. He was the elemental male, this stranger she'd married, strong, and powerful, and beautiful to see.

The breeze caught at her hair and whipped it free of the pins she'd carefully replaced during the drive from the airport. She put her hand up to catch the wild curls and suddenly Damian was there, beside her.

"Are you all right?"

Laurel nodded. He was so close to her that she could smell the sun and salt on his skin, and the musky aroma of his sweat. She imagined pressing her lips to his throat, tasting him with the tip of her tongue.

"Yes," she said, "yes, I'm fine."

His hand fell on her shoulder. "You'd tell me if you felt ill, wouldn't you?"

"Damian, really, I'm okay. The nausea is all gone, and you know that Dr. Glassman gave me a clean bill of health."

"And the name of a physician on Crete," he said, and smiled at Laurel's look of surprise. "I told her where I was taking you, and she approved."

He wouldn't have taken her on this trip otherwise. Still, out here on the sea, with the wind blowing and the waves rising to slap against the hull, he was struck again by his bride's fine-boned delicacy.

"Go on," she said, with a little smile that might almost have been real, "Sail your boat. I don't need watching."

His lips curved in a smile. He bent his head and put his lips to her ear, and she shuddered as she felt the soft warmth of his breath.

"Ah," he whispered, "you are wrong, my beautiful wife. Watching is exactly what you need, if a man is to feed his soul."

She tilted her head back and looked at him and when she did, he wrapped his hand around the back of her neck, bent his head and kissed her, hard, on the mouth.

"Leave your hair loose for me," he said, and then he kissed her again before scrambling lithely back to the helm.

Laurel waited until her heartbeat steadied, then raised her head and found Damian looking at her. This was the way a flower must feel, she thought dazedly, as its tightly closed petals unfurl beneath the kiss of the sun.

His final words whispered through her head. Leave your hair loose, he'd said, just like the night they'd made love, just before he'd undressed her, with such slow, sweet care that her heart had almost stopped beating.

But that night was far behind them, and it had no meaning.

Her shoulders stiffened. Defiantly she raised her arms and began to pin up her hair again.

And then the wind gusted, and before she could prevent it, the pins sailed from her hand and disappeared into the sea.

Her shoulders stiffened. Defiantly she raised her arms and began to pull up her again.

And then the wind gusted, and before she could prevent it the pins snapped and the disappeared into the sea...

CHAPTER NINE

THE ISLAND ROSE before them an hour later.

"Actos," Damian said, coming up beside Laurel. She knew, from the way he said it that this was their destination.

She shaded her eyes with her hand and gazed over the narrowing strip of blue water that separated the *Circe* from a small, crescent-shaped harbor. No yachts bobbed at anchor here; the few boats moored were small, sturdy-looking fishing vessels. Square, whitewashed houses topped with red tile roofs stood clustered in the shadow of the sun-baked, rocky cliffs that rose behind them. Overhead, seabirds wheeled against the pale blue sky, their shrill cries echoing over the water.

All at once, Laurel thought of how she had wept last night, as she'd thought of the unknown days and years that lay ahead, and she shuddered.

Damian put his arm around her and drew her against his side.

"What is it? Are you ill?"

"No. No, I told you, I'm fine."

He stepped in front of her, leaned back against the rail of the boat and drew her between his legs. His body felt hard and hot, and the faint male smell of his skin rose to her nostrils. Another tremor went through her. This man was her husband.

Her husband.

"You *are* ill! You're as white as a sheet." His mouth twisted. "I should have realized. The motion of the boat..."

"Damian, really, I'm okay. It's just—too much sun,

136

maybe.'' She smiled brightly. ''I'm used to the concrete canyons of New York, remember?''

''I wasn't thinking. We should have made this trip in two days instead of one.'' The wind ruffled her hair and he caught a strand of it in his fingers. It felt silky, and warm, and he fought to keep from bringing it to his lips. ''I should have considered your condition when I made these plans.''

His hand dropped to the curve of her shoulder and he stroked his thumb lightly against her neck. She had the sudden desire to close her eyes, lean into the gentle caress and give herself up to his touch.

The realization frightened her, and she gave herself up, instead, to a sharp response.

''You should have considered a lot of things, Damian, but you didn't, and here we are.''

His hand fell away from her. ''Yes,'' he said, ''and here we are.''

When Laurel had come to Greece before, it had been to do a cover for *Femme*. They'd shot it on a tiny island that had stunned her with its natural beauty.

Actos was not such a place.

If the island was beautiful, she was hard-pressed to see it. A rusted Ford station wagon was waiting for them at the dock, its mustachioed driver as ancient and gnarled as an olive tree. He and Damian greeted each other quietly, though she noticed that when they clasped hands, the men looked deep into each other's eyes and smiled.

The old man turned to her and took off his cap. He smiled, bowed and said something to Damian.

''Spiro says he is happy to meet you.''

''Tell Spiro I am glad to meet him, too.''

''He says you are more lovely than Aphrodite, and that I am a very fortunate man to have won you.''

''Tell him Aphrodite's an overworked image but that I

thank him anyway for being such a charming liar, and that you are not fortunate, you are a scheming tyrant who blackmailed me into marriage.''

Damian laughed. "That would not upset Spiro. He still remembers the old days, when every man was a king who could as easily take a woman as ask for her.''

The old man leaned toward Damian and said something. Both men chuckled.

Laurel looked from one to the other. ''What did he say now?''

''He said that your eyes are cool.''

''It is more than my eyes that are cool, Damian. And I fail to see why that should make the two of you smile.''

''Because,'' he said, his smile tilting, ''Spiro tells me there is a saying in the village of his birth. A woman who is cold in the day fills the night with heat.''

A flush rose in her cheeks. ''It's amazing, how wrong an old saying can be.''

''Is it, my sweet wife?''

''Absolutely, my unwanted husband.''

Spiro muttered again and Laurel rolled her eyes.

''I feel like the straight man in a comedy act,'' she snapped. ''Now what?''

Damian moved closer to her. ''He thinks there is more than coolness in your eyes,'' he said softly. ''He says you do not look like a happy woman.''

''A clever man, this Spiro.''

''It is, he says, my responsibility to make you happy.''

''Did you tell him you could have done that by leaving me alone?''

Damian's slow smile was a warning, but it came too late. His fingers threaded in her hair and he bent his head and kissed her.

''Kissing me to impress the old man is pathetic,'' Laurel said, when he drew back. She spoke calmly and told herself that the erratic beat of her pulse was the result of weariness, and the sun.

Damian kissed her again, as gently as he had when she'd said 'No' at their wedding.''

"I kiss you because I want to kiss you," he said, very softly, and then he turned away and helped Spiro load their luggage into the old station wagon, while Laurel fought to still her racing heart.

A narrow dirt road wound its way up the cliffs, through groves of dark cypresses and between outcroppings of gray rock. They passed small houses that grew further and further apart as they climbed. After a while, there were no houses at all, only an occasional shepherd's hut. The heat was unrelenting, and a chorus of cicadas filled the air with sound.

The road grew even more narrow. Just when it seemed as if it would end among the clouds, a house came into view. It was made of white stone with a blue tile roof, and it stood on a rocky promontory overlooking the sea.

The house, and the setting, were starkly simple and wildly beautiful, and Laurel knew instantly that this was Damian's home.

A heavy silence, made more pronounced by the shrill of the cicadas and the distant pound of the surf, filled the car as Damian shut off the engine. Behind them, the car door creaked as Spiro got out. He spoke to Damian, who shook his head. The old man muttered in annoyance, doffed his cap to Laurel and set off briskly toward the house.

"What was that all about?"

Damian sighed. "He will be eighty-five soon, or perhaps even older. He's rather mysterious about his age." He got out of the car, came around to Laurel's door and opened it. "Still, he pretends he is a young man. He wanted to take our luggage to the house. I told him not to be such an old fool."

Laurel ignored Damian's outstretched hand and stepped onto the gravel driveway.

"So you told him to send someone else to get our things?"

Damian looked at her. "There is no one else at the house, except for Eleni."

"Eleni?"

"My housekeeper." He reached into the back of the wagon, picked up their suitcases and tossed them onto the grass, his muscles shifting and bunching under the thin cotton T-shirt. "Besides, why would I need anyone to do such a simple job as this?"

Her thoughts flashed back to Kirk, and the staff of ten who'd run his home. She'd never seen him carry anything heavier than his attaché case, and sometimes not even that.

"Well?" Damian's voice was rough. "What do you think? Can you survive a week alone with me, in this place?"

A week? Alone, here, with Damian? She didn't dare tell him what she really thought, that if he had set out to separate her from everything safe and familiar, he had succeeded.

"Well," she said coolly, "it's not Southampton. But I suppose there's hot water, and electricity, at least."

Out of the corner of her eye, she saw Damian's jaw tighten. Good, she thought with bitter satisfaction. What had he expected? Tears? Pleas? A fervent demand he take her somewhere civilized? If that was what he'd hoped for, he'd made an error. She wasn't going to beg, or grovel.

"I know it would please you if I said no." His smile was curt as he stepped past her, hoisted their suitcases and set off for the house. "But we have all the amenities you wish for, my dear wife. I know it spoils things for you, but I am not quite the savage you imagine."

The house was almost glacial, after the heat of the sun-baked hillside. White marble floors stretched to meet white painted walls. Ceiling fans whirred lazily overhead.

Damian dumped the suitcases on the floor and put his hands on his hips.

"Eleni," he roared.

A door slammed in the distance and a slender, middle-aged woman with eyes as dark as her hair came hurrying toward them. She was smiling broadly, but her smile vanished when she saw Damian's stern face. He said a few words to her, in Greek, and then he looked at Laurel.

"Eleni speaks no English, so don't waste your time trying to win her to your cause. She will show you to your room and tend to your needs."

The housekeeper, and not Damian. It was another small victory, Laurel thought, as he strode past her.

Eleni led the way up the stairs to a large, handsome bedroom with an adjoining bath.

Laurel nodded.

"Thank you," she said, "*efcharistó.*"

It was the only word of Greek she remembered from her prior trip. Eleni smiled her appreciation and Laurel smiled back at her, but when the door had shut and she was, at last, alone, her smile faded.

She had set out to irritate Damian and somehow, she'd ended up wounding him. It was more of a victory than she'd ever have hoped.

Why, then, did it feel so hollow?

The cypresses were casting long shadows over the hillside. Soon, it would be night.

Damian stood on the brick terrace and gazed at the sea. He knew he ought to feel exhausted. It had been a long day. An endless day, following hard on the heels of an endless week—a week that had begun with him thinking he'd never see Laurel again and ending with his taking her as his wife.

His wife.

His jaw knotted, and he lifted the glass of chilled *ouzo* to his lips and drank. The anise-flavored liquid slipped easily down his throat, one of the few pleasurable experiences in the entire damned day.

It still didn't seem possible. A little while ago, his life had been set on a fixed course with his business empire as its center. Now, in the blink of an eye, he had a wife, and a child on the way—a wife who treated him, and everything that was his, with such frigid distaste that it made his blood pressure rumble like the volcanos that were at the heart of these islands.

So she didn't like this house. Hell, why should she? He knew what it was, an isolated aerie on the edge of nowhere, and that he'd been less than forthright about its amenities, which began, and just about ended, with little more than electricity and hot water. She was a woman accustomed to luxury, and to the city. Her idea of paradise wasn't likely to include a house on top of a rocky hill overlooking the Aegean, where she was about to spend seven of the longest days of her life trapped with the fool who'd forced her into marriage.

Damian frowned and tossed back the rest of the *ouzo*.

What the hell had he been thinking, bringing her here? God knew this wasn't the setting for a honeymoon—not that this was going to be one. Spiro, that sly old fox, had slapped him on the back and said that it was about time he'd married. Damian had told him to mind his own business.

This wasn't a marriage, it was an arrangement…and maybe that was the best way to think about it. Marriage, under the best of circumstances, was never about love, not once you scratched the surface. It was about lust, or loneliness, or procreation. Well, in that sense, he and Laurel were ahead of the game. There was no pretense in their relationship, no pretending that anything but necessity had brought them to this point in the road.

Damian refilled his glass and took a sip. Viewed reasonably, he really had no cause to complain. Not about having a child, at least. The more he'd thought about it the past week, the more pleased he'd been at the prospect of fatherhood. He'd enjoyed raising Nicholas, but the boy had come into his life almost full-grown. There'd be a special pleasure in holding an infant in his arms, knowing that it carried his name and his genes, that it would be his to mold and nurture.

His mouth twisted in a wry smile. And, despite all the advances of modern science, you still needed a woman to have a baby. A wife, if you wanted to do it right, and as wives went, Laurel would be eminently suitable.

She was beautiful, bright and sophisticated. She'd spent her life rubbing elbows with the rich and famous; to some degree, she was one of them herself. She'd be at ease as the hostess of the parties and dinners his work demanded, and he had no doubt that she'd be a good mother to their child.

As for the rest…as for the rest, he thought, the heat pooling in his loins, what would happen between them in bed would keep them both satisfied. She would not deny him forever. She wouldn't want to. Despite her protestations, Laurel wanted him. She was a passionate woman with a taste for sex, but she was his now. If she ever thought to slake her thirst with another man, he'd—he'd…

The glass splintered in his hand. Damian hissed with pain as the shards fell to the terrace floor.

"Dammit to hell!"

Blood welled in his palm. He cursed again, dug in his pocket for a handkerchief—and just then, a small, cool hand closed around his.

"Let me see that," Laurel said.

He looked up, angry at himself for losing control, angry at her for catching him, and the breath caught in his throat.

How beautiful his wife was!

She was wearing something long, white and filmy; he thought of what Spiro had said, that she looked like Aphrodite, but the old man was wrong for surely the goddess had never been this lovely.

Laurel must have showered and washed her hair. It hung loose in a wild cloud of dark auburn curls that tumbled over her shoulders as she bent over his cut hand.

"It isn't as bad as it probably feels," she said, dabbing at the wound with his handkerchief.

He felt a fist close around his heart. Yes, it was, he thought suddenly, it was every bit as bad, and maybe worse.

"Come inside and let me wash it."

He didn't want to move. The moment was too perfect. Laurel's body, brushing his. Her hair, tickling his palm. Her breath, warm on his fingers…

"Damian?" She looked up at him. "The cut should be— it should be…"

Why was he looking at her that way? His eyes were as dark as the night that waited on the rim of the sea. There was a tension in his face, in the set of his shoulders…

His wide shoulders, encased in a dark cotton shirt. She could see the golden column of his throat at the open neck of the shirt; the pulse beating in the hollow just below his Adam's apple; the shadow of dark, silky hair she knew covered his hard-muscled chest.

A chasm seemed to open before her, one that terrified her with its uncharted depth.

"This cut should be washed," she said briskly, "and disinfected."

"It is not necessary." His voice was low and throaty; it made her pulse quicken. "Laurel…"

"Really, Damian. You shouldn't ignore it."

"I agree. A thing like this must not be ignored."

Her eyes met his and a soft sound escaped her throat. "Damian," she whispered, "please…"

"What?" he said thickly. He lifted his uncut hand and pushed her hair back from her face. "What do you want of me, *kalí mou*? Tell me, and I will do it."

Kiss me, she thought, and touch me, and let me admit the truth to myself, that I don't hate you, don't despise you, that I—that I…

She let go of his hand and stepped back.

"I want you to let me clean this cut, and bandage it," she said briskly. "You've seen to it that we're a million miles from everything. If you developed an infection, I wouldn't even know how to get help."

Damian's mouth twisted.

"You are right." He wound the handkerchief around his hand and smiled politely. "You would be stranded, not just with an unwanted husband but with a disabled one. How selfish of me, Laurel. Please, serve yourself some lemonade. Eleni prepared it especially for you. I will tend to this cut, and then we shall have our dinner. You will excuse me?"

Laurel nodded. "Of course," she said, just as politely, and she turned and stared out over the sea, watching as a million stars fired the black velvet sky, and blinking back tears that had risen, inexplicably, in her eyes.

She woke early the next morning.

The same insect chorus was singing, accompanied now by the soaring alto of a songbird. It wasn't the same as awakening to an alarm clock, she thought with a smile, or to the honking of horns and the sound of Mr. Lieberman's footsteps overhead.

Dressed in a yellow sundress, she wandered through the house to the kitchen. Eleni greeted her with a smile, a cup of strong black coffee and a questioning lift of the eyebrows that seemed to be the equivalent of, "What would you like for breakfast?"

A bit of sign language, some miscommunication that resulted in shared laughter, and Laurel sat down at the marble-topped counter to a bowl of fresh yogurt and sliced strawberries. She ate hungrily—the doors leading out to the terrace were open, and the air, fragrant with the mingled scents of flowers and of the sea, had piqued her appetite. She poured herself a second cup of coffee and sipped it outdoors, on the terrace, and then she wandered down the steps and onto the grass.

It was strange, how a night's sleep and the clear light of morning changed things. Yesterday, the house had seemed disturbingly austere but now she could see that it blended perfectly with its surroundings. The location didn't seem as forbidding, either. There was something to be said for being on the very top of a mountain, with the world laid out before you.

Impulsively she kicked off her sandals and looped the straps over her fingers. Then she set off toward the rear of the house, where she could hear someone—Spiro, perhaps—beating something with what sounded like a hammer.

But it wasn't the old man. It was Damian, wearing denim cutoffs, leather work gloves, beat-up sneakers and absolutely nothing else. He was wielding what she assumed was a sledgehammer, swinging it over and over against a huge gray boulder.

His swings were rhythmic; his attention was completely focused on the boulder. She knew he had no idea she was there and a part of her whispered that it was wrong to stand in the shadow of a cypress and watch him this way…but nothing in the world could have made her turn away or take her eyes off her husband.

How magnificent he was! The sun blazed down on his naked shoulders; she could almost see his skin toasting to a darker gold as he worked. His body glistened under a fine layer of sweat that delineated its muscled power. He grunted softly each time he swung the hammer and she found herself catching her breath at each swing, holding it until he brought the hammer down to smash against the rock.

Her thoughts flashed two years back, to Kirk, and to the hours he'd spent working out in the elaborate gym in the basement of his Long Island home. Two hours a day, seven days a week, and he'd still not looked as beautifully male as Damian did right now.

She thought of how strong Damian's arms had felt around her the night they'd made love, of how his muscles had rippled under her hands...

"Laurel."

She blinked. Damian had turned around. He smiled, put down the hammer and wiped his face and throat with a towel that had been lying in the grass.

"Sorry," he said, tossing the towel aside and coming toward her. "I didn't mean to wake you."

"You didn't. I've always been an early riser."

He stripped off his gloves and tucked them into a rear pocket.

"I am, too. It's an old habit. If you want to get any work done in the summer here, you have to start before the sun is too high in the sky or you end up broiled to a crisp. Did you sleep well?"

Laurel nodded. "Fine. And you?"

"I always sleep well, when I am home."

It was usually true, though not this time. He'd lain awake half the night, thinking about Laurel, lying in a bed just down the hall from his. When he'd finally dozed off, it was only to tumble into dreams that had left him feeling frustrated. He'd figured on working that off this morning through some honest sweat, but just the sight of his wife, standing like a barefoot Venus with the wind tugging at her hair and fluttering the hem of her sundress, had undone all his efforts.

Laurel cleared her throat. "What are you doing, anyway?"

"Being an idiot," he said, and grinned at her. "Or so Spiro says. I thought it would be nice to plant a flower garden here."

"And Spiro doesn't approve?"

"Oh, he approves. It's just that he's convinced that I will never defeat the boulder, no matter how I try." He bent down, picked up a handful of earth and let it drift through his fingers. "He's probably right but I'll be damned if I'll give in without a fight."

She couldn't imagine Damian giving in to anything without a fight. Wasn't that the reason she was here, as his wife?

"Besides, I've gotten soft lately."

He didn't look soft. He looked hard, and fit, and wonderful.

"Too many days behind a desk, too many fancy lunches." He smiled. "I can always find ways to work off a few pounds, when I come home to Actos."

"You grew up here, in this house?"

Damian laughed. "No, not quite. Here." He plucked her sandals from her hand and knelt down before her. "Let me help you with these."

"No," she said quickly, "that's all right. I can..." He lifted her foot, his fingers long and tan against the paleness of her skin. Her heart did another of those stutter-steps, the foolish ones that were coming more often, and for no good reason. "Damian, really." Irritation, not with him but with herself, put an edge on her words. "I'm not an invalid. I'm just—"

"Pregnant," he said softly, as he rose to his feet. His eyes met hers, and he put his hand gently on her flat stomach. "And with my child."

Their eyes met. It was hard to know which burned

stronger, the flame in his eyes or the heat in his touch. Deep within her, something uncoiled lazily and seemed to slither through her blood.

"Come." He held out his hand.

"No, really, I didn't mean to disturb you. You've work to do."

"The boulder and I are old enemies. We'll call a truce, for now." He smiled and reached for her hand. "Come with me, Laurel. This is your home, too. Let me show it to you."

It wasn't; it never would be. She wanted to tell him that but he'd already entwined his fingers with hers and anyway, what harm could there be in letting him walk her around?

"All right," she said, and fell in beside him.

He showed her everything, and she could tell from the way he spoke that he took a special pride in it all. The old stone barns, the pastures, the white specks in a lower valley that he said were sheep, even the squawking chickens that fluttered out of their way...it all mattered to him, and she could see in the faces of the men who worked for him, tilling the land and caring for the animals, that they knew it, and respected him for it.

At last he led her over the grass, down a gentle slope and into a grove of trees that looked as if they'd been shaped by the wind blowing in from the sea.

"Here," he said softly, "is the true heart of Actos."

"Are these olive trees? Did you plant them?"

"No," he said, with a little smile, "I can't take any credit for the grove. The trees are very old. Hundreds of years old, some of them. I'm only their caretaker, though I admit that it took years to restore them to health. This property had been left unattended for a long time, before I bought it."

"It wasn't in your family, then?"

"You think this house, this land, was my inheritance?" He laughed, as if she'd made a wonderful joke. "Believe me, it was not.'' His smile twisted; he tucked his hands into his back pockets and looked at her, his gaze steady. ''The only thing I inherited from my parents was my name—and sometimes, I even wonder about that.''

''I'm sorry,'' Laurel said quickly. ''I didn't mean to pry.''

''No, don't apologize. You have the right to know these things about me.'' A muscled knotted in his jaw. ''My father was a seaman. He made my mother pregnant, married her only because she threatened to go to the police with a tale of rape, and left her as soon as I was born.''

''How terrible for her!''

''Don't waste your pity.'' He began walking and Laurel hurried to catch up. Ahead, a low stone wall rose marked the edge of the cliff, and the bright sea below. ''I doubt it happened as she described it. She was a tavern whore.'' His voice was cold, without inflection; they reached the wall and he leaned against it and stared out over the water. ''She told me as much, when she'd had too much to drink.''

''Oh, Damian,'' Laurel said softly, ''I'm so sorry.''

''For what? It is reality, and I tell it to you not to elicit your pity but only because you're entitled to know the worst about the man you've married.''

''And the best.'' She drew a deep breath and made the acknowledgment she'd refused to make until this moment. ''Your decision about this baby—our baby—wasn't one every man would choose.''

''Still, it was not a decision to your liking.''

''I don't like having my decisions made for me.''

A faint smile curved over his mouth. ''Are you suggesting that I am sometimes overbearing?''

Laurel laughed. ''Why do I suspect you've heard that charge before?''

The wind lifted his dark hair and he brushed it back off his forehead. It was a boyish gesture, one that suited his quick smile.

"Ah, now I see how things are to be. You and Spiro will combine forces to keep me humble."

"You? Humble?" She smiled. "Not unless that old man is more of a miracle worker than I am. Who is he, anyhow? I got the feeling he's more than someone who works for you."

Damian leaned back, elbows on the wall, and smiled.

"What would you call a man who saves not only your life, but your soul?" A breeze blew a curl across her lips. He reached out and captured the strand, smoothing it gently with his fingers. "Spiro found me, on the streets of Athens. I was ten, and I'd been on my own for two years."

"But what happened to your mother?"

He shrugged. It was a careless gesture but it couldn't mask the pain in his words.

"I woke up one morning, and she was gone. She left me a note, and some money... It didn't matter. I had been living by my wits for a long time by then."

"How?" Laurel said softly, while she tried to imagine what it must have been like to be ten, and wake up and find yourself alone in the world.

"Oh, it wasn't difficult. I was small, and quick. It was easy to swipe a handful of fruit or a couple of tomatoes from the outdoor markets, and a clever lad could always con the tourists out of a few drachma." The wind tugged at her hair again, and he smoothed it back from her cheek and smiled. "I was quite an accomplished little pickpocket, until one winter day when Spiro came into my life."

"You stole from him, and he caught you?"

Damian nodded. "He was old as Methuselah, even then, but strong as an olive tree. He gave me a choice. The police—or I could go with him." He smiled. "I went with him."

"Damian, I'm lost here. Didn't you have a sister? Nicholas—the boy who married my niece—is your nephew, isn't he?"

"It's how his mother and I thought of each other, as brother and sister, but, in truth, we weren't related. You see, Spiro brought me here, to Actos, where he lived. The summer I was thirteen, an American couple—Greeks, but generations removed—came to the island, searching for their roots. Spiro decided I needed a better future than he could provide and, since I'd learned some English in Athens when I'd conned tourists, he convinced the Americans to take me to the States."

"And they agreed?"

"They were good people and Spiro played on all their Greek loyalties. They took me home with them, to New York, and enrolled me in school. I studied hard, won a scholarship to Yale..." He shrugged. "I was lucky."

"Lucky," she said softly, thinking of the boy he'd been and the man he'd become.

"Luck, hard work...who knows where one begins and the other ends? The only certainty is that if it hadn't been for Spiro, I would be living a very different life."

She smiled. "I'll have to remember to thank him."

"Will you?" His dark, thick lashes drooped over his eyes, so that she couldn't quite see them. "If he'd left me on the streets, I'd never have stormed into your life and turned it upside down."

"I know."

The words, said so softly that they were little more than a whisper, hung in the air between them. Damian framed Laurel's face in his hands. Her eyes gave nothing away, but he could see the sudden, urgent beat of her pulse in the hollow of her throat.

"*Mátya mou,*" he whispered.

"What does that mean? *Mátya mou*?"

Damian bent his head and brushed his mouth gently over hers. "It means, my dearest."

She smiled tremulously. "I like the sound of the words. Would it be difficult, to learn Greek?"

"I'll teach you." His thumb rubbed lightly over her bottom lip. "I'll do whatever makes you happy, if you tell me what's in your heart."

A lie would have been self-protective, but how could she lie to this man, who had just opened himself to her?

"I—I can't," she said. "I don't know what's in my heart, Damian. I only know that when I'm with you, I feel—I feel…"

His mouth dropped to hers in a deep, passionate kiss. For one time-wrenching moment, Laurel resisted. Then she sighed her husband's name, put her arms around his neck and kissed him back.

CHAPTER TEN

LAUREL'S KISS almost undid him.

It was not so much the heated passion of it; it was the taste of surrender he drank from her lips.

She had been his, but only temporarily on that night in New York. Now, holding his wife in his arms on a wind-swept hill above the Aegean, Damian made a silent vow. This time, when he made love to her, she would be his forever.

Was he holding her too closely? Kissing her too hard? He knew he might be and he told himself to hold back—but he couldn't, not when Laurel's mouth was so soft and giving beneath his, not when he could feel her heart racing, and he knew that her desire burned as brightly as his. Desire, and something more.

He couldn't think. All he could do was feel, and savor, and when she moaned softly and pressed herself against him, so that he could feel her body molded to his, he almost went out of his head with need.

"Damian," she whispered. Her voice broke. "Damian, please…"

He thrust his hands into her hair, his thumbs tracing the delicate arch of her cheeks, and lifted her face to his. Her eyes were dark with desire; color stained her cheeks.

"Tell me," he murmured, just as he had that first time, and he moved against her so that she caught her breath at the feel of him. "Say it, *o kalí mou*."

Laurel brushed her lips against his. "Make love to me," she sighed, and he caught her up in his arms and carried her to a stone watchtower that was a part of the wall.

The tower was ancient, older, even, than the wall. A

thousand years before, it had been a place from which warriors safeguarded the island against pirates. Now, as Damian lay his wife down gently on a floor mounded with clean, sweet-smelling hay, he knew that the battle that would be fought here today was one in which there would be no way to tell who was the conqueror and who the conquered.

He told himself to undress her slowly, despite the hunger that beat within him. But when she moved her hands down his chest, down and down until she cupped his straining arousal, the last semblance of his control slipped away.

"Now," he said fiercely, and he tore away her sundress.

Beneath, she was all lace and silk, perfumed flesh and heat. He tried again to slow what was happening but Laurel wouldn't let him. She lifted her head, strained to kiss his mouth; she stroked his muscled shoulders and chest, drew her hand down his hard belly, and then her fingers slid under the waistband of his shorts. Damian groaned; his hands closed over hers and together, they stripped the shorts away.

At last, they lay skin against skin, heat against heat, alone together in the universe.

"Damian," Laurel said brokenly, and he bent his head to hers and kissed her.

"Yes, sweetheart, yes, *o kalóz mou.*"

And then he was inside her, thrusting into the heart of her, and in that last instant before she shattered in her husband's arms, Laurel, at last, admitted the truth to herself.

She was in love, completely in love, with Damian Skouras.

A long time later, in the white-hot blaze of midday, they made their way to the house.

Someone—Eleni, probably—had closed the thin-slatted blinds at all the windows so that the foyer was shadowed and cool. Everything was silent, except for the soft drone of the fan blades rotating slowly overhead.

Laurel looked around warily. "Where's Eleni?"

"Why? Do you need something?" Damian pulled her close and kissed her, lingeringly, on the mouth. "Let me get whatever it is. I've no wish to share you with anyone else just now."

"I don't need anything, Damian. I was just thinking…" She blushed. "If she sees us, she'll know that we—that you and I—"

Damian smiled. Bits of hay were tangled in his wife's hair, and there was a glow to her skin that he knew came from the hours she'd spent in his arms.

"What will she know, *keería mou*, except that we have made love?"

"What does that mean? Keerya moo?"

"It means that you are my wife." He pressed a kiss into her hair. "And a husband may make love to his wife whenever he chooses." He put his hand under her chin and gently lifted her face to his. "On Actos, in New York…anywhere at all, so long as she is willing. Do you agree?"

"Only if the same rules apply for the wife."

Damian's eyes darkened. "Has no one ever told you that democracy was invented here, in these islands?"

Laurel smiled. "In that case…"

She rose on her toes, put her mouth to her husband's ear and whispered.

Damian laughed. "I couldn't have put it better myself," he said, and he lifted her into his arms, carried her up the stairs and into his bedroom.

The days, and the nights, flew past. And each was a revelation.

Damian, the man who could do anything from saving a

dying corporation to making an endless assault against a boulder, turned out to have a failing.

A grave one, Laurel said, with a solemnity she almost managed to pull off.

He didn't know how to play gin rummy.

He was, he assured her, an expert at baccarat and chemin de fer, and he admitted he'd even been known to win a dollar or two at a game of poker.

Laurel wasn't impressed. How could he have reached the age of forty without knowing how to play gin?

"Thirty-eight," he said, with only a glint in his eye, and then he said, well, if she really wanted to teach him the game, he supposed he'd let her.

He lost six hands out of six.

"I don't know," he said, with a sigh. "Gin just doesn't seem terribly interesting."

"Well, we could try playing for points. I'll keep score, or I can show you…what's the matter?"

"Nothing. It's just… I don't know. Points, scoring…it seems dull."

"Okay, how about playing for money?"

"A bet, you mean? Yes, that would be better."

"A nickel a hand."

Damian's brows lifted. "You call that interesting?"

"Maybe I should tell you that I'm the unofficial behind-the-runways-from-Milan-to-Paris gin rummy champion."

"So? What's the matter? Afraid of losing your title?"

Laurel blew her hair back out of her eyes. "Okay, killer, don't say I didn't warn you. We'll play big time. A dime a hand."

Damian's smile was slow and sexy. "I've got a better idea. Why don't we play for an article of clothing a hand?"

Laurel's eyes narrowed. "You sure you never played gin before?"

"Never," he said solemnly, and dealt out the cards.

Half an hour later, Laurel was down to a pair of jeans

and a silk teddy. Her sandals, belt, shirt, even the ribbon she'd used to tie back her hair, lay on the white living-room carpet.

"No fair," she grumbled. "You *have* played gin before."

Damian gave her a heart-stopping smile and fanned out another winning hand. He leaned back against the cushions they'd tossed on the floor and folded his arms across his chest. "Well?"

Laurel smiled primly and took off an earring.

"Since when is an earring an article of clothing, *keería mou*? An article of clothing for each losing hand, remember?"

Her heart gave a little kick. "You wouldn't really expect me to—"

He reached out a lazy hand, drew his fingertip lightly over her breasts, then down to the waistband of her jeans. "Your game and your rules," he said huskily. "Take something off, sweetheart."

Laurel's eyes met his. She rose to her feet, undid the jeans and slid them off.

"Your turn is coming," she said, "just you wait and see."

He smiled and dealt the cards. It pleased her to see that his hands were unsteady. Surely he would lose now.

"Gin."

Laurel ran the tip of her tongue over her lips, and Damian's eyes followed the gesture. Heat began pooling in her belly.

"Damian, you're not going to make me…"

Their eyes met again. She swallowed dryly, then got to her knees. Slowly she hooked a finger under one shoulder strap and slid it off. She slid off the second. There were three satin ties on the teddy, just between her breasts, and she reached for them.

Damian's breathing quickened, but his eyes never left hers.

"One," she said softly. "Two. Three..."

With a throaty growl, he tumbled her to the carpet. And then, for a long, long time, the only sounds in the room were the sighs and whispers of love.

He refused to believe that she could cook.

They discussed it, one afternoon, as Laurel sat in a field of daisies with Damian's head in her lap.

She reminded him, indignantly, of the bread he'd found rising in her kitchen. He reminded her, not very gallantly, that it had resembled a science experiment gone bad.

Laurel plucked a handful of daisies and scattered them over his chest.

"I'll have you know that I make the most terrific sourdough bread in the world."

"Uh-huh."

"What do you mean, 'uh huh'? I do. Ask George. He loves my bread."

"George," Damian scoffed. "The man's besotted. He'd say it was great even if it tasted like wet cardboard."

Laurel dumped more daisies over him. "He is not besotted with anyone but his own wife."

Damian sat up, reached for her hand and laced his fingers through hers. There was something he had to tell her, something he should have told her sooner. It meant nothing to him, but she had the right to know.

"It's good, for a man to be besotted with his wife," he said softly.

She smiled and brushed a daisy petal from his hair. "Is it?"

"Did I ever tell you," he asked, catching her hand and raising it to his mouth, "that I was married before?"

Laurel's teasing smile vanished. "No. No, you didn't."

"Well, I was. For a grand total of three weeks."

"What happened?" She tried another smile and hoped this one worked. "Don't tell me. The lady served you a slice of wet cardboard, called it sourdough bread and you sent her packing."

"Nothing so simple. It turned out we had nothing in common. She wanted my name and my money, and I..."

"And you? What did you want?"

"Out," he said, with a little laugh, "almost from the beginning. The marriage was a complete mistake. I think we both knew it."

"Why did you marry her, then?" A chill crept into Laurel's heart, and she gave him a stiff smile. "Was she pregnant, too?"

She regretted the ugly words as soon as she'd said them, but it was too late to call them back. Damian sat up, his face cold and hard.

"No. She was not pregnant. Had she been, I can assure you, I would still be married to her."

"Because it would have been your duty." Laurel stood up and dusted the grass from her shorts. "Of course," she said, and started briskly toward the house, "I almost forgot how noble you are, Damian. Sorry."

"*Theé mou!*" Angrily he clasped her shoulders and spun her around. "What is the matter with you, Laurel? Are you angry with me for having divorced a woman I did not love? Or for admitting that I would have done the right thing by her, if I'd had to?"

"I'm not angry with you at all." Her smile was brittle. "I'm just—you can't blame me for being curious, Damian. After all, I only just found out you have an ex-wife."

"I told you, the relationship was meaningless. We met, we thought we were in love, we got married. By the time we realized what we'd done, it was too late."

"Yes, well, that's what happens, when a person marries impetuously."

"Dammit, don't give me that look!"

"What look? It's the only one I've got—but how would you know that?"

"Don't be a little fool!" Damian glared at her, his face dark with anger. "There is no comparison between this marriage and the other. I married you because—because..."

"Because I was pregnant."

"Yes. No. I mean..." What did he mean? Of course he'd married her because she was pregnant; why deny it? What other reason could possibly have made him ask Laurel to be his wife?

"You needn't explain." Laurel's voice was frosty, a perfect match to her smile. "We both know what an honorable man you are. You married me for the sake of our child, and you'll stay married to me for the same reason. Isn't that right?"

Damian's jaw knotted. "You're damned right," he growled. "I'm going to stay married to you, and you to me, until as the man said, 'Death do us part.'"

He pulled her into his arms and kissed her just as he had the day he'd announced he was going to make her his wife. For the first time since they'd made love in the tower overlooking the sea, Laurel didn't respond. She felt nothing, not desire, not even anger.

"You are my wife," Damian said. Stone-faced, he held her at arm's length and looked down into her face. "And nothing more needs to be said about it."

Laurel wrenched free of his grasp. "How could I possibly forget that, when you'll always be there to remind me?"

She swung away and strode up the hill, toward the house. Damian's hands knotted at his sides. Dammit, what was wrong with her? He thought they'd gotten past this, that Laurel had made peace with the circumstances of their marriage, but it was clear that she hadn't.

Had she been pretending, all those times they'd made

love? Had she lain in his arms, touching him, kissing him, and wishing all the while that he'd never forced her into becoming his wife? Because he had. Hell, there was no denying it. He'd given her about as much choice in the matter as the rocks below gave to the ships they'd claimed, over the centuries.

His mouth twisted. So what? They were man and wife. She had to accept that. As for this afternoon's pointless quarrel…she'd get over it when he took her to bed, tonight.

He took a deep breath, stuck his hands into his pockets and stood staring out to sea.

She hadn't been pretending, when they made love. He would have known if those sweet sighs, those exciting whispers, had been false.

Of course, he would… Wouldn't he?

Laurel sat at the dressing table in the bedroom where she'd spent her first night as Mrs. Damian Skouras, staring at her reflection in the mirror.

She hadn't been back in this room since then. Every night—and a lot of long, wonderful mornings and afternoons—had been spent in Damian's bed.

Her hand trembled as she picked up a silver-backed brush and ran it over her hair.

What had gotten into her today? Damian had been married before. Well, so what? She'd had a relationship before, too, and even if Kirk hadn't treated it as a marriage, she had. She'd been faithful, and loving, and when she'd found out that he'd deceived her, her heart couldn't have been more broken than if she had been Mrs. Kirk Soames. She'd loved Kirk every bit as much as if—as if—

A choked cry burst from her lips and she dropped the brush and buried her face in her hands.

It wasn't true. She'd never really loved Kirk, she knew that now. What she felt for Damian made her feelings for Kirk seem insignificant.

And that was what this afternoon's performance had been all about, wasn't it?

"Wasn't it?" she whispered, lifting her head and staring at her pale face and tear-swollen eyes in the mirror.

Damian had told her he'd been married before, that it had been an impetuous marriage and hadn't worked out, and all she'd been able to think was that he'd married her the same way, impetuously, because it had been the right thing to do.

How she'd longed for him to deny it!

I married you because I love you, she'd wanted him to say, because I'll always love you.

But he hadn't. He'd married her because he wanted his child to have a father, and even though part of her knew how right, how decent, that was, another part of her longed to hear him say he'd married her for love.

She picked up the hairbrush again and stared at her reflection.

But he hadn't. She was Damian's wife, but not his love. She had his name, and his interest in bed, but if she made many more scenes like the one she'd made today, she probably wouldn't even have that, and never mind the Until death do us part promise. Her mouth turned down with bitterness. She knew all about men like Damian, and promises of fidelity. Oh, yes, she knew all about—

"Laurel?"

Her gaze flew to the mirror just as the bedroom door opened. Damian stood in the doorway, wearing a terry cloth robe. She knew from the experience of the past week that he had nothing on beneath it. His hair was tousled, his eyes were dark and she wanted nothing so much as to jump up and hurl herself into his arms.

Pride and pain kept her rooted in place.

"Yes, Damian," she said. She smiled politely, put down the brush and turned around.

"Are you feeling better?"

She'd missed dinner, pleading a headache. It would never have done to have told him the truth, that what ached was her heart.

"Much better, thank you. Eleni brought me some tea, and aspirin."

He nodded and stepped further into the room. "It's late."

"Is it? I hadn't noticed."

He paused beside her and lifted his hand. She thought, for a moment, he was going to touch her hair and if he had, that would have been her undoing. She'd have sighed under his hand like a kitten—but he didn't. He only reached out, straightened the dressing table mirror, then put his hand into his pocket.

"Are you coming to bed?"

Laurel turned away and looked into the mirror again. He'd asked the question so casually but then, why wouldn't he? So far as he was concerned, her place was in his bed. Not only was she his wife, but she'd made it clear she wanted to be there. Her throat constricted as she remembered the things they'd done together in that bed.

Why was it that loving a man who didn't love you, knowing he'd *never* love you, could suddenly make those things seem cheap?

"Actually," she said, picking up the brush again, "I thought I'd sleep in here tonight."

"In here?" he repeated, as if she'd suggested she was going to spend the night on an ice floe in the North Sea.

"Yes." Briskly, she drew the brush through her hair. "I still have a bit of a headache."

"Shall I phone the doctor Glassman recommended on Crete?"

"No. No, I don't need a doctor."

"Are you sure? Laurel, if you're ill—"

"I'm fine. The baby's fine." She smiled tightly at him in the mirror. "It's just an old habit of mine, Damian. Sometimes, I need a night to myself. Kirk used to say—"

"Kirk?" he said, and the way he said it made her heart stop.

Don't, she told herself, oh, don't do this...

"A man I used to live with. Well, actually, a man I thought about marrying. Didn't I ever tell you about him?"

"No," he said coldly, "you did not."

She looked into the mirror again and what she saw in his face terrified her. The brush clattered to the mirrored top of the dressing table and she swung toward him.

"Damian," she said quickly, but it was too late. He was already at the door.

"You're right," he said, "a night apart might be an excellent idea for the both of us. I'll see you in the morning."

"Damian, wait..."

Wait? He stepped into the hall and slammed the door after him. She wouldn't want him to wait, if she knew how close he was to smashing his fist into the wall. He stormed into his bedroom, kicked the door shut, then flung open the french doors that let out onto the terrace. The black heat of the Agean night curled around him like a choking fog.

All right, so she'd lived with a man. So what? It didn't matter a damn. She'd married him, not Kirk, whoever in hell Kirk might be.

Married him under protest. Under the threat of losing her child to him. Under the worst kind of blackmail.

Damian spun around and slammed his fist against the wall. It hurt like hell, and he winced and put his knuckles to his mouth, tasted the faint tang of blood, and wished to God it was Kirk's blood instead of only his own. What sort of name was that, anyway? A stupid name, befitting a man foolish enough to have let Laurel go.

Any man would want her. Would desire her. Would fall in love with her.

And, just that simply, Damian saw the truth.

He loved Laurel. He loved his wife.

"I love her," he said to the night, and then he laughed out loud.

What a fool he'd been, not to realize it sooner.

And maybe, just maybe, she loved him, too.

He lifted his face to the moonless sky, as if the answer might be there, in the blazing light of a million stars that dotted the heavens.

It would explain so much, if she did.

The softness of her, in his arms. The passion she could never hide when he touched her. Even her reaction earlier today, when he'd so clumsily told her that he'd been married before.

His heart filled with hope. Maybe what had seemed like anger had really been pain. Maybe she'd felt the same jealousy at his mention of a former lover that he'd felt at the mention of Kirk.

But if she loved him, would she have chosen to sleep alone tonight? Would she have taken such relish in telling him she'd lived with another man and almost married him?

Damian took a deep breath. He'd always prided himself on knowing how to chart a direct path from A to B, but tonight he felt as if he were going in circles.

There was only one thing to do, by God, go back into Laurel's room, confront her, drag her from that bed if he had to, shake her silly or kiss her senseless until she told him what she felt for him...

The telephone rang. Damian cursed and snatched it up.

"Whoever you are," he snapped, "you'd better have a damned good reason for calling."

It was Hastings, his personal attorney, phoning from New York.

Damian sat down on the edge of the bed. Hastings was not a man given to running the risk of waking his most important client in the middle of the night.

"I'm afraid we have a problem, Mr. Skouras."

Damian listened and, as he did, the look on his face went from dark to thunderous.

"Gabriella is suing me for breach of promise? Is she crazy? She hasn't got a case. What do you mean, she's going to sell her story to 'The Gossip Line' unless I meet her demands? Who'd give a crap about...? What's my marriage got to do with...?" His face went white. "If she drags my wife down into the mud, so help me God, I'll—"

Hastings spoke again. According to Gabriella, Damian had made promises. He'd said he'd marry her. He'd been not just her only lover but her first lover, since her divorce, and her last.

Damian took a stranglehold on the telephone cord. "All right," he said abruptly, rising to his feet and shrugging off his robe. "Here's what I want you to do." He rattled off a string of commands. Hastings repeated them, then asked a question, and Damian glared at the phone as if he could see the attorney's face in it. "How the hell do I know who to contact? That's why you're on retainer, Hastings, because you're the legal eagle, remember? Just get the information by tomorrow. That's right, man. Tomorrow. I'll see you in New York."

Rage and determination propelled him through the next few minutes. He phoned Spiro on the intercom, called his pilot on Crete—and then he hesitated.

Should he wake Laurel, to tell her he was leaving? No. Hell, no. The last thing he needed right now was to explain to his wife that his vindictive former mistress was trying to stir up trouble by selling a story to some TV gossip show featuring herself as an abandoned lover—and Laurel as a scheming, pregnant fortune hunter.

Spiro could deal with it. The old man could tell her he'd been called to New York on urgent business. She wouldn't like it, but how long would he be gone? A day? Two, at the most. Then he'd be back, on Actos, and he'd take his wife in his arms, tell her he loved her and pray to the gods

that she would say she loved him, too. And if she didn't—
if she didn't, he'd make her love him, dammit, he'd kiss
her mouth until all memory of Kirk whoever-he-was had
been wiped from her mind and her soul, and then they'd
begin their lives together, all over again.

He just had to see her once, before he left. The house
was quiet, as he left his room; no light spilled from beneath
Laurel's closed door. Damian opened it and slipped inside.

She lay on her back, fast asleep.

How lovely she was. And how he adored her.

"*Kalí mou*," he murmured, "my beloved."

He bent and brushed his mouth gently over hers. She
stirred and breathed a soft sigh, and it was all he could do
to keep from lying down beside her and gathering her into
his arms.

First, though, there was Gabriella to deal with.

Damian's jaw hardened as he left his wife's room and
quietly shut the door after him.

And deal with the bitch, he would.

CHAPTER ELEVEN

LAUREL AWAKENED to bright sunlight and a memory as ethereal as a wisp of cloud.

Was it a dream, or had Damian really entered her room in the middle of the night, kissed her and called her his beloved?

It seemed so real...but it couldn't have been. They'd quarreled, and even though he'd held out a tentative olive branch, she'd rejected it.

She sat up, pushed aside the light sheet that covered her and scrubbed her hands over her face.

Rejected his peace offering? That was putting it mildly. She'd damn near slapped his face, then rubbed his nose in her relationship with Kirk for good measure.

Laurel puffed out her breath. What on earth had possessed her? The man she loved—the only man she'd ever loved—was Damian.

She dressed quickly, with little care for how she looked. All that mattered was finding a way to rectify the damage she'd caused last night. Damian didn't love her, not yet, but she knew that he cared for her—at least, he had, until she'd instigated that ugly scene.

Well, there was only one way to fix things.

She had to tell Damian the truth. To hell with pride, and the pain that would come of admitting she loved him without hearing that he loved her, too. She'd go to him, tell him that Kirk had never meant a damn to her, that no one had or ever would, except him.

Her heart was racing, as much with apprehension as with anticipation. After Kirk, she'd promised she'd never leave herself so vulnerable to any man again. But Damian wasn't *any* man. He was her husband, her lover—he was the man she would always love.

Laurel squared her shoulders and stepped out into the hall.

He wasn't in his bedroom. Well, why would he be? It was past eight o'clock, late by his standards, and there'd been nothing to make him linger in bed today. She hadn't been lying in the curve of his arm, her head pillowed on his shoulder; he hadn't whispered a soft, sexy "good morning" and she hadn't given him a slow, equally sexy smile in return.

He wasn't in the kitchen, either, nor on the terrace, sipping a second cup of coffee while he and Spiro conferred on what might need doing today.

Eleni was there, though, out on the terrace, busily watering the urns filled with pansies and fuchsias and impatiens.

"*Kaliméra sas.*"

Laurel smiled as she stepped outside. "*Kaliméra sas*, Eleni. Where is Mr. Skouras, do you know?"

Eleni's brows lifted. "Madam?"

"My husband," Laurel said. "Have you any idea where..." She sighed, smiled and shook her head. "Never mind. I'll find him, I'm sure."

But she didn't. He wasn't at the barns, or strolling along the wall, or hammering at the boulder.

"*Kaliméra sas.*"

It was Spiro. He had come up behind her, as quietly as a shadow.

"*Kaliméra sas*," Laurel said, and hesitated. The old man spoke no English and she spoke no Greek beyond the few words she'd picked up during the week. Still, it was worth a try. Damian had to be here somewhere. "Spiro, do you know where Mr. Skouras is?"

The old man's bushy brows lifted questioningly.

"I'm trying to find Damian. Damian," she repeated, pointing at the platinum wedding band on her left hand, "you know, my husband."

"Ah. Damian. *Né*. Yes, I understand."

"You *do* speak English, then?"

"A little bit only."

"Believe me, your English is a thousand times better than my Greek. So, where is he?"

"Madam?"

"Damian, Spiro. Where is he?"

The old man cleared his throat. "He leave island, madam."

"Left Actos? For Crete, you mean?"

"He is for New York."

Laurel stared at him. "What do you mean, he's... No, Spiro, you must be mistaken. He wouldn't have gone to New York without me."

"He is for New York, madam. Business."

"Business," she repeated and then, without warning, she began to weep. She cried without sound, which somehow only made her tears all the more agonizing for Spiro to watch.

"Madam," he said unhappily, "please, do not cry."

"It's my fault," she whispered. "It's all my fault. We quarreled, and I hurt him terribly, and—and I never told him—he doesn't know how much I—"

She sank down on a bench and buried her face in her hands. Spiro stood over her, watching, feeling the same helplessness he'd felt years ago, when he'd come across a lamb who'd gotten itself caught on a wire fence.

He put out his hand, as if to touch her head, then reached into his pocket instead, pulled out an enormous white handkerchief, and shoved it into her hands.

"Madam," he said, "you will see. All will be well."

"No." Laurel blew her nose, hard, and rose to her feet.

"No, it won't be. You don't understand, Spiro. I told Damian a lie. An awful lie. I said cruel things…"

"You love him," the old man said gently.

"Yes. Oh, yes, I love him with all my heart. If only I'd gone to him last night. If only I hadn't been so damn proud. If only I could go to him now…"

Spiro nodded. It was as he'd thought. Something had gone wrong between Damian and his bride; it was why he had left her in the middle of the night.

"Where are you going at such an hour?" Spiro had asked.

Damian's reply had been sharp. "New York," he'd said, "and before you ask, old man, no, Laurel does not know I'm going, and no, I am not going to tell her."

"But what shall I tell her, when she asks?"

"Tell her whatever seems appropriate," Damian had said impatiently, and then he'd motioned Spiro to cast off the line.

The old man frowned. Damian and this woman loved each other deeply, any fool could see that, but for reasons that were beyond him to comprehend, they could not admit it.

"Spiro."

He looked at the woman standing beside him. Her eyes were clear now, and fierce with determination.

"I know that you love Damian," she said. "Well, I love him, too. I have to tell him that, Spiro, I have to make him understand that there's never been anyone but him, that there never could be."

Tell her whatever seems appropriate…

The old man straightened his shoulders. "Yes," he said. He put his gnarled hand on Laurel's shoulder. "Yes, madam. You must tell him—and I will help you to do it."

New York City was baking in brutal, midsummer heat.

It had been hot on Actos, too, but there the bright yellow

sun, blue sea and pale sky had given a strange beauty to the land.

Here, in Manhattan, the sun was obscured by a sullen sky. The air was thick and unpleasant. And, Damian thought as the doors of the penthouse elevator whispered open, it had been one hell of a long day.

He stripped off his jacket and tie, dumped them on a chair and turned up the air conditioner. A current of coolness hissed gently into the silent foyer. Stevens and his housekeeper were both on vacation; he had the place to himself. And that was just as well.

Damian closed his eyes and let the chill envelope him as he undid the top buttons of his shirt, then rolled back his cuffs. He was in no mood to pretend civility tonight, not after dealing with Gabriella. The hour he'd spent closeted with her and their attorneys had felt like an eternity. Even the cloying stink of her perfume was still in his nostrils.

"Are you certain you're up to a face-to-face meeting?" Hastings had asked him.

Damian had felt more up to putting his hands around Gabriella's throat, but he'd known this was the only thing that would work. She had to be confronted with the information he'd ordered gathered but, more than that, she had to see for herself that he would follow through.

For the next sixty minutes, while Gabriella wept crocodile tears into her lace handkerchief and cast him tragic looks, he'd tried to figure out what he'd ever imagined he'd seen in her.

The bleached hair. The artful but heavy makeup. The clinking jewelry—jewelry he'd paid for, from what he could tell—all of it offended him. The sole thing that kept him calm was the picture he held in his mind, of Laurel as he'd last seen her, asleep at Actos, in all her soft, unselfconscious beauty.

Finally he'd grown weary of the legal back-and-forth, and of Gabriella's posturing.

"Enough," he'd said.

All eyes had turned to him. In a voice that bore the chill of winter, he'd told Gabriella what she faced if she took him on and then, almost as an afterthought, he'd shoved the file folder across the conference table toward her.

"What is this, darling?" she'd said.

For the first time, he'd smiled. "Your past, *darling*, catching up to you."

She'd paled, opened the folder...and it was all over. Gabriella had called him names, many that were quite inventive; she'd hurled threats, too, but when her attorney peered over her shoulder at the contents of the folder, the list of names of the men she'd been involved with, the photos culled from the files of several private investigators including one of her, topless, sitting between the thighs of a naked man on a palm tree lined beach, he'd blanched and walked out.

Damian smiled, went to the bar and poured himself a shot of vodka over a couple of ice cubes.

"To private investigators," he said softly, and tossed back half his drink.

Glass in hand, he made his way up the stairs to his bedroom, the room where he'd first made love to his wife. And it *had* been love; he knew that now. It was illogical, it was almost embarrassingly romantic, but there wasn't a doubt in his mind that he'd fallen in love with Laurel at first sight.

He couldn't wait to tell her that.

As soon as he got back to Actos, he was going to take her in his arms and tell her what had been in his heart all the time, that he loved her and would always love her, that it didn't matter what faceless man she'd loved in the past because he, Damian Skouras, was her future, and the future was all that mattered.

He put down his drink, stripped off the rest of his clothes

and stepped into the bathroom. His plane was waiting at the airport. Just another few hours, and he'd be home.

He showered quickly. There wasn't a minute to waste. The sooner he left here, the sooner he'd be in Laurel's arms.

But there was one stop to make first.

He knotted a bath sheet around his waist, ran his fingers carelessly through his damp hair and retrieved his drink from the bedroom.

He was going to go to Tiffany's. He'd never given his wife an engagement ring. Well, he was going to remedy that failing right away. What would suit her best? Diamonds and emeralds? Diamonds and sapphires? Hell, maybe he'd solve the problem by buying her a whole bucketful of rings.

He grinned as he headed down the stairs. Another drink—ginger ale, because he wanted a clear head for this—and then he'd phone Tiffany's, see if they were open. If they weren't...what was the name of that guy he'd met last year? He was a Tiffany Veep, or maybe he was with Cartier or Harry Winston. Damian laughed out loud as he set his glass down on the bar. It didn't matter. Laurel wouldn't care where the ring was from, she wouldn't give a damn if it came from Sear's, not if she loved him, and he was closer and closer to being damned sure that she—

What was that?

Damian frowned. He could hear the soft hum of the elevator, see the lighted panel blinking as the car rose.

What the hell? He certainly wasn't expecting anyone, and the doorman would not send someone up without...

Unless it was Laurel.

His heart thudded.

That was impossible. She was on Actos. Or was she? Spiro hadn't approved of his hasty departure. In the old days, the old man had never hesitated to do what he thought best, even if it meant overriding Damian's wishes. Of course, a lot of years had gone by since then.

On the other hand, Spiro could still be stubborn. If he thought it wise to take matters into his own hands...

The elevator stopped, and Damian held his breath. The doors opened—and Gabriella stepped out of the car.

"Surprise," she said in a smoky contralto.

The sight of her, draped in hot pink that left nothing to the imagination and with a crimson smile painted on her lips, twisted his gut with such savage rage that it left him mute for long seconds. Then he drew a deep, painful breath and managed to find his voice.

"I'm not going to bother asking how you talked your way past the doorman," he said carefully. "I'm just going to tell you to turn around, get back into that elevator and get the hell out."

"Damian, darling, what sort of greeting is that?" Gabriella smiled and strolled past him, to the bar. "What are you drinking, hmm? Vodka rocks, it looks like. Well, I'll just have a tiny one, to keep you company."

"Did you hear me? Get out."

"Now, darling, let's not be hasty." She lifted her glass, took a sip, then put it down. "I know you were upset this morning, but it's my fault. I shouldn't have tried to convince you to come back to me the way I did."

"Convince me to...?" Damian put his fists on his hips. "Let's not play games, okay? What you tried was blackmail, and it didn't work. Now, do us both a favor and get out of here before it gets nasty."

Gabriella licked her lips. "Damian," she purred, "look, I understand. You married this woman. Well, you had no choice, did you? I mean, the word is out, darling, that your little Laurel got herself pregnant."

He came toward her so quickly that she stumbled backward. "I'll give you to the count of five," he snarled, "and then I'm going to take you by the scruff of your neck and toss you out the door. One. Two. Three…''

"Dammit," she said shrilly, "you cannot treat me like this! You made promises."

"You're a liar," he said flatly. "The only promise you've ever heard from me is this one. Go through that door on your own, or so help me…"

"Don't be a fool, Damian. You'll tire of her soon enough." Gabriella's hand went to the sash at her waist and pulled it. The hot pink silk fell open, revealing her naked body. "You'll want this. You'll want me."

Later, Damian would wonder why he hadn't heard the elevator as it made its return trip but then, how could he have heard anything, with each thud of his heart beating such dark fury through his blood?

"Cover yourself," he said, with disgust—and then he heard the sound of the elevator doors opening.

He saw Gabriella's quick, delighted smile and somehow, he knew, God, he knew…

He spun around and there was Laurel, standing in the open doors of the elevator.

"Laurel," he said, and when he started toward her, she threw up her hands and the look in her face went from shock to bone-deep pain.

"No," she whispered, and before he could reach her, she stabbed the button and the doors closed in his face.

And Damian knew, in that instant, that his last chance, his only chance, at love and happiness was gone from his life, forever.

CHAPTER TWELVE

RAIN POUNDED at the windows; late summer lightning split the low, gray sky as thunder rolled across the city.

Inside Laurel's kitchen, three women sat around the table. Two of them—Susie and Annie—were trying to look anywhere but at each other; the third—Laurel—was too busy glaring at her cup of decaf to notice.

"I *hate* decaffeinated coffee," Laurel said. "What is the point of drinking coffee if you're going to take out all the caffeine?"

Susie's gaze connected with Annie's. "Here we go again," her eyes said.

"It's better for you," she said mildly. "With the baby and all."

"I know that. For heaven's sakes, I'm the one who decided to give up coffee, aren't I? It's just that it's stupid to drink stuff that smells like coffee, looks like coffee, but tastes like—"

"Okay," Annie said, getting to her feet. She smiled brightly, whisked the coffee out from under Laurel's nose and dumped it into the sink. "Let's see…" She opened the cabinet and peered inside. "You've got a choice of herbal tea, cocoa, regular tea—"

"Regular tea's got as much caffeine as coffee. A big help you are, Annie."

Annie's brows shot skyward. "Right," she said briskly. She shut the cabinet and opened the refrigerator. "How about a nice glass of milk?"

"Yuck."

"Well, then, there's ginger ale. Orange juice." Her voice

178

grew muffled as she leaned into the fridge. "There's even a little jar of something that might be tomato juice."

"It isn't."

"V8?"

"No."

"Well, then, maybe it's spaghetti sauce."

"I don't remember the last time I had pasta."

Annie frowned and plucked the jar from the shelf. "It's not a good idea to keep chemistry experiments in the—"

Laurel shot to her feet. "Why did you say that?"

"Say what?" Annie and Susie exchanged another look. "Laurel, honey, if you'd just—"

"Just because a person finds something strange in another person's kitchen is no reason to say it looks like a— it looks like a..." Laurel took a deep breath. "Sorry," she said brightly. She looked from her big sister to her best friend. "Well," she said, in that same phony voice, "I know the two of you have things to do, so—"

"Not me," Susie said quickly. "George is downstairs, glued to the TV. I'm free as a bird."

"Not me, either," Annie said. "You know how it is. My life is dull, dull, dull."

"Dull? With your ex hovering in the background?" Laurel eyed her sister. "What's that all about, anyway? You're not seriously thinking of going down that road again, are you?"

For one wild minute, Annie considered telling Laurel the whole story...but Laurel's life was complicated enough. The last thing she needed was to hear someone else's troubles.

"Of course not," she said, with a quick smile. "Why on earth would I do that?"

"Good question." Laurel shoved back her chair, rose from the table and stalked to the sink. "If there's one truth in this world," she said, as she turned on the water, "it's that men stink. Oh, not George, Suze. I mean, he's not a man..."

Susie laughed.

"Come on, you know what I'm saying. George is so sweet. He's one in a million."

"I agree," Susie said. She sighed. "And I'd have bet my life your husband was, too."

Laurel swung around, eyes flashing. "I told you, I do not wish to discuss Damian Skouras."

"Well, I know, but you said—"

"Besides, he is not my husband!"

"Well, no, he won't be, after the divorce comes through, but—"

"To hell with that! A man who—who forces a woman into marriage isn't a husband, he's a—a—"

"A no-good, miserable, super-macho stinking son of a bitch, that's what he is!" Annie glared at her sister, as if defying her to disagree. "And don't you tell me you don't want to talk about it, Laurel, because Susie and I have both had just about enough of this nonsense."

"What nonsense? I don't know what you're talk—"

"You damn well *do* know what we're talking about! It's two months now, two whole months since I got that insane call from you, telling me you'd married that—that Greek super-stud and that you'd found him in the arms of his bubble-brained mistress a week later, and in all that time, I'm not supposed to ask any questions or so much as mention his name." Annie folded her arms and lifted her chin. "That is a load of crap, and you know it."

"It isn't." Laurel shut off the water and folded her arms, too. "There's nothing to talk about, Annie."

"Nothing to talk about." Annie snorted. "You got yourself knocked up and let the guy who did it strong-arm you into marrying him!"

Laurel stiffened. "Must you say it like that?"

"It's the truth, isn't it?"

After a minute, Laurel nodded. "I guess it is. God, I almost wish I'd never gone to Dawn's wedding!"

Susie sighed dramatically. "That must have been some wedding." Annie and Laurel spun toward her and she flushed. "Speaking metaphorically, I mean. Hey, come on, guys, don't look at me that way. It must have been one heck of a day. Annie's ex, coming on to her..."

"For all the good it's going to do him," Annie said coldly.

"And didn't you say that friend of yours, Bethany, met some guy there and ended up having a mad affair?"

"Her name's Stephanie, and at the risk of sounding cynical, I don't think very much of mad affairs, not anymore." Annie jerked her chin toward Laurel. "Just look where it got my sister."

"I know." Susie shook her head. "And Damian seemed so perfect. Handsome, rich—"

"Are you two all done discussing me?" Laurel asked. "Because if you aren't, you'll have to continue this conversation elsewhere. I told you, I will not talk about Damian Skouras. That chapter's over and done with."

"Not quite," Annie said, and looked at Laurel's gently rounded belly.

Laurel flushed. "Very amusing."

"Can we at least talk about how you're going to raise this baby all by yourself?"

"I'll manage."

"There are financial implications, dammit. You said yourself you're at the end of your career."

"Thank you for reminding me."

"Laurel, sweetie—"

"Don't 'Laurel sweetie' me. I am a grown woman, and I made a lot of money over the years. Trust me, Annie, I saved quite a bit of it."

"Yes, but children cost. You don't realize—"

"Dammit," Laurel said fiercely, "now you sound just like him!"

"Who?"

"Damian, that's who. Well, you sound like his attorney, anyway. 'Raising a child is an expensive proposition,' she said in a voice that mimicked the rounded tones of John Hastings. "'Mr. Skouras is fully prepared to support his child properly.'"

Susie and Annie exchanged looks. "You never told me that," Susie said.

"Me, neither," Annie added.

Laurel glared at the two women. "It doesn't matter, does it? I'm not about to take a penny from that bastard."

"Yes, but I thought... I mean, I just figured..." Susie cleared her throat. "Not that being willing to support his kid makes me change what I think of the man. Running off that way, going back to his mistress after a week of marriage... It makes me sick just to think about it"

Annie nodded. "You're right. How he could want that idiotic blonde instead of my beautiful sister..."

"He didn't." Susie and Annie looked at Laurel, and she flushed. "I never said that, did I?"

"You said he left you, for the blonde."

"I said he went back to New York and that I found him with her. I never said—"

"So, he didn't want to take up where they'd left off?"

"I don't know what he wanted." Laurel plucked a sponge from the sink, squeezed it dry and began wiping down the counter with a vengeance. "I never gave him the chance to tell me."

"What do you mean, you never...?"

"Look, when you find your husband with a naked blonde, it's not hard to figure what's going on. I just turned around and walked out. Don't look at me like that, Annie. You would have, too."

Annie sighed. "I suppose. What could he possibly have

said that would have made things better? Besides, if he'd really wanted to explain, he'd have called you or come to see you—''

''He did come here.''

Annie and Susie looked at each other. ''He did? When?''

''That same night.''

Susie looked shocked. ''You see what happens when George and I take a few days off? Laurel, you never said—''

''I wouldn't let him in. What for? We had nothing to say to each other.''

''And that was it?'' Annie asked. ''He gave up, that easily?''

Silence fell on the kitchen and then Laurel cleared her throat.

''He phoned. He left a message on my machine. He said what had happened—what I'd seen—hadn't been what it appeared to be.''

''Oh, right,'' Annie said, ''I'll just bet it—''

''What did he say it had been?'' Susie asked, shooting Annie a warning look.

''I don't remember,'' Laurel lied. She remembered every word; she'd listened to Damian's voice a dozen times before erasing it, not just the lying words but the huskiness, hating herself for the memories it stirred in her heart. ''Some nonsense about his bimbo threatening to drag my name through the mud unless he paid her off. Oh, what does it matter? He'd have said anything, to get his own way. I told you, he was determined to take my baby.''

''Well, it's his baby, too.'' Susie swallowed hard when both women glared at her. ''Well, it is,'' she said defiantly. ''That's just a simple biological fact.'' She frowned. ''Which brings up an interesting point. How come he's backed off?''

Annie frowned, too. ''Good question. He has backed off, hasn't he?''

Laurel nodded. She pulled a chair out from the table and sank into it. "Uh-huh. He has."

"How come? Not that I'm not delighted, but why back off now, after first all but dragging you into marriage?"

Laurel folded her hands on the tabletop.

"He—he called and left another message."

"The telephone company's best pal," Susie said brightly.

"He said—he said that he had no right to force me into living with him. That he understood that I could never feel about him as I had about Kirk—"

"Kirk?" Annie's brows arched. "How'd that piece of sewer slime get into the picture?"

"He said he'd been wrong to make me marry him in the first place, that a marriage without love could never work."

"The plot thickens." Susie leaned forward over the table. "I know you guys are liable to tar and feather me for this, but Damian Skouras isn't sounding like quite the scuzzball I'd figured him for."

Annie reached out and clasped her sister's hand. "Maybe you should have taken one of those phone calls, hmm?"

"What for?" Laurel snatched back her hand. "Don't be ridiculous, both of you. I called him and left him a message of my own. I said it didn't matter what had been going on or not going on with the blonde because I agreed completely. Not only could a loveless marriage never work, a marriage in which a wife hated the husband was doomed. And I hated him, I said. I said that I always had, that he had to accept the fact that it had been nothing but sex all along… Don't look at me that way, Annie! What was I supposed to believe? That that woman appeared at his door, uninvited, and stripped off her clothes?"

"Is that what he claimed?"

"Yes!"

Annie smiled gently. "It's possible, isn't it? The lady didn't strike me as the sort given to subtle gestures."

Laurel shot up from her chair. "I don't believe what's going on here! The two of you, asking me to deny what I saw with my own eyes! My God, it was bad enough to be deceived by Kirk, a man I'd thought I loved, but to be deceived by Damian, by my own husband, the only man I've ever really loved, is—is…" Her voice broke. "Oh God, I *do* love him! I'll never stop loving him." She looked from Susie to Annie, and her mouth began to tremble. "Go away," she whispered. "Just go away, and leave me alone."

They didn't, not until Laurel was calmer, not until she was undressed and asleep in her bed.

Then they left because, really, when you came right down to it, what else was there to do?

What else was there to do? Damian thought, as he attacked the boulder outside his house overlooking the Aegean with the sledgehammer.

Nothing. Nothing but beat at this miserable rock and work himself to exhaustion from sunup to sundown in hopes he'd fall into bed at night and not dream of Laurel.

It was a fine plan. Unfortunately it didn't work.

He had not seen Laurel, or heard her voice, in two months—but she was with him every minute of the day, just the same. The nights were even worse. Alone in the darkness, in the bed where he'd once held his wife in his arms, he tossed and turned for hours before falling into restless, dream-filled sleep.

He had considered returning to New York, but he could not imagine himself sitting behind a desk, in the same city where Laurel lived. And so he stayed on Actos, and worked, and sweated, and oversaw his business interests by computer, phone and fax. He told himself that the ache inside him would go away.

It hadn't. If anything, it had grown worse.

He knew that Eleni and Spiro were almost frantic with worry.

"Is he trying to kill himself?" he'd heard Eleni mutter just that morning, as he'd gone out the door. "You must speak to him, Spiro," she'd said.

Damian's mouth thinned as he swung the sledgehammer. If the old man knew what was good for him, he'd keep his mouth shut. He'd interfered enough already. Damian had told him so, on his return to Greece.

"Was it you who permitted my wife to leave the island and follow me to New York?" he'd demanded.

Spiro had stiffened. "*Né*," he'd said, "yes, it was I."

Damian's hands had balled into fists. "On whose authority did you do this thing, old man?"

"On my own," Spiro had replied quietly. "The woman was not a prisoner here."

A muscle had knotted in Damian's cheek. "No," he'd said, "she was not."

Spiro had waited before speaking again.

"She said that she had something of great importance to tell you," he'd said, his eyes on Damian's. "Did she find you, and deliver her message?"

Damian's mouth had twisted. "She did, indeed," he'd replied, and when Spiro had tried to say more, he'd held up his hand. "There is nothing to discuss. The woman is not to be mentioned again."

She had not been, to this day. But that didn't mean he didn't think about her, and dream about her. Did she dream of him? Did she ever long for the feel of his arms and the sweetness of his kisses, as he longed for hers?

Did she ever think of how close they'd come to happiness?

Damian's throat constricted. He swung the hammer hard, but his aim wasn't true. His vision was blurred—by sweat, for what else could it be?—and the hammer hit the rock a glancing blow.

"Dammit," he growled, and swung again.

"Damian," Spiro's voice was soft. "The rock is not your enemy."

"And you are not a philosopher," Damian snapped, and swung again.

"What you battle is not the boulder, my son, it is yourself."

Damian straightened up. "Listen here," he said, but his anger faded when he looked at the old man. Spiro looked exhausted. Sweat stained his dark trousers and shirt; his weathered face was bright red and there was a tremor in his hands.

Why was the old fool so stubborn? The heat was too much for a man his age. Damian sighed, set the sledgehammer aside and stripped off his work gloves.

"It is hot," he said. "I need something to drink."

"There is a bottle of *retsina* in my jacket, under the tree."

Damian plucked his discarded T-shirt from the ground and slipped it on.

"I know the sort of *retsina* you drink, old man. The sun will rot our brains quickly enough, without its help. We will go up to the house. Perhaps we can convince Eleni to give us some cold beer."

"*Né.*" Spiro smiled. "For once, you have an excellent idea."

It took no convincing at all. Eleni took one look at them, rolled her eyes and brought cold beer and glasses out to the terrace. Damian ignored the glasses, handed one bottle to the old man and took the other for himself. He leaned back against the railing and took a long drink. Spiro drank, too, then wiped his mustache with the back of his hand.

"When do you return to New York?" he said.

Damian's brows lifted. "Are you in such a rush to get rid of me?"

"You cannot avoid reality forever, Damian."

"Spiro." Damian's voice was chill. "I warn you, do not say anything more. It is hot, I am in a bad mood—"

"As if that were anything new."

Damian tilted the beer bottle to his lips. He drank, then set the bottle down. "I am going back to work. I suggest you go inside, where it is cooler."

"I suggest you stop pretending you do not have a wife."

"I told you, we will not discuss her."

"And now I tell you that we must."

"Dammit, old man—"

"I saw how happy she made you, Damian, and how happy you made her."

"Are you deaf? I said that we would not—"

"You loved her. And you love her still."

"No! No, I do not love her. What is love anyway, but a thing to make men idiots?"

Spiro chuckled and folded his arms. "Are you saying I was an idiot to put up with you, after I found you on the streets of Athens? Be careful, or I will have to take a switch to your backside, as I did when you were a boy."

"You know what I mean," Damian said, stubbornly refusing to be taken in. "I'm talking of male and female love, and I tell you that I did not *love* her. All right? Are you satisfied now? Can I get back to work?"

"She loved you."

"Never." Damian's voice roughened. "She did not love me, old man. She despised me for everything I am and especially for forcing her into a marriage she did not want."

"She loved you," Spiro repeated. "I know this, for a fact."

"She loved another, you sentimental old fool."

"It is not sentiment or foolishness that makes me say this, Damian, it is the knowledge of what she told me."

Damian's face went pale beneath its tan. "What the hell are you talking about?"

"It is the reason I sent her after you. She said she loved you deeply."

For one sweet instant, Damian felt his heart might burst from his chest. But then he remembered the reality of what had happened: the swiftness with which Laurel had accepted the ugly scene orchestrated by Gabriella, the way she'd refused even to listen to his explanation...and the message he'd found on his answering machine, Laurel's cool voice saying that she'd never stopped hating him, that what they'd shared had been nothing but sex...

"You misunderstood her, old man. You speak English almost as badly as she spoke Greek."

"I know what she told me, Damian."

"Then she lied," Damian said coldly. He picked up the bottle and drained it dry. "She lied, because it was the only way she could get you to agree to let her leave the island, and you fell for it. Now, I am going to work and you are going to stay out of the sun before it bakes your brain completely. Is that clear?"

"What is clear," the old man said quietly, "is that I raised a coward."

Damian spun toward him, his eyes gone hard and chill. "If any other man but you dared say such a thing to me," he said softly, "I would beat him within an inch of his life."

"You are a coward in your heart, afraid to face the truth. You love this woman but because she hurt you in some fashion, you would rather live your life without her than risk going after her."

"Damn you to hell," Damian roared, and thrust his face into the old man's. "Listen, Spiro, and listen well, for I will say this only once. Yes, I love her. But she does not love me."

"How do you know this?"

"How? How?" Damian's teeth glinted in a hollow laugh. "She told me so, all right? Does that satisfy you?"

"Did you ever tell her that you loved her?"

"Did I ever...?" Damian threw his arms skyward. "By all the gods that be, I cannot believe this! No, I never told her. She never gave me the chance. She came bursting into my apartment in New York, found me with another woman and damned me without even giving me an opportunity to explain."

Spiro's weather-beaten face gave nothing away. "And what were you doing with this woman, my son? Arranging flowers, perhaps?"

Damian colored. "I admit, it did not look good..."

"You were not arranging flowers?"

"What is this? An interrogation? I had just come out of the shower, okay? And the woman—the woman was trying to seduce me. I just admitted, it did not look good." He took a deep breath. "But Laurel is my wife. She should have trusted me."

"Certainly she should have trusted you. After all, what had you ever done to make her distrustful, except to impregnate her and force her into a marriage she did not want?"

"How did you—"

"Eleni says that there is a look to a woman's face, when she is carrying a child. Any fool could see it, just as any fool could see that when you first brought her here, neither of you was happy." Spiro smiled. "But that changed, Damian. I do not know how it happened, but you both finally admitted what had been in your hearts from the beginning."

"All right. Yes, I fell in love with her. But nothing is that simple."

"Love is never simple."

Damian turned and clasped the railing. He could feel his anger seeping away and a terrible despair replacing it.

"Spiro, you are the father I never knew and I trust your advice, you know that, but in this matter—"

"In this matter, Damian," the old man said, "trust your heart. Go to her, tell her that you love her. Give her the chance to tell you the same thing."

Damian's throat felt tight. He blinked his eyes, which seemed suddenly damp.

"And if she does not?" he said gruffly. "What then?"

"Then you will return here and swing that hammer until your arms ache with the effort—but you will return knowing that you tried to win the woman you love instead of letting her slip away." Spiro put his hand on Damian's shoulder. "There is always hope, my son. It is that which gives us the will to go on, *né*?"

Out in the bay, a tiny sailboat heeled under the wind. The sea reached up for it with greedy, white-tipped fingers. Surely it would be swallowed whole...

The wind subsided as quickly as it had begun. The boat bobbed upright.

There is always hope.

Quickly, before he could lose his courage, Damian turned and embraced the old man. Then he headed into the house.

They were wrong. Dead wrong.

Laurel pounded furiously at the lump of sourdough.

What did Annie and Susie know, anyway? Annie was divorced and Susie was married to a marshmallow. Neither of them had ever had the misfortune to deal with a macho maniac like Damian Skouras.

Damn, but it was hot! Too hot for making bread but what else was she going to do with all this pent-up energy? Laurel blew a strand of hair out of her eyes, wiped her hand over her nose and began beating the dough again.

They were driving her crazy, her sister and her friend. Ever since yesterday, when she'd been dumb enough to break down in front of them and admit she'd loved Damian, they hadn't left her alone. If it wasn't Annie phoning, it was Susie.

Well, let 'em phone. She'd given up answering. Let the machine deal with the cheery ''hi''s and the even cheerier ''Laurel? Are you there, honey?''s.

This morning, in a fit of pique, she'd snatched up the phone, snarled, ''No, I'm not there, *honey*,'' and slammed it down again before Annie or Susie, whichever it was, could say a word. Why listen to either of them, when she knew what they were going to say? They'd both said it already, that maybe she'd misjudged Damian, that maybe what he'd told her about the blonde was the truth.

''I didn't,'' Laurel muttered, picking up the dough and then slamming it down again. ''And it wasn't.''

And anyway, what did it matter? So what, if maybe, just maybe, Blondie had set him up? He'd left her, damn him, in the middle of the honeymoon, he'd gone off without a word.

Because you hurt him, Laurel, have you forgotten that?

No, she thought grimly, no, she had not forgotten. So she'd hurt him. Big deal. He'd hurt her a heck of a lot more, not telling her where he was going or even that he was going, not saying goodbye...

Not loving her, when she loved him so terribly that she couldn't shut her eyes without seeing his face or hearing his voice or—

''Laurel?''

Like that. Exactly like that. She could hear him say her name, as if he were right here, in the room with her...

''Laurel, *mátya mou*...''

Laurel spun around, and her heart leaped into her throat. ''Damian?''

Damian cursed as her knees buckled. He rushed forward, caught her in his arms and carried her into the living room. ''Take a deep breath,'' he ordered, as he sat down on the sofa with her still in his arms. "You're not going to pass out on me, are you?"

"Of course not," she said, when the mist before her eyes cleared away. "I never pass out."

"No," he said wryly, "you never do—except at the sight of me."

"What are you going here, Damian? And how did you get in?"

"That George," he said, smoothing the hair back from her face with his hand. "What a splendid fellow he is."

"George gave you my spare key? Dammit, he had no right! *You* had no—"

"And I see that I got here just in time." A smile tilted at the corner of his mouth. "You've been doing experiments in the kitchen again."

"I've been making bread. And don't try to change the subject. You had absolutely no right to unlock the door and—"

"I know, and I apologize. But I was afraid that you'd leave me standing in the hall again, if I asked you to let me in."

"You're right, I would have done exactly that." Laurel put her hands on his shoulders. "Let me up, please."

"I love you, Laurel."

Hope flickered in her heart, but fear snuffed it out.

"You just want your child," she said.

"I want *our* child, my darling wife, but more than that, I want you. I love you, Laurel." He took her face in his hands. "I adore you," he said softly. "You're the only woman I have ever loved, the only woman I will ever love, and if you don't come back to me, I will be lost forever."

Tears roses in Laurel's eyes. "Oh, Damian. Do you mean it?"

He kissed her. It was a long, sweet, wonderful kiss, and when it ended, she was trembling.

"With all my heart. I should have awakened you that

night and told you I had to leave, but you were so angry and I—I was angry, too, and wounded by the knowledge that you'd once loved another.''

Laurel shook her head. ''I didn't love him. I only talked about Kirk to hurt you. I've never loved anyone, until you.''

''Tell me again,'' he whispered.

She smiled. ''I love you, Damian. I've never loved anyone else. I never will. There's only you, only you, only—''

He kissed her again, then leaned his forehead against hers.

''What I told you about Gabriella was the truth. I didn't ask her to my apartment. She—''

Laurel kissed him to silence. A long time later, Damian drew back.

''We'll fly to Actos,'' he said, ''and ask that interfering old man to drink champagne with us.''

Laurel linked her arms around her husband's neck and smiled into his eyes.

''Did anybody ever tell you that you can sound awfully arrogant at times?''

Damian grinned as he got to his feet with his wife in his arms.

''Someone might have mentioned it, once or twice,'' he said, as he shouldered open the bedroom door.

Laurel's pulse quickened as he slowly lowered her to the bed.

''I thought we were going to Actos,'' she whispered.

''We are.'' Damian gave her a slow, sexy kiss. ''But first,'' he said, as he began to undo her buttons, ''first, we've got to get reacquainted.''

Laurel sighed as he slipped off her blouse. ''And how long do you think that's going to take, husband?''

Damian smiled. ''All the rest of our lives, wife.''

Slowly he gathered her into his arms.

EPILOGUE

NO ONE ON THE ISLAND of Actos had ever seen anything quite like it.

There were always weddings, of course, young people and life being as they are, but even the old women at the fish market, who usually argued about everything, agreed on this.

There had never been a wedding the equal of Damian and Laurel's.

Of course, as the old women were quick to point out, the Skourases were already married. But the ceremony that had joined them meant nothing. It had been performed all the way across the sea, in America, and—can you imagine?—a judge had said the words that had made them man and wife, not a priest.

No wonder they had chosen to be wed all over again, and in the proper way.

The day was perfect: a clear blue sky, a peaceful sea, and though the sun shone brightly, it was not too hot.

The bride, the old ladies said, was beautiful in her lacy white gown. And oh, her smile. So radiant, so filled with love for her handsome groom.

Handsome, indeed, one of the crones said, and she added something else behind her wrinkled hand that made them all cackle with delight.

It was just too bad the bride wasn't Greek…but she was the next best thing. Beautiful, with shining eyes and a bright smile, and Eleni had told them that she was learning to think like one of them, enough so that when her groom had teasingly warned her that marriage in a Greek church

195

was forever, she'd smiled and put her arms around him and said that was the only kind of marriage she'd ever wanted.

And so, in a little church made of whitewashed stone, with the sun streaming through the windows and baskets of flowers banked along the aisle and at the altar, and with friends and relatives from faraway America flown over for this most special of days, Laurel Bennett and Damian Skouras were wed.

"Yes," Laurel said clearly, when the priest asked—in English, at Damian's request—if she would take the man beside her as her husband, to love and honor and cherish for the rest of her days. And when Damian offered the same pledge, he broke with tradition by looking deep into his wife's eyes and saying that he would cherish forever the woman he had waited all his life to find.

The old ladies in black wept, as did the two stylishly dressed American women in the front pew. Even old Spiro wiped his eyes, though he said later that it was only because a speck had gotten into one.

Retsina and *ouzo* flowed, and bubbly champagne flown in from France. Everyone danced, and sang; they ate lobster and red snapper and roast lamb, and the men toasted the bride and groom until none could think of another reason to raise his glass.

It was, everyone said, an absolutely wonderful wedding—but if you'd asked the bride and the groom what part was the most wonderful, they'd have said it came late that night, when the crickets were singing and the air was heavy with the scent of flowers and they were alone, at last, on their hilltop overlooking the sea.

The groom took his bride in his arms.

"You are my heart," he said, looking deep into her eyes, and she smiled so radiantly that his heart almost shattered with joy.

"As you are mine," she whispered, and as the ivory

moon climbed into the black velvet sky, Damian swept Laurel into his arms and carried her up to their bedroom.

The next morning, Laurel awoke to the ring of the sledge-hammer.

She dressed quickly and went outside, to where the boulder stood.

"Damian," she called, and her husband turned and smiled at her.

"Watch," he said.

He swung the hammer against the boulder. The sound rang like a bell across the hilltop, and the rock crumbled into a thousand tiny pieces.

THE DIVORCEE SAID YES!

the subtle answer—"Dighten the knife as you'd look
where it got too—what not one you wanted to make to
your own child

It certainly was.........parents marriage
had ended in divorce.

of Orleans......as much to........
....
turning in space and the sun across......
....

"......." said gently come out..........

Annie..........said gently come out......

....
....

Give me one.........
....
Well, right..............

....

I know I lol......
....

became onto the folka.

....
....

....

....

her.................love...........

Blame her, Dawn, and I know her for the boy.

CHAPTER ONE

IT WAS HER DAUGHTER'S wedding day, and Annie Cooper
couldn't seem to stop crying.

"I'm just going to check my makeup, darling," she'd
told Dawn a few minutes ago, when her eyes had begun to
prickle again.

And now here she was, locked inside a stall in the ladies'
room of a beautiful old Connecticut church, clutching a
handful of soggy tissues and bawling her eyes out.

"Promise me you won't cry, Mom," Dawn had said,
only last night.

The two of them had been sitting up over mugs of cin-
namon-laced hot chocolate. Neither of them had felt sleepy.
Dawn had been too excited; Annie had been unwilling to
give up the last hours when her daughter would still be her
little girl instead of Nick's wife.

"I promise," Annie had said, swallowing hard, and then
she'd burst into tears.

"Oh, Moth-ther," Dawn had said, "for goodness'
sake," just as if she were still a teenager and Annie was
giving her a hard time about coming in ten minutes after
curfew on school nights.

And that was just the trouble. She *was* still a teenager,
Annie thought as she wiped her streaming eyes. Her baby
was only eighteen years old, far too young to be getting
married. Of course, when she'd tried telling that to Dawn
the night she'd come home, smiling radiantly with Nick's
engagement ring on her finger, her daughter had countered
with the ultimate rebuttal.

"And how old were *you* when *you* got married?" she'd
said, which had effectively ended the discussion because

the whole answer—"Eighteen, the same as you, and look where it got me"—was not one you wanted to make to your own child.

It certainly wasn't Dawn's fault her parents' marriage had ended in divorce.

"She's too young," Annie whispered into her handful of Kleenex, "she's much, much too young."

"Annie?"

Annie heard the door to the ladies' room swing open. A murmur of voices and the soft strains of organ music floated toward her, then faded as the door thumped shut.

"Annie? Are you in here?"

It was Deborah Kent, her best friend.

"No," Annie said miserably, choking back a sob.

"Annie," Deb said gently, "come out of there."

"No."

"Annie." Deb's tone became the sort she probably used with her third-graders. "This is nonsense. You can't hide in there forever."

"Give me one good reason why I can't," Annie said, sniffling.

"Well, you've got seventy-five guests waiting."

"A hundred," Annie sobbed. "Let 'em wait."

"The minister's starting to look impatient."

"Patience is a virtue," Annie said, and dumped the wet tissues into the toilet.

"And I think your aunt Jeanne just propositioned one of the groomsmen."

There was a long silence, and then Annie groaned. "Tell me you're joking."

"All I know is what I saw. She got this look on her face—you know the look."

Annie clamped her eyes shut. "And?"

"And, she went sashaying over to that big blond kid." Deborah's voice turned dreamy. "Actually I couldn't much blame her. Did you see the build on that boy?"

"Deb! Honestly!" Annie flushed the tissues down the toilet, unlocked the stall door and marched to the sink. "Aunt Jeanne's eighty years old. There's some excuse for her. But you—"

"Listen, just because I'm forty doesn't mean I'm dead. *You* may want to pretend you've forgotten what men are good for, but I certainly haven't."

"Forty-three," Annie said, rummaging in her purse. "You can't lie about your age to me, Deb, not when we share a birthday. As for what men are good for—believe me, I *know* what they're good for. Not much. Not one damn thing, actually, except for making babies and that's just the trouble, Dawn is *still* just a baby. She's too young to be getting married."

"That's the other thing I came in to tell you." Deb cleared her throat. "He's here."

"Who's here?"

"Your ex."

Annie went still. "No."

"Yes. He came in maybe five minutes ago."

"No, he couldn't have. He's in Georgia or Florida, someplace like that." Annie looked at her friend in the mirror. "You're sure it was Chase?"

"Six-two, dirty-blond hair, that gorgeous face with its slightly off-center nose and muscles up the yin-yang..." Deb blushed. "Well, I notice these things."

"So I see."

"It's Chase, all right. I don't know why you're so surprised. He said he'd be here for Dawn's wedding, that he wouldn't let anyone else give his daughter away."

Annie's mouth twisted. She wrenched on the water, lathered her hands with soap and scrubbed furiously.

"Chase was always good at promises. It's the follow-through he can't manage." She shut off the faucet and yanked a paper towel from the dispenser. "This whole thing is his fault."

"Annie…"

"Did he tell Dawn she was making a mistake? No. He most certainly did not. The jerk gave her his blessing. His blessing, Deb, can you imagine?" Annie balled up the paper towel and hurled it into the trash can. "I put my foot down, told her to wait, to finish her education. *He* gave her a kiss and told her to do what she thought best. Well, that's typical. Typical! He could never do anything that wasn't just the opposite of what I wanted."

"Annie, calm down."

"I really figured, when he didn't show up for the rehearsal last night, that we'd gotten lucky."

"Dawn wouldn't have thought so," Deb said quietly. "And you know that she never doubted him, for a minute. 'Daddy will be here,' she kept saying."

"All the more proof that she's too young to know what's good for her," Annie muttered. "What about my sister? Has she shown up yet?"

"Not yet, no."

Annie frowned. "I hope Laurel's okay. It's not like her to be late."

"I already phoned the railroad station. The train came in late, or something. It's the minister you've got to worry about. He's got another wedding to perform in a couple of hours, over in Easton."

Annie sighed and smoothed down the skirt of her knee-length, pale green chiffon dress. "I suppose there's no getting out of it. Okay, let's do it… What?"

"You might want to take a look in the mirror first."

Annie frowned, swung toward the sink again and blanched. Her mascara had run and rimmed her green eyes. Her small, slightly upturned nose was bright pink, and her strawberry blond hair, so lovingly arranged in a smooth, sophisticated cap by Pierre himself just this morning, was standing up as if she'd stuck her finger into an electric outlet.

"Deb, look at me!"

"I'm looking," Deb said. "We could always ask the organist if he knows the music from *Bride of Frankenstein.*"

"Will you be serious? I've got a hundred people waiting out there." And Chase, she thought, so quickly and so senselessly that it made her blink.

"What's the matter now?"

"Nothing," Annie said quickly. "I mean…just help me figure out how to repair some of this damage."

Deb opened her purse. "Wash your face," she said, taking out enough cosmetics to start her own shop, "and leave the rest to me."

Chase Cooper stood on the steps of the little New England church, trying to look as if he belonged there.

It wasn't easy. He'd never felt more like an outsider in his life.

He was a city person. He'd spent his life in apartments. When Annie sold the condo after their divorce and told him she was moving to Connecticut, with Dawn, it had damn near killed him.

"Stratham?" he'd said, his voice a strangled roar. "Where the hell is that? I can't even find it on a map."

"Try one of those big atlases you're so fond of," Annie had said coldly, "the ones you look in when you're trying to figure out what part of the country you'll disappear into next."

"I've told you a million times," Chase had snapped, "I have no choice. If I don't do things myself, they get screwed up. A man can't afford that, when he's got a wife and family to support."

"Well, now you don't have to support me at all," Annie had replied, with a toss of her head. "I refused your alimony, remember?"

"Because you were pigheaded, as usual. Dammit, Annie, you can't sell this place. Dawn grew up here."

"I can do what I like," Annie had said. "The condo's mine. It was part of the settlement."

"Because it's our home, dammit!"

"Don't you dare shout at me," Annie had yelled, although he hadn't shouted. Not him. Never him. "And it's not our home, not anymore. It's just a bunch of rooms inside a pile of bricks, and I hate it."

"Hate it?" Chase had repeated. "You hate this house, that I built with my own two hands?"

"You built a twenty-four story building that just happens to contain our particular seven rooms, and you made a million trillion bucks doing it. And, if you must know, yes, I hate it. I despise it, and I can hardly wait to get out of it."

Oh, yeah, Chase thought, shuffling uneasily from one foot to the other and wishing, for the first time in years, that he hadn't given up smoking, oh, yeah, she'd gotten out of the condo, all right. Fast. And then she'd moved herself and Dawn up to this—this pinprick on the map, figuring, no doubt, that it would be the end of his weekly visits with his daughter.

Wrong. He'd driven the hundred-and-fifty-plus miles each way every weekend, like clockwork. He loved his little girl and she loved him, and nothing that had happened between Annie and him could change that. Week after week, he'd come up to Stratham and renewed his bond with his daughter. And week after week, he'd seen that his wife—his former wife—had built herself a happy new life.

She had friends. A small, successful business. And there were men in her life, Dawn said. Well, that was fine. Hell, there were women in his, weren't there? As many as he wanted, all of them knockouts. That was one of the perks of bachelorhood, especially when you were the CEO of a construction company that had moved onto the national scene and prospered.

Eventually, though, he'd stopped going to Stratham. It was simpler that way. Dawn got old enough so she could take a train or a plane to wherever he was. And every time he saw her, she was lovelier. She'd seemed to grow up, right before his eyes.

Chase's mouth thinned. But she hadn't grown up enough to get married. Hell, no. Eighteen? And she was going to be some guy's wife?

It was Annie's fault. If she'd paid a little less attention to her own life and a little more to their daughter's, he wouldn't be standing here in a monkey suit, waiting to give his little girl away to a boy hardly old enough to shave.

Well, that wasn't quite true. Nick was twenty-one. And it wasn't as if he didn't like the kid. Nick—Nicholas, to be precise—was a nice enough young man, from a good family and with a solid future ahead of him. He'd met the boy when he'd flown Dawn and her fiancé to Florida to spend a week with him on his latest job site. The kids had spent the time looking at each other as if the rest of the world didn't exist, and that was just the trouble. It *did* exist, and his daughter hadn't seen enough of it yet to know what she was doing.

Chase had tried to tell her that, but Dawn had been resolute. In the end, he had no choice. Dawn was legally of age. She didn't need his consent. And, as his daughter quickly told him, Annie had already said she thought the marriage was a fine idea.

So he'd swallowed his objections, kissed Dawn, shaken Nick's hand and given them his blessing—as if it were worth a damn.

You could bless the union of two people all you wanted, but it didn't mean a thing. Marriage—especially for the young—was nothing but a legitimate excuse for hormonal insanity.

He could only hope his daughter, and her groom, proved the exception to the rule.

"Sir?"

Chase looked around. A boy who looked barely old enough to shave was standing in the doorway of the church.

"They sent me out to tell you they're about ready to begin, sir."

Sir, Chase thought. He could remember when he'd called older men "sir." It hadn't been so much a mark of respect as it had been a euphemism for "old man." That was how he felt, suddenly. Like an old, old man.

"Sir?"

"I heard you the first time," Chase said irritably and then, because none of what he was feeling was the fault of the pink-cheeked groomsman, he forced a smile to his lips. "Sorry," he said. "I've got the father-of-the-bride jitters, I guess."

Still smiling, or grimacing, whichever the hell it was, he clapped the boy on the back and stepped past him, into the cool darkness of the church.

Annie sniffled her way through the ceremony.

Dawn was beautiful, a fairy-tale princess come to life. Nick was handsome enough to bring tears to whatever eyes weren't already streaming, though not to his former guardian's, who stood beside him wearing a look that spoke volumes on his handsome face.

Chase was wearing the same look. Her ex was not just dry-eyed but stony-faced. He'd smiled only once, at Dawn, as he'd handed her over to her waiting groom.

Then he'd taken his place beside Annie.

"I hope you know what in hell you're doing," he'd muttered, as he'd slipped in next to her.

Annie had felt every muscle in her body clench. How like him, to talk like that here, of all places. And to blame her for—what? The fact that the wedding wasn't being held in a church the size of a cathedral? That there wasn't room for him to invite all his big-shot clients and turn a family event into a networking opportunity?

Maybe he thought Dawn's gown was too old-fashioned, or the flower arrangements—which she, herself, had done—too provincial. It wouldn't have surprised her. As far as Chase was concerned, nothing she'd ever done was right. She could see him out of the corner of her eye, standing beside her, straight and tall and unmistakably masculine.

"Isn't Daddy gorgeous in formal wear?" Dawn had gushed.

A muscle twitched in Annie's cheek. If you liked the type, she supposed he was. But she wasn't a dumb kid anymore, to have her little heart sent into overtime beats by the sight of a man's hard body or equally hard, handsome face.

There had been a time, though. Oh, yes, there'd been a time that just standing next to him this way, feeling his arm brush lightly against her shoulder, smelling the faint scent of his cologne, would have been enough to—would have been enough to—

Bang!

Annie jumped. The doors at the rear of the church had flown open. A buzz of surprise traveled among the guests. The minister fell silent and peered up the aisle, along with everybody else, including Dawn and Nick.

Somebody was standing in the open doorway. After a moment, a man got up and shut the door, and the figure moved forward.

Annie let out a sigh of relief. "It's Laurel," she whispered, for the benefit of the minister. "My sister. I'm so relieved she finally got here."

"Typical Bennett histrionics," Chase muttered, out of the side of his mouth.

Annie's cheeks colored. "I beg your pardon?"

"You heard me."

"I most certainly did, and—"

"Mother," Dawn snapped.

Annie blushed. "Sorry."

The minister cleared his throat. "And now," he said in tones so rounded Annie could almost see them forming circles in the air, "if there is no one among us who can offer a reason why Nicholas Skouras Babbitt and Dawn Elizabeth Cooper should not be wed…"

A moment later, the ceremony was over.

It was interesting, being the father of the bride at a wedding at which the mother of the bride was no longer your wife.

Dawn had insisted she wanted both her parents seated at the main table with her.

"You can keep your cool, Daddy, can't you?" she'd said. "I mean, you won't mind, sitting beside Mom for a couple of hours, right?"

"Of course not," Chase had said.

And he'd meant it. He was a civilized man and Annie, for all her faults—and there were many—was a civilized woman. They'd been divorced for five years. The wounds had healed. Surely they could manage polite smiles and chitchat for a couple of hours.

That was what he'd thought, but reality was another thing entirely.

He hadn't counted on what it would be like to stand at the altar, with Annie standing beside him looking impossibly young and—what was the point in denying it—impossibly beautiful in a dress of palest green. Her hair had been the wild cluster of silky strawberry curls she'd always hated and he'd always loved, and her nose had been suspiciously pink. She'd sniffled and wept her way through the ceremony. Well, hell, his throat had been pretty tight there, once or twice. In fact, when the minister had gone through all that nonsense about speaking up or forever holding your peace, he'd been tempted to put an arm around her and tell her it was okay, they weren't losing a daughter, they were gaining a son.

Except that it would have been a lie. They *were* losing a daughter, and it was all Annie's fault.

By the time they'd been stuck together at the head of the receiving line as if they were a pair of Siamese twins, he'd felt about as surly as a lion with a thorn in its paw.

"Smile, you two," Dawn had hissed, and they'd obeyed, though Annie's smile had been as phony-looking as his felt.

At least they'd traveled to the Stratham Inn in separate cars—except that once they'd gotten there, they'd had to take seats beside each other at the table on the dais.

Chase felt as if his smile was frozen on his face. It must have looked that way, too, from the way Dawn lifted her eyebrows when she looked at him.

Okay, Cooper, he told himself. Pull it together. You know how to make small talk with strangers. Surely you can manage a conversation with your ex-wife.

He looked at Annie and cleared his throat. "So," he said briskly, "how've you been?"

Annie turned her head and looked at him. "I'm sorry," she said politely, "I didn't quite get that. Were you talking to me?"

Chase's eyes narrowed. Who else would he have been talking to? The waiter, leaning over to pour his champagne?

Keep your cool, he told himself, and bared his teeth in a smile.

"I asked how you've been."

"Very well, thank you. And you?"

Very well, thank you... What was with this prissy tone?

"Oh, I can't complain." He forced another smile, and waited for Annie to pick up the ball. She didn't, so he plunged into the conversational waters again. "Matter of fact, I don't know if Dawn mentioned it, but we just landed a big contract."

"We?" she said, in a tone that could have given chilblains to an Eskimo.

"Well, Cooper Construction. We bid on this job in—"

"How nice," she said, and turned away.

Chase felt his blood pressure shoot off the scale. So much for his attempt at being polite. Annie was not just cutting him dead, she was icing the corpse, craning her neck, looking everywhere but at him.

Suddenly a smile, a real one, curved across her mouth.

"Yoo hoo," she called softly.

Yoo hoo? *Yoo hoo*?

"Hi, there," she mouthed, and waved, and damned if some Bozo the Clown at a nearby table didn't wave back.

"Who is that jerk?" Chase said before he could stop himself.

Annie didn't even look at him. She was too busy looking at the jerk, and smiling.

"That 'jerk,'" she said, "is Milton Hoffman. He's an English professor at the university."

Chase watched as the professor rose to his feet and threaded through the tables toward the dais. The guy was tall, and thin; he was wearing a shiny blue serge suit and he had on a bow tie. He looked more like a cadaver than a professor.

He had a smile on his face, too, as he approached Annie, and it was the smile, more than anything, that suddenly put a red film over Chase's eyes.

"Anne," Hoffman said. "Anne, my dear." Annie held out her hand. Hoffman clasped it in a pasty, marshmallow paw and raised it to his lips. "It was a beautiful ceremony."

"Thank you, Milton."

"The flowers were perfect."

"Thank you, Milton."

"The music, the decorations...all wonderful."

"Thank you, Milton."

"And you look exquisite."

"Thank you, Milton," Chase said.

Annie and the Prof both swung their heads toward him. Chase smiled, showing all his teeth.

"She does, doesn't she?" he said. "Look great, I mean."

Annie looked at him, her eyes flaming a warning, but Chase ignored it. He leaned toward her and hooked an arm around her shoulders.

"Love that low-cut neckline, especially, babe, but then, you know how it is." He shot Hoffman a leering grin. "Some guys are leg men, right, Milty? But me, I was always a—"

"Chase!" Color flew into Annie's face. Hoffman's eyes, dark and liquid behind horn-rimmed glasses, blinked once. "You must be Anne's husband."

"You're quick, Milty, I've got to give you that."

"He is *not* my husband," Annie said firmly, twisting out of Chase's embrace. "He's my *ex-husband*. My *former* husband. My once-upon-a-time-but-not-anymore husband, and frankly, if I never see him again, it'll be too soon." She gave Hoffman a melting smile. "I hope you've got your dancing shoes on, Milton, because I intend to dance the afternoon away."

Chase smiled. He could almost feel his canine teeth turning into fangs.

"You hear that, Milty?" he said pleasantly. He felt a rush of primal pleasure when he saw Hoffman's face turn even paler than it already was.

"Chase," Annie said, through her teeth, "stop it."

Chase leaned forward over the table. "She's a wonderful dancer, our Annie. But if she's had too much bubbly, you got to watch out. Right, babe?"

Annie opened and shut her mouth as if she were a fish. "Chase," she said, in a strangled whisper.

"What's the matter? Milt's an old pal of yours, right?

We wouldn't want to keep any secrets from him, would we, babe?''

"Stop calling me that!''

"Stop calling you what?''

"You know what,'' Annie said furiously. "And stop lying. I've never been drunk in my life.''

Chase's lips curved up in a slow, wicked smile. "Sweetheart, come on. Don't tell me you've forgotten the night we met.''

"I'm warning you, Chase!''

"There I was, a college freshman, minding my own business and dancing with my girlfriend at her high school's Valentine Day dance—''

"You were never innocent,'' Annie snapped.

Chase grinned. "You should know, babe. Anyway, there I was, doing the Mashed Potato, when I spied our Annie, tottering out the door, clutching her middle and looking as if she'd just eaten a bushel of green apples.''

Annie swung toward Milton Hoffman. "It wasn't like that at all. My date had spiked my punch. How was I to know—''

A drumroll and a clash of cymbals drowned out her voice.

"...and now,'' an oily, amplified voice boomed, "Mr. and Mrs. Nicholas Babbitt will take their very first dance as husband and wife.''

People began to applaud as Nick took Dawn in his arms. They moved onto the dance floor, gazing soulfully into each other's eyes.

Annie gave Milton a beseeching look.

"Milton,'' she said, "listen—''

"It's all right,'' he said quickly. "Today's a family day, Anne. I understand.'' He started to reach for her hand, caught himself, and drew back. "I'll call you tomorrow. It was...interesting to have met you, Mr. Cooper.''

Chase smiled politely. "Call me Chase, please. There's

no need to be so formal, considering all we have in common.''

Annie didn't know which she wanted to do more, punch Chase for his insufferable behavior or punch Milton Hoffman for being so easily scared off. It took only a second to decide that Chase was the more deserving target. She glared at him as Hoffman scuttled back to his seat.

"You are lower than a snake's belly," she said.

Chase sighed. "Annie, listen—"

"No. No, *you* listen." She pointed a trembling finger at him. "I know what you're trying to do."

Did she? Chase shook his head. Then, she knew more than he did. There wasn't a reason in the world he'd acted like such a jerk just now. So what if Annie was having a thing with some guy? So what if the guy looked as if he might faint at the sight of a mouse? So what if he'd had a sudden, blazing vision of Annie in bed with the son of a bitch?

She could do what she wanted, with whom she wanted. It sure as hell didn't matter to him.

"Are you listening to me?" she said.

Chase looked at Annie. Her face was still shot with color. It arced across her cheekbones and over the bridge of her nose, where a scattering of tiny freckles lay like sprinkles of gold. He remembered how he used to kiss those warm, golden spots after they'd made love.

"I know what you're up to, Chase. You're trying to ruin Dawn's wedding because I didn't do it the way you wanted."

Chase's eyebrows leaped into his hairline. "Are you nuts?"

"Oh, come off it!" Annie's voice quavered with anger. "You wanted a big wedding in a big church, so you could invite all your fancy friends."

"You *are* nuts! I never—"

"Keep your voice down!"

"I am keeping it down. You're the one who's—"

"Let me tell you something, Chase Cooper. This wedding is exactly the kind Dawn wanted."

"And a damn good thing, too. If it had been up to you, our daughter might have ended up getting married on a hillside in her bare feet—"

"Oh, and what that would have done to Mr. Chase Cooper's image!"

"—while some idiot played a satyr in the background."

"Sitar," Annie hissed. "It's called a sitar, Cooper, although you probably know a lot more about satyrs than you do about musical instruments."

"Are we back to that again?" Chase snarled, and Annie's color heightened.

"No. We are not 'back' to anything. As far as I'm concerned—"

"...the bride's parents, Mr. and Mrs. Chase Cooper."

Annie's and Chase's gazes swung toward the bandstand. The bandleader was smiling benevolently in their direction, and the crowd— even those who looked a bit surprised by the announcement—began to applaud.

"Come on, Annie and Chase." The bandleader's painted-on smile widened. "Let's get up on the dance floor and join the bride and groom."

"Let's not," Chase growled, under his breath.

"The man's out of his mind," Annie snapped.

But the applause had grown, and even the wild glance for help Annie shot toward Dawn, still swaying in the arms of her groom, brought only an apologetic shrug of her daughter's shoulders.

Chase shoved back his chair and held out his hand.

"All right," he said grimly, "let's do it and get it over with."

Annie's chin jerked up. She rose stiffly and put her hand in his.

"I really hate you, Chase."

"The feeling, madam, is entirely mutual."

Eyes hot with anger, Annie and Chase took a couple of deep breaths, pasted civilized smiles on their lips and swung out onto the dance floor.

CHAPTER TWO

IMPOSSIBLE, miserable woman!

That was what she was, his ex-wife, what she'd turned into during the years of their marriage. Chase held Annie stiffly in his arms, enough space between them to have satisfied even starchy Miss Elgar, the chaperone at Annie's Senior Prom.

"Propriety, please," Miss Elgar had barked at any couple daring to get too close during the slow numbers.

Not that she'd approved of the Frug or the Mashed Potato, either. It was just that she'd figured those insane gyrations were safe.

Even all these years later, Chase smiled at the memory. Safe? A bunch of horny kids shaking their hips at each other? And no matter what the old witch thought, the sweetly erotic, locked-in-each-other's-arms slow dancing went on behind her back just the same, in the hallway, in the cafeteria downstairs, even in the parking lot, where the music sighed on the warm spring breeze.

That was where he'd taken Annie, finally, out to the parking lot, where they'd danced, locked in each other's arms, alone in the darkness and so crazy about each other after four months of dating that nothing else had mattered.

That was the night they'd first made love, on an old patchwork blanket he'd taken from the back of his beat-up Chevy and spread on the soft, sweet-smelling grass that grew up on Captree Point.

"We should stop," he'd kept saying, in a voice so thick it had seemed to come from somebody else, though even as he'd said it, he'd been undoing Annie's zipper, removing her gown and baring her beautiful body to his eyes and mouth and touch.

"Yes," Annie had whispered, "oh, yes," but her hands had been moving on him, even as she'd spoken, trembling as she'd undone his silly bow tie, sliding his white dinner jacket from his shoulders, opening his shirt buttons and smoothing her fingers over his hot skin.

The memories surrounded him, as if it were a gentle fog coming in over the sea. Chase made a soft sound in the back of his throat. His arm tightened around his wife; the hand that had been holding hers in stiff formality curled around her wrist, bringing her hand to his chest.

"Chase?" she said.

"Shh," he whispered, his lips against her hair. Annie held herself rigid a second longer, and then she sighed, laid her head against his shoulder and gave herself up to the music and to the memories that had overcome her.

It felt so good to be here, in Chase's arms.

When was the last time they'd danced together this way, not because dancing was what you did at the endless charity functions they'd attended so Chase could "network" with the movers and doers of the business community but simply because there were few things as pleasurable as swaying slowly in each other's arms?

Annie closed her eyes. They'd always danced well together, even back in her high school days at Taft. All those senior parties, the last-minute Friday night get-togethers in somebody's basement rec room the weekends Chase came home from college, and the dance at Chase's fraternity house, when her parents had let her go up for Spring Weekend. The school formals, with Elgar the Dragon Lady marching around, trying to keep everybody at arm's length.

And the night of her senior prom, when they'd finally gone all the way after so many months of fevered kisses and touches that had left them trembling in each other's arms.

Annie's heartbeat quickened. She remembered Chase taking her out to the parking lot, where they'd moved oh, so slowly to the music drifting from the school gym, and the way Chase had kissed her, filling her with a need so powerful she couldn't think. Wordlessly they'd climbed into his ancient Chevy and made the long drive to the Point, with her sitting so close beside him that they might have been one.

She remembered the softness of the blanket beneath her, after they'd spread it over the grass, and then the wonderful hardness of Chase's body against hers.

"I love you so much," he'd kept saying.

"Yes." She'd sighed. "Yes."

They shouldn't have done it. She'd known that, even as she was opening his shirt and touching him, but to stop would have been to die.

Oh, the feel of him as he'd come down against her naked flesh. The smell of him, the taste of his skin. And oh, that mind-shattering moment when he'd entered her. Filled her. Become a part of her, forever.

Except it hadn't been forever.

Annie stiffened in the circle of her husband's arms.

It had been sex, and eventually, it hadn't been anything at all. He was her ex. That's who Chase was. He wasn't her husband anymore. He wasn't the boy she'd fallen head over heels in love with, nor the man who'd fathered Dawn. He was a stranger, who'd been more interested in his business than in coming home to his wife and child.

More interested in bedding a twenty-two-year-old secretary than the wife whose body had begun to sag and bag.

A coldness seized Annie's heart. Her feet stopped moving. She jerked back and flattened her palms against her former husband's chest.

"That's enough," she said.

Chase blinked his eyes open. His face was flushed; he looked like a man rudely awakened from a dream.

"Annie," he said softly, "Annie, listen—"

"The by-request dancing's over, Chase. The dance floor's filled with people."

He looked around him. She was right. They were on the perimeter of the floor, which was packed with other couples.

"We've played out the necessary charade. Now, if you don't mind, I've reserved the rest of my dance card for Milton Hoffman."

Chase's expression hardened. "Of course," he said politely. "I want to touch bases with some people, too. I see you broke down and invited some of my old friends and not just your own."

"Certainly." Annie's smile would have turned water to ice. "Some of them are my friends, too. Besides, I knew you'd need something to keep you busy, considering that you made the great paternal sacrifice of not asking to bring along your latest little playmate. Or are you between bimbos, at the moment?"

Chase had never struck a woman in his life. Hell, he'd never even had the urge. Men who hit women were despicable. Still, just for an instant, he found himself wishing Annie were a man, so he could wipe that holier-than-thou smirk from her face.

He did the next best thing, instead.

"If you're asking if there's a special woman in my life," he said, his gaze locked on hers, "the answer is yes." He paused for effect, then went for broke. "And I'll thank you to watch the way you talk about my fiancée."

It was like watching a building collapse after the demolition guys had placed the dynamite and set it off. Annie's smirk disintegrated and her jaw dropped.

"Your—your…?"

"Fiancée," he said. It wasn't a complete lie. He'd been dating Janet for two months now, and she hadn't been at all subtle about what she wanted from the relationship. "Janet Pendleton. Ross Pendleton's daughter. Do you know her?''

Know her? Janet Pendleton, heiress to the Pendleton fortune? The blond, blue-eyed creature who turned up on the *New York Times* Sunday Society pages almost every week? The girl known as much for the brilliance she showed as vice president at Pendleton as for having turned down a million-dollar offer to lend her classic beauty to a series of perfume ads for a top French company?

For the barest fraction of a second, Annie felt as if the floor was tilting under her feet. Then she drew herself up and pasted a smile on her lips.

''We don't move in the same circles, I'm afraid. But I know who she is, of course. It's nice to see your tastes have gone from twenty-two-year-olds to females tottering on the brink of thirty. Have you told Dawn yet?''

''No! I mean, no, there hasn't been time. I, ah, I thought I'd wait until she and Nick get back from their honey—''

''Milton. There you are.'' Annie reached out and grabbed Milton Hoffman's arm. She was pretty sure he'd been trying to sneak past her and Chase undetected, en route to the line at the buffet table, but if ever there'd been a time she'd needed someone to cling to, it was now. ''Milton,'' she said, looping her arm through his and giving him a dazzling smile, ''my ex has just given me some exciting news.''

Hoffman looked at Chase, his eyes wary behind his tortoiseshells. ''Really,'' he said. ''How nice.''

''Chase is getting married again. To Janet Pendleton.'' *Could your lips be permanently stretched by a smile?* ''Isn't that lovely?''

''Well,'' Chase said, ''actually—''

''I suppose it's the season for romance,'' Annie said, with a silvery laugh. ''Dawn and Nick, Chase and Janet Pendleton...'' She tilted her head and gazed up into Milton Hoffman's long, bony face. ''And us.''

Hoffman's Adam's apple bobbed so hard it almost dislodged his bow tie. It was only a week ago that he'd asked Anne Cooper to marry him. She'd told him how much she liked and admired him, how she enjoyed his company and his attention. She'd told him everything but yes.

His gaze leaped to her former husband. Chase Cooper had taken his father's construction firm and used his engineering degree and his muscles to turn it into a company with a national reputation. He'd ridden jackhammers as they bit deep into concrete foundations and hoisted pickaxes to reduce the remainder to piles of rubble. Hoffman swallowed hard again. Cooper still had the muscles to prove it. Right now, the man looked as if he wanted to use those muscles to pulverize him.

"Chase?" Annie said, beaming. "Aren't you going to wish us well?"

"Yes," Chase said, jamming his hands into his pockets, balling them so hard they began to shake. "I wish you the best, Annie. You and your cadaver, both."

Annie's smile flattened. "You always did know the right thing to say, didn't you, Chase?" Turning on her heel, she propelled herself and Milton off the edge of the dance floor and toward the buffet.

"Anne," Milton whispered, "Anne, my dearest, I had no idea…"

"Neither did I," Annie whispered back, and smiled up into his stunned face hard enough so he'd have to think the tears in her eyes were for happiness and not because a hole seemed suddenly to have opened in her heart.

Married, Chase thought. His Annie, getting married to that jerk.

Surely she had better taste.

He slid his empty glass across the bar to the bartender.

"Women," he said. "Can't live with 'em and can't live without 'em."

The bartender smiled politely. "Yes, sir."

"Give me a refill. Bourbon and—"

"And water, one ice cube. I remember."

Chase looked at the guy. "You trying to tell me I've been here too many times this afternoon?"

The bartender's smile was even more polite. "I might have to, soon, sir. State law, you know."

Chase's mouth thinned. "When I've had too much to drink, I'll be sure and let you know. Meanwhile, make this one a double."

"Chase?"

He swung around. Behind him, people were doing whatever insane line dance was this year's vogue. Others were still eating the classy assortment of foods Annie had ordered and he hadn't been permitted to pay for.

"I've no intention of asking you to foot the bill for anything," she'd told him coldly, when he'd called to tell her to spare no expense on the wedding. "Dawn is my daughter, my floral design business is thriving and I need no help from you."

"Dawn is my daughter, too," Chase had snarled, but before he'd gotten the words out, Annie had hung up. She'd always been good at getting the last word, dammit. Not today, though. He'd gotten it. And the look on her face when he'd handed her all that crap about his engagement to Janet made it even sweeter.

"Chase? You okay?"

Who was he kidding? He hadn't had the last word this time, either. Annie had. How could she? How *could* she marry that pantywaist, bow-tie wearing, gender-confused—

"Chase, what the hell's the matter with you?"

Chase blinked. David Chambers, tall, blue-eyed, still wearing his dark hair in a long ponytail clasped at his nape the same way he had since he'd first become Chase's personal attorney a dozen years ago, was standing alongside him.

Chase let out an uneasy laugh.

"David." He stuck out his hand, changed his mind and clasped the other man's shoulders. "Hey, man, how're you doing?"

Chambers smiled and drew Chase into a quick bear hug. Then he drew back and eyed him carefully.

"I'm fine. How about you? You all right?"

Chase reached for his drink and knocked back half of it in one swallow.

"Never been better. What'll you have?"

Chambers looked at the bartender. "Scotch," he said, "a single malt, if you have it, on the rocks. And a glass of Chardonnay, please."

"Don't tell me," Chase said with a stilted smile. "You're here with a lady. I guess the love bug's bitten you, too."

"Me?" David laughed. "The wine's for a lady at my table. As for the love bug... It already bit me, remember? One marriage, one divorce...no, Chase, not me. Never again, not in this lifetime."

"Yeah." Chase wrapped his hand around his glass. "What's the point? You marry a woman, she turns into somebody else after a couple of years."

"I agree. Marriage is a female fantasy. Promise a guy anything to nab him, then look blank when he expects you to deliver." The bartender set the Scotch in front of David, who lifted the glass to his lips and took a swallow. "The way I see it, a man's got a housekeeper, a cook and a good secretary, what more does he need?"

"Nothing," Chase said glumly, "not one thing."

The bartender put a glass of Chardonnay before David, who picked it up. He turned and looked across the room. Chase followed his gaze to a table where a cool-looking, beautiful brunette sat in regal solitude.

A muscle knotted in David's jaw. He took another swallow of Scotch.

"Unfortunately," he said, "there is one other thing. And it's what most often gets poor bastards like you and me in trouble."

Chase thought of the feel of Annie in his arms on the dance floor, just a couple of hours ago.

"Poor bastards, is right," he said, and lifted his glass to David. "Well, you and I both know better. Bed 'em and forget 'em, I say."

David laughed and clinked his glass against Chase's. "I'll drink to that."

"To what? What are you guys up to, hidden away over here?"

Both men turned around. Dawn, radiant in white lace and with Nick at her side, beamed at them.

"Daddy," she said, kissing her father's cheek. "And Mr. Chambers. I'm so glad you could make it."

"I am, too." David held his hand out to her groom. "You're a lucky man, son. Take good care of her."

Nick nodded as the men shook hands. "I intend to, sir."

Dawn kissed Chase again. "Get out and circulate, Daddy. That's an order."

Chase tossed her a mock salute. The bridal pair moved off, and he sighed. "That's the only good thing comes of a marriage. A kid, to call your own."

David nodded. "I agree. I'd always hoped..." He shrugged, then picked up his drink and the glass of white wine. "Hey, Cooper," he said, with a quick grin, "you stand around a bar long enough, you get maudlin. Anybody ever tell you that?"

"Yes," Chase said. "My attorney, five years ago when we got wasted after my divorce was finalized."

The men smiled at each other, and then David Chambers slapped Chase lightly on the back.

"Take Dawn's advice. Circulate. There's a surprising assortment of good-looking single women here, in case you hadn't noticed.''

"For a lawyer," Chase said with a chuckle, "sometimes you manage to come up with some pretty decent suggestions. What's with the brunette at your table? She spoken for?''

David's eyes narrowed just the slightest bit. ''She is, for the present.''

"Yeah?''

"Yeah,'' the attorney said. He was smiling, but there was a look in his eye that Chase recognized. He grinned.

"You dirty dog, you. Well, never mind. I'll—what did my daughter call it? Circulate. That's it. I'll circulate, and see what's available.''

The men made their goodbyes. Chase finished his drink, refused to give the bartender the satisfaction of telling him he wouldn't pour him another, and circulated himself right out the door.

Annie kicked off her shoes, put her feet up on the old chintz-covered ottoman she kept promising herself she'd throw out and puffed out a long, deep sigh.

"Well,'' she said, "that's over.''

Deb, seated opposite her on the sofa, nodded in agreement.

"Over and done with.'' She flung her arms along the top of the sofa and kicked off her shoes, too. "And I'll bet you're glad it is.''

"Glad?'' Annie pursed her lips and blew a very unladylike raspberry. "That doesn't even come close. I'll bet Custer had an easier time planning the battle at Little Bighorn than I had, planning this wedding.''

Deb arched a dark, perfect eyebrow. "Bad analogy, if you don't mind my saying so.''

"Yeah.'' Annie heaved another sigh. "But you know what I mean. The logistics of the whole thing were beyond belief. Imagine your daughter walking in one night and calmly announcing she's going to get married in two months and wouldn't it be wonderful if she could have the perfect wedding she'd always dreamed about?''

Deb stood, reached up under her chiffon skirt and wriggled her panty hose down her legs.

"My daughter's in love with the seventies," she said, draping the hose around her throat like a boa. "If I'm lucky, she'll opt for getting married on a hilltop somewhere, with the guests all invited to bring... What's the matter?''

"Nothing." Annie shot to her feet and padded to the kitchen, returning a moment later with a bottle of champagne and a pair of juice glasses. "He accused me of wanting that, you know."

"Know what? Wanting what? Who accused you?"

"You mind drinking this stuff out of juice glasses? I know you're supposed to use flutes, but I never got around to buying any."

"We can drink it out of jelly jars, for all I care. What are you talking about, Annie? Who accused you of what?"

"Chase. Mr. Ex." Annie undid the wire around the foil, then chewed on her lip as she carefully worked the cork between her fingers. It popped with a loud bang and champagne frothed out. Some of it dripped onto the tile floor. Annie shrugged and mopped it up by moving her stockinged foot over the small puddle. "A few weeks ago, he called to talk to Dawn. I had the misfortune to answer the phone. He said he'd gotten his invitation and he was delighted to see I hadn't let my instincts run amok." She held out a glass of wine, and Deb took it. "Amok," she said, licking her fingertips, "can you imagine? And all because when we were first married, I threw a couple of parties in the backyard behind the house we lived in."

"I thought you lived in a condo."

"We did, eventually, but not then. Chase knew somebody who got us this really cheap rental in Queens."

Deb nodded. "What kind of parties did you throw?"

"Outdoor parties, mostly."

"So?" Deb made a face. "Big deal."

Annie's lips twitched. "Well, it was wintertime."

"Wintertime?"

"Yes. See, the thing was, the house was so small, the mice pretty much ran it. And—"

"Mice?"

Annie sank down on the chair again. "It wasn't much of a house, but then, we didn't have much money. I'd just graduated from high school and the only job I could find was at the local Burger King. Chase had transferred to City College. The tuition was lots cheaper and besides, that way he could work construction jobs for his father a couple of days a week." She sighed. "We were dead broke. Believe me, we found a million ways to save money!"

Deb smiled. "Including having parties outdoors in midwinter."

Annie smiled, too. "Oh, it wasn't that bad. We'd build a fire in a barbecue in the backyard, you know? And I'd make tons and tons of chili and homemade bread. We'd put on a huge pot of coffee, and there'd be beer for the guys..."

Her voice drifted away.

"A far cry from today," Deb said. She reached for the champagne bottle and refilled both their glasses. "Bubbly, caviar, shrimp on ice, boneless beef with mushrooms..."

"*Filet de Boeuf Aux Chanterelles*, if you please," Annie said archly.

Deb grinned. "*Pardonnez-moi, madam.*"

"No joke. Considering what that stuff cost, you'd better remember to give it its French name."

"And you didn't let Chase pay a dime, huh?"

"No," Annie said sharply.

"I still think you're nuts. What're you trying to prove, anyway?"

"That I don't need his money."

"Or him?" Deb said softly. Annie looked at her and Deb shrugged. "I saw you guys on the dance floor. Things looked pretty cozy, for a while there."

"You saw the past worm its way into the present. Trust me, Deb. That part of my life is over. I don't feel a thing for Chase. I can't quite believe I ever did."

"I understand. A nostalgia trip, hmm?"

"Exactly. Brought on by my little girl's wedding…" Annie paused, swallowed hard and suddenly burst into tears.

"Oh, sweetie." Deb jumped from the couch and squatted down beside Annie. She wrapped her arms around her and patted her back. "Honey, don't cry. It's not so unusual to still have a thing going for your ex, you know. Especially when he's hunky, the way Chase is."

"He's getting married," Annie sobbed.

"Chase?"

"To Janet Pendleton."

"Am I supposed to know her?"

"I hope not." Annie hiccuped. "She's rich. Gorgeous. Smart."

"I hate her already." Deb put her hand under Annie's chin and urged it to rise. "Are you sure?"

"He told me so." Annie sat back, dug a hanky out of her cleavage where she'd stuffed it after the ceremony and blew her nose. "So I told him I'm marrying Milton."

"Milton? As in, Milton Hoffman?" Deb rocked back on her heels. "My God, you wouldn't!"

"Why not? He's single, he's dependable and he's nice."

"So is a teddy bear," Deb said in horror. "Better you should take one of those to bed than Milton Hoffman."

"Oh, Deb, that's not fair." Annie got to her feet. "There's more to a relationship than sex."

"Name it."

"Companionship, for one thing. Similar interests. Shared dreams."

"And you can have enough of those things with Milton to make you forget all the rest?"

"Yes!" Annie's shoulders slumped. "No," she admitted. "Isn't that awful? I like Milton, but I don't love him."

Deb heaved a sigh as she stood up. "Thank you, God. For a minute there, I thought you'd gone around the bend."

"Not only am I sex-obsessed—"

"You're not. Sex is a big part of life."

"—but I've used poor Milton badly. Now I've got to call him up and tell him I didn't mean it when I introduced him to Chase as my fiancé."

"Wow," Deb said softly. "You certainly have had a busy day."

"A messy day, is what you mean."

"Don't kill me for saying this, but maybe you should rethink things. I mean, I know he's getting married and all, but maybe you do still have a thing for your ex."

"I wouldn't care if he were living in a monastery!" Annie's eyes flashed. "I do not have a 'thing' for Chase. I admit, I'm upset, but it's because my baby's gotten herself married."

"You know what they say, Annie. We only raise children to let go of them once they grow up."

Annie tucked the hanky back into her cleavage, picked up the champagne bottle and headed for the kitchen.

"It's not letting go of her that upsets me, Deb. It's that she's so young. Too young, I'm afraid, to make such a commitment."

"Well," Deb said, folding her arms and leaning against the door frame, "you were young when you got hitched, too."

Annie sighed. "Exactly. And look where it led me. I thought I knew what I was doing but it turned out I didn't.

It was hormones, not intelligence, that—'' The phone rang. She reached out and picked it up. "Hello?"

"Annie?"

"Chase." Annie's mouth narrowed. "What do you want? I thought we said all we needed to say to each other this afternoon."

Across town, in his hotel room, Chase looked at the boy standing at the window. The boy's shoulders were slumped and his head was bowed in classic despair.

Chase cleared his throat.

"Annie... Nick is here."

Annie's brows knotted together. "Nick? There? Where do you mean, there?"

"I mean he's here, in my room at the Hilton."

"No. That's impossible. Nick is on a plane to Hawaii, with Dawn..." The blood drained from Annie's face. "Oh God," she whispered. "Has there been an accident? Is Dawn—"

"No," Chase said quickly. "Dawn's fine. Nothing's happened to her, or to Nick."

"Then why—"

"She left him."

Annie sank down into a chair at the kitchen table. "She left him?" she repeated stupidly. Deb stared at her in disbelief. "Dawn left Nick?"

"Yeah." Chase rubbed the back of his neck, where the muscles felt as if somebody were tightening them on a rack. "They, uh, they got to the airport and checked in their luggage. Then they went to the VIP lounge. I upgraded their tickets, Annie, and bought them a membership in the lounge. I knew you wouldn't approve, but—"

"Dammit, Chase, tell me what happened!"

Chase sighed. "Nick said he'd get them some coffee. Dawn said that was fine. But when he came back with the coffee, she was gone."

"She didn't leave him," Annie said, her hand at her heart, "she's been kidnapped!"

"Kidnapped?" Deb snapped. "Dawn?"

"Did you call the police? Did you—"

"She left a note," Chase said wearily. Annie heard the rustle of paper. "She says it's not that she doesn't care for him."

"Care for him?" Annie's voice rose. "People *care* for—for flowers. Or parakeets. She said she loved Nick. That she was crazy about him."

"...not that she doesn't care for him," Chase continued, "but that loving him isn't enough."

"Isn't—?"

"Isn't enough. She says she has no choice but to end this marriage before it begins."

Annie put her hand over her eyes. "Oh God," she whispered. "That sounds so ominous."

Chase nodded, as if Annie could see him.

"Nick's beside himself, and so am I." His voice roughened with emotion. "He's looked for her everywhere, but he can't find her. Dear God, If anything's happened to our little girl..."

Annie's head lifted. As soft as a whisper, the front door opened, then closed. Footsteps came slowly down the hall.

"Mom?"

Dawn stood in the doorway, dressed in the going-away suit they'd bought together, the corsage of baby orchids Annie had pinned on the jacket's lapel sadly drooping. Dawn's eyes were red and swollen.

"Baby?" Annie whispered.

Dawn gave Annie a smile that trembled, and then a sob burst from her throat.

"Oh, Mommy," she wailed, and Annie dropped the phone and opened her arms. Her daughter flew across the room and buried her face in her mother's lap.

Deb picked the phone up from the floor.

"Chase?"

"Dammit to hell," Chase roared, "who is this? What's going on there?"

"I'm a friend of Annie's," Deb said. "You and Nick can stop worrying. Dawn's here. She just came in."

Chase flashed an okay sign to Nick, who hurried to his side.

"Is my daughter okay?"

"Yes. She seems to—"

Chase slammed down the phone, and he and Nick ran out the door.

CHAPTER THREE

THE MOON HAD RISEN, climbed into a bank of clouds, and disappeared.

Sighing, Chase switched on the lamp beside his chair and wished he could pull a stunt like that. Maybe then people would stop looking at him as if he might just come up with a solution to an impossible situation.

But the simple truth was that impossible situations required improbable solutions, and he didn't have any. His mind was a blank. At this point, he wasn't even sure what day it was. The only thing he knew for certain was that a few hours ago, he'd been the father of—the bride. Now he was the father of—what did you call a young woman who'd gotten to the airport and then told her brand-new husband that they'd made an awful mistake and she wanted out?

Smart. That was what Chase would have called her, twenty-four hours ago, when he'd have given just about anything if Dawn had decided to put her wedding off until she was older and, hopefully, wiser.

Chase closed his eyes wearily. But his daughter *hadn't* decided to put off her wedding. She'd gone through with it, which put a different spin on things. More than canceling arrangements with the church and the caterer were involved here. Dawn and Nick were bound together, in the eyes of God and in accordance with the laws of the state of Connecticut.

Severing that bond was a lot more complicated than it would have been a few hours ago. And it sure didn't help that Dawn kept weeping and saying she loved Nick with all her heart, it was just that she couldn't, wouldn't, mustn't stay married to him.

Chase put his hand to the back of his neck and tried to rub the tension out of his muscles. He had no idea what she was talking about, and neither did Nick, the poor, bewildered bastard. Not even Annie understood; Chase was certain of that, and never mind the way she'd kept saying, "I understand, sweetheart," while she'd rocked Dawn in her arms.

"*What* do you understand?" Chase had asked her in exasperation, when she'd come hurrying out of the bedroom after she'd finally convinced Dawn to lie down and try to get some sleep. Annie had shot him one of those men-are-so-stupid looks women did so well and said she didn't understand *anything*, but she wasn't about to upset Dawn by telling her that.

"Dammit, Annie," Chase had roared, and that had done it. Nick had come running, Dawn had started crying, Annie had called him a name he hadn't even figured she knew...hell, he thought wearily, it was a good thing Annie didn't have a dog, or it would have gotten in on the act and taken a chunk out of his ankle.

"Now see what you've done," Annie had snarled, and the door to Dawn's room had slammed in his bewildered face.

Chase groaned. He was tired. So tired. There'd been no sound from behind the closed door for hours now. Annie and his daughter were probably asleep. Even Nick had finally fallen into exhausted slumber on the sofa in the living room.

Maybe, if he just put his head back for a five-minute snooze...

"Dammit!"

Chase's head bobbed like a yo-yo on a string. That was just what he'd needed, all right. Oh, yeah. Nothing like a little whiplash for neck muscles that already felt knotted.

"Stupid chair," he muttered, and sprang to his feet.

For a minute there, he'd forgotten he wasn't in the den

he and Annie had shared for so many years. Annie had dumped all the old furniture when she'd bought this house. She'd filled these rooms with little bits and pieces of junk. Antiques, she called them, but junk is what the stuff was. Delicate junk, at that. Sofas and tables with silly legs, chairs with no headrests...

"You kick that chair, Chase Cooper, and I swear, I'll kick you!"

Chase swung around. His ex-wife stood in the entrance to the room. She'd exchanged her mother-of-the-bride dress for a pair of jeans and a sweatshirt and from the way her hair was standing on end and her hands were propped on her hips, he had the feeling her mood wasn't much better than his.

Too bad. Too damned bad, considering that she was the one had gotten them into this mess in the first place. If only she hadn't been so damned permissive. If only she'd put her foot down right at the start, told Dawn she was too young to get married—

"It deserves kicking," he grumbled, but he stepped aside and let her swish past him, snatch up the chair cushions and plump them, as if that might remove any sign he'd sat there. "How's Dawn?"

"She's asleep." Annie tucked the cushions back in place. "How's Nick? I assume he's still here?"

"Yes, he's here. He's asleep, in the living room."

"And he's okay?"

"As okay as he can be, all things considered. Has our daughter told you yet just what, exactly, is going on?"

Annie looked at him. Then she ran her fingers through her hair, smoothing the curls back from her face.

"How about some tea?" Without waiting for his answer, she set off for the kitchen. "Unless you'd prefer coffee," she asked, switching on the overhead fluorescent light.

"Tea's fine," Chase said, blinking in the sudden glare. He sank onto one of the stools that stood before the kitchen counter, watching as Annie filled a kettle with water and put it on the stove. "Has she?"

"Has she what?" Annie yanked open the pantry door. She took out a box of tea bags and put it on the counter. "Would you like a cookie? Of course, I don't have those hideous things you always preferred, with all that goo in the middle."

"Just tea," he replied, refusing to rise to the bait. "What did Dawn say?"

Annie shut the pantry door and opened the refrigerator. "How about a sandwich? Swiss? Or there's some ham, if you prefer."

"Annie..."

"You'd have to take it on whole grain bread, though, the kind you always said—"

"—that I wouldn't touch until somebody strapped a feed bag over my face and a saddle on my back. No, thank you very much, I don't want a sandwich. I don't want anything, except to know what our daughter told you and what it is you don't want to tell me." Chase's eyes narrowed. "Has Nick mistreated her?"

"No, of course not." Annie shut the refrigerator door. The kettle had begun to hiss, and she grabbed for it before it could whistle. "Hand me a couple of mugs, would you? They're in that cupboard, right beside you."

"He doesn't seem the type who would." Chase grabbed two white china mugs and slid them down the counter to Annie. "But if he's so much as hurt a hair on our daughter's head, so help me—"

"Will you please calm down? I'm telling you, it isn't that. Nick's a sweetheart."

"Well, what is it, then?"

Annie looked at him, then away. "It's, ah, it's complicated."

"Complicated?" Chase's eyes narrowed again. "It's not—the boy isn't..."

"Isn't what? Do you still take two sugars, or have you finally learned to lay off the stuff?"

"Two sugars, and stop nagging."

Annie dumped two spoonfuls of sugar into her ex's tea, and stirred briskly.

"You're right. You can wallow in sugar, for all I care. Your health isn't my problem anymore, it's hers."

"Hers?"

"Janet Pendleton."

"Janet Pen…" He flushed. "Oh. Her."

Annie slapped the mug of tea in front of him, hard enough so some of the hot amber liquid sloshed over the rim and onto his fingers.

"That's right. Let your fiancée worry about your weight."

"Nobody's got to worry about my weight," Chase said, surreptitiously sucking in his gut.

He was right, Annie thought sourly, as she slid onto the stool next to his. Nobody did. He was still as solid-looking and handsome as he'd been the day they'd married—or the day they'd divorced. Another benefit of being male. Men didn't have to see the awful changes that came along, as you stood at top of the yawning chasm that was middle age. The numbers that began to creep upward on your bathroom scale. The flesh that began to creep downward. The wrinkles that Janet Pendleton didn't have. The sags Chase's cute little secretary hadn't had, either.

"…make him normal. That's not what happened with Dawn and Nick, is it?"

Annie frowned. "What are you talking about?"

"Reality, that's what. I was telling you that I just heard about this guy, married a girl even though he knew he was a switch hitter, hoping that having a wife would make him normal—"

Annie choked over her tea. "Good grief," she said, when she could speak, "you are such a pathetic male stereotype, Chase Cooper! No, Nicholas is not, as you so delicately put it, a 'switch hitter.'"

"You're sure?"

"Yes."

"Yeah, well, it might not hurt to ask."

"Nick and Dawn have been living together, the past three months. And Dawn hasn't so much as hinted at any problem in bed. Quite the contrary." Annie blushed. "I dropped in a couple of times—not in the morning, or late at night, you understand—and I could pretty much tell, from the time it took them to get to the door and the way they looked, that things were perfectly fine in that department." She looked down at her tea. "I don't drop by without calling first, anymore."

"What do you mean, they've been living together?"

"Just what I said. Didn't Dawn tell you? They took an apartment, in Cannondale."

"Dammit, Annie, how could you permit our daughter to do that?"

"To do what? Move in with the man she was going to marry?"

"Didn't you tell her no?"

"She's eighteen, Chase. Legally of age. Old enough to make her own choices."

"So?"

"What do you mean, 'so'?"

"You could have told her it was wrong."

"Love is never wrong."

"Love," Chase said, and shook his head. "Sex, is more like it."

"I asked her to take her time and think it through, to be sure she was doing the right thing. She said she'd done that, and that she was."

"Sex," Chase said again.

Annie sighed. "Sex, love...they go together."

"Yeah, well, they could have had the one and still waited

for the other, until after the wedding.'' Chase glowered into his tea. ''But I suppose that's too old-fashioned.''

''It was, for us.''

Chase looked up sharply. Color swept into his face. ''What we did, or didn't do, has nothing to do with this situation.''

''That's where you're wrong.'' Annie stood. She picked up her mug of tea, cupped it with both hands and walked to the deep bow window that overlooked the garden. ''I'm afraid we have everything to do with this situation.''

''What are you talking about?''

''Do me a favor, will you? Shut off the light. My head's pounding like a drum.''

''You want some aspirin?''

Annie shook her head. ''I already took some.'' She sat down on the sill, her knees drawn up to her chin, her eyes on the darkness beyond the glass. ''You want to know what Dawn said? Okay, I'll tell you, but you're not going to like it.''

''I don't like much of anything that's already happened today,'' Chase said, getting to his feet and walking toward her. ''Why should this be any different?''

''The first thing she said was that she loves Nick.''

''Uh-huh.'' Chase folded his arms and leaned back against the window frame. ''Why do I get the feeling we're about to play, 'good news, bad news'?''

''She said she knows that he loves her.''

''That's the good news, right?''

Annie nodded. ''The bad news is that she ran away from him for the same reason.''

Chase's brows knotted. ''Let me be sure I'm following this. Our daughter fell in love, got engaged, moved in with the guy, married him, went off with him on her honeymoon…and then decided to bolt because it dawned on her that she loves him and he loves her?''

Annie sighed. "Well, it's a bit more complicated than that."

"I'm relieved to hear it. For a second there, I thought I was going completely nuts. What's the rest?"

"She's afraid."

"She's afraid," Chase said, trying to stay calm. He had the feeling they were moving into the sort of emotional deep water that women swam through effortlessly and men found way over their heads. "Of what?"

"Of them falling out of love."

"Annie." Chase sat down on the sill, his knee brushing hers. "You just said, girl loves boy. Boy loves girl. They're just starting out. There's no reason for her to think—"

"She's afraid of what's going to happen."

Chase waited, but Annie said nothing. He could almost see the water rising.

"What's going to happen?" he said carefully.

Annie shrugged. "Their love will shrivel up and die."

"That's ridiculous."

"I said the same thing."

"And?"

"And, she said…" Annie swallowed hard. "She said she'd watched us today, at the wedding."

"Us?" Chase nodded, as if he had a clue as to what they were talking about. The only thing he was sure of was that the water was definitely getting deeper. And rougher. "As in you, and me?"

"Us," Annie repeated, "as in you, and me. She said it hurt her to see how we hated being forced into each other's arms, on the dance floor."

"Well, of course we did. Nobody warned us that was going to happen. Did you explain that to her?"

"I did."

Chase thought back to the moment when Annie had gone into his arms. He thought beyond that, to when he'd suddenly realized how good it had felt to have her there, and he cleared his throat.

"We managed, didn't we?"

"Sure. I pointed that out to her."

"And?"

"And, she said it was sad, that—that we'd had to pretend we enjoyed dancing together again." Annie's cheeks grew warm. She could clearly recall the instant when being held in Chase's arms had gone from being an unwanted chore to being—to being... She took a deep breath. "I told her it was nothing for her to worry about."

"And?"

"And, that was it."

"What was it? I don't know what the hell you're talking about."

Annie put her mug on the sill beside her. Then she linked her hands together in her lap.

"That was what triggered it."

"Triggered what? I still don't know what—"

"Dawn said she was standing at the airport ticket counter, just standing there, you know, while Nick checked their luggage through and confirmed their seats, and all of a sudden it struck her that what was really so sad about you and me was that once upon a time, we must have loved each other a great deal."

"She'd have liked it better if we hadn't?"

Annie swallowed. Her throat felt uncomfortably tight. "She said—she said that she realized, for the first time, that you and I must have felt just the way she and Nick feel. You know, as if we were the only two people on the whole planet who'd ever loved each other so much."

"Lovers always feel that way," Chase said gruffly.

"She said that if her mother and father could go from feeling like that to—to feeling the way we do about each other now, then she didn't want any part of the process that got them—that got us—to this point."

Chase stared at his ex-wife. Her eyes were glassy with unshed tears and her mouth was trembling. Was she remembering, as he was, how it had once been between them? The joy? The passion? After a long minute, he cleared his throat again.

"What'd you say?"

"What could I say?"

"That our mistakes don't have to be hers, for starters."

Annie waved her hand in a sad little gesture of dismissal.

"Did you tell her that she was probably tired and jittery, and overdramatizing things?"

"Yes."

"Good."

"I thought so, too." Annie sighed. "But Dawn said she was just being pragmatic. She said she'd rather end things between her and Nick now, while they still cared for each other, than wait until—until they hated each other."

"God, Annie. We don't hate each other. You told her that, didn't you?"

Annie nodded.

"And?"

"And she said I was kidding myself, that love and hate were two sides of the same coin, that there was no middle ground, once people who'd been in love fell out of love."

Chase blew out his breath. "My daughter, the philosopher."

Annie looked up, her eyes filling again. "What are we going to do?" she whispered.

"I don't know."

"Dawn's heart is breaking. There's got to be something! We can't just let her walk away from Nick. She loves him, Chase. And he loves her."

"I know. I know." Chase shoved his hand through his hair. "Let me think for a minute."

"Our daughter's terrified of marriage, and it's our fault!"

Chase shot to his feet. "That's crap."

"It's the truth."

"It isn't. It's bad enough we couldn't make *our* marriage work but I'll be damned if I'm going to feel guilty for the failure of Dawn's marriage. You hear me, Annie?"

"The entire house will hear you," Annie hissed. "Keep your voice down, before you wake the kids."

"They're not 'kids.' Didn't you just tell me that? Our daughter was old enough to decide she was ready to get married even though, according to you, you tried to talk her out of it."

"According to me?" Annie leaped up, her hands on her hips. "I *did* try to talk her out of it! But you'd already caved in and given her the 'follow your heart' baloney. You told her to do what she wanted!"

"That's not true." Chase strode toward Annie, his eyes blazing. "I begged her to think and think again. I said she was too damned young to take such a serious step—and guess what? I was right."

Annie's shoulders slumped. "Okay, okay. So we both tried to convince her to wait. So maybe she should have listened to us. But she didn't."

"No. She didn't. She did her own thing. And then she sees us dancing and all of a sudden, she turns into Sigmund Freud and figures out that she's made a terrible mistake."

"Chase, please! Keep your voice—"

"She has an epiphany, brought on by seeing us dancing. Why not by a gum wrapper on the floor at the airport, or the electrical energy from an overhead wire?"

"This is not something to joke about, dammit!"

"Maybe it was some guy at a piano, playing a three-handed version of 'The Man That Got Away.'" Chase lifted his arms to the sky, then dropped them to his sides. "What was wrong with her hearing the day her old man tried to give her some advice?"

"It was advice I'd tried to give her, too," Annie said coldly. "I keep telling you that."

"What was the use of my talking," Chase said, ignoring her, "if she wasn't listening? She did what she wanted and now she thinks she can lay it off on our divorce?" Chase's mouth thinned. "I don't think so."

"She's not trying to lay anything off. She's upset."

"*She's* upset? What about everybody else? Does she think we're busy yakking it up and having an all-around good time?" Chase's face darkened. "Do you know what it was like, having Nick turn up at the door to tell me Dawn had run off and he couldn't find her? Do you have any idea at all of what that kid and I went through?"

"Yelling won't help, Chase."

"Neither will playing the patsy." Chase rammed his fist against the wall. "If only you'd put your foot down sooner."

"Dammit," Annie said fiercely, "I did!"

"I don't know what you did. I wasn't here for the past five years, remember?"

"And whose fault was that?"

Chase and Annie glared at each other, and then Annie blew out her breath.

"This is pointless. There's no sense bringing up the past. Dawn needs our help. We can't let her walk away from Nick and her marriage for the wrong reasons."

"I agree. Damn, if only she'd made do with simply moving in with Nick. Why'd she have to rush into marriage?"

"A little while ago, you were furious because she *had* moved in with him!"

"Didn't you teach her any self-control? If she hadn't let her hormones get the best of her—"

"How dare you? How *dare* you talk about self-control? If you'd had any self-control at all, we might still be married!"

"I'm tired of defending myself against that old charge, Annie. Besides, if you hadn't treated me as if I had leprosy—"

"That's right. Blame it on me."

"I don't see anybody else in this room to blame it on."

"I hate you, Chase Cooper! I hate you, do you hear? And I regret every time I ever let you touch me!"

"Liar!"

"Liar, am I?"

Chase reached out, caught Annie's shoulders and yanked her to him. "You were like warm butter, in my arms, right from the beginning."

"Only because I was so innocent!" Annie set her teeth and tried to twist free. "I was a baby when we met. Or have you forgotten that?"

"You were the hottest baby I'd ever seen. The first time I kissed you, you were like fireworks going up. All I could think of was having you to myself, for the rest of my life."

"Except when you found out there was more to life than bed."

"Oh, yeah," he said, his lips pulling back from his teeth, "yeah, you sure taught me that lesson. 'Not now, Chase. I'm not in the mood, Chase.'"

"And whose fault was that, do you think?"

"You didn't see me rolling over and turning my back to you, did you, babe?"

"Don't 'babe' me," Annie said furiously. "And if I rolled away from you, it was for a darn good reason. I didn't feel anything anymore. Did you expect me to pretend?"

"Is that what you do when you're with Hoffman? Do you pretend he turns you on?"

Annie's hand shot through the air, but Chase caught her wrist before she could connect with his jaw.

"You know damn well you didn't have to pretend when I made love to you," he growled, "even at the end. You were just too proud to admit it."

"Poor Chase. Can't your ego take the truth?"

"I'll show you 'truth'!"

"No," Annie said, but it was too late, Chase had already pulled her into his arms, and brought his mouth to hers.

His kiss was filled with anger and Annie struggled against it, pounding her fists against his shoulders, trying desperately to tear her mouth from his.

And then, deep within her, something seemed to let go.

Maybe it was the stillness of the night, curling just outside the window. Maybe it was the unyielding tension of the endless day. Suddenly anger gave way to a far more dangerous emotion. Hunger. The hunger that had been between them in the past and that she'd believed dead.

Chase felt it, too.

"Annie," he whispered, against her mouth. His hands swept into her hair, lifting her face to his. With a sigh of surrender, her arms went around his neck, her lips parted beneath his, and she gave herself up to him and to the kiss.

It was like a dance once learned and never forgotten. Their bodies shifted, moving against each other with an ease that came of passion long-ago shared. Their heads tilted, their lips met, their tongues sought and tasted. Annie clasped her hands behind Chase's neck; he slid his slowly down her body, cupped her bottom and lifted her into him. She whimpered when she felt the hardness of him against her; he groaned when he felt her tilt her hips to his.

For long moments, they were lost to everything but each other. Then, breathing hard, they stepped apart.

Annie's skin felt hot when Chase cupped her face in his hands and brushed a light kiss on her lips. He wanted to lift her into his arms and carry her into the darkness.

"Annie?" he whispered, and she smiled and clasped his wrists with her hands.

"Yes." She sighed…

Suddenly the kitchen blazed with light.

"Mom? Dad? What on earth are you doing?"

Annie and Chase spun around. Dawn and Nick stood in the doorway, openmouthed with shock.

CHAPTER FOUR

IT WAS, Annie thought, the question of the decade.

What *were* they doing, she and her former husband?

Her cheeks, already scarlet, grew even hotter.

Making out as if they were a pair of oversexed kids, that was what. She and Chase had been wrapped around each other as if it were years and years ago, when he'd just brought her home from a date. In those days, not even an hour spent parked on that little knoll half an hour's drive north of the city, steaming up the windows of Chase's old Chevy, had been enough to keep them from wanting just one more kiss, one more caress.

"Mother?"

Dawn was still staring at them both. She looked as if finding her parents kissing was only slightly less shocking than it would be if she'd found the kitchen populated with little green men saying, "Take me to your leader."

And, Annie thought grimly, it was all Chase's fault.

He'd taken advantage of her distress, capitalized on her already-confused emotions. And for what possible reason?

To shut her up.

It was the same old ploy he'd used during the years that their marriage had been falling apart. She'd try to talk about what was wrong and Chase, who was perfectly happy with their marriage as it was, would say there was nothing to discuss. And if she persisted, he'd shut her up by taking her in his arms and starting to make love.

It had worked, but only for a very little while, when she'd still been foolish enough to think those kisses meant he loved her. Eventually she'd figured out that they meant nothing of the sort. Chase was just silencing her, in the most direct way possible, using what had always worked best between them.

Sex. Raw, basic, you-Jane, me-Tarzan sex.

But sex, no matter how electric, just wasn't enough when the rest of the relationship had gone wrong. It had taken her a while to realize that, but realize it she had.

He was playing the same ugly game tonight. And she'd made it easy. Responding to him, when she knew better. Kissing him back, when she didn't feel anything for him. Whatever had seemed to happen, in his arms just now, was a lie. She *didn't* feel anything for Chase, except anger.

"Mother? Are you all right?"

Annie took a deep, deep breath.

"Fine," she said, and cleared her throat. "I'm perfectly fine, Dawn."

A puzzled smile broke across Dawn's mouth. She looked from Annie to Chase.

"What were you guys doing?"

Annie waited for Chase to respond, but he remained silent. That's right, she thought furiously. Let me be the one to figure out something to say. He knew, the rat, that she wouldn't tell Dawn the truth, wouldn't say, "Well, Dawn, your no-account old man was on the losing end of an argument so he did what he always used to do whenever that happened..."

"Well," Annie said, "well, your father and I were, ah, we were talking about you. And Nick. And—and—"

"And your mother began to cry, so I put my arms around her to comfort her."

Annie swung toward Chase. He was standing straight and tall, the portrait of honor, decency and paternalism in his chinos, open-collared shirt and long-sleeved, forest-green cashmere sweater. His hair was a little ruffled and he had end-of-day stubble on his jaw, but on him—she hated to admit—it looked good.

She, on the other hand, was a mess. Old jeans. Old

sweatshirt. Hair that had been allowed to dry without benefit of a dryer or a brush, and a face that was painfully free of even the most basic makeup.

"Your poor mother is very upset," Chase said, putting his arm around Annie's shoulders and giving her his best "chin-up" smile. "She needed a shoulder to cry on. Isn't that right, Annie?"

"Right," Annie said, through a smile that was all clenched teeth. What else could she do? Blurt out that Chase was lying? That the two of them had been standing in the dark, locked in a kiss that had left her knees buckling, because he was a manipulative bastard and she was too long without a man? That was the truth, wasn't it? The real truth. She'd never have responded to him if she hadn't been living like a nun.

"Really?" Dawn looked at them both again, and then the faint smile that had been lifting her lips trembled and fell. "I understand. It was foolish of me to think... I mean, when I saw you guys kissing, I thought... I almost thought... Oh, never mind."

"Kissing?" Annie said, with a slightly wild laugh. She stepped carefully out of Chase's encircling arm, went to the stove and began making what had to be the hundredth pot of tea she'd made this evening. "Kissing, your father and me?"

"Uh-huh." Dawn slouched to the table, pulled out a chair and dropped into it. She propped her elbows on the table and rested her chin in her cupped hands. "Kissing. Just goes to show how utterly dumb I can be."

"No," Nick said quickly. Everyone looked at him. It was the first word to come out of his mouth since he and Dawn had switched on the light. His fuzz-free cheeks pinkened under the scrutiny of his bride and her parents. "You aren't."

"I am. Getting married when anybody with half a brain

could see it was a mistake, because marriage doesn't last. We all know that.''

"We don't know any such thing," Nick said, hurrying to her. He squatted beside her chair and reached for her hands, taking them gently in his.

"Just look around you, Nicky. Your guardian, your uncle Damian? Divorced. My parents? Divorced. Even Reverend Craighill—"

"The guy who performed the ceremony?" Chase said.

Dawn nodded.

"How do you know that?"

"I asked him. The poor man's been divorced twice. Twice, can you imagine?"

Chase shot a look at Annie. "No," he said tightly, "I certainly can't."

"Don't look at me that way," Annie snapped. The tea-kettle let out a piercing whistle and she snatched it from the stove. "What has the man's marital history to do with anything?"

"A minister who can't keep his wedding ring on ought to consider going into some other kind of work," Chase growled.

"No," Dawn said, "he's in the right kind of work, Daddy. He's a reminder of reality." She sighed again. "I just wish I'd been smart enough to realize all this before today instead of being so darned dumb."

"Sweetheart, stop saying that." Nick clasped her shoulders. "You were smart to fall in love with me, smarter still to marry me." He shot an accusatory look at Chase and Annie. "As for thinking you saw your folks kissing when we turned on the light—you were right."

Dawn's head came up. "I was?"

"Absolutely. I saw them, too."

"No," Annie said.

"We weren't," Chase added.

"Not at all," Annie argued, waving her hand in her ex's

direction. "Dawn, your father already explained what happened. I was upset. He was trying to comfort me."

"You see, Nicky?" Dawn's eyes filled with tears. "They weren't kissing. Oh, how I wish they had been."

Annie frowned. "You do?"

"Of course." Dawn snuffled and wiped the back of her hand across her nose. Annie and Chase both reached for the paper towels, but Nick pulled a handkerchief from his pocket and handed it to his wife, who blew into it. "See, when I saw you in Daddy's arms, well, when I thought I saw you in his arms, it was such a big thing that I felt happy for the first time since Nick and I got to the airport. I figured, just for a second, I admit, but still, I figured..."

"You figured what?" Annie said, softly, even though she already knew, even though it broke her heart to think that her daughter still harbored such useless dreams, such futile hopes. She went to Dawn's side, looped her arm around her shoulders and kissed the top of her head. "What, darling?"

Dawn took a shuddering breath. "I figured that a miracle had occurred today," she whispered, "that you and Daddy had finally realized what a mistake you'd made in splitting up and that you still loved each other."

There was a pained silence. Then a soft sob burst from Annie's throat.

"Oh, Dawn. Darling, if it were only that simple!"

"You can't judge the future of your marriage by the failure of ours," Chase said gruffly. "Sweetie, if you and Nick love each other—"

"What does that prove? You and Mom loved each other, once."

"Well, sure. Of course we did, but—"

"And then you fell out of love, like everybody else."

"Not everybody, sweetie. That's an awfully broad state—"

"It must have been awful, knowing you'd loved each other and then having things fall apart."

Chase looked at Annie. Help me with this, his eyes flashed, but she knew she had no more answers now than she'd had five years ago.

"Well," he said carefully, "yes, yes, it wasn't pleasant. But that doesn't mean—"

"You guys did your best to keep me out of it, but I wasn't a baby. I used to hear Mom crying. And I saw how red your eyes were sometimes, Daddy."

Nick got to his feet and stepped back as Chase reached for his daughter's hand.

"We never meant to hurt you, Dawn. We'd have done anything to keep from hurting you."

"You don't understand, Daddy. I'm not crying over the past, I'm crying over the future. Over what's almost definitely, positively, absolutely going to happen to Nicky and me. I don't know why it took me so long to realize. We'll—we'll break each other's hearts, is what we'll do, and I'd rather walk away now than let that happen."

Annie smoothed her daughter's hair from her forehead. "Dawn, honey, I can point to lots of marriages that have succeeded."

"More fail than succeed."

"I don't know where you got that idea."

"It's not an idea, it's a fact. That Family Life course I'm taking at Easton, remember? My instructor showed us all these statistics, Mom. Marriage is a crapshoot."

Annie gritted her teeth, silently calling herself a fool for having convinced Dawn that she ought to at least attend classes at the local community college, now that she wasn't going to go away to school as they'd planned.

"There's an element of risk in anything that's really worthwhile," Chase said.

Annie gave him a grateful look. "Exactly."

"So, when people get married, they should be aware that

they're taking a gamble?'' Dawn said, looking from her mother to her father.

Annie opened her mouth, then shut it. ''Well, no. Not exactly,'' she said, and cleared her throat. ''People shouldn't think that.'' She looked at Chase again. *Say something*, was written all over her face.

''Of course not,'' Chase said quickly. ''A man and a woman should put all their faith in their ability to make their marriage succeed.''

''And if that turns out not to be enough?''

''Then they should try harder.''

Dawn nodded. ''And then they should give up.''

''No! What I mean is…'' It was Chase's turn to look at Annie for support. ''Annie? Can you, ah, explain this?''

''What your father is saying,'' Annie said, stepping gingerly onto the quicksand, ''is that sometimes a man and a woman try and try, and they still can't make a relationship work.''

''Like you and Daddy.''

Annie could feel the sand shifting, ever so slowly, under her feet.

''Well, yes,'' she said slowly, ''like us. But that doesn't mean all marriages are failures.''

Dawn sighed. ''I guess. But other people's marriages don't mean much to me right now. All I could think of today was how wonderful it would be if you guys got back together again.'' She buried her nose in Nick's handkerchief and gave a long, honking blow. ''And then, when I saw you guys kissing…when I *thought* I saw you kissing…''

''We were,'' Chase said. Annie's head sprang up as if somebody had jabbed her with a pin. He saw the look of disbelief she flashed him but hell, there was no reason to lie about something as simple as a kiss. He laced his fingers through Dawn's and smiled gently at her. ''You didn't imagine that, sweetheart. You and Nick were right. I was kissing your mother. And she was kissing me back.''

Dawn's tearstained face lit.

"You mean…'' She looked at them, her lips trembling. "I was right? You guys are thinking of getting together again?''

"No,'' Annie said quickly. "Dawn, a kiss doesn't mean—''

"It doesn't mean they've reached any decisions,'' Nick said. "Right, Mrs. Cooper?''

Oh, Nick, Annie thought unhappily. She rose to her feet and put her hand on his arm. "Look, I know what you both would like to hear me say, but—''

"Just say there's a chance,'' Nick said, his eyes pleading with hers for time, for hope, for understanding. "Even a little one.''

Annie could feel the delicate pull of the quicksand at her toes. "Chase,'' she said urgently, "please, say something!''

Chase swallowed hard. It was years since Annie had looked at him this way, as if he were her knight in shining armor. Dawn, too. He couldn't remember his daughter turning to him since she'd stopped skinning her knees playing softball.

Both his women needed him to come to their rescue.

It was a terrific feeling. Unfortunately he hadn't the faintest idea how to do it.

Think, he told himself, dammit, man, think! There had to be something…

Dawn's eyes filled again. "Never mind. You don't have to spell it out for me. I'm old enough to understand that a kiss isn't a commitment.''

Annie let out a breath that felt as if she'd been holding forever.

"That's right,'' she said.

"It was stupid of me to think that you guys were going to give it another try.''

Annie smiled at Chase over their daughter's head.

"I'm glad you understand that, sweetie."

"There are no second chances, not in this life." Dawn wiped her nose and looked at the trio gathered around her. "That's from Kierkegaard. Or maybe Sartre. One of those guys, I forget which."

"Your philosophy course," Annie said grimly, mentally ripping in half the tuition check she'd just mailed to Easton Community College.

"Of course there are," Chase said sharply.

"No," Dawn said, sighing, "there aren't. Just look at you two, if you want a perfect example."

"All right," Chase said, "I've had enough."

"Chase," Annie said, "don't say anything you'll regret."

"Mr. Cooper, sir, as Dawn's husband—"

"Dawn Elizabeth Cooper... Dawn Elizabeth *Babbitt*, you're behaving like a spoiled child." Chase nudged Nick aside, put his hands on his hips and glared down at his daughter. "This is all nonsense. Marriage statistics, divorce statistics, and now quotes from a bunch of dead old men who wouldn't have been able to find their—"

"Chase," Annie said sharply.

"—their hats on their heads, when they were still alive and kicking." Chase squatted down in front of Dawn. "You and Nick love each other. That's the reason you got married. Right?"

"Right," Dawn said, in a small voice. "But, Daddy—"

"No, you listen to me, for a change. I gave you your turn, now you give me mine." Chase took a deep breath. "You loved each other. You got married. You took some very important vows, among them the promise to stay together through the bad times as well as the good. Think about that promise, Dawn." He took her hands in his and looked into her teary eyes. "It means, you've always got to give it a second chance. It means, love doesn't die, it only gets lost sometimes, and if you loved each other once, there's always damn good reason to think you can find it again.''

Dawn nodded, the tears streaming down her face.

''Exactly,'' she said. ''That's why, when I saw you and Mom together I thought, isn't it wonderful? They've decided to give themselves another chance.''

''Dawn,'' Nick said, ''please, darling. You're upset.''

''I am not,'' Dawn said in a shaky whisper.

''Let's get out of here. Let's give *us* a chance.''

''What for? So we can break our hearts someplace down the road?'' A sob caught in her throat. ''You're asking me to take a terrible gamble, Nick, and to do that would take a miracle.''

''Yes!'' The word seemed to leap, unbidden, from Chase's throat. Every head in the room snapped in his direction.

''Yes?'' Annie said. ''Yes, what?''

Chase stared at his former wife's pale face. It was a terrific question. What had he said yes to? Despite all his arguments, he knew his daughter was right. A frighteningly high percentage of marriages failed. And the breakup, when you'd loved someone as deeply as he'd once loved Annie, was the worst pain imaginable.

But how could he let his daughter and her groom fail before they'd even tried? Nick had the right idea. He and Dawn had to get away from here. They had to be alone and unpressured. They had to go on their honeymoon, and Chase could think of only one way to make that happen.

His daughter wanted a miracle? Okay. He'd give her one.

''Yes, you were right, about your mother and me.''

''No,'' Annie said. ''Chase, don't!''

''We didn't want to say anything until we were certain, because it isn't certain yet, you understand, it's far from certain, in fact, it's very, very uncertain and altogether iffy—''

"Chase!" Annie cried, her voice high and panicked, but hell, he'd gone too far to stop now.

So he ignored Annie, gave Dawn his most ingratiating smile and shot a quick prayer in the direction of the ceiling, just in case anybody who kept track of white lies was listening.

"No promises," he said, "and absolutely no guarantees because, frankly, I don't think the odds are too good but yeah, your mother and I have decided to at least talk about giving things between us a second chance."

CHAPTER FIVE

CHASE WATCHED as Annie paced the length of the living room.

It was almost hypnotic. She went back and forth, back and forth, pausing before him each time just long enough to give him a look that had gone from anger to disbelief to a glare that would have brought joy to the heart of the Medusa.

Aside from a quick burst of fury after Dawn and Nick had left, she had yet to say anything to him, but that was hardly reassuring. Another explosion was just a matter of time. Her white face, thinned mouth and determined pacing told him so. And he could hardly blame her.

What in heaven's name had impelled him to do such a stupid thing? To even suggest there was a possibility of reconciliation had been crazy. It was wrong. Hell, it was unfair. Dawn, falsely convinced she'd had her miracle, had gone off with hope in her heart...

But at least she'd gone. That was what he'd wanted, after all, to give his daughter time to be alone with her husband, time to realize that the future of her marriage was not linked to the failure of his and Annie's.

Just because one generation screwed things up didn't mean the next one would, too.

Chase felt the weight lifting from his shoulders. What he'd done had been impetuous, perhaps even outrageous. But if it gave Dawn time to find her own way through the minefield of life and marriage, it was worth it. Who had he hurt, really? When the kids got back from their honeymoon—happy, he was certain, and concentrating on their future instead of his and Annie's—he'd explain that he'd misled them, just a little bit.

"And just how do you think she's going to feel, when you tell her you lied?"

Chase looked up. Annie had come to a stop in front of him. Her sweatshirt inexplicably but appropriately featured a picture of Sesame Street's Oscar the Grouch. Her face was white, her eyes shiny and she was so angry she was trembling.

Angry—and incredibly beautiful.

A lifetime ago, she used to tremble that way when she lay in his arms. When he touched her. When he stroked her breasts, and her belly. When he moved between her silken thighs...

"Do you hear me, Chase Cooper? How do you think our daughter will feel, when she finds out her miracle is a bucket of hogwash?"

Chase frowned. "It isn't as bad as that."

"You're right. It's worse."

"Look, I was just trying to help her."

"Hah!"

"Okay, okay. Maybe I made a mistake, but—"

"Maybe?" Her voice shot up the scale, her eyebrows to her hairline. "*Maybe* you made a mistake?"

"The words just came out. I didn't mean—"

"Can't you even admit you were wrong?"

"I already did. I said maybe I made a mistake."

Annie snorted. "You still don't see it, do you! A 'mistake' is when a person forgets an appointment. Or dials a wrong number."

"Or says something, in the heat of the moment, that he thinks might—"

"You lied, Chase. There's a big difference. But I'm not surprised."

Chase rose to his feet. "And what, exactly, is that supposed to mean?"

"Nothing," Annie said coldly, and turned away.

"Dammit!" He grabbed her shoulder and swung her around to face him. "If there's one thing I never could stand, it was that word. 'Nothing,' you always say, but even an idiot can tell you really mean 'something.'"

Annie smiled sweetly. "I'm happy to hear it."

Dark color swept into his face. He clutched her tighter and leaned toward her.

"You're pushing your luck, babe."

"Why?" Her chin lifted. "What are you going to do, huh? Slug me?"

Annie saw Chase's eyes narrow. What had made her say such a thing? They had quarreled, yes. Fought furiously with words. By the time they'd agreed to divorce, they'd hurled every possible bit of invective at each other.

But he'd never hit her. He'd never raised his hand to her. She'd never been afraid of him physically and she wasn't now.

It was just that she was so angry. So enraged. He was, too. And just a little while ago, when he'd been mad and she'd been mad, he'd ended up hauling her into his arms and kissing her until her toes had tingled.

For Pete's sake, woman, are you insane? Are you trying to tick him off so he'll kiss you again?

She stiffened, then twisted out of his grasp.

"This isn't getting us anywhere," she said. She walked to the sofa and sat down. "I just wish I knew what to do next."

"Why should we have to 'do' anything?" Chase said, sitting down in the chair.

"Dawn's going to have such expectations..."

Chase sighed and leaned forward, his elbows on his knees. He put his head in his hands.

"Yeah."

"How could you? How *could* you tell her that?"

"I don't know." He straightened up and passed his hand

over his face. "Exhaustion, maybe. I haven't slept in— what year is this, anyway?"

"To tell her such nonsense—"

"Yeah, yeah," he said, "okay, you made your point." He frowned and shifted his backside on the cushion of the contraption Annie called a chair, where he'd spent the last hour being tortured. "What's this damn chair stuffed with, anyway? Steel filings?"

"Horsehair, which should be just right, considering that you are, without question, the biggest horse's patootie I ever did know!"

Chase gave a bark of incredulous laughter. "Patootie? Goodness gracious, land's sakes alive, Miss Annie, what out and out vulgarity!"

"Dammit, Chase—"

"Oh my. Better watch yourself, babe. Your language is slipping."

"Don't 'babe' me. I don't like it. Just tell me what we're supposed to do now."

Chase winced as he got to his feet. He rubbed the small of his back, then massaged his neck, and walked slowly to the window.

The sun was a slash of lemon yellow as it rose in the deep woods behind the house. Dawn was almost here—and *his* Dawn was almost there, in Hawaii, beginning her honeymoon with Nick. He smiled and thought of sharing the play-on-words with Annie, but he suspected she might not see the humor in the situation.

"We wait until the kids come home," he said, turning around and looking at Annie, "and then we tell—*I* tell them—that I should never have claimed we were going to give things another try."

"The truth, you mean."

"The whole truth, and nothing but the truth. Yes."

Annie nodded. She stood up and walked toward the kitchen. Chase followed her.

"I suppose that will clear your conscience."

Chase eased onto a stool at the counter.

"Look, I know it won't be that easy, but—"

He winced as Annie slammed a cupboard door shut.

"Unfortunately," she said, "it won't do a thing for mine."

"If you're going to make another pot of coffee or tea—"

"That's exactly what I'm going to do."

"Not for me." He put a hand against his flat belly. "The last dozen cups are still gurgling around in my stomach."

"Maybe you'd rather have something else. Hot chocolate?"

Chase's brows lifted. "Well, yeah, that might be—"

"Hemlock, perhaps. A nice, big cup."

"There's no need to behave like that, Annie."

"No?"

"No." He stood up, went to the refrigerator and opened it. "Isn't there any beer?"

"There is not." Annie slid under his arm and slammed the fridge door shut. "I," she said self-righteously, "do not drink beer."

Chase looked at her. "I'll just bet the poetry pansy doesn't drink it, either."

"The…?" Annie flushed. "If you mean Milton—"

"How about some diet Coke? Or is that beneath you, too?"

Annie shot him an angry glare. Then she stalked to the pantry door and pulled it open.

"Here," she said, jamming the can of soda at him. "Have a Coke, even though it's only six in the morning. Maybe it'll clear your head enough so you can come up with a plan that'll work."

"I already did." Chase yanked the pull tab on the can and made a face as he downed a mouthful of warm soda. "I told you," he said, as he took a tray of ice cubes from the freezer, dumped some into a glass and added the Coke.

"When the kids come back from their honeymoon, I'll tell them that we stretched the truth a little for their own good."

"We?" Annie said, in an ominously soft voice.

"Okay. Me. I did it. I stretched the truth."

"You're stretching it now, Chase. Say it. You lied."

Chase took a long drink, then put the cold glass against his forehead.

"I lied. All right? Does that make you feel better?"

"Yes." Annie frowned. "No." She looked at him for a long minute. Then she turned and stared at the coffee, dripping slowly from the filter basket into the carafe. "You lied, and what did I do?"

"Look, I don't know what you're trying to accomplish here, Annie, but we just went around with this, remember? I was the black-hearted horse's whatever-you-called-me that started us on this path into the pits of hell." He sighed, then laid the hand clutching the glass of Coke over his heart. "You want me to swear I'll come clean? I will. You want my word I'll make it crystal clear you didn't do anything? I'll do that, too."

Annie folded her arms over her chest. "But I did."

"Did what? God, I have been up for more hours than there are in a day, and my brain is starting to whimper. What's wrong now? I said I'd tell Dawn it was all my idea. I can't do any more than that, babe, can I?"

Annie plunked herself onto a stool. "Don't call me that," she said, but without her usual fire. She sighed deeply. "You can't tell her I'm not part of it because the truth is that I was."

"Was what?" Chase said, trying to keep his patience. He looked at his half-filled glass of soda, and wondered if there was more caffeine in it or in a cup of coffee. "I'm tired," he muttered. "I need to lie down, Annie. I'm worse than tired. I could have sworn I heard you say—"

"I did." Annie put her elbows on the counter and

scrubbed her face with her hands. "I said, I'm as responsible for this mess as you are."

"Don't be ridiculous. I was the one who lied."

"At least you're admitting that it *was* a lie." She sighed, scrubbed her face again and then looked up at him and folded her hands neatly on the countertop. "Dawn's going to ask me why, if I knew you were lying, I didn't say anything."

"Well, you'll tell her the truth."

"Which is?"

"Which is..." Chase frowned. "I don't know what we're talking about anymore! The truth is the truth."

"The truth isn't the truth. Not exactly. I mean, I heard you tell her that we're thinking about a reconciliation. I could have said 'That isn't so, Dawn. Your father's making it up.'"

Chase felt a tightening in his chest.

"But you didn't," he said.

"I didn't." Annie looked at him, then at her hands, still folded before her. "I kept quiet."

"Why?" Her hair had fallen forward, curling around her face. He fought the urge to reach out and touch the soft, shining locks.

Annie sighed. "You'll call me crazy."

"Try me."

"Because, in my heart, I knew it was the only way to get her to stop comparing herself and Nick to us. It was a foolish thing for her to be doing. Just because you and I—because we fell out of love, doesn't mean they will, too." She looked up, her expression one of defiance. "Well?"

Something indefinable swept through him. Relief, he told himself. Hell, what else could it be?

"I won't call you crazy." He smiled. "But you've got to admit, you're up to your backside in the murky waters of what's a lie and what's a fib, the same as me."

Annie nodded. "Well then, when they get back, we both admit that we fudged the truth and hope for the best."

"I suppose."

Annie's mouth trembled. "Dawn's going to be hurt. And angry."

"She'll get over it."

"We never lied to her about anything, Chase. Even when—when we finally decided to end our marriage, we told her the truth."

Chase looked at his ex-wife.

"Well," he said carefully, "perhaps there's another way." He watched as Annie wiped her hands over her eyes. "I mean..." He forced his lips into a tight smile. "I mean, we could agree to go ahead with a reconciliation."

"What?"

"Not a real one, of course," he said quickly. "A pretend one. You know, spend some time together. Go out for dinner, talk. That kind of thing."

Annie stared at him. Her eyes were wide and very dark. "Pretend?"

"Well, sure." Chase spoke briskly, almost gruffly. "Just so we could look the kids straight in the eye and say yeah, we tried..."

"No."

"No?"

Annie shook her head. "I—I couldn't."

"Why not?"

Annie struggled to find an answer. Why not, indeed? What would it take, for her to spend the week of Dawn's honeymoon dating—pretending to date—her former husband? They could avoid pushing the buttons that stirred up old animosities and pain. They could shake hands, as if this were a business deal, and pretend, for their daughter's happiness.

But she couldn't do it. A week, seeing Chase? Seven days, smiling at him over dinner? Seeing his face, hearing his voice? Walking at his side? No. It would be too—too—

"It would be wrong," she said brusquely.

"Annie…"

"There's no reason to compound one lie with another." She rose, picked up the coffeepot and dumped the contents into the sink. "You were right. One more mouthful of caffeine and I'm going to start twitching."

"Annie…"

"What?" She swung around and faced him. "It wouldn't work," she said flatly. "Not for you, not for me—not for anybody else."

"Who else? Nobody'd need to know."

Annie drew herself up. "What about your fiancée?"

"My…?"

"Janet Pendleton. How would you explain it to her?"

Chase frowned. Another lie, coming back to bite him in the tail. "Well," he said, "well, I'd just tell her—I'd say…" His eyes focused on Annie's. "I'll tell her whatever it is you'd tell your pansy poet."

Annie flushed. "That's one thing about you, Chase Cooper. You always did have a way with words. I thought I told you, Milton is a professor at the college."

"He's a limp-wristed twit, and I'll bet anything you're taking one of his dumb courses. What is it this time? How To Speak Sixteenth-Century English In A Twenty-First Century World? Fifty Ways To Turn Simple Thoughts Into Total Obfuscation?"

"Obfuscation," Annie said, batting her lashes. "I'm impressed."

"Yeah, well, I'm not. How can you be so gullible? Flocking to dumb courses given by jerks with too many initials after their names…"

"You have a lot of initials after your name, Mr. Cooper. But, of course, you're not a jerk."

"You're damn right, I'm not. At least I've got some

calluses on my hands. I know the meaning of honest labor.''

''Sorry, Chase. You've lost the right to use that word. 'Honest' does not apply, after the whopper you told our daughter.''

''Is that how you met him?''

''Who?''

''Hoffman. Am I right? Did you take a course he taught?''

''Milton is a Shakespearean scholar with an outstanding reputation.''

''In what? Seducing married women?''

Annie's eyes flashed. ''I am not a married woman. Yes, I took a course he taught and yes, he writes poetry. Beautiful poetry, which I'm sure is beyond your comprehension. Unfortunately, since I know it'll disappoint you to hear this, Milton is not gay.''

Chase folded his arms over his chest. ''I suppose you speak from personal experience,'' he said, and felt his stomach clench.

Annie barely hesitated. Why worry about telling a lie to the master of the art? ''Of course,'' she said, with a little smile.

Chase's jaw tightened. This was a moment for some cleverly sarcastic remark. Unfortunately, his mind was a blank. No, that wasn't true. It had filled with an image of Annie in Hoffman's arms, of his fist connecting with Hoffman's narrow jaw.

''How nice for you both,'' he said coldly.

Annie tossed her head. ''We think so.''

''So, when's the big day?''

''What big...?'' She swallowed. ''You mean, the wedding?'' She shrugged and mentally crossed her fingers. ''We, ah, we haven't set an actual date yet. And you?''

''And me, what?''

''When are you and Janet tying the knot?''

Knot was right. Chase could feel the noose, slipping around his throat.

"Soon."

"This summer?"

"It depends. I've got this project starting in Seattle."

"And, of course, that comes first."

"It's an important job, Annie."

"I'm sure it is. And I'm sure Janet understands that."

"She does, yes. She knows it takes twenty hours out of a twenty-four-hour day to take a firm like the one my old man left me to the top."

"Better her than me."

"You're damned right!"

They glared at each other, both of them remembering—just in case it had slipped their minds—how glad they were not to be living with each other anymore, and then Chase turned away.

"I've got a plane to catch," he said.

"That's it. Just take off. Turn your back on the mess you made."

"Dammit, what would you like me to do? I'm due in Seattle for a site inspection tomorrow afternoon. Hell, what am I talking about?" Frowning, he pushed back the sleeve of his sweater and checked his watch. "It's *this* afternoon."

"Run away," Annie said coldly, folding her arms, "before we've even finished talking or found a solution to the problem *you* created."

"Fine. You want to talk? You can drive me to my hotel so I can pick up my things. Then you can drive me to the airport."

Fifteen minutes to his hotel, Annie thought, eyeing him narrowly, and then forty more to Bradley Airport. One hour, more or less. Surely she could survive that much time in his company if it meant they might come up with a plan.

"All right," she said, then hesitated. Maybe she should go upstairs and change…? No. What for? Chase deserved to be driven to the airport by a woman in an Oscar the Grouch sweatshirt.

"Well?" she said impatiently, sweeping her car keys from a hook on the wall. "What are you waiting for, Chase? Let's go."

Annie waited in her car while Chase collected his suitcase from his hotel room.

Offering to drive him to the airport hadn't been such a great idea.

They hadn't come up with one single good idea during the time it had taken them to get here. And sitting so close to Chase in the bucket seats of her little Honda made her, well, uncomfortable. He was too big for the car. His thigh was right there, an inch from her own. His shoulder brushed hers, on a tight turn, and his after-shave wafted in the air.

The sooner she got rid of him, the better.

"Okay," she said, once he was seated beside her again, "what airline?"

"West Coast. Something like that." He dug into his pocket as she pulled the car into traffic. "Here's the ticket. West Coast Air, that's it."

"How original," Annie said with a tight smile. "Must be new. What terminal is it at? A or B?"

"What do you mean, A or B?"

"Bradley's got two terminals," she said patiently. "One's A. One's B. I need to know which we're going to."

"We're not going to Bradley."

Annie looked at him. "We're not?"

"I'm flying out of Logan. In Boston. I thought you understood that."

Boston. A two-hour drive, instead of forty minutes. Annie's hands felt sweaty on the steering wheel.

"Boston," she said faintly. "I don't think…"

"My flight leaves at noon. Will we make it? Maybe I

should phone the airline. If there's another flight in an hour or two, we could stop for a bite to eat first.''

"Don't be silly.'' Annie glanced at the dashboard clock. "I'll get you there in plenty of time,'' she said, and jammed her foot to the floor.

They got to the airport with twenty minutes to spare.

Annie stopped her car at a stretch of curb marked No Parking. Chase opened his door and got out.

"Well,'' he said, "thanks for the lift.''

She nodded. "You're welcome.''

"Sorry we didn't come up with a solution.''

"Yes. Me, too.''

"As soon as the kids get home…''

"I'll call you.''

"We'll figure out something, by then.''

"Sure.''

"Dawn's a good kid. She'll understand, if we decide to make a clean breast of things.''

"Chase. Your plane.''

"Oh. Right. Right.'' Chase slammed the car door. "Well…''

"Goodbye,'' Annie said. She stepped on the gas and drove off.

A block away, she pulled to the curb. Her heart was racing and her eyes felt grainy.

Why had they quarreled over so many silly things? Why had they sniped at each other?

"Because you're mismatched,'' she whispered, answering her own questions. "You were always mismatched. It's just the sex that kept you from realizing the truth—''

Annie frowned. What was that, on the floor in front of the passenger seat? She bent down and scooped a long white envelope from the floor.

It was Chase's airline ticket.

"Damn," she said, and threw the car into a rubber-burning U-turn.

He wasn't in the terminal, or maybe he was. There were people milling around everywhere; how could she be certain?

Annie raced to look at the Departures screen. Where had he said he was going? Seattle, that was it. On West Coast Air. There it was. Gate Six.

She flew through the ticket area, through the lounge, toward the gate. She almost stopped at the security checkpoint when the guard asked to see her ticket, but then she remembered that was the reason she was here, that she *had* a ticket clutched in her hand, and she waved it at him and hurried through.

Where was Chase?

There! There he was! Her relief at finding him diminished everything else, including how he'd managed to clear security without a ticket.

"Chase," she yelled, "Chase!"

He turned at the sound of her voice. "Annie?" She saw his face light. "Annie," he said again, and opened his arms.

She told herself later that she hadn't meant to run to him, that she'd simply been going too fast to stop. But the next thing Annie knew, she was locked in Chase's embrace.

"Annie," he said softly, "baby."

And then her arms were around his neck and his hands were in her hair and they were kissing.

"Chase," she whispered shakily, "your ticket…"

"It's okay," he said, against her lips. "Don't talk. Just kiss me."

She did, and it was just the way it had always been. The sweetness of the kiss. The sheer joy of it, and then the rush of excitement that came of being in Chase's arms…

"Mom! Dad! Isn't this incredible?"

Annie and Chase sprang apart. Dawn and Nick were

standing perhaps three feet away. Nick looked a little surprised, but Dawn's face showed only absolute delight.

Annie recovered first.

"Dawn?" she said. "And Nick. What are you doing here?"

"Yes." Chase cleared his throat. "We thought you'd, ah, we thought you'd flown out hours ago."

"Well, there was a delay. Weather. Something like that. Nothing serious."

"Great," Chase said heartily. "I mean, that's too bad. I mean... Listen, I wish I could stay and talk to you guys, but my plane—"

"We were just walking around to kill time. Are you on this flight to Seattle?"

"Yes. And it's going to be leaving in a couple of minutes, so—"

"Sure." Dawn came forward and gave them each a hug. "I think it's wonderful," she said, smiling at her parents. "You two, doing this."

"Dawn," Annie said, "baby..."

"Annie," Chase said carefully.

She looked at him. He was right. This was hardly the time to tell their daughter about their subterfuge.

"What, Mom?"

"Just—just keep an open mind, okay? About—about your father and me."

Dawn nodded and settled into the curve of her husband's arm.

"I will."

"Good. That's good. Because—"

"I just want you both to know how much this means to me, seeing that you're so serious about giving yourselves another try."

Chase frowned. "Well, we are, of course. But—"

"I'll accept whatever decision you reach, especially now that I see you're putting so much effort into this."

Annie and Chase stared at their daughter.

"Going off together, to Seattle. That's wonderful."

"Oh," Annie said, "but Dawn—"

"I had my doubts, you know? Whether you were really trying to work things out or if, well, if you were just trying to make me feel better." Dawn smiled. "Now I know, whatever happens, it's for real."

The loudspeaker crackled. "Last call for West Coast Air, Flight 606 to Seattle."

Dawn looped her arms through those of her parents.

"Come on," she said, "Nick and I will see you off."

"No," Annie said, rushing her words together, "really, kids, it isn't necessary."

But they were already marching across the lounge in lockstep, Annie on one side of Dawn, Chase on the other. When they reached the boarding gate, Dawn kissed them goodbye.

"I love you, Mom," she whispered as she pressed her cheek to Annie's.

"Dawn. Baby, you don't understand…"

"I do. And I know, in my heart, this is right."

"Folks?" Everyone looked up. The attendant at the gate was managing to smile and look stern at the same time. "Hurry, please, if you wish to make this flight."

"Chase?" Annie said desperately, as his hand closed over her elbow.

"Just walk," he muttered through his teeth, and steered her forward.

"No. This is impossible!"

"So is turning back. Walk, smile—and when we get on that plane, behave yourself."

"In your dreams, Cooper. Have you forgotten? I don't have a ticket."

Beside her, Chase made a sound that might have been a laugh.

"Sorry," he said, "but I'm afraid you do."

"Don't be silly! I have *your* ticket. I tried to tell you that."

Annie waved the envelope in his face, then went white as her ex-husband plucked an identical envelope from his jacket pocket.

"And I bought another one," he said. "I tried to tell *you* that."

"No," Annie whimpered.

"Yes."

Annie's feet felt as if they'd been nailed to the floor. Chase's hand tightened on her elbow.

"The clerk will notice the names! She'll see that I can't possibly be—"

Chase plucked the envelope from Annie's limp hand and yanked out the contents.

"Hurry," the attendant said, and the next thing Annie knew, she was seated beside him in the first-class cabin of a 747 as it lifted off into a bright, early-morning sky.

CHAPTER SIX

"I CANNOT BELIEVE THIS!"

Chase sighed, tilted back his seat and closed his eyes. Little men with hammers were dancing around inside his head, trying to beat their way out.

"I absolutely, positively cannot believe this!"

"So you've said, a hundred times this morning. Or maybe it was last night. I can't imagine why, but I seem to have lost track of time."

"To think I let you get me into this incredible mess—"

"Annie. Do us both a favor, will you? Lay off."

"—this *impossible* mess! And there you are, lying back with your eyes closed, relaxing, taking it easy, acting as if nothing out of the ordinary were happening!"

Chase's fingers tightened around the arms of his seat. Okay, she was upset. Upset enough so he could damn near feel her quivering with anger and indignation beside him but hell, he was upset, too.

He'd made a monumental screwup, lying to his daughter in the first place and now, as with most lies, he was getting in deeper and deeper. It didn't thrill him to know that, probably sooner than later, he was going to have to let his little girl down.

"Do you care? No. Uh-uh. You do not. No, sir, not Mr. Chase Cooper. He's as cool as a cucumber. He just sits there, as calm as he pleases!"

But first he was going to have to listen to Annie telling him what he already knew, that he was an idiot for having gotten them into this mess in the first place.

"—just drives me crazy! I'm sitting here, wound up like

277

a spring, thinking about what a hideous mess we're in, but do you worry about it?''

"Annie, trust me. I'm worrying."

"You are not," Annie said coldly. "If you were worrying, you couldn't eat a mouthful. But you tore into your meal like a starving man at a banquet table."

"You're damned right I did. I was hungry. I haven't eaten a thing since the caterer fed me that tenderized shoe leather and slippery toadstool concoction at the wedding."

"Shoe leather? Toadstool?" Annie quivered with indignation. "That just shows what you know."

Chase looked at Annie. He thought of replying, then thought better of it. Hell, he thought wearily, she was right. What *did* he know?

Enough to have built Cooper Construction into what it was today—but not enough to have saved his own marriage. And now he, of all people, was trying to save his daughter's. There was a joke in there someplace, if only he could manage to see it.

He put his head back and let Annie's angry tirade wash over him. He was too tired to argue, or even to answer. He hadn't felt this exhausted since the early years of their marriage, when he'd spent his days working and his evenings taking courses in finance and administration and whatever else he'd figured might help him grow his business into something he and Annie could be proud of.

He could still remember coming home late at night, too tired to see straight—but not too tired to go into Annie's arms, or to sit across the kitchen table from her and talk about everything under the sun, from some problem at a job site to politics to Annie's day flipping burgers at the King.

When had it all started to go wrong? He'd tried and tried to figure it out, but there hadn't been any one day or any one event. Things had changed, that was all, little by little, and so subtly that even now, after all this time, he couldn't put his finger on it. He only knew that at some point, Annie had stopped waiting up for him.

Not while he was still in school. No, it was after that. When he was scrambling for jobs, taking on work two, three hours from home; he'd drive back at night, so worn-out he could barely make it, because he didn't want to be away from Annie...until he'd figured out that there wasn't any point because the only thing she'd say when she heard his key in the lock was "Don't track mud on the floor, Chase," and then she'd tell him his meal was in the microwave and she'd go off to bed.

Hours later, after he'd eaten his dried-out dinner and pored over plans and specs for the next day, he'd trudge upstairs and find her asleep or pretending to be, lying far over on her side of the mattress, her back to him, her spine so rigid he couldn't bring himself to touch her.

He'd thought things might improve when the money finally started coming in. He bought Annie extravagant gifts, things he'd always longed to give her, and sent her chocolates and huge bouquets of roses.

"Thank you," she'd say politely, and he'd feel as if he'd somehow failed her.

He'd still spent long hours on job sites—he was a hands-on kind of man, not the sort to sit behind a desk and anyway, if you wanted to stay on top of things, you had to be there, in the flesh. He knew he'd arrived when he began getting invited to all kinds of functions. Chamber of Commerce dinners. Charity affairs. Things he couldn't afford to turn down, because if you didn't network, some other guy would and then you'd lose the jobs you'd worked so hard to get—the jobs that bought the things he wanted Annie and Dawn to have. The things Annie had done without, for so long.

So he started accepting invitations. He didn't know how it would be, mingling with the doers and shakers; he was nervous, at first, and excited, but Annie was neither.

"Am I expected to go with you?" she asked, the first time he tossed a cream-colored charity ball announcement on the kitchen table.

Her response hurt. He'd still been foolish enough, in those days, to have hoped she'd get some pleasure at how he'd moved them up in the world.

"Yes," he'd said, speaking coldly to hide his disappointment. "You're my wife, aren't you?"

"Certainly," Annie had answered, and she'd gone out, bought a gown and all the stuff to go with it, had her hair done and sailed into the gilded hotel ballrooms and wood-paneled meeting rooms of their new life as if she'd never flipped hamburgers or burped a crying baby.

Lord, he'd been so proud of her. He'd been as nervous as a cat inside, wondering if he'd fit in, but not Annie. She'd brimmed with self-confidence. And she'd been so beautiful, so bright. He'd ached to keep her stapled to his side but he hadn't done it, not once he'd realized she didn't need him to shore her up. He knew how hard she'd worked in the background, all those years. It was little enough to do, to back off and let her shine on her own. Just as long as he was the guy who took her to the party and brought her home, he was happy.

What an idiot he'd been! It had turned out she'd hated spending those evenings with him. His first clue had come when she'd started saying no, she couldn't attend this function or that dinner because she'd signed up for some artsy-fartsy course that had no practical use except to make the very clear point that what she really wanted was a life apart from his.

He found himself devoting more time to business, spending days at a clip away from home. What did it matter? Dawn was slipping into her teenage years. Her life centered around her friends. As for Annie...Annie was never there. She was neck-deep in courses that only emphasized the growing differences between them.

How To Appreciate Haiku. Understanding Jasper Johns, whoever in hell Jasper Johns was. Batik-Making. And then, finally, what had seemed like a trillion courses in flower arranging and design and the next thing he'd known, he had a suitcase in his hand and it was goodbye, twenty years of marriage—well, there'd been that mess at the end that had finished things off, when his secretary had thrown herself into his arms, but he hadn't done a thing to encourage it, no matter what Annie thought.

Peggy had been lonely. As lonely as he was. Some quiet talk, a couple of suppers after they'd been poring over figures for hours in the office, followed by his seeing her into a taxi, never anything more personal than that. That was why nobody had been more surprised than he when Peggy had suddenly launched herself into his arms one night. And wouldn't you know that would be the one night in who knew how many years Annie had picked to come waltzing into the office?

Chase sighed. Not that it mattered anymore. He and Annie were long divorced. He'd made a new life for himself. A pleasant one and yes, he supposed—okay, he knew— that Janet would be delighted to be part of that life, if he asked her.

He'd been happy. Content.

Until today.

Until he'd taken Annie into his arms on that dance floor and felt things, remembered things, he didn't want to feel or remember. Until he'd opened his mouth and jammed his own big foot right into it. And now here he was, heading for Seattle, listening to Annie go on and on about what he'd done, and he had another couple of hours of listening ahead of him before their plane landed and he got her on a flight headed in the other direction.

"...could at least show some concern!"

Chase looked at his ex. Annie was staring straight ahead, her face flushed, her arms crossed over her middle.

"Listen," he said, "what would you like me to do? Get down on my knees and beg for forgiveness?"

She made a humphing sound and lifted her chin a notch.

"Maybe you want me to stand up and tell all these people what a chump I am."

Annie humphed again.

"Just tell me, all right? Say, 'Chase, here's what you've got to do if you want me to shut up.' And I'll do it, Annie, so help me, I'll do it, because I am tired unto death of listening to you bitch and moan!"

That got her attention. She swung toward him, her blue eyes flashing.

"Bitch and moan? Me?"

"Yes, you. Complain and nag, complain and nag, and all because I made one mistake."

"I am not complaining or nagging. I am merely stating the obvious. Yes, you made one mistake. A biggie. And now here we are, off on a trip to Portland—"

"Seattle."

"Dammit, what's the difference?"

"Portland's in Oregon. Seattle's in Washington. There's a big difference."

"Well, excuse me. I suppose I'd know the difference, if I had a college degree, but forgive me, I don't."

"Are you going completely nuts? What's a college degree got to do with this?"

What, indeed? Annie bit her lip. "Nothing."

"You're damn right," Chase said. "Now why don't you do us both a favor? Put back your seat, shut your eyes and try to get some rest."

"Oh, yes, that's easy for you to say but then, everything's easy for you to say! Otherwise, you'd never have gotten us into such a mess in the first place. How could you? How could you have told Dawn—"

"That's it," Chase said grimly, and he hauled Annie into his arms and kissed her. She was too surprised to fight him, and he took advantage of it, making the kiss long and deep. "Now," he said, drawing back just far enough so he could look straight into her eyes, "are you going to keep quiet? Because if you start babbling again, so help me, I'll kiss you until you shut up."

Annie's cheeks flooded with color.

"I hate you, Chase Cooper," she hissed.

Chase let her go. "What else is new," he said tiredly, and then he shut his eyes, told himself not to think about how good it had felt to kiss her because then he'd start remembering what making love had been like, before they'd turned away from each other, how it had been powerful and tender, wild and serene, and so much more than he'd ever imagined a basically simple physical act could be.

Stop it, he told himself angrily, and he tumbled into a deep, troubled sleep.

Annie watched with disgust as Chase slept beside her.

He was snoring softly, and from the look on his face she could tell that he was sleeping the sleep of the innocent.

Well, why be surprised? That was how he'd dealt with any kind of problem, before their divorce.

"By sleeping," she muttered, and scrunched down lower in her seat.

There'd been times, as soon as she'd realized their marriage was in trouble, when she'd spent half the day just thinking about what was going wrong, trying to put a name to it, to come up with an explanation and maybe a solution. Then she'd wait for Chase to come home, so they could talk.

What a slow learner she'd been!

How could you talk to a man who came dragging through the door hours late? Who pretended he'd been trudging around job sites or driving back from one when the simple truth was that he didn't come home because he had nothing to say to you anymore?

Was it her fault that she'd married him so young, before she'd had a chance to go to college, the way he had?

There'd been a brief time, after Cooper Construction had begun to grow, when she'd dared let herself dream that things were getting better.

But they hadn't. Things had gotten worse, instead, starting the night Chase had come home and told her, with a smug smile, that he'd been invited to a big-deal dinner. He wanted to go. It was, he'd said, a terrific opportunity.

He made it sound like an invitation to paradise.

"Do you want me to go?" she'd asked, and just for a minute, she'd looked into his eyes and prayed for him to say that all he really wanted was for them to love each other as they once had.

Instead he'd gotten a closed-up look on his face and said that she was his wife. Of course, he wanted her to go.

What he'd meant was that it was expected of her. Accompanying him to the party was part of her job description, like cooking the meals he never came home to share or warming his bed when he reached for her.

So she'd gone out and bought herself the right clothes, had her hair done the right way, and gone with him to the damned Chamber of Commerce party. Whatever. She couldn't really remember anymore. Not that it mattered. The dozen or more functions she'd attended on Chase's arm were all equally dull and dreary, and he didn't even stay with her during the evening. It was always the same. He'd introduce her, then go off on his own. Networking, not even making the slightest pretense that he enjoyed her company because the truth was, he didn't.

That was when she'd decided she was tired of playing the demure, domesticated backup to Chase's Captain of Industry. He had his degrees and his construction company; she could have something of her own, too.

An education. In things that would never interest him. He'd made that accusation, once, when he'd come home from a trip and she'd paused only long enough to acknowledge his presence before hurrying out the door to a lecture on haiku.

"Dammit," he'd roared, "is that how you pick courses from the catalog, Annie? Do you look the list over and say, hey, that's a good one! Maybe my big dumb husband won't even know what the name of the course means."

"However did you know?" she'd said with a chilly smile, and then she'd flounced out the door, but quickly, so that she wouldn't cry in front of him or say, Chase, please, what's happened to us? I love you. Tell me that you still love me.

It wasn't true, of course, about the courses. She took the ones that sounded interesting: haiku because the description in the catalog sounded so spare and elegant. The one on Jasper Johns because one of Chase's clients had mentioned having a Johns collection, and the one on batik-making because she'd seen a dress in the window of a shop and been fascinated by the swirling colors.

She took the flower-arranging courses simply because there'd been a time in their lives when they were broke and desperately in love, and Chase had bought her a single red rose, because it was all he could afford, and she'd cherished it more than the huge bouquets that came, impersonally, by messenger once he'd struck it rich.

Oh, how much more wonderful that single rose had been!

He'd come home with it in his hand, years and years ago, along with wine and two tickets to the Virgin Islands, and when he'd offered her the rose he'd smiled shyly and said it was almost as beautiful as she was.

She could still remember how she'd gone into his arms.

"I'm sweaty, babe," he'd said huskily. "I need a shower."

And she'd said yes, he did, and she'd started to undress

him, and a minute later they'd been naked, in the shower together.

Her skin tingled now, just remembering what it had been like, the long, slow soaping of each other's bodies, the kissing and touching, the way they'd ended up making love right there, under the spray, Chase's arms hard around her, her legs tight around his waist, him saying her name against her mouth, over and over, and she crying out as they came together in explosive release.

Tears stung behind her lids. It was stupid, thinking about things like that. Especially about sex, because that brought her straight to what had finally ended their marriage.

She'd been taking a class in dried flower making and design. She'd done some nice work, she knew that, but one night the instructor had asked her to wait after she dismissed the class. Then she'd asked Annie's permission to enter one of her flower arrangements in a juried show.

Annie had said yes. And she'd been so happy and excited that she'd forgotten how long it had been since she and Chase had shared good news. She'd jumped into her car, driven to Chase's office building, found the front door unlocked and sailed down the hall, straight into his office...

Annie shuddered.

She could still see them now, her husband and his secretary, the girl with her arms around Chase's neck and his around her waist, their bodies pressed together...

That was it. The marriage was over.

Chase had tried to explain, to worm out of the truth, but Annie wasn't stupid. She'd endured enough pain, watching the man she loved slip slowly but steadily away from her all those years.

And ''loved'' was the right word. That night, as Chase and his secretary sprang guiltily apart, Annie knew that whatever she'd once felt for her husband was gone. Deader than a daffodil that's been squashed by a truck.

''Annie,'' Chase had said, ''Annie, you have to listen.''

"Yes, Mrs. Cooper," the young woman had pleaded, "you must listen!"

Listen? Why? There was nothing to talk about.

She'd felt suddenly very calm. The decision was out of her hands, thanks to Chase and the weeping girl.

"I want a divorce," she'd told him, and she'd even managed a cold smile for the secretary. "He's all yours," she'd said, and then she'd turned on her heel and marched out.

Things had gone quickly, after that. Her sister, Laurel, had recommended an attorney, although Laurel had done her best to convince Annie not to act so hastily. But there was nothing hasty in Annie's decision. She and Chase had been heading for this moment for years.

The divorce had been civilized. Chase's attorney was an old friend, David Chambers, who kissed her cheek and treated her with courtesy during their one face-to-face over a conference table. Chase wanted her to have the condominium. Half their savings. Half of everything. Child support, and generous alimony.

Annie said she didn't want the money. Her lawyer, and his, told her not to be stupid. She had a child to support. They were right, she knew, so she accepted everything except the alimony. As for the condo—it was filled with ugly memories. She sold it as soon as she could, moved to Stratham and began a new life. A career. She'd cut herself off from the past, and damned successfully. She'd made friends. She'd dated. And now she had Milton Hoffman, who wanted to marry her.

And then Chase had come along, spoiling everything with a stupid lie.

Annie chomped down on her lip.

Who was she kidding? Her life had started slipping off the tracks hours before Chase had told that dumb lie and the truth was, she understood that he'd done it not out of stupidity but out of love for their daughter.

The lie hadn't put her on this collision course with disaster.

The dance had. That silly dance at the wedding.

Annie tried not to remember. The warmth of Chase's arms encircling her. The beat of his heart against hers. The feel of his lips against her hair, against her skin. The feeling that she had come home, that she was where she'd always belonged.

Oh God.

She took a long, shuddering breath.

Stop it, she told herself fiercely, and she put her head back, shut her eyes and willed herself to sleep.

A change of pitch in the jet's engines woke Chase hours later.

He yawned, tried to remember where he was—and went completely still.

Annie was asleep, with her head on his shoulder. She was tucked close against him, her face against his neck, just the way she used to back in the long-ago days when they'd cuddle up together on the sofa to watch Sunday football.

"You watch," she'd say, "I don't mind. I'll read."

But after a little while, she'd sigh. The book would slip from her hands. She'd put her head on his shoulder and sigh again, and he'd sit there with her asleep beside him, unwilling to move or to give up these sweet moments even if every muscle in his body ached.

A feeling of almost unbearable tenderness swept over him. She was dreaming, too. Looking down, into her face, he could see the little smile on her lips.

Was she dreaming about him?

"Annie?"

Annie sighed. "Mmm," she said.

"Babe, it's time to wake up."

She smiled and cuddled closer. "Mmm," she whispered, "Milton?"

Milton?

Milton Hoffman? That was the man in his wife's dream? That was why she was smiling and cuddling up so close to him?

Chase felt his heart turn to ice.

Hoffman. That poor excuse for a man. That effete jerk. That was who Annie wanted. That was the kind of man she'd always wanted.

Why hadn't he seen it before?

Milton Hoffman, Professor of English, Shakespearean Authority and All-round Chrome Dome, never had mud on his wing tips. He never had to leave the house before dawn and come home, dragging his tail, long after dark. He never had to wonder if anybody noticed the shadow of dirt under his fingernails because ol' Milton had never had dirt under his fingernails, not in this lifetime.

Chase sat up straight. Annie's head bobbed; she made a little purring sound and nuzzled closer.

"Annie," he said coldly. "Wake up."

"Mmm."

Annie sighed. She was at that point where you know you're dreaming, but you're not quite ready to give up the dream. Not this dream. She was too interested in seeing how it would end.

She had been sitting in a classroom, with Milton on his knees beside her. He'd just proposed, and she was earnestly explaining why she had to turn him down.

I like you very much, Milton, she said, *and I respect you and admire you.*

But he wasn't Chase. His kisses had never stirred her the way Chase's did. His touch didn't set her on fire.

"Annie? Wake up."

"Milton," she said, and then she opened her eyes and saw Chase glaring at her from two inches away.

Annie jerked back, her face coloring. How long had she been asleep? How long had she been lying snuggled up against Chase as if she were a teenager in a drive-in theater—if there still were such places?

No wonder Chase was looking at her that way. God, she'd probably drooled all over him.

"Sorry." She put her hands to her hair and smoothed it back from her face. "I, ah, I guess I dozed off."

"And dreamed of Prince Charming," Chase said, with a tight little smile.

"Prince…?"

"Good old Milty. Your fiancé."

Annie stared at Chase and remembered her dream. "Did I—did I say anything?"

"What's the matter, Annie? Afraid I might have heard the dialogue that went with an X-rated dream?"

"It wasn't X-rated! I was just dreaming that—that…"

"Don't waste your breath." Chase's voice was chill. "I'm not interested."

Annie stiffened. "Sorry. I almost forgot. Nothing I ever had to say was of much interest to you, was it?"

"Mr. Cooper? Mrs. Cooper?" The flight attendant smiled down at them both. "We'll be landing in just a few minutes. Would you put your seat-backs up, please?"

"With pleasure," Chase said.

"I'm buying a return ticket the instant we touch down," Annie snapped, without looking at him.

"You won't have to. Believe me, it'll be my pleasure to buy you the ticket and to see you to the plane."

It was a fine idea. Unfortunately it didn't work.

The next plane to Boston was completely booked.

"Providence, then," Chase said. "Bradley…"

One by one, he rattled off the names of airports. One by one, the clerk at the ticket counter shook her head.

"We've had lengthy delays all morning," she said. "Fog

here, thunderstorms in the Midwest...'' She smiled apologetically. ''I might be able to get your wife—''

''Ex-wife,'' Annie said.

''Whatever. I might be able to get her out of here tomorrow afternoon.''

''Yeah,'' Chase grumbled, ''okay.''

''Not okay!''Annie glared at him, as if it was his fault she was in this predicament. ''What am I supposed to do until tomorrow afternoon? Sit around the airport?''

''I'll get you a hotel room.''

''Good luck.''

Annie and Chase looked at the ticket clerk, whose shoulders rose and fell in a helpless shrug.

''On top of all the delays, there're two major conventions in town.'' She leaned forward and lowered her voice to a confidential whisper. ''My boss tried everything he knew to get a room for a VIP just a little while ago, and even he couldn't come up with anything.''

Annie had a mental picture of herself joining the rows of exhausted travelers draped over every available seat in the terminal.

''Don't worry,'' Chase said quickly. ''I'm sure my client's arranged a room somewhere for me. You can have it just as soon as I get in touch with him.''

As if in response, an electronically amplified voice rang out, paging Mr. Chase Cooper.

Chase took Annie's arm, drew her aside and picked up a courtesy phone.

''Yes?'' He listened, then sighed and rolled his eyes as if to say this was just one more problem he didn't need. ''Mr. Tanaka,'' he said politely. ''No, no, I didn't see your man holding up my name at the arrivals gate.'' He glared at Annie, who glared right back. ''I was, ah, preoccupied.''

''Who is it?'' Annie hissed.

Chase turned away. ''Well, that's very kind of you, Mr. Tanaka. Sending a car for me...thank you.''

"Is it somebody from Seattle?" Annie said, dancing in front of him. "Ask him if he knows of a hotel that might have a room."

Chase sighed. She was right. Kichiro Tanaka, his new client, was a wealthy and well-connected businessman. He had major investments in the southwest, and now he'd turned his attention to the coast. For all Chase knew, the guy might even own a hotel in this city.

"Mr. Tanaka… Yes, I'll meet your driver at the exit. In just a moment. But first—I wonder if you might be able to help me out with a small problem?"

Annie's mouth thinned. That's what she was, all right. A small problem. It was all she'd ever been, as far as Chase was concerned.

"Well…" Chase rubbed the back of his neck. "My, ah, my wife accompanied me to Seattle."

"Ex-wife," Annie snapped.

Chase glared at her and slapped his hand over the mouthpiece of the phone.

"Do you really want me to start explaining what you're doing here to a stranger?"

Annie colored. After a second, Chase cleared his throat and spoke again.

"She didn't intend to stay, though. Yes, well, I suppose that's one way of looking at it."

"What is?" Annie demanded.

"Charming. Yes. Yes, that she'd fly all this distance, just so we could spend a few hours more together."

Annie opened her mouth, stuck the tip of her finger inside and pretended to gag.

"The problem, Mr. Tanaka, is that all the flights have been delayed. It's probable Annie won't be able to leave until tomorrow and I've been told all the hotels are solidly booked… Really?"

"Really, what?" Annie said.

"That's fine. Yes, of course. At the exit area, in a couple of minutes. Thank you, sir. I'll…we'll see you soon."

"What?" Annie said again.

Chase hung up the phone and grabbed her hand.

"Come on. We've got to meet the car and driver he sent for me."

"Hot stuff," she muttered. "A car and a driver, all for you."

"And a suite, all for us." His smile was quick and shiny. "So stop complaining."

Annie looked at him as they hurried toward the escalator. "You mean…?"

"I mean, luckily for you, he says there's more than enough room for the both of us."

"Not in one hotel room, there isn't."

"Didn't you hear what I said?" They'd reached the lower level, and Annie hurried to keep up with Chase's long stride. "He says we'll have a living room, bedroom, kitchen and bathroom all to ourselves."

"Well, that's good news," Annie snapped, as Chase thrust her out the door ahead of him.

"Damn right. The last thing I feel like doing is curling up in a hotel lobby tonight while you take over my bed."

"Such gallantry. But—"

"But what?" Chase snapped in her ear as a black limousine slid to the curb. The driver got out, executed a perfect salute and opened the rear door. "Just get into the car, Annie. We can endure each other's company a little while longer. As tempting at the thought of leaving you at the airport is, I can't bring myself to do it."

As tempting as it was, staying at the airport for endless hours didn't appeal to her, either.

"All right," she snapped back. "But you better hope this suite is the size of Yankee Stadium. Otherwise, you may find yourself sleeping in the lobby anyway!"

*   *   *

It wasn't the size of Yankee Stadium—although it was close.

But it wasn't a suite, Annie thought an hour later, as she stared around her in shock. And it certainly wasn't a hotel.

The limo had not taken them to one of the high-rise buildings in downtown Seattle. It had whisked them to a pier, where they'd boarded a sleek motorboat.

"Chase," Annie had said, over the roar of the boat's engines, "where are we going?"

Chase, who'd been starting to think he knew the answer, looked at the pilot.

"Tell me that we aren't going to the island," he said.

The pilot grinned. "Sure enough, we are."

Chase groaned.

Annie looked at him as he gripped the railing and stared out over the churning water. She'd read the one, silent word on his lips and the tips of her ears had turned pink.

Now, standing in this room, she half wanted to say the word herself.

The wisps of fog that had drifted across the boat's bow during their journey had lifted as they'd neared their destination. Annie had glimpsed an island, a place of towering green trees sloping down to a rocky shore. High among the trees, as if it were an eagle soaring out over the water, there was a lodge. It was a magnificent sight, a sculpture of redwood and glass. It was a fabulous aerie, commanding a view of the Sound in isolated splendor.

Wooden steps led up the craggy face of the cliff. Annie had climbed them, refusing Chase's outstretched hand and instead clasping the wooden railing, telling herself that when they reached the top, she'd see something more than that one structure. A hotel. A cluster of buildings. A resort...

But there was only the lodge, and when Chase opened the door and went inside, she followed.

The rooms they passed through were spectacular. There

was a kitchen, white and shiny and spotless. A bathroom, complete with a deep Jacuzzi and a stall shower built against a glass wall so that it seemed open to the forest. There was a living room and as Annie stepped into it, sunlight suddenly poured through the huge skylight overhead, so that the white walls and pale hardwood floor seemed drenched in gold.

Mr. Tanaka's ancient heritage showed in the room's elegant yet simple lines: the woven tatami mats on the floor, the handsome shoji screen that served as a backdrop for a low, black-lacquered table and the plump, black-and-white silk cushions that were strewn on the floor before the fieldstone fireplace. Sliding glass doors, flanked by tall white vases filled with pussy willows, opened on to the deck.

But it was the bedroom that made Annie gasp, and mentally repeat Chase's muttered profanity. Their absent host's living room had been serenely Japanese—but Mr. Tanaka had very Western tastes when it came to his sleeping quarters.

The floor was covered with white carpet so deep and lush it made Annie's toes curl longingly inside her sneakers. One wall was mirrored; one was all glass and gave out onto the forest and the Sound. The furnishings themselves were spare and handsome. There was a teak dresser. A matching chest. A bentwood rocking chair.

And a bed.

One enormous, circular bed, elevated on a platform beneath a hexagonal skylight, and swathed in yards and yards of black-and-white silk.

CHAPTER SEVEN

ANNIE TOLD HERSELF to calm down.

Count to ten. To twenty. Concentrate on finding the peaceful center within herself. Wasn't that what she'd spent six weeks trying to learn when she'd taken that Zen philosophy course last winter?

Take a deep breath. Hold it. One. Two. Three. Four.

Annie let out her breath. It wasn't working. All she could see was the bed. All she could think about was Chase, standing next to her with a look of bland innocence on his face.

"Damn," she said, and when that clearly wasn't going to be anywhere near enough to relieve her anger, she gave up Zen for reality, swung around and punched her ex-husband in the belly. It was a hard belly—he'd always had a great body, and apparently that hadn't changed, which somehow only made her more furious—and she felt the jolt of the blow shoot straight up her arm and into her shoulder. But it was worth it to see the look of shock that spread across his face.

"Hey," he said, dancing back a step. Not that Annie's reaction entirely surprised him. She looked as if she could have happily murdered him. Well, hell, he understood that. He'd have happily murdered good old Kichiro Tanaka, given the opportunity. "Hey, take it easy, will you?"

"Take it easy?" Annie slapped her hands on her hips and glared at him, her chest rising and falling with each quick, huffy breath. "Take it easy?" she repeated, her voice shooting out of its normal range into a ragged soprano.

"Yeah." Chase rubbed his midsection. "There's no need to get violent over what's obviously a mistake."

"Oh, it's a mistake, all right." She blew a breath that lifted the curls dangling over her eyes. "A big mistake, Cooper, because if you think, even for one minute, that I— that you and I—that the two of us are going to share that— that bed, that we're going to relive old times—"

"Babe…"

"Don't 'babe' me!"

"Annie, you don't think…"

"But I do. I think. I always have, even though you never credited me for having a brain in my head when we were married."

Chase almost groaned. Here they went again, plunging right into deep water.

"Listen," he said carefully, "I know you're upset. But—"

"That's it. Tell me I'm upset. That way, I'll shut my mouth and you won't have to listen to the truth."

"Annie…"

"Let me tell you something, Chase Cooper. That might have worked years ago, but not now. I am not the dumb little thing you always thought I was."

"Annie, I never thought—"

"Yes, you did, but it doesn't matter a damn anymore."

"I swear, I didn't."

"'Oh, *Ba-aabe*,'" she said, cruelly mimicking his voice, "'I'm so sorry, but you don't mind if I go out, do you? I've got to attend a meeting of the—the Sacred Sons of the Saxophones tonight.'"

Despite himself, Chase laughed. "The what?"

"Don't try and joke your way out of this, Cooper!" Annie took a step forward, her index finger uplifted and wagging an inch off his nose. "You can't change the facts."

"What facts?"

"I'm talking about our so-called marriage, that's what!

And how you used to treat me as if I never had a thought in my head.''

''I still don't know what the hell you're talking about!''

''Well, let me refresh your memory. Think back to the good old days, when you used to drag me to all those horrible dinners and charity things.''

''Like the Sacred Sons of the Saxophones?''

''I just said, don't try and laugh your way out of this, Chase. I am dead serious.''

''About what?''

She had to give him credit; he'd managed to put on an expression of total bewilderment. If she hadn't known better, she'd have thought he meant it.

''I know how you worried that your poor little wifey wouldn't be able to hold her own.''

''What?''

''And then, when it turned out I could, you just—just left me, dumped me into a—a seaful of sharks and took off by yourself.''

''Annie, you're crazy. I never—''

''Was that when you looked around and decided you could have lots more fun if you left me at home?''

Chase's expression went from bewilderment to confusion. ''One of us is losing her mind,'' he said, very calmly. ''And it sure as hell isn't me.''

Annie's chin rose pugnaciously. ''Hah,'' she said, and folded her arms.

''You think I was glad when you stopped going to those dinners and things with me, so I could go by myself and have a wild old time?''

''You said it, not me.''

''Damn, but your spin on ancient history is truly amazing!''

''What's the matter, Chase? Can't you stand the truth?''

''Am I supposed to have forgotten that I stopped taking

you with me because you made it clear how much you hated going?''

Annie flushed. ''Don't try and twist things. Okay, maybe I didn't care for those stuffy evenings—''

''Finally, the woman speaks the truth!''

''Why would I have enjoyed them? We were only there so you could grab yourself another headline in the business section of the newspaper!''

Chase's eyes narrowed. ''We were there so I could land myself jobs, Annie. Jobs, remember? The stuff that put bread on the table?''

''Give me a break, Chase! We had plenty of money by then. You were just—just getting your ego stroked.''

A muscle knotted in his cheek.

''Go on,'' he said softly. ''What else have you saved up, all these years?''

''Only that when I finally said I didn't want to go anymore, instead of trying to change my mind, which any intelligent man would have done, which *you* would have done, at one time—''

Chase gave a short, desperate laugh. ''Are we both speaking the same language here, or what?''

''Instead of doing that,'' Annie said, ignoring the interruption, ''you simply shrugged your shoulders and agreed. And that was that.''

''You're telling me that I should have tried to talk you into doing something you obviously hated?''

''Don't make it sound as if you don't understand a word I'm saying, Chase. I won't buy it.''

''And I won't buy you making me into some kind of Neanderthal who cheered when my wife signed off and let me go play with the rest of the boys,'' Chase said grimly. ''No way, babe, because that's *not* how it was, no matter what you say!''

''Yeah, well, that's your story and you're stuck with it.''

''No!'' Chase grabbed her wrist as she started past him. ''No, it damn well is not 'my story.' It's fact. Did you expect me to get down on my knees and beg you to spend your evenings with me, instead of with one dumb textbook after another?''

"Right. Lay everything off on me, even my wanting to better myself. That's typical. Everything was my fault, never yours."

"Better yourself? *Better* yourself?" he said, bending toward her, his eyes dark and dangerous. "So that you could do what, huh? Tell me that you knew more about haiku than I knew about building houses?"

"That's not the way it was and you know it," Annie said angrily, as she tried to pull her arm from his grasp. "You couldn't bear to see me turning into a whole person instead of just being Mrs. Chase Cooper."

"Wasn't being my wife enough to make you happy?"

"Being the woman who cooked your meals and cleaned your house and raised your child, you mean," Annie said, her voice trembling. "Who waited up nights while you built your empire. Who got told to buy fancy dresses and jewelry so she could be dragged to Chamber of Commerce meetings as a reflection of her husband's importance!"

Chase could feel a humming in his ears. He let go of Annie's wrist and took a step back.

"If that's what you believe," he said, his voice so low and dangerous that it made the hair lift on the back of Annie's neck, "if you really think that's what you meant to me, my once-upon-a-time-wife, then it's a damn good thing our marriage ended when it did."

Annie stared at his white face and pinched lips. "Chase," she said, and held out her hand, but it was too late. He'd already whirled away from her and disappeared down the hall.

Unbelievable!

Chase walked along the gravel path that led from the lodge into the trees.

It was more than unbelievable. It was incredible, that Annie should have hated him so. Hated being married to him, and for so many years.

He tucked his hands into his pockets and slowed his pace, scowling at a squirrel that scolded him from beneath the branches of a cedar.

He knew a lot of guys who'd been divorced. They were everywhere: at his health club, at the board meetings he sat in on...it seemed as if you couldn't throw a stick in New York or San Francisco or any city in the whole U.S.A. without hitting some poor bastard who'd gone from being a family man to being a guy who thought a microwave meal was gourmet dining.

The happy bachelor image, the divorced stud with a little black book full of names and addresses, was the stuff of movies. It wasn't reality or if it was, then he'd missed something. The divorced men he met were almost invariably just like him, guys who'd once had it all and now had nothing but questions.

When had it all started to go wrong? And why? And then there was the biggest question of all.

What could they have done to change it?

Most of them had answers, even if they didn't much like them. Chase never had. Try as he would, he'd never really been able to pinpoint when things had started going downhill, or why. As for changing it...how could you change something when you didn't know what it was that needed changing?

He'd been the best kind of husband he'd known how to be, working his butt off to give Annie a better life. A life she deserved, and now it turned out she'd not only hated all the years of hard work, but she'd also resented them.

A bitter taste filled his mouth.

"What does she think?" he muttered, kicking a pinecone out of the way. "Does she think I enjoyed working like a slave? Does she think I had a good time, busting my back-side all day and cracking books half the night?''

Maybe. Annie had just proved that she was capable of thinking damn near anything, when it came to him.

The land was sloping upward. The trees were pressing in from either side, and a cool, salt-scented breeze was blowing into his face. Chase drew it deep into his lungs, lowered his head and trudged on.

At least it was all out in the open, now. Annie had been as remote about their split-up as the sphinx. He couldn't even remember which of them had said the words first, he or she; he only knew that except for that one awful scene at the end, when Annie had come bursting into his office and seen poor Peggy embarrassing them both—except for that, their separation had been the most civilized thing on record.

No harsh words. No screaming matches. No accusations. Nothing. They had both been polite and proper about the whole thing. His attorney had even joked about it.

''I had a law prof used to say that the only man who never raises his voice during divorce proceedings is a man whose almost-ex-wife's already slit his throat,'' David had said, and Chase had grinned and said that David, with his own strikeout, certainly ought to know.

Chase shook his head. No, Annie hadn't killed him when she'd thought she'd caught him being unfaithful. She'd waited, and let him suffer for five long years, and now she'd plunged a dagger right into his heart.

It shouldn't have hurt, not when she wasn't his wife any-more. Not when she didn't mean a damn thing to him any-more.

Chase stepped out of the woods. He was standing on a high, rocky cliff overlooking the dark green Pacific.

Who was he kidding? Annie meant everything to him. She always had, and she always would.

*   *   *

Annie sat on the edge of the circular bed, her hands folded in her lap.

Well, she'd finally gotten everything out of her system. She'd let it all hang out; wasn't that what the kids used to say? She'd dredged up all the anger and pain she'd thought was long gone and dumped it right into Chase's lap.

She sighed, fell back against the pillows and put her arm over her eyes.

Who was she kidding? Neither the hurt nor the rage was long gone. They weren't gone at all. Hardly a week went by that something didn't make her remember how miserable her marriage had been, how much she'd despised Chase.

It was just a good thing she'd finally gotten it out in the open.

Tears welled in her eyes.

It wasn't true. Her marriage hadn't been miserable. Not the first years, anyway. She'd been so crazy in love, so happy, that sometimes she'd had to pinch herself to make sure she wasn't dreaming.

And she'd never despised Chase. Heaven knew, that would have made things a lot easier. Then, when she'd finally acknowledged the truth, that he'd outgrown her and that he didn't love her anymore, it wouldn't have hurt so badly.

Annie sighed, stood up, and walked to the window wall. The view was spectacular: the deep green water in one direction, and a stand of windblown cypresses stretching off in the other. The ancient trees looked as if they'd been there forever, protecting the house and keeping it safe.

A smile moved across her lips.

That was how she'd always felt about Chase. They'd met so young that there were moments she'd felt as if she'd known him all her life. And her safe haven had always been within his arms.

It had come as a shock to her to learn that other women

didn't feel that way about their husbands. She could still recall sitting on a bench at a little playground years ago. Dawn must have been two, maybe three; she was playing with a bunch of kids and the mothers sat around watching, keeping an eye on things while they chatted about this and that.

Eventually the talk had turned to husbands.

"He drives me nuts," one woman said, "coming in the door at night like some kind of conquering hero, and I'm supposed to hum a couple of bars of Hail to the Chief while I pull off his shoes, stoke the fire and serve him a meal straight out of *Gourmet* magazine."

There'd been some laughter, some groans and lots of general agreement. Annie had been too flustered to do much of anything except sit there and think how sad it was that all those women didn't feel as she did, waiting for the sound of her husband's key in the lock so that she could fly into his arms.

Her throat tightened. She leaned her head forward and pressed her forehead against the cool glass.

When had it all started to change? When had eager anticipation turned to annoyance? When had the clock on the wall become not a way to count off the minutes and hours until Chase's arrival but an infuriating reminder of his lateness?

All the things she'd just said to him…how long had they been waiting to come out?

She'd hurt him, she knew. But he'd hurt her, too. Dragging her to those business affairs, with her all gussied up to prove his success.

That was the way it had been, wasn't it?

Wasn't it?

And he'd said such awful things just now. Implying that she'd studied stuff just so she could show him his ignorance of the fine arts…

Annie snorted and turned her back to the window. What

a lie! She'd never done that. How could she? Chase was the one with the college degrees; she was the meek little wife with nothing but a high school diploma. It wasn't her fault if she'd taken an interest in obscure poetry and Indonesian art and things that were beyond his comprehension...

Things that were beyond his comprehension.

She drew a deep, shuddering breath.

No. Never. She wouldn't have studied anything for such a shabby reason. She'd enjoyed the poetry, the art; she'd improved herself with the vocabulary courses and the Great Books series, and if Chase just happened to be overwhelmed by the books she left open on the kitchen table, it wasn't anything deliberate on her part.

A muffled sob burst from Annie's throat.

"I never meant to hurt you, Chase," she whispered.

Never.

She'd loved him, with all her heart. She loved him still. That was the awful truth of it, and there wasn't a damn thing she could do about it now because he didn't love her, not anymore.

Their marriage was over. Chase was engaged to another woman, and she—she was going to have to go on without him.

It was just that it was going to be harder, now.

It was always harder, once you knew the truth.

Chase knocked on the open bedroom door.

"Come in," Annie said politely.

He stepped into the room.

She was sitting in the rocker, her hands folded neatly in her lap. Her face was pale but her features were composed, and she smiled when she saw him.

"Hi."

"Hi."

"Did you go for a walk?"

"Yeah, I did." He hesitated. "Listen, about all that stuff we said before. I'm really sorry—"

"Me, too. There's no reason to quarrel over the past."

Chase nodded. "No reason at all."

They smiled at each other, and then Annie cleared her throat. "So," she said briskly, "I'll bet the island's beautiful."

"It is. I was here before. Tanaka bought the place from some computer megamillionaire. He flew me out to see it after he'd signed the papers. He wanted to know what I thought of his plan."

"What plan?" Annie asked politely.

"He's going to tear this place down, build a kind of retreat."

"Ah." She looked down, and plucked a bit of thread off her jeans-clad leg. "Buddhist?"

Chase smiled. "Top-class hotel, would be closer to the mark. What he's got in mind is a kind of hideaway for his executive staff. You know the sort of thing—elegant but rustic. Simple food, prepared by a Cordon Bleu chef. Simple suites, with a Jacuzzi in every bathroom and a wet bar in every sitting room. Simple pleasures, starting with a nine-hole golf course, tennis courts and an Olympic-size swimming pool."

"A bigger, even more elaborate version of this, you mean."

"Yeah." Chase grinned. "Incredible, isn't it?"

"Incredible's the word, all right. So, you're going to build this Shangri-la for him?"

"Well, not quite the way he'd envisioned it, no. I told him that he'd ruin the feeling of the land and the sea, if he went overboard on the luxuries."

"No wet bars?"

Chase grinned. "And no suites, no golf courses, no tennis courts, and why put in a pool when Puget Sound's outside your door?"

"That's darned near a pool in the bathroom already," Annie said, smiling. "Heaven knows, it's too big for just one pers…" Color swept into her face. Her eyes met Chase's, and she looked quickly away. "I'll, uh, I'll bet you had a tough time, convincing him."

Chase shrugged. "Well, it took a while, yes."

Silence filled the room. Finally Annie spoke.

"Chase?"

"Yes?"

"Well…well…" She took a deep breath. "Listen, I know it'll be embarrassing for you to have to admit to your Mr. Tanaka that you and I ended up in the plane together by mistake, but you're going to have to do it. Tell him anything you want. Whatever's easiest for you. Lay it off on me, if you like. Say that I suddenly thought of something important back home."

"Your fiancé," Chase said politely. "I could say you forgot about him. How's that sound?"

Annie refused to acknowledge the gauntlet, much less stoop to pick it up.

"I don't care what you say. Just—just get me off this island, please."

Chase nodded. She was right. They both needed to leave this place. "I'll take care of it."

"You could tell him the same thing," Annie blurted as he turned toward the door. He looked at her, and she ran the tip of her tongue over her lips. "You know," she said, because it was too late to back down, "that you have to get back to your fiancée, too."

Chase looked at his ex-wife. Sitting on the edge of the rocker, ankles crossed, hands locked together, with the rays of the late-afternoon sun streaking her hair with gold, she looked soft, sweet and undescribably vulnerable. He saw himself going to her, taking her in his arms, kissing her and telling her that she was the only woman he'd ever wanted, the only woman he'd ever loved.

"Chase?"

"Yeah," he said gruffly. "Uh, the thing is—we've both forgotten something."

"I don't think so," Annie said, fighting against the tears that inexplicably threatened. "Believe me, Chase, we haven't forgotten a thing."

"No flight back until tomorrow, babe. No hotel rooms, either."

"Oh." Annie chewed on her lip. "Well, that's okay. I'll wait at the airport."

"That's not a good idea."

"It's a fine idea." Annie smiled brightly. "I've always liked airports. I can buy myself half a dozen magazines and a hot dog, curl up in a corner and—"

"Listen, we'll stay right where we are. But we'll start over. New ground rules. No talking about the past, or about us. Okay?"

"The past, and us, are the only things we've got," Annie said quietly. "I don't see how we can avoid talking about them."

Chase looked at her for a long moment. Then he sighed and ran his fingers through his hair.

"I'll go find the guy who brought us here. He can take us back to shore. And I'll phone Tanaka and see if he can pull some strings to get you a room somewhere. Or I'll stay with you at the airport, until you can get a flight out."

"That won't be necessary."

"Look, we can argue about it later. Right now, let me just put the wheels in motion."

"What'll you tell him? Your Mr. Tanaka? About why we want to leave the island, I mean?"

His mouth twisted. "Don't start worrying about how I handle business at this late date, Annie. It's my problem, not yours."

Chase strode from the room and slammed the door after him. Annie sat back in the rocker. She was shaking, and she felt like crying, which was stupid. It only proved how much pressure she'd been under, the last couple of days.

She took a deep breath, heel-and-toed the rocker into motion and settled in to wait for her liberation from this island, Chase, and a thousand unwanted memories.

"He's gone."

Annie blinked her eyes open and swung her legs to the floor.

"Who?" she said, in a hoarse voice. She frowned and rubbed her hands over her eyes. "Who's gone?"

Chase leaned back against the wall and folded his arms. His face looked as if it had been chipped from granite.

"The guy who brought us here."

Annie's head was swimming. "I'm not—I'm not following you. The guy with the boat, you mean?"

"Uh-huh."

"How can he be gone? *Where* could he have gone? He couldn't have walked to…" Her breath caught at the expression on Chase's face. "You mean, he took the boat?"

"You've got it."

Annie stared at him. "We're stuck here?"

"Right again."

"Well—well, phone your Mr. Tanaka. Tell him—"

"Will you stop calling him that? He is *not* my Mr. Tanaka." Chase glowered at her. "Anyway, I already tried to phone him."

"And?"

"And," he said, shrugging his shoulders, "it's not a regular phone they've got here, it's a radio thing."

"So?"

"So, it doesn't seem to work."

Annie bit her lip and fought down a rising tide of hysteria. "If this is your idea of some kind of joke, Chase…"

"Do I look like I'm joking?" Chase smiled tightly. "The

guy left a note, in the kitchen. It seems we're trapped until tomorrow."

"That's impossible. Why would he strand us here?"

"I don't know why. I don't much care, either. All I know is that we're going to have to make the best of things, until the jerk with the boat shows up tomorrow morning at eight."

"At eight," Annie repeated, through lips that felt numb. She looked at her watch. Sixteen hours to get through. Sixteen hours, alone with her ex-husband.

"Just get this through your head," Chase said. Annie looked up. "This setup. This—this honeymoon hotel. I assure you, it wasn't my idea."

"I certainly hope not. Because if it was, you're in for a heck of a disappoint—"

Annie gasped as Chase grabbed her shoulders and hauled her to her feet.

"Lady, I have taken all the insults I'm going to take! I promise you, I'm not so desperate for a woman to warm my bed that I'd go to all this trouble to arrange it."

He was right, and she knew it. Her accusation had been dumb. He couldn't have arranged this fiasco if he'd wanted to.

And he was right about all the rest, as well. Chase wouldn't have to resort to subterfuge, to get a woman into his bed. He was—what had Deb called him, the day of the wedding? Hunky, that was it. He was hunky and he always had been, especially now that he was in his prime. Chase was a man who'd turn women's heads without even trying.

No wonder she spotted his photo in the paper so often, with some smiling bimbo on his arm.

Except they weren't bimbos. She might as well admit that, too, while she was going for the truth. She liked to tell herself they were, but the women in the photos with her ex-husband were invariably beautiful and elegant.

Like Janet Pendleton, who was going to become his wife.

Annie's throat felt raspy. It was silly, but she felt like crying.

"You're right," she said.

"You're damned right I am."

"This entire thing—our getting on that plane in the first place, and now our getting stuck here is—just, what's the word? Karma."

Chase could hardly believe it. Annie, holding out an olive branch? It seemed inconceivable but hell, most of what had happened during the past forty-eight hours fell into that very same category. If it was an olive branch, what did he have to lose if he accepted it? If he was going to spend the night in that rocker—and he was—it would be a lot better for the both of them if they weren't at each other's throats.

"Karma," he said, as he lifted his hands from her shoulders. "Don't tell me. You're taking a course in Eastern religions."

Annie smiled and shook her head. "I bought a computer. That's what the guy who installed it said. It's karma if you can get a computer to work right, and karma if you can't."

"You bought yourself a computer?"

"For business. But it's turned out to be fun, too. The Internet, that kind of thing."

"Uh-huh. Who showed you how to use it? The pan…Hoffman?"

"I taught myself. Well, with a little help from Dawn."

"Really." Chase smiled. "Maybe you'll give me some pointers, sometime. I'm still all thumbs at anything more complicated than punching up a spreadsheet."

"Sure."

Their eyes met and held, and then Chase made a show of looking around at the room. "I'm really sorry about this. The accommodations, I mean. I never dreamed Tanaka would dump us out here."

"It's a bit much, I admit." Annie smiled. "But it's beautiful, too. Maybe this is what hotels are like, wherever it is he comes from.''

Chase grinned. ''He's from Dallas, babe—I mean, Annie. No, I suspect he figured we wanted to spend some private time together.''

Annie laughed. ''Cupid Tanaka, huh?''

''So it would seem.''

Again, silence closed around them. Annie sat down on the edge of the rocker.

''So,'' she said briskly, ''what're you going to do? Tear this place down, then build the retreat he wants from scratch?''

''Something like that.''

''I'll bet the final result will be spectacular.''

''Livable, anyway,'' Chase said, leaning back against the wall and folding his arms.

Annie smiled. ''Don't be modest, Chase. I know your work is well thought of. I see your name—the company's name—in the papers all the time. You've made it to the top.''

''So they tell me.'' His tone was flat, and so was his smile. ''To tell you the truth, the only thing I've noticed is that if that's where I am, it's not all it's cracked up to be.''

''Aren't you happy?''

''Are you?''

She stared at him. Why was she hesitating? Of course, she was happy. She had her house. Her business. Friends. Interests. A life that was comfortable, not one in which she was expected to play a role.

''Annie?''

She looked up. Chase had moved closer. She had only to reach out her hand, if she wanted to touch him.

''Are you happy?'' he asked softly.

She wanted to say that she was. To tell him what she'd just told herself, how her life had taken on shape and meaning.

Instead she found herself thinking how wonderful it had felt when they'd kissed. She wanted to tell him that though she'd made a good life for herself, there was an emptiness to it that she hadn't even been aware of until she'd gone into his arms on the dance floor.

But to say any of that would have been stupid. Chase was out of her life; she was out of his. That was the way they both wanted it. Hadn't they proved that a few hours ago, when they'd gone at each other, hammer and tong? Whatever she thought she'd felt since the wedding was an aberration.

"Yes," she said, with a smile that felt as if it were stretching her lips grotesquely, "certainly, I'm happy. I've never been more content in my life."

A curtain seemed to drop over Chase's eyes.

"Of course," he said politely. "You're happy, with your business and your fiancé."

Annie nodded. "And so are you."

"Yeah. And so am I."

They looked at each other and then Chase walked to the door.

"Well," he said briskly, "I think I'll go check out the refrigerator. There's bound to be enough food for a couple of meals there, or in the freezer."

"All the conveniences, hmm? Even way out here."

"Everybody's got a different definition of roughing it, I guess."

"So I see. If you'd told me we'd end up in a cabin on an island a million miles from civilization, I'd have imagined a one-room shack with a propane stove on the porch and an outhouse in the back."

Chase smiled. "Like the place we rented that summer after we got married. Remember? The outdoor sun-shower, the one-hole, no-flush john..."

Annie laughed. "How could I forget? We bought that

funny set of pots and pans that were supposed to fit inside each other, and those sleeping bags…"

"Boy, we were dumb," Chase said, laughing, too. "We must have spent, what, an hour or more trying to figure out how to zip the bags together because we sure as hell weren't going to sleep apart…" His words trailed off. "Damn," he said softly, "I haven't thought of that weekend in years."

Neither had Annie. Just remembering made her throat constrict.

"I—I think I'll go freshen up," she said. "And then—and then, maybe I'll take a walk, too. Just to clear my head. The flight was so long, and—and everything's been so hurried…"

"Yeah. Sure." Chase swallowed dryly. "You go on. Wash up, walk around, whatever. I'll check out the supplies."

"I'll come give you a hand in a few minutes." She gave a quick, brittle laugh. "I wish I had a hairbrush with me, or even some lipstick. I feel like a complete mess."

Chase thought of telling her the truth, that she didn't need a brush or cosmetics because she was already more beautiful than any woman he'd ever known.

Hell, he thought, and he pulled open the door, stepped out into the hall and strode away from temptation as fast as he could without breaking into a run.

CHAPTER EIGHT

CHASE GLANCED at his watch.

The Tanaka Hotel wasn't as perfect as it looked, he thought wryly. The freezer and the refrigerator had turned out to be surprisingly empty. Someone must have emptied things out, in preparation for the day the cabin would be demolished.

Still, there'd been some usable stuff in the pantry and he'd been able to come up with the makings for an improvised meal. Now, he was peeling potatoes and onions but his thoughts were elsewhere. Fifteen minutes had gone by since he'd heard the front door open, then shut as Annie had gone off on her walk.

Maybe he ought to go look for her.

Not that there was anything to worry about on this island. It was wild and isolated, but nothing here could harm her. There were no predatory animals, not of a size to be a problem. No bears, or coyotes...

Well, he supposed there probably were snakes, though the odds of Annie meeting up with one on the neatly kept gravel path that traversed the island were remote.

Spiders, though. There were definitely spiders—he'd seen some Class A specimens the first time Tanaka had brought him out here. They'd been the size of a child's fist but they were harmless.

It was just that Annie had a thing about creepy crawlies.

He'd learned that the winter he'd scored his first really big contract. On his way home after he'd landed the deal, he'd stopped to buy Annie a box of chocolates. There was a kid on the corner near the subway, selling single red roses; Chase had selected the prettiest one he could find and just then, he'd spied a travel agency across the street. There was a big, bright poster in the window.

Come To The Virgin Islands, it said.

Under the words was a picture of a smiling couple, holding hands under a fiery tropic sun and gazing lovingly into each other's eyes.

Chase hadn't hesitated. He'd trotted across the street and straight into the travel agency. A bored clerk had looked up from a scarred wooden desk.

"We're just about to close," she'd said. "Why don't you come back tomorrow and—"

"That poster. The one in the window." He'd been too young, and too flushed with excitement, to phrase his question with any subtlety. "How much would it cost for me to take my wife to the Virgin Islands?"

The clerk had looked at the rose in his hand and the chocolates under his arm, and maybe at him, too, all youthful, eager anticipation, cleaned up but wearing, as he had in those years, the chambray shirt, jeans and work boots he felt most comfortable in. She'd sighed, but something that might have been a smile had lit her tired face.

"Come and sit down," she'd told him. "I have a couple of packages here that just might interest you."

So he'd gone home to Annie with one perfect red rose, a box of candy, a contract that made all his, and her, sacrifices worthwhile—and reservations at a resort on Saint John Island.

Neither the poster nor the travel agent had exaggerated the beauty of the islands. To this moment, he remembered the shock of first seeing the pale sky, white sand and crystal-clear blue water.

"It's the color of your eyes," he'd whispered to Annie, as he held her in his arms that first night, in their wonderful hideaway overlooking the sea. Compared to this, the place had been a shack—but oh, how happy they'd been there!

Chase smiled to himself. That night had been what he'd come to think of as the Night of the Spider.

He and Annie had made love on the secluded terrace of their little house, cocooned in a black velvet bowl of night sky.

"I love you," he'd whispered, after she'd cried out in his arms and he'd spent himself in her silken heat. Annie had sighed and kissed him, and then they must have fallen asleep, there in the darkness with the soft whisper of the surf seeming to echo the beats of their hearts.

Sometime during the night, he'd awakened to a shriek.

"Annie?" he'd shouted, and though it had taken only a couple of seconds to race through the little house and find her in the bathroom, his adrenaline must have been pumping a mile a minute by the time he got there.

Annie, white-faced, was standing on the closed toilet, trembling with terror.

"Annie? Babe," he'd said, pulling her into his arms. "What is it? What happened?"

"There," she'd said, in a shaky whisper, and she'd pointed an equally shaky hand toward the tub.

"Where?" Chase had responded. All he saw was the porcelain tub, the bath mat, the gleaming white tile...

And the spider.

It was big, as spiders went. Definitely the large, economy size. And it was hairy. But it was only a spider, for God's sake, and in the time it had taken him to get from the bedroom to Annie, he'd died a thousand deaths, imagining what might have happened to her.

So he'd reacted the only way he could, scooping the spider up with a towel, marching to the back door, dumping the thing into the sandy grass and then returning to his wife, slapping his hands on his hips and asking her what in hell was wrong with her, to shriek like a banshee because she saw some little spider that was probably more afraid of her than she was of it.

Annie had slapped her hands on her hips, too, and matched his angry glower with one of her own.

"That's it," she'd said, "take the spider's side instead of mine!"

"Are you nuts? I'm not taking—"

"You just think how you'd feel, if you'd come in here, turned on the light and found that—that thing waiting for you!"

"It wasn't 'waiting' for you. It was minding its own business."

"It was waiting for me," Annie had insisted, "tapping its eight trillion feet and waiting for—"

Chase had snorted. "Eight trillion feet?" he'd said, choking back his laughter, and suddenly Annie had started to laugh, too, and the next thing he'd known, his wife was in his arms.

"I know it's dumb," she'd said, laughing and crying at the same time, "but I'm scared of spiders. Especially big ones."

"Big?" Chase had said, cupping her face in his hands and smiling into her eyes. "Hey, that thing was big enough to eat Chicago." He'd stopped smiling then, and told her what was in his heart, that his anger had only been a cover-up for the fear he'd felt when he'd heard her scream, that if he ever lost her—that if he ever lost her, his life would have no meaning...

"Hi."

He swung around. Annie was standing in the doorway, smiling, and only force of will kept him from going to her, taking her in his arms, and telling her that—telling her that...

"Sorry I took so long, but I lost track of the time."

Chase expelled his breath and looked away from her.

"Were you gone long?" he said, with a casualness he didn't feel. "I hadn't noticed."

"I walked through the woods." Annie came closer,

peered over his shoulder at the potatoes and onions and picked up a paring knife. "This is some beautiful place. I hate to think of it overrun with guys in three-piece suits."

Chase forced a smile to his lips. "They won't wear three-piece suits when they come here. They'll wear plaid Bermudas, black socks and wing tips."

Annie laughed, picked up a potato and began peeling it. "Same difference." They worked in silence for a few minutes, and then she spoke again. "I saw an interesting spider on the deck."

Chase looked up. "That's strange. I was just thinking about... Did you say, 'interesting'?"

"Uh-huh. It was..." She hesitated. "It was big. You know. Impressive."

"Impressive, huh? And you didn't scream? Seems to me I can remember the days when creepy crawlies weren't exactly your favorite creatures."

Annie blew an errant curl off her forehead. "They still aren't. But I took this course last year..."

"Why doesn't that surprise me?"

"It was about insects," she said with dignity.

That *did* surprise him. "You? Taking a course about bugs?"

Annie flushed. "Well, why not? I figured it was stupid to be scared of things with more than four legs. I decided, maybe if I understood them better, I might not jump at the sight of an ant."

"And?"

She shot him a sideways look and an embarrassed smile. "And, I learned to respect creepy crawlies like crazy. There are a heck of a lot more of them than there are of us, and they've been here longer."

Chase nodded. "I can almost hear the 'but' that's coming."

She laughed and reached for another potato. "But, I'm

still not in the mood for a one-to-one relationship with anything that needs eight legs to cross a room.''

Chase grinned. "It's nice to know that some things never change.''

Annie's smile dimmed. "Yes. Yes, it is.''

They worked in silence for a couple of minutes, Annie peeling potatoes, Chase slicing onions, and then Chase spoke.

"Annie?''

"Mmm?''

"I, ah, I wanted to tell you... I just hope you know...'' He swallowed. "I didn't mean what I said before. About you taking all those courses to take digs at me, I mean.''

Annie felt her cheeks redden. "That's okay.''

"No. It's not okay. I know you enjoy learning all that stuff. The poetry, the art... It's just not my thing. Heck, if I'd had to take anything but the minimum liberal arts stuff to get my engineering degree, I'd never have managed. I'd probably still be digging ditches for a living.''

Annie smiled and shook her head. "You know that's not true.'' She glanced at him, then put all her concentration on the potato she was peeling. "Anyway, maybe—maybe there was some truth to what you said. I mean, I didn't pick those things to study because I thought they'd, you know, be about stuff you wouldn't enjoy. I do like poetry, and art, and all the rest.'' She bent her head so that her hair fell around her face, shielding it from his view. "But I have to admit, when you looked puzzled about some eighteenth century poet, well, it made me feel good.'' She looked up suddenly, her eyes bright and shiny. "Not because I felt smarter or anything but because—because it was a way of proving that I could hold my own, you know? That even though I was only a housewife, that didn't mean I was—''

"*Only* a housewife?''

Annie shrugged as she dumped the potato on the counter and reached for another.

"That's what I was."

"Only a housewife," he said, and laughed. "That's a hell of a description for the woman who kept our home running smoothly, who raised our child, who entertained all the clowns I had to butter up while I was trying to get Cooper Construction moving."

"I guess I wasted an awful lot of time in self-pity."

"That's not what I meant. If anybody wasted time, babe, it was me. I should have told you how proud I was of all the things you did. But I was too busy patting myself on the back, congratulating myself for building Cooper Construction into something bigger than my father had ever dreamed. Something that would…"

Something that would make you proud of me, he'd almost said, but he stopped himself just in time. It was too late to talk about that now.

"Well, what's the difference?" he said briskly. "It's all water under the bridge." He concentrated on slicing the onions, and then he cleared his throat. "At least now I know that you didn't take all those classes just to get away from me."

"You weren't home often enough for me to worry about getting away from you," Annie said, a little stiffly.

"You could have had your degree by now," he said, wisely deciding it was the better part of valor to avoid a minefield than to attempt to cross it. "If you'd taken a concentration in one area, I mean."

"I don't need it." Annie peeled the last potato, put down her knife and wiped her hands on a towel. "All those horticulture courses paid off." A note of pride crept into her voice. "Flowers by Annie is a success, Chase. I've had to hire more people, and I'm thinking of maybe trying my hand at landscape design."

"That's wonderful."

"The truth is, I don't think I ever really wanted a degree. The thought of taking a bunch of formal classes didn't have any appeal. I just figured, well, I'd improve myself a little. Learn some stuff. You know.''

"You didn't need improving," Chase said. He knew he sounded angry, but he couldn't help it. The only thing he didn't know was whether he was angry at Annie or himself. Improve herself? His Annie?

"I did. I just had this high school education…''

Chase dropped his paring knife, clasped her shoulders and turned her to face him.

"You were the valedictorian of your graduating class, dammit! The only reason you didn't go to college was because we got married, right after you graduated high school.''

"I know. But—''

"We talked about it, remember? We tried to figure out if we could both go to college and still get married, and we decided we'd never be able to afford that.'' His mouth twisted. "So I went. You didn't. You took those miserable jobs, flipping hamburgers—''

"First, I flipped fish filets," Annie said with a shaky smile. "And then french fries. Hamburgers were a step up.''

"Dammit, Annie, you gave up what you could have had, for me. Don't you think I know it?''

"I gave up nothing. I wanted to do it.''

"Whatever we had—whatever I have, today—I owe to you.''

"You don't owe me anything, Chase. You never did. Don't you understand?'' Annie took a deep breath. "I didn't want a college degree half as much as I wanted to marry you.''

"Yes.'' Chase's voice roughened. His hands slid up her throat and he buried them in her hair as he tilted her face to his. "That was all I could think of, too. Marrying you. Making you mine. So I did the selfish thing.''

"You didn't!''

"I did, dammit!" His eyes searched her face, his gaze brushing her mouth before lifting again. "I let you give up your hopes and dreams so that I could have *my* dream."

"It was important to you. Becoming an engineer, making a success of yourself...."

"My dream was to have you. Only you. And, once I did, to give you the things you'd missed out on when we first got married, because you'd had to make so many sacrifices."

"They weren't sacrifices," Annie said, as the tears rose in her eyes. "I loved you, Chase. I wanted to help you succeed."

"And I only wanted to make you proud of me."

They fell silent.

If only I'd known, Annie thought...

If only I'd understood, Chase thought...

Was it too late? he wondered. Could you turn back the years? Could that be something this beautiful, confident woman in his arms might even want to do? She'd turned into someone else, his Annie, a stranger with a life of her own.

Was it too late? Annie wondered. Was it possible to roll back time? They were two different people now, she and this handsome, wonderful man who had once been her husband. He had moved into a high-powered world that was eons removed from her quiet country life.

And then, there was Janet Pendleton. The woman Chase was engaged to marry. The woman he loved.

Tears stung Annie's eyes. What an idiot she was! How could she have forgotten? They'd moved on, the both of them, and Chase had found someone to replace her, in his heart and in his life.

She swallowed hard. Chase was looking at her so strangely. Oh, how tempting it was to let herself believe, just for an instant, for a heartbeat, that he still loved her. But she knew that he didn't. What she saw in his eyes was regret for the pain they'd caused each other, and compassion—but not love.

Not anymore.

"Annie." His voice was soft, almost tender. "Annie," he said, "I'm so sorry."

"Don't be," she said quickly. Compassion was one thing, but pity was another. Pity was the last thing she wanted from Chase. "There's no point. It's spilt milk, you know?" It wasn't easy, but she smiled. "And nobody should ever waste tears over spilt milk."

"It's not that simple."

"But it is." Annie spoke quickly, rushing her words, hurrying to keep him from offering her another apology. What she wanted from him, needed with all her heart, was something she wouldn't think about, wouldn't admit to thinking about, even to herself. "It's very simple," she said, with another little smile. "It looks as if us spending time together was a good idea, after all."

"Yes. I agree."

"If we hadn't, we'd never have gotten this chance to— to make peace with the past."

"Can you forgive me, for hurting you?"

"Of course." It was easier to smile, now that she knew it was the only choice left to her. "As long as you can forgive me, too, because I wasn't blameless. And then, we get on with our lives. With—with our new relationships."

The tiny flame of hope in Chase's heart flickered and died.

"Milton Hoffman." His voice was toneless.

"And your Janet Pendleton. Yes."

Chase could see the radiance in Annie's smile. It lit her eyes. Funny, but a couple of minutes ago, he'd foolishly let himself think the light in her eyes was for him.

"We're very fortunate people," she said softly. "Some never find love once but we—we found it twice."

Chase stared at the stranger who had once been his wife.

He thought of pulling her into his embrace and kissing her until that smile for Milton Hoffman was erased from her lips. He thought of kissing her until all she could think of was him.

But, in the end, he did what he knew was right.

"That's true," he said, touching his hand to her hair, because he couldn't keep from doing it. He kept the touch light, though, so that it matched his smile. "We're very lucky, the both of us."

He let go of her, turned away and reached blindly for a peeled onion. Annie watched, her heart breaking, as he sliced into it. She felt the sting of tears again and she scrubbed the back of her hand furiously over her eyes.

"Damned onions," she said, with a choked laugh. "You're slicing them but I'm suffering. Isn't that silly?"

Chase, lost in his own thoughts, nodded. "Yeah."

"So," she said briskly, "what are we having for supper, anyway? Onion and potato pie?"

Somehow, he forced his attention back to the kitchen, and the mundane chores they were performing. He smiled, put down the knife, wiped his hands on the towel and opened the door of the cabinet just over the sink.

"*Voilà,*" he said, whipping around to face Annie and holding out a small, round can as if he were a sommelier presenting her with a bottle of fine wine.

"Tuna? That's it? That's all you could find in this kitchen?"

"There's another half a dozen, right on the pantry shelf."

"I don't believe it. All this, and Mr. Tanaka eats canned tuna?"

"I don't think sushi would have much of a shelf life." Chase grinned. "Less than thrilling, huh?"

"You're sure there isn't anything else?"

"A couple of cans of evaporated milk. A bottle of corn oil. Some soup—"

"Cream of mushroom?" she asked hopefully.

"Yeah. I think so."

Annie sighed. "Get me the soup and the evaporated milk, Cooper. Then step aside and let an expert get to work."

"You mean, you can do something clever with this stuff?"

"I can try."

Chase grinned as he plucked the other cans from the shelves, opened them and put them on the counter.

"I should have known. I'd almost forgotten how inventive you were with Spam, the first couple of years after we were married."

"Inventive?" Annie said, as she drained the tuna into the sink.

"Sure. Seems to me I can remember Spam casserole, sautéed Spam, grilled Spam…"

"A can of Spam, a couple of onions and some potatoes."

"Which recipe was that?"

"All of them," Annie said, laughing. She dug around in the shelves beneath the stove, took out a skillet and put it on a burner. "I kept giving the same concoction different names, to keep us from going whacko."

"Now she tells me. So, what's on the menu tonight?"

"How about Tuna Surprise?"

"What's the Surprise?"

"Managing to turn this mess into something edible," Annie said, and laughed. "Here. Start dicing the potatoes. I'll heat up some oil and slice the rest of the onions."

"Suppose you supervise while I do the work. It's my fault we're stuck out here, in the tail end of nowhere, so it's only fair I get to make dinner."

"Let's face it, Cooper. We're trapped in a place most people would kill for, so stop apologizing and start dicing."

Annie splashed some oil into the skillet, then leaned past Chase and placed it on the burner. Her breast brushed lightly across his arm, and he felt himself harden like stone. Desire, an overpowering need for her, for Annie, the mother of his child and the passion of his youth, surged through his blood, pumping hard and hot, and pooled low in his belly.

He jerked away. As he did, his elbow knocked against the knife and it clattered to the floor.

"Damn," he said, as if it mattered, as if anything mattered but wanting to take his wife in his arms.

Milton Hoffman's face, the face of the man she loved, rose before him as if it were an apparition. Hoffman, who couldn't love Annie as much as he did because, dammit, he *did* love her. Not again, but still. He'd never stopped loving her, and it was time to admit it.

"Annie," he said in a low voice.

Annie looked up. The temperature in the kitchen felt as if it had gone up ten degrees.

The message was there, in Chase's eyes. Her heart leaped in her chest. She told herself not to be a fool. What was happening here wasn't real. Reality was the papers that had legally severed their marriage. It was a woman named Janet, waiting for Chase back in New York.

On the other hand, hadn't some philosopher said reality was what you made of it?

"Annie?" Chase whispered. He reached toward her and she swayed forward, her eyes half-closed...

The smell of burning oil filled the kitchen.

Annie swung around, grabbed the skillet and dumped it into the sink.

"We'll have to start over," she said, with a shaky laugh. She looked at Chase. "With the cooking, I mean."

Chase nodded. Then they turned away from each other and made a show of being busy.

Annie fried more onions, parboiled the diced potatoes and put together a tuna casserole.

Chase made the coffee and opened a package of crackers and a box of cookies.

When everything was ready, they carried their meal into the living room, arranged it on the low, lacquered table and sat, cross-legged, on the black-and-white cushions. They ate in silence, as politely and impersonally as if they were strangers who'd been asked to share a table in a crowded coffee shop.

Afterward, they cleaned up together. Then Annie took a magazine from a stack she'd found in the kitchen.

Chase said he'd take another walk.

Annie said she'd read.

But she didn't. The black-and-white cushions didn't offer much in the way of comfort. Besides, her thoughts kept straying away from the magazine, to the hours looming ahead. There was an entire night to get through. She and Chase, sharing this cabin. And that bedroom.

How would she manage?

She jumped when Chase stepped into the living room.

"Sorry," he said. "I didn't meant to startle you."

"That's okay." She folded her hands over the closed magazine, her fingers knotted tightly together. "I was thinking," she said carefully. "I mean, it occurred to me…"

"What?"

Annie took a breath.

"Well, there is one advantage to being here by ourselves."

Chase looked at her. His eyes were burning like coals. "There's a definite advantage."

There was no mistaking his meaning. Annie felt her heart swell, as if it were a balloon, until it seemed to fill her chest.

"What I mean," she said, speaking with care, "is that there's no one here to know what our arrangements are. We wouldn't have to explain anything…" Her words stuttered to a halt. "Don't look at me that way," she whispered.

Chase shut the door, his eyes locked on hers. "Do you want to make love?"

The directness of the question stole her breath away. She shook her head. "No! I didn't say—"

"I want you, Annie."

His voice was rough and his face seemed to have taken on an angularity, but she knew what she was really seeing was desire. She knew, because this was how he'd looked, years ago, when their need for each other had been an unquenchable thirst. They'd be talking, or just sitting and reading or watching TV, and suddenly she'd feel a stillness in the air. And she'd look up, and Chase would be watching her, and what she saw in his eyes would make her breasts swell so that she'd feel the scrape of her bra against her nipples, feel the dampness bloom between her thighs...

"Babe," he said thickly, "I want you so much I can't think straight."

It seemed to take forever before she could draw enough strength to answer.

"We can't," she said, in a voice that sounded like a stranger's.

"Why? We're adults. Who is it going to hurt, if we do what we both want to do?"

Me, she'd thought, me, Chase, because if I go to bed with you, I'll be forced to admit the truth to myself, that I still—that I still—

"No," she said, her voice rising in a cry that seemed to tremble in the air between them. "No," she repeated, and then, because it was the only safe thing she could think of, she took another breath and lied again, the same way she had when they'd been preparing dinner. "It wouldn't be fair to—to Milton."

"Milton." The name was like an obscenity on Chase's lips.

"That's right. Milton. I'm engaged, and so are you. What I meant about nobody knowing what we do tonight, nobody asking questions, was that there's no reason for us to share the bedroom."

"I see."

She waited for him to say something else, but he didn't.

"Surely, in this entire house, there's another—"

"No."

"No?"

"Look around you, dammit. There's no sofa. There's not even a chair, except for the rocker in the bedroom."

Annie stared at him, wondering why he sounded so angry.

"Well," she said, looking up at the ceiling, "what's on the second—"

"Did you see a staircase?"

"Well—well, no. No, I didn't. But—"

"That's because there aren't any rooms above us. There's just a storage loft, full of boxes. And bats."

"Bats?" Annie said, with a faint shudder.

"Bats," Chase repeated coldly, furious at her, at himself, at Dawn, at Kichiro Tanaka and the city of Seattle and the Fates and whoever, whatever, had put him into this impossible situation. His lips drew back from his teeth. "The bats eat the spiders. The *impressive* ones, the size of dinner plates."

"In other words, you're telling me we'll have to make the best of things."

"A brilliant deduction."

Annie tossed aside the magazine and shot to her feet. "Listen, Cooper, don't be so high-and-mighty! I'm not the one who got us stuck out here, and don't you forget it."

"No," he snarled, "I won't forget it. If you'd put your foot down in the first place, if you'd told our daughter, flat out, that she couldn't marry Nick—"

"That's it," Annie said, stalking past him.

"Don't you walk out on me, lady."

"I'm going to find something else to read," she snapped, over her shoulder. "Even the label on a can of tuna would be better than trying to have a conversation with you."

"You're right," Chase snapped back, shouldering past her. "I might even take my chances and try swimming to the mainland. Anything would be an improvement over an evening spent in your company!"

Annie sat on the rocker in the bedroom. She looked at her watch.

Chase had been gone a long time. Surely he hadn't really meant that. He wouldn't have really tried to swim the cold, choppy water...

The bedroom door opened. She looked up and saw Chase.

"Sorry," he said briskly. "I should have knocked."

"That's all right. I, uh, I was just sitting here and—and thinking."

"It's been a long day. I don't know about you, but I'd just as soon turn in and get some sleep."

"That's what I was thinking about. Our sleeping arrangements. We can share the room."

"We *are* sharing it," he said coldly. "I thought I'd made that clear. There isn't a hell of a lot of choice."

"You did. And I—I agree. It's not a problem," Annie said, rushing her words together. "The bed's the size of a football field. I'll take the right side. You can have... What are you doing?"

Chase was yanking open closet doors. "There've got to be linens here somewhere... Here we go." He reached inside, took out an armful of bedding, tossed a blanket to Annie and then draped another over the rocker.

"You're going to sleep in the chair?"

"That's right." He sat down, tucked a pillow behind his

head and stretched out his legs. "I wouldn't want to sully your reputation."

"Chase, please. I never meant—"

He reached behind him, hit the switch on the wall and the room was plunged into darkness. Annie closed her eyes. Tears seeped out from beneath her lashes.

"Chase?" she whispered, after a long time.

"What?"

"Nothing," she said, and rolled onto her side.

I love you, Chase, she thought, because there was no harm in saying it now, to herself, even as she wondered how she was going to get through the endless night.

"Good night, Annie," Chase said, and he shifted uneasily, trying to find a comfortable position even though he knew there was no such thing, not in a wooden rocker, not with the granddaddy of all headaches in permanent residence behind his temples—and not with the only woman he would ever love sleeping a hand's span away.

He could smell her perfumed scent, hear the softness of her breathing. All he had to do was reach out and he'd be able to touch her warm, silken skin.

How in hell was he ever going to get through the night?

CHAPTER NINE

CHASE CAME AWAKE with a start. The room was inky black; he could hear the light patter of rain against the roof.

Where was he? Not at home, that was for sure.

Memory came back in a rush. The crazy flight to Seattle. The motorboat, speeding across the water. The island. The cabin. The bedroom...

This bedroom.

And Annie. Annie, asleep in a bed inches from where he sat.

Don't think about that. About Annie. Think about something else. Anything else.

Chase grimaced. He could think about how it would be a miracle if he ever managed to stand upright again. Now, that was a topic worth considering.

Gingerly, hands clasping the arms of the wooden rocker, he eased himself up so that his back was straight. Not that caution would make much difference. His spine felt as brittle as china, and it ached like hell. The rest of him didn't feel much better.

Whistler's Mother be damned, he thought grimly. Wooden rocking chairs were not made for comfort, or for sleeping.

It was chilly in here, too. It didn't help that the blanket he'd draped over himself was somewhere on the floor. Wincing, he bent down and felt around until he found it. Then he dragged it up to his neck and told himself that this night couldn't last forever.

What time was it, anyway? Chase raised his arm and peered at the place on his wrist where he knew his watch ought to be. The lighted dial was faint; he had to squint to

333

see it clearly. It had to be, what? Three, maybe four in the morning?

Bloody hell! It was eleven twenty-five. He'd been asleep, if you could call it that, all of two hours.

Wearily he closed his eyes, started to put his head back and remembered, just in time, that if he did, he'd whack his skull against the wall. He'd done it a couple of times already. For all he knew, that was what had awakened him in the first place.

Eleven twenty-five. Unbelievable! If he were in Seattle right now, he'd be wide-awake. He'd be sitting up in a nice, soft bed, with a pillow tucked between him and the head-board, and he'd be reading. Or watching TV. Making notes for the next day's meetings. Whatever. The one sure thing was that he wouldn't be sitting in the most uncomfortable chair man had ever invented, with no place to rest his head. Or his legs. As for his butt…men, he'd decided, were not born with enough padding where it counted.

Another couple of hours, he'd end up a chiropractor's dream.

Dammit, who was he kidding? Another couple of minutes, he'd end up out of his skull. Forget the chair, and the discomfort of trying to sleep in it. Forget the night chill that had seeped into the room. Forget the soft whisper of the rain.

None of that was the reason he was awake.

The reason, plain and simple, was Annie.

How was he supposed to get through the night trapped in this room with her?

Chase told himself he ought to be ashamed for his lecherous thoughts. Not that they were his fault. It was Annie who was to blame.

Damn. Oh damn. Why couldn't he admit the truth? There was no way to lay this off on Annie. She hadn't planted these pictures in his head. She couldn't possibly know he was sitting here with an aching back and a sizzling libido.

She was sound asleep. He could tell by the soft, steady whisper of her breath. If he'd been having raunchy dreams—and he had—it was nobody's fault but his own.

One dream, in particular, had been very real.

It had started with him sitting right here, in this chair, when he'd heard Annie sigh his name.

Chase, she'd said, and suddenly moonlight had streamed into the room, casting an ivory glow on the bed.

Annie had sat up and opened her arms to him.

Chase, she'd whispered, *why are you sitting over there? Come to bed, darling, with me, where you belong.*

Chase rubbed his hands over his eyes.

"Give us a break, Cooper," he muttered. "What are you, a pimply-faced kid?"

A grown man could share a room with a woman for the night without coming unglued, especially when she was the very woman he'd divorced five long years ago. He could get through twenty-four hours without letting himself think he'd fallen for her all over again because the truth was, he hadn't.

Of course he hadn't.

It was just the pressure of the last few days, that was all. Things were catching up. The wedding. Dawn's running away. His emotional and physical exhaustion. Taken all together, it was a prescription for disaster.

Then, too, his ex was still a very attractive woman. His type of woman, which was only logical considering that he'd been married to her, once upon a time. But he'd also left her, or they'd left each other, to be exact, and for very good reasons.

Chase sat back carefully in the rocker.

So, okay, she could still push all the right buttons. And yeah, his stupid male hormones were still programmed to make his equally stupid male anatomy straighten up and salute. That didn't mean he had to sit here having thoughts that were beginning to make going out into the rain for an impromptu shower seem like a pretty good idea.

He had to concentrate on the reality of the situation. Annie was in love with another man, and if he wasn't actually feeling the same way about Janet, well, he could. He would. It was just a matter of letting it happen. And then the story of Annie and Chase would be over, once and for all.

Dawn was a big girl now. She'd understand that life wasn't a fairy tale that ended with the words, "And they lived happily ever after."

Chase sighed. He felt better already. There'd be no more dreams tonight. Why, even if that last silly dream were to come true, if Annie were to suddenly stir and whisper his name, he wouldn't—

"Chase?"

Annie's voice, as soft and sweet as an early June morning, turned that firm conviction into an instant lie.

"Chase? Are you awake?"

Was he awake? He couldn't imagine why she had to ask. Couldn't she hear the thunder of his heart?

He heard the rustle of the bed linens as she turned toward him. Her face was a pale, perfect oval; her eyes were wide and gleaming. Her hair curled around her face and neck, falling in a gentle curve to her shoulder.

How he'd always loved to kiss her there, in the satin-softness of that curve.

Chase cleared his throat. "Hi," he said. "Sorry if I woke you."

Annie shook her head. "You didn't. Not really. I had a silly dream—"

She broke off in the middle of what she'd been about to say, grateful for the lack of light in the room because it meant Chase couldn't see the blush she knew was spreading over her face. It was bad enough she'd had the dream in the first place. She certainly wasn't going to describe it to him.

Why would any woman in her right mind tell her ex-husband about an erotic dream—especially when she, and he, had been its stars?

"What dream?"

"I don't remember."

"But you just said—"

"What's that I hear? Rain?"

Annie sat up against the pillows and drew the blanket up to her chin. Her arms and shoulders were bare. Chase's heart lifted into his throat. Was she naked under that blanket?

"Yes," he said in a voice that sounded more like a croak but hey, a man had to be happy for what he could manage and right now, managing even that much was a miracle.

Annie sighed. "Mmm. It sounds wonderful, doesn't it? It makes it seem so cozy in here."

Cozy? Chase almost groaned. "Yeah," he said, "oh, yeah, cozy's the word."

"What time is it, anyway? Is it close to morning? I could make us some coffee."

"It's almost twelve."

"Twelve? How could that be? It's so dark..." Annie gave an incredulous laugh. "Twelve at *night*? You're joking."

"I wish I were."

Annie's head drooped. There was still an entire night, stretching ahead. Hours and hours of lying here, knowing she had only to reach out her hand to touch the man who'd once been her husband.

No. This was impossible. She could never survive until morning...

Of course she could. She wasn't foolish enough to still think herself in love with Chase. That nonsense had faded away while she'd slept. What she felt was lust, pure and simple. Hey, she could admit it. This was the end of one century and the start of another. Women were allowed to have sexual feelings. They were encouraged to have them, according to the talk shows on TV and the supermarket tabloids.

And she had them. Oh, yes, she did. Chase had always been—probably always would be—the kind of man who could turn her on with a look, but wanting sex with a man didn't necessarily have anything to do with loving him, despite what she'd told Chase when they'd talked about Dawn and Nick, just yesterday.

The truth was, sex was all a matter of hormones and libido. Love was a separate thing entirely. Everybody said so, even Milton, who'd earnestly assured her that it was okay if she didn't feel anything for him physically. They could still have a good life together, he'd said.

Maybe he was right.

"Annie?"

She blinked and lifted her head. Her eyes had grown accustomed to the lack of light in the bedroom. She could see Chase clearly now, sitting in the rocker and watching her.

"What are you thinking?"

"Nothing," she said quickly, "only that—that it's amazing if Mr. Tanaka ever manages to get any sleep in this bed. The mattress feels as if it's stuffed with steel."

Chase laughed. "Welcome to the Chamber of Horrors. Did President Kennedy really sit in one of these godawful chairs to ease the pain in his back?"

"I don't think he tried to substitute a rocker for a bed," Annie said, smiling.

"Well, that's why he got to be president. The guy was smart."

Annie laughed. It was such a light, easy sound that it made Chase smile. There was a time they'd laughed a lot together. Not over anything special. Just something one would see or hear and say to the other, or something that would happen when they were together.

It felt good, making her laugh again. Everything about today had felt good, even the moments they'd been going at each other. An argument with Annie was better than an evening of smiles from any other woman, especially if the argument ended, as it so often had, in the old days, with her in his arms...in his arms, and wanting him as much as he wanted her.

What would she do, if he went to her now? If he shucked off his clothes, pulled back the blankets and got into the bed with her? He knew just how she would smell, like a blend of perfume and honey and cream. And how she would feel, the heat of her breasts and belly, the coolness of her hands and feet.

He smiled, remembering. Lord, she had the iciest hands and feet in the world!

It was a game they'd often played, on chilly nights like this. They'd get into bed, he'd take her in his arms and she'd wrap one leg around his, dance her toes over his calf while she slid her hand down his chest and he'd say, very sternly, Annie, you stop that right now, and she'd ask why and he'd say because she was positively frigid.

"Frigid?" she'd say, indignantly.

"Frigid," he'd insist, and then he'd roll her onto her back and whisper, "but I know a way to fix that..."

Chase shot to his feet.

"Here," he said gruffly, dumping the blanket he'd been using on Annie's bed. "Take this. It's gotten a little chilly in here."

"I'm fine. Anyway, I can't take your blanket."

"Sure you can."

"But what'll you use?"

A snowbank, if he could find one. What he needed was not to warm up but to chill down.

"I'm, ah, I'm not tired."

"Not tired? Chase, that's impossible. We've had an awful day. An endless day—"

"You've got that right."

"And you've only had, what, two hours sleep? That's not enough."

"Yeah, well, maybe I'm overwound. Or maybe it's just that I'm not in the mood to turn into a human pretzel."

"You're right." Annie reached for his discarded blanket. In one quick motion, she dropped her own blanket, wrapped his around her shoulders, and rose from the bed. Chase had a glimpse of ivory-colored skin and nothing more. "So you take the bed. I'll take the chair."

"Don't be ridiculous."

"I'm smaller than you are."

She was. Definitely. Smaller, and fragile. Wonderfully fragile. Make that feminine. The top of her head barely brushed his chin. If he dipped his head, he could rub his chin against her hair. Her soft, shiny hair.

"I can tuck my legs up under me and I'll be perfectly comfortable, Chase. You'll see. Come on. Switch places with me."

Switch places? Climb into the bed, still warm from her body? Put his head on the pillow, still fragrant with her scent? He shook his head and moved back, until the seat of the rocker dug into the backs of his legs.

"No."

"Honestly, you're such a chauvinist! This is hardly a time to worry about being a gentleman."

He had to fight hard to keep from laughing. Or groaning. One or the other, or maybe both. Is that what she thought this was all about? Him trying to be a gentleman? He wondered what she'd think if she knew the real direction of his thoughts, that it was all he could do to keep from picking her up, tossing her onto the bed and tearing away that blanket so he could see if she was wearing anything under it.

"That's it," he said.

"What's it?"

Chase cupped Annie's shoulders, trying not to think

about the feel of her under his hands, and moved her gently but firmly out of his way.

"Chase?" Her voice rang with bewilderment as he opened the door. "Where are you going?"

To hell in a handbasket, he thought.

"To heat up some coffee," he said. "Go back to sleep, Annie. I'll see you in the morning."

He slipped out of the room, shut the door after him and leaned back against it.

The torture of the chair was one thing. A man could deal with that. But the torture of being so close to Annie was something else.

Saints willingly martyred themselves, not men.

Annie stared at the door as it swung shut. Then she sighed and sank down on the edge of the bed.

"Stupid man," she muttered. "Let him suffer, if he wants."

It was ridiculous of him to have turned down her offer.

"Brrr," she said, and burrowed under the covers.

Of course, he'd been uncomfortable in that chair. Chase was six foot two; he'd weighed 190 pounds for as long as she could remember, all of it muscle. Hard muscle.

There was no denying that he'd always been a handsome man.

Beautiful, she'd called him once, after they were first married. They'd been lying in each other's arms after a long, lazy afternoon of love, and suddenly she'd risen up on her elbows, gazed down at him and smiled.

"What?" he'd said, and she'd said she'd never thought about it before, but he was beautiful.

"Goofball," Chase had said, laughing. "Men can't be 'beautiful.'"

"Why can't they?" she'd said, in a perfectly reasonable tone, and then, in that same tone, she'd gone on to list all his attributes, and to kiss them all, too. His nose. His mouth. His chin. His broad shoulders. His lightly furred chest. His flat abdomen and belly...

"Annie," he'd said, in a choked whisper, and seconds later he'd hauled her up his body, into his arms and taken her into the star-shot darkness with him again.

"Dammit!"

Annie flung out her arms and stared up at the skylight, where the light rain danced gently against the glass. What was wrong with her tonight? First the dream that had left her aching and unfulfilled. And now this ridiculous, pointless memory.

"You're being a ninny," she said out loud.

She wasn't in love with Chase; hadn't she already admitted that? As for the sex... Okay. So sex with him had always been good.

Until he'd ruined it, by never coming home to her.

Until she'd ruined it, by treating him so coldly.

Annie threw her arm across her eyes.

All right. So she wasn't as blameless as she liked to think. But Chase had hurt her so badly. Nothing had prepared her for the pain of watching him grow out of her life, or of finding him with his secretary...

Or for the pain of losing him.

The truth was that she'd never stopped wanting him. Her throat tightened. Never. Not then. Not all the years since. If he'd taken her in his arms again tonight, if he'd kissed her, stroked his hand over her skin...

The door banged open. Annie grabbed for the blanket and sat up, clutching it to her chin. Chase stood framed in the doorway. Light streamed down the hall, illuminating his face and body with shimmering rays of gold.

"Annie."

His voice was soft and husky. The sound of it sent her heartbeat racing. Say something, she told herself, but her throat felt paralyzed.

"Annie." He stepped into the room, his eyes locked on

hers. "I lied," he said. "It isn't the chair that kept me from sleeping. It's you."

It was a moment for a flippant remark. A little humor, a little sarcasm; something along the lines of, "Really? Well, it's good to know I'm giving you a bad time."

But she didn't want to toss him a fast one-liner.

She wanted what he wanted. Why keep up the pretense any longer?

They were two adults, alone on an island that might just as easily have been spinning in the dark reaches of space instead of being just off the Washington coast. Going into Chase's arms, loving him just for tonight, would hurt no one.

He has a fiancée, a voice inside her whispered. *He belongs to another woman now.*

"Annie? I want to make love to you. I *need* to make love to you. Tell me to go away, babe, and I will, if that's what you really want, but I don't think it is. I think you want to come into my arms and taste my kisses. I think you want us to hold each other, the way we used to."

The blanket fell from Annie's hands. She gave a little sob and her arms opened wide.

Chase whispered her name, pulled off his clothes and went to her.

He kissed her mouth, and her throat. He kissed the soft skin behind her ear and buried his face in that sweet curve of neck and shoulder that felt like warm silk.

She'd been wearing something under the blanket, after all. A bra and panties, just plain white cotton, but he thought he'd never seen anything as sexy in his life. His hands had never trembled more than they did as he unfastened the bra and slid the panties down Annie's long legs.

"My beautiful Annie," he murmured, when she lay naked in his arms.

"I'm not," she said, with a little catch in her throat. "I'm older. Everything's starting to sag."

Her breath caught as Chase bent and kissed the slope of her breast.

"You're perfect," he whispered, his breath warm against her flesh. "More beautiful than before."

His hands cupped her breasts; he bent his head and licked her nipples. It was the truth. She'd gone from being a lovely girl to being a beautiful woman. Her body was classic in its femininity, lushly curved and warm with desire beneath his hands and his mouth. Annie smelled like rosebuds and warm honey, and she tasted like the nectar of the gods.

She was a feast for a man who'd been starving for five long, lonely years.

"Chase," she whispered, when he kissed his way down her belly. Her voice broke as he parted her thighs. "Chase," she said again.

He looked up at her, his eyes dark and fierce. "I never forgot," he said. "The smell of you. The heat." His hands clasped her thighs. Slowly he lowered his head. "The taste."

Annie cried out as his mouth found her. It had been so long. Five years of lonely nights and empty days, of wanting Chase and never admitting it, of dreaming of him, of this, and then denying the dreams in the morning.

I love you, she thought fiercely, Chase, my husband, my beloved, I adore you. How could I have ever forgotten that?

He kissed her again and she shattered against the kiss, tumbling through the darkness of the night, and just before she fell to earth he rose up over her and thrust into her body with one deep, hard stroke.

"Chase," she cried, and this time, when she came, he was with her, holding her tightly in his arms as they made the breathless free fall through space together.

The last thing she saw, just before she fell asleep in his arms, was the crescent moon, framed overhead in the skylight, as the clouds parted and the gentle rain ceased.

*   *   *

She awakened during the night, to the soft brush of Chase's mouth against her nape.

It was as if the years had fallen away. How many times had she come awake to his kisses, and to his touch?

"I never stopped thinking about you," he whispered.

I never stopped loving you, was what he wanted to say, but he wanted to look into her eyes when he did, to read her answer there.

So he spoke to her with his body instead, burying himself in her heat, one hand on her breast and the other low across her belly, moving within her, matching his rhythm to hers, until he groaned and she cried out. Then he turned her into his embrace, kissed her and slipped inside her again, still hard, still wanting her, and this time when she came, she wept.

"Did I hurt you?" he said softly, and for an instant she almost told him that the pain would come in the morning, when the sun rose and the night ended, and all of this would be nothing more substantial than a dream.

But that would be wrong. This *was* a dream, and she knew it. So she smiled against his mouth and said no, he hadn't hurt her, and then she sighed and put her head on his shoulder.

"Annie?"

"Mmm?"

"I've been thinking." He kissed her, and she could feel the smile on his lips. "We ought to try out that tub."

"Mmm," she said again. She yawned lazily. "First thing in the morning..."

And she drifted off to sleep.

Sunlight woke them—sunlight, and the hornet buzz of the motorboat.

Annie jumped up in bed, heart pounding.

"What...?"

Chase was already pulling on his chinos and zipping up his fly.

"It's okay, babe," he said. "I'll take care of things."

She nodded, put her hands to her face and pushed back her hair. Chase started for the door, hesitated, and came back.

"Annie," he said, and when she looked up, he bent to her and kissed her. "It was a wonderful night," he said softly.

She nodded. "Yes. It was."

For a minute, she thought he was going to say something more but then he turned away and snagged his shirt from the chair just as a knock sounded at the front door.

"Okay, okay," he yelled, "hold your horses. I'm coming." He swung back one last time, just before he opened the door. "Wonderful," he said. "And I'm never going to forget it."

Annie smiled, even though she could feel tears stinging her eyes.

Chase's message had been gallant, to the point and painfully clear.

It had been a wonderful night. But it was morning now, and what they'd shared was over.

CHAPTER TEN

ANNIE STARTED DOWN the steps of her sister's apartment building just as the skies opened up.

It had been raining, on and off, for most of the sultry August afternoon but half an hour ago the sky had cleared and so the cloudburst took her by surprise. She gave a startled yelp and darted back into the vestibule of the converted brownstone.

Wonderful, she thought, as fat raindrops pounded the hot pavement. Just what she needed. A steamy day, and now a hard rain. By the time she got to the subway entrance, she'd be not only drenched but boiled.

Annie looked over her shoulder. Should she ring the intercom bell? She could ask Laurel to buzz her in, go back upstairs and keep her sister company a while longer.

No, she thought, and sighed. That wouldn't be such a good idea. Laurel might have fallen asleep by now. She'd promised she was going to lie down and take a nap, right after Annie left. Heaven knew she looked as if she needed the rest.

Laurel was going through a bad time.

Hell. A bad time was putting it mildly.

Annie hadn't wanted to leave her, not even when it began to get late and it looked as if she might miss the last train for Stratham.

"You're sure you're okay?" she'd said to Laurel.

"I'm fine," Laurel had replied.

The sisters both knew it was a lie.

Laurel was not fine. She was pregnant and alone and desperately in love with a husband who'd maybe two-timed her or maybe hadn't, depending on whose story you believed. Either way, it broke Annie's heart to see her little sister looking so beautiful and feeling so sad.

"Men," Annie muttered with disgust.

Not a one of them was worth a penny. Well, her son-in-law was an exception. Annie's features softened. Nick was a sweetheart. But the rest of the male species was impossible.

She blew her curls away from her forehead. The vestibule was turning into a sauna. She'd have to make a run for it soon, even though she could still hear the rain beating down as if the heavenly floodgates had opened and Noah was giving the last call for the Ark.

Boy, it was really coming down. People always said it rained hard in the Pacific northwest, but the night she'd been there, the rain had been as soft as a lover's caress.

Annie frowned. What nonsense! She hadn't wasted a minute thinking about that awful night, and now it had popped into her head, wrapped in a bit of purple prose that would make any levelheaded female retch.

It was the rain that had done it. And spending the day with Laurel. What was the matter with the two of them? Were the Bennett sisters doomed to go through life behaving like idiots?

No way. Laurel would pull herself together, the same as she'd always done. As for her... Annie straightened her shoulders. She was not going to think about that night, or Chase. Why would she? She wasn't a masochist, and only a masochist would want to remember making a fool of herself, because that was what she'd done on that island.

Falling for her ex's lying, sexy charm, tumbling into his arms, inviting him into her bed and making it embarrassingly clear that she'd enjoyed having him there...so clear that he'd figured she'd be only too happy to offer a repeat performance.

Chase had phoned with that in mind several times since. She'd talked with him the first time, because she knew they'd had to agree on what to tell Dawn when she and Nick returned from Hawaii.

"What do you want to tell her?" Chase had asked, neatly dumping the problem into her lap.

"The truth," Annie had answered, "that you lied and I was dumb enough to go along with it—but that would probably be a mistake. So why don't we settle for something simple. Like, we spent the weekend together and it just didn't work out."

"We didn't spend the weekend together," Chase had said. "It was only one night. But it doesn't have to end there."

Apparently behaving like an idiot once didn't keep you from behaving like one all over again. Annie's heart had done those silly flip-flops that she hated and she'd waited, barely breathing, for him to say he loved her.

But he hadn't.

"I know you don't want to get involved again," he'd said in the same, reasonable tone a TV pitchman might have used selling used cars, "but you have to admit, that night was—it was memorable."

"Memorable," Annie had repeated calmly.

"Yes. And I'd like to see you again."

She could still remember how she'd felt, the pain and the rage twisting inside her so she hadn't been sure which she wanted to do first, cry her eyes out or kill him.

"I'll just bet you would," she'd said, with dignity, and then she'd hung up the phone, poured herself a double sherry and toasted the brilliance she'd shown on having removed Mr. Chase Cooper from her life five long years ago.

At least he'd been up-front about what he wanted. And talkative, especially compared to the silent act he'd put on that morning on the island. He hadn't said more than half a dozen words to her, after the guy had come to fetch them with the motorboat.

Not that she'd given him the chance to say much of anything. She'd done something foolish by sleeping with Chase but she wasn't stupid: that remark about what a wonderful night it had been wasn't anything but code for "Thanks for the roll in the hay, babe," and she knew it. The quick brush-off had almost broken her heart, but she'd sooner have died than let Chase know it. So she'd put on what she'd figured was a look of morning-after sophistication, as if one-night stands were part of her life, and ignored him until they reached the airport, where she'd smiled brightly, shaken his hand and said it had been a delightful evening and she hoped his meeting with Mr. Tanaka went well.

Then she'd marched off, bought herself a ticket back to Connecticut, and done her weeping alone in the back of a nearly empty jet throughout the long flight home.

Sex, that was all Chase had wanted. But that was okay. Sex was all she'd wanted from him, too. She understood that now. Five years was a long time for a healthy woman to go without a man. And, she thought coldly, Chase was good in bed. It was just too bad that even in this era of female liberation, she'd had to delude herself into thinking she loved him before she could sleep with him.

Well, it wouldn't happen again, despite his eager hopes for a repeat performance. Let him wrestle between the sheets with his fiancée—not that being engaged had stopped him that night. Why would it? Fidelity wasn't his strong suit. He'd certainly proved that, five and a half years ago.

"Sex-crazed idiot," Annie muttered, just as the door swung open and an elderly gentleman shuffled in.

"I *beg* your pardon," he said, while water dripped from his bushy white eyebrows.

Annie's face turned bright pink. "Not you," she said hastily. "I didn't mean... I was talking about..."

Oh, what was the use. She took a deep breath, yanked open the door and plunged out into the deluge.

The train to Stratham was half an hour late, thanks to the weather, and a good thing, too, because it took her twice as long as it should have to get to Penn Station.

She snagged a seat, even though the train was crowded, but her luck ran out after that. The guy who sat down next to her was portly enough to overflow his seat and part of hers, too. And he was in a chatty mood. He started with the weather, went on to the current political scene without stopping for breath. He was coming up fast on the problems of raising teenagers in today's troubled world when Annie made a grab for somebody's discarded newspaper, mumbled "Excuse me," and buried her nose in what turned out to be the business section.

It was rude, perhaps, but she just didn't feel like small talk with a stranger. Her visit with Laurel had upset her, on more than one level. She and Laurel and Susie, Laurel's neighbor, had sat around the kitchen table, drinking coffee and talking, and of the three, only Susie had a husband who'd lived up to his marriage vows.

Annie stared blindly at the newspaper. What was it with men? And with women, for that matter? Didn't they learn? How much grief did it take before you finally figured out that men were just no…

Her breath caught.

Was that a photo of Chase? It certainly was. It was Chase, all right, smiling at the camera and looking pleased with himself and with the world, and why shouldn't he? Standing right beside him, looking gorgeous and as perfect as a paper doll, was Janet Pendleton.

Annie's eyes filled with tears, although she couldn't imagine why. Chase certainly didn't mean anything to her.

"Damn you," she said, in a quavering whisper.

The man beside her stiffened.

"Were you speaking to me, madam?"

She looked up. The guy was looking at her as if she'd just escaped from the asylum.

Annie blinked back her tears.

"You're a man, aren't you?" she said.

Then she crumpled the newspaper, dumped it on the floor, rose from her seat and made her way through the train, to the door.

It was raining in Stratham, too.

Well, why not? The perfect ending to a perfect day, Annie thought grimly, as she made her way through the parking lot to her car. It didn't even pay to run, not when she was wet through and through. What could another soaking possibly matter?

By the time she pulled into her driveway, she was shivering, sniffling, and as close to feeling sorry for herself as she'd ever come. A hot shower and getting into her old terry-cloth robe and a pair of slippers helped. Supper seemed like a good idea, too, but banging open cabinet doors and peering into the fridge didn't spur any creative juices. Finally she gave up, took a diet meal from the freezer and popped it into the microwave.

She was just putting it on the kitchen counter when the doorbell rang.

Annie looked at the clock. It was after seven. Who'd be dropping by at this hour? Unless it was Dawn. A smile lit her face. Dawn and Nick lived only half an hour away and sometimes they dropped in for a quick visit. Everything was fine on that front, thank goodness. Dawn had returned from her honeymoon glowing with happiness, and she'd taken the news that her parents' supposed reconciliation had failed in her stride.

"I'm so sorry, Mom," she'd said, hugging Annie, "but at least you guys tried."

But the visitor at the door wasn't Dawn. It was Deborah

Kent, standing in the rain, clutching an enormous box from Angie's Pizza Palace.

"Well?" Deb demanded. "Do I get asked in, or do I have to sit in my car and pig out on all ninety billion calories of an Angie's Deluxe without any help?"

Annie's bleak mood lifted a little. "What kind of friend would I be if I let you suffer such a fate?" she said, taking the box from Deb's hands. "Come on in."

"The kind who ignores repeated phone calls," Deb grumbled as she peeled off her raincoat. "This thing is soaked. You want me to hang it in the laundry room, or what?"

"Just drape it over the back of that chair," Annie said as she headed for the kitchen.

"It'll drip on the floor."

"Trust me, Deb. The floor won't mind. Come and make yourself comfortable while I grab a couple of plates and some napkins."

Deb's eyebrows lifted when she saw the sad little box that had just come out of the microwave oven.

"I see I interrupted an evening of gourmet dining," she said, moving the thing aside with a manicured fingertip.

"Mmm." Annie took two diet Cokes out of the refrigerator and put them on the counter. "You can't imagine what a sacrifice it's going to be to eat a slice of Angie's Deluxe instead."

"A slice?" Deb opened the box, dug out a huge triangle of pizza and deposited it on Annie's plate. "A half of an Angie's Deluxe, is what I'm figuring on." She dug in again and lifted out a piece for herself. "So what's new in your life, anyway?"

"Oh, nothing much." Annie hitched a hip onto a stool. "How've you been?"

"And well you might ask," Deb said indignantly. "For someone's who's supposed to be my best *amiga*, you sure haven't paid much attention to me lately. Don't you ever return phone calls?''

"Of course I do. I've just been busy, that's all. Mmm, this pizza is to die for. And to think I was going to make a meal out of two hundred calories of fat-free, flavor-free yuck. So what if I'll have to give up eating for the rest of the week? This is definitely worth the sacrifice.''

"Don't try and pull my leg, Annie Cooper. I can tell a fib from the truth.''

"Cross my heart and hope to gain two inches around my hips,'' Annie said, ''this is delicious.''

"And can the innocent act.'' Deb slipped another piece of pizza from the box. "Nobody could be as busy as you claim to be, not unless you've given up eating and sleeping. You've turned into the 'no' girl. No, you don't want to go to the movies, not even when Liam Neeson's on the screen. No, you don't want to go to the mall, even if Lord and Taylor's got a fifty percent clearance.''

"I'm sorry, Deb. Really, I am, but as I said, I've been—''

"And,'' Deb said, stealing a slice of pepperoni from the pizza still in the box, "instead of sharing the good stuff with me, which is the duty of a true-blue friend, you let me find it out all on my own.''

Annie's smile stiffened. Nobody knew what had happened on that island. Nobody even knew she'd gone away with Chase, except for Dawn and Nick.

"What 'good stuff'?''

"You know.''

"I don't, or I wouldn't be asking. Come on, Deb. What are you talking about?''

Deb shoved aside her plate and pulled the tab on her can of soda.

"Well, for openers, when were you going to tell me you gave Milton Hoffman the old heave-ho?''

"Oh. That.''

"Yeah. That. Not that I wasn't happy to hear it. Milton's a nice guy, but he's not for you."

"Where did you hear—"

"I bumped into him at the Stop And Shop the other day." Deb leaned closer. "Did you know that he eats low-fat granola?"

I'm not surprised, Annie said to herself, then scowled for thinking something so unkind.

"Well, so what?" she said staunchly. "That doesn't make him a bad person. Besides, if you wanted to know if I was still seeing him or not, you could have just asked me. You didn't have to buttonhole poor Milton."

"I did not buttonhole poor Milton! He was standing in front of the cereal display, looking unhappy, and I wheeled my cart up to his and said he might want to try the oatmeal, or maybe the All-Bran, depending on his needs. I mean, who knows what's going on under that shiny suit? And he gave me this look that reminded me of a basset hound I once had... Did I know you then? He was the dearest little dog, but—"

"Dammit, Deb, what did Milton say?"

"He just asked if I'd seen you around lately. And I said well, I'd gone to lunch with you a few weeks back. And he said that was more than he'd done. And I said—"

"Whoa." Annie held up her hands. "Let me simplify things, okay? Milton's a lovely man. A delightful man. But..."

"But?"

"But, we're just friends."

"He seemed to think you'd once been something more." Deb picked up another piece of pizza. "Like, you'd maybe had serious plans."

"No! We never..." Annie put her hands over her face. "Oh gosh. I feel terrible."

Deb gave a delicate burp. "The pizza's a killer, I admit, but it's not *that* bad."

"Not the pizza. Milton."

"You led him on," Deb said, clucking her tongue.

"No. Yes. Damn! I suppose I did," Annie said, and told Deb about what had happened at the wedding, and how she'd put on an act for Chase's benefit. "But I cleared things up the next week," she added quickly. "I explained that—that I'd said some things I hadn't really meant and—and…"

"You broke his little heart," Deb said solemnly, and then she grinned and lightly punched Annie in the arm. "Don't look like that! I'm exaggerating. Milton looked absolutely fine. Happier than I've ever seen him, to tell the truth, and halfway through our chat a woman came waltzing over from the produce aisle and looped her arm through his. Her name's Molly Something-or-other, she's new in the English department and it didn't take a genius to figure out what's happening between them when she dropped her head of cabbage into the cart next to his box of granola."

Annie sighed with relief. "I'm glad."

"Milton said to say hi if I saw you, so here I am, saying hi."

"Honestly, Deb—"

"Honestly, Annie, why didn't you tell me you went off and spent the weekend after the wedding with your gorgeous ex?"

Annie turned bright red to the roots of her hair. "What are you talking about?"

"Dawn told me." Deb reached for a piece of pizza, bit into it and chewed thoughtfully. "I met her in the detergent aisle."

"Have you ever considered changing supermarkets?" Annie said sweetly. "What else did my darling daughter tell you?"

"Only that you and Chase went out of town in hopes of a reconciliation, and that it didn't work out. Is that about it?"

"Yes," Annie said. "That's about it."

Deb, who was nobody's fool, eyed her best friend narrowly.

"Maybe your baby girl bought that story," she said, "but I have a few years of observing the human condition on her."

"Meaning?"

"Meaning, you want to tell me what really happened?"

"Nothing happened."

"Annie," Deb said.

The doorbell rang. Annie sent up a silent prayer of thanks.

"Don't think you're off the hook," Deb called as Annie hurried from the kitchen. "I have every intention of picking up the inquisition as soon as you get back." Her voice rose. "You hear?"

Annie rolled her eyes. "I hear," she said, as she flung the door open.

A boy stood on the porch. Rain glittered on his hair and shoulders, and on the yellow panel truck in the driveway.

"Mrs. Annie Cooper?"

Annie looked at the long white box clutched in his arms.

"*Ms.* Annie Cooper," she said. "And I don't want them."

The boy frowned and looked at the tag clipped to the box.

"This is 126 Spruce Street, isn't it?"

"It is, and you're to take those flowers right back where they came from."

"They're roses, ma'am. Long-stemmed, red—"

"I know what they are, and I do not want them." Annie reached behind her and took her pocketbook from the hall table.

"But—"

"Here," she said, handing the boy a ten-dollar bill. "I'm sorry you had to come out in such miserable weather."

"But, ma'am…"

"Good night."

Annie shut the door. She sighed, leaned back against it and closed her eyes.

"What was that about?"

Her eyes flew open. Deb was standing in the hall, staring.

"Nothing. It was a—a mix-up. A delivery of something or other, but the kid had the wrong—"

"I heard the whole thing, Annie. He had the right house and the right woman. He also had a humongous box of roses, and you told him to take them away."

Annie's chin lifted. "I certainly did," she said, marching past Deb into the kitchen. "You want a glass for that Coke, and some ice?"

"I want to know if I'm going crazy. Somebody sends you long-stemmed roses and you don't even want to take a look? You don't even want to ask who they're from?"

Annie took two glasses from the cabinet over the sink and slammed them down on the counter.

"Chase," she said grimly.

"Chase what?"

"Chase sent the roses."

"How do you know? You didn't even—"

"He's been doing it for weeks."

"Your ex has been sending you roses for weeks?"

"Yes. And I've been refusing them." Annie sat down at the counter and picked up her slice of pizza. "Your pizza's going to get cold, if you don't eat it pretty soon."

Deb looked down at her plate, then at Annie.

"Let me get this straight. You went away with your ex, he's been sending you roses ever since, and you really expect me to believe nothing happened between you?"

"That's exactly what I expect you to believe," Annie said, and she burst into tears.

Half an hour later, the pizza had been forgotten, the diet Cokes had been replaced by a bottle of Chianti, Annie's eyes and nose were pink and Deb had heard the whole story.

"The bastard," she said grimly.

"Uh-huh," Annie said, blowing her nose into a paper towel.

"The skunk!"

"That's what he is, all right. Taking me to bed and then telling me how terrific it was—"

"Was it?"

Annie blushed. "Sex was never our problem. Well, not until the very end, when I was so hurt and angry at him for never coming home...."

"Other women, huh?"

"No." Annie blew her nose again. "I mean, not then. At the end, there was somebody, even though Chase said there wasn't."

"Yeah," Deb said, "that's what they always say. So, if it wasn't some foxy broad, why didn't the oaf come home nights?"

"Oh, he came home. Late, that's all. He took all these courses, see, so he could learn the things he needed to build up the business he'd inherited from his father. He worked crazy hours, too. Most days, he'd leave before sunrise and not get back until seven, eight at night."

"Uh-huh."

"And then, when things took off and the company really began to grow, he went to all these parties. Chamber of Commerce things. You know, the sort of stuff you read about in the paper."

"And he left you home. God, the nerve of the man!"

"No. I mean, he took me with him. And then I decided I didn't want to go to these things anymore."

"I can imagine the rest. The jerk went by himself and that's when he began to fool around. He met this society type with a pedigree and a face like an ice sculpture and she was lots more appealing than the house mouse he'd left at home, right?''

"Well—well, no. He didn't meet anybody. Although, eventually, he—he got involved with his secretary.''

"How disgustingly trite. His secretary! Will men never learn?''

"He said it wasn't what it seemed to be, but I knew.''

"Of course, you knew. Lipstick on his collar, receipts from motels you'd never been to in his pockets, charge account statements for flowers and candy and perfume...''

"No.''

"No?''

Annie shook her head. "Well, bills for flowers and candy and perfume, yes. For my birthday, or Christmas, or sometimes just for no reason at all.''

"Really,'' Deb said, arching an eyebrow.

"I'd never have known, except I just—I showed up at his office when he didn't expect me and there she was, wound around him like—like a morning glory vine on a fence post.''

"And Chase said he was just taking a speck of dust out of her eye,'' Deb said, shaking her head.

Annie looked up, her mouth trembling. "Chase said it wasn't what it looked like. His secretary said it, too. She cried and begged me to believe her, she said Chase had never even looked at her cross-eyed but I—''

"But you?''

"But I knew. That he—that she... Because, you know, I'd stopped turning to him in bed, when he reached for me. I couldn't help it.'' A sob ripped from Annie's throat. "I loved him so much, Deb. So terribly much!''

"Oh, Annie, you poor soul,'' Deb said, "you still do.''

"I don't,'' Annie said, and she began to weep uncontrollably.

Deb stood up, went to Annie's side and put her arm around her.

"Oh, honey, I never realized. You're crazy about the man."

"No," Annie said in a choked whisper, and then she pulled out of her friend's embrace and threw her arms into the air. "Yes," she said, "and isn't that pathetic? It's true. I *am* crazy about him. I love him with all my heart. I'd even forgive him that fling with his secretary."

"If there was a fling." Annie shot her a look, and Deb shrugged. "Well, it's a possibility, isn't it? I mean, all those stories about bosses and their secretaries...if half of 'em were true, the American economy would grind to a halt. Anyway, why would she have put up such a denial?"

"I don't know. I don't know anything, anymore, only that somewhere along the line, Chase and I lost each other. And I know now that it wasn't all his fault. We were so young when we got married, Deb. I thought marriage was just a fairy tale, you know, the prince rides off with the maiden and they live happily ever after. But it isn't like that. You have to work at a marriage, talk about your goals and your problems."

"And you guys didn't."

Annie shook her head. "No," she said, her voice muffled as she wiped her nose again.

"Well, it's never too late."

"It is." Annie dumped the wet paper towel into the trash and peeled another one off the roll. "It's way too late."

"What about the reconciliation attempt?"

"I told you. It wasn't for real. We just went through the motions, for Dawn."

"But you made love."

"I made love. Chase—Chase just figures we slept together." Annie flashed Deb a fierce look. "And don't you dare tell me it's the same thing."

Deb smiled sadly. "Trust me, Annie. Even I know that it isn't. Well, what happened when the weekend was over? Didn't he suggest seeing each other again?"

"He did." Annie's expression hardened. "He phoned a dozen times. Sure, he wants to see me. For sex. Not for anything else."

"You don't think it would help to see him? Tell him how you feel?"

"No! God, no! It's bad enough I *showed* him how I feel. In bed, I mean. I..." Annie shook her head. "I don't want to talk about it anymore. There's no point. Talking's not going to change—"

The telephone rang. Deb waited for Annie to reach for it.

"Do you want me to take that?" she said, after the phone had rung three times.

Annie shook her head. "Let the machine pick up. I'm not fit to talk to anybody."

The answering machine clicked on.

"*Hi,*" Annie's disembodied voice said. "*It's me, but I can't take your call right now. Leave a message and your number, and I'll give you a ring soon as I can.*"

"Very original," Deb said with a smile.

Annie smiled back at her, but her smile disappeared at the sound of Chase's voice.

"Annie? Annie, it's me. Please, babe, pick up if you're there."

"Speak of the devil," Deb whispered.

"Okay," Chase said, and sighed. "But I've got to tell you, it's a problem. How does a guy find out why his ex-wife won't talk to him, if she won't talk to him?"

Annie folded her arms. "He knows why," she hissed to Deb.

"Here's the deal," Chase said, and cleared his throat. "I'm in Puerto Rico. I've got this new client... Hell, Annie, you don't want to hear the whole story. The thing is, I'm flying back to New York tonight. Matter of fact, I'm at the airport down here, right now."

"Fascinating," Annie muttered. "Now he's going to give me his itinerary."

"I'll only be in New York for a couple of days before I head back down to San Juan, and then I'm liable to be gone for a while. And I figured, if there was any last chance you'd see me again…"

"Sleep with him, he means," Annie said, glowering at the telephone.

"I know I've said some of this before, babe, maybe a hundred times to that damn machine of yours, but I guess one last try can't hurt, so here goes. Annie, I know we didn't intend to get involved again. I know we went away together because I dug us into a hole with Dawn. But I thought—I really thought that night we spent together was incredible. And—"

"And we ought to try it again," Annie said coldly. She tried smiling brightly at Deb but it didn't work. Her smile trembled and tears glittered in her eyes.

"And I knew I didn't have any right to ask you to take me back, Annie. That's what I kept thinking, all the way back to Seattle. You've made a new life for yourself, and you've found a new guy, and I could tell you regretted what had happened, the minute you woke up that morning. You were so quiet, with that same shuttered look you had the last few years we were married."

"Annie?" Deb said uncertainly. "Are you hearing this?"

"Annie," Chase said, his voice roughening, "dammit, babe, I love you! If you really want the pansy poet instead of me, you're gonna have to look me in the eye and tell me so. You're gonna have to say, 'Chase, I don't love you anymore. What happened in that cabin was all pretense. I don't want to marry you again and live with you forever…'" Chase drew a ragged breath. "Dammit," he said, "I'm no good at this! You want sensitive, stick with the poet. You want a guy who's never stopped loving you, who'll love you until the day he dies, you don't have to look any further than me."

"Chase," Annie whispered, "oh, Chase..."

"The only lie I told you that entire weekend was when I said I was engaged to Janet Pendleton. Janet's a nice woman. I like her. But I don't love her. I told her that, a few days ago. I could never love anyone, except you."

"Annie," Deb said desperately, "pick up the phone!"

"They're calling my flight, babe, but hell, I'm not getting on! I changed my plans. I'm gonna fly to Boston instead. I'll be at your door in a few hours and I'm warning you, if you don't open it when I ring that bell, so help me, I'll bust it dow—"

Annie made a dive for the phone, but it was too late. All she heard when she picked it up was a dial tone.

"Annie," Deb said, "what are you going to do?"

Annie's smile glittered. "Boston," she said, "here I come."

It was raining in Boston, too.

All flights, departing and arriving, were delayed, the soothing voice over the public address system kept repeating.

The terminal was jammed with weary travelers. Bodies were draped everywhere as people tried to snatch some sleep. There were lines at the ladies' rooms, at the snack counters, at the newsstands. Babies screamed, irate passengers argued with overworked ticket agents and Annie noticed absolutely none of it.

She kept up her vigil at Gate Nine, her eyes glued to the arrivals board, waiting. And waiting.

She wasn't even sure she was waiting in the right place and if she wasn't—if she wasn't, she'd just about run out of options.

It had seemed such a wonderful idea, to go to Boston and meet Chase as he arrived. She'd pictured his face, when he saw her waiting for him; she'd imagined running to him and having his arms close around her.

Halfway to Logan Airport, it had occurred to her that she had no idea what airline Chase was flying.

Her foot had eased off the accelerator. Maybe she should go back.

Back? To pace from one room to another? To go crazy as she waited? No. She couldn't do that. That was why she'd thrown on jeans, sneakers and a T-shirt in the first place, and dashed to her car. She needed to be doing something, or she'd go crazy.

She had to see Chase the minute he stepped off the plane, had to fly into his arms and tell him she had never stopped loving him.

So she'd stepped down, hard, on the pedal again.

By the time she'd reached the airport, she'd had a plan. Well, a plan of sorts.

She'd gone to the first information desk she saw.

"Excuse me," she'd said politely, "but could you tell me what flights are coming in this evening from Puerto Rico?"

"What airline?" the clerk had asked, and Annie had smiled and said, unfortunately, she really didn't know what airline. Was that a problem?

It was, but not an insurmountable one. Annie knew the time Chase's New York-bound flight had boarded. If he'd managed to get himself ticketed on a flight to Boston instead, it would have to have gone out sometime after that.

That narrowed things down a bit, the clerk said.

There were only three possible flights Chase could have taken. They were on three different airlines, and they came in minutes apart. Annie's plan, therefore, was simple. She'd wait for the first flight and if Chase wasn't one of the deplaning passengers, she'd rush to the next gate and wait again. If necessary, she'd do the same thing a third time.

"Good luck," the clerk had called, as Annie had hurried away.

The plan had seemed logical.

Now, she was beginning to wonder.

Flight one had arrived and disgorged what had looked like a full load of passengers.

Chase had not been among them.

Annie had hurried to the next gate. She'd gotten there out of breath, but with two minutes to spare before the door had opened and the arriving passengers had started streaming into the terminal.

She'd watched faces, standing on tiptoe, keeping her fingers crossed and silently chanting Chase's name like a mantra, but it hadn't helped. The last travelers walked into the terminal but he wasn't among them, either.

Now she was at the final gate, waiting for the third and last plane.

What if Chase wasn't on it?

Annie's hands began to tremble. She thrust them deep into the pockets of her jacket.

Maybe he hadn't been able to change his flight plans. Planes could be sold out. You couldn't just change your plans at the last minute and assume you could get a ticket.

For all she knew, Chase might be landing in New York at this very minute. He might be phoning her, and reaching her answering machine again. It was late; he'd know she'd be home at this hour of the night.

When she didn't take the call, would he assume she'd gotten his message and wasn't interested?

Annie chewed on her lip.

There was another possibility she hadn't even considered until now. Chase could have hung up the phone and suddenly realized that it would be easier if he flew to Bradley Airport, in Hartford. He might be on his way to her house right now. What if he got there and banged on the door? What if she wasn't there to answer?

Would he think she was out, with Milton Hoffman?
Would he think she'd gotten his message and didn't want
to see him?

"Oh God," she whispered, "please, please, please…"

God didn't seem to be listening. The last few stragglers
had emerged from the ramp that led to the plane.

Chase wasn't one of them.

Tears spilled down Annie's cheeks.

Maybe the simple truth was that he'd changed his mind.

A sob burst from her throat. A couple standing nearby
looked at her curiously. She knew how she must look, in
her ratty outfit, with her hair all curly and wild from the
rain and now with tears coursing down her face, but she
didn't care.

Nothing mattered, now that she'd lost Chase a second
time.

She turned, jammed her hands into her pockets and
started walking.

"Annie?"

What fools they'd been, the two of them. So in love, and
so unable to connect about the things that really mattered.

"Annie?"

There would never be another love in her life. Chase
would stay in her heart, forever.

"Annie!"

Hands closed around her shoulders, hands that were familiar and dear.

"Chase?" Annie whispered, and she spun around and
saw her husband.

They stared at each other wordlessly, and then Chase
opened his arms and gathered her in. She threw her arms
around his neck and they clung to each other, oblivious to
the people watching and smiling, to the noise and the announcements.

A long minute later, Chase led Annie off into a corner.

"Annie, darling." He took her face between his hands.

She was so beautiful. So perfect. His eyes blurred as he bent and brushed his lips against hers. "I'm sorry, sweetheart," he whispered. "I never meant to hurt you. I always loved you, Annie. Everything I did, babe—the long hours, the networking, the meetings—it was all for you. I wanted you to have everything. I wanted you to be proud of me, to be glad you were my wife."

Annie put her hands over his and smiled through her tears.

"I was always proud of you. Don't you know that? I wouldn't care if you dug ditches, just as long as you loved me."

Chase gathered her close and kissed her. "Annie Bennett Cooper," he whispered against her mouth, "will you marry me?"

"Oh, yes," Annie said, "oh, yes, Chase, oh, yes."

"Tonight, babe. We can get right on a plane, fly to the Caribbean and get married on Saint John Island."

"That's a wonderful idea," she said, and kissed him.

Chase looped his arm around her shoulders. "Come on. Let's find the ticket counter."

Halfway to the escalator, he came to a stop.

"Wait here a minute," he said. He brushed a kiss over her mouth, and hurried into one of the shops that dotted the terminal.

Annie looked in the window. A huge vase stood behind the glass, filled with red roses. As she watched, Chase pulled out his wallet and spoke to the clerk. Seconds later, he stood before Annie again, holding one perfect red rose in his hand.

"Do you remember that night, years ago?" he asked. "I'd gotten my first big break, and I brought you one rose…"

Did she remember? Annie's smile trembled. "Yes."

"I love you as much now as I did then, babe." His voice turned husky. "If it's possible, I love you even more."

Annie took the rose from him.

"I'll never stop loving you, Chase," she whispered, and she went into her husband's arms.

EPILOGUE

IT WAS THE DAY AFTER Christmas, and the Cooper clan was gathered in Annie and Chase's living room.

"There's no way your father and I can eat all these leftovers by ourselves," Annie had said, when she'd phoned Dawn and asked if she and Nick would come by for dinner.

"You don't have to convince me, Mom," Dawn had replied, with a smile in her voice. "If there's one thing I still don't love about being a wife, it's cooking."

Now, as Annie sat on the sofa beside her husband, with his arm curled tightly around her shoulders, she looked around her at her family and knew that she had never been happier.

Dawn and Nick were sitting cross-legged beside the big spruce tree Chase had wrestled through the door last week.

"It'll never fit," he'd groaned, as he'd lugged the tree toward the living room.

"Of course it'll fit," Annie had insisted, and it had—after Chase had lopped off two feet with a saw.

Annie's sister, Laurel, was there, too, standing under the sprig of mistletoe Chase had hung in the living room entryway. Annie smiled. Laurel and her gorgeous husband, Damian, were kissing each other as if nobody else existed. As Annie watched, Damian drew back a little, smiled at Laurel and lay his hand gently on her huge belly. He said something that brought a rosy flush to Laurel's cheeks.

Annie smiled and looked away, toward her friend, Deb, who was sitting before the fireplace, deep in conversation with a man—a very nice man—whom she'd met a couple of months ago.

"In the supermarket?" Annie had asked teasingly.

Deb had blushed. "In the library, but if you tell that to anybody, I'll deny everything."

Annie sighed and put her head on Chase's shoulder. What a difference a few months could make. She'd been so unhappy this past summer, and now—and now, her heart was almost unbearably filled with joy.

"Babe?"

She looked up. Chase smiled at her.

"You think it's time to tell them our plans?"

Annie smiled back at her husband. They'd been married for months now, and every day still felt like part of their honeymoon.

"Yes," she said. "Let's."

Chase grinned and kissed her. Then, holding her hand and drawing her up with him, he rose to his feet.

"Okay, everybody," he said, "listen up."

Everyone turned and looked at Chase and Annie. Chase cleared his throat.

"Annie and I had a problem..."

Long, deep groans echoed around the room.

Chase laughed and drew Annie closer.

"The problem was, where were we going to live? Annie had this old house that she loved. And I had a condo that I was pretty happy with, in New York."

"Don't tell us," Deb said. "You guys have decided to pitch a tent on a beach, in Tahiti."

Chase and Annie laughed along with everybody else, and then Chase held up his hand.

"And then, there was Annie's flower business and my construction company. As I say, we had a problem." He looked down at his wife and smiled. "Tell 'em how we solved it, babe."

"Well," Annie said, "when we thought about it, it was really a cinch."

"I told you," Deb said. "The tent, on the beach in Tahiti."

"We bought an island," Annie said, "off the Washington coast."

Dawn scrambled to her feet. "*An* island, Mom? Or *your* island?"

Annie blushed. "Our island. Your father spoke to Mr. Tanaka and convinced him that there was another island for sale up the coast that would be much more to his liking."

"I'm going to build us a house," Chase said.

"Isn't there a house there already?"

Chase and Annie smiled at each other. "Yes," Annie said softly, "a very handsome one...but we've decided we want something of our own. Something—something cozier." She looked at the people gathered around them. "Chase will build our house, and I'm going to put in a garden, and after that, we're going to combine forces. Cooper and Cooper, Landscape and House Design." She grinned. "Please notice that I get top billing."

Everyone laughed, and then Dawn clapped her hands.

"Well," she said, "as long as it's announcement time, I have one of my own." She smiled happily. "I'm going back to school. I signed up for the spring semester."

Annie let out a shriek. "Oh, baby, that's wonderful news!"

Nick smiled proudly and put his arm around his wife's waist. "It is, isn't it? Dawn will have her degree four years from now, and then—" A blush stole over his handsome features. "And then," he said, ducking his head, "we're going to start a family."

"Way to go, Nick," Damian called out. He winked at his wife, who stood smiling in the circle of his arms. "Of course, by then Laurel and I will probably be working on baby number two, or maybe three."

Everyone whistled and cheered.

"All right," Deb said briskly, "that's enough of this nonsense. You guys don't have a monopoly on good news, you know." She took a deep breath, looked up at the smiling man at her side and looped her arm through his. "Arthur and I have decided to tie the knot. And before anybody says we're tying it around each other's throats, let me make it perfectly clear that what I mean is, he's asked me to marry him." Deb's voice softened. "And I said I would so—it's too late to back out, Arthur, because now I've got witnesses."

In the laughter and good-natured banter that followed, it was simple for Annie and Chase to drift off into the kitchen, alone.

Chase took Annie in his arms.

"You know," he said, "after all these happy announcements, I've been thinking…"

She smiled up at him. "Yes?"

"Well," he said, "well…"

"Well, what?"

Chase smiled back at her. "Maybe we ought to reconsider those plans for the new house. I mean, heck, right down the hall from where our bedroom's going to be—wouldn't that be a great place to put a nursery?"

Annie looked deep into the eyes of her husband. Then she smiled, looped her arms around his neck, brought his head down to hers and kissed him.

THE GROOM SAID MAYBE!

CHAPTER ONE

DAVID CHAMBERS sat in the back row of the little Connecticut church and did his best to appear interested in the farce taking place at the altar.

He had the sneaking suspicion he wasn't managing to pull it off very well, but then, how could he?

Lord, what utter nonsense!

The glowing bride, the nervous groom. The profusion of flowers that made the chapel look like a funeral parlor, the schmaltzy music, the minister with the faultless vocal cords intoning all the trite old platitudes about loving and honoring and cherishing one another...

David frowned and folded his arms. He felt as if he were sitting through the second act of a predictable comedy, with act three—The Divorce—lurking in the wings.

"Dawn and Nicholas," the minister said, his voice ringing out with emotion, "today you embark upon the greatest adventure of your young lives..."

Beside David, a woman with a helmet of dark hair sat clutching her husband's arm with one hand and a frilly handkerchief with the other. She was weeping silently and wearing a look that said she was having the time of her life. David's blue eyes narrowed. Other women were sobbing, too, even the bride's mother, who certainly should have known better than to be moved by such saccharine sentiment.

Any human being over the age of thirty should have known better, dammit, especially the ones who'd been divorced, and their number was legion. David suspected that if a voice suddenly boomed down from the choir loft and demanded that all those who'd lost the marriage wars stand up, the shuffling of feet would drown out the cherub-faced man at the altar.

"Nicholas," the minister said, "will you take Dawn to be your lawful wife?"

The woman next to David gave a choked sob. David looked at her. Tears were streaming down her cheeks but her mascara was intact. Amazing, how women came prepared for these things. The makeup that didn't run, the lace hankies…you never saw a woman carrying a hankie except at weddings and funerals.

"In sickness and in health, for richer or for poorer…"

David slouched in his seat and tuned out the drivel. How much longer until it was over? He felt as if he'd spent the last week airborne, flying from D.C. to Laramie, from Laramie to London, from London to D.C. again, and then to Hartford. His eyes felt gritty, his long legs felt as if they'd been cut off at the knees thanks to the hour and a half he'd had to spend jammed into the commuter plane that had brought him to Connecticut, and sitting in this narrow wooden pew wasn't helping.

The church dated back to 1720, some white-haired old lady who might have stepped out of a Norman Rockwell painting had confided as he'd made his way inside.

David, suspecting that two and a half centuries of history would boil down to pews so closely packed that he'd end up feeling exactly the way he felt now, had offered what he'd hoped was a polite smile.

"Really," he'd said.

The smile hadn't worked. He knew, because the old lady had drawn back, given him a second, narrow-eyed stare that had swept over him from head to toe, taking in his height, his ponytail, his stirrup-heeled, silver-tooled boots, and then she'd raised her eyes to his and said, "Yes, really," in a tone that had made it clear what she thought of a Westerner invading this pristine corner of New England.

Hell.

Maybe she was right. Maybe he shouldn't have come to the wedding. He was too tired, too cynical, too old to pretend that he was witnessing a miracle of love when the truth was that those two kids up there had about as much chance of succeeding at the thing called wedlock as a penguin had of flying to the moon.

The bride lifted worshiping eyes to her young man. Her smile trembled, full of promises. Pledges. Vows…

And right about then, David suddenly thought of the world's three biggest lies.

Every man knew them.

The check is in the mail.

Of course, I'll respect you in the morning.

Trust me.

Lie number one, at least, was gender neutral. As an attorney with offices in the nation's capitol, David had spent more time than he liked to remember sitting across his desk from clients of both sexes, either of whom had no trouble looking you straight in the eye and swearing, on a stack of Bibles, that whatever sums were in dispute were only a postal delivery away. And they usually were—so long as you assumed United States mail was routed via Mars.

The second lie was unabashedly, if embarrassingly, male. If pressed, David would have had to admit offering it himself, back in the days of his callow, hormone-crazed youth.

The memory made him smile. He hadn't thought of Martha Jean Steenburger in years, but he could picture her now, just as clearly as if it had happened yesterday.

Martha Jean, home for the summer after her freshman year at college, somehow much, much older than her eighteen years and as gloriously endowed as any sixteen-year-old boy stumbling into manhood could imagine. Martha Jean, eyeing him with interest, making him blush as she took in the height and muscle he'd added since she'd last seen him. She'd flashed him a hundred-watt smile across the barbecue pit at the Steenburgers' July Fourth party and

David had gulped hard, then followed her swaying, denim-clad backside to the calf barn and up into the hayloft, where he'd nervously tried to plant a kiss on her parted lips.

"But will you respect me in the morning?" Martha Jean had said with a straight face, and when he'd managed to stutter out that of course he would, she'd chortled in a way that had made him feel dumb as well as horny and then she'd tumbled him back into the hay and introduced him to paradise.

Ah, but the third lie... The dark scowl crept over David's face again. It, too, was supposed to be strictly male, but any man over the age of puberty knew that women told it just as often and with devastating effect, because when a woman said, "Trust me," it had nothing to do with sex and everything to do with love. That was what made it the most damnable falsehood. For all he knew, it had started as a whisper made by a ravishing Eve to a defenseless Adam, or a promise breathed in the ear of Samson by Delilah. It might even have been the last vow made by Guinevere to Arthur.

Trust me.

How many males had done just that, over the centuries? Millions, probably—including David.

"Well, they probably mean it, when they say it," a fraternity brother had once told him. "Something about the female of the species, you know what I mean?"

It was as good an explanation as any, David figured. And all it took was one trip through the marriage mill for a man to learn that when a woman said a man could trust her, what it *really* meant was that he'd be a fool if he did. It was a hard lesson to learn, but he'd learned it.

Damn right, he had.

Put in the most basic terms, marriage was a joke.

Not that he'd given up on women. Taken at face value, he liked them still. What man wouldn't? There was nothing as pleasurable as sharing your bed and your life with a beautiful woman for a few weeks, even a few months, but when the time came to end a relationship, that was it. He wanted no tears, no regrets, no recriminations. Women didn't fault him for his attitude, either. David figured it was because he was completely up-front about his intentions, or his lack of them. He wasn't a man who made promises, not of forever-after or anything even approximating it, but he'd yet to meet a woman who'd walked away after he'd shown interest in her.

Jack Russell, one of his law partners, said it was because women saw David as an irresistible challenge. He said, too, that the day would come when David changed his mind. A wife, according to Jack, had a civilizing influence on a man. She'd run your home, plan your parties, help entertain your clients and generally get your life in hand. David agreed that that was probably true, but a good secretary and an inventive caterer could do the same things, and you didn't have to wonder what day of the week they'd turn your life upside down.

Love, if it even existed, was too dependent on men trusting women and women trusting men. It sounded good but it just didn't work...and wasn't that a hell of a thing to be brooding over right now?

David sighed, stretched his legs out as best he could, and crossed his booted ankles.

Jet lag, that was his problem, otherwise why would he be thinking such stuff? The kids standing at the altar today deserved the benefit of the doubt. Not even he was jaundiced enough to be convinced this bride would do a Jekyll and Hyde after the honeymoon ended. The girl was the daughter of an old friend. David had watched her develop from a cute kid with braces on her teeth to charming young womanhood...and he'd watched her father and mother end up in divorce court. In fact, he'd represented Chase in the divorce.

There was just no getting away from it. Marriage was an

unnatural state, devised by the female of the species to suit her own purposes, and—

Bang!

What was that?

David sat up straight and swung around. The church doors had flown open; the breeze had caught them and slammed them against the walls.

A woman stood silhouetted in the late afternoon sun. A buzz of speculation swept up and down the aisles.

"Who's that?" the weeper beside him hissed to her husband. "Why doesn't she sit down? Why doesn't someone shut those doors?"

Why, indeed? David sighed, got to his feet and made his way to the rear of the church. This was going to be his day for charitable works. Annie had kissed him hello and whispered that she'd seated him with a special friend of hers.

"She's no one for you to fool around with, David," she'd said with a teasing smile. "Her name is Stephanie Willingham, and she's a widow. Be nice to her, okay?"

Well, why not? He'd been hard on the old lady outside the church but he'd make up for it by being nice to this one. He'd chat politely with the widow Willingham, maybe even waltz her once around the room, and then he'd cut out, maybe give Jessica or Helena a call before he flew back to D.C. On the other hand, he might just head home early. He had some briefs to read before tomorrow.

The woman who'd caused the commotion nodded her thanks. She was the bride's aunt; he'd met her a couple of times. She was a model, and probably accustomed to making theatrical entrances. He gave her a polite nod as she made her way past him.

David shut the doors, turned—and found himself looking straight at the most beautiful woman he'd ever seen.

She was seated in the last pew, as he had been, but on the opposite side—the groom's side—of the church. Her face was triangular, almost catlike in its delicacy; her cheekbones were high and pronounced. Her eyes were brown, her nose was straight and classic and her mouth was a soft, coral bow that hinted at endless pleasures. Her hair was the color of dark chocolate and she wore it drawn back from her face in an unadorned knot.

With heart-stopping swiftness, David found himself wondering what it would be like to take out the pins that held those silken strands and let her hair tumble into his hands.

The image was simple, but it sent a jolt of desire sizzling through his blood. He felt himself turn hard as stone.

Damn, he thought in surprise, and at that instant, the woman's eyes met his.

Her gaze was sharp and cold. It seemed to assess him, slice through the veneer afforded him by his custom-made suit and dissect his thoughts.

Hell, he thought, could she tell what had happened to him? It wasn't possible. His anatomy was behaving as if it had a will of its own, but there was no way for her to know...

But she did. She knew. He was sure of it, even though her eyes never left his. Nothing else could explain the flush that rose in her face, or the contemptuous expression that swept over it just before she turned away.

For what seemed an eternity, David remained frozen. He couldn't believe he'd had such a stupid reaction to the sight of a stranger, couldn't recall a woman looking at him with such disdain.

Primal desire gave way to equally primal rage.

He saw himself walking to where she sat, sliding into the empty seat beside her and telling her that he wouldn't have her on a bet—or better still, he could tell her that she was right, just looking at her had made him want to take her to bed, and what did she intend to do about it?

But the rules of a civilized society prevailed.

He drew a deep breath, made his way to his seat, sat

down and fixed his attention on whatever in hell was happening at the altar because he was, after all, a civilized man.

Damn right, he was.

By the time the recessional echoed through the church and the bride and groom made their way out the door, he had had forgotten all about the woman...

Sure he had.

Stephanie Willingham stood at the marble-topped vanity table in the country club ladies' room and stared at her reflection in the mirror.

She didn't *look* like a woman who'd just made a damn fool of herself. That, at least, was something to be grateful for.

She took a deep breath, then let it out.

How much longer until she could make a polite exit?

Long enough, she thought, answering her own question. You couldn't sit through a wedding ceremony, hide in the powder room during the cocktail hour, then bolt before the reception without raising a few eyebrows. And that was the last thing she wanted to do because raised eyebrows meant questions, and questions required answers, and she had none.

Absolutely none.

The way that man, the one in the church, had looked at her had been bad enough. Those cool blue eyes of his, stripping her naked....

Stephanie's chin lifted. Despicable, was the only word for it.

But her reaction had been worse. Her realization that he was looking at her, that she knew exactly what was going on inside his head...that was one thing, but there was no way to explain or excuse what had happened when a rush of heat had raged through her blood.

Color flooded her cheeks at the memory.

"What is the matter with you, Stephanie?" she said to her mirrored image.

The man had been good-looking. Handsome, she supposed, in a hard sort of way—if you liked the type. Expensively put together, but almost aggressively masculine. The hair, drawn back in a ponytail. The leanly muscled body, so well-defined within the Western-cut suit. The boots. Boots, for goodness' sake.

Clint Eastwood riding through Connecticut, she'd thought, and she should have laughed, but she hadn't. Instead, she'd felt as if someone had lit a flame deep inside her, a flame that had threatened to consume her with its heat, and that was just plain nonsense.

She didn't like men, didn't want anything to do with them ever again. Why on earth she should have reacted to the man was beyond her, especially when the look on his face had made clear what he was thinking.

Exhaustion, that had to be the answer. Flying in from Atlanta late last night, getting up so early this morning—and she'd had a bad week to begin with. First the run-in with Clare, then the meeting with Judge Parker, and finally the disappointing consultation with her own attorney. And all the while, doing what she could not to show her panic because that would only spur Clare on.

Stephanie sighed. She should never have let Annie talk her into coming to this wedding. Weddings weren't her thing to begin with. She had no illusions about them, she never had, not even before she'd married Avery, though heaven knew she wished only the best for Dawn and Nicholas. She'd certainly tried to get out of coming north, to attend this affair. As soon as the invitation had arrived, she'd phoned Annie, expressed her delight for the engaged couple, followed by her regrets, but Annie had cut her short.

"Don't give me any of that Southern cornpone," Annie had said firmly, and then her voice had softened. "You have to come to the wedding, Steffie,'' she'd said. ''After all, you introduced Dawn and Nicholas. The kids and I will be heartbroken if you don't attend.''

Stephanie smiled, put her hands to her hair and smoothed back a couple of errant strands. It had been a generous thing to say, even if it was an overstatement. She hadn't really introduced the bride and groom, she'd just happened to be driving through Connecticut on her way home after a week on Cape Cod—a week when she'd walked the lonely, out-of-season beach and tried to sort out her life. A drenching rain was falling as she'd crossed the state line from Massachusetts to Connecticut and, in the middle of it, she'd gotten a flat. She'd been standing on the side of the road, miserable and wet and cold, staring glumly at the tire, when Dawn pulled over to offer assistance. Nick had come by next. He'd shooed Dawn away from the tire and knelt down in the mud to do the job, but his eyes had been all for Dawn. As luck would have it, Annie had driven by just as Nick finished. She'd stopped, they'd all ended up introducing themselves and laughing in the downpour, and Annie had invited everyone for an impromptu cup of hot cocoa.

Stephanie's smile faded. Avery would never have understood that a friendship could be forged out of such a tenuous series of coincidences, but then, he'd never understood anything about her, not from the day they'd married until the day he'd died....

''Mrs. Willingham?''

Stephanie blinked and stared into the mirror. Dawn Cooper—the former Dawn Cooper—radiant in her white lace and satin gown, smiled at her from the doorway.

''Dawn.'' Stephanie swung toward the girl and embraced her. ''Congratulations, darlin'. Or is it good luck?'' She smiled. ''I never can remember.''

''It's luck, I think.'' The door swung shut as Dawn moved toward the mirror. ''I hope it is, anyway, because I think I'm going to need it.''

"You've already got all the luck you'll need," Stephanie said. "That handsome young man of yours looks as if he— Dawn? Are you all right?"

Dawn nodded. "Fine," she said brightly. "It's just, I don't know…it's just, I've been waiting and waiting for this day and now it's here, and—and—" She took a deep breath. "Mrs. Willingham?"

"Stephanie, please. Otherwise, you'll make me feel even older than I already am."

"Stephanie. I know I shouldn't ask, but—but… Did you feel, well, a little bit nervous on your wedding day?"

Stephanie stared at the girl. "Nervous?"

"Yes. You know. Sort of edgy."

"Nervous," Stephanie repeated, fixing a smile to her lips. "Well, I don't—I can't recall…"

"Not scared. I don't mean it that way. I just mean… Worried."

"Worried," Stephanie said, working hard to maintain the smile.

"Uh-huh." Dawn licked her lips. "That you might not always be as happy as you were that day, you know?"

Stephanie leaned back against the vanity table. "Well," she said, "well…"

"Oh, wow!" Dawn's eyes widened. "Oh, Mrs.…oh, Stephanie. Gosh, I'm so sorry. That was such a dumb thing to ask you."

"No. Not at all. I'm just trying to think of…" *Of what lie will sound best.* "Of what to tell you."

She hadn't been nervous the day she'd married Avery, or even scared. Terrified was more accurate, terrified and desperate and almost frantic with fear…but, of course, she could never tell that to this innocent child, never tell it to anyone, and the fact she was even thinking about the possibility only proved how frazzled her nerves really were.

Stephanie smiled brightly. "Because, you understand, it

was such a long time ago. Seven years, you know? Seven—''

Dawn grasped Stephanie's hands. "Forgive me, please. I'm so wrapped up in myself today that I forgot that Mr. Willingham's—that he's—that you're a widow. I didn't mean to remind you of your loss."

"No. No, really, that's all right. I'm not—"

"I am such an idiot! Talking without thinking, I mean. It's my absolutely worst trait. Even Nicky says so. Sometimes, I just babble something before I've thought it through and I get myself, *everybody,* in all kinds of trouble! Oh, I am *so* sorry, Stephanie! Can you forgive me?"

"There's nothing to forgive," Stephanie said gently, smiling at the girl.

"Are you sure?"

"Absolutely."

"No wonder you looked so sad when I came into the room. It must be so awful, losing the man you love."

Stephanie hesitated. "I suppose it is," she said after a minute.

"I can just imagine. Why, if anything ever happened to Nicky...if anything were to separate us..." Dawn's eyes grew suspiciously bright. She laughed, swung toward the mirror, yanked a tissue from the container on top of the vanity table and dabbed at her lashes. "Just listen to me! I am turning into the most maudlin creature in the whole wide world!"

"It's understandable," Stephanie said. "Today's a very special one for you."

"Yes." Dawn blew her nose. "I feel like I'm on a roller coaster. Up one minute, down the next." She smiled. "Thanks, Stephanie."

"For what?"

"For putting up with me. I suppose all brides are basket cases on their wedding days."

"Indeed," Stephanie said with another bright, artificial smile. "Well, if you're sure you're okay…"

"I'm fine."

"Would you like me to look for your mother and send her in?"

"No, don't do that. Mom's got enough to deal with today. You go on and have fun. Did you pick up your table card yet?"

Stephanie paused at the door and shook her head. "No. No, I didn't."

"Ah." Dawn grinned. "Well, if I remember right, Mom and I put you at a terrific table."

"Did you?" Stephanie said with what she hoped sounded like interest.

"Uh-huh. You're sitting with a couple from New York, old friends of Mom's and Dad's. You know, from when they were still married."

"That sounds nice."

"And my cousin and her husband. Nice guys, both of them. He's an engineer, she's a teacher."

"Well," Stephanie said, still smiling, "they all sound—"

"And with my uncle David. Well, he's not really my uncle. I mean, he's Mr. Chambers, but I've known him forever. He's a friend of my parents'. He's this really cool guy. Really cool. And handsome." Dawn giggled. "He's a bachelor, and very sexy for an older man, you know?"

"Yes. Well, he sounds—"

The door swung open and two of Dawn's bridesmaids sailed into the room on a strain of music and a gust of laughter. Stephanie saw her opportunity and took it. She blew a kiss at Dawn, smoothed down the skirt of her suit, and stepped into the corridor.

Her smile faded.

Terrific. Annie had put her at a table with an eligible bachelor. Stephanie sighed. She should have expected as much. Even though her own marriage had failed, Annie had all the signs of being an inveterate matchmaker.

"Oh," she'd said softly when she'd learned Stephanie was widowed, "that's so sad."

Stephanie hadn't tried to correct her. They didn't know each other well enough for that. The truth was, she didn't know *anyone* well enough for that. Not that anyone back home thought of her as a grieving widow. The good people of Willingham Corners had long-ago decided what she was and Avery's death hadn't changed that. At least, nobody tried to introduce her to eligible men...but that seemed to be Annie's plan today.

Stephanie gave a mental sigh as she made her way to the table where the seating cards were laid out. She could survive an afternoon with Dawn's Uncle David. He'd surely be harmless enough. Annie was clever. She'd never met Avery but she knew he'd been in his late fifties, so she'd matched Stephanie with an older man. A sexy older man, Stephanie thought with a little smile, meaning he was fifty- or sixty-something but he still had his own teeth.

She peered at the little white vellum cards, found hers and picked it up. Table seven. Well, that was something, she thought as she stepped into the ballroom. The table would be far enough from the bandstand so the music wouldn't fry her eardrums.

Stephanie wove her way between the tables, checking numbers as she went. Four, five... Yes, table seven would definitely be away from the bandstand out of deference to Uncle David, who'd probably think that the dance of the minute was the merengue. Not that it mattered. She hadn't danced in years, and she didn't miss it. She just hoped Uncle David wouldn't take it personally when she turned out to be a dud as a table partner.

Table seven. There it was, tucked almost into a corner. Most of its occupants were already seated. The trendy-looking twosome had to be the New Yorkers; the plump, sweet-faced woman with the tall, bespectacled man were sure to be the teacher and the engineer. Only Uncle David was missing, but he was certain to turn up at any second.

The little group at table seven looked up as she dropped her place card beside her plate.

"Hi," the plump woman said—and then her gaze skittered past Stephanie's shoulder, her eyes rounded and she smiled the way a woman does when she's just seen something wonderful. "And hi to you, too," she purred.

"What a small world."

Stephanie froze. The voice came from just behind her. It was male, low, and touched with satirical amusement.

She turned slowly. He was standing inches from her, the man who'd sent her pulse racing. He was every bit as tall as he'd seemed at a distance, six-one, six-two, easily. His face was a series of hard angles; his eyes were so blue they seemed to be pieces of sky. Clint Eastwood, indeed, she thought wildly, and she almost laughed.

But laughing wouldn't help. Not now. Not after her gaze fell on the white vellum card he dropped on the table beside her.

Stephanie looked up.

"Uncle David?" she said in a choked whisper.

She remembered the way he'd looked at her the first time they'd seen each other. The smoldering glance, the lazy insolence of his smile... There was nothing of that about his expression now. His eyes were steely; the set of his mouth gave his face a harsh cast.

"And the widow Willingham." A thin smile curved across his mouth as he drew Stephanie's chair out from the table. "It's going to be one hell of a charming afternoon."

CHAPTER TWO

STEPHANIE sat down.

What else could she do? Everyone at the table was watching them, eyes bright with curiosity.

David Chambers sat down beside her. His leg brushed hers as he tucked his feet under the table. Surreptitiously, she moved her chair as far from his as she could.

He leaned toward her. "I carry no communicable diseases, Mrs. Willingham," he said dryly. "And I don't bite unless provoked."

She felt her face turn hot. His voice had been low-pitched; no one else could have heard what he'd said, but they'd wanted to—she could see it in the way they leaned forward over the table.

Say something, Stephanie told herself. Anything.

She couldn't. Her tongue felt as if it were stuck to the roof of her mouth. She cleared her throat, moistened her lips…and, mercifully, an electronic squeal from the bandstand microphone overrode all conversation in the ballroom.

The guests at table seven laughed a bit nervously.

"Those guys could use a good sound engineer," the man with the glasses said. He grinned, rose and extended his hand toward David. "Too bad that's not my speciality. Hi, nice to meet you guys. I'm Jeff Blum. And this is my wife, Roberta."

"Call me Bobbi," the plump brunette chirped, batting her lashes at David.

The other couple introduced themselves next. They looked as if they'd both been hewn out of New England granite, and had the sort of names David always irreverently thought of as Puritan holdovers.

"Hayden Crowder," the man said, extending a dry, cool hand.

"And I'm Honoria," his wife said, smiling. "And you folks are?"

"David Chambers," David said when Stephanie remained silent. He looked at her, and the grim set of his mouth softened. Okay. Maybe he was overreacting to what had happened when he'd first seen her, and to her reaction to it.

Actually, when you came down to it, *nothing* had happened—nothing that was her fault, or his. A man looked at a woman, sometimes the moment or the chemistry was just right, and that was that—although now that he was seated next to the widow Willingham, he thought wryly, he couldn't for the life of him imagine why his hormones had gone crazy back in that church. She was a looker, but so were half a dozen other women in the room. It was time to stop being an ass, remember his manners and get through the next few hours with something approaching civility.

"And the lady with me," he said pleasantly, "is—"

"Stephanie Willingham. Mrs. Avery Willingham," Stephanie blurted. "And I can assure all of you that I am not here with Mr. Chambers, nor would I ever choose to be."

Bobbi Blum looked at her husband. Hayden Crowder looked at his wife. All four of them looked at Stephanie, who was trying not to look at any of them.

Ohmygod!

What on earth had possessed her? It was such an incredibly stupid thing to have said, especially after the man seated beside her had made an attempt, however late and unwanted, at showing he had, at least, some semblance of good manners.

"Do tell," Bobbi Blum said with a bright smile. She sat

back as the waiter set glasses of champagne before them.
"Well, that's certainly very, ah, interesting."

Honoria Crowder shot a brilliant smile across the table.
"Champagne," she said briskly. "Isn't that nice? I always
say champagne's the only thing to serve at weddings, isn't
that right, Hayden?"

Hayden Crowder swallowed hard. Stephanie could see
his Adam's apple bob up and down in his long, skinny
neck.

"Indeed you do, my dear."

"Oh, I agree." Jeff Blum, eager to do his part, nodded
vigorously. "Don't I always say that, too, Bobbi?"

Bobbi Blum turned a perplexed smile on her husband.
"Don't you always say what, dear?"

"That champagne is—that it's whatever Mrs. Crowder
just said it was."

"Do call me Honoria," Honoria said.

Silence settled over the table again.

Stephanie's hands were knotted together in her lap.
Everyone had said something in an attempt to ease the tension—everyone but David Chambers.

He was looking at her. She could feel the weight of his
gaze. Why didn't he say something? Why didn't *she* say
something? A witty remark, to take the edge off. A clever
one, to turn her awful words into a joke.

When was the band going to start playing?

As if on cue, the trumpet player rose to his feet and sent
a shattering tattoo of sound out into the room.

"And now," the bandleader said, "let's give a warm
welcome to Dawn and Nicholas!"

The Crowders, then the Blums, looked toward the dance
floor as the introductions rolled on. Stephanie breathed a
small sigh of relief. Perhaps David Chambers's attention
was on the newlyweds, too. Her hand closed around her
small, apricot-silk purse. Carefully, she moved back her

chair. Now might be the perfect time to make another strategic retreat to the ladies' room…

"Leaving so soon, Mrs. Willingham?"

Stephanie froze. Then, with as much hauteur as she could manage, she turned her head toward David Chambers. His expression was polite and courteous; she was sure he looked the picture of civility—unless you were sitting as close to him as she was, and you could see the ridicule in his eyes.

Okay. It was time to take a bite, however small, of humble pie.

"Mr. Chambers." She cleared her throat. "Mr. Chambers, I suppose—what I said before—I didn't mean…"

He smiled coolly and bent toward her, his eyes on hers.

"An apology?"

"An explanation." Stephanie sat up straight. "I was rude, and I didn't intend to be."

"Ah. What did you intend to be, then?" His smile tilted and he moved closer, near enough to make her heartbeat quicken. For one foolish instant, she'd thought he was going to kiss her.

"I simply meant to make it clear that you and I were not together."

"You certainly did that."

"I'm sure Annie meant well, when she seated us this way, but—"

"Annie?"

"Annie Cooper. Surely, you know—"

"You were seated on the groom's side."

"I know both the bride and the groom, Mr. Chambers."

"But you're Annie's guest."

"I can't see of what possible interest it could be to you, sir."

Neither could David—except that it had occurred to him, as he'd gone down the receiving line, that word had it that the groom's uncle, Damian Skouras, had a mistress in attendance at the wedding. Perhaps Stephanie Willingham was she. Or perhaps she was a former mistress. Or a future one. It was a crazy world out there; there was no telling what complications you got into when you drew up guest lists. He'd avoided the problem, his one time in the matrimonial sweepstakes. You didn't draw up a guest list when you said "I do" at city hall.

"Humor me, Mrs. Willingham," David said with a chilly smile. "Why did you choose to sit on the groom's side?"

"What do you do for a living, Mr. Chambers?"

"I don't see what that has to do with my question."

"Suppose you humor *me,* and answer it."

David's frown deepened. "I'm an attorney."

"Ah. Well, I suppose that explains it."

"Explains what?" David said, his eyes narrowing.

"Your tendency to interrogate."

"I beg your pardon, Mrs. Willingham. I did not—"

"I must admit, I find it preferable to your tendency to strip a woman naked with your eyes."

The band segued from a bouncy rendition of "My Girl" to a soft, sighing "Stardust." Stephanie's words rose clearly over the plaintive opening notes.

A strangled gasp burst from Honoria Crowder's lips. Her champagne glass tipped over and a puddle of pale golden wine spread across the white tablecloth.

"Oh, my," Honoria twittered, "how clumsy of me!"

Bobbi Blum snatched at a napkin. "Here," she said, "let me get that."

Saved by the spill, Stephanie thought hysterically. She smiled blindly at the waiter as he served their first course. The Crowders and the Blums grabbed their oyster forks and attacked their shrimp cocktails with a fervor she suspected was born of the desire to leap to their feet and run from what was turning into the kind of encounter that ends with one of the parties bleeding.

If you had any brains, Stephanie told herself, you'd do the same...

Instead, she picked up her fork and began to stuff food into her mouth because if she was chewing and swallowing, maybe—just maybe—she'd stop saying things that only made this impossible mess messier.

"I don't."

Stephanie's head snapped up. She looked at David, and the smug little smile on his face sent a chill straight into the marrow of her bones.

"Don't what?" Bobbi Blum said, and everyone leaned forward in eager anticipation.

"Don't have a tendency to strip women naked with my eyes." His smile tilted, and his gaze swept over Stephanie again, sending a flood of color to her cheeks. "Not indiscriminately, that is. I only focus that sort of attention on beautiful women who look to be in desperate need of—"

Music blared from the bandstand.

Forks clattered to the table.

The Crowders and the Blums pushed back their chairs and rushed to the dance floor.

Stephanie sat very still, though she could damn near feel the blood churning in her veins. She thought about slugging the man beside her, but that wouldn't be fair to Annie, or Dawn, or Nicholas. Besides, ladies didn't do such things. The woman—the girl—she'd once been might have. Would have. Steffie Horton would have balled up her fist and shot a right cross straight to David Chambers's square jaw.

A tremor went through her. Steffie Horton would have done exactly what Stephanie Willingham had been doing all afternoon. She'd have been rude, and impolite; she'd have spoken her mind without thinking. She might even have reacted to the heat in a stranger's eyes. It was in her genes, after all. Avery had been wrong about a lot of things, but not about that.

What was wrong with her today? She was behaving

badly. And even when David Chambers had held out an olive branch—a ragged one, it was true, but an olive branch nevertheless—she'd slapped it out of his hand.

Stephanie took a deep breath and turned toward him.

"Mr. Chambers…"

Her words caught in her throat. He was smiling…no, he wasn't. Not really. His lips were drawn back from his teeth in a way that reminded her of a mastiff Avery had owned when she'd first married him and gone to live in the house on Oak Hill—when she'd still been young enough, stupid enough, to have thought their arrangement could work.

"Oh," she'd said, "just look at your dog, Avery. He's smiling at me."

And Avery had guffawed and slapped his knees and said that he'd truly picked himself a backwoods ninny if she thought that was a smile, and maybe she'd like to offer the mastiff her hand and see if it came back with all the fingers still attached.

"Yes?" David said politely. "Did you have something you wanted to say?"

"No," Stephanie said just as politely. "Not a thing."

He nodded. "That's fine. I think I've just about run out of conversation, myself—except to point out that, with any luck at all, we'll never have the misfortune to meet again." His wolfish smile flickered. "Have I left anything out?"

"Not a thing. In fact, I doubt I could have put it better."

David unfolded his napkin and placed it in his lap. Stephanie did the same.

"*Bon appétit*, Mrs. Willingham," David said softly.

"*Bon appétit*, Mr. Chambers," Stephanie replied, and she picked up her fork, speared a shrimp, and began to eat.

More toasts were drunk, the wedding cake sliced. The Blums and the Crowders continued to make themselves scarce, appearing only from time to time and then just long enough to gobble down a few mouthfuls of each course as it was served.

"We just adore dancing," Bobbi Blum gushed between the *Boeuf aux Champignons* and the salad.

"Same with us," Hayden Crowder said as his wife sat smiling uneasily beside him. "Why, we never sit very long at these shindigs, no matter who's seated at our table, do we, honey?"

"Never," Honoria said, and jumped to her feet. "We never stay seated, no matter what."

David watched with a thin smile as both couples hurried off. Then he pushed his plate aside, tilted back his chair and folded his arms over his chest.

"Well," he said after a minute, "this is one wedding they're never going to forget."

Stephanie glanced up. "No. I suppose not."

Across the dance floor, the Blums and the Crowders were standing in a little huddle, looking back at table seven as if they expected either the police or the men with strait-jackets to show up at any minute.

David couldn't help it. He laughed.

Stephanie's lips twitched. "It isn't funny," she said stiffly—and then she laughed, too.

He looked at her. Her cheeks had taken on a delicate flush and there was a glint in her dark eyes that hadn't been there before. She looked young, and beautiful, and suddenly he knew that he'd been kidding himself when he'd told himself she wasn't the most beautiful woman in this room, because she was. She was more than beautiful, she was indescribably gorgeous.

And he'd been sniping at her for the past hour. Damn, he had to be crazy! Everything he'd done had been crazy, since he'd laid eyes on her. He should have sat down beside her, introduced himself, asked her if he could see her again. He should have told her she was the most beautiful woman he'd ever met....

He could still do all of that. It wasn't too late and, heaven knew, it was the best idea he'd had in the past couple of hours.

"Mrs. Willingham. Stephanie. About what happened earlier..." Her face lifted toward his. David smiled. "In the church, I mean."

"Nothing happened," she said quickly.

"Come on, let's not play games. Something happened, all right. I looked at you, you looked at me..."

"Mr. Chambers—"

"David."

"Mr. Chambers." Stephanie folded her hands in her lap. "Look, I know this isn't your fault. I mean, I know Annie probably set this up."

"Probably?" He laughed. "Of course, she set this up. You're unattached. You *are* unattached, aren't you?"

Stephanie nodded. "I'm a widow."

"Yeah, well, I'm divorced. So Annie took a look at her guest list, saw my name, saw yours, and that was it. It's in her blood, though I can't imagine why, considering her own record."

Color flooded Stephanie's face. "I assure you, Mr. Chambers, I have absolutely no wish to marry, ever again."

"Whoa!" David held up his hands. "One step at a time, Mrs. Willingham—and before anybody takes that step, let me assure *you* that I'd sooner waltz Mrs. Blum around the dance floor for the next three weeks than ever do something as stupid as tying another knot. Not in this lifetime. Or any other, for that matter."

Stephanie tried not to smile. "There's nothing wrong with Mrs. Blum."

"She dances on her husband's feet," David said, "and she outweighs the both of us." Stephanie laughed. His smile tilted, and his gaze dropped to her mouth. "You have a nice laugh, Stephanie."

"Mr. Chambers..."

"David. Surely we've insulted each other enough to be on a first-name basis."

"David, maybe we did get off on the wrong foot, but—"

"So did Mrs. Blum."

She smiled again, and his heart lifted. She really did have a nice smile.

"Let's just forget it, shall we?"

"I'd like that, very much—especially since it was all my fault."

"That's kind of you, David, but, well, I was to blame, too. I—I saw the way you were looking at me in the church, you know, when you went to shut the doors, and—and I thought…" She took a deep breath. "All I'm trying to say is that I didn't mean to be so—so—"

"Impolite?" he asked innocently. "Judgmental? Is that the word you're looking for?"

Laughter glinted in her eyes.

"You're pushing your luck," she said. "Putting words in my mouth that way."

He thought of what he'd like to do with that mouth, how badly he wanted to taste it, and cleared his throat.

"Ah," he said, shaking his head sadly, "and here I thought the widow Willingham was about to offer a full apology for her behavior. So much for the mystique of Southern good manners."

"My manners are usually impeccable. And how can you be so certain I'm from the South?"

He chuckled. "'An' how can you be so suhtain Ah'm from th' South?'" he said.

Stephanie tried not to smile, but it was impossible. "I'm glad my accent amuses you, Mr. Chambers."

"I promise you, Mrs. Willingham, I'm not laughing at you. Matter of fact, I like your drawl. It's very feminine."

"If you're waiting for me to say I like the sound of your Montana twang, Mr. Chambers—"

"Montana?" David slapped his hand over his heart.

"Good God, woman, you do know how to wound a man. I'm from Wyoming."

"Oh."

"Oh? Is that all you can say, after you accuse me of being from a state where the cows outnumber the people three to one?" He grinned. "At least, in Wyoming, we only have one critter that walks upright for every two point something that moos."

Stephanie laughed politely. "My apologies."

"Apologies accepted. And, just for the record, I have no accent."

Her smile was warm and open this time. He had an accent; she was sure he knew it as well as she did. His voice was low and husky; it reminded her of high mountains and wide open spaces, of a place where the night sky would be bright with stars and the grassy meadows would roll endlessly toward the horizon....

"Gotcha," he said softly.

Stephanie blinked. "What?"

"You smiled," David said with a little smile of his own. "Really smiled. And I agree."

"Agree about what?" she said in total confusion.

"That we got off to the wrong start."

She considered the possibility. Perhaps they had. He seemed a nice enough man, this friend of Annie's. There was no denying his good looks, and he had a sense of humor, too. Not that she was interested in him. Not that she'd ever be interested in any man. Still, that was no reason not to be polite. Pleasant, even. This was just one day out of her life. One afternoon. And what had he done, when you came down to it? Looked at her, that was all. Just looked at her, and even though she hated it, she was accustomed to it.

Men had always looked at her, even before Avery had come along.

Besides, she wasn't guiltless. For one heart-stopping instant, for one quick spin of the planet, she'd looked at David and felt—she'd felt…

"Stephanie?"

She raised her head. David was watching her, eyes dark and intense.

"How about we begin over?"

He held out his hand. Stephanie hesitated. Then, very slowly and carefully, she lifted her hand from her lap and placed it in his.

"That's it," he said softly. His fingers closed around hers. They were warm, and hard, and calloused. That surprised her. Despite what he'd said about being from the west, despite the cowboy boots and the ponytail and the incredible width of his shoulders, everything about him whispered of wealth and power. Men like that didn't have hands that bore the imprint of hard work, not in her world.

He bent his head toward hers. She knew she ought to pull back but she couldn't. His eyes were still locked on hers. They seemed to draw her in.

"You're a very beautiful woman, Stephanie."

"Mr. Chambers…"

"I thought we'd progressed to David."

"David." Stephanie ran the tip of her tongue over her lips. She saw him follow the motion with his eyes and the tiny flame that had come to life hours before sprang up again deep within her. A warning tingled along her skin. "David," she said again, "I think—I think it's nice that we made peace with each other, but—"

"We should be honest, too."

"I am being honest. I don't want—"

"Yes. You *do* want." His voice had taken on a roughness. A huskiness. It made the trembling flame within her burn brighter. "We both do."

"No!"

He could feel the sudden tension radiating from her fingers to his. Don't be a fool, David told himself fiercely.

There was plenty of time. The longer it took to go from that first beat of sexual awareness to the bed, the greater the pleasure. He'd lived long enough to know that.

But he couldn't slow down. Not with this woman. He wanted her, now. Right now. He wanted her beneath him, her body naked to his hands and mouth, her eyes liquid with desire as he touched her, entered her.

"Come with me," he said urgently. "I have a car outside. We'll find a hotel."

"You bastard!" She tore her hand from his. "Is that what the past few minutes were all about?"

"No," he said, trying to deny it, as much to himself as to her. He felt as if he were standing on the edge of a precipice, that the slightest gust of wind could come by and send him tumbling out into space. He'd met women before, wanted them, but not like this. Not with a need so fierce it obliterated everything else. "Stephanie—"

"Don't 'Stephanie' me!" She shoved back her chair. Her face was flushed; she glared at him, her mouth trembling. "You've wasted your time, Mr. Chambers. I know your game."

"Dammit, it isn't a game! I saw you, and I wanted you. And you wanted me. That's why you're so angry, isn't it? Because you felt the same thing, only you're afraid to admit it."

"I'm not afraid of anything, Mr. Chambers, especially not of a man like you."

It was a lie. She *was* afraid; he saw it in her eyes, in the feverish color in her cheeks.

"I know your type, sir. You see a woman like me, your mind goes rolling straight into the gutter."

"What?" he said with an incredulous little laugh.

"As for what I want… You flatter yourself. I'd no more want you in my bed than I'd want a cottonmouth moccasin there! Why would I? Why would any woman in her right mind want to subjugate herself to a—a—"

"Hey, guys, how's it going?"

Stephanie clamped her lips together. She and David both looked up. Annie Cooper stood over them, smiling happily.

"Annie," David said after a minute. He cleared his throat. "Hello."

"I hated to interrupt," Annie said, smiling. "You two were so deep in conversation."

Stephanie looked at David, then at Annie. "Uh, yes. Yes, we were." She smiled brightly. "It's a lovely wedding, Annie. Really lovely."

Annie pulled out a chair and sat down. "So," she said slyly, "I figured right, hmm?"

"Figured right?"

"About you guys." Annie grinned. "Dawn and I were doing the seating chart and Dawn said to me, 'Mom, except for Nicky, the best-looking man at the wedding is going to be Uncle David.' And I said to her, 'Well, except for you, my gorgeous, too-young-to-be-a-bride daughter, the most beautiful woman at the wedding is going to be your very own cupid, Stephanie.'"

"Annie," David said, "listen—"

"So my brilliant offspring and I put our heads together and, *voilà*, we put the pair of you at the same table." Annie smiled. "Clever, if I say so myself, no?"

"No," Stephanie said. "I mean, I'm sure you thought it was, Annie, but—"

Annie laughed. "Relax, you two. We won't expect you to announce your engagement or anything. Not today, anyway... My gosh, Stef, I'm making you blush. And David...if looks could kill, I'd be lying in a heap on the floor." A furrow appeared between her eyes. "Don't tell me we goofed! Aren't you two having a good time? Haven't you hit it off?"

"We're having a terrific time," Stephanie said quickly. "Aren't we...David?"

David smiled tightly and shoved back his chair. "Better

than terrific,'' he said. "Excuse me for a minute, will you? I'm going to get myself a drink. Annie? Stephanie? Can I bring you ladies something?"

"Nothing for me, thank you," Annie said. "I'm on overload as it is."

A bludgeon, Stephanie thought. "White wine," she said, because Annie was looking at her expectantly.

David nodded. "Be right back."

Damn, he thought grimly as he made his way across the ballroom, damn! Why in hell was he making such a fool of himself with Stephanie Willingham? She was wild as a mustang and beautiful as a purebred, and okay, there wasn't another woman in the place who could hold a candle to her, but either he'd read the signs wrong and she wasn't interested, or she liked to play games. Whichever it was, why should he care? The world was filled with beautiful women and finding ones who were interested had never been a problem. They seemed to go for his type, whatever that was.

It was just that there was something about Stephanie. All that frost. Or maybe the heat. It was crazy. A woman couldn't be hot and cold at the same time, she couldn't look at a man as if she wanted to be in his arms one minute and wanted to slap him silly the next unless she was a tease, and instinct told him that whatever she was, she was not that.

What he ought to do was walk right on past the bar, out the door and to his car. Drive to the airport, catch the shuttle back to D.C....

David's brows lifted. He began to smile.

"Chase?" he called.

There was no mistaking the set of shoulders in front of him. It was his old pal, Chase Cooper, the father of the bride.

Chase turned around, saw David, and held out his hand.

"David," he said, and then both men grinned and gave each other a quick bear hug. "How're you doing, man?"

"Fine, fine. How about you?"

Chase lifted his glass to his lips and knocked back half of the whiskey in it in one swallow.

"Never been better. What'll you have?"

"Scotch," David said to the bartender. "A single malt, if you have it, on the rocks. And a glass of Chardonnay."

Chase smiled. "Don't tell me that you're here with a lady. Has the love bug bitten you, too?"

"Me?" David laughed. "The wine's for a lady at my table. The love bug already bit me, remember? Once bitten, twice shy. No, not me. Never again."

"Yeah." Chase nodded, and his smile flickered. "I agree. You marry a woman, she turns into somebody else after a couple of years."

"You've got it," David said. "Marriage is a female fantasy. Promise a guy anything to nab him, then look blank when he expects you to deliver." The bartender set the Scotch in front of David, who lifted the glass to his lips and took a drink. "Far as I'm concerned, a man's got a housekeeper, a cook, and a good secretary, what more does he need?"

"Nothing," Chase said a little too quickly, "not one thing."

David glanced back across the ballroom. He could see Stephanie, sitting alone at the table. Annie had left, but she hadn't bolted. It surprised him.

"Unfortunately," he said, trying for a light touch, "there *is* one other thing a man needs, and it's the thing that most often gets guys like you and me in trouble."

"Yeah." Chase followed his gaze, then lifted his glass and clinked it against David's. "Well, you and I both know how to deal with that little problem. Bed 'em and forget 'em, I say."

David grinned. "I'll drink to that."

"To what? What are you guys up to, hidden away over here?"

Both men turned around. Dawn, radiant in white lace, and with Nick at her side, beamed at them.

"Daddy," she said, kissing her father's cheek. "And Mr. Chambers. I'm so glad you could make it."

"Hey." David smiled. "What happened to 'Uncle David'? I kind of liked the honorary title." He held out his hand to Nicholas, said all the right things, and stood by politely until the bridal couple moved off.

Chase sighed. "That's the only good thing comes of a marriage," he said. "A kid of your own, you know?"

David nodded. "I agree. I'd always hoped..." He shrugged. "Hey, Cooper," he said with a quick grin, "you stand around a bar long enough, you get maudlin. Anybody ever tell you that?"

"Yes," Chase said. "My attorney, five years ago when we got wasted after my divorce was finalized."

The men smiled at each other, and then David slapped Chase lightly on the back.

"You ought to circulate, man. There's a surprising assortment of good-looking single women here, in case you hadn't noticed."

"For a lawyer," Chase said with a chuckle, "sometimes you manage to come up with some pretty decent suggestions. So, what's with the brunette at your table? She spoken for?"

"She is," David said gruffly. "For the present, at least."

Chase grinned. "You dirty dog, you. Well, never mind. I'll case the joint, see what's available."

"Yeah." David grinned in return. "You do that."

The men made their goodbyes. Chase set off in one direction, David in the other. The dance floor had grown crowded; the band had launched into a set of sixties' standards that seemed to have brought out every couple in the room. David wove between them, his gaze fixed on

Stephanie. He saw her turn and look in his direction. Their eyes met; he felt as if an electric current had run through his body.

"Whoops." A woman jostled his elbow. "Sorry."

David looked around, nodded impatiently as she apologized. The music ceased. The dancers applauded, and the crowd parted.

Table seven was just ahead. The Blums were there, and the Crowders.

But Stephanie Willingham was gone.

CHAPTER THREE

THE only thing worse than leaving Washington on a Friday was returning to it on a Monday.

Every politician and lobbyist who earned his or her living toiling in the bureaucratic fields of the District of Columbia flew home for the weekend. That was the way it seemed, anyway, and if Friday travel was a nightmare of clogged highways, jammed airports and overbooked flights, Mondays were all that and more. There was something about the start of the workweek that made for woefully short tempers.

David had made careful plans to avoid what he thought of as the Monday Morning Mess. He'd told his secretary to book him out of Hartford on a late Sunday flight and when that had turned out to be impossible, he'd considered how long it would be before he could make a polite exit from the Cooper wedding reception and instructed her to ticket him out of Boston. It was only another hour, hour and a half's drive.

A simple enough plan, he had figured.

But nothing was simple, that Sunday.

By midafternoon, hours before he'd expected to leave Stratham, David was in his rented car, flooring the pedal as he flew down the highway. He was in a mood even he knew could best be described as grim.

Now what? He had hours to kill before his flight from Boston, and he had no wish whatsoever to sit around an airport, cooling his heels.

Not ever, but especially not now. Not when he was so annoyed he could have chewed a box of nails and spit them out as staples.

There was always the flight out of Hartford, the one he'd turned down as being scheduled too early. Yes. He'd head for Bradley Airport, buy a ticket on that flight instead.

Maybe he should phone, check to see if there was an available seat.

No. What for? Bradley was a small airport. It didn't handle a lot of traffic. Why would a plane bound for D.C. on a Sunday afternoon be booked up?

David made a sharp right, skidded a little as he made up his mind, and took the ramp that led north toward the airport.

The sooner he got out of here, the better. Why hang around this part of the world any longer than necessary?

"No reason," he muttered through his teeth, "none at all."

He glanced down, saw that the speedometer was edging over sixty. Was fifty-five the speed limit in Connecticut, or was it sixty-five? Back home—back in his *real* home, Wyoming—people drove at logical speeds, meaning you took a look at the road and the traffic and then, the sky was the limit.

But not here.

"Hell," he said, and goosed the car up to sixty-five.

He'd done what had been required, even if he had left the reception early. He'd toasted the bride and groom, paid his respects to Annie, shaken Chase's hand and had a drink with him. That was enough. If other people wanted to hang around, dance to a too loud band, tuck into too rich food, make a pretense of having a good time, that was their business.

Besides, he'd pretty much overstayed his welcome at table seven. David figured the Blums and the Crowders would make small talk for a month out of what had gone on between him and Stephanie, but they'd also probably cheered his defection.

The needle on the speedometer slid past seventy.

"Leaving so soon?" Bobbi Blum had asked, after he'd made a circuit of the ballroom and then paused at the table just long enough to convince the Blums and the Crowders that he really was insane. Her voice had been sweet, her smile syrupy enough to put a diabetic into a coma, but the look in her eyes said, "Please, oh, please, don't tell us you're just stepping outside to have a smoke."

Maybe it had something to do with the way he'd demanded to know if any of them had seen Stephanie leave.

"I did," Honoria had squeaked, and it was only when he'd heard that high-pitched voice that reality had finally made its way into David's overcooked brain and he'd realized he was acting like a man one card short of a full deck.

And for what reason? David's mouth thinned, and he stepped down harder on the gas pedal.

It wasn't Honoria's fault—it wasn't anybody's fault—that he'd let Stephanie Willingham poison his disposition before she'd vanished like a rabbit inside a magician's hat.

"Give us a break, Chambers," he muttered.

Who was he trying to fool? It was somebody's fault, all right. His. He'd homed in on Stephanie like a heat-seeking missile and that wasn't his style. He was a sophisticated man with a sophisticated approach. A smile, a phone call. Flowers, chocolates...he wasn't in the habit of coming on to a woman with all the subtlety of a cement truck.

He could hardly blame her for leaving without so much as a goodbye.

Not that he cared. Well, yeah, he cared that he'd made a fool of himself, but aside from that, what did it matter? David's hands relaxed on the steering wheel; his foot eased off the pedal. The widow Willingham was something to look at, and yes, she was an enigma. He'd bet anything that the colder-than-the-Antarctic exterior hid a hotter-than-the-Tropics core.

Well, let some other poor sucker find out.

He preferred his women to be soft. Feminine. Independent, yes, but not so independent you felt each encounter was only a heartbeat away from stepping into a cage with a tiger. The bottom line was that this particular babe meant nothing to him. Two, three hours from now, he'd probably have trouble remembering what she looked like. Those dark, unfathomable eyes. That lush mouth. The silken hair, and the body that just wouldn't quit, even though she'd hidden it inside a tailored suit the color of ripe apricots.

Apricot. That was the shade, all right. Not that he'd ever consciously noticed. If somebody had said, "Okay, Chambers, what was the widow wearing?" he'd have had to shrug and admit he hadn't any idea.

Not true. He *did* have an idea. His foot bore down on the accelerator. A very specific one. His brain had registered all the pertinent facts, like the shade of the fabric. And some nonpertinent ones, like the way the jacket fit, clinging to the rise of her breasts, then nipping in at her waist before flaring out gently over her hips. Or the way the skirt had just kissed her knees. He'd noticed the color of her stockings, too. They'd been pale gray. And filmy, like the sheerest silk.

Were they stockings? Or were they panty hose? Who was it who'd invented panty hose, anyway? Not a man, that was certain. A man would have understood the importance of keeping women—beautiful, cool-to-the-eye women—in thigh-length stockings and garter belts. Maybe that was what she'd been wearing beneath that chastely tailored suit. Hosiery that would feel like cobwebs to his hands as he peeled them down her legs. A white lace garter belt, and a pair of tiny white silk panties....

The shrill howl of a siren pierced the air. David shot a glance at the speedometer, muttered a quick, sharp word and pulled onto the shoulder of the road. The flashing red lights of a police cruiser filled his rearview mirror as it pulled in behind him.

David shut off the engine and looked in his mirror again. The cop sauntering toward him was big. He was wearing dark glasses, even though the afternoon was clouding over, as if he'd seen one old Burt Reynolds' movie too many. David sighed and let down his window. Then, without a word, he handed over his driver's license.

The policeman studied the license, then David.

"Any idea how fast you were tooling along there, friend?" he asked pleasantly.

David wrapped his hands around the steering wheel and blew out a breath.

"Too fast."

"You got that right."

"Yeah."

"That's it? Just, 'yeah'? No story? No excuse?"

"None you'd want to hear," David said after a couple of seconds.

"Try me," the cop said. David looked at him, and he laughed. "What can I tell you? It's been a slow day."

A muscle clenched in David's jaw. "I just met a woman," he said. "I didn't like her. She didn't like me, and I think—I know—I pretty much made an ass of myself. It shouldn't matter. I mean, I know I'll never see her again...but I can't get her out of my head."

There was a silence, and then the cop sighed.

"Listen," he said, "you want some advice?" He handed David his license, took off his dark glasses and put his huge hands on the window ledge. "Forget the babe, whoever she is. Women are nothing but grief and worry."

David looked at the cop. "That they are."

"Damn right. Hey, I should know. I been married seven years."

"I should, too. I've been *divorced* seven years."

The two men looked at each other. Then the cop straightened up.

"Drive slowly, pal. The life you save, and all that..."

David smiled. "I will. And thanks."

The cop grinned. "If guys don't stick together, the babes will win the war."

"They'll probably win it anyway," David said, and drove off.

A war.

That's was what it was, all right.

Men against women. Hell, why limit it? It was male against female. No species was safe. One sex played games, the other sex went crazy.

David strode into the departures terminal at the airport, his garment carrier slung over his shoulder.

That was what all that nonsense had been today. A war game. The interval with the policeman had given him time to rethink things, and he'd finally figured out what had happened at that wedding.

Stephanie Willingham had been on maneuvers.

It wasn't that he'd come on too hard. It was that she'd been setting up an ambush from the moment in church when they'd first laid eyes on each other. He'd made the mistake of letting his gonads do his thinking and, bam, he'd fallen right into the trap.

On the other hand... David frowned as he took his place on the tail end of a surprisingly long line at the ticket counter. On the other hand, the feminine stratagems she'd used were unlike any he'd ever experienced.

Some women went straight into action. They'd taken the equality thing to heart. "Hello," they'd purr, and then they'd ask a few questions—were you married, involved, whatever—and if you gave the right answers, they made it clear they were interested.

He liked women who did that, admired them for being

straightforward, though in his heart of hearts, he had to admit he still enjoyed doing things the old-fashioned way. There was a certain pleasure in doing the pursuing. If a woman played just a little hard to get, it heightened the chase and sweetened the moment of surrender.

But Stephanie Willingham had gone overboard.

She hadn't just played hard to get. She'd played impossible.

The line shuffled forward and David shuffled along with it.

Maybe he really wasn't her type. Maybe she hadn't found his looks to her liking.

No. There was such a thing as modesty but there was such a thing as honesty, too, and the simple truth was that he hadn't had trouble getting female attention since his voice had gone down and his height had gone up, way back in junior high school.

Maybe she just didn't like men. Maybe her interests lay elsewhere. Anything was possible in today's confused, convoluted, three-and-four-gender world.

No. Uh-uh. Stephanie Willingham was all female. He'd bet everything he had on that.

What was left, then? If she hadn't found him repugnant, if she wasn't interested in women...

David frowned. Maybe she was still in love with her husband.

"Hell," he said, under his breath. The elderly woman standing in front of him looked around, eyebrows lifted. David blushed. "Sorry. I, uh, I didn't expect this line to be so long..."

"Never expect anything," the woman said. "My Earl always said that. If you don't expect anything, you can't be disappointed."

Philosophy, on a ticket line in Connecticut? David almost smiled. On the other hand, it was probably good advice. And he'd have taken it to heart, if he'd needed to.

But he didn't, because he was never going to see Stephanie Willingham again. How come he kept forgetting that?

End of problem. End of story. The line staggered forward. By the time David reached the ticket counter, he was smiling.

"Mrs. Willingham?"

Honoria Crowder let the door to the ladies' room of the Stratham Country Club swing shut behind her.

"Mrs. Willingham? Stephanie?"

Honoria peered at the line of closed stalls. Then she rolled her eyes, bent down and checked for feet showing under the doors. A pair of shiny black pumps peeped from beneath the last door on the end.

"He's gone," she said.

The door swung open and Stephanie looked out. "You're sure?"

"Positive. The coast is clear. Mr. Chambers left."

"You saw him go?"

"With my very own eyes, Stephanie. He gave us the third degree and when we'd convinced him you'd left, he did, too."

"I'm terribly sorry to have put you through all this, Mrs. Crowder."

"Honoria."

"Honoria." Stephanie hesitated. "I know my behavior must seem—it must seem..." Odd? Bizarre? Strange? "Unusual," she said. "And I'm afraid I really can't explain it."

"No need," Honoria said politely.

It was a lie. Honoria Crowder would have sold her soul for an explanation. She'd felt like a voyeur, watching the sparks bounce between the Chambers man and this woman. She'd said as much to Hayden, even added that anybody standing too close could almost have gotten singed. Hayden had given one of his prissy little smiles as if he had no idea what she was talking about—but Bobbi Blum, who'd turned out to be lots more perceptive than she'd looked, had leaned over as she'd danced by in her husband's arms and whispered that what Honoria had just said was God's honest truth.

"I'm not sure if those two are going to haul off and slug each other senseless, or if they're going to grab hold of each other and just…" She'd blushed. "Just, you know…"

Honoria knew. She wouldn't have put it quite so bluntly, but yes, that about summed things up. The Willingham woman and that man had turned out to be the entertainment of the day.

"It isn't as if I was afraid of him, you understand."

Honoria blinked. "Beg pardon?"

"That man. David Chambers." Stephanie cleared her throat. "I, uh, I wouldn't want anyone to think he'd, you know, threatened me or anything."

"Oh. Well, no, no, actually I didn't—"

"It's just that he…that I…that I felt it was best if…if…"

If what, Stephanie? Why are you acting like such an idiot? Why are you hiding in the ladies' room, as if this were prom night and you'd just discovered that your slip was showing?

Stephanie grabbed for the doorknob. "Thanks again."

The door swung shut, and that was it. Honoria Crowder sighed, washed her hands, and headed back to table seven.

"Fascinating," Bobbi Blum said when Honoria told her the latest details over decaf and wedding cake.

"Interesting," Honoria corrected.

Bobbi leaned closer. "Wasn't he just drop-dead gorgeous?"

Honoria opened her mouth and started to correct her there, as well. Drop-dead gorgeous was such a New York kind of phrase. It was overblown. Overdone. Overdramatic…

But my goodness, it was accurate.

That build. Those eyes. The hair. The face... Honoria's inborn New England sense of reticence deserted her, and she sighed.

"Drop-dead gorgeous, indeed," she murmured.

David Chambers surely was.

The wonder of it was that Stephanie Willingham hadn't seemed to notice.

Stephanie got into her rented Ford, snapped the door locks, and turned on the engine. She checked the traffic in both directions, then pulled out of the parking lot.

She felt badly, leaving this way, never even saying good-bye or thank-you to Annie, but if she'd done either, Annie would have wanted to know why she was leaving so early, and what could she possibly have said?

I'm leaving because there's a man here who's been coming on to me.

Oh, yeah. That would have gone over big, considering that Annie had clearly hoped for exactly that to happen.

Stephanie frowned as she approached the on-ramp to the highway. She slowed the car, checked right, then left, and carefully accelerated.

If Annie only knew. If she only had an idea of what had gone on. The way David Chambers had looked at her, as if he wanted to—to—

He'd even said as much! Oh, if Annie only knew. If she knew that he'd told her he wanted to make love to her, that it was what she wanted, too.

Stephanie's heart did a quick flip-flop.

How dare he?

"How *dare* he?" she muttered.

She hadn't wanted any such thing. Never. Not with this—this self-satisfied, smug cowboy or with any other man. She shuddered. Not since Avery—not since her husband had...

Was that the airport exit? Had she missed it? There was a sign, but she'd gone by too fast to read it.

Too fast?

She frowned, looked down at the speedometer. Sixty. She was doing sixty? The speed limit in this state was fifty-five—she'd made a point of asking at the car rental counter at the airport. She never drove above the limit. Never. Not when she was back home in Georgia; not when she was on vacation.

Stephanie eased her foot from the pedal and the speedometer needle dropped back to a safe and sane fifty. Not that she'd been on many vacations. Actually, there'd been just the one, to Cape Cod. She really hadn't much wanted to go. It had been her attorney's idea.

"You need to get away," he'd said firmly, making it sound as if he were concerned for her welfare when really he'd just wanted her out of the way. But she'd been too naive to figure that out, so she'd agreed that, yes, a change of scene would do her good.

Of course, she hadn't wanted to be away from Paul for any great length of time. Not that her brother minded. He never seemed to notice anymore if she was there or not, but what did that matter? She would be there for him, always.

Always.

Just thinking about Paul drove all the idiocy about David Chambers from her head. She had more important things to worry about than her irrational response to a man with a sexy smile, knowing eyes and softly seductive words.

There! Straight ahead. The sign for the airport. And, beyond it, the exit ramp.

Stephanie slowed the car and put on her turn signal indicator. Carefully, she made her way toward Bradley and an earlier flight than she'd planned.

Surely, there would be one.

And after that...after that, there'd be Clare and the mess

waiting for her at home, but what was the point in thinking about it now?

Things would work out. They just had to.

David smiled at the ticket clerk.

"Excellent," he said, and whipped his platinum charge card from his wallet.

"Which was it, sir? Window or aisle?"

"Aisle. Definitely. Even in first class, I can use the leg-room."

The clerk smiled and batted her lashes at him. "Here you are, Mr. Chambers. Have a pleasant flight."

At the far end of the airport, Stephanie smiled and walked straight up to the ticket counter.

Seconds later her smile was gone. The only direct flight to Atlanta was the one she was ticketed on. It didn't leave for another four hours.

"I'm really sorry, Mrs. Willingham," the clerk said. "Unless..." The woman's fingers flew over the keyboard of her computer. "Let me just check something." She looked up, beaming happily. "I've got one seat on a flight to Washington, where I can put you on a connecting flight to Atlanta. It's a window seat—"

"That's fine."

"And it's in first class."

Stephanie hesitated, thinking of the cost, thinking, too, of how Avery would have laughed at her for hesitating, but you didn't change the habits of a lifetime that easily.

"Mrs. Willingham?" The clerk looked at the wall clock. "The plane's about to board."

Stephanie nodded. "I'll take it."

The flight was leaving from the opposite end of the terminal. It wasn't easy, rushing to get to it with high heels on.

Fortunately, she only had a garment bag to carry. That made things easier. Still, by the time she reached the gate, the lounge area was empty, and the attendant was just starting to shut the door that led to the boarding ramp.

"Wait," Stephanie cried.

The man turned, saw her hurrying toward him, and swung the door wide.

"Almost missed it," he sang out cheerfully as she shoved her boarding pass at him.

Stephanie ran down the ramp. The flight attendant smiled when she saw her coming.

"Almost missed it," she said as Stephanie stepped into the cabin and showed her her ticket stub. "Seat 3-A. Right over here, Mrs. Willingham. Why don't you give me your luggage and I'll tuck it away for you?"

Stephanie smiled her thanks, collapsed into her seat, and puffed out her breath.

Maybe it was just as well she'd had to go with such last-minute arrangements. She sighed, kicked off her shoes and stretched out her legs. She'd almost forgotten the luxury of first class. The soft, wide seat. The legroom. She turned her face to the window and shut her eyes. Mmm. This was exactly what she needed. Peace. Quiet. The opportunity to purge the arrogant, overbearing, disgustingly macho David Chambers from her mind...

The handsome, vital, sexy David Chambers from her mind.

She felt someone sit down in the seat beside her, heard the faint clink of a seat belt—heard a sharply indrawn breath.

"I don't believe it," a man's husky voice growled softly. "I leave my seat for two minutes, and I come back to this? Great God Almighty, I don't care how small the world is, I can't be this unlucky twice in one day."

Stephanie shot upright. It couldn't be... But it was. David was sitting in the aisle seat, looking at her with the same horrified disbelief she knew must be stamped across her face.

A sob of desperation burst from her throat, and she fumbled for the buckle of her seat belt.

"Stop the plane," she yelped, but it was too late.

Even as the words left her lips, the sleek jet lifted into the late afternoon sky and headed toward Washington, D.C.

CHAPTER FOUR

"IS THERE a problem, madam?"

David dragged his gaze from Stephanie's flushed face. The flight attendant stood over them, brows lifted, a concerned smile stapled to her lips.

Yes, he thought, reading her look, you're damned right there's a problem.

"Madam?"

"No," David said before Stephanie could answer. "There's no problem." He smiled, too, though it felt as if the attempt might crack his skin. "We're fine."

"We? *We?*" Stephanie fumbled madly with her seat belt. "There is no *we,* there's only me and this—this—" She glared at the attendant. "I want out of here!"

"Madam, if you would just calm down—"

"Either that or I want you to stop this plane. Take it back to—"

She gasped as David's hand clamped hard around her wrist. "You'll have to forgive my, ah, my wife's outburst."

"Your wife? Your *wife?* I am not—"

"She's taken all the courses. Fearless Flyers, Flight Without Fright...all of them." His tone was the embodiment of compassion and tolerance. "None of it's worked. She's still terrified of flying."

"That's a lie! It's all lies. I am not terrified of flying, and you are not my—"

"Darling." David turned his smile, feral and sharp with warning, in Stephanie's direction. "If you don't calm down, this charming young lady is going to have to tell the pilot that he's got a disturbed passenger on board and they'll call to have an ambulance waiting at the gate, just the same as last time. Isn't that right, miss?''

"Another lie! I am not—"

The breath hissed from Stephanie's lungs as David's fingers tightened around her wrist.

"You wouldn't want that to happen again, would you, darling?"

"I am not disturbed." Stephanie glared at the flight attendant. "Do I look disturbed? Do I?"

"No," the girl said in a way that clearly meant just the opposite. "But, ah, perhaps it would be best if I went up front and spoke with the captain."

"I'm certain that won't be necessary, miss." David looked at Stephanie again. "Darling," he said through his teeth, "I'm sure if you just calm down, you'll feel better. You don't want them to turn this plane around and take us back to Hartford, do you?"

Stephanie glared at him. He was right, and she knew it. She pulled her hand from his, turned away sharply and stared out the window.

"That's my girl."

Stephanie swung toward him. "I am most definitely *not* your…"

Her eyes met those of the flight attendant's. The only time Stephanie had seen a person look at another in quite the same fashion was the Fourth of July when Johnny Bullard had gotten drunk on White Lightning, pulled off all his clothes in the middle of the town square and announced to the gathering crowd that he was a rocket and he was going to blast off.

Oh, hell!

"Never mind," she said glumly, and turned her face to the window again.

"She'll be fine now," David said.

"Are you sure, sir? Because if there's going to be a problem—"

"There won't be, will there, dearest?"

Not until I figure out a way to get even, there won't be...

"Darling?" David said. "Will there be a problem?"

"No," Stephanie said coldly.

The attendant produced another thousand-watt smile. "Thank you, ma'am. Now, if you'd just buckle your seat belt? I'm afraid we've been told to expect some bumpy weather ahead."

"For the rest of the passengers, or just for the man sitting next to me?" Stephanie said sweetly.

"I'm sure this young lady doesn't want to get in the middle of our private little spat, darling." David leaned toward her, a warning light glinting in his eyes. "Would you like me to buckle your belt for you?"

"Not unless you want to lose both your hands," she said through her teeth as she snapped the edges of the seat belt together.

David looked up at the flight attendant. "Thank you for your concern. You can see that we're fine now, Miss—" He peered at her badge, then gave her a dazzling smile. "Miss Edgecomb."

Stephanie watched bitterly as the girl's knees almost buckled under the sexy force of that smile. Oh, if she only knew what a no-good, scheming rat David Chambers really was.

"Yes, sir," Miss Edgecomb said. "And if I can be of any further help..."

"Of course. I'll be sure and let you know."

She bent down and whispered something. Stephanie couldn't hear it and didn't much want to, but David's easy laughter set her teeth on edge. She swung toward him, glaring, once they were alone.

"That was certainly a charming scene you orchestrated."

David put his seat back. "I'd love to take credit for it," he said, shutting his eyes, "but you're the one deserves all the applause."

"You have her convinced I'm crazy!"

"Sorry, but you get full credit for that, too."

"What did she say to you just now? Did she offer her sympathy?"

"She said that it might be a good idea to tank you up to the eyeballs with medication next time we fly."

"How generous of her."

"I said I hadn't known you'd intended to fly with me this time, that your presence had come as a delightful surprise."

"Oh, yeah. I'll just bet it did!"

"Meaning?"

"Do me a favor, Mr. Chambers. Don't try and play me for a fool. Do you really think I'm so naive I wouldn't realize you'd followed me?"

David blinked open his eyes. "Maybe she's right. Maybe you *are* nuts. Either that, or you're the most conceited broad I ever met."

"I am neither crazy nor conceited. And I no more appreciate being called a 'broad' than I appreciate having you follow me!"

"You really believe that?"

"No," she purred, "of course not. You just happened to turn up at the same airport, at the same time, and got yourself ticketed on the very same flight and, oh, yes, what an extra little coincidence, you ended up sitting right beside me." Stephanie sniffed. "I repeat, sir, I am neither naive, nor am I a fool."

David sighed. Her accent was back, that faint softening of vowels along with the way she had of addressing him as "sir" when the truth was the name she really had in mind was a lot less polite. She'd blushed the last time he'd commented on her drawl, which certainly made it worth commenting on again.

But he wasn't about to encourage this conversation. It had been a long day, he was tired, his disposition was so frazzled it was damn near nonexistent. The last thing he felt like doing was stepping into the ring and going another round with Stephanie Willingham, no matter how intriguing the possibility.

"The very idea," she muttered, "thinking you could pull off something so downright crass!"

"Mrs. Willingham," he said wearily, "I suggest again, calm down."

"What did you do, sir? Tail me from the country club?"

"Tail you?" He laughed in a way that sent the color sweeping back into Stephanie's face. "I think you've seen one bad detective movie too many."

"I do not watch detective movies, sir, bad or otherwise."

"Listen, Mrs. Willingham—"

"Dammit! Stop calling me that!"

David's mouth twisted. "Okay, Scarlett. Whatever you say. You want to think I came after you? Think it. Think whatever you like, so long as you shut up."

"It was sheer good fortune that placed you in the seat beside me. Is that what you'd like me to believe?"

"No, I would not."

She shot him a quick, mirthless smile. "That's something, anyway."

David opened one eye and looked in Stephanie's direction. "Good fortune would have put me down in the cargo hatch. Strapped to the wing. If luck had anything to do with this, I'd be on a rocket to Mars. I'd be anywhere but here."

"Ha."

He stabbed impatiently at the button that returned his seat to an upright position. There was to be no rest for him, he could see that. Bad weather was closing in on all sides: from the woman beside him, who obviously wasn't going to shut up until they touched down in D.C., and from the oily gray clouds that surrounded the plane. They were headed into a storm. The plane was starting to buck like a horse with a burr under its saddle. It was, he thought grimly, an apt metaphor for how he felt.

"Try and get this into your head, Scarlett," he growled, leaning toward her. "I'm just about as thrilled with our seating arrangements as you are, so here's my suggestion. Shut that pretty mouth of yours. That way, we can forget all about each other. How's that sound?"

"Like the first intelligent thing you've said," Stephanie said, fixing him with a cold look.

She folded her hands and did her best to ignore him. But it wasn't easy. How could she ignore him when each time the plane took a bone-jarring bounce—something it was doing with unsettling frequency—his shoulder brushed against hers? The scent of his cologne was annoying, too, that clean, outdoorsy aroma of leather and pine forests. She glanced at him from the corner of her eye. His profile might have been sculpted in granite. That chiseled forehead. That straight nose. The firm, full mouth and the strong, square chin.

His chin had stubble on it. So did his jaw. Her fingers curled into her palms. She could almost imagine the feel of that stubble under the soft stroke of her hand...

Stephanie sat up straighter.

"There must be an empty seat somewhere on this plane," she said angrily.

"No."

"No? No? What do you mean, no?"

"I mean exactly what I said. The plane's as full as a can of sardines."

"Wonderful." Stephanie folded her arms.

"Look, we'll be in Washington soon. And then we'll never have to set eyes on each other again."

"Thank goodness for that."

"I'm not going to argue, Scarlett." David shot her a quick look. "Frankly, I can hardly wait to be rid of you."

"Oh, do be frank, sir," Stephanie said coldly. "Considering that you've spent the afternoon being the soul of discretion, I imagine that a little frankness would be soothing.''

David gritted his teeth. What in hell had he done to deserve being saddled with such an impossible woman? She was gorgeous, yes, maybe even more now than before, where their surroundings demanded she at least try to maintain a civilized veneer. Her eyes were bright, her cheeks red, and her breathing had quickened so that her breasts rose and fell in a way a man couldn't possibly ignore. She was clever, too, and more than willing to stand up to him despite her look of fragility.

But she was impossible. Stephanie Willingham was a short-tempered, sharp-tongued, opinionated hellion. She wouldn't appreciate the comparison, but she reminded him of a wild mare he'd brought down from the high summer pastures a couple of years before.

The filly had been a beautiful animal, with fine bones, a soft, silky mane and tail—and the disposition of a wildcat. His men had tried everything to gentle her, but nothing had worked. They'd have to break her spirit, his foreman finally said...but David had refused to let that happen. He'd wanted the horse to accept the saddle, and him, not out of fear but out of desire.

So he'd taken up the challenge. He'd talked softly to the filly, offered her treats from his hand despite the sharp nips she'd given him. He'd stroked her neck, the rare occasions she'd permitted it. And at last, early one morning, instead of greeting him with wildly rolling eyes and bared teeth, the mare had come slowly to the fence, buried her velvet muzzle in the crook of his shoulder and trembled with pleasure as he touched her.

''Well?''

He looked up. Stephanie was glaring at him in defiance. Somewhere along the line, her dark hair had begun to escape its neat, nape-of-the-neck knot. Strands of it curled lightly against her ears and throat.

I could tame you, he thought, and he felt the swift surge of hot blood race through his veins.

"Well, what?" he said very softly.

Something in his voice, in the way his blue eyes were boring into her, made Stephanie's pulse beat quicken.

"Nothing," she said.

"Come on, Miss Scarlett, don't chicken out now." David smiled silkily. "You were going to tell me something, and I'd like to hear it."

Don't say anything, a tiny voice within Stephanie's head whispered. He's baiting you, and he's dangerous. You're playing out of your league here....

A tingle of excitement danced over her skin.

"Only," she said, carefully and very deliberately, "only that you're the most arrogant, ill-mannered, self-centered male I've ever had the misfortune to—"

She gasped as his hand closed around her wrist.

"Am I?"

His voice was low and rough. Stephanie felt as if she could hardly breathe. Her thoughts flew back to when her grandmother had still been alive. She'd been sent to live with her one summer. She was three, four, too young, anyway, to know the difference between honey that came from a jar and the stuff that oozed from a broken, bee-laden comb lying beneath Gramma's old pin oak.

"Leave it be, child," Gramma had cried as she'd reached for the comb, but Stephanie had already brought it to her mouth. The moment was forever frozen in time: the candied kiss of the welling honey, and then the fierce, painful sting of the bee.

She thought of it now, that dizzying combination of sweetness and danger, as David bent toward her. Should she force herself to face him down...or should she leap from her seat and run for her life, never mind that the plane was dipping and rising like a roller coaster, or that the flight attendant would probably call ahead and have the men in the white coats waiting.

No. Why should she run? There was nothing to be afraid of. What could happen here, in this public place?

Anything. The word whispered through her like a hot wind.

David's eyes smoldered with heat. She could almost scent his anger on the air. No, she thought, her heart giving another giddy kick, not his anger. His masculinity. His awareness of her not as a foe but as a woman.

The plane was carrying them into a velvet darkness. As if from a great distance, she heard the disembodied voice of the captain requesting that all passengers be sure they were buckled in. The cabin lights blinked on and off, on and off, and she caught a glimpse of lightning zigzagging like flame outside the window.

Somewhere in the cabin behind her, a woman's voice rose in fear. Stephanie knew she ought to be afraid, too, of the storm raging just beyond the fragile shell of their aircraft, but the only storm she could think about was the one that had been building between David and her from the moment they'd met.

He undid his seat belt, his gaze never leaving her face. A soft whimper rose in her throat and it took all her strength to suppress it.

"Do you like playing games, Scarlett?" He moved closer; his thumb rolled across her bottom lip, the tip of it just insinuating itself into her mouth. He tasted of heat, of salt. Of passion. "That's what we've been doing all day, isn't it? Playing games." His gaze fell to her mouth; she felt the hungry weight of it, like a caress, before his eyes met hers again. "No more games, Stephanie," he said gruffly, and he kissed her.

She made no sound, moved not an inch. But the moan she'd managed to hold back moments ago slipped through the kiss. She felt a tremor pass through him and then he thrust one hand into her hair, tipped her head back, and parted her lips with his.

There was no time to think. All she could do was react—and respond. Stephanie whimpered softly, wound her arms around David's neck, and opened her mouth to his kiss.

The lights in the cabin blinked out. Blackness engulfed them. The plane lifted, then dropped as if there were a hole in the sky. They were alone on the dark, wild sea of the heavens, and at its mercy.

Stephanie wasn't afraid. She felt the strength of David's arms as they encircled her, felt the racing pound of his heart against hers, and when his hand slid under the jacket of her suit and cupped her breast, she cried out in pleasure.

"Yes," he whispered. "Oh, yes."

She felt the nip of his teeth. Her head fell back as he pressed his lips to her throat and when he brought her hand to him, settled it against the powerful thrust of his arousal, she arched against him.

This was wrong. It was insane. She knew that, knew it well. But to stop what she felt, what David was making her feel, was impossible. His hunger was fierce, but so was hers. She had to assuage it, had to give in to it, had to touch and be touched....

The lights in the cabin blazed on. The plane rocked one last time, then settled onto a steady course.

It was all Stephanie needed to return her to reality.

She gave a muffled cry and tried to break free, but David wouldn't let her. He clasped her face between his hands, his mouth hot and demanding on hers...and despite everything, the cabin lights, and the voice of the captain assuring the passengers that they were okay, despite all that, she almost gave herself up again to the passion, the intoxication of this stranger's kiss.

"No!" Stephanie slammed her fists against his chest, tore her mouth from his. "Stop it," she said, her voice trembling, and David blinked his eyes, like a man awakening from a deep dream.

He drew back and stared into the flushed face of this woman he'd met only hours before. Her eyes were huge and glazed; her mouth was swollen from his kisses and her hair had come undone so that dark strands curled lightly around her face.

"You're despicable," she hissed as she twisted away from him, as far as she could get.

A muscle knotted in David's cheek. He sat back, his hands curled tightly around the armrests of his seat. Despicable? Crazy might be a better word.

"Mrs. Willingham..." he said.

Mrs. Willingham? He really *was* crazy, addressing a woman he'd damn near ravaged with such formality. And what was he going to say to her? I'm sorry? Hell, he was not. Not sorry, not apologetic, not any of those things because she'd wanted what had happened as much as he had.

"Ladies and gentlemen." The amplified voice of the flight attendant interrupted his thoughts. "The captain has asked me to tell you that we are on our approach to Dulles and we should be on the ground in just a few minutes."

A thin cheer of relief rose from the passengers. David felt like cheering, too, but it had nothing to do with having survived the storm. He'd survived something else entirely.

He was a man who'd known his fair share of women. Okay, more than his fair share, some would say. He was not a stranger to the fever that could flare like wildfire between two consenting adults.

But nothing like this had ever happened to him before. If the lights hadn't come on, if Stephanie hadn't stopped him, he'd have taken her there, in the darkness. In the hot little universe they'd created. He'd have ripped off her panties, buried himself deep in her heat until—until...

He'd been out of control, and he knew it. And it scared the hell out of him.

Life—his life—was all about control. Control of the self. It was how he'd gone from being a kid enduring life in a foster home to a man with a law degree and a well-regarded practice. He'd only made that one slip, when he'd let himself think he was in love, let himself trust a woman who wasn't to be trusted....

The plane touched down with a thump. There was scattered applause, a few whistles, but David was already on his feet, reaching for his garment bag, making his way up the aisle to the door.

"Sir? Mr. Chambers?" The flight attendant smiled and sent a darting look over his shoulder. "Isn't your wife—"

"She isn't my wife," David said fiercely. "She isn't anything, not to me."

He left the flight attendant's voice behind him, left everything behind him. Whatever it was that had happened to him in that airplane cabin was over. And he sure as hell was never going to think about it again.

CHAPTER FIVE

THERE were few certainties in life.

Stephanie knew that. It was, in fact, the very first certainty.

The others ranged from the sublime to the ridiculous.

For instance, she knew that a pair of cardinals would rebuild the old nest deep within the shelter of the rhododendron outside the back door, come every spring.

They were there now, on this bright, warm morning, the male in his bright plumage chirping encouragement to the female as she flew off for more twigs.

"I don't know that it's the same pair, ma'am," the gardener had said when he'd found her watching them that first spring, seven long years ago. "Might be younguns of the first two what built that nest."

It didn't matter. If it was a new generation doing the building, that only made what was happening all the sweeter. Somebody, even if that somebody had wings and feathers, believed in home and family.

And then there were the other constants, the ones that were not so pleasant.

The way the good townsfolk of Willingham Corners looked at her whenever she drove into town. Not that it was very different from how they'd always looked at her, the men with sly smiles that made her skin crawl, the women with condemnation tightening their mouths.

Well, that was surely going to change, and soon. Smirks would replace the smiles, and the looks of condemnation would be replaced by ones that said morality had, at last, triumphed.

Stephanie glanced at the dining room table, and the letter

lying on it. Oh, yes. Just wait until the town heard about that.

They'd probably celebrate.

Stephanie Willingham, Mrs. Avery Willingham, was going to lose the roof over her head and the ground under her feet. She was going to lose everything.

Everything—including the one thing that mattered, that she had bartered her soul to possess.

She should have known Avery would renege on his promise. His word had never been any good—another of life's little certainties, Stephanie thought with a bitter smile, but one she'd only learned after they'd made their unholy bargain.

There wasn't even any point in telling herself that the documents Avery's sister had produced were forgeries. It would have given Avery as much pleasure to have arranged the situation as it had given Clare to hint at it. It was the cruelty of the thing that had convinced her, the "joint tenancy" provisions carefully devised to make Clare Avery's heir—and to leave Stephanie with absolutely nothing.

Oh, yes, the documents were legitimate. It was Avery's final gift—which only emphasized the last certainty.

Men were a bunch of double-dealing bastards.

They'd lie to get what they wanted and then fix it so that their promises were worth about as much as they were.

Stephanie put her hand to her forehead. Except for Paul. Paul was different, and not just because he was her brother. Paul was kind, and caring; he'd always been there for her, when she was little. No one else had been. Not her father, whom she'd never known. Not her mother, who'd wandered out of her children's lives like a wisp of smoke.

And not Avery. God, certainly not Avery.

Stephanie put her back to the window and looked down blindly into the cup of rapidly cooling coffee cradled between her palms. Avery, with his talk of being the father she'd never had. With his compassionate gifts—the food basket on Thanksgiving, the visits to the specialists for Paul, the big box of books she'd hungered for but couldn't afford to buy. And then the greatest gift of all, the one she'd believed would be the start of a better life, for her and for Paul...a year's tuition for Miss Carol's Secretarial School.

"It's too much, Mr. Willingham," Stephanie had said. "I can't let you do this."

"Sure you can, darlin'." Avery had put a beefy arm around her shoulders in fatherly fashion. "You learn to type, take dictation, an' I'll give you a job, workin' for me."

Working for him, Stephanie thought, and shuddered.

Oh, how he'd hooked her. Set out a lure she couldn't resist and reeled her in like a fish all ready for the skillet.

How could she have been so naive? So stupid? So pathetically, painfully dumb?

Not that the answers mattered anymore. It was true, fate had intervened. Paul had become more and more withdrawn but still, it was she who'd agreed to make a contract with the devil.

There was no one to blame but herself...

Just as she was to blame for what had happened two weeks ago, on what should have been a pleasant, peaceful Sunday afternoon.

Stephanie shut her eyes against the humiliating memory. That she'd let a stranger do those things to her—that she'd let *any* man do those things to her—was inconceivable. None of it made sense. She knew what men were and what they wanted. What they always wanted, whether they were old and fat, like Avery, or young and handsome, like David Chambers.

Sex. That was what men wanted. And sex was—it was...

Stephanie shuddered again, despite the warmth of the morning sun on her shoulders. Sweat. Grasping hands. Hot breath on your face and wet lips smothering you, and the feel of bile rising in the back of your throat...

Except, it hadn't been like that with David. When he'd kissed her. Touched her. Cupped her breast and made her moan. She could still remember the taste of him, the feel of his mouth, warm against hers, his kiss hinting at pleasures she'd never imagined...

"Missus Willingham?"

Stephanie spun around. Mrs. Cross stood in the doorway. The straw hat she wore for marketing days was on her head; her suitcase was in her hand.

"I'm leavin'," she said coldly. "Thought I'd let you know."

Stephanie nodded. "I understand. I'm sorry I haven't been able to pay you the last few weeks, but—"

"Wouldn't stay under this roof, money or no money," the housekeeper said. "Town knows what you are now, missus, what with Mr. Avery fixin' things for all to see."

Coffee sloshed over the rim of Stephanie's cup and onto her hand, but she didn't so much as blink.

"I'll send you a check for what I owe you, Mrs. Cross." Her voice was clear and steady. She'd be damned—*damned*—if she'd break down now. "You may have to wait for your money, but you'll get it all, I promise."

"Don't want nothin' from you, missus."

Mrs. Cross turned on her heel and marched off. Stephanie didn't move as she listened to the housekeeper's footsteps stomp the length of the marbled hall, but after the front door slammed shut, she pulled a chair out from the table and sank down into it.

"And a good thing you don't, Mrs. Cross," she whispered shakily, "because I don't have anything left to give."

Her eyes burned with unshed tears. She blinked hard, then drew a deep breath.

"All right," she said briskly, and scrubbed her hands over her face.

What was done, was done. There was no sense in brooding over things, or in playing a game of "What if?" What was it her mother used to say? It was hard to remember; it seemed such a long, long time ago...

"No use cryin' over spilled milk, Steffie. Just mop it up an' get on with your life."

The advice still held. She had to get on with her life, put aside what the town thought, what Avery had done...put aside, as well, all memories of whatever it was that had happened between her and David Chambers. He wasn't even worth thinking about. For all his looks and money and charm, he was nothing but another member of the brotherhood, a lying, sneaking, self-centered, testosterone-impaired, no-account rat—and the only good news about that Sunday was that it was over, and she'd never see the man's face again.

Stephanie swiped her hand across her eyes one last time, then reached for the letter from Clare's attorneys. Not that she needed to read it. She'd paced the floor with it the last ten days; its message was embedded in her brain.

Dear Mrs. Willingham: Please be advised that it is the wish of our client, Clare Willingham, that you vacate her property no later than Friday the thirteenth.

"Such a propitious date, don't you think?" Clare had purred, when she'd phoned to have the pleasure of delivering the news, firsthand.

Stephanie's throat constricted. She cleared it, then read the next sentence aloud into the silence of the room.

"Please be advised that the stipend paid to your account will cease as of that date, as well."

That was the phrase that had made her begin to tremble.

That was when she'd known she was lost.

She'd tried fighting it. Months ago, as soon as Clare had started dropping hints that Stephanie's days at Seven Oaks were limited, she'd gone to see Amos Turner, who had a law office in town.

"I don't give a damn about the house," she'd told him. "I only want what's rightfully mine. Avery promised to

ut a specified amount of money into my checking account
ach month.''

"How much?" Turner asked with an oily smile.

Stephanie took a deep breath. "Twenty-five hundred dol-
ars.''

The lawyer smiled. "My, my, my," he purred, "that
urely is a lot of money for a man to provide his wife as
n allowance.''

"It wasn't an allowance."

"No? What was it then, my dear?"

Payment. Payment for selling her soul…

"I don't see how that's germane, Mr. Turner," she said
oolly.

Turner's beady eyes glistened. "Must be nice, havin'
uch a value put on yourself," he said, tilting back his chair
o that his fat belly protruded like an island in a sea of
hiny black worsted.

Stephanie flushed but she refused to give an inch. What
vas the point? The town had made up its mind about her
a long time ago.

"Bet you earned every bit of that money, too," he'd
aid, and she'd looked him squarely in the eye and assured
im that he was damned right. She had.

Such brave talk, she thought now. Her mouth trembled.
And so useless. Turner had folded like an accordion after
a meeting with Clare and, she had no doubt, with Clare's
heckbook. Judge Parker had proved no obstacle to the pro-
eedings, either.

And so it was over. She had nothing. No roof over her
ead, no money—and no way to pay for Paul's care.

Panic sent her heart thump-thumping in her chest.

There had to be something she could do. She was
Avery's widow, wasn't she? A widow had certain rights.
Sure, the Willinghams owned this town, but they didn't rule
he world.

Stephanie rose to her feet. She'd met an attorney once,

at one of the dinner parties she'd hosted for Avery. The man didn't practice here, he practiced...where? Washington. That was it. What was his name?

Hustle? Fussell?

Russell. That was it. Jack Russell, like the breed of dog. She'd blurted that out when they'd been introduced, and Avery's arm had tightened around her waist and he'd pinched her, where no one could see. She'd tried to stammer out an apology but Russell had bowed over her hand and assured her, in a drawl thicker than hers, that he had no objection to being compared to a handsome, feisty little terrier, especially when the comparison was made by such a beautiful woman.

Russell had smiled at her the entire evening. Not the way other men did. His smile had been kind, and generous, and tinged, she'd thought, with a little sadness.

"If this old ogre ever mistreats you, my dear," he'd said, kissing her cheek at evening's end, when she and Avery stood at the ornate front door to bid their guests goodnight, "you just give me a call and I'll come to your rescue."

Avery had laughed in that way that made her skin crawl just to remember it.

"Not to worry," he'd said. "I know exactly how to treat a gal like this."

Stephanie blocked out the memory and hurried to the library, where Avery had kept his address book. There was no point in thinking about the past. It was the present that mattered and perhaps, if she were very, very lucky, Jack Russell could help her face that present and survive it.

She leafed through the book, found Russell's name and a Washington, D.C., telephone number.

"No use crying over spilled milk, Steffie," she whispered.

Then she took a deep breath and reached for the telephone.

*　*　*

Life had taught David a series of lessons.

Red wine was better than white.

Old Porsches were better than new ones.

Springtime in the nation's capitol was glorious.

But not this year, David thought as he sat with his back to his desk and stared out his office window.

The weather was mild. The sky was clear. The cherry blossoms were delivering their annual show, a little late, but the tourists didn't much care.

And still, he was in a foul mood.

Everybody had told him so, including his secretary. He'd never liked Miss Murchison much; he knew he'd hired her in a moment of weakness, when sympathy for her acne, mousy looks and weight problem had overruled logic.

What he hadn't counted on was that she couldn't type much faster than he could, or figure out how to turn on her computer without bringing down the entire system. She had her hat and coat on by five o'clock, promptly, and never mind that she'd known, right up front, that he sometimes would need her to put in an additional hour or so, for which her salary more than compensated.

Yesterday, after she'd taken an entire afternoon to type two letters and topped the day off by whining, "But, Mr. Chambers, do you know what time it is?" when, at twenty minutes of five, he'd asked her to please retype one of the letters she'd managed to get chocolate stains on, he'd finally exploded.

He said that he knew exactly what time it was. It was time for her to find a new job. Time for her to inflict herself on somebody else...

David shut his eyes and groaned.

So much for doing things that seemed right at the time you did them. He'd ended up with a weeping Miss Murchison and a knot in his belly.

"Don't cry, for God's sake," he'd said helplessly, and then he'd done his best to soothe her hurt feelings by writing out a check for three months' severance pay and handed it over along with a rambling tale about his rotten mood being caused by a headache that simply refused to go away. Miss Murchison, who'd managed a swift recovery once she had his check firmly in her hand, had sniffed and said that any man who'd had a rotten headache for two weeks' straight was a man with a problem.

She was right. He *did* have a problem, and its name was Stephanie Willingham. The woman was in his head, night and day, and wasn't that ridiculous? Okay, so he'd been attracted to her. Okay, so he'd come on to her...

David groaned again and slumped back in his chair. To hell with all that. He'd behaved like a jerk, and he knew it. Kissing her in that airplane. Touching her. Damn near ravishing her... Who knew what he'd have done if the lights hadn't come back on when they did?

Why? Because she was good-looking? So were half the women on the planet. So were all the women in his little black book, and he'd never made a fool of himself with any of them.

Maybe he needed a break. Yes, that was it. This town was great. He loved its pace, its excitement, the realization that he was practicing high-powered law in the very heart of the western world, but sometimes it got to be too much. The crowds. The cars. The day that began at six and ended after midnight, if you added in the dinners and parties and charity affairs he had to attend.

"We work our tails off," Jack Russell had told him when David had come on board more than a dozen cherry-blossom seasons ago, and the esteemed law firm of Russell, Russell and Hanley had become Russell, Russell, Hanley and Chambers. "But if you like living on the edge, David, you'll love it here."

David had smiled and said he was sure he would.

"No place prettier than D.C. in the springtime," Jack had said as David's gaze went to the cherry trees out on the street, and David had smiled again and asked Jack if he'd ever seen Wyoming this time of year.

"No," Jack had replied. "Bet it's all snow and cold winds."

Snow, David thought, staring out the window. Probably. The mountains ringing his ranch would still bear their winter cloaks…and yet, if he saddled a horse and went riding, he knew he'd see the signs of rebirth all around. The rosy tinge birch branches get when the sap begins to flow. Green shoots seeking the sun's warmth where the snow had blown away. Calves butting their heads against their mothers' bellies and colts, still gawky on their long, ungainly legs…

"Hell," David muttered, and swiveled his chair back toward his desk.

Sitting here and staring out the windows was not going to get any work done. And he had a lot of work to do. Tons of it, from the look of his appointment book, with "hire a secretary" right on top.

It was just that he was in the darkest mood. The Cooper wedding had taken place two weeks ago but the memory of Stephanie Willingham wouldn't go away. And never mind all that stuff he'd been telling himself about damn near ravishing her. Who was he trying to kid? The widow Willingham, she of the icy words and the hot mouth, had sizzled as soon as he'd looked at her. And when he'd touched her—when he'd touched her…

David mouthed an oath, rose to his feet and stalked across his office. There was a carafe of fresh coffee on an antique mahogany sideboard and it took him a couple of seconds to remember that this was not the pale slop Miss Murchison had passed off as coffee but a pot he'd brewed for himself. He poured a cup, took a sip, and plunked himself down on one of a pair of small leather sofas.

Enough of this crap. He'd been dragging his butt for days, alternately chewing himself out for the idiotic way he'd behaved with Stephanie and fantasizing over what might have happened if they hadn't been in a plane but in his town house. It was time to move on to something else.

What he needed was a good, swift dose of reality. A workout in his gym. A couple of games of racquetball, maybe, or half an hour trading jabs with a punching bag…

Or a weekend at home.

David put down his cup, rose and strolled to the window. Yes. That would do it. A couple of afternoons spent digging fence posts or stringing wire after the damages of the winter would put him on track again. Hard work and sweat went a long way toward reminding a man of what really mattered in the overall scheme of things. That conviction had taken him home nearly every weekend after he'd first come east to practice law.

Reality, he had known instinctively, would always lie to the west, in Wyoming.

It was unfortunate that his wife—his ex-wife—had figured it to be just the opposite. The real world, Krissie had insisted, was in Georgetown. The cocktail parties and dinners, the tweedy weekends spent at elegant old homes in the Virginia countryside—all the stuff that made him wince, made her smile.

Krissie's idea of a cozy evening at home involved twenty or thirty of her closest friends.

A muscle knotted in David's cheek. It had not been that way when they'd been dating.

Back then, she'd professed to love the things he loved. The ranch, and riding out to the purple hills. Quiet meals by the fireside and afterward, soft music on the CD player, and freshly made popcorn…and long hours spent in each other's arms.

It was going to be like a fairy tale. One man, one woman. One love, forever after.

What a fool he'd been. Women said what a man wanted to hear when they were setting the snare that would trap him. His wife had lied about everything, what she liked, what she disliked...

About fidelity.

He'd tolerated all of it. Everything—right up until the day he'd come home early and found her in bed with another man. That he hadn't killed the son of a bitch and thrown Krissie into the street bare-ass naked was less a reflection of his forbearance than an indication of how little she'd meant to him by then.

The divorce had been swift and nasty, the recovery lengthy and painful. But recover he had, and the lessons he'd learned had stuck.

Women were not to be trusted. They said one thing, meant another, and the man who didn't keep that always, *always,* in mind deserved what he got.

David smiled. That wasn't to say that women didn't have their uses. He liked women. He liked the way they sounded, and the way they smelled. He liked the softness of their laughter, the curved lushness of their bodies...

Stephanie had a lush body. Her skin had been soft as silk, hot as flame under his hands. And the taste of her mouth...he'd never known a taste like it. So honeyed. So sweet. So exciting...

David swung away from the window, his breathing harsh. What in hell was he doing, thinking about her? It was crazy. Crazy! The world was filled with women. Obliging women, who didn't say "no" when they meant "yes"—and yet his thoughts were possessed by one who did just that.

Stephanie.

He'd even phoned Annie Cooper, late last week, and after a few minutes of inconsequential chitchat, he'd brought Stephanie's name into the conversation, asked Annie about her, then braced himself for the teasing he'd figured he was sure to get. But Annie had seemed preoccupied. She'd said she didn't know Stephanie very well, only that she was a widow whose husband had died fairly recently.

"Is it important?" she'd said, adding that if it was, she could always give Stephanie a call.

"No," David had said quickly, "no, it's not important at all."

Annie, completely out of character, had let the subject go. He'd hung up the phone, reached for his Rolodex file, had his hand on the card of the private investigator the firm sometimes used before he'd realized that he was behaving like a certifiable nutcase.

David sighed, sat down behind his desk and picked up a pencil. Instead of reaching for the private investigator's card, he'd reached for his own private address book. He'd made some phone calls, then spent the next few evenings pleasantly, in the company of half a dozen bright, beautiful females. He'd taken them out, he'd taken them home—one at a time, he thought, with a little smile...

His smile faded. And then, despite the promises in their eyes, he'd kissed them gently, eased their arms from his neck, said goodnight and gone home, alone, to lie in his bed and dream of a woman he would never see again, never wanted to see again...

"Hell," he said through his teeth, and snapped the pencil in two.

"Careful, lad. Got to watch that temper."

David jerked his head up. Jack Russell stood in the doorway, smiling, thumbs tucked into the pockets of his old-fashioned vest.

"Jack." David mustered a smile. "Good morning."

"It is that." Jack strolled into the room, sat down on the chair across from David's desk, and glanced at the window. "Though, I must say, the cherry blossoms aren't all they should be this year."

"Nothing is all it should be," David said flatly. Jack shot

him a quizzical look, and he managed another smile. "What can I do for you this morning?"

"Well, for openers, you can tell me where you were last night."

"Where I was last..." David puffed out his breath. "The Weller cocktail party! Jack, I'm sorry."

"That's all right. I made your apologies to our host and hostess, and told them you were up to your neck in work."

"I owe you one."

Jack chuckled. "You owe me several. I've protected your *gluteus maximus* more than once in the past couple of weeks."

"Yeah. Well, you know how it is. I've been...busy."

"Preoccupied, might be a better word. Something on your mind?"

"Listen, just because I blew a couple of appointments..."

"Six," Jack said, ticking them off on his fingers. "Three dinners, one round of drinks, one embassy do and that charity auction last weekend."

"I told you," David said brusquely, "I've been—"

"Busy. Yes, I know." Jack leaned back in his chair and crossed his arms. "Who's the lucky young woman?"

"The baloney I have to put up with," David said, forcing a smile to his lips, "because I'm the only bachelor around here..."

"And deservedly so, according to my better half. Mary says you need a wife."

David laughed. "You tell Mary that what I need is a secretary. Somebody to keep my appointments straight and type more than ten words a minute. I fired Murchison, did you hear?"

"Certainly. The other secretaries are taking up a collection."

"Yeah," David said, and sighed. "Well, I'm sure she'll

appreciate the flowers, whatever it is they send her. Tell them they can count on me for my share.''

Jack chuckled. ''The collection's for you, David. They figure you deserve a bouquet for tolerating her as long as you did.'' Jack pursed his lips. ''So, now what?''

''Well, I've arranged for a temp. Next week, I'll phone that agency we always use...''

''I meant, what about you? Murchison's not around to irritate you and everybody else. So, now will you stop going around looking like a hound dog with a tick under its tail?''

David grinned and leaned back in his chair. ''Uh-oh.''

''Uh-oh, what?''

''When you start tossing out the down-home maxims— even though you haven't lived in that little dot on the map you call home for three decades—it's always a bad sign. Means you're going to tell me something you figure I won't want to hear.''

''Four decades,'' the older man said modestly, ''and Macon, Georgia, is hardly a dot on the map. Still, roots is roots, as my ol' granpappy used to say.''

''Your 'ol' granpappy' was a supreme court justice.''

Jack mimed being shot in the heart. ''A direct hit! Nonetheless, roots is—''

''—Roots. Yeah. I know.'' David's smile tilted. ''To tell the truth, I'm pretty much overdosed on things south of the Mason-Dixon line, as of late.''

''Is that why you've been as grouchy as a boll weevil at harvesttime the past couple of weeks?''

''Jack...''

''Okay, okay, I'll keep my store of country wisdom to myself.''

''Good. Now, what is it you need to tell me that I'm not going to like?''

Jack leaned forward, his hands on his knees. ''You recall a situation last year? The Anderson mess, where the old man died intestate and suddenly three cousins turned up with three different wills?''

"Sure. We represented the old guy's son, and we won. Don't tell me one of the cousins hired himself another lawyer!''

"No, no. It's just that this reminds me a bit of that situation. Man kicks off. Leaves behind a wife but no will, and then it turns out he held his entire estate in joint tenancy with his sister, who now has, of course, full rights of survivorship.''

"Was he trying to defraud his widow?''

Jack shook his head. "The court says no. The widow ends up without a dime.''

"Ouch," David said, picturing a white-haired old lady turned out onto the streets.

"Ouch, indeed. I just got the call a little while ago, from the wife of the dead man. He was an old friend... Well, no. He wasn't a friend. Not at all. An acquaintance, you might say, from a town twenty, twenty-five miles from Macon.''

"And?''

"And, she's penniless. The widow's not surprised—says she should have figured he'd leave her nothing.''

David's eyebrows rose. "No love lost in the relationship, I gather?''

"None.'' Jack rose to his feet and paced around the office, his hands in his pockets. "I only met the lady once, years ago. Can't say I remember much about the meeting, except that she was a tiny little thing, seemed kind of sad.''

"She wants you to represent her?''

"Well, she asked if I'd look things over, see if she's not at least entitled to the monthly stipend her husband had been giving her. I didn't ask too many questions because I could see there might be a conflict of interest. You see, the dead man's sister was a school friend of Mary's. Same sorority, all that nonsense. Bottom line is that I know Clare rather well." Jack smiled. "I don't like her, but I know her. So it's a problem."

"Well, if you told that to the widow…"

"I told her this wasn't our cup of tea. Too messy. That's the truth, even if she had a chance of collecting something. Purty young thang from the backwoods—"

"The sister?"

"The widow."

"Ah. I thought—well, from what you'd said, I assumed she was an older woman."

"Young," Jack said. "Very young. And more than pretty, as I recall. The story just about rocked the town. Beautiful girl—eighteen, nineteen years old—marries a man pushing sixty with both hands. Little lady's got swamp grass between her toes, he's from the town's first family."

"She traded sex for money and power. Jack, that's the world's oldest profession. Second oldest, when people make it legit with a marriage license."

"The sister agrees. According to her, that's how the girl got a marriage ring on her finger. Bed for board, so to speak. But, says Sis, her brother wasn't a complete fool. He had no intention of providing for the girl beyond the here and now."

"The girl knew this?"

"She says she didn't. Says her hubby promised she'd be taken care of on a monthly basis, even after his death. She makes no bones about it, David. Kind of boasted to me that she'd insisted on it before she'd agree to marry him." Russell sat down again and crossed his legs. "Amazing, how cold-blooded some members of the so-called gentler sex can be, don't you think?"

David smiled tightly. "You're asking the wrong man that question, Jack."

"Sorry. I'd forgotten about that ex-wife of yours."

"Actually," David said, "I wasn't thinking of her at all. Well, go on. What is it you want from me? If it's my opinion, I don't see much of a chance for appeal or reversal. I suppose the girl could sue, on the grounds that she's been defrauded of her rights to the estate.''

"She did, and the matter was decided against her. She says she doesn't care about anything but getting the monthly allowance her husband promised.''

"How much was it?''

"I don't know. I told you, I didn't ask too many questions.''

"Well, whatever it was, fifty bucks or five hundred, I hope you told her the chances of that happening were slim to none.''

"I tried. But she started crying…''

David gave a wry smile. "I'll bet.''

"I ended up promising I'd drive down and talk to her—but then I realized how it would look, considering my connections to the sister.''

"Damn right.''

"So,'' Jack said with a little smile, "I'm asking you to do me a favor.''

"Jack, for heaven's sake…''

"It's not a big thing, David. Tomorrow's Friday. You can fly to Atlanta in the morning, cab to her house, be back before dinner.''

David frowned. "You're leaving out the part where I tell her not to be greedy, to be grateful for the cash, jewelry, furs, whatever it is she's got squirreled away.''

"Yes—except you might try doing it a little more gently.''

"Why? To prove that lawyers have hearts?''

"That's a cold attitude, counselor.''

"I'm feeling cold lately, Jack. And realistic.''

"Look, we do pro bono work all the time, and that's all I'm suggesting here, an hour of free advice for a young woman who needs it. I have to admit, I feel sorry for her, even knowing she married for money.''

"Sold herself, you mean."

"I suppose. Still, there's something about her. She has this vulnerability... What?" Jack said when David's mouth crooked in a half-smile.

"I knew a rancher once, said the same thing about a yearling grizzly cub just before it mauled him."

Jack laughed. "You see? Sometimes, nothing will do but a down-home sentiment." He sat down again and leaned forward. "Look, we both know the girl's a manipulative little gold digger, but she did keep her end of the deal, or so I gather. She stayed with Avery, right to the end."

"Such dedication," David said, folding his arms and tilting back in his chair.

"Don't be so hard-hearted. She's broke. She has no skills, no talents, well, none other than a secretarial course she took one time, before she married." Jack chuckled. "There's an idea. Maybe you should offer her a job."

"You're leaving a skill out, Jack. The one that got her a wedding ring."

"Ah, yes." Russell gave a deep sigh. "Amazing, what a man will put himself through, and all so he can get one particular woman into his bed."

An image of Stephanie Willingham flashed through David's head.

"Amazing," he said coolly. "Okay, I'll talk to her."

"Thank you, David."

"Don't thank me," David said, and smiled. "I'll get my pound of flesh out of you, Jack. I'll make you go to the Sheratons' house party next weekend, instead of me."

Jack laughed. "Still running away from Mimi Sheraton? I wish I could oblige, but Mary's already made plans."

"Terrific."

"It will be. Just take out that little black book of yours and find yourself a playmate to take along for the weekend. That should stop Mimi."

David snorted. Mimi Sheraton, daughter of a senator and

married to a client who was husband number three—or was it four?—was stunning and about as subtle as a shark. Assertive women were fine—but one that groped you under the table while you were talking with her husband was definitely a turnoff.

"The only thing that would stop Mimi," he said, "would be the announcement of my death."

Jack laughed again. "Or of your engagement."

"Same thing."

The men smiled at each other, and then David reached for a pen and paper.

"Okay," he said. "I'll fly down to Atlanta tomorrow. No need to let grass grow on this."

"No need at all." Jack dug into his pocket and pulled out a slip of paper. "And I just happen to have the lady's address and phone number right here."

"All I need now," David said, glancing at the paper as he took it from his partner's outstretched hand, "is her name."

"Oh. Oh, right. I thought I'd... Her name is Willingham."

David stiffened, and his fingers tightened around the pen. "It's what?"

"Willingham. Stephanie Willingham." Jack closed one eye in a slow, deliberate wink. "I don't know what today's terminology is but when I was a young and callow youth, we'd have described her as one hell of a piece of—"

"I know the phrase," David said. He tried to smile but from the look on the older man's face, he suspected he wasn't succeeding. "Believe me, Jack—it hasn't changed."

It was insane, agreeing to see Stephanie again. It was even more insane, not telling Jack the truth.

Talk about a breach of ethics... David's hands tightened on the steering wheel of his Porsche as he turned off the highway at the exit for Willingham Corners. He'd driven down instead of flying, telling himself that the hours on the road would clear his head.

Even a first-year law student would know that what he was doing was improper. He was the wrong man to deliver legal advice to the widow Willingham.

I already know her, he should have said to Jack. I've had a run-in with her.

A run-in? Hell, he'd almost ripped off her clothes.

It wasn't too late to turn back. To head for the nearest phone, call Jack, tell him…what?

Hello, Jack. Listen, I spent an afternoon trying to seduce the grieving widow, so I'll have to disqualify myself from this case.

But there was no case. He was only a messenger and if Stephanie had any faint hopes of going into a courtroom again, she'd change her mind once he'd laid out the facts.

David smiled thinly, and tromped down on the gas.

CHAPTER SIX

DUST rose into the air as Stephanie lugged her suitcase down from the shelf in the attic.

She sneezed, wiped her nose on the sleeve of her sweatshirt, and dumped the suitcase on the floor.

This was not the best place to spend an already warm May morning. The attic was airless and hot. Dust and cobwebs clung to every surface, spiders skittered in the corners and every now and then she caught the sound of mice behind the walls.

Stephanie shivered, despite the heat. She hoped they were mice, anyway.

The attic was depressing, too. It wasn't the kind of place that made you want to open old trunks and delve through the contents, despite the fact that it was a repository of cast-off furniture and knickknacks that dated back two centuries. Under ordinary circumstances, she'd probably have been fascinated by the stuff—but these weren't ordinary circumstances, and never had been.

"You have married into a fine old family," Clare had said on their wedding day, "but you will never be part of it."

Stephanie smiled grimly as she slammed the attic door behind her and edged her way down the steep wooden steps with her suitcase in her hand.

"I'll do my best to fit in," she'd said—but that was when she was still naive, when she'd believed in Avery's promises and in his kindness.

"Your best could never be good enough," Clare had replied with a brittle smile, and Stephanie, stung, had started to answer but Avery's hand had tightened painfully on hers and he'd drawn her into a corner. It had been the first indication of what her life as his wife was really going to be.

"Lesson one," he'd said with a phony smile plastered to his face so that anyone watching would think he was only whispering sweet nothings in her ear. "Don't you never sass my sister, you understand?"

Oh, yes, she'd understood. Avery had lied...but what could she do about it? He was all that stood between her and despair.

Stephanie carried the suitcase down the hall and into her bedroom. The lies, at least, were over now. She had no place to live, no money, and her brother's bills to meet, but at least she didn't have to pretend anymore. That was something to be grateful for, although she hadn't done much to keep up the pretense that she was glad to be Avery's wife the last couple of years. It hadn't been necessary. Avery had been too sick to appear in public very often. There'd been no reason to smile when he told a vulgar joke, or try not to shudder when he put his arm around her.

There'd been no reason to do much of anything—but she'd done it anyway, slept in the room next to his, as she'd done from the beginning; tended him when he woke during the night, gave him his medicines and fed him his meals and cleaned up his messes when he'd refused to let the nurses do it, because, after all, she'd given her word.

If only Avery had adhered to the same philosophy.

No. Stephanie opened the suitcase and stared down at the things inside it. She wouldn't think about that. She wouldn't think about anything, not until she spoke with Jack Russell's associate.

A woman from his office had phoned late yesterday. Mr. Russell was sending a colleague to meet with her, she'd said. Not Mr. Russell himself? Stephanie had asked, trying not to let her disappointment show. No, the woman had said briskly. An associate. A gentleman, who'd be paying a courtesy call in late afternoon.

After she hung up the phone, Stephanie realized she'd neglected to ask the gentleman's name. Not that it mattered. She was in no position to make demands on Mr. Russell. So long as he wasn't sending the office boy, she'd be satisfied. Russell's firm was well-respected. Avery had said as much once, in a left-handed way.

"Ol' Jack's the one man in Washington I've never been able to buy," he'd said with a wheezing laugh.

Stephanie blew a tangle of curls off her forehead. As far as she was concerned, there couldn't have been a better recommendation.

"Okay," she muttered, "let's see what's still usable here."

A musty smell wafted from the suitcase as she opened it. Stephanie wrinkled her nose, went to the windows and threw them open. Then she bent over the neatly folded clothing she'd put away seven long years ago...

And groaned.

The smell came from mildew, though that wasn't the worst of it. Something had gnawed a tiny hole in the corner of the lid, just big enough to have given the moths and mice a treat. Two dresses, both made on an ancient sewing machine, a pair of polyester slacks that could almost pass for wool, the blouses she'd put away with such care...all ruined.

"Burn that garbage," Avery had ordered the day she'd first come to this house.

The thought of tossing out what little remained of her old life, her real life, had terrified her. So, instead, she'd committed her first act of defiance and stashed the suitcase in the attic.

Stephanie sank down on the edge of the bed. It was silly, she knew, but she really had wanted to leave with nothing that wasn't her own. In view of the mess she'd found inside the suitcase, her choice was reduced to the jeans, sweatshirt and sneakers she was already wearing.

"Hell," she whispered, and shot to her feet.

It was even sillier, to sit here and waste time worrying about it.

"On to Plan Two, Steff," she said briskly.

She wiped her grimy hands on the seat of her jeans, then pulled open the closet door. Designer clothing crowded the rack from one wall to the other. Stephanie put out a hand, then drew it back.

"You're being an idiot," she muttered. "Clothing is clothing, that's all it is."

Exactly. And the cold truth was that she'd worked long and hard for her keep.

"Damn right," she said, and she began stripping garments from their hangers. Not too many—just enough until she found a job. Found a way to earn money for herself...

For Paul.

But how? How? She didn't need much to live on, but the costs of keeping her brother safe, and well, and reasonably content...

Why was she wasting time on a line of thought that wouldn't accomplish anything?

She worked quickly, folding things and placing them on the bed. Shoes, underwear, a sweater...

The sound of tires crunching on the bluestone gravel driveway drifted up through the opened windows.

Stephanie glanced at her watch and frowned. Who could that be? It was early afternoon; Russell's man wasn't due until much later and she wasn't expecting anyone else...

Clare.

Of course. It would be her sister-in-law, come to gloat, to remind her that she had to be out of here by midnight.

The doorbell rang. Stephanie shot a look into the mirror. She was a mess. She had no makeup on, her hair seemed to have forgotten its morning touch of the comb. Her sweatshirt was grimy, her jeans were torn and she'd snagged a couple of fingernails wrestling the suitcase from the attic.

She looked like hell—and hell was exactly what Clare deserved.

She took a deep breath and headed for the stairs.

David stood on the porch, his hands tucked into the back pockets of his chinos, whistling softly through his teeth as he surveyed the scene around him.

Big white house, colonnaded porch, a driveway you damn near needed a map to negotiate and enough Spanish moss dripping from the trees to gladden the heart of the entire Confederate army.

Nice. Very nice—assuming that living on the set of *Gone with the Wind* was your idea of a good time. It sure as hell wasn't his and somehow, he wouldn't have thought it suited the widow Willingham, either, but then, what he knew about the woman could fit in a thimble with room left to spare.

Frowning, he jabbed the doorbell again. Wouldn't it be a bitch if she wasn't in? He knew he was early, knew he probably should have phoned from his car, but there'd been no way to precisely estimate his arrival time…

Who was he kidding? He hadn't phoned because he was damned well certain Stephanie would have told him what he could do with his impending visit, had she known about it. And then she'd have seen to it that Jack knew the details, as well. All the details, including the embarrassing ones. So David had instructed his temp to offer no names to Mrs. Willingham.

"Just tell her to expect a visit from a member of Mr. Russell's firm," he'd said.

The woman's brows had taken a barely perceptible lift but, unlike the late, unlamented Miss Murchison, she hadn't asked any questions.

"Yes, sir," she'd replied, and now here he was, unembarrassed...and, thanks to the hour, unexpected.

David stepped off the porch and gave the house the once-over again. Windows were open upstairs; he could see draperies billowing gently under the warm caress of the spring breeze. Okay. One last try. He climbed the steps, crossed the porch, and pressed the bell, listening as the chimes echoed distantly through the rooms.

All right. Enough was enough. He'd head back to the highway. Or to his car. Yes, that's what he'd do, phone Jack and tell him what he should have told him in the first place, that he was the wrong man to deal with the beautiful young widow with the vulnerable air and the disposition of a tigress...

The door swung open. Stephanie Willingham stood before him, her hands on her hips.

"You know what, Clare?" she was saying. "As far as I'm concerned, you can take this miserable house and—"

She broke off, her face reflecting shock. Not that David really noticed. He was pretty much in shock, himself.

This wasn't the stunning, sophisticated woman he'd been dreaming about . Stephanie looked about as sophisticated as a teenager. And she was—there was no other word to describe her—a mess. Her face was smudged and makeup-free; her hair was a mass of ringlets. She was wearing a sweatshirt that was a couple of sizes too large and a pair of jeans that had definitely seen better days.

And she was definitely not as beautiful as he'd remembered.

She was more beautiful, so lovely that the shock of seeing her almost stole his breath.

As it was, it damn near stole his hand, which he'd rested on the doorjamb.

"You," Stephanie said, and slammed the door in his face.

He moved fast, got his hand out of the way just in time

and replaced it with his shoulder, wincing when the door threatened its removal.

"Okay," he said, "calm down."

"How dare you? How *dare* you?"

"Mrs. Willingham...Stephanie..."

She called him a name, one that made his eyes widen.

"Get out of here! You hear me? You—get—out—of— here—right—now," she said, punctuating each word with a shove against the door.

"Hey. Hey, don't do that. You're going to slice my arm off at the shoulder."

"That'll be a good start, you—you..."

"Look, I know you're not glad to see me, but—"

"Not glad? *Not glad?*" Her voice flew up the scales. "Get off my porch. Get out of my driveway. Get—"

"Dammit, woman, listen to me!"

"No, Mr. Chambers. You're the one has to do the listening." Her eyes narrowed coldly. "I've got a shotgun right at my side."

"Oh, for crying out loud..."

"My late husband always said a loaded gun was a man's best friend, but believe me, this gun's got nothing against being a woman's best friend, too."

"Listen, there's a perfectly logical explanation for—"

"You get yourself out of this doorway, down those steps and into your car or so help me Hannah, I'll blow your head off!"

Did she really have a gun? David hadn't seen any, but what did that prove? Not seeing a weapon didn't mean there wasn't a weapon. That was urban survival lesson number one.

"Mrs. Willingham," he said in his finest, most conciliatory-courtroom manner, "you're overreacting."

"Move, Mr. Chambers!"

"Stephanie, dammit because—"

"One-one thousand. Two-one thousand. Three-one thou—"

"What are you doing?"

"I'm counting. You have five seconds, sir. Two more, in other words, and if I'm not looking at your backside by then, I'm going to fire."

David sighed. "Jack Russell," he said, and the instant he saw her eyebrows knot together in puzzlement, he twisted hard, freed his shoulder and threw all his weight against the door.

She had the advantage of leverage. He, however, he had a multiplicity of advantages. He had weight. Height. Muscle. And the growing conviction that if she really did have a gun, she wouldn't hesitate to use it.

The wood groaned. Stephanie shrieked. And then the door gave and he barreled through the opening and damn near through her, too. She shrieked again as his momentum carried him forward, onto her. Together, they fell against the wall.

David's elbow hit first. Dimly, in the back of his mind, he was aware of a lancet of pain and the knowledge that his arm would probably hurt like hell later on.

Mostly, he was aware of her.

Of Stephanie. Her softness, and the fullness of her breasts, braless apparently, beneath the oversize sweatshirt. Of the silky brush of her hair against his mouth. The faint incredibly sexy aroma of woman and flowers and sweat...

And of her knee, as she aimed it straight for the most vulnerable part of his anatomy.

David cursed and sidestepped just in time. She caught him in the thigh instead of where she'd been aiming, but it was close enough so that he got the message.

There was no gun—his brain had registered that fact right away—but that didn't mean she wasn't hell-bent on murder.

"Okay," he said grimly as she struggled to get a thumb

in his eye and a knee to his groin. His hands closed on her wrists; he lifted her arms and pinned them to the wall above her head. "Okay, Scarlett, that's enough!"

"I'll scream," she panted. "And everybody in this house will come running. The maid. The butler. The chauffeur. The cook. The housekeeper..."

"Funny not a one of them came running when I was leaning on that doorbell," David said with a mirthless smile, "or when you were screaming up a storm, a couple of minutes ago."

Color drained from her face. "They're—they're all busy."

"Busy." He smiled silkily. "Of course. Why didn't I think of that? No well-trained servant would interrupt his or her work to respond to a doorbell or, heaven forbid, a woman's bloodcurdling screams."

"They're all here, I'm telling you."

"Sure they are."

"I've only to call them—"

"Call."

"—And they'll come running."

"Tripping over each other's feet, as they rush to your aid, right?"

"Yes. No. I mean—"

"I know what you mean, Scarlett. I'm just not buying. You've told one tall tale too many. First a loaded rifle—"

"A shotgun," Stephanie said with surprising dignity.

"And now a bunch of stalwart servants near at hand." David grinned. "You've certainly got a fine imagination."

Color seeped back into her face, along the elegant, high arches of her cheeks.

"And you've got your nerve, coming here!"

"I've been trying to tell you, I'm here for a reason...and not the one you think."

But he was having increasing trouble, remembering the reason for his visit. The supposed reason because, the truth was, he'd been searching for an excuse to find this woman ever since he'd turned his back on her in that airplane and walked away.

He could see the swiftness of her pulse beating in the hollow of her throat. She wasn't frightened of him anymore; the magic words—Jack Russell—had taken care of that. She was just wary now, and angry.

And so damn gorgeous.

She was breathing rapidly, and not even the fullness of the sweatshirt could disguise the rise and fall of her rounded breasts. He was still holding her hands locked above her head; the position of her arms tilted her body forward ever so slightly and his weight was still on her— it had been the only way to keep that knee from getting him where he lived—and now, for the first time, he registered the fact that her hips were angled toward his, that her pelvis was tight against him.

Heat rose in his loins and raced through his blood; he saw her pupils enlarge as she felt the immediacy of his arousal against her. The pulse in her throat beat faster, and his heart raced along with it. She knew what was happening, and she was responding to it. She wanted him, wanted what he knew now he had never stopped wanting.

He slid his hands up her throat, to her face. Her skin felt cool against his fingertips. His thumb slid across her mouth, and her lips parted.

God, he was on fire!

He whispered her name, his voice husky and thick with need. The sound of it seemed to startle her. He felt her stiffen against him, and saw the sudden contraction of her pupils.

"Don't," she said. "Please, don't." And even in the escalating fever of his desire, David recognized the fear in that soft, breathless plea.

It stunned him.

He'd known many women over the years. Some had

claimed to adore him, one—his former wife—to despise him, but none had ever feared him. It was a new experience, and an ugly one.

There was nothing lower than a man who inspired fear in women.

And Stephanie wasn't just afraid. She was terrified.

His hands slid to her shoulders. He felt her start to tremble.

"Listen to me. I'm not going to hurt you. I'd never hurt you—"

"Let go of me!"

He did, immediately, although what he really wanted to do was take her into his arms, hold her close, promise her that no one would ever hurt her, not so long as he was there...

"Now, get out of my house." She pointed her finger at the door. Her hand was shaking, but her voice was clear and steady.

"Jack Russell asked me to talk to you."

"I don't believe you!"

"Jack told me you'd phoned him about a legal problem. He asked me if I'd come down and discuss it with you."

Her eyes narrowed. "Why would he do that? And how do you know Mr. Russell?"

"He and I are partners in the same law firm. He told me you needed legal advice."

She stared at him, speechless, and then she gave a choked laugh.

"Let me get this straight. You're his errand boy?"

David's mouth thinned. "I'm no one's errand boy. Jack asked me to talk to you and I said I would, as a favor. To Jack," he added with deliberate emphasis.

Was he telling her the truth? she wondered. Probably. He couldn't have found out about her call to Russell any other way. Not that it changed the facts. Given the choice between finding Godzilla and David Chambers on her doorstep, she'd have opted for the reptile, and never mind that it wasn't the one who had the law degree.

Stephanie stood as straight and tall as her five feet, four inches permitted.

"Well, you've done it. You've come here to see me—and now you can go home." Her chin tilted. "You can inform Mr. Russell that you did as he'd requested, and that I sent you packing."

"No loss, Scarlett. I always thought this was a complete waste of time. I told Jack straight off that you haven't got a case."

"Thank you for your opinion, Mr. Chambers. And good-bye."

"I'll give Jack your regards."

"You do that."

He nodded, stepped out onto the porch, started toward the steps... Hell, he thought angrily, and swung toward her.

"I was wrong."

"Indeed you were."

"It *is* a loss. Mine—considering that I've already wasted the day."

"What a pity," she said sweetly.

"Yeah. I'm sure it breaks your heart that I expected to be back home on my ranch just about now."

"My goodness," she purred. "I didn't know they had ranches up there in the nation's capitol." And she laughed softly in a way that made him want to walk over, grab her and shake her until she stopped laughing...

Or grab her and kiss her until she melted in his arms.

A muscle knotted in David's cheek.

"It seems to me you've got a choice here," he said, his tone brusque. "You can feel smug about knowing my weekend's shot to hell, thanks to you, or you can come down off that high horse and tell me your story." David swept back his tweed jacket and slapped his hands onto his hips. "Your choice, though frankly, I don't give a damn what you decide."

He didn't, either; Stephanie could see it in his stance. And in his face. That hard, handsome face that she'd thought of so many times during the past days and nights, although why she should have was beyond her.

Everything about him was exactly as she'd remembered. His hair was drawn back in that sexy ponytail; his skin had that golden tanned look that nobody had ever gotten from a bottle or a sunlamp. The well-tailored dark suit, snowy-white shirt and silk tie of two weeks ago had given way to a gray tweed jacket, a pale blue cotton sweater and a pair of chino trousers. His boots were dark brown this time, and scuffed just enough so they looked as if they'd seen real use. Not that they would have. She could just imagine his ranch, with yards of manicured lawn and hot-and-cold running servants, and a big, paneled den lined with the heads of dead animals where he sat pretending to be a Western Hero while outside, other men sweated and worked their butts off on his behalf...

"—Your mind."

Stephanie blinked. "I didn't...what did you say?"

"I said..." He glanced purposefully at his watch. "Make up your mind. If I'm going to be heading back to Washington, I'd just as soon get started." He smiled coolly. "Maybe I can get back in time to do something pleasant with my Friday night."

Call some woman, he meant. Take her someplace cozy for dinner, then bring her back to his place, take her in his arms...

Which was none of her business. Absolutely none.

"Well?" he demanded. "What's it going to be?"

Not that he needed to ask. David almost smiled. Stephanie's face was like an open book. She wanted to tell him to go. Maybe it was more accurate to say that what she really wanted was to push him down the steps and off the porch.

But she also wanted him to stay. That didn't surprise him. She'd called Jack for help; to turn that help away now would be stupid, and whatever else she was, the widow Willingham was not dumb.

He shot back his sleeve, looked at his watch again, and that did it.

"You're right," she said, the words rushed together as if she knew that if she didn't say them quickly, she'd never manage to say them at all. "I suppose I've no choice in the matter."

"There's always a choice, Scarlett. I'm sure you've been around long enough to know that."

She smiled bitterly at the thinly veiled condemnation in his voice. How smug he was. How sure of himself. How totally, completely, thoughtlessly male.

She thought of telling him so, of adding that if he really believed there were always choices, he'd either been born with a silver spoon in his mouth or with an IQ rivaling that of a slug.

Stephanie turned on her heel and strode toward an arched doorway at the end of the enormous hall. "Very well, Mr. Chambers. I'll give you ten minutes."

"No."

Incredulous, she spun toward him. "No? But you just said—"

"*You* are not giving me anything," David said in a clipped tone. "Let's be sure we understand that from the start." He eyed her stonily. "I'm the one who's giving *you* something. And if you can't get that straight, I'm out of here."

Her face bloomed with color. "I do not like you, Mr. Chambers," she said. "Let us be sure *you* understand that!"

He laughed. "Why, Scarlett, darlin', you just about break mah heart."

"I'd take that as a compliment—except we both know you haven't got a heart." Stephanie jerked her head toward the doorway. "We can talk here, in the parlor."

David hesitated. *Step into my parlor, said the spider to the fly...*

"Are you coming, sir? Or have you suddenly changed your mind?"

Change it, David told himself. *Don't be an idiot, Chambers.*

"Don't be silly," he said with a tight smile. "I wouldn't miss our little talk for anything."

And he sauntered down the hall and stepped past her, into the parlor.

CHAPTER SEVEN

THE room suited the house, or perhaps it suited David's expectations.

It was big and overdone, a relic of a bygone era. And it was meant to impress, assuming you were the sort who'd be impressed by dark velvet sofas and chairs that looked as if they'd buckle under a person's weight. Lamps topped with fringed silk shades fought for space on tables crowded with an army of gilt cupids and porcelain shepherdesses.

"Sit down, Mr. Chambers." Stephanie yanked open the top drawer of a mahogany rolltop desk. "That green love seat's probably the most comfortable spot, and you can turn on the lamp beside it."

David looked at the love seat in question. "Comfortable" was not a word he'd have used to describe it, but then, compared to the other chairs and sofas in the cavernous room, he figured she might have been right. He ran his hand over the rectangle of white lace centered on the headrest.

"Antimacassars," he said with a little laugh. "I didn't think they made them anymore."

Stephanie turned toward him, a sheaf of papers in her hand. Something that resembled a smile pulled at the corners of her lips. "*They* don't, but Clare does."

"Your sister-in-law?"

"Correct. Antimacassars aren't popular items in today's world. I'm surprised you'd even know the word."

"I had an aunt who had antimacassars draped over every chair and sofa in what she called 'the front room.'" David strolled to a fireplace that looked big enough to house a family of four, tucked his hands into the back pockets of his chinos and put one booted foot up on the hearth. "The room was off-limits, but sometimes, when we were visiting, I used to sneak inside. It was kind of like stepping into a time warp. Chairs that creaked when you sat down, lampshades hung with dusty..." He frowned, as if he'd just realized what he was saying, and cleared his throat. "Not that this is anything like Aunt Min's front room," he said quickly. "This is, well, it's...interesting."

"Don't try and be polite, Mr. Chambers. It would be too out of character. Besides, there's no need to mince words. This room is not interesting. It's ugly. Everybody knew it, except for my husband." She tapped the stack of papers on the edge of the desk, squared off the edges and handed them to him. "This is all the correspondence I've had with my lawyer, with the judge, with Dawes and Smith..."

"Clare's attorneys?"

"That's right."

David fanned through the documents. "Impressive."

"But meaningless. I'd lost the battle before the first shot was fired."

"Yes. Jack told me your husband and his sister held all his property jointly. That means—"

"I know what it means," Stephanie said impatiently. "I also know what Avery promised me—"

"Money," David said.

"The money I'm entitled to." Her face pinkened but her head was high. "As for what I meant about losing the battle before the first shot was fired...you should be aware that there isn't a person in this county who wanted me to collect a dime from my late husband's estate."

"What people want has little to do with what the law determines."

Stephanie laughed. "Mr. Chambers, look around you. You're standing in Avery Willingham's home, in the town named for his great-great-great-grandfather. Maybe I left out a great or two—I never did get it straight. My husband owned this town and the people in it. Everyone admired him and revered him—''

"Everyone," David said, his eyes on her face, "except for you."

Stephanie's gaze never wavered. "Have you come here to pass judgment, sir, or to tender advice? If it's judgment, I've had enough to last a lifetime and you can just turn around and go straight out the door. If it's advice, I suggest you read through those papers and then tell me what you think."

David smiled. "I gather you're not an advocate for delicate Southern womanhood, Mrs. Willingham."

"Delicacy is an indulgence," Stephanie said coolly, folding her arms, "and I have neither the time nor the patience for it."

"No." His tone was the chilly equal of hers. "Not with your husband's assets at stake."

She didn't so much as blink. "That's right. So, what's it going to be? Are you going to read those documents or are you going to leave?"

Amazing, he thought. This woman only gave the appearance of fragility. Under that delicate exterior, she had a strength he admired, even if he didn't admire the greed that drove it.

"Well? What's it going to be, Mr. Chambers?"

Logic and reason told him that his best bet would be to dump the papers on the nearest table, but he'd put in long hours on the road to get here. What would be the point in walking out now? Besides, he was doing this for Jack, not for the widow Willingham. So he walked to the love seat she'd designated as comfortable, undid the buttons on his jacket and cautiously eased his six-foot-two-inch frame onto the bottle green velvet.

"Brew me a pot of strong coffee and give me an hour," he said, "and then we'll talk."

Stephanie fought to keep the relief from showing on her face. For a minute or two, she'd thought David might really drop her papers into her arms and march out the door. And she hadn't wanted that, despite her threats. She needed his advice...and needing his advice was surely the sole reason she'd want anything whatsoever to do with this man.

She watched as he began reading the first page. After a minute, he frowned, half rose, shrugged off his jacket and tossed it aside. Then he sat back and pushed up the sleeves of his cotton sweater, all the while never taking his eyes from the page.

He'd already forgotten her presence. Well, she was accustomed to that. Avery used to do the same thing... No. It wasn't the same. Her husband had deliberately ignored her. It had been a way of showing her her proper place in his life, but David was oblivious to her because he'd lost himself in reading the documents. His brow was furrowed in concentration, and those piercingly blue eyes were fixed on the printed page.

Her gaze fell to his hands. They were powerful, and very masculine. His forearms were muscular and lightly dusted with dark hair. He should have looked as out of place as a weight lifter at a tea party, perched on the ridiculous love seat with his boots planted firmly on the flowered rug, but he didn't. He looked—he looked big, and wonderfully rugged, and he dominated the room with his presence.

"Do I get that coffee or not?"

She started at the brusqueness of his voice. He looked up, his expression unreadable, and then he gave her a smile that could only be described as patronizing.

"Or is making coffee a skill you haven't mastered?"

"You'd be shocked at the skills I've mastered," Stephanie said with frigid disdain.

No, David thought as she swept from the room, hell, no, he wouldn't...and then he took a deep breath, forced his mind back from where it was threatening to wander, and focused on the law.

The law, at least, always made sense.

*   *   *

He was barely aware of Stephanie placing a silver serving tray on the table beside him. He reached out, located the cup of coffee by feel, and took a sip. It was black, hot and strong, and surpassingly good. He acknowledged it with a curt nod.

The next time he surfaced, the cup, and the pot, were both empty. Stephanie was sitting across from him, her feet crossed at the ankles, her hands folded tightly in her lap.

"You drank it all," she said. "Do you want me to make more?"

David shook his head, rotated his shoulders, and lifted the papers from the cushion beside him.

"No, that's fine. I'm done reading." He rose and walked to the secretary.

"And?" Stephanie said. "What do you think?"

He swung around and faced her. He could see her fingers knotting together. She was apprehensive, and he could hardly blame her. She'd invested half a dozen years, maybe more, in a project named Avery Willingham, and now she was about to be cut out of the payoff.

"And," he said with a smile as bright as a shark's, "your chances of changing the judge's decision range from slim to none."

"I don't want to change his decision. I thought you understood that. Clare can have everything. I only want what I'm entitled to."

"Nothing. That's what you're entitled to, in the eyes of the law."

Stephanie nodded. Her face gave nothing away. "Well, then, I guess that's—"

"There was no pretense about it, I have to give you that much," David said, his voice harsh.

"No pretense?"

"About why you decided to snag Willingham." He jerked his head toward the secretary, and the documents.

"It was a tradeoff, plain and simple. He put money in the piggy bank, and you gave him what he wanted. I have to hand it to you, Scarlett. You look like a throwback to Jane Austen, but the truth is that you've got a cash register where most people have a heart."

Stephanie flushed and rose to her feet. "Contrary to the sleazy little script you've worked up, Mr. Chambers, I did not set out to *snag* Avery. I knew him for many years. I worked for him, as his secretary." David snorted and she stalked toward him, eyes flashing with anger. "I was a damn good secretary, too!"

"Until you looked around and saw that there was a chance at a better-paying job."

"You're like all the rest. You know it all, and don't give a damn for the truth!"

"Tell it to me, then," David said, his laughter suddenly gone. "Give me something to go on, something that makes this look like anything but what it is."

"Prove my innocence, you mean? I thought lawyers were supposed to defend their clients, regardless of guilt or innocence."

"You've got your facts twisted, Scarlett. You're not my client, remember? As for guilt or innocence…there's none at issue here."

"Then why do you expect me to defend myself to you?"

"I don't."

"Good. Because I don't intend to." Stephanie slapped her hands on her hips. "But I'll tell you this much. I was Avery's secretary for a year. And then…" Her throat constricted as she swallowed. "And then he said what he really needed was a wife. Someone to run his home and entertain his guests."

David's smile was wolfish. "And I'll bet you were even better at providing entertainment than you were at taking dictation."

"In return," she said, refusing to be drawn into the game, "Avery agreed to—to compensate me. It was his idea, all of it. The marriage, the terms...and the money."

"And you jumped at the offer."

Stephanie thought of the shock she'd felt when Avery had proposed the arrangement, of how she'd agonized over it; of how he had reassured her that it was the only way she could ensure proper care for Paul...

And of his promise that nothing between them would change.

"Is this how the law is practiced on your turf, Mr. Chambers?" Her voice was cool and steady. It had to be. She would show no weakness, ever again. "Do lawyers get to be judge and jury, too?"

He smiled in a way that made her want to take a step back.

"No. They don't." He began moving toward her and she couldn't help it, she did take a step back, then another, until her shoulders hit the wall. "Frankly, I've always thought that was unfortunate. After a while, most lawyers can pretty much tell if a client's telling them the truth—or a load of bull."

"I'm not your client, remember?"

"It's a good story, Scarlett, and you tell it well. But the simple truth is that you conned Avery Willingham into marriage. Well, maybe that's a bit harsh." His smile sent shivers up her spine. "What you did was set out the bait. Then you settled back, waited—"

"Get out of my house!"

"What's the problem? Is the truth too rough for your delicate tastes?" Darkness filled his eyes. "Or is there another truth, one that I've somehow missed? If there is, tell it to me now."

Of course, there was another truth. The *only* truth. But she had made a promise to Paul, one she would not break.

"The late Mr. Willingham bought you." His voice was

flat and harsh. "Twenty-five hundred bucks a month, deposited into an account in your name. That was the deal."

"Yes," she said. "That was the deal."

David nodded calmly, even though he felt as if someone had punched him in the gut. He looked down into those chocolate eyes. What had he expected? That she'd weep? That she'd spill some incredible tale explaining that she'd been forced into the marriage? He'd come to this house, knowing the truth. She'd sold herself to the highest bidder. She'd gone to a man's bed for money...

But it was desire that would have brought her to his bed, had he asked. She'd moaned with need in his arms, returned his kisses with a passion he still remembered, and he hadn't bought those moments with coins dropped into a till. He could make her moan again, want him again, even now. All he had to do was reach out for her...

David cursed under his breath. He strode past her, took a couple of deep breaths, just enough to be sure he had himself under control again, then turned around.

"You wanted my legal advice, and here it is." His eyes met hers. "Remember that old saw about shutting the barn door after the horse is gone?"

"Meaning?"

"Meaning, it's too late. You should have consulted a lawyer before you agreed to marry Willingham."

"Avery was a lawyer," she said softly. "He assured me that he'd take care of everything."

"Yeah, well, he certainly did. He fixed it so the gravy train stopped the day he died."

"I thought—I hoped my—my arrangement with my husband could be construed as a kind of contract," Stephanie said softly.

"You mean, an oral contract?" David shook his head. "You'd need a disinterested witness, or at least a set of circumstances that would make a reasonable person think such a contract might have been possible. Your best hope would be to find a judge who'd take pity on you and agree that a man couldn't cut his wife off without a dime...but you've already traveled that route.''

She nodded, put her hands into the pockets of her jeans and looked down at the floor. For the very first time, there was the slump of defeat in her shoulders. Despite what he knew about her, David felt a twinge of sympathy.

"Do you think Mr. Russell would agree with your opinion?''

"Yes," he said, because there was no point in lying.

"Well." She swallowed, lifted her head, and looked him squarely in the eye. "Thank you for your trouble, Mr. Chambers.''

"You could contact another attorney, not the one who represented you before, ask if he'd take the case on.''

"No. You've made it very clear that it would be an impossible battle, and besides, no one around here would touch this." She held out her hand. "Again, I thank you for your trouble—''

"I suppose," David said, "I could get you a stay, so that you wouldn't have to vacate the house by today.''

She drew back her hand, tucked it into her pocket, and shook her head. "There's no sense in delaying the inevitable.''

"Do you have a place to go?''

"Of course," she said instantly, the lie tripping from her tongue with amazing ease, but there wasn't a way in the world she was going to let anyone—David, especially—know how bad her situation was.

"And you have something stashed away to live on." His smile was quick and unpleasant. "All that money, going into your account month after month... It must have piled up a tidy bit of interest by now.''

Lying the second time was even easier. "Certainly," she said briskly. She brushed by him and made her way toward the hall. "Thank you for your time, and please thank Mr.

Russell, too. Now, if you don't mind, I have a great deal to do—"

"I just keep wondering," David said, "did you give your husband value for his money?"

She swung toward him, her face drained of color. "That's none of your business!"

"Actually, it is."

What in the name of heaven are you doing, Chambers? a voice inside him whispered in amazement, but he ignored it. The grim truth was, he'd passed the point of no return two weeks ago, on the plane to Washington.

"It's very much my business," he said. "As your attorney—"

"One of us is crazy, Mr. Chambers. You've just gone out of your way to make it clear that you are *not* my attorney."

"Semantics," he said, mixing first-year law with any-year gibberish. "I've given you legal counsel, haven't I?"

"You have, yes, but—"

"Then, I'd be negligent if I didn't ask if you'd kept your part of what you say may have been an oral contract."

"But you just said—"

"I know what I said." He didn't. He didn't even know what he was saying now. He only knew that he had to touch her again, that something was stretching and stirring deep within a hidden, primitive part of him. She looked so lost, so alone. "I need more information," he said reasonably, as he walked toward her, stopping when they were inches apart. "About your relationship with Willingham."

He looked down into Stephanie's puzzled, upturned face. At the dark eyes that could shine with an innocence he knew to be a sham, then cloud over with desire in a heartbeat. He reached out and ran the back of his hand along her cheek. She jerked away, like a skittish colt.

"Did he please you?" he said gruffly. "Aside from the money, I mean. Were you happy with him?"

"You've no right to ask me such—"

"Did you tremble when he touched you?"

He put his hand against the curve of her cheek, dropped it to her throat. His fingers were hot against her skin and she caught her breath, stiffening herself against his touch, trying to deny what it made her feel because it was impossible. She couldn't—she mustn't...

"You trembled when I touched you," he said, his voice low and rough. "Just as you are now."

"Stop," she said, but her voice was a thready whisper. "David, stop."

His gaze dropped to her mouth. Her lips parted, as he'd known they would. He felt the rush of heat racing through his body, felt the tension spreading until his nerve endings seemed to hum. He said her name, drew her into his arms, thrust his hands into her hair and tangled his fingers in its sensuous weight.

"David," she whispered, and her breath caught. "David?"

"Yes," he said, drowning in what he saw in her eyes. "That's right. David. Only David..."

He kissed her. Or she kissed him. In the end, it didn't matter. The fusion was complete. Mouths, bodies... Where did she begin and he end? He didn't know, didn't care, didn't want to think about it because nothing else mattered but the feel of Stephanie, warm and willing, in his arms.

CHAPTER EIGHT

NOTHING mattered, but being in David's arms.

Stephanie felt weightless, as she melted into him. All rational thought was gone.

The feel of him. The warmth of his body. The touch of his hot, hungry mouth on hers. She was spinning, spinning, like a planet around an incandescent sun.

She heard him whisper her name as he slid his hands up her body, cupped her face and held her willingly captive to his kiss. He said something against her mouth. She couldn't understand the words but she knew what he must be asking, and her answer was in the way she touched him and moved against him.

"Scarlett." His voice was urgent as he cupped her bottom, lifted her into the heat and hardness of his arousal, urged her to feel the raw, masculine power she had unleashed.

The reality should have terrified her, as it had in the past. But what she felt was excitement. This was—David was—every half-forgotten dream of her girlhood. He was a million unfulfilled wishes, and more.

"Tell me what you want," he said. He cupped her breast, pressed his mouth to her throat. "Say that it's me, Scarlett. Say—"

"Well, heavens to Betsy! Now, isn't this a charmin' sight?"

They sprang apart. Instinctively, David put Stephanie behind him as they turned toward the hall.

He saw a woman in the arched doorway. His lawyer's mind made a fast inventory. She was, perhaps, two decades older than Stephanie with a heavily made-up face, a mane of frizzy hair whose platinum color could only have come from a bottle, and eyes a shade of green that had to have started life on an optician's workbench. She was poured into a leopard-print cat suit that was at least a size too small. And a cat, David thought, was what she looked like, one that had just opened its mouth and swallowed a live canary.

Stephanie stepped out from behind him. "Clare?"

Avery Willingham's sister. David's eyes narrowed.

"In the flesh," Clare said. Smiling, she strolled toward them, breasts jiggling under the clinging cat suit. "And who, pray tell, is your charmin' visitor?"

Stephanie moved forward, and the women met in the center of the room. Her mouth still bore the faint swelling that was the imprint of his kisses, her cheeks were still flushed, but somehow she'd managed to take on an aura of composure and command. Even to his jaundiced eye, it was a remarkable performance.

"What are you doing here, Clare?"

Clare smiled. "What am I doin' here? she asks. This is my house, missy. I don't need a reason to be in it."

"It isn't yours, not until midnight."

Clare shrugged. "A technicality."

"Until then," Stephanie said calmly, "please ring the doorbell if you wish to come in."

"I did, missy." Clare batted her heavily mascaraed lashes at David. "But there was no answer. 'Course, I understand the reason. You were...busy. You and Mister..."

"Chambers," David said. "David Chambers."

"A pleasure, Mr. Chambers. I'm awfully sorry if I interrupted anythin', but I had no idea Stephanie would be entertainin' a gentleman, this bein' such a busy weekend for her an' all."

David put his hand lightly on Stephanie's shoulder. Her posture was rigid but she was trembling; he could feel it through his fingertips.

"What do you want, Clare?" she said.

"Why, just to make sure things are as they should be." The blonde gave David a last slow smile, then began circling the room, brushing long, fuchsia-lacquered fingernails over the gilt cherubs and porcelain shepherdesses. "All of this is mine now, missy, these precious heirlooms that've been passed from one generation of Willin'hams to another. You just remember that."

"How could I forget?"

"You're to take nothin', you understand that? Not a single thing."

"You've nothing to worry about, Clare. I don't want any of this—this stuff. I intend to leave with nothing but the same suitcase I brought here."

"Just you make sure there's nothin' in that suitcase but the junk you brought to this fine house, missy, you got that?"

Stephanie stepped out from under David's hand. She wasn't shaking anymore; he was sure of it.

"Your attorney already did an inventory," she said.

"An' how do I know that would stop you from takin' my things?" Clare's eyes looked like bright green beads. "Trash like you is capable of anythin'."

"Go home, Clare." Stephanie's voice was low but firm. "You can do all the gloating you want, come midnight."

"And that big bedroom closet of yours, the one my brother kept filled. All that stuff's mine now. You just be sure an'—"

"The clothing is Mrs. Willingham's."

Both women looked at David. "I beg your pardon?" Clare said.

"I'm Mrs. Willingham's attorney, and I said the clothing belongs to her. It's her personal property."

Clare laughed. "Still not givin' up, are you, missy? Well, you're too late, Mister Attorney. The case has been settled."

"Whether it has or has not, Mrs. Willingham has certain rights. I've come here to make sure she is able to exercise them without interference."

Clare tossed back her peroxide mane. "Really. An' here I could have sworn you and my beloved sister-in-law were…well, I won't use the word. I'm too much a lady."

"Is that right?" David smiled lazily. "I'd have thought a lady would have known that breaking into a house was against the law."

"Don't be ridiculous! Seven Oaks belongs to me."

"Not until midnight."

"I have a key!"

David's brows rose. "Did you give this woman a key, Mrs. Willingham?"

Stephanie stared at him in amazement. In all these months, this was the first time anyone had ever come to her defense. Even Amos Turner, whom she'd paid for his legal services, had never said a word on her behalf except in judge's chambers.

Stephanie swallowed dryly. "No," she said. "No, I—"

"My client says she did not give you a key," David said pleasantly, "and I can attest to the fact that you neither asked permission to enter nor received it. Where I come from, that makes you an intruder until the time the court order takes effect."

Clare shot a baleful look at Stephanie. "You better tell this hotshot lawyer of yours that he's bein' stupid! Maybe he doesn't understand who I am!"

"He knows who you are," Stephanie said calmly. "And I suspect he knows what you are, too."

Clare's plump face took on a purplish tinge.

"I don't know what game you two think you're playin'," she snapped, "but it isn't goin' to change one little thing. I'm tellin' you right here an' now, Miss High an' Mighty, you'd best be out of here by tonight."

"With pleasure."

"I heard about that call you made to the judge—"

"There's no need to go into details," Stephanie said quickly.

"Cryin' about needin' time to find a place to live and a job, moanin' about not havin' any money—"

"I said I don't want to discuss this now, Clare."

"You came to Seven Oaks with nothin', and you're gonna leave with nothin'. You can sleep on the street, for all I care!"

"Is it true?" David said quietly, his eyes locked on Stephanie's.

"It's none of your affair."

"Stephanie, answer me! Do you have money, and a place to live?"

"She has nothin'," Clare said with ill-concealed glee. "Nothin' a-tall!"

"Dammit," David growled, "tell her she's wrong!"

Stephanie glared at him. "I can't, David. She's right. Now, are you satisfied?"

David's eyes narrowed. What in hell had she done with all the money Willingham had paid her? Not that it mattered to him. He'd come to her rescue a minute ago because it was the proper thing to do. No decent lawyer would stand by and let her give up property that was rightfully hers. But the rest of it, what happened to her after this...she was correct. It was none of his affair.

"Just you make sure there's nothin' of mine accidentally falls into your suitcase, when you leave my house."

"I wouldn't take anything from this house, Clare. I don't *want* anything that belonged to the Willinghams. Haven't you got that straight yet?"

"What *you'd* best get straight, missy, is that I expect everythin' I deserve. You hear?"

Stephanie looked at Clare, at the pudgy, selfish face and the piggy eyes. She'd had years of looking at that face, of listening to that whining voice.

"I hear," she said...and then, with a graceful movement of her hand that could almost have been accidental, she swept a tabletop's worth of ugly cupids and shepherdesses crashing to the floor.

No one moved. No one even breathed. Clare, Stephanie and David all looked down at the floor.

Stephanie was the first to raise her head.

"Oh, my," she said sweetly, "just look at what I've done. I don't know how I could have been so clumsy."

Clare, as puffed as a chicken ruffling its feathers, took a step forward. "Why, you—you—"

"Accidents will happen," David said, trying not to laugh. He looked at Stephanie, whose eyes were bright with defiance, and he felt a strange lurch inside his chest. "Isn't that right, Mrs. Willingham?"

"That's a fact," she said pleasantly.

"Accident?" Clare glared at them both. "That was no accident. She did it on purpose!"

"So sue her." David's smile held all the warmth of an iceberg.

"What for, wise guy? Your precious client is broke, or have you forgotten that?"

A muscle knotted in David's cheek. "No," he said quietly, "I haven't forgotten. Send the bills to me."

"David," Stephanie said, "this isn't necessary."

"It surely is!" Clare snatched David's business card from his outstretched hand. "The cost of replacin' these things will be horrendous. They're—"

"Priceless heirlooms, passed from one generation of Willinghams to another." David nodded, looked down and frowned as something caught his eye. He bent and scooped up the broken base of one of the cupids. "'Made in Taiwan,'" he read, with a lift of his eyebrows. Smiling politely, he handed the bit of porcelain to a crimson-faced Clare. "As I said, Ms. Willingham, buy yourself some new 'heirlooms' and send the bill to my firm."

''David,'' Stephanie hissed, ''I told you, it isn't neces- sary. I can repay Clare for the figures.''

''When?'' Clare demanded.

''Yes,'' David said evenly. ''When?''

''Well—well, I'll contact her, as soon as I'm settled.''

''As soon as you have a place to live,'' he said, his voice hardening, ''and some money to buy groceries, you mean.''

Stephanie flushed. ''Where I live, and how, is no one's concern but mine.''

''It's the court's concern,'' David said sharply, ''or it should have been. Your lawyer must have been sitting on his brain when he argued this case.''

''Dammit, I don't want to discuss this! I made my living as a secretary before. I can do it again. I'll go to—to Atlanta. I'll get a job and I'll reimburse Clare down to the last penny.''

That was when it came to him. The idea was simple, obvious and logical, when he thought about it. It was an excellent, if temporary, solution to more than one prob- lem—assuming he ignored the voice shouting, *Are you nuts?* inside his head.

''You're right,'' he said. ''You'll reimburse her.''

Stephanie nodded. He could tell, from the look on her face, that she'd been prepared for more argument.

''Well, I'm glad we agree.''

''I'll tell payroll to advance you your first month's pay, and you can send her a check.''

Her face went blank. ''What?''

David's hand curled around her elbow, the pressure of his fingers firm. ''It's not an unusual procedure,'' he said, knowing that it was an impossible one. Russell, Russell, Hanley and Chambers offered many benefits to its employ- ees, but acting as a bank was not one of them. ''After all, now that we've found you a good job—''

''We have?''

''As my secretary.''

Stephanie's mouth dropped open. "As your..."

"My secretary. Exactly."

"No! David—"

"And," he said, his eyes warning her not to try and defy him, "now that I've had time to think about it, I'm advising you to leave your clothing right where it is."

Stephanie's look changed from one of confusion to outright disbelief. "Why on earth would I do that?"

"Well," he said, "I could invent some legal mumbo-jumbo by way of explanation, but the simple fact is that I'd imagine it'll be an endless source of amusement for you, envisioning Ms. Willingham trying to shoehorn her corpulent self into your things."

There was a second of silence. Then Clare called David a name that made his eyebrows shoot into his hairline, and Stephanie laughed.

She had, he thought, a wonderful laugh. It was free, and easy, and when he looked at her, he suddenly had the feeling that this was the first time she'd laughed, really laughed, in years.

"Stephanie?" he said, and held out his hand.

Stephanie looked at his hand. She thought of her sad old suitcase, lying open on the bed upstairs, and that the only clothes in this entire house that were salvageable and really hers were the ones she was already wearing.

"Stephanie?" David said again, "shall we leave?"

Don't be stupid, she told herself, Stephanie, don't be an idiot...

"Yes," she said, and she smiled, took his outstretched hand, and walked away from Seven Oaks, and Clare, and the terrible memories of a life she'd never, ever wanted.

The day had started with soft breezes and bright sunshine, but as they drove away from Seven Oaks, it began to drizzle. By the time they reached the highway, the drizzle had turned into a downpour.

Stephanie sat rigid and silent, the euphoria of her departure gone. *What have I done?* she kept thinking, and when David turned on the windshield wipers, they offered not an answer but a command.

Go back, they sang as they swooped across the glass. *Go back, Stephanie, go back.*

"How about some music?" David said.

She jumped at the sound of his voice. He hadn't spoken a word until now, either. She looked at him, at the stern mouth and firm jaw. He was a man accustomed to getting what he wanted.

Out of the frying pan, into the fire, Steffie. Go back, go back, go back.

"Stephanie?"

Music. He was asking her if she wanted to hear—

"Yes." She swallowed dryly. "Music would be fine."

He reached out and punched a button on the dashboard. Dark, deep chords and arpeggios resonated through the car.

"Sorry," he said quickly, and punched another button. Rachmaninoff gave way to Paul Simon. "I like classical stuff, but, I don't know, at the moment, Rachmaninoff seems..."

Melodramatic, at the very least. Stephanie folded her hands tightly together in her lap. Here she was, fleeing one nightmare for what might just as easily be another.

"Do you like Simon? The old stuff, I mean, that he wrote and recorded with Art Garfunkel."

It was such an inane conversational thread; if she hadn't known better, she'd have suspected David was having second thoughts, too. But if he were, if he'd changed his mind about offering her a job, he'd have pulled off to the side of the road and told her so. Bluntly. If there was one thing she knew about David Chambers, it was that he didn't pull his punches. He said what he was thinking, took what he wanted without hesitation...

Her heart gave an unsteady thud. And she was running off with him?

The wipers swooshed across the windshield. *Oh, Steffie,* they sang. *Go back, go back, go back.*

Windshield wipers were strange things.

They swept across the glass, back and forth, back and forth, and after a while you could set a tune to them. Lyrics, too.

David's hands tightened on the steering wheel.

Unfortunately, he didn't much care for the words to this particular song. Not the one drifting from the car's speakers; Simon and Garfunkel were singing about Mrs. Robinson, and that was just fine. It was the lyric only he could hear that was the problem.

Cray—zee, the wipers sang, *Oh, man, you are crayay—zeeee...*

Damn right. How else to explain why he was driving along with Stephanie Willingham tucked into the seat beside him—although not even an optimist would describe her as looking "tucked in." She looked about as relaxed as he felt. Her back was straight as a board, her hands were clenched in her lap, and her mouth was a tight little knot. People sitting in dental waiting rooms looked happier than she did, and who could blame her? He wasn't in the best of moods himself.

What in hell had possessed him? He'd gone down to Georgia because Jack had asked him to. Okay, maybe there'd been more to it than that. Maybe he'd gone to find what the shrinks called closure, a way of signing off on the experience of a couple of Sundays ago. Okay, so there was no "maybe" about it. He'd driven to Willingham Corners to take a cold look at Stephanie and get her out of his head. That had been step one. Step two was supposed to have been letting her bend his ear with her tale of woe, which would have led to the good part, when he chucked her under the chin and said, hey, he was sorry but she was fresh out of luck, and out of suckers...

Now here he was, top contender for the Sucker of the Year award.

Okay. Stephanie hadn't trapped him into this mess. Not directly. He'd managed to do that by himself. But she'd helped. Damn right, she had. David's jaw tightened. Instead of listening to Simon and Garfunkel, they ought to be humming strains from the *The Merry Widow*. That's what his passenger was, a widow who wouldn't even bother to pretend she was grieving, who claimed not to have a cent to her name or a job or a place to take shelter...

Claimed? It was probably true, otherwise she'd never have gone with him. So what? Those were her problems, not his. Stephanie had made her bed. Now she could lie in it.

Or in his. His bed. His arms. And he could kiss her until she went all soft and breathless, as she had before Clare had burst into the room, and perhaps then he could seek out and find that sweetness that seemed to be waiting just for him, only for him.

Cray—zee, the wipers blades whispered. *You are cray— zee...*

Think about the case. Concentrate on the law. What were the facts? Could a man leave his wife with zero bucks when he had plenty? Had Avery Willingham simply given Stephanie a raw deal? Had he bought her favor for cold, hard cash, married her, shown her off to the world but arranged it so that when he toddled off this planet, there was nothing for her to inherit?

But she was entitled to something, wasn't she? The court should have seen that.

On the other hand, how come Stephanie was broke? At the rate of a couple of thou per month, the little bride should have had time to amass a pretty decent retirement fund.

David frowned.

Where was the money? What had she done with it? It was a great question. How come he'd neglected to ask it?

David's frown deepened. Because he was the wrong person to handle this case, that was why. His involvement was too personal. Too—too something. Call it what you wanted, it was not going to work. A lawyer and a client worked best when there was some space between them, not when they started out with a history that involved damn near making it in the cabin of an airplane.

There was a way out. He'd get Stephanie to Washington, check her into a hotel and phone Jay O'Leary. Or Bev Greenberg. Or any of the half a dozen juniors at the firm. One of them would be more than happy to take the case, and, come to think of it, wasn't one of the pool secretaries going on maternity leave next week?

"That's it," David murmured.

"Excuse me?"

He looked at Stephanie. "Nothing," he said, and smiled. "Nothing at all."

Still smiling, he turned up the volume on the radio and began humming along with Paul and Art.

Nothing? Nothing at all?

Stephanie stared blindly out the window.

Something was going on in David's head, and she knew damn well it couldn't be classified as "nothing."

A few minutes ago, he'd looked like a man on his way to his own execution. Now he was the portrait of contentment, from his smug little smile to the fingers tapping against the steering wheel to the abominable, off-key humming. What did *he* have to feel so good about?

Nothing she could think of.

As for her, she was beyond feeling, unless you wanted to dwell strictly on the panic she felt growing inside her as the minutes, and the miles, flew by.

What on earth was she doing here? It had seemed such a wonderful exit, walking straight out the door of that hideous mausoleum and leaving Clare looking even more slack-jawed than usual.

So she'd done it. *Shall we leave?* this man—this arrogant, oh-so-quick-to-condemn man—had said. And she had. She'd followed him blindly and now here she was, heading for no place, with nothing to her name but the grungy clothes on her back, a handful of change that she'd scooped off her dresser this morning, and a comb.

Well, that's good, Steff. You have a comb, at least. That ought to be a big help when you get to D.C. and find out that this man has no real intention of helping you. For all you know, he's going to tell you that your "secretarial" duties will begin, and end, in his bedroom.

"Stop the car!"

David looked at Stephanie. She had a wild look in her eyes and she was already fumbling with her seat belt. He cursed, twisted the wheel hard to the right and pulled onto the grassy shoulder of the road. The car behind them shot past, horn blaring.

"Dammit," he roared, "what the hell are you doing?"

Flinging open the door, that was what she was doing. Hurling herself out like a human projectile and then sprinting for the nearby woods. David undid his seat belt and chased after her.

She was easy enough to catch. Not that she wasn't fast on her feet; it was only that he was faster. Four years as a running back on a much-needed football scholarship at Yale still guaranteed that. He reached her just as she entered the treeline, tackled her and brought her down in a tangle of arms and legs. They rolled down a shallow embankment and landed in a pile of last fall's leaves, Stephanie on her back, David straddling her.

"Dammit, Stephanie…"

"Don't you 'Stephanie' me, you—you—"

Words weren't enough. She made a fist and punched him, as hard as she could, in the belly. He grunted, grabbed for her wrists, forced her arms over her head and pinned them to the ground.

"Let go of me!"

"Not if you're going to pretend I'm a punching bag."

"Let—go—of—me, you—you…"

"Are you nuts? What did I do, to rate this?"

"You were born with the wrong chromosomes. Let go!"

"Will you behave if I do?"

"Yes," she said.

Only a fool would have believed her, and David had committed his last foolish act an hour ago, when he'd walked her out the door and into his life.

"You're pretty fast with the punches," he said as she struggled beneath him. "What'd you do, grow up in a gym?"

"No," she panted. "I grew up with a brother who believed in women being able to defend themselves against men like you!"

"Men like me?" David gave a short, sharp laugh. "Yup, you're right. You sure as hell need to know how to defend yourself against an s.o.b. like me. Why, just look at what I've done in the past hour. Defended you against—"

"You didn't defend me," Stephanie huffed, trying to shove his weight off her. "Why would you? I don't need defending."

"Need it or not, I defended you. And I offered you free legal advice—"

"Some advice. You told me I've got as much chance of getting anything out of the estate as a—a cottonmouth has of getting petted."

"It was not only free advice, it was excellent advice. Plus, I gave you a job."

"Ha."

"Listen, lady, maybe typing letters isn't half as exotic

as what you used to do to earn your daily bread, but most women in your position would be grateful for it.''

"And what is *that* supposed to mean, huh? 'Most women in my position'? Just what, exactly, is *my* position, Mr. Chambers?''

It was a question fraught with many possibilities but, just then, David could only see one of them. Stephanie's position was directly under his, and even though he was angry, even though hanging on to her was like hanging on to a football at the bottom of a pileup, he knew suddenly that if she kept moving the way she was, they were both going to be in trouble.

"Okay," he said, "here's what I'm going to do."

"Oh, I know what you're going to do," Stephanie said fiercely.

"I'm going to stand up," David said, ignoring her. "Take it nice and easy, understand? Then we'll talk."

"We are done talking! I should never have listened to you in the first place. Walking me right past Clare and out of that house, and I never stopped to ask why!''

"I'm a sucker for appeals from the SPCA, too," David said grimly. "Dammit, don't do that!''

"You're no better than Avery, you—you liar!''

"Did he lie to you? Your husband?''

"Don't call him that," Stephanie said through her teeth. "And yes, he lied to me. I told you that. He said—he said he'd take care of my—my needs as long as it was necessary, but he didn't.''

"What needs?" David said softly, and suddenly everything around them seemed to stop.

Stephanie looked up into David's face. His eyes were sapphire dark and locked on hers. The rest of him was locked on her, too. Chest to chest. Hip to hip. Thigh to thigh…

Warmth suffused her skin. Her heart gave an unsteady thump. Desperately, she tried to dislodge him.

"Don't..." David caught his breath. "Don't do that."

"Do what? Dump you on your head? Damn you, David!"

"That," he said, biting back a groan as she moved again. "Hell, that. You're the one who was busy talking about all those male chromosomes. What must I do, draw you a diagram?"

His body gave up the struggle and reacted to hers. He saw comprehension dawn in her eyes and she went absolutely still.

That had stopped her, he thought grimly. She wasn't fighting him anymore...not that he was thinking about her fighting him. All he could think about now was her softness. Her heat. Her scent.

"Let go," she said.

He would. He'd let go of her wrists, gather her into his arms and take her angry mouth in a long, hungry kiss—except, she wasn't angry. She had a look to her he'd seen in the eyes of a stray cat he'd found haunting the back alley when he was a kid, a cat so feral and afraid it had never let him get close enough to help it.

"Let me up," she said. "Right now."

The words were strong, but that didn't disguise the fear. Hell, it was more than that, it was something he didn't even want to put a name to. He drew back, his hands still holding hers.

"I'm not going to hurt you."

"Just—just get off me."

Her eyes glittered with unshed tears. He took a deep breath and fought against the unreasonable desire to kiss those tears away.

"Promise me you won't run?"

She nodded stiffly.

"Let me hear you say it. Tell me you're not going to run like a scared rabbit."

"I was not running like a scared rabbit."

He decided against arguing the point. He released her, rolled off her and stood up. He held out his hand, but Stephanie ignored the gesture, rose on her own and began dusting off her jeans.

"Maybe you'd like to tell me where you thought you were going," he said.

She sniffed, wiped her nose on her sleeve, and shrugged. "Home."

"Home," he repeated.

His tone incredulous. Not that she could blame him. Where was home, exactly? It was just that anywhere was safer than here, when she didn't trust this stranger or his promises...when she didn't trust herself when he touched her.

"That's right. Home. I told you. Home. To Willingham Corners."

"Ah, yes. Willingham Corners. And that house." David folded his arms and fixed her with an interested look. "How stupid of me. Come to think of it, didn't the Yankees burn Tara?"

She gave a choked little laugh. "It's true. I thought of Tara, too, the first time I saw Seven Oaks."

David smiled. "When I rang the doorbell, that's what I half expected to hear. Dah-daaah-dah-dah...you know. That music."

"You almost did," Stephanie said. "For a time, Avery actually thought about it."

"But you managed to talk him out of it?"

"Me? Talk Avery out of something?" Her laugh was without humor this time. "I didn't even try. He just got sidetracked, I guess. Not that it mattered to me. It was his house, not mine."

"Strange way to feel, about a house that's your home, isn't it?"

"Seven Oaks was never my home. It belonged to my husband, and I...I..." Her voice trailed away.

"And you belonged to him, too."

Anger flashed in her eyes. "Are we back to that?"

"We never left it."

"What do you want me to say, David? That it wasn't an arrangement I was proud of? Okay. It wasn't." Her shoulders slumped. "Look, I don't expect you to understand."

"Try me."

"I…I don't see how it matters."

"If I'm going to represent you," he said, waving a mental goodbye to his junior partners because, hell, this case was too complex for them, "the arrangement you keep referring to matters a great deal. I need to know the specifics."

"You know them. Avery deposited money in my name each month—"

"Did your sister-in-law hate you from the beginning?"

Stephanie shrugged. "No more than anyone else in town."

David nodded. "I got that feeling from the documents I read. And yet, you were going back there, where Clare's probably already changed the locks, and the good townsfolk are probably holding a party to celebrate the removal of the grasping, scheming, hard-hearted widow of the town's fair-haired patriarch."

"You don't believe in pulling your punches, do you, Mr. Chambers?"

"We've made too much progress to go back to such formality now, Mrs. Willingham. And no, I don't believe in pulling my punches. That is how they see you, isn't it?"

Stephanie lifted her chin. "Everyone does. Including you."

David reached out and plucked a leaf from her hair. "Change my opinion, then."

"How? By listing my virtues?" She drew herself up. "I am not about to defend myself to you or anybody, sir."

He smiled. "I like the way you say that."

"Say what?"

"Sir." His smile tilted. "It's very old fashioned, and polite—and yet, I get the feeling what you're really doing is calling me a four-letter word." He reached out and took another bit of leaf from her hair, his hand lingering against the dark curls. "Avery wasn't a nice guy, was he?"

"He was a rat," Stephanie said in a whisper.

"Because he cut you off without a cent?"

"Because he lied," she said sharply. "He lied about everything, and once I was trapped, once I realized, he just laughed and said I'd have to live with it."

She spun away, her arms wrapped around herself. David turned her to face him.

"Did he hurt you?"

She looked up. His eyes had gone as flat as his voice.

"He didn't beat me, if that's what you mean." She shook her head. "He was just—he got his kicks out of inflicting other kinds of pain. He was mean-tempered. Vindictive. He must have been the kind of little boy that pulled wings off bugs, you know?" She touched the tip of her tongue to her lips. "I suspect lots of people would agree, if it didn't mean bucking Clare and siding with me. Most folks would sooner shake hands with a rattlesnake than admit to having anything in common with Bess Horton's girl."

David's gaze swept over her face. It was bright with defiance.

"Is that your maiden name? Horton?"

She nodded.

"And what is it people have against your mother?"

Stephanie looked down and brushed a speck of dirt he couldn't see off her jeans.

"They don't have anything against her, anymore," she said brusquely. "She's gone."

"Gone where?"

She shrugged. "I've no idea."

"And the brother you mentioned? Where is he?"

"He's…" She hesitated. "He's around."

"Why didn't you leave Avery Willingham, if he was such a bastard?"

"I didn't know what he was like. Not at first. And besides…"

"Besides, there was the money." His tone was cold and accusatory.

"Yes," she said, so faintly that he had to strain to hear it.

"And it's all gone," he said.

She nodded.

"How? How could it be gone? What did you do with it?"

"I spent it."

"All of it? On what?"

"That's none of your—"

"Do you want me to represent you, or don't you?"

She stared at him. "Why would you do that? You don't like me. You don't believe anything I say. Why would you take me on?"

"Because I'm a lawyer," he said quickly. Too quickly. What was he getting into here? Nothing he couldn't get out of, he told himself, answering his own question. "And I believe that every person in this country is entitled to the protection of the law."

"I couldn't pay you."

"Our office does pro bono work all the time," he said, trying to think straight. It wasn't easy. She was touching the tip of her tongue to her bottom lip again. Her tongue was a pale, velvety pink, and her mouth was—her mouth was— "But I need some answers first. Like, what happened to the money in your account?"

Stephanie thought of Paul, who'd been her courage and her strength when the town had pointed its fingers at Bess Horton and her dirty-faced, ragamuffin offspring. Who'd raised her, after their mother left. Who sat now in his room at Rest Haven, unable to do the things he used to do, and of the pride that was all he had left.

Swear to me, Steff, he'd said, *swear you won't ever tell anybody about me.*

She swallowed dryly and looked at David. "I spent the money."

"Gambling?" She shook her head. "Drinking?" She shook her head again. "Do you do coke? Heroin? Dammit, Scarlett." He shook her, hard. "It couldn't have just trickled through your fingers."

"It's gone," she said, her eyes on his. "That's all I can tell you."

"And now you want more," he said softly.

"I want what's rightfully mine. What Avery promised me."

It was the answer David had expected. Only a miracle would have made her say that she didn't want anything, now that she'd met him. Nothing but him, his kisses, his arms around her...

He stepped back, his hands curling into fists that he buried in his pockets, his anger as much for himself as for her.

"I'll take you to D.C.," he said. "To my place." He almost laughed at her strangled yelp of indignation. "There's a housekeeper's apartment in my town house. Bath, bedroom, small sitting room—and a lock on the door. All that's missing is a housekeeper. Mine sleeps out, not in."

"And what will you expect in return?" she asked coldly.

"Your presence at my office, five days a week from nine to five."

"Why are you doing this for me, David?"

He thought again of the stray cat he'd tried to help, all those years ago.

"It's for me," he said briskly. "Your case is interesting. Well?" He held out his hand. "Deal?"

Stephanie drew a deep breath. What choice was there? Slowly, she placed her hand in his.

"Deal," she said.

David's fingers closed around hers. Shake her hand, he told himself, do it in an impersonal way...

But his arms were already gathering her to him and she was yielding, melting, soft and warm as honey, into his embrace. He kissed her, kept kissing her, while time stopped. And when he finally let her go, he looked at his watch, then said, in a voice so calm that it amazed even him, "We'd better get moving."

David started for the car. Stephanie stood motionless.

Go back, the voice within her whispered.

He turned and looked at her. "Well?" His tone was brusque, almost impatient. "Are you coming?"

Steffie, don't do this...

Stephanie nodded. "Yes," she said, and followed him.

CHAPTER NINE

THE arrangement wasn't going to work.

Once again, David sat in his office, his back to his desk and his gaze fixed blankly on the cherry trees that lined the walk. The pink blossoms were falling almost as fast as his disposition, but then, it wasn't often a man had to admit defeat.

What had ever possessed him to think his crazy scheme had any chance at success?

Poverty was the curse that had been passed from one generation of Chamberses to the next, not insanity. And yet, he'd behaved like a certifiable lunatic. What else could you call a man who saw a woman he knew he shouldn't want, wanted her anyway, and told himself it wouldn't be any kind of problem to bring her into his life? Into his office? Hell, into his home?

David muttered a word that would have curled Miss Murchison's hair, if she'd been around to hear it. But, mercifully, Murchison was gone—and Stephanie was all too torturously here. After six days—five and a half, if you wanted to be exact—he was ready to admit that he'd made one huge mistake.

It had seemed so simple. Install Stephanie in the small apartment in his town house. Hire her as his secretary. See her in the office, where she'd at least make no more a mess of things than the memorable Miss Murchison, not see her at all at home, because the apartment had its own private entrance, as well as an entrance just off the kitchen...

"Great plan," David said to the cherry trees...except, something had gone wrong between the planning and the execution.

On the surface, things were going fine. Much to his surprise, Stephanie was as good a secretary as she'd claimed. His office had been transformed. His files were all up to date, his appointment calendar was accurate, the notes he scribbled during meetings or court proceedings were typed and organized so quickly it made his head spin. He'd even given up brewing his own coffee. Why wouldn't he, when Stephanie's was so much better?

She was pleasant to have around, too. Everybody said so, from the kid in the mail room straight up to the partners. Even Jack Russell, whose shocked expression made it clear he'd swallowed a mouthful of objections on learning the identity of David's new secretary, had admitted that much.

"Great improvement over the Grump," Jack had commented, "but—"

"I know all the 'buts,'" David had said, with the easy air of a man who was convinced he'd thought a problem through and solved it. "Not to worry, Jack. It's temporary."

"Temporary," Jack had replied thoughtfully, and David had nodded.

"Temporary, and practical."

"In that case," Jack had said with a smile, "I'll save my comments until you ask to hear them."

David scowled and turned his chair away from the window.

He could only imagine what Jack's comments would be if he knew that Stephanie wasn't only working for him but that she was living with him. Living under his roof, anyway. He hadn't lied about that part of it, he simply hadn't mentioned it because he'd known how that bit of information would have been received.

"There's no need to talk about our living arrangements," he'd told her gruffly, when they'd reached his home in Georgetown last Saturday.

"I'm not a fool, David," she'd said coolly. "People will

talk, as it is. You many find this difficult to believe, but my reputation is as important to me as yours is to you."

"It isn't that. It's just—I wouldn't want it to seem as if—"

"No. Neither would I."

"Dammit," David said, and rose to his feet.

All he'd done was give a job and a place to live to a woman who needed them. The loan of some money, too, so she could show up at work in something other than a pair of jeans and a sweatshirt. He'd have done as much for anybody else in the same situation...

Who was he kidding? He'd come within inches of compromising his professional ethics. You didn't give a woman legal advice, employ her, take her into your home and all the time, every damn minute of every night and every day, want to take her in your arms and make love to her, without knowing you were walking a painfully fine line between what was right and what was wrong.

He never saw her, except in the office. Stephanie left before he did each morning, because she insisted on taking public transportation to work.

"Don't be stupid," he'd said brusquely. "I'll drive you."

"And do what? Drop me off a block away?"

"Well," he'd said, "well..."

"I can manage on my own, thank you. And I'll be punctual."

She was that. She was at her desk, ready to work the second he came through the door.

"Good morning, Mr. Chambers," she'd say, and she never so much as smiled or paused to say a word that wasn't business-related after that, even though he—even though he...

David mouthed another oath, jammed his hands into his trouser pockets and paced the length of his office.

She left at the end of the day, meaning she left only when he finally said, "Go home, Mrs. Willingham."

"Yes, sir," she'd say, and he'd sit in his office with the door partly open, watching as she straightened up her desk, collected her purse and perhaps a light sweater, then went out into the twilight. He had to force himself to sit still and not follow after her. There was no point. He'd tried that, the other evening after they'd worked an hour late.

"I'll drive you home," he'd said briskly, but Stephanie had shaken her head.

"Thank you, but I prefer going home alone."

The way she'd phrased it had been like a slap in the face. He'd felt a thrum of anger deep in his bones. For one crazy second, he'd thought of pulling her into his arms, kissing her until that cool smile left her mouth and her heart raced against his.

The windshield wipers had been right. He'd been crazy to do this, crazier still if he went on doing it.

Okay, then. He'd keep her on as his secretary. For a while, anyway. But he'd find her a different place to live. Someplace where he didn't have to lie awake nights, thinking of her sleeping just a few doors away. Where he didn't have to step into the hall in the morning and catch the faint whiff of her perfume. Where he didn't have to be strained to the limit by her presence.

"To the freaking limit," he said under his breath.

It had been fine, that first evening. Things had been brisk. Businesslike. He'd handed her the keys, pointed her toward the apartment, told her she was free to change things around as she liked and not to hesitate to let him know if she needed anything, and then he'd turned his back and walked away.

"No problem," he'd told himself smugly.

And there hadn't been. Not until somewhere around three or four o'clock, when he'd awakened from a dream hot enough to have left his heart pounding and his mouth dry...a dream in which Stephanie had starred.

It hadn't helped when he'd been shaving the next morning and he'd heard the faint hiss of water in the pipes. What was that? he'd wondered—and then he'd known. It was the shower running in her apartment.

"So what?" he'd said out loud.

The answer, to his chagrin, had come at once, in the mental image of Stephanie, wrapped in a towel, her skin dewy, her hair wet and curling around her face.

The swiftness of his physical reaction had both stunned and angered him. Hell, what was this crap? He wasn't some half-baked kid, operating at the mercy of runaway hormones. He was an adult male, fully in control of his own life. Rational. Intelligent. Pragmatic.

David rubbed his hand over his forehead. If he'd been any of those things, he'd never have gotten into such a mess. He'd have gone to Seven Oaks, delivered his message, and headed home. Okay, maybe he'd have offered to check out the subtleties of inheritance law or suggested an attorney she might contact...

"David?"

"What?" he snarled, swinging toward the door. Jack Russell stood in the opening, eyebrows lifted in inquiry.

"I knocked, David, but there was no answer. Are you all right?"

David blew out his breath. "I'm fine."

"Are you sure? If this isn't a good time, I can come back later."

"No, it's fine." He smiled, or hoped he did. "Come on in."

Russell shut the door behind him. "I just wanted to touch bases, let you know that the UPT deal went through, as you'd said it would." Jack shook his head as he looked around David's office. "Amazing. I just can't get over it.

Your Mrs. Willingham. Such a remarkable find. She's been here only a week and look at what she's accomplished.''

"A great deal. But she's not *my* Mrs. Willingham.''

"Ah. Simply a figure of speech, I assure you. It *is* amazing, though. Five short days, to have done so much. Such efficiency. And so unexpected, in such an attractive package. Altogether, quite a remarkable find.''

David leaned back against his desk, arms folded. "So you already said.''

"And so I'm saying again. Truly, David, this is, well, it's—''

"Amazing.''

"Yes.''

"And remarkable.''

"Yes, that, too. And—''

"Unexpected. Where are we going with this?''

Jack's brows rose again. "With what? I merely said—''

"You said it all a minute ago.''

"So? Can't I repeat myself? As my ol' granpappy used to say…''

"Uh-huh.''

"Anythin' worth sayin' is worth sayin' twice. Well, I'm saying it twice. The lady's talents are outstanding.''

"Are you forming a chapter of the Stephanie Willingham Fan Club?''

Jack laughed, walked to one of the leather love seats, and sat down.

"My, oh, my, counselor. We are testy today, aren't we?'' He undid the buttons on his vest, sighed and folded his hands in his lap. "In that case, perhaps I should follow granpappy's advice and cut to the chase.''

David smiled tightly. "Granpappy and I agree, for once. Please do.''

"Here it is, then. There's talk. And please, David, do us both the courtesy of not asking, talk about what?''

David's eyes narrowed. "I'm afraid you have me at a disadvantage, Jack. I *do* have to ask. Talk about what?"

"About her. Stephanie."

"What is there to talk about? I thought the consensus was that she's doing a good job."

"An excellent job." Russell lifted his hand and examined his fingernails. "The talk isn't about her work, David."

David leaned away from the desk. "Talk is cheap, Jack. You should know that."

"Yes, but is it true?" Russell looked up, the air of affability gone. "Is she living in your house?"

"Yes," David said coldly. "She is."

"My God, David..."

"Did whomever's busy spreading gossip bother adding that she's living in a separate apartment?"

Russell shook his head in dismay. "I don't believe this! How could you put yourself in such an untenable position? I didn't say anything when you brought her to the office, but—"

"I hired her to do a job."

"But taking her to live with you—"

"She isn't living with me! She's living in an apartment that happens to be located in my house."

"Surely, you must realize how this looks." Russell got to his feet. "For heaven's sake, man—"

"And even if she were living with me, the day I have to ask you or anybody else to vote on what in hell I do with my personal life is the day—"

"Whoa. Calm down. I'm not questioning your personal life. I'm questioning your sanity, and please don't tell me you don't see any problem with people thinking that you're sleeping with your secretary—a secretary whose reputation has preceded her."

"Listen, here, Jack..." David glared at the older man—and then he groaned, sank into the chair behind his desk and buried his head in his hands. "I've made a total screw-up of this thing."

"Yes," Russell said gently, "you have, indeed."

David looked up. "I'm not sleeping with Stephanie," he said quietly. "You, of all people, should have known I wouldn't muddy the waters that way."

"I never thought you were, but not everyone in this office is so clear-minded about these things. Apparently, somebody noticed that the home address she gave on the employment forms is the same as yours, and...well, you know. People talk."

"Yeah." David let out a deep sigh. "She said they would."

"She was right." Jack nodded toward a file on David's desk. The name "Stephanie Willingham" was scrawled across the cover. "Have you taken her on as a client? I thought we'd agreed—"

"We didn't 'agree,' Jack. You said this case wasn't to our liking. Anyway, I've only been doing some research."

"And?"

"And, Willingham and his sister dotted all the i's and crossed all the t's. Her chances of getting a piece of that estate are nonexistent."

"Well, then..."

"She's broke. Penniless. I couldn't turn my back on her."

"Yes." Russell smiled faintly. "Just as I said, do you remember? There's a certain vulnerability to her. But you can't take her on as your private charity, David."

David's expression turned cool. "Are you trying to tell me whom I can and cannot employ?"

"No. Of course not."

"That's good. That's damn good."

"I'm telling you that I think you've shown an error in judgment, moving this woman into your home."

"When she can afford another place, she'll get one."

"You're making a mistake, David."

"It's my mistake to make, Jack."

"Slow down, will you? I'm not trying to tell you how to run your life."

"Aren't you?"

"David, I'm not a fool. I know you're the reason half of Washington thinks of us first when they think of a top-flight law firm."

"Don't patronize me, Jack. I don't like it."

"I'm not patronizing you, I'm speaking the truth."

"What is it, then? You can't have grown so complacent that you're afraid the firm will be embarrassed—"

"Dammit, David! You're not talking to a wet-behind-the-ears kid here, with his eyes fixed on the Holy Grail!" Jack shook his head. "I'm concerned about you. You, the man. Not you, the attorney."

"There's nothing to be concerned about."

"I think there is. And I feel responsible. I was the one who got you into this mess. Why, you'd never have laid eyes on this woman if I hadn't—"

"I'd already laid eyes on her," David said abruptly, "two weeks before you mentioned her name, and before you ask, no, I do not want to explain what I'm talking about."

"David, my boy—"

"I'm not your boy, Jack. I'm not anyone's 'boy.' I'm a grown man, and while I appreciate your concern, what I do with my life is my affair."

"Oh, hell. Mary warned me I'd do this all wrong. Look, I don't care about cheap gossip around the coffee machine. I care about you, David. I love you like a son. I just don't want to see you hurt by a woman who—a woman who—" Jack threw his arms wide. "Dammit, man, I don't even know how to describe Stephanie!"

David looked into the face of his old friend and mentor.

Suddenly his anger drained away. He got to his feet and came around his desk.

"That's all right, Jack," he said quietly. "I don't know how to describe her, either."

The two men looked at each other for a few seconds. Then Russell smiled and clapped David on the shoulder. They walked slowly toward the door.

"Just don't get yourself in too deep, okay?"

David almost laughed. How deep was that? he wanted to say. Any deeper, he'd drown.

"Not to worry," he said lightly. "I'll know when it's time to bail out."

"You want some last advice?"

David smiled. "No. But that won't stop you from giving it."

"The lady's beautiful, bright, and broke. And okay, maybe she got a raw deal. But do yourself a favor. Write her a glowing letter of recommendation, hand her a copy of the employment ads, and say goodbye."

"I'll consider it."

"That's the spirit." Russell smiled. "I'm glad you'll be getting your mind off all this for the weekend."

"What about the week…" David clapped his hand to his forehead. "Damn! The Sheraton house party. I'd almost forgotten."

"Check your calendar. I'm sure the efficient Mrs. Willingham has it listed."

"Oh, hell. The last thing I feel like doing is taking on Mimi Sheraton."

"Interesting choice of words," Jack said, chuckling.

"An entire weekend, avoiding that barracuda."

Jack opened the door. "I keep telling you, my boy. What you need is an excuse even our Mimi can't ignore."

"Yeah. Like my name on the obituary page."

"Or on the society page. An announcement, that you're

to be married." Jack winked. "Mary's advice, but I tend to agree."

"Tell Mary, thanks a bunch." David grinned. "Women just like to see men lassoed and branded. Well, not me. Once was more than enough."

Russell laughed. "Too bad you can't just phone that rental company we used for that Fourth of July party last year. You know, the one that rents dishes, chairs, tables...see if they have a division called Rent-A-Fiancée."

"Thanks, counselor," David said, smiling. "Be sure and send me a bill for your sage advice."

He was still smiling when he shut the door.

"Rent-A-Fiancée," he said as he strolled back to his desk. Too bad there wasn't such a thing. But he could try another approach. He could call one of the women he'd been seeing, invite her to go to the Sheratons with him. Yes, there was a down side to that. With his luck, the lady in question might end up thinking his intentions were more serious than they were, but it was worth a shot. Anything was better than spending the weekend trying to avoid Mimi and dark hallways—

"Mr. Chambers?"

David turned around. Stephanie looked at him from the doorway. God, how beautiful she was!

"Sir? Do you—can you spare a minute?"

He sighed. It was just as well. He supposed he had to tell her that the gossip had begun. She had the right to know.

"Of course," he said. "Come in and sit down, Mrs. Willingham."

Stephanie nodded, shut the door behind her and stepped into the room.

She hadn't wanted to do this.

David had done enough for her. A job, a place to live, a loan. She couldn't ask him. She couldn't. On the other hand, what choice was there? Rest Haven had phoned again last night. The director had been pleasant, but firm. She was already a month behind in payments. They couldn't wait any longer.

"Your brother's care is costly, Mrs. Willingham," the director had said.

As if she didn't know that already.

She knew it was useless but, during her lunch hour, she'd gone to the bank where she'd opened an account, and asked for a loan. To his credit, the loan officer hadn't laughed in her face. In desperation, she'd phoned Amos Turner. He hadn't been as kind. She'd hung up the phone, face burning, the sound of the lawyer's laughter ringing in her ears. And then she'd suffered the worst humiliation of all. She'd called Clare, who'd listened, let her talk on and on until she was near begging before Clare had laughed hysterically and hung up the phone.

So Stephanie had steeled herself for what had to be done. There was no other choice. She had to ask David to lend her the money.

"How much?" he said, with the kind of smile that suggested this was a joke.

"Five thousand," Stephanie said, with no smile at all. "I know it's an enormous amount of money, but I'll repay you the second you get me my share of Avery's—"

"Why in heaven's name do you need five thousand bucks?"

She hesitated. The bank loan officer had asked her the same question, in just the same tone of voice.

"I—I don't think that's important."

David laughed.

"You've got a lot of brass, Scarlett, I'll give you that much. Five thousand bucks, and it's not important?"

"It is. I mean, the amount is. And the reason I need it is. But—"

"But it's none of my business. Right?"

The tip of her tongue snaked out between her lips. He tried not to notice.

"I understand that you'd like some answers, David. But—"

"It doesn't matter." He sat down, leaned forward across his desk and folded his hands on the polished cherrywood surface. "I've gone over your case a dozen times, and I have to tell you, I can't see any way around the judge's decision."

Stephanie blanched. "But you said—"

"I said I'd give it my best shot. Well, I have. We could petition the courts, make a case for your having been left destitute." His eyes fixed on hers. "I could probably get you a couple of hundred a week for a year or two, long enough for you to get back on your feet."

"It isn't enough!" She could hear the thread of panic in her voice and she swallowed hard before she spoke again. "I need—"

"Five thousand dollars." His smile was remorseless. "I heard you the first time. Well, Scarlett, I'm afraid you're just going to have to accustom yourself to a simpler life-style."

"Dammit! I don't want the money to—to… I need it."

His eyes went flat and cold. "For what?"

"I can't—"

"You can," he said, and he reached out, clasped her wrist and rose to his feet. Defiance glittered in her eyes but her mouth was trembling. Jack was wrong, he thought. Vulnerable wasn't the word to describe her. He remembered the feral kitten, how it had spit and refused to be stroked…and yet, how clearly it had needed the gentling touch of a loving hand. He looked into Stephanie's beautiful face and thought, just for a moment, that he could see straight into her wounded soul.

"David?" she whispered, and then she was in his arms. She gave a soft cry as he gathered her to him; her body sank into his. Her slender arms looped around his waist in a gesture that seemed equal parts desire and despair.

His heart hammered. He knew he had only to caress her, lift her into his arms, carry her to the love seat, and she would be his. But she had been Avery Willingham's, too. Would she belong to any man, for the right price?

He reached behind his back, grasped her wrists and drew her arms to her sides. It was the hardest thing he'd ever done in his life. Knowing that made him even angrier.

"Okay," he said, his voice harsh. "I get the message. You're broke, you need a bundle of cash, and you don't know how to get it."

He heard the indrawn hiss of her breath. "That's an over-simplification."

"Let's not argue the semantics of this, Scarlett, all right?" He cocked his head and looked at her. "Did you ever do any acting when you were in school?"

Stephanie stared at him as if he'd lost his mind. Hell, he thought, maybe he had.

"Acting?"

"Yeah. You know, playacting."

"I don't see what that has to do with anything."

"Humor me. Just answer the question."

"No. Well…" Her brow furrowed. "Well, once. In sixth grade. We did *Sleeping Beauty,* for spring assembly."

"Okay," he said briskly, as if what he was about to propose wasn't completely, totally, absolutely insane. "Okay, then, here's the deal." He walked away from her, to his desk, sat down behind it as if putting distance between them could make what came next sound like the rational suggestion of a rational man. "I'm going to a house party this weekend, in the Virginia countryside. A client's hosting it. Lots of people networking, pretending to have a good time." He shot her a humorless smile. "It's hard to explain, unless you've been to one of these things."

"Buffet breakfasts on the sideboard," Stephanie said.

"Drinks around the fireplace. You don't have to explain. Avery was big on trying to impress the right people. But I still don't see—"

"My client's wife will have one other item on the agenda." David sat back, his eyes on Stephanie's. "She's on the make."

"David, I'm sorry, I'm just not following you."

"She'll seat me next to her at dinner," he said bluntly, "and while her right hand's holding her salad fork, her left will be searching for my lap."

He thought, just for a second, that she was going to laugh. Her eyes widened; her mouth twitched. He remembered the last time—the only time—Stephanie had laughed, how wonderful it had made him feel, and he almost smiled...and then he remembered that she had just come to him for five thousand bucks, with no explanation other than that she needed it, and his smile faded before it began.

"So, I'm going to take Jack Russell's advice. He says my only salvation is to take my fiancée with me."

There wasn't even a hint of a smile on her lips now.

"Your... Well, of course. I'm sure he's right. A fiancée is certain to put you off-limits."

David nodded. The office seemed to fill with silence.

"There's only one problem. I don't have a fiancée. So here's my proposal. You need five thousand dollars, I need an actress. Sound workable to you?"

The color drained from Stephanie's face. "You mean, you want me to... You're joking!"

"I've never been more serious."

"No," she said quickly. "No, I couldn't."

"Sure you could." He got to his feet and walked toward her, moving slowly, his eyes never leaving hers. "All you have to do is pretend you're back in sixth grade."

"It wouldn't be right."

"Think of it as a kind of collateral on the loan, if it makes you feel better."

"David, it's crazy." Her eyes narrowed. "Are you figuring I'll go to this house party and sleep with you? Because if you are—"

"My motives are purely self-protective, Scarlett. Mimi Sheraton's husband's a nice guy. He deserves better than having me tell him what his wife's doing." Don't touch her, David told himself. It's bad enough you've made this crazy offer... But a stray curl lay against Stephanie's cheek, and he couldn't help it; he reached out and let it slip around the tip of his finger. "It wouldn't be so difficult, pretending you and I were lovers, would it?"

"David, this is crazy. You can't expect—"

He bent his head and kissed her. Nothing touched but their mouths and yet Stephanie felt something warm and sweet stir and spread its wings, deep in the hidden recesses of her heart.

He lifted his head, his eyes locked on hers. "Say you'll do it," he said gruffly, and he held his breath, waiting, until, at last, in a voice he could hardly recognize, she said that she would.

CHAPTER TEN

THE Sheraton house made Seven Oaks look like an impostor.

Not that the house was another Tara. David had told her it was a Virginia farmhouse, but when had a farmhouse looked like a cross between Buckingham Palace and the Taj Mahal?

"I'll bet nobody with manure on his boots ever got further than that porch," Stephanie murmured as David took their luggage from the back of his Porsche.

David's brow lifted. "Manure, Scarlett?"

"Manure, David. I'm sure you'll be amazed to hear we have our fair share of the stuff back home in Georgia."

He grinned. "Not quite as much as there is in our esteemed capitol, but why quibble? You're right. The only thing rural about this place is Mimi's little speech to newcomers about the purity of the bucolic ethos she demanded of her architect and interior designer."

Stephanie laughed. "She doesn't really say that!"

"Heck, for all I know, she might be right—assuming the *ethos* of a Virginia farm in the seventeen hundreds included gold faucets in all the johns, a dining room that seats fifty, and hot and cold running servants." David hoisted both their overnight bags under one arm. "Here comes one now. Just watch."

Stephanie looked toward the house again. A young man dressed in a white jacket and dark trousers was coming briskly toward them.

"Welcome to Sheraton Manor, madam. May I help you with your luggage, sir?"

"Thank you," David said, "but I can manage myself."

521

"I'm sure you can, sir, but—"

"James," David said. "Your name *is* James, isn't it? I believe we went through a similar dance the last time I was here."

"Yes, sir. I mean, my name is James, sir. And I—"

"And you are here to anticipate my every need." David smiled and clapped a hand on James's shoulder. "The thing of it is, James," he said conversationally, "I had a job picking up after people when I was just about your age."

James stared at him. "You, sir?"

"Me. And when I finally had enough money to quit, I promised myself I'd never, in this lifetime, ask any man to do something for me that I was capable of doing for myself. Can you understand that, Jimmy?"

For an instant, a boy seemed to replace the proper young man.

"I certainly can...sir."

David smiled and held out his hand. There was a bill tucked inside it. "Glad we understand each other, son."

The boy's eyes widened. "Yes, sir. And I hope you have a very pleasant weekend. You and your lady both."

Stephanie, who'd been smiling at this exchange, suddenly frowned. "I am not—"

"I'm sure we will." David took her arm. "Won't we, Scarlett?"

Their eyes met and held, and finally she nodded stiffly. "Yes."

David smiled. "See you around, Jimmy," he said, and he headed toward the house, his hand still clasping Stephanie's.

"You don't have to hang on to me," she said coldly. "I'm not going to run away."

"You're not going to convince Mimi Sheraton that you and I are an item, either, despite what I told her on the phone. Not if you turn to stone each time someone refers to us as a couple."

"He said—James said—"

"That you were my lady."

"Yes. And I'm not."

David stopped, dropped the suitcases and spun Stephanie toward him. "Let's get the ground rules straight here, Scarlett. You've agreed to act the part of the woman I'm engaged to marry."

"I understand that." She glared at him. "That doesn't mean...I just don't like the way he said what he said. As if I were your—your—"

"My what?"

"I don't know." And she didn't. What had the boy said that was so terrible? What was the difference between being David's lady and his fiancée?

"He made it sound as if we were lovers," David said matter-of-factly.

Stephanie flushed.

"I suppose he did. And that isn't what we agreed to."

"I see."

"I hope you do, David, because—"

"This is damn near the twenty-first century, Scarlett, and we are both adults. If we were really engaged to be married, I can promise you, we'd be lovers."

"Fortunately for me, we are not *really* anything."

"Listen, Scarlett..."

"David! Yoo-hoo. David, here I am!"

David looked around. Stephanie did, too. A woman stood on the porch. Her auburn hair was lacquered into artful disarray, her makeup was impeccable, and her smile was brilliant.

"Oh, my," Stephanie whispered, "all she needs is a baton and a bathing suit!"

"Mimi," David said under his breath, and gave a quick wave of his hand.

"Sweetie, hurry on up here so I can say a proper hello!"

Stephanie's mouth twitched. "Sweetie?"

"Exactly," David said out of the side of his mouth. "And if you think Miss America's going to be put off by you, me, and chastity, you'd better think again."

"I'm not going to sleep with you," Stephanie said quickly.

His smile sent a wave of heat curling straight down to her toes. "Is that a dare, Scarlett?"

"It's a statement of fact, Rhett."

"David?" Mimi waggled a coral-taloned finger in their direction. "Are you going to make me come down to you?" She laughed and tossed her head, but not one hair so much as shifted. "You know what the sun does to my skin, sweetie."

Stephanie cocked an eyebrow. "Goodness to Betsy, *sweetie*, whatever does it do?"

"That's it," David said grimly.

"No," Stephanie said. "David—"

But he'd already pulled her into his arms. "Smile," he said. "Act as if you're enjoying this." And his mouth covered hers.

Act, he'd said...but she didn't have to act. Not when the touch of his lips sent her heart bumping against her ribs, when the earth tilted so that she had to curl her fingers into his jacket and hang on.

"You see?" he said, when he'd finished kissing her. His smile was as cool as if they'd done nothing more than shake hands. "You can carry this off, if you put your mind to it."

He picked up their luggage and took her hand, the pressure of his fingers exerting a clear message. Live up to our bargain, he was saying, or pay the penalty...and yet, if having him take her in his arms and kiss her was the penalty, did she really want to resist it?

Mimi Sheraton was all smiles as she greeted David, all ᵈish purrs as she air-kissed Stephanie on both cheeks, but

neither the smiles nor the purrs disguised the fact that
Stephanie was about as welcome at Sheraton Manor as
she'd been at Seven Oaks.

Mimi tried to be subtle. She pushed herself between
them, linked arms and led them into a foyer big enough to
double as a dance hall, playing the role of perfect hostess
to the hilt, chattering nonstop as she led them up a wide
staircase. They paused at the top, and Mimi turned her
smile on Stephanie.

"You must tell me, dear. However did you land this
gorgeous man?"

"I'm afraid you'll have to ask him," Stephanie said air-
ily.

"It was all rather sudden, wasn't it?" Mimi clutched
their arms again and started down the hall. "I mean, how
long have you and David known each other?"

Stephanie looked past their hostess to David for help, but
he was strolling along, seemingly intent on studying the
carpet that seemed to stretch for miles into the distance.

"You must be the reason he hasn't been available the
past couple of weeks," Mimi said, answering her own
question. She flashed her killer smile. "You know, darling,
there are going to be scores of ladies out for your scalp.
Even I, a happily married woman, was stunned when David
phoned yesterday and told me the news."

Stephanie laughed gaily. "You'll defend me, won't you,
Mimi? As a happily married woman."

Mimi chuckled. "Of course! Ah. Here we are." She
drew their little party to a halt and opened the door on a
sea of blue. "The Blue Room for you, David, sweetie."
She leaned toward him, batting her lashes. "I'm just across
the hall, remember?"

David smiled politely. "How could I possibly forget?"

"And your girlfriend—"

"Fiancée."

"Fiancée. Of course. That's what I meant. She's in the Ruby Room in the West Wi—"

"No."

Mimi's smile faltered. "No?"

David looked down at Mimi's hand, clutching his elbow. Gently, he peeled it loose, moved to Stephanie's side, and put his arm around her.

"Scarlett and I wouldn't want to be separated, not even for one night. Would we, darling?"

"Scarlett," Mimi said with a little laugh, "isn't that charming?"

"Charming," Stephanie said through her teeth. She looked at David. "Of course we wouldn't want to be separated, lover. But if those are the arrangements our hostess has made…"

"Then," David said, "I'm afraid she'll just have to unmake them." He looked at Mimi. "That isn't a problem, is it?"

Mimi cleared her throat. "Well…well, I suppose… Scarlett—I mean, Stephanie can have the room next to yours."

"Do the rooms connect?"

Stephanie resisted the urge to slap that little smile from David's handsome face. "It really isn't necessary—"

"Yes, it is," David said, and kissed her.

Mimi made a strangled sound. "Cocktails in an hour," she chirruped, and fled.

Stephanie glared at her opened suitcase.

"I," she said to it, "am going home." All David's talk, about needing to thwart Mimi Sheraton's plans. "Liar," Stephanie muttered.

What did he think? That he'd purchased a playmate for the weekend? Well, he was in for one hell of a nasty surprise…although, it was true, Mimi did seem to have her ˪ts set on David.

Stephanie sat down on the edge of the bed. Actually, even a trout snapping at a mayfly would have shown more finesse, but that didn't mean David had to make such a display of kissing her or of his intention of supposedly slipping into her bed tonight, when the house lay silent and sleeping.

Didn't he care what people thought?

Stephanie flopped back against the pillows. Of course, he cared. He *wanted* them to think exactly what Mimi was thinking. That was the purpose of all of this. And she had no right to complain. She'd agreed to play this dumb game. David was lending her five thousand dollars to go along with it, and who was she kidding? He was *giving* her the money because she'd probably be a hundred years old before she saved enough to pay him back.

Oh, lord. What a mess. She *hated* the way Mimi Sheraton had looked at her, *hated* the cheap way she'd felt...

Be honest, Steffie. What you really hate is how you crumple each time David kisses you.

She sat up. There was only one thing to do. She'd have to tell him this ridiculous deal was off. No playing his girlfriend.

No five thousand dollars.

What would become of Paul?

He had never turned his back on her, not even after their mother left. Not that Bess's leaving had made a difference. Bess hadn't paid much attention to either of them, and Stephanie had done the cooking, cleaning, washing and ironing ever since she could remember.

Paul was the one whose life had changed. He'd been forced to grow up fast. He'd quit school and become their breadwinner, and even though he was younger than she by eleven months, he'd turned into her big brother and father all in one. He'd even given up his music, the thing he loved most, rather than leave her alone to face Willingham Corners and the world it represented.

How could she have left *him,* after his accident? It hadn't even been much of an accident. His car skidded off the road one rainy night and hit a tree. The fender got crumpled and Paul got a bump on his head, but a few weeks later, he'd started to change. He began to have headaches, and hear noises, and sometimes he didn't know who she was or where he was...

"Swear to me, Steff," he'd begged when he was lucid. "Swear you won't ever tell anybody what's happened to me. They'll say it's 'cause I'm a Horton, 'cause I'm our mama's son."

So she'd sworn. And she'd never gone back on her word—except when, in desperation, she'd told Avery Willingham.

Stephanie rose to her feet. Paul needed her help, as she had once needed his. She didn't regret the sacrifice she'd made, marrying Avery, even though he'd lied when he'd promised to treat her like a daughter. It was this sacrifice that was the difficult one. Pretending to be in love with David was hard. No. That was wrong. The pretending wasn't hard. Why would it be? David was—he was... A woman would find it easy to love him. He was wonderful, everything she'd ever wanted, ever hoped and prayed for.

Stephanie's breath caught. No, she thought, no, please, no...

"No," she said, and hurried to the door that connected their rooms. She couldn't go through with this. She'd take a train, go to Rest Haven. She'd plead with the doctors. With the director. They'd understand. They had to, because she couldn't do this, couldn't spend this weekend with David, pretending to be his lover.

"David?" she called, and knocked on the door. "David, are you there?" She knocked again, waited, and then, carefully, she opened the door.

David's clothing lay strewn across the bed. Beyond, the

bathroom door stood ajar. She could hear the sound of running water.

He was showering. Well, she'd sit down and wait until…until what? Until he walked, naked, into the room? Her heart banged into her throat. She could imagine how he'd look, his skin golden and glistening with drops of water, his hair loose around his face. He'd be magnificent to look at, broad-shouldered and lean-hipped, his muscles taut…

Stephanie fled to the safety of her own room, and locked the door behind her.

"Chambers, you lucky son of a gun!" The newest, youngest Supreme Court justice paused en route to the bar and slapped David lightly on the back. "You certainly have found yourself a winner."

"That I have," David said. He smiled and took a sip of his cognac. A winner, he thought, and took another sip. Maybe the cognac would take the edge off. Something had to, or he was going to explode.

The evening wasn't going quite the way he'd imagined.

It had seemed such a fine plan—telling Mimi he was engaged, bringing Stephanie along and making it clear he was out of circulation. He'd been so sure of its logic.

What an idiot he was.

Everything had seemed fine. Well, not fine, really. Kissing Stephanie hadn't been so clever. He'd done it for Mimi's benefit, but he'd been the one who'd ended up standing under a cold shower, thinking thoughts he knew better than to think, trying but not succeeding in not imagining what would happen if Stephanie climbed into the shower with him.

But the shower had helped. He'd cooled down, had a stern heart-to-heart with himself in the bathroom mirror as he'd shaved, gotten all spiffed up in his white dinner jacket and black trousers and marched to the door that led into Stephanie's room.

"All ready?" he'd said pleasantly when she'd opened the door...and that had been the end of him, because one look at her and he knew it was all over.

She was simply gorgeous.

There were other ways to describe how she looked, in a creamy slip of a dress with her hair loose and shining and hanging down her back, but why come up with a bunch of useless adjectives when one would do?

He'd sent her shopping in Georgetown, with instructions to buy whatever she thought would make Mimi Sheraton take notice.

"I'll repay the cost of whatever I purchase," she'd said stiffly, and he hadn't bothered arguing. What was the point, when she already owed him five thousand bucks and had to know, as he did, that she could probably never repay it?

But when he saw her, he knew it wasn't only Mimi who'd take notice, it would be every man on the premises.

"Will I do?" she'd said as dispassionately as you'd ask somebody if they wanted their coffee black or with cream.

"Sure," he'd said with a shrug, while some evil presence in his primitive male brain urged him to grab her and drag her into his cave. His civilized brain argued that it didn't have to be a cave. His bed would do. But even in his demented state, he knew she wouldn't let him get away with it. So he'd compromised by pulling her into his arms and kissing her. She hadn't protested. He hadn't given her the chance, though it had pleased him, when the kiss ended, to see how her eyes glittered.

"Just wanted to be sure you had the right look," he'd said briskly, as if kissing her had been part of some careful plan, and then he'd put his arm around her waist and led her down to the party.

Half an hour later, he knew he'd made a mistake. Not in figuring the dampening effect Stephanie would have on Mimi. That seemed to be working just fine. David took a swig of his cognac. No, his mistake had been in thinking he could bring Stephanie into a roomful of men, turn her loose and not go crazy watching what happened.

The men circled her like bees around the sweetest flower in the garden.

The jerk from *The Washingtonian* had damn near drooled into his cold sorrel soup. A lecherous congressman from California had all but dipped his tie into his blackened tuna. And when the fat cat financier from Boston had put his hand on Stephanie's, David had come close to grabbing him by the throat and telling him to back off because, dammit, she belonged to him.

All these s.o.b.'s thought she was his fiancée. They had no right to hover around her. She had no right, either, to laugh and listen with rapt attention to every stupid story they told. She had no right to have a good time with anybody but him. Didn't she know she was his? Well, supposed to be his. For the night. For the weekend. Hell, for as long as he wanted. Didn't she know that?

Just now, she was holding court with a group of men who pretty much ran the world, according to the American press, and they were lapping up her every word—including the congressman from California, who'd just casually slipped his arm around her waist.

David's eyes narrowed. He tossed back the rest of his cognac and put down the snifter.

"Easy," a male voice said.

He swung around. Tom Sheraton had come up beside him.

"She can handle things, that girlfriend of yours." Tom smiled. "But the sooner you put a wedding band on her finger, the sooner those fools will get the message."

"Yeah," David said through his teeth. "If you'll excuse me, Tom…"

"So, when's the happy occasion?"

"The? Oh. Well, we only just got engaged…" David frowned. The congressman whispered something in

Stephanie's ear. She tossed back her head and laughed. "Uh, as I was saying, we just got engaged, so…" The syndicated political columnist standing on Stephanie's other side leaned in, too, and offered a comment. She smiled and turned toward him, at the same time neatly dislodging the old goat's arm. "As I was saying, we really haven't had time to…" Dammit, was there no end in sight? A movie star with a mane of blond hair, a thousand-watt smile and a penchant for the-cause-of-the-day, deftly shouldered the columnist aside and took Stephanie's arm. He said something, she nodded, and the two of them started toward the terrace.

Enough, David thought. "Great party, Tom," he said, and he strode up to Stephanie and lay a proprietorial hand on her shoulder.

"David," she said with a little smile, "have you met Gary?"

David looked at the actor. "No."

"Well, let me intro—"

"Stephanie, could I see you for a minute?"

Stephanie frowned. "Yes, but first—"

"I want to talk to you."

"I understand, David, but—"

"Forget the 'but's,' Scarlett." David clamped his arm around her waist. "You're coming with me, and now."

He saw the flash of anger in her eyes but he moved quickly, herding her out the door and onto the terrace before she could protest. His luck ran out as soon as they stepped outside; she twisted free of his arm and glared at him.

"What kind of performance was that?"

"You're the one who's been giving a performance, madam, starting with the hors d'oeuvres and working straight through the coffee and cake."

"I don't know what you're talking about." She stalked

down the stone steps and into the garden, with him on her heels. "How dare you drag me off that way?"

"I did not 'drag' you off, though believe me, I was tempted." David grabbed her arm and spun her toward him. "Since when does a man have to beg his fiancée for a minute of her time?"

"I was talking to someone, or hadn't you noticed? Gary was telling me a funny story about something that happened on the set of his last film, and—"

"Gary," David said, "wouldn't know a funny story unless somebody pointed it in his direction and told it to bite him on the ankle."

"For your information, Gary not only acted in that film, he directed it. And wrote the script."

"A, a piece of wood shows more acting talent than he does. B, he couldn't direct a dog to lift its leg at the nearest tree, and C, can you really write a script with crayons?"

"Oh, that's hilarious, David. Very funny. And, by the way, I would remind you, I am *not* your fiancée."

"You are, for the weekend."

"And what a mistake that was," Stephanie said, blowing a curl out of her eyes.

David's gaze narrowed. "Meaning?"

"Meaning, I agreed to help you out of a tight spot. I didn't agree to become your property. Now, if that's all—"

David clamped a hand around her wrist as she started to turn away.

"Where do you think you're going?"

"To my room, to pack. I have decided to return to the city."

"No way, Scarlett. We made a deal, remember?"

"It was a bad one, and I am terminating it."

"You didn't quit when Avery Willingham bought your services."

He saw the color drain from her face and cursed himself for being a fool. That wasn't what he'd meant to say. The truth was, he didn't know what he'd meant to say. He only knew that it was safer to be angry at her than to admit the truth, that he was hurting because she'd ignored him all night and that the hardest thing he'd ever done in his life was to keep smiling while he shared her with a roomful of people.

"You're right," she said, "I didn't." Her voice trembled, but she met his eyes with unflinching determination. "I'm an honest whore, David. I sold myself to you and to him, and both times I got exactly what I deserved."

"Damn you," he growled. His fingers bit into her wrist and he moved closer to her. "I want some answers. Why, Scarlett? Why did you marry a man you despised?"

"This isn't the time."

"It damn well is. Tell me the truth."

"Please." She shook her head, grateful for the darkness of the night, knowing that what he saw in her eyes now could be her undoing. "Let go of me, David. We both know this was a mistake. I'll pack my things and make some excuse to Mimi—"

"Scarlett. Look at me."

She shook her head again but the pressure of his hand was persistent.

"I need to know the reason." He thought he could see the telltale glimmer of tears in her eyes, and he bent his head and brushed his lips over hers. "Don't shut me out, Scarlett. Please. Let me help you."

Silence filled the moment. It stretched between them, shimmering with a quality as ephemeral as the moonlight, and then the tears rolled down her cheeks.

"I have a brother." She spoke in a whisper; David had to lean closer to hear her words. "My little brother. He's always been—he means everything to me, David. He's all I have, all I ever had, and—and he's ill. Terribly ill. He needs special care, and it costs a small fortune. Avery
He was wonderful. He helped me find the right place

for Paul. He even lent me money for his care, but it grew more and more costly and eventually, Avery said—he suggested…''

She trembled, and David drew her closer.

"It's all right," he said softly.

"But it isn't. Don't you understand? I married Avery because he said—he said it was the only way he could guarantee Paul would always be cared for properly. He said he'd—he'd treat me as he always had, that he'd be my friend…." She shuddered. "He lied," she whispered. "About everything."

About everything. The words echoed in David's brain. God, what had Avery Willingham done to her?

"Sweetheart." He drew her close, stroked her hair as she buried her face against him. Her body was racked with sobs, and it broke his heart. "Sweetheart, don't cry."

She pulled back in his embrace and looked up at him, eyes wide, mouth tremulous.

"I was supposed to be his hostess. His companion. His social secretary. He said—he said he'd never touch me." She drew a deep, shaky breath. "But he lied. After a while, he—he came to my room…"

"Hush," David said, and told himself that wanting to beat the crap out of a dead man was possibly blasphemous and undoubtedly insane. "It's over now, Scarlett. Try and forget."

"And then, he died. And Clare came, and she laughed and laughed, and she told me Avery had never intended to leave me anything, that as it was, he'd kept me around longer than he'd intended, but it was only because he'd gotten sick—''

David kissed her. Her lips were cold, her skin icy, but he kept kissing her until he felt the warmth returning to her flesh.

"I know what you must think of me," she whispered. "But I trusted Avery. And I couldn't see any other way—''

"What I think," David said fiercely, "is that you're a fine, brave woman. And that I'm an idiot for making you cry."

"I should never have come with you this weekend. It was bad enough I let you give me a job, and a place to live. But going away with you..." Her eyes met his. "I wouldn't have slept with you, David."

"I know."

"My situation with Avery, wrong as it might have been, was different."

David nodded. "You were his wife."

"Yes. And I was a good wife, strange as that may sound. So you can see why I—why I can't live up to my end of our bargain." She swallowed hard, and tried not to think about where she could turn for the money she needed, nor about what it would be like, never to see David again. "I'm not for sale anymore."

His thumbs traced patterns along her cheekbones.

"I know," he said, as calmly as if he'd intended this, as if he weren't about to say something that would make everything he'd done up till now seem meaningless. "That's why I want to marry you."

model with superior stallid... one that wouldn't disappoint in tough situations. A car that was a joy to drive...

Stephanie filled the bill. She was... beautiful. She was bright, able and no trouble. She'd... respected at her job. She had no more dbubitile... poor marriage than he had.

It made perfect sense that would work... Andy... that was all he asked. They didn't...

CHAPTER ELEVEN

WHICH of them had he startled the most, Stephanie...or himself?

And yet, as soon as David had spoken the words, he knew they made sense.

He'd avoided the truth for years, but here it was, staring him in the face. It was time he got himself a wife.

Mary and Jack Russell were right. A man in his position needed one, and she couldn't be just any wife. He needed a woman who'd understand the social, as well as the business, aspects of his lifestyle. She'd have to entertain clients, give dinner parties and feel at ease with the people he dealt with, despite their titles and importance on the Washington scene. Until now, he'd relied upon whatever woman was in his life at the moment to play hostess, but that wasn't the same as having a wife to oversee the planning—or to sit beside you on the sofa when the evening ended, kick off her shoes and share a quiet moment.

Not that he'd expect that of Stephanie. It had never really been like that with Krissie and he wasn't foolish enough to think it would be any different this time around, but at least this arrangement would be an honest one, with all the expectations out in the open.

He'd learned from his mistakes. The first time he'd married, he'd been young and foolish; he'd thought you chose a woman with your heart. He knew better now. Choosing a wife was like choosing a car. He always bought Porsches, as much for their beauty and performance as for their workmanship. An intelligent man could apply the same standards to his choice of a mate. You wanted a good-looking model with superior ability, one that wouldn't disappoint in tough situations.

Stephanie filled the bill. She was beautiful; she was bright, she'd understand what would be expected of her, and she had no more illusions about marriage than he did.

There it was. He needed a wife. She needed a provider. It was an arrangement that would work. All he had to do was convince Stephanie, who was staring at him as if he'd just suggested they spend the weekend on Mars.

"Did you say...did you ask me to marry you, David?"

"Yes," he said calmly, "I did."

"Marry?" she said, looking bewildered. Well, he couldn't blame her for that. "You, and me?"

"That's right, Scarlett. You, and me."

"This is a joke, right?" Stephanie started to smile, then read the answer in his eyes. "My God! You're serious!"

"I am, indeed."

"Why?" She hesitated, then touched the tip of her tongue to the center of her bottom lip. "You aren't say-ing—you don't mean... You haven't—"

"Fallen in love with you?" He smiled and shook his head, as if she'd made a sad attempt at humor. "Of course not."

"Well, that's a relief," Stephanie said, giving the same little smile in return, because it was better than wondering why her pulse was racing.

"Love doesn't enter into this." He folded his arms; his expression grew serious. "That's what makes my proposal so reasonable."

"Reasonable?" She shook her head. "To you, maybe. Why on earth would we want to marry? I don't under-stand."

There was a trill of laughter from the house. David frowned and looked over his shoulder. The party had spilled onto the terrace.

"Let's walk," he said brusquely, and took her elbow.

She didn't move, and he jerked her forward. She hurried to match his pace as he drew her deeper into the garden. "All right," he said when they'd left the house far behind, "let me put this so you *can* understand."

"I wish you would."

"A couple of months ago, I arranged for a corporate merger."

She gave a brittle laugh. "You see us as the new Procter and Gamble?"

"Each of the companies had different strengths," he said, deciding her nervous attempt at humor didn't merit a response. "One had—I suppose you'd call it power. The other had, well, a certain flair for doing things."

"Let me guess," Stephanie said. "You've got the power. And I've got—what did you call it? Flair?"

A breeze ruffled the rosebushes behind them and blew a strand of hair across her cheek. David reached out and tucked it behind her ear.

"For lack of a better word, yes."

"David, I still have no idea what you're talking about."

"I'm trying to explain the benefits of marriage. Let me try by telling you what I stand to gain." He cleared his throat. "Being a bachelor in this town isn't easy."

Stephanie smiled. "Do that many Mimi Sheratons pop out of the woodwork?"

"I know it must seem amusing, but trust me, Scarlett, it's not. And then there are the Annie Coopers, and the Mary Russells—Jack's wife—ladies who wake up in the morning and ask themselves, what man can I marry off today?" He sighed. "It gets to you, after a while."

"I'm sure it does," Stephanie said politely.

David scowled. "Look, I know I'm not making a good job of this..."

"No," she said, even more politely, "you're doing fine. You want a wife, to keep you safe from matchmakers and predatory females. Or is there more?"

"This isn't funny, Scarlett. I'm serious."

"I can see that. Go on. You said there was more."

"Well, there are my professional responsibilities."

"I'm already working as your secretary, David. What more could I possibly—"

"Okay. Okay, I'm making this sound like—like—"

"Like a merger. But then, that's exactly what you said it was."

"Hell!" David put his fists on his hips and glared at her. "Why must you make this so difficult? I'm talking about the kind of life I live. There are parties. Dinners. All kinds of functions…"

"And you need a wife, to oversee them."

"Yes," he said with a relieved smile. At last, she was getting it. "That's right, I do."

"So you said to yourself, 'Self, I need a wife. One who can plan a dinner party, make small talk, you know the routine.' And your Self said, 'Well, there's always Stephanie Willingham. She's done this kind of thing before.'"

"No," David said quickly, "it wasn't like that."

"Of course it was." Stephanie flashed a quick smile. "Think of the benefits, David. No on-the-job training needed. Right?"

"Dammit, Scarlett—"

"No. No, really, I understand. Truly, I do." Her voice quavered a little, which was dumb. Why would it upset her, that David would offer her the same arrangement she'd had before? It made absolute sense—for him. "But, what's that saying? Been there, done that. And I'd be a fool to do it again."

"I'm not suggesting a repeat of your first marriage. I'm not Willingham. Haven't you figured that out by now?"

"I hoped I had," she said, speaking carefully, not wanting to let him know how hurt she was. "But here you are, making me the same offer."

''The hell I am!''

''You are! There's no difference.''

''Sure there is.''

''Name one.''

''For starters, I'll direct Jack to write a pre-nup, guaranteeing you a generous income for the rest of your life, no matter what happens to me.''

''I don't need your money. It's for—''

''Your little brother. I understand that. I'm just pointing out that you wouldn't be left destitute, if I weren't around. And I won't dole money out to you, month by month. I'll deposit...'' He paused and did some quick mental math. ''I'll put five hundred thousand dollars into your checking account, Monday morning.''

Stephanie stared at him. Half a million dollars? He was serious! But why?

''Why?'' she said. ''Why would you do all that, David? You're not a man who needs to—to buy a wife.''

Why? he thought. It was a good question. Could he answer it, without looking too deeply inside himself?

''Because you and I can be up-front about what each of us expects from this marriage,'' he said.

''You want a relationship that's so—so cold-blooded?''

''I was married before. We were in love, or so I thought,'' he said bluntly. ''It was a disaster.''

''What happened?''

An image flashed through David's mind, of Krissie, in bed with her lover. It still hurt. The fact of the adultery, yes, and the divorce...but it was the betrayal that had devastated him.

He shrugged. ''It turned out we each had different ideas about marriage.''

''Lots of people are divorced, David. They don't end up trying to—to buy a spouse.''

''Are you being deliberately dense? I'm not trying to buy you!''

"Really?" Stephanie folded her arms. "Well, that's how it sounds to me."

"Then you're not paying attention or you'd understand that I'm outlining a marriage in which each of us contributes something of value."

"What I understand," Stephanie said, "is that I won't make the same mistake twice." She stepped back, her head at a proud angle. "Thank you for your offer, David, but I'm not interested."

"Scarlett, you're not thinking. You're—"

"Damn you!" She flew at him, moving so fast that he didn't have time to duck, and pounded her fists against his shoulders. "A marriage *needs* feelings! *I* need feelings. I need—"

"I know what you need," David said, and pulled her into his arms.

His mouth was warm, his arms strong. She struggled against him for the time it took her heart to take one suddenly erratic beat and then she admitted the truth to herself, that she was struggling not against David but against what she felt, and she wound her arms around his neck and kissed him back with all the hunger inside her.

"Marry me," he whispered.

She hesitated, and he kissed her again.

"Scarlett. Just take a deep breath and say yes."

Stephanie looked at him. Then she took the breath he'd suggested.

"Yes."

They left the Sheraton house without making their good-byes, and drove to Georgetown.

David's house was dark, and silent. The sound of the door, shutting behind them, echoed against the night.

Stephanie could hear the thud-thud of her own heart. She was trembling. She'd accused David of being crazy, but she was the crazy one. What had she agreed to? She, of all people. Why would she agree to this marriage? To become this stranger's wife? She couldn't go through with the marriage, or with what would come next. It was one thing to feel the stir of desire in David's embrace but to act upon it, to think, even for a moment, she'd feel what a woman was supposed to feel when a man touched her...

"David," she said urgently, "I think—"

"Don't think," he said, and took her in his arms.

He kissed her over and over, each kiss deeper, hungrier, than the last until she was clinging to his shoulders.

"Scarlett," he whispered, and swung her into his arms.

Stephanie looped her hands behind David's head. A pale ribbon of creamy light streamed in through the window. In its faint illumination, she could see the need etched into his face.

"I've never wanted a woman as I want you, Scarlett," he said softly.

"David." She swallowed audibly. "I can't...I'm not...I don't much like sex. You have the right to know that. I'll disappoint—"

His kiss silenced her. "Never," he whispered, and carried her up the stairs.

She had not been in his bedroom until this night.

It was austere, what little she could see of it in the shadowed dark, what little she could concentrate on, other than the hot pounding of her own blood.

David put her down, slowly, beside the bed.

"There's nothing to be afraid of, Scarlett." He cupped her face in his hands, bent his head and brushed his mouth gently over hers.

"I'm not afraid," she said, "I know you won't hurt me."

It wasn't true. He *would* hurt her. Not physically. She knew that. He was nothing like Avery, who had taken pleasure from the pain of others. But she was vulnerable to

David in other ways, ones that could result in a far deeper pain, because she felt—she felt—

"David." She caught his hands as he reached for her. "This is a mistake. We shouldn't marry."

"We can be happy," he said gruffly. "Did you ever think of that?"

She wanted to. Oh, she wanted to. He saw it in her eyes, the hope, the desire...

"Scarlett?" he said, and she went into his arms.

He undressed her slowly, baring her skin to his mouth and hands inch by silken inch. She was even more beautiful than he'd imagined, her breasts high and rounded, her waist slender, her hips almost as narrow as a boy's. She felt like silk, tasted like vanilla, smelled like some exotic flower. By the time she lay naked in his arms, he was breathing hard and fast.

"Scarlett." He reached out, traced the tip of his finger down her throat, over the swell of her breast, down, down, down until it rested just above the soft curls that guarded her feminine self. "You are so beautiful, Scarlett. So perfect..." His hand moved, dipped between her thighs, and she gasped and caught hold of his wrist.

"David." Her voice was thready. "I don't... Could we pull up the blankets?"

"Are you cold, love? I'll warm you."

Love. He had called her "love."

"No." She shook her head, wondering why there should be a sudden dampness on her cheeks. "I'm not cold, David. I'm—it's the way you're looking at me. I feel—embarrassed."

He smiled. "That's because you're undressed and I'm not. But we can fix that."

He rose to his feet, his eyes never leaving hers, and stripped off his clothing. The body he revealed was beautiful and powerful. Even the frightening part, that most masculine part, was beautiful. He lay down beside her again, his hair loose, floating like a dark curtain around their faces as he took her in his arms.

"Better?" he whispered.

She nodded. His skin was hot, his body hard. She could feel his arousal against her belly and she waited for the excitement to ebb and the panic to start, but it didn't. Instead, she felt a throbbing heat begin to spread between her thighs.

"David," she said unsteadily. "You're so beautiful."

He laughed softly. "How can a man be beautiful, sweetheart?" Her breath caught as he bent and tongued her nipple. "This is beautiful," he whispered. His head dipped lower; he kissed her belly. "And this." He moved again, and she moaned as she felt the heat of his breath between her thighs. "And this," he said, his voice gruff. "Open for me, Scarlett," he said.

And she did.

She shattered at the first kiss, arching against his mouth. Surely she'd have flown into the sky, into the night, if his hands hadn't been curved around her hips, holding her against him. Just as she was falling back to earth, he rose above her and kissed her mouth. She tasted the miracle of their shared passion on his tongue.

"David," she said in a whisper so filled with awe and joy that it was almost his undoing. "David, please…"

"Yes," he said, and he entered her, trying to do it gently, slowly, wanting to pleasure her and not hurt her, wanting to give her everything, not just his body and his seed but his heart.

She cried out in wonder, moved against him, and he let go of everything, the taut control and the anger that had defined his life for so long. He sank into Stephanie's welcoming heat and let himself, at long last, find happiness.

She said she could cook.

"Red beans and rice," she said, "hush puppies, fried

catfish…'' She looked over her shoulder at him and smiled. ''Except I don't see any of those things in these cabinets, David.''

David smiled back. It was near dawn. They were in his kitchen, Stephanie was at the stove and he was straddling a chair, his chin resting on his folded arms. Hunger had driven them from the bed. Nothing else could have. He'd made love to her all night, and he still wanted her so badly he ached. But the ache was worthwhile, if it meant watching his future wife search the shelves. She was wearing the white shirt he'd discarded when they'd arrived home last night. Just the shirt. Nothing more.

''It doesn't cover very much, David,'' she'd said, blushing as he buttoned her into it.

''It covers everything,'' he'd said, lying through his teeth, because hell, he was not a saint, he was a man. Seeing the sweet curve of her breasts, the faint darkness at the juncture of her thighs; enjoying the length of her legs and the occasional glimpse of her backside as she reached for something on the top shelf, was more than he could possibly pass up.

By God, he was lucky! It amazed him, to have found this woman. She was everything a man could hope for. Beautiful. Bright. Capable. And sexy enough to steal his breath away, even though she didn't know it.

''I don't much like sex,'' she'd said, but she'd been incredible in bed. Warm. Eager. Giving. Everything he had done to her, for her, she had wanted to do in return. She'd gone from restraint to recklessness, and it had driven him half out of his head. Even thinking about it made things happen to his anatomy.

That bastard, Willingham. He'd never deserved Stephanie. Whatever he'd done to her… No. He couldn't think about it. It was just a good thing the man was dead because if he wasn't—if he wasn't…

"Bacon and eggs?"

David blinked. Stephanie was looking at him inquiringly. She had a skillet in one hand and a package of bacon in the other, and he knew she wanted him to tell her what he wanted for breakfast, but God, all he really wanted to tell her was that he loved her, that he'd always loved her, that fate or kismet or whatever you wanted to call it had brought them together at that wedding...

"David?"

He took a deep breath. "Fine," he said calmly. "Sounds great. I'll do the toast and coffee."

And work on regaining his equilibrium, along with his sanity. This wasn't love, it was lust.

"Let me just get down this bowl," Stephanie said, and reached high to the top shelf.

David kicked back his chair. "To hell with breakfast," he said.

The skillet, and the bacon, fell from her hands. "Yes," she said, and then she was in his arms again, where he knew she had always belonged.

He broke the news to Jack over lunch on Monday.

"You're nuts," Jack said flatly.

"Maybe," David said, smiling.

Jack lifted his martini. "Wonderful. I tell the groom he's crazy and the groom says, 'Maybe.'"

"I'm also happy."

"Even better. My ol' granpappy used to say—he used to say..." Jack gulped half his martini. "Who knows what the old so-and-so used to say? What *I* say is that you're loco. The lady gets a bank account. What do you get?"

"A wife. Ask Mary. She'll tell you it's an equitable trade."

"Did you check her out? Did you check out the sick brother?"

"No," David said tightly. "I told you, this all happened very suddenly."

"Think about the lady's past, David. She married for money once before. Now, she's doing it again. For all you know, the *brother* could be a gambling habit. He could be drugs."

"She's not on drugs, Jack. And she's not a gambler."

"Well, then, he could be a lover with expensive tastes."

"Watch what you say," David said coldly. "This time next week, Stephanie will be my wife."

Jack refused to back down. "Look, phone Dan Nolan. Let him do a little research. I'm surprised you haven't already done it."

David's eyes narrowed. Stephanie, supporting a lover? He'd never even thought...

He rose quickly, slapped a few bills on the table. "I've got a meeting," he said when Jack started to protest, "and I'm running late."

"What kind of groom says 'maybe' when you tell him he's crazy?" Jack Russell demanded of his wife, late that night.

Mary patted her husband's hand. "The kind who's not ready to admit he's in love."

Jack snorted. "Don't be ridiculous. He's infatuated."

"He's in love," Mary said. "All we can do now is hope he doesn't get hurt."

That evening, before she left the office, Stephanie phoned Rest Haven. Paul's nurse took the call. Paul didn't want to speak to her. He was depressed. Stephanie almost laughed. Paul was always depressed, but she understood. This was worse than usual. It was not a good sign.

"Call me, if anything happens," she said. Then she hung up the phone and stared blindly at the wall.

Paul had been doing so well. Was he going to have a relapse? It didn't matter. She still had to tell David more about him. Soon, David would be her husband. He'd be paying for Paul's care. And she wanted no secrets between her and the man she—the man she...

"Ready?"

She looked up. David was standing in the doorway. His smile had an edge that unnerved her.

"David? What is it? Is something wrong?"

David hesitated. Yes, he wanted to say, something *was* wrong. He'd spent the afternoon pacing his office and finally, half an hour ago, he'd put in a call to Dan Nolan, asked him to check on Stephanie and find out what he could about her brother. If she had a brother. If Jack hadn't put his finger on the truth...

Enough!

"No," he said. "It's just been a long day. Let's go home."

An uneasy silence lay between them through dinner and on into the evening. Finally, David put aside the papers he'd been trying to read and looked at Stephanie.

"Scarlett?"

She looked up from her book. There was a strained look on her face.

"Yes?"

David thought of the call he'd made to Dan Nolan. He regretted it, now. He had questions, yes, but he should have asked them of Stephanie. This was supposed to be an honest relationship.

"What, David?"

Ask her, he told himself. Tell her you need to know more about her brother, that you want to meet him...

"Nothing," he said after a minute. "Just..." He took her hand. "It's late," he said. "Let's go up."

He undressed her slowly in the darkness of the bedroom, loving the sounds she made as he touched her, the scent of desire that rose from her skin. His concerns fell away from him as they went into each other's arms. This was right. *She* was right. This could work…

The phone rang.

"David? The telephone…"

"Let it ring," he said, but he sighed, kissed her gently, turned on the bedside lamp and lifted the receiver.

Stephanie sat up against the pillows, the blanket to her chin. David was turned away from her, the blanket at his waist. His naked shoulders and back were pale gold in the faint gleam of the light. The call couldn't be for her, yet she knew it was. Paul, she thought, it's Paul.

David turned and looked at her. He held out the telephone.

"It's a man," he said. His face was expressionless. "He won't give his name. He wants to talk to you."

Stephanie took the phone. "Hello?"

It *was* Paul. His voice was calm, controlled. He said the nurse had given him Stephanie's new phone number.

"Where are you?" Stephanie said.

He told her. He'd slipped out of Rest Haven. He was in a motel.

Stephanie nodded. Rest Haven was a care facility, not a prison.

"I need you, Sis," Paul said.

She looked at David. There was still no expression on his face.

"I'll come in the morning," she said. "Meanwhile, you should—"

"I need you now."

She looked at David again. Then she reached for the pad and pencil on the nightstand.

"Tell me where you are," she said, and wrote it down. She licked her dry lips. "I'll come." The phone went dead, and she handed it to David, who hung it up.

"David? I—I have to go to my brother."

David's eyes were as flat and dull as the sea before a storm. "At this hour?"

"Yes."

"Why? What's the problem?"

"He's ill. Look, I know you have questions, but I can't explain now." She started to rise, remembered she was naked under the blanket, and knew she couldn't endure the feel of his cool gaze on her skin. "Could you—would you turn around, please?"

David's jaw clenched. "Such modesty, Scarlett," he said with a hard smile, but he turned his back and she rose quickly and began pulling on her clothes.

She heard a noise behind her. David had flung back the blanket. He was dressing.

"What are you doing?"

"What does it look like I'm doing?" He yanked a sweat-shirt from a drawer and tugged it over his head. "I'm getting dressed."

"No, David. It isn't necessary."

He looked at her. "I'm not going to let you go out, alone, in the middle of the night."

"I'll be fine. I'll call a cab."

"I can drive you wherever it is you're going."

"No!" She thought of Paul, as he would be now, knowing how much worse things could get if he were to be upset. "No, David, really. You don't have to."

"I know that. I *want* to go with you."

"But *I* don't want you with me!" The words fell between them like stones. Stephanie caught her breath. "David. I didn't mean that the way it sounded."

"You'll find the number of a cab company programmed into the phone downstairs," he said coldly. Then he walked into the bathroom, and shut the door.

The motel looked like a set from a cheap movie.

Paul was in the last room. He lay in bed, under the

covers, with his arm over his eyes, and he was as bad as she'd ever seen him. His clothing lay discarded on the floor.

"Paul?" she said softly.

He didn't respond. She sighed, shut the door behind her, and went to him. She knew what to do. She'd sit beside him, cradle him in her arms, tell him how much she loved him and hope against hope that her words would sink in…and that, when she explained, David would understand. She thought of how he'd looked at her and a shudder racked her body.

She would not lose David. She could not lose him, and it hadn't a damn thing to do with needing money, or what he'd miraculously made her feel in bed.

It was time to admit the truth. She was in love with David, and she could only hope that he might love her, too, someday.

David paced up and down his living room.

What in hell did Stephanie think she was doing? Going off in the middle of the night to see her sick brother? Telling him, hell, *shrieking* at him, that she didn't want him to go with her?

If it was a brother, he thought grimly.

For all he knew, Jack was right. There was no brother. There was a man, yeah, but not one related to her. It would explain so much. So much. The reason she needed money, that she'd tolerated Willingham's abuse…

That she was so good, so incredibly good, in bed.

David stopped pacing. He felt cold, as if the marrow of his bones were turning to ice. Women lied. Krissie had taught him that. They were faithless. Krissie had taught him that, too.

But Krissie, at least, hadn't married a man for money.

Why hadn't he asked Nolan to check on Stephanie before this? He needed something to go on…

And then he remembered. She had scrawled something on the notepad.

He ran up the stairs, snatched up the pad. The impression left by the pencil was deep and clear. David read it, and the coldness seeped away. Rage, white-hot and glowing, replaced it.

"Damn you, Stephanie," he whispered.

And then he was out of the house, in his Porsche, roaring toward the Elmsview Motel.

"Paul," Stephanie said. "Paul, please, can you hear me?"

She shifted closer to her brother, lifted his head and cradled it against her shoulder. "Please, Paul. Talk to me."

Paul made a strangled sound. He rolled over, clutched her tightly and buried his face in her breast.

"Oh, Paul," she said softly. She bent her head, kissed his hair. "Darling, I love you. You know I do. No matter what happens, I'll always be here for you. I love you, Paul. I love…"

The door slammed against the wall, and the stink of the highway suddenly filled the room. Stephanie turned quickly and saw David standing in the doorway.

"David? David, what are you doing here?"

His gaze swept over the room, taking in the discarded clothing, the rumpled bed, the man in her arms. Something hot and dark twisted inside him.

"Such a trite question, Scarlett. At least I don't have to ask it of you. We both know what *you're* doing here."

"No. Whatever you're thinking…"

David's hands knotted into fists. The man, the scurvy bastard, had barely moved. The urge to stride across the room, drag Stephanie from the bed by the scruff of her lying neck, beat the crap out of her lover, roared through him like a tidal wave. But, if he did, he'd never stop. He'd beat her lover until he was a bloody pulp, and then he'd turn on Stephanie and he'd—he'd…

God, oh, God, what did you do when the woman you loved tore out your heart?

He blinked hard, forcing the red haze to clear from his eyes.

"Not to worry, Scarlett." From somewhere, he dredged up a smile. "We were both playing games. You just got careless before I did, that's all."

Her face, her lovely face, became even paler than it already was.

"What games?"

He laughed. "You didn't really think I was going to marry you, did you? Hey, a man will do a lot of things to get a woman into his bed, but marry her? Not me, baby. I'm not a fool like Willingham."

She recoiled, as if she'd been struck. He turned on his heel, victorious, and strode from the sleazy little room, telling himself he'd forever remember this moment.

But it wasn't true. He got into his car, shut the door and pounded his fists against the steering wheel while the tears coursed down his face, knowing that what he'd always remember was the agony of Stephanie's betrayal.

It would be with him for the rest of his life.

CHAPTER TWELVE

THERE was no place on earth as beautiful as Wyoming in June. David had always thought so, even when he was a kid growing up in a clapboard shack in a cowtown slum.

He'd come a long way since then, a hell of a long way. The thought brought a smile to his face for the first time in days, but then, he'd almost always found something to make him smile, when he was up here, on the ridge that overlooked the Bar C Ranch.

Night was coming. Purple shadows were already stretching their long fingers over the mountains. A red-tailed hawk, still seeking his dinner, drifted on silent wings across the canyon.

David's horse snorted and danced sideways with impatience. He reached forward and patted the velvet-soft neck.

"Easy, boy," he said softly.

The horse had had enough of sunsets. And so had he. It was getting him nowhere, sitting on this damned bluff every evening, watching the mountains and the hawk... and imagining.

He frowned, tugged at the reins, and turned for the trail that led down to the valley, and home.

"Stupid," he muttered.

Stupid was the word. What else could you call a man who'd been lucky enough to avoid disaster by the thinnest margin, who'd come within a whisper of tying himself to a woman who lied and cheated as easily as some people breathed? What was such a man, if not stupid, when he ended up thinking about her, remembering each detail of her face, instead of being forever grateful he'd gotten away with his skin intact?

There was no reason to think about Stephanie anymore. She was out of his life, and he was thankful for it.

"Thank heavens you came to your senses," Jack had said when David had brusquely informed him that the wedding was off, and he hadn't argued. Jack was right.

Then, why couldn't he get her out of his head?

It was almost dark now. His horse knew the trail well but still, the animal's ears were pricked forward and he made his way with care. That was fine. David was in no rush to get back to the house. His housekeeper would have supper waiting, he'd go through the charade of telling her how fine the meal was, move the stuff around on his plate a little so it looked as if he'd done more than pick at it, and then he'd go sit in the parlor, build a fire to ward off the chill that still settled on the mountains, even in June. He'd read, or work on some legal stuff he'd brought with him...pretend to read, or work, to be accurate. And then he'd look at the clock, tell himself it was time for bed, and go upstairs, alone, to toss and turn in the big canopied bed where he'd once imagined himself lying with Stephanie in his arms.

David frowned. Where in hell had that bit of nonsense come from? He'd never even thought of bringing her here. She wasn't the outdoors type—was she? He really didn't know. And, dammit, he really didn't care.

Why didn't he stop thinking about her?

His horse whinnied and David realized they'd come out of the trees. Dusk had settled over the valley. The house, nestled against the spectacular mountain backdrop, looked cozy and warm. It had the look and feel he'd always thought a home should have, even years ago, when he'd only been able to dream about living in a place like this.

He couldn't recall much about the house where he'd been born. His folks had been poor; they'd died when he was just a little kid and he'd gone to live in a foster home where the man he was ordered to address as ''Dad'' thought beatings and poverty were necessary for the good of the soul. That house he could remember with utmost clarity. The rooms had been uniformly gray, but neither the surroundings nor the people had been able to ruin the view.

The view had been David's salvation.

If you scrambled up the drainpipe to the flat roof, you could see past the streets and the clutter to the mountains. He'd spent a lot of time on that roof, looking at the mountains, telling himself that someday he'd live up there, in a place where you could almost reach up and touch the sky. It had seemed an impossible dream but he was living proof that dreams could, indeed, come true. Everything here was his. The valley, the house, the mountains—all of it.

Luck, hard work, a combination of things had secured him this existence. The football scholarship had come first, then an academic scholarship to Yale Law, and, at last, a career he loved. So he'd had a failed marriage along the way. Those things happened to lots of people. He'd been bitter, but he'd survived. And, until a couple of weeks ago, he'd figured he had everything a man could possibly want in life.

Now, he knew better.

What he needed was someone to share all this with. No. Not someone.

Stephanie.

David's jaw tightened. That was crazy. He didn't need her. Why would he?

It infuriated him, that he should even think of her. What a time she must have had, not to have collapsed with laughter when he'd asked her if she had any acting experience. Experience? She had enough to open her own drama school. She'd spent her years with Willingham at stage center. As for the short time she'd spent with him…damn, but she'd outdone any performance he'd ever watched on the Broadway stage.

It wasn't as if he'd really loved her. Oh, sure, he'd been infatuated. He'd even sat outside that fleabag motel, convinced he'd never get over her, but he had. It didn't hurt to think about her anymore. What thinking about her did was make him angry.

"Angry as hell," he said, and the horse danced nervously again.

No man liked to be played for a fool, and that was exactly what Stephanie had done to him.

He'd admitted that to Jack.

"She played me for a fool," he'd said over a three-bourbon lunch.

Jack had sighed and shaken his head; he'd looked down into his drink and over the heads of the diners at the next table, anywhere but at David, and he'd said, in a voice that could have rung with self-righteous satisfaction but didn't, "I tried to warn you, David."

Yes. Oh, yes. Jack had tried to warn him, but he'd been so sure. So convinced. So damn positive he'd found…

What?

What had he thought he'd found? An honest woman? Stephanie had never been that. A woman with simple tastes? No way. A woman who loved him? Absolutely not. Well, that was something, wasn't it? She hadn't ever claimed to love him. And a good thing, too, because he'd have called her on it. He'd have known she was handing him a load of crap because a woman who loved a man didn't lie, didn't cheat, didn't weep crocodile tears.

It was just that he couldn't forget. Her laugh. Her smile. The way she'd get that glint in her eye and stand up to him, no matter what…

The way she whispered his name when they made love, in a voice hushed with emotion. The way she returned his kisses. The way she curled into him when she slept, with her head on his shoulder and her arm across his chest, as if she never wanted to let him go...

"Dammit," he snarled.

Startled, the horse reared up on its hind legs. When its hooves touched the ground, David dug in his heels and leaned forward. He knew better than to hope he could leave his memories behind, but maybe, if he was lucky, he could ride and ride and ride, until he was just too tired to think anymore.

Riding helped.

So did working hard every day, from sunrise until sunset. He knew his men were asking each other questions behind his back. Even his foreman, who knew him as well as anybody and knew, too, that he'd always worked as hard as any of the hands, started looking at him strangely.

Nobody would ask him any questions, though, partly because he was the boss, mostly because you just didn't do that. In the West, a man's thoughts were his own. And that was just as well, David told himself as he sweated over what had to be his millionth fence posthole of the afternoon, because anybody getting a look at what he was thinking would have run for cover.

Why had he ever gone to the Cooper wedding? Why had he sat at table seven? Why had he let Jack talk him into going to Georgia?

Because he was an idiot, that was why. David grunted and jammed the digger into the soil. Because he was an unmitigated, unrepentant ass, that was why.

"David?"

He looked up. His foreman was standing in front of him, his hands on his hips.

"What?" he snapped.

"You have a phone call." The foreman looked down

at the ground, then up at David. "You're also about to dig that next hole right through your foot."

David looked at the posthole digger, then at his boot. He cursed, tossed the digger aside and wiped the sweat out of his eyes.

"I'm not in such a great mood lately," he said.

His foreman raised his eyebrows. "Do tell."

The two men looked at each other.

"I guess it shows."

"Nah."

His foreman grinned. David smiled back.

"Thanks for the message," he said.

The foreman nodded. "Sure." He watched his boss stride toward the house. Then he sighed, shrugged his shoulders, and headed back to the barns.

The house was cool and quiet. David nodded to his house-keeper and signaled that he'd take the call in the library. He shut the door after him, took the phone from the desk, and put it to his ear.

"This had better be good, Jack," he said.

He heard his partner laugh.

"That's quite a greeting, David. How could you be so sure it's me?"

"No one else would be foolhardy enough to call me here." David cocked a hip against the edge of his desk. "What do you want, Jack? I told you, when I left, that I was going to take a few weeks off."

"I know, but…" Jack cleared his throat. "I thought you might want to hear this."

"Hear what? The only open file I've got is that Palmer thing, and I explained—"

"It's not about the office, David." Jack cleared his throat again. "It's about the Willingham woman."

David's heart dropped. "What about her? Has something happened to her? Is she—"

"No, no, it's not about her. Not exactly. It's...the report came in."

"What report?"

"The one from Dan Nolan. You asked him to do a check on her, remember?"

David closed his eyes. A sharp pain lanced just behind his eyes. "Yeah," he said, rubbing the bridge of his nose. "I remember. Listen, do me a favor, Jack. Burn it."

"Well, I was going to, David. But then Dan phoned, and he said some things..."

"What things?"

"Look, I think you might be interested in what he found out."

"Yeah, well, I'm not. Just take the report and—"

"I sent it out this morning, David. By courier."

David sighed. "No problem. I'll chuck it out when it arrives."

But he didn't.

The report arrived early the next morning. David took it into the library, along with a mug of black coffee. He sat down at his desk, tilted back his chair, put his feet up and studied the envelope as it lay on his desk. Then he sat up straight, drank the coffee, and squared the edge of the envelope with the edge of the desk. It was a standard number nine tan manila envelope, no different than a thousand other envelopes...

He dreaded opening it.

"Dammit, Chambers, stop being a jerk."

He moved quickly, grabbing the envelope and ripping it open. A slim white folder was inside. Dan's letter was attached but he ignored it, looked at the folder and took a deep breath.

There it was, waiting for him. The story of Stephanie's life. Not as many pages as he'd have figured, but quantity wasn't everything, quality was.

His smile was bittersweet.

Read it, he told himself, and put an end to thinking about her. He took another deep breath.

"'And the truth shall set you free,'" he murmured.

He opened the folder.

An hour later, he sat with the pages of the report scattered on the desktop.

"Oh, Scarlett," he whispered. "Scarlett, my love."

By midday, he was seated in the cockpit of a chartered plane, headed for Willingham Corners, Georgia. The pilot, a man he'd known most of his adult life, chattered on and on about the world and the weather, but all David could think about was Stephanie, and how much he loved her...

And how badly he had failed her.

Stephanie sat shelling peas on the tiny porch of the house she'd grown up in.

It was a warm, lazy afternoon. Fat honeybees buzzed among the roses; an oriole trilled from the lowest branch of a magnolia. It was a perfect June day—or it would have been, if she weren't so angry.

"Idiot," she muttered, snapping open a pod and slipping the peas into the bowl in her lap.

She wasn't just angry. She was furious, and at herself. She had been, for weeks.

She blew a strand of hair out of her eyes and picked up another pea pod.

Oh, she'd wasted some time on stupidity, crying over losing David, but that hadn't lasted long. Why would it? You couldn't lose what you'd never had, and she had never "had" David. Why would she have wanted to have him? What had she seen in him, anyway? He was a liar, a cheat, and a scoundrel, just like all the rest of them.

"Avery incarnate," she mumbled, and slammed the peas into the bowl.

To think she'd imagined herself in love with such a rat.

To think she'd wanted to marry him. To think she'd slept with him...

Except, she hadn't slept with him. She'd made love with him, and yes, there was a difference. A wonderful difference. Otherwise she'd never have felt the things she'd felt, never have died and been reborn in his arms.

"Nonsense," she said briskly.

And it *was* nonsense. She'd been vulnerable, that was all. David had come along when she was having a difficult time. He'd shown her what she'd thought was kindness, but it had turned out to be nothing but a scheme to get her into his bed.

It was hard to believe any man would go to such lengths just to seduce a woman, especially a man like David. Stephanie's throat constricted. She'd been so sure it was all real. The kindness. The decency. The concern.

The love. Oh, David's love. His kisses and caresses. His whispered promises. His tenderness.

Stephanie gave herself a little shake.

"Stop it," she said sternly.

The lies, for that was what they'd been, were all behind her. David was the past. The future...well, she wasn't sure just what the future was, but it was shaping up. She smiled and brushed her hand over her eyes. Things were definitely going to get better. Paul, for one. He *was* better. New medications had made a big improvement. And a day after she'd pleaded with Rest Haven's management board, explained how desperate she was, they'd come up with an incredible proposal. They'd halve the cost of Paul's care, if she'd agree to replace the administrative assistant to the manager, when she retired in two weeks.

So now, here she was, spending a quiet time at the old family homestead before beginning her new job. Yes, life was good. It was fine. It was...

Oh, God, it was a mess, because David, damn him, had broken her heart. Who was she kidding? She hated him.

Despised him. But that didn't keep her from dreaming about him, from longing for the comfort of his arms—

"Scarlett?"

The bowl tumbled from her lap and Stephanie shot to her feet. She spun around, her hand to her breast, knowing, *knowing*, that she had to be imagining the sound of David's voice...

But she wasn't.

"David," she whispered, and her heart kicked against her ribs.

He stood no more than twenty feet away, not moving, not talking, just looking at her. What was he doing here? How had he found her?

What did he want?

"You," he said, and she knew she must have spoken the last question aloud.

Her heart did another little tumble. Don't, she told herself. Oh, Steffie, don't. He's lying. He must be lying. And even if he isn't, you know what he believes. What he thinks...

"I love you, Scarlett."

Her mouth began to tremble. "No," she said, and shook her head. Her hands were trembling, too, and she stuck them deep into the pockets of her old jeans. "Please, don't say that."

"I don't deserve another chance," he said as he started slowly toward her. "I know that. I failed you, sweetheart. When you needed me the most, I wasn't there."

"No." Stephanie shook her head again. "Don't, David. I can't—I can't bear it."

"I didn't trust you. I knew it, and I told myself that was fine, that a man had to be a fool to trust a woman." He stopped at the foot of the porch steps and looked into her eyes. They were shining with tears and he resisted the desire to reach out, pull her down into his arms and kiss the tears away. "I love you," he said again. "I want you to be my wife."

Stephanie took a step back. "This isn't fair," she whispered. "To say these things and—and not mean them..."

He smiled. "I'm a lawyer, Scarlett. Would a lawyer tell a lie?"

"Isn't that what they do?" she said, her head lifting with defiance.

David sighed. "Well, yeah. Sometimes, I guess, but only by omission."

"*You* lied. And not by omission. You know you did."

He climbed the steps slowly, watching as she backed away from him, drinking in her beauty and the sweetness of her face, his heart suddenly blazing with hope because he knew, he *knew,* that she loved him just as much as he loved her.

"You're right," he said softly. Her shoulders hit the wall of the little clapboard house that looked strangely like the one he'd grown up in, and he smiled again, knowing she couldn't get away from him now, that he'd never let her get away from him again. "I did lie," he said, reaching out to touch her hair. "That's what I've come here to tell you."

"Don't—don't do that," she said, trying to pull away from him. He wouldn't let her. He just came closer, until she had to tilt her head to look up into his eyes, those wonderfully blue eyes. "What do you mean, that's why you've come here?"

He stroked his hand over her hair, along her cheek. He cupped her shoulders with his palms and drew her unyielding body toward his.

"I came to tell you that I lied about everything, Scarlett." He put his hands into her hair and lifted her face to him. "About not meaning it, when I proposed marriage."

"It doesn't matter," she said stiffly. "I wouldn't have—I never wanted to—please, David. Don't do that."

He did it, anyway; he bent his head and brushed his mouth gently over hers. Stephanie held still. She didn't breathe. She wouldn't let him know what was happening to her, what his touch was doing to her...

A sob burst from her throat.

"Damn you," she whispered. "You broke my heart, David. Wasn't that enough? Have you come here to do it again?"

"I came here to tell you that I love you," he said, "that I've always loved you...and to beg your forgiveness."

Stephanie looked up at him, her eyes wide.

"I love you, Scarlett. That's why I came up with that whole crazy scheme about why we should marry. I was too afraid to tell you the truth."

"Afraid? Of what?"

"Of getting hurt. Of you saying you didn't love me."

"Oh, David." Stephanie smiled through her tears. "I love you with all my heart. But—but that night—the things you said..."

David kissed her. "Lies," he whispered, brushing the tears from her cheeks with his thumbs. "I saw you with another man and I went crazy with jealousy."

"It was Paul. My brother."

"I know that now."

"He's been sick for years, David, ever since he hit his head, a long time ago. I know I should have taken you to meet him. I wanted to, but Paul had—"

David kissed her again, holding her closely in his arms, so that she could feel the accelerated beat of his heart.

"You don't have to explain. I know everything, Scarlett, including what a fool I was, and if you let me, I'll spend the rest of my life proving how much I adore you. Will you marry me?"

Stephanie wrapped her arms around David's neck.

"Yes," she said, her eyes shining, and David lifted her into his arms and carried her away from Willingham Corners forever.

They were married on the ranch, in Wyoming, on a gloriously warm and bright Sunday afternoon, two months later.

It would have been sooner, but it had taken time for David to arrange for Paul's admittance to a San Francisco clinic where remarkable progress was being made with injuries such as his.

"Anything you want to bet," David said softly to his bride on the morning of their wedding, "Paul will be well enough to celebrate our first anniversary with us here, on the Bar C."

Stephanie smiled, leaned up and kissed his cheek. She had no doubt it would happen, just the way David said. David always told the truth, and she trusted him with all her heart.

The wedding was small but perfect. All the guests said so, even Mary Russell, when she could stop weeping long enough to talk.

"You're being silly," Jack whispered to his wife, but he was smiling when he said it, and thinking what a lucky man he was to have her.

Annie couldn't come, but Stephanie promised to send pictures.

"You'll be a beautiful bride," Annie had promised, and everyone agreed that she was.

She wore a long, full gown of white silk with tiny silver flowers trimming the bodice, and carried a bouquet of baby's breath and tiny white and purple orchids. David wore a Western-cut tuxedo and black leather boots, and all the women sighed and said there'd never been a more handsome groom.

And when the day ended, and all the guests had left, he

lifted Stephanie before him onto the saddle of his horse, just as she was, in all her bridal finery, and they rode up into the mountains, to watch the sun go down.

David turned her face up to his. "I love you, Scarlett."

Stephanie smiled radiantly. "I love you, too, my beloved husband," she murmured.

David kissed his bride. At long last, he was truly home.